THE ADVERSARIES

BOOKS BY EDWARD LINN

Veeck a/ *in Wreck*
The Adversaries

THE ADVERSARIES

Saturday Review Press / E. P. Dutton & Co., Inc.

NEW YORK

Published simultaneously in Canada by
Doubleday Canada Ltd., Toronto.

Library of Congress Catalog Card Number: 73–79529

ISBN 0–8415–0281–1

1 2 3 4 5 6 7 8 9 10

PRINTED IN THE UNITED STATES OF AMERICA

Design by Tere LoPrete

to my own Ruthie
my own jewel

THE ADVERSARIES

BOOK I

An Act of Magic

"The Supreme Court says it doesn't matter whether you did it. You open that door and all winds blow in . . ."

> *From the Journal of James J. Ambose*
> *First Assistant District Attorney*
> *Brederton County*

Tuesday, June 15
4:12 A.M.

Sam Tabor woke up slowly, drifting in and out of sleep in that long, weightless moment that is so warm and comfortable and sheltered. The phrase had come into his head, it seemed, along with the first faint ray of consciousness . . . *the vanquished of* . . . and he kept running it round and round in a circle, the end back into the beginning, tagging the first word onto the last, the *at* on the *swami.*

The philosophical message was there—the revelation—in such absolute clarity that he knew very well (drifting in and out of consciousness) that this time he would not lose it as he always seemed to lose these early morning messages. Either lose it or remember it so fragmentarily that what had seemed so important would be nothing, would be gibberish, would be stupid, would be false. Would be lies. This time it had such a sweet rhythm, such a sweet, airless merry-go-round rhythm, that even while he drifted back and forth, in and out, he was able to hold onto it. Even when a black splotch would squeeze down upon him, blotting part of it out, the mind, through this new perception it had of itself, would pick it up again, all by itself, rolling on, rhythm on wheels, clickety-clack . . . *I was young* . . . and he knew that this time he was indeed peering around hidden corners, searching the vast, illuminated skies. For once, his mind was accepting itself, congratulating itself, applauding itself. At last.

And then—fool!—he lost it. Fool!

Through sheer will and expanding consciousness he had held off, *fought* off, sleep and then, like a fool ("Self-indulgence and sloth," *she* used to say), lost it while he was telling himself how brilliant he was. Fool again; fooled again—fool, fool, fool.

The heart, sick of itself—sickened—missed a beat, lifting him one more layer out of sleep, up through the cloudy membrane, and—don't move; don't even breathe—there it was again, the sweet refrain, pulsating anew, struggling back to life, blip-blip, inhale-exhale, clickety-clack . . . *At that time. . . .*

The jolt of the missed heartbeat had lifted him physically, sitting him up, over onto his feet, stumbling to the bureau. The hand, reaching for the chain on the dim lamp, somehow closed upon Vera's eyebrow pencil (that was a *good* sign; if he'd had to go searching for a pen it might have been too late) and still half-asleep,

3

dark more than light, he wrote the words along the border . . . *At that time I was* . . . of a package of Vera's hair curlers.

Gotcha! Caught! Impaled! Immortal!

Vera was breathing heavily, not quite a snore, and he thought momentarily about giving her a good shove, the way he used to when they were sleeping together and her snoring kept him awake. He was still thinking about it when he found himself back in bed wondering how much more time he had to sleep. But before he could look at the alarm clock on the night table between the beds, the membrane had clouded over again and he was drifting back, cuddled to himself, snug within himself. He could not remember ever being happier. Out of all the people on the earth he had been selected to become the carrier of this powerful and liberating message, a message of such overwhelming dynamism and force as to be instantly recognizable and clearly understood by the most brilliant minds and the most simple. Dr. Shtogren would know, he thought, and immediately he pictured Dr. Shtogren finding out about it from another source (*not* Vera). From the *television screen*. Sam Tabor on television being introduced by the President ("Ladies and gentlemen of the world"). He saw Dr. Shtogren sitting with Vera, he in front, she in back, just the two of them in what looked like the show-up room down at the police station, and Dr. Shtogren saying, "Well, I never knew . . . I had no idea." And Vera saying, "Why, of course, didn't you know? But how could you? Nobody knew. Even I didn't know. But now we know. Now everybody knows."

They would know at last. They would recognize his undoubted goodness, his unrecognized genius, the purpose of his life. "Deserted, scorned and despised," said *Time*. "And yet he went on, enduring the blows, surviving the worst, awaiting the moment."

He slept so heavily and peacefully that for the first time in years the click of the alarm clock didn't awaken him. The ringing was still in his ears, his hand still on the button, when the memory of the written message came back to him. As eager as he was to find out what the hell it had been all about, he lay there very quietly, his hand on the alarm and his eyes on his wife as she stirred, snorted and finally turned over onto her back.

What surprised him most of all was that it was so short. He would have sworn that there had been . . . maybe not a paragraph but certainly something more than this short, nothing sentence. In a wavering, barely legible scribble, running up the side border and curving back across the top, were the words:

At that time I was young and the vanquished of the swami.

He grimaced. He had to laugh at himself. The crazy thoughts that come to you in the night, and the crazier interpretations you put on them. He remembered it all so vividly, right down to those final intimations of immortality before he fell asleep ("Ladies and gentlemen of the world"), that he blushed for himself.

He blushed for himself, too, because he had to admit how disappointed he was that it had turned out to be not a message of hope for all of humanity (or whatever the hell he had been expecting) but only this poor piece of gibberish.

And yet . . .

And yet, were the words really so crazy when you studied them carefully, or were they only . . . well, rather obscure. Abstruse. Challenging. Were they not, when you came to think about it, very odd words to have come to him so unbidden? *Swami*. In his whole life, he would bet that he had never once used

4

the word "swami." If forced on pain of death to come up with a definition, what would he say? All right: "A swami is a special kind of fortuneteller with a turban." God, there was a great definition for you. "Ladies and gentlemen of the world. Sam Tabor will now give you the definition of 'swami.' "

And yet, now wait a minute, there *was* a kind of mysticism there that was not wholly out of whack with that feeling of what? . . . prophecy? . . . that had been over him during the night. He wasn't so far gone that he was going to make anything of this—not in broad daylight, for godsake—and yet, just to play with it a little, he read it over again, mouthing the words slowly.

"Vanquished" was an odd word, too. Who used words like "vanquished" these days? Vanquished was something the old Norsemen used to do to their enemies. There came to his mind—what a thing to remember; god, how his mind was racing—a highschool teacher who had sprung a vocabulary test on them one morning. One of the words was "transparent" and everybody had written, "Something you can see through." The teacher—Mahoney? Maloney? Maroney —that prick, had flunked them all and told them (so proud he was that he had tricked them) that "transparent" was not "something" at all, it was the "property" of the something you saw through.

Now, why should he remember that so vividly at this time—it must have been forty years ago—unless he was in a state of heightened sensitivity, a moment of truth-finding? Could it be—just as an idea to play with—that he was being given one more clue, one final chance to find some kind of meaning in the whole experience? Was he being told that if he could wipe away the conventional thoughts he would be able to see through the conventional definitions? *See through!* Against his better judgment he felt a rising excitement. Was he being told that he had within himself some special property by which . . .

He groaned aloud. Looking into the bureau mirror, he pointed a finger at himself and announced, "You have a special property, all right, which I, and I alone, can see through. Your special property, Sam-you-vell my boy, is that you are the world's own fool."

Still peering in the mirror, still pointing, his mood underwent a sudden change. It was as if a cloud had suddenly passed over the sun, darkening and dampening his whole mood. Studying himself more carefully in the shadowed mirror, *looking* at himself, he saw Sam Tabor clear. Jowly, heavy stubble. Balding. He ran a hand through his sparse and thinning hair. Badly balding now. And no wonder . . .

Look at yourself! A man who slept in his underwear. That said it all, didn't it? Vera used to hate it when he came to bed in his underwear. A man who didn't bother to take off his dirty underwear, she would tell him, had no respect for himself or for his wife. (Laziness and sloth would be his undoing, *she* used to say.)

Looking at Vera now, through the mirror, he could see that she was still lying flat on her back, spread-eagled, one leg sticking out under the thin cover. She was, he could see now, wearing the short black nightgown she wore only when she wanted to let him know that she wanted it. How come he hadn't noticed that last night? To hell with her. The separate beds had been her idea. Dr. Shtogren had suggested it to him (as a temporary measure . . . suuuure), but Sam knew whose idea it had been, all right. If she wanted it, she knew where his bed was. Damn right. The thought was so pleasing to him that he lifted an eyebrow mockingly, rubbed his fingers along the stubble of his beard and drawled into the mirror, "If you want it, baby, you know where my bed is." It came out just the way he had hoped it would; coolly indifferent, devastatingly amused.

He was still feeling so good about it after he had finished shaving that he reached for the after-shave lotion and applied it to his cheeks with the slap and rhythm of a man beating on a big bass drum. "Clickety-click, clickety-clack," he sang. "If you want it, baby, you gotta wait till I get back."

To catch the bus for work, Sam had to walk only two blocks down his own street and slightly less than a full block up the main thoroughfare. "If the R22 bus comes first, it will be a *good* day for me," he told himself. "If it comes second, it will be a nothing day, and if it comes third (a pleasing thought came to him) . . . if it comes third, I had better consult the swami."

The first of the big green municipal buses came rolling across the intersection while he was still a good ten strides from the corner, and he could see by the sign on the side window that it was R22. Still, he stopped at the corner to buy his paper, and even paused to give careful consideration to the carefully considered observation that though there was still a snap of morning coolness in the air, the sun would be burning it out quick enough and they could be expecting another bitch. "A bitch," Sam agreed, having perused the skies and sniffed at the air. "That's just what I was thinking just now. Another bitch."

With the line down to almost nothing, he strolled, confident and unhurried, past the crowd waiting for the other buses, reached the door just as the last man was stepping up onto the platform and was able to board without breaking stride. A *very* good sign. Yes, indeed. It was going to be one of the *good* days.

On the front page of the *Morning Globe* was a picture of the Chief Justice of the United States, David Boone Wilcke, being greeted outside the terminal building of Lowell Airport by a mob of angry, placard-carrying citizens. One hideous-looking old woman with a particularly maniacal look on her face seemed ready to swing her placard at him, while two of the deputies from Sheriff Stringfellow's office closed in on her. The placard, which could just barely be made out, bore the rather cryptic message:

The Word of God
or
the word of man?

Behind her, a young and rather good-looking man was carrying a sign, raised high for the camera, which proclaimed:

Communists and
Criminals
Belong in Jail

The accompanying news story confirmed that the woman had in fact jabbed her placard at the Chief Justice before the deputies had moved in, amidst the jeering of a hostile and abusive crowd, to place her under arrest. In the overrun Bob Stringfellow was quoted as saying that the size of the waiting crowd had come as a complete surprise in that neither the Chief Justice's flight nor arrival time had been publicized.

The sense of outrage that filled Sam Tabor as he read the story was not so much on behalf of the Chief Justice, whom he felt rather neutral about, as at this latest example of the lack of respect being shown toward the courts of which he himself was, in his own small way, a representative.

There had been a great deal of talk down at the courthouse these past few days about the Chief Justice's acceptance of the invitation to address the local Bar

Association's annual dinner, and not everyone had viewed it as a signal honor. Jim Ambose, for one—Sam Tabor thought, breaking out into a grin—had undoubtedly found a great deal to say.

8:32 A.M.

Jim Ambose, the first assistant district attorney, was seated in the rear-wall booth of the Buckminster Restaurant, his dark, deep-set eyes glowering at the approaching FBI agent, Bernie Rogell.

Rogell, a beefy man, was wearing the regimental uniform of the Lowell office, a tweed suit buttoned a little too tightly across his midsection. He was also wearing, as he slid into the seat across from Ambose, the smug, triumphant look Ambose had been expecting. "You sent for me, Jim?" he asked innocently.

"Goddamn bureaucratic crap," Ambose snorted. "Goddamn de-part-mental protocol. You tell that Ber-tram Chester he's getting worse down there with his goddamn dipsy-doo than the State Department." With Rogell just sitting back, grinning at him comfortably, Ambose hunkered his big shoulders forward. In parched and measured tones he said, "If I ever get to talking to the director, I'll let him know what a bunch of goddamn social butterflies he's got down here. You can take a crack squad of FBI agents is what I always say and with their combined inves-ti-ga-tive talents they couldn't track a three-legged elephant across a snowbank."

"You know," Rogell said, "that's just what Mr. Chester warned me. That you were going to turn all your charm on me. He seems to think you want a favor or something. Hope you haven't lost any of your elephants lately, Jim, because that happens to be one of our weaker services."

Ambose reached into his shirt pocket for a small, flat metal container, opened the lid and selected a small, very dark cigar. Without really taking his eyes off Rogell, he rolled the little cigar around in his lips. "This isn't really the FBI down here, anyway," he said in a flat challenging drawl. "It's an outpost of the Knights of Columbus. Tell me something, Bernard, do you got to be Irish or Italian to get into the Bureau or is it enough to graduate from the Jesuits?" He rolled the little cigar around between his lips. "Or are they still doing it the old-fashioned way where you have to buy an indulgence from the Pope?"

"Beats me, chum. I'm French and what's a Jesuit?" The waitress had come alongside to take Rogell's order, and Ambose noted with satisfaction that despite the flippant answer Rogell had not been able to control a quick, anxious glance in her direction.

Jim Ambose had been unhappy enough—a not unaccustomed state—about having to call the Justice Department in the first place. The unhappiness had increased by leaps and bounds when they appointed Rogell as liaison man and proceeded to go through all this rigamarole about finding a neutral meeting ground halfway between the courthouse and the Federal Building.

He knew what they were doing, of course, and—being a man who prided himself on objectivity—he couldn't say he blamed them. The last time Jim Ambose had spoken to Rogell he had been throwing him out of his office, along with the U.S. Attorney, Bert Chester, who had refused to allow Rogell to testify for the state in a bank robbery case.

And that was one conflict, Ambose had to admit, that had not come as a direct and inevitable result of the goddamn decisions of Chief Justice David Boone Wilcke and the Idiot Court. With both the state and the federal government having jurisdiction on bank robbery cases, there was a long-standing agreement whereby the state would prosecute if the local cops made the arrest and the U.S. Attorney would assume jurisdiction if the FBI made the arrest. On the case in question, the city burglary division had made the arrest, and Rogell had hustled right down to the police station. Standard operating procedure. Even Ambose would admit that nobody could be more efficient than the FBI when it came to getting a man to the police station to question a suspect after the local police had made the pinch. Or, for that matter, in picking him up after he had been questioned and released.

What tore it this time was that the thieves had been so eager to explain to Rogell where their plans had gone awry that not all the warnings about their constitutional rights could shut them up. Five minutes later, when Cap LaPorte arrived for his own interrogation, the place was crawling with lawyers, and the thieves had been instructed to clam up.

Given such admittedly unique circumstances, Ambose had expressed a wholly unwarranted confidence that the FBI would allow Rogell to testify for the state. Chester insisted that he had instructions from Washington to hold to the established policy of not permitting FBI agents to testify in nonfederal cases, which was another way of saying that the only way the confessions could be used would be for Ambose to turn the trial over to the Justice Department.

Ambose had damn well let him know that he had a few long-standing policies of his own. Like trying his own cases. He had not only thrown them both out of his office, he had sworn a holy oath to have any FBI agent who came within fifty feet of the courthouse arrested for loitering. "And that goes for you, too!" he had shouted after them. "Don't either of you come back unless I send for you!"

Soon enough he had sent for them. The day of the trial he subpoenaed Rogell and the confessions, which, as he well knew, meant only that Chester would have to take the stand, out of the presence of the jury, and put the Justice Department's policy on the record. But as happy as it made Ambose to harass the FBI, that wasn't why he had done it. Judge Elijah Chobodian had put the subpoena under seal and warned the press to print nothing that would jeopardize the defendants' right to a fair trial. But the press knew. And once the trial was over, there was nothing to prevent them from printing it.

The ironic part of it, as Ambose would reflect later, was that if the bums had got off, everybody would have been coming around to cry with him. Instead, the jury came back with "all the time," thirty years for both defendants, and while that could have been taken as a testimonial to Ambose's brilliance as a prosecutor, it was also rather conclusive evidence that Rogell's testimony had not been absolutely essential.

District Attorney Hilliard Nevins had thereupon summoned him to his office to make it abundantly clear that he, not Ambose, would be the man who dealt with the Justice Department from now on. "I am telling you for the last time that we are going to have a good working relationship with the FBI here," Nevins had growled. "We've always had it and we're going to keep on having it. The guidelines have been laid down to my complete satisfaction and if you don't find them to your liking I think I can do something about facilitating your resignation."

Nevins had put him on probation—for only the fifth or sixth time that month —and he had also sent around a memo stating that when the district attorney was out of the office, DeWitt Pawley, the number three man, would be in charge.

It had not been easy, then, for Ambose to call upon the U.S. Attorney for help less than three weeks later—and on another bank robbery case at that. Having reestablished a position of strength, to his own satisfaction at least, he told Rogell, "Look, we've had our disagreements and we'll have them again. But there's one thing we can both agree on. When law enforcement officers get into a hassle nobody benefits except the thieves."

Rogell was willing enough to go along with that.

"All right," Ambose said, "let's stop farting around. Did Chester send you here to hear me out or to see how much you can make me squirm?"

Rogell pursed his lips and rocked his hand back and forth. "A little of this, a little of that. Keep talking."

The new case was getting under way that morning with a pretrial hearing on "probable cause" on what had seemed like a solid collar. The problem was that Thomas P. Mallon had suddenly come into the case, claiming illegal search and seizure, and with Harrison T. Davies on the Bench, Ambose had developed a very bad feeling about it. Davies had been overturned three times in three successive sessions of the state Court of Appeals, and the only way he could make sure he wasn't overturned again would be to find for the defense. The state legislature, in their unspeakable wisdom, had given the prosecution no right of appeal at all. Ambose had such a bad feeling about it that he had swallowed his pride and asked for a supporting brief from the U.S. Attorney.

"I broke Tommy Mallon in," he told Rogell, "and I can read him. He's thinking that with Harry Davies sitting, anything's worth a shot. With your ordinary idiot, I don't think he'd even bother. And if there was no money in the case, you can be damn sure he wouldn't. He figures he's got enough small, nit-shit, piddling things to throw at Davies to maybe make him think a second time, because once this guy thinks another time—hell, once he has to think at all—you know he's going to panic. You know Harry. If his IQ was as high as his Wasser-mann he'd be twice the judge and half the man."

All in the world he wanted Chester to do was to notify Davies that he was going to be putting a supporting brief from the Justice Department of the U.S. of A. into his hand, so that when Tommy Mallon began waving the Supreme Court of the U.S. of A. at him, Davies would know he was on safe grounds.

Choosing his words with care, Rogell said, "It is my honest impression that Mr. Chester is in complete agreement with you that Mallon's petition is wholly without merit."

"Oh, for chrissake," Ambose said, turning his head away.

"It is my impression, first of all, that Mr. Chester doesn't want to stick his head into a state case. It is my impression, second, that he doesn't think you need anything from him on Garrett–Kehoe. Any more than you needed those confessions you got all jumping up and down about. I mean, if only you didn't get so hard-headed, Jim. You got them with the money, you got them with the guns, you got them with the masks and—what was it they were wearing—rubbers? Holy Mother of Mercy, Ambose, you got them in everything except technicolor."

"Sneakers," Ambose said. "And will you for once do me a favor and stop talking like a diplomat. Just tell it to me like you were told to tell it to me, and I'll tell it to you the way I want you to tell it back to Chester." He noted, and not without pleasure, the grim set of Rogell's mouth at being reminded that he was, after all, only a messenger, but because it griped him to have to be doing

9

this through a flunky, he found himself saying, "I don't expect the U.S. Attorney to read the cases. He's too busy kissing ass in Washington for that. But he could at least read the newspapers. These judges are throwing everything out. You got federal judges standing on their heads they're so panicked about being tipped over anymore. What do you think it does to a birdbrain like Davies?"

Still smarting, Rogell told him that Mr. Chester would undoubtedly reply that Harrison Davies was Ambose's problem not his.

"He would, huh?" Jim Ambose placed the heels of both palms against his plate and with an almost elaborate lack of haste pushed it away from him. "Just so there'll be no misunderstanding between us, I want to put it on the record that for all I care they could turn all the bank robbers in the world loose and send them to safe-cracking school for postgraduate work on the latest electronic timing devices. That's their business, the legislators and the judges. I'm interested in only one thing. In doing my job . . . being allowed to." His voice had changed. "When I started in this business twelve years ago, I didn't have any idea what I was doing. I admit that. But I went in there every day, day after day, and I got my asshole turned inside out by every smart defense lawyer in this state, and a lot of them —and I don't mind admitting it—that weren't so smart, either. But I learned. I learned, see? And after a couple of years it got to where I could reach in and do some twisting of my own. A couple of more years and I could walk into my office in the morning, pick up a brief, read it quick and tell you just what the case was worth. And then go into court an hour later and get every day, month or year that could be got out of it.

"All right." He shrugged. "Maybe twice a year a jury goes crazy, but that's part of the game—it's what keeps you on your toes. And maybe more than twice a year a judge is got to, but I can usually smell that kind of a deal coming up. And if I don't smell it before I walk in, I can sure as hell smell it before the pretrial motions are done with."

He could see that Rogell was rather taken aback by this unexpected burst of confidence. And rather flattered, too. Which was exactly what Ambose had in mind. Ambose sort of hunched over toward him, the big shoulders bowed. "I'll tell you something, Bernie. The way I feel, I feel like they've taken twelve years of my life and flushed it down the can. I don't know what's happening in there anymore. They've changed the rules on me so much that I go into court these days and half the time I don't have any idea what I'm doing."

The sideways glance Rogell shot at him demonstrated his complete disbelief. "You wanna give me a signed affidavit on that? Because I'll run right down to the Bar Association with it and get rich."

"What I'm telling you is that I don't give a damn anymore! I don't have any wife or daughter I have to worry are they safe on the streets at night. But . . . let . . . me . . . know, huh? If they want me to stand on my left foot, shove beans up my nose and whistle 'Dixie,' all they got to do is tell me. But don't tell me 'left foot' one day and 'right foot' the next. And don't *you* sit there looking so damn smug and smart-ass and tell me you don't feel the same way. We may have our disagreements but we're looking for the same thing."

"Oh, you mean you're waiting for your pension, too?" You could see that he had realized instantaneously what a lousy joke that was. "Look," he said. "I know how you feel. We're getting them thrown out of the federal courts, too. We had one a couple of weeks ago you wouldn't believe. I don't think I'd be talking out of school if I said that Mr. Chester was really jumping up and down himself after that one." He paused and cleared his throat. "As I understand the position of the U.S. Attorney, and I believe I understand it correctly, he does not see anything in the Garrett case at this time of such a nature as to justify departmental intervention. But if you're still worried after today's hearing, he'll be willing to meet with you personally and reassess the situation."

That told Ambose all he had to know. That Chester was willing to reestablish the old relationship once Ambose was willing to admit he had been well and truly chastised. All at once it occurred to him to wonder whether Chester hadn't already talked the whole thing over with Nevins. Well, if Chester didn't know by now that while Hilliard Nevins might sit in the big office and give out the quotes, Jim Ambose was the man you had to see when it came to the bruising, then Mr. Chester would have to have that fact of life rammed home to him.

"Ho-kay," he said. "So Chester thinks I owe him one."

He was satisfied that Rogell had not failed to pick up the message that as far as Jim Ambose was concerned it was now their side that owed him one.

9:30 A.M.

The district attorney's office occupied the entire top floor of the six-story courthouse building. Jim Ambose, strolling along in the pleasant morning air, had turned his mind to the upcoming hearing, and since a hearing called for little more than a rebuttal of the defense position, he had concentrated mostly upon his opening remarks and his tactics. For the most part he had been trying to decide whether to hit Mallon hard or to really throw him off balance by playing it cool and professional.

Since Ambose had been the only person in the elevator, it was natural enough, preoccupied as he was, that he would step out when the elevator stopped. Too late he saw that it had stopped, for some incalculable reason, not on the sixth floor but the fifth. Annoyed, he whacked the UP button hard with the side of his fist, and then, with a heavy shrug of resignation, decided that walking up one flight wasn't going to kill him. The stairwell was only a few yards up the hall. Just beyond the Bureau of Missing Persons.

Across the corridor, on the other side of the stairwell, was something called the Young Adults Service, which could have meant anything but which was in this jurisdiction a special probation office for juvenile delinquents. The county prided itself on a fashionably enlightened attitude toward juvenile delinquents. Instead of being shipped off to reform school after their first conviction, they were allowed to remain at home or, if a suitable home was lacking, they were placed in a foster home. If they reported in regularly and were able to get through their probation period without getting into any more trouble, the conviction was wiped off the books and they became eligible to return to the Young Adults Service on their next "first" conviction. (Farther down the hall was the New Horizons Institute, a corollary service that took the kids who were either illiterate or hopelessly behind in their schoolwork and tried to teach them reading, writing and anything else they might be able to absorb. The institute was an accredited part of the city school system, and was supported by both private and public funds.)

Behind the desk in the outer office of the Young Adults Service a blonde in her thirties, compact in hand, was putting herself through the final lip-pursing, pro-file-studying, blemish-flicking paces of the morning. Alongside her, on the still uncluttered desk, a huge tan handbag lay open. As soon as she realized that someone had come in, she snapped the compact shut and dropped it, guiltily, into the bag. Upon seeing that it was Jim Ambose, she became even more flustered, noticeably flustered, her hand flicking tentatively along her hair as if she were afraid every strand might not be in perfect order.

"Caroline," Ambose said, "I want you to do something for me."

Resting her head against her hand, she looked up at him wistfully. "I thought you'd never ask."

"There's a woman in Missing Persons now," he said. "A woman wearing a red suit. I've got to be in Judge Davies' court in a few minutes, but when you see her come out I'd take it as a favor if you'd ask Sam to hold her questionnaire for me."

"Me and Sam," she said, holding up two crossed fingers. "For good old me, Sam will do anything." Especially, she added, since he was required by statute to keep a carbon on file anyway.

There was an awkward pause, for it had been some time since Ambose had been in this office or, for that matter, alone with Caroline. "I intend to drop in for a few minutes to watch you and Tommy Mallon, Jim. You know, root for the home team." She inclined her head toward the main office in back. "If the boss ever gets here and I don't get tied down with too many of my rotten kids."

"If you miss it," he said, "you won't have missed anything. It's just a routine hearing. Just a couple of lawyers talking to a judge."

Jim Ambose, who liked few women, liked Caroline Beyner. There had been a time, a couple of years back, when he had been sorely tempted, and he could guess that she had never been able to understand why he had let it go. He had heard that she'd been sleeping around with this one and that, which wasn't unusual—was, in fact, the norm—in this courthouse. It wasn't until he heard her name coupled with Judge Parks that he had realized how fond he had been of her.

Looking at her more critically now, as a woman who had shacked up with Judge Parks, he could see that she—like the woman in red across the corridor—was beginning to show the wear and tear. He wondered if her friends still called her "Bunny." It was a name that fit her well, he had always thought. As why shouldn't it? For wasn't it safe to assume that she, like any other Bunny, had chosen that nickname for herself back in her early teens, and that seeing herself as a Bunny (or wanting so bad to be seen as one) had gone to work with a vengeance to shape her personality to fit her own self-image. It fit this Bunny well: rather short, rather cuddly, more than friendly, small puggish nose, which she had, as a girl, undoubtedly practiced wrinkling.

She had gotten up from behind the desk, smoothing her skirt carefully, and as she came toward him he could see that though the body was a little stockier, the face a little puffier, she still looked pretty good. Damn good. If Parks had dumped her, he must have gotten himself tied up with something very nice, very quickly. The old bastard must have been on a winning streak.

This place, he thought, was getting to be an open, out-and-out whorehouse. And then, because he looked upon himself as a student of human behavior, not excluding his own, he thought, By god, Jimbo, if you're not getting to be a righteous sonofabitch.

Back in his apartment, locked in a desk in his workroom, unseen by any eye save his own, were stacks of journals in which he had through the years written down in meticulous detail his observations of the law, of human nature, of mankind. In those journals he had made some comment on almost every case he had ever tried, and, at times, a single case had taken up many, many pages. His favorite journal was entitled "Observations, Aphorisms and Maxims." Although it had been years since he had made his entry on "righteousness," he not only heard its echo but could see it written out, about two-thirds down the page, about a quarter of an inch into the book. He had written, and he was sure he could remember it accurately, "Listen for the subject on which a man becomes most righteous and you will discover the subject upon which he feels most inadequate."

"Bunny," he said, "you're looking better than ever."

He could see that she took the "Bunny" for what it was, an expression of renewed interest. "Any time you want to do anything about it," she said, laughing, "the door is always open, and these kids we have in here wouldn't even stop to notice."

"A wise old man once told me," Jim said, holding it to the same flippant tone, "not in the shade of your own apple tree."

"Ah yes," she said, flicking her eyes at him, "especially when there are other pastures. Juicier fruit."

If she had missed his meaning, what did it matter? It hadn't been a wise old man and it hadn't been any figure of speech. There was no way on earth he could tell her that Hilliard Nevins had laid down an ultimatum after that thing with that slut in the law library, that bitch on wheels. The dark eyes tightened just at the thought of her. Talk about probation. That was where he was really on probation. In perpetuity. Nevins had fixed everything up for him, sure enough —and it just might have been Jim's biggest mistake to let him. After Nevins had placed the affidavits and medical report into his office vault he had warned Ambose that if he ever got himself involved with another woman in the courthouse, he was out. Not only out of the DA's office but, if Nevins had anything to say about it, out of town. Not a word had ever been said about it again, not even when Nevins was doing everything except making a flat commitment to recommend Ambose as his successor when he decided to retire. Which, as they both knew, meant when he got his federal judgeship.

Having, through the accumulated accidents of this young day, found himself in this office with Caroline, he regretted that he had left her to a pig like Parks. Taking another look at her, he thought to himself, Why not? It had happened so long ago. It was probably a dead issue, more in his own mind by now than in Hilliard's. What could Nevins really do at this stage of the game, anyway? With all Ambose knew about him by now, what would he dare to do?

Which really meant, now that he had been forced to think about it, what would he, Jim Ambose, dare to do? Everything was going along so well. Exactly the way he had planned. He was, after all, a realist. Why rock the boat?

He became aware that Bunny was looking past him, out to the corridor. "As much as I hate to break up any rejection of this generous offer of my person," she said, "your woman in red. That must be her leaving now."

He patted her affectionately on the cheek. "Be a good girl, Bunny," he said, "and I'll take you to lunch."

Sam Tabor handed over the questionnaire without hesitation. "I sure hope she ain't in any trouble, Jim," he said. "She seemed like a very nice lady."

Unable to resist it, Ambose told him that he wasn't really at liberty to say. "All I am free to say at this moment is that an FBI agent and I have been tailing her since breakfast."

"Well, I'll be darned. You just can't tell these days, can you?"

Ambose hastened to assure him it was always possible that they were on a false trail. "You go ahead and make out your report to the sheriff," he said, "and I'll make out my report to the FBI."

The Bureau of Missing Persons (courthouse division) and the two agencies across the corridor were the last remnants of an ambitious and highly publicized Social Reorganization Convention, which had been convened during the regime of the late, unlamented Mayor George Curraine, known, derisively, to those who liked him as "George the Good," and, scornfully, to those who disliked him as "Georgie Dum-Dum."

Curraine's great—and perhaps only—virtue was that he was so well aware of his limitations that he gathered platoons of professors and social planners around him. Which was fine when the professors were economists and political scientists, but disastrous when they were psychologists and social reformers.

The great adventure of his administration had been the aforementioned convention called to remove from government control—which meant from police jurisdiction—all purely social and moral problems, such as drugs, gambling, prostitution, divorce and abortion, with prison reform and anything else that came to mind thrown in.

It had been most amusing for the professional politicians and other cynics to watch those innocents leading themselves to the slaughter. The drug traffic paid off everybody in government (with the possible exception of the governor himself). Gambling, almost everybody. Divorce proceedings provided a prime source of income for many of the leading figures in the Bar. Sex, in all its varieties and variations, belonged to the Church, which was not about to relinquish its claim on the devil to anyone, let alone to a band of overeducated troublemakers who did not even look upon the devil as evil.

Out of it all, in the end, the reformers had been left with the juvenile delinquents, the illiterates and the runaway husbands, since nobody had ever made, or could figure out any way of making, any money out of them.

As an adjunct to their study on divorce, Curraine's professors had discovered that 78 percent of all missing persons were husbands running away from wives. And since they deemed it both demeaning and humiliating for the deserted woman to have to go to the police station and tell a gruff cop that her husband had got sick of her, the office was moved to the courthouse (with the rest of the package) and placed under a trained and sympathetic social worker. (It had originally been named the Department of Domestic Affairs, and the enabling bill had been drawn up and was being rushed through the city council before the loud guffaws reached the ears of the professors. With no time for any more creative thinking, they had been forced to the ultimate humiliation of calling it what it really was.)

As happy as the police department was to be rid of the runaway husbands, the

14

fact remained that it was still a police matter in almost every other state, which meant that the circulars still had to be sent through regular police channels. The courthouse division was therefore placed under the jurisdiction of the sheriff's office. While Sam Tabor was a social worker by choice and by training, he was, by title, a sheriff's deputy, charged to their table of organization, budget and pension plan. He filed all his questionnaires with the sheriff's office, which whipped them right over to the police station.

So ended, in a comedy of confusion, the great professorial assault upon the divorce laws.

9:55 A.M.

Judge Harrison Davies poked his bushy head out of the door of the private little bathroom at the far side of his chambers. "It's about goddamn time, Jim," he bellowed. "How we gonna keep the wheels of justice turning if the forces for good within the community are always half an hour late. I hope you've got an excuse that will be acceptable to this Honorable Court."

"Well, what happened," Ambose said, "was that I kept going around to all the wrong courts. I didn't know you had this hearing, Harry. I thought you were up in the capital being impeached."

Davies was rubbing some kind of hair tonic into his hair, and there was a towel wrapped around his neck. He gave him an open-mouthed, eye-popping grin, shocked but appreciative. "Haw," he said. "They dang well gotta catch you before they can impeach you. I know all about that kind of thing from reading up on the Con-sti-tu-tion."

The judge's chambers were well filled. As Davies' secretary, Mrs. Coles, had told Jim (leave it to Davies to have a grandmotherly secretary with blue-gray hair), "Go on in and join the party. Regular clambake."

DeWitt Pawley had been standing just inside the door when Jim entered, his hand extended in his characteristic courtroom gesture. ". . . and I say to you, ladies and gentlemen of the jury, that David Boone Wilcke himself would be the first to defend every man's right to free assemblage and peaceful picketing." The clear, beautifully trained voice suddenly changed, tightening and twanging into his well-known imitation of Uncle Rabble, the character with whom Pawley entertained at all parties and not infrequently dropped, to the delight of the knowledgeable, into the middle of a hot and heavy courtroom exchange. "But I tell you, cousin, those crazy old ladies has got to go."

Behind him, on the judge's brown leather couch, the little redheaded kid from the DA's office, Mollineaux, was sitting very quietly, holding the Garrett–Kehoe file on his lap. Ambose liked to have the new kids look and listen, but this one was too damn polite, too unassertive.

Off to the side, just beyond the opening into the judge's law library, was the man Pawley had been gesturing toward. Tommy Mallon. Tommy was seated on the arm of the matching leather chair, his palms flat against the leather and his legs held out stiffly. He flashed Jim that boyish smile of his and continued to push himself up off the arm, as if he were a gymnast and it were a gym horse. Tommy had been short and thin when he first came into the DA's office eight years earlier; he had been short and square when he left four years later to open his own office.

15

And now, it seemed to Ambose, he had suddenly gone to fat. The double chin was no longer a promise or a shadow, it was there, a visible clump, testifying to success, the good life, a pervading softening of the fiber and the passage of time. "Goddamn," Ambose said, scowling at him, "I've come across nothing but fat slobs all day. Isn't anybody growing thin anymore?"

Mallon must have been counting the pushups, because he indicated with a quick shake of the head that he didn't want to be distracted. "We were just— ugh—talking about the reception the—aaaahhh—Chief Justice got in arriving in what is known, among my intellectual peers, as 'Our Town.' I, for one, was proud to see that our nuts are as nutty as anybody else's nuts." He was grunting every time he pushed himself up and sighing every time he settled back down. "There were certain parties, whom I am forbidden by Canon 27 from publicizing any further, who hold that they detected your fine hand behind the overenthusiastic reception. I assured them, out of my long friendship and high personal regard, that if you'd had anything to do with it the old bat would have aimed at a more exotic portion of his anatomy and would never have been taken alive." He lowered himself, finally, for the last time, let his shoulders collapse, flipped the edge of a finger across his forehead and, letting his tongue hang out, began to pant like a puppy dog.

"In case you don't understand all that high-flown technical language, cousins," Pawley said, "he means she'd have speared him right in the tes-*ti*cles."

A roar went around the room, because they all knew he was referring to one of the more famous Ambose stories, a story still passed on by local lawyers to visiting firemen. Ambose, in prosecuting a rape–murder, had led the medical examiner to testify to "the bruises and lacerations of the anus," and not satisfied that the bestiality of the act had been fully brought home, kept after him to explain exactly what those bruises and lacerations had indicated to him. The medical examiner, sweating profusely, had answered with such phrases as "it indicates to me that the anus had been forced" and "evidently a violent incursion had taken place." At last Ambose had turned to the jury box and, in the primmest and most delicate of tones, had said, "In case you don't understand all that high-flown medical language, ladies and gentlemen, the doctor means he rammed it up her asshole."

From the bathroom there came the sound of the toilet flushing. Judge Davies hollered out, "Chobodian was sitting, wasn't he, Jim? I always meant to ask you, did the Old Man ever say anything to you about it? Like hauling it over the coals?"

"Not until it was over," Jim said.

After it was over old Chobodian had summoned him into his chambers and glared at him over his glasses. "Mr. Ambose, you have once again caused me to reassess one of my basic beliefs regarding human behavior. For thirty years now I have been advancing the theory that profanity and vulgarity may be viewed as nothing more than the fool's cap of a gross mentality or a limited vocabulary. In your case, however—and you may rest assured that you have finally convinced me—vulgarity is quite clearly sufficient unto itself."

From the bathroom the disembodied voice called out, "Good for the Old Man. Did you have any answer for that, I'll just bet?"

"Sure did," said Ambose. "Quick as a wink I said, 'Yes, sir,' and executed the well-known military maneuver of getting my ass the hell out of there."

"Speaking of getting the hell out of here," Pawley said, "I can see that you are eaten up with curiosity as to why I am here in this select gathering. I have been instructed by the district attorney to inform you that he would like a word with you and, finding our Mr. Mollineaux pacing impatiently in your office, I took his hand in mine and conducted him hither." Without pausing, he continued, "In the event you can't see your way clear to humoring Mr. Nevins today, I can tell him I have already told you that he wants you at the Bar Association dinner this evening without fail. Also without rancor. We are to be seated along with a spanking catch of dignitaries at something called, curiously enough, the district attorney's table, and Mr. Nevins would wish you to be informed that he would definitely not appreciate any unauthorized indexing of either the IQ or the SQ —the latter connoting the Syphilis Quotient—of the esteemed Chief Justice."

Ambose heard him out with an obligatory scowl, although everyone knew that nothing pleased him more than to be looked upon as the bad boy, the irreconcilable, of the district attorney's office. "You can tell Hilliard I wouldn't miss the chance of hearing the Great White Father for anything. I've got it good that he's going to go all the way tonight and tip over the Sermon on the Mount. Because it was delivered to a nonintegrated group, see. Not a WASP on the whole damn hill."

"A very poorly drawn document from a legal point of view," Mallon offered sagely. "The man left himself no out at all. Took the sins of all mankind upon his head in return for a few spikes, a hatful of thorns and some long-distance bleeding. Where, gentlemen, is the consideration? Where, I ask you, is the *quid pro quo*?"

Jim Ambose was nodding vigorously. As easily as that the old communication had been set up between them. "No reciprocity," he agreed. "What I want to know is where were all those smart Jewish lawyers?"

"Good thing for Him," Mallon said, "that the prophet David has finally come along, after two thousand years, to get him off the schneid."

From the sofa young Mollineaux had cleared his voice a couple of times. "Aren't you forgetting," he offered tentatively, "that there was a five-day escape clause in there?"

Pawley came wheeling around, low to the ground, leveling a finger at him. "This boy is going to be one of the great ones! Sits there and waits for his opening and then . . ." He jabbed three times. "Boom, boom, boom."

DeWitt Pawley's lower lip had a natural pucker that gave him a sort of clown's look even in repose. You laughed at him, you took him as a clown at your peril. Although Pawley had come into the district attorney's office three years after Ambose, his rise had been so rapid that they were, to all intents and purposes, on the same level. Everybody had expected some kind of strain to develop between them, and everybody had been disappointed.

Ambose held Dee Pawley in high regard. For one thing, it tickled him that Pawley was, probably without being aware of it, everything that Hilliard Nevins would have so dearly loved to be. Dee Pawley was not only Ivy League, he looked, talked and quacked Ivy League. If it rained clothes from some Salvation Army in the sky, the clothes that fell upon Dee Pawley would appear to have been custom-made for him by a team of Savile Row tailors. There was about him the casual bearing of the natural aristocrat—confident and unassuming—that made it no problem at all for him to meet the surliest hood or the most influential citizen on their own terms and—as far as anyone could see—not only treat them as equals but consider them to be *his* equals.

17

But most important of all to their peaceful coexistence, the areas into which Pawley moved were never the areas that Ambose had staked out for himself. For while Pawley tried some cases, and was a good enough lawyer, his sphere of power lay in the administrative side of the office, in the pretrial negotiating and the appeals. The two areas of the law that bored Ambose almost to death.

Ambose was therefore able to look upon himself as the combat leader—it pleased him to view himself that way—with Pawley handling the lines of communications. Pawley, after varying degrees of consultation with Nevins, would decide whether to bring a case to trial or take a plea of guilty for a reduced sentence. Once the case had been filed for trial, it was Ambose who took over and assigned it to a particular judge's court (which meant to the assistant DA assigned regularly to that court) or, if it were a major case, to either himself or one of the senior assistant district attorneys. It was Ambose who, with varying degrees of participation from the lawyer handling the case, then assigned the investigator, screened the information coming in and decided what the trial lawyer had to know and what he didn't have to know.

Pawley and Ambose got on so well, then, because Ambose did not look upon Pawley as a competitor in the reach for day-to-day power and influence, but rather as a buffer between himself and all the damn time-consuming paper work. And, by the very nature of his duties, as a buffer between Ambose and Hilliard Nevins. For if there was no strain between Pawley and Ambose, there was a constant field of irritation flowing between Nevins and Ambose. Ambose preferred to stay out of Nevins' way as much as possible and the feeling was mutual. While Nevins was eager to pile up a winning record to cite to the electorate every fourth year, he did not necessarily want to know everything that Ambose was doing to enable him to compile that record.

Pawley was not only the buffer between them, he was also the bridge. The office needed a man who could speak Ambose's language as well as Nevins'; it was as simple as that. That was the real role a younger DeWitt Pawley had staked out for himself, and it was a role that had carried him far.

Of course, there was something else that was not that simple. While Ambose recognized that he would need Pawley, or someone like him, to help him run the shop when he became district attorney, he also recognized that Pawley—who had far more credits with the Bar Association—could very easily become a dangerous opponent when it came to getting the nomination. But Ambose was not wholly without friends, either, and time was on his side.

In his seven years of real power in the DA's office Ambose had sent scores of bright young lawyers out into private practice. For a Lowell lawyer to be told that his adversary in an upcoming trial was an old "Ambose boy" was tantamount to saying, "Watch out, this guy has been hand-trained and licensed to kill."

Even those who had not really been looked upon as Ambose boys during their apprenticeship in the DA's office would sometimes find themselves traveling under his colors after they had left, and since it was an identification that was both flattering and useful, it was not very difficult to convince themselves that they had been much closer to him than they really had. It was, for one thing, a great icebreaker to be able to tell the client over lunch about Ambose's cruder and racier tactics, since it not only permitted the client to feel he was getting inside information but also let him know that his attorney had once been with the DA's office. (If he wanted to draw the inference that his attorney had some kind of influence around the courthouse . . . well, what harm was there in that?) There was more to it than that, though. Although almost all of the young assistant DA's went into civil rather than criminal practice, most clients felt that criminal lawyers were the real trial lawyers and it reassured them no end to have a lawyer with such a solid background.

The Ambose boys, real and ersatz, were just beginning to make their voices heard in Bar Association politics. Hardly within hailing distance of making policy, to be sure, but a strong and growing cadre. Tommy Mallon alone was a man for any of the old Brahmins to contend with. As a realist, Ambose knew that he had made far too many enemies to have any chance of getting the Bar Association's support. By the time the issue arose, however, he felt that his boys would most certainly have enough muscle to prevent the Bar Association from vetoing his selection. And now that he had been assured of Hilliard Nevins' support, nothing short of a Bar Association veto could stop him.

Judge Davies, having washed, shaven and taken care of the call of nature, was now bursting with energy and—almost an hour after court was supposed to be convened—crackling with impatience. He was a vigorous man in his early fifties. The heavily peppered gray hair was so thick that it was almost impossible for it to hold a part without the liberal application of hair tonic. In his neat gray suit he looked like any successful businessman. Probably the head of the sales department. And yet, seated on the Bench, the black robe covering all but the gray hair, a remarkable transformation would take place. If you saw Harry Davies during a trial, leaning forward, intent to all purposes upon the proceedings, he would strike you as the very embodiment of wisdom and justice. You had to know Harry Davies to know that there was a far, far better chance that he was thinking of broads and booze.

But he was immensely popular with the voters, not surprising when you understood that he was one of the rare judges who mixed socially at a civic-club level and who belonged to almost every social or service club in the county. The voters were flattered that he treated them as equals. They would say about him that he was a regular guy, much as if they were talking about one of those priests who plays softball. And if, from time to time, word reached them that lawyers of the community found grievous fault with him, these citizens (most of whom thought of themselves, really, as his friend) were sure it was because the judge was too regular for those stuffed shirts, had too much common sense for those nit-picking, overeducated fools, was too much the champion of the common man.

Nobody, of course, pays very much attention to the names of the judges listed on the voting machine (once a judge was on the Bench, the political parties—by agreement with the Bar Association—nominated him jointly) but, in election after election, more levers were always pulled for Judge Harrison Davies than for any other candidate for the judiciary. There had been elections when he had received more votes than anybody running for any county office.

"If the district attorney's office has finished reading off its orders for the day," Harry Davies said, rubbing his hands together impatiently, "may we proceed to the courtroom and get on to the hearing. I know I don't have to add," he told Ambose, "that I'd just as soon be treated with the respect that my freshly pressed black robe, graying hair and distinguished public service deserve."

Mallon pushed himself up one last time, grinned his bright, puppy-dog grin and in a meek, piping little voice, he said, "Me, Jim. I'll take whatever I can get."

Peterson, Davies' bailiff, had materialized out of the woodwork to help the judge on with his robe. Peterson gave Ambose the creeps. You never saw him except when he was needed, and then he'd be there by the judge's side, leaving you with the feeling that he had been lurking outside the door listening to everything that was being said.

"If we can have a moment of silence," Davies said, "I will now invoke the Judges' Prayer." Cupping his hands in the attitude of prayer, he looked to the ceiling and implored, "May all my errors be irreversible ones."

To get to his courtroom Davies had only to walk through his secretary's office, directly alongside his own. He would stop there momentarily to grab a quick smoke while the lawyers were settling themselves in the courtroom, then step out through the door at the other side of the office. That door opened directly onto the courtroom behind a guard rail that extended all the way across to the far wall, closing off the Bench area from the well of the Bar. Up a couple of steps and Harry Davies was onto the ramp only a few strides from the Bench, from the seat of power, from the throne.

In those black robes, from that exalted perch, Harry Davies would look down, king of all he surveyed, and dispense justice. Good old Harry Davies, in a sudden paroxysm of good will, could look with understanding and compassion upon the frightened petty thief and, with a word and an admonishing smile, send him out of the courtroom free as a bird, making the sun to smile upon the scraggly, uncomfortably coiffured wife and bringing tears of happiness to the gray, weather-beaten mother. Or, if Harry Davies was of a mood; if the defendant was sullen, murky, shifty of eye; if he caught Harry Davies' eye the wrong way; if, to get right down to it, Harry Davies didn't like the way your hair was parted, mister, then Harry Davies could, yessiree, give you just about all the trouble you could handle for the next few years.

The three lawyers left his chambers by the front door and turned down the narrow corridor just outside the secretary's office. The door at the end of the corridor would open onto the area in front of the Bar railing, the area known among the members of the local Criminal Bar as "The Pit" or, to those purists who held to original derivations, "Jim Ambose's Snake Pit."

As they were about to open the door and step into court, Mallon slapped Jim heavily on the shoulder. "It was like old times in there, James. I was telling this young man before you came that he's getting an opportunity you couldn't buy for a million dollars."

Tommy Mallon had come to Jim Ambose as an unimposing kid, boyish and bubbly, but it had become apparent very quickly that this boy's brain was a superior instrument, washed by a richer blood. What Ambose had learned by trial and error, this boy knew by instinct. Once in court, the playfulness was replaced by a total concentration. The boyish charm, if it appeared at all, was a tactic controlled by a stop-start switch.

Tommy Mallon was one of the very few Ambose boys who had gone into criminal law. Having got their trial experience, most of them would go into corporation law or personal injury law or be scooped up by the insurance companies. It was true enough, of course, that the Criminal Bar was the least prestigious of the branches open to an experienced trial lawyer and, except in rare instances, the least remunerative. But that wasn't why Ambose's boys stayed away from it. Ambose's boys would tell you, almost to a man, that while life wasn't as interesting as it had been in the DA's office, "I couldn't look Jim Ambose in the eye if

I went into criminal law and did the things we all know that criminal lawyers have to do."

Tommy Mallon was different. When he left the DA's office, after only three years, there was not the slightest question but that he would go into criminal law. He was, as everyone said, the one criminal lawyer who could handle Jim Ambose. Knowing Ambose's game as well as he did, Mallon heard nothing, saw nothing, reacted to nothing. It was as if he had consigned Ambose to some cage beyond his purview.

Tommy was in everything. He was in real estate, politics, banking and god only knew what else. You could be sure that it would be lost in a maze of companies and corporations, and the usual labyrinth of trusts. If he died tomorrow, his affairs would never be straightened out. It always amused Ambose how these smart lawyers could be so brilliant in beating the income tax (why have all that specialized knowledge and all those great contacts if you don't put them to use?) that when they died their executors were never able to find all their assets. And that most of what they did find went directly to the Internal Revenue Bureau. The bureau, which was not exactly made up of blithering idiots either, had been sitting back patiently all those years, knowing full well that the time would come when it would be handing the estate the full tax bill, plus penalties.

Tommy had his share of the mob guys, too. But as Ambose had reason to know, he was too smart to permit himself to be put on a retainer. When they wanted him they had to come to his office and report to his secretary and sit on the client's side of his desk and ask him if he'd take the case. Each case separate. With the money up front.

When he took the ordinary man in trouble, he demanded access to his financial records, complete with income tax returns. His rule of thumb on a murder case was "everything you have," and it was amazing how often he got it.

And yet, personally, Tommy Mallon was little different from the bubbly kid who had first walked into Ambose's office. Not only with Ambose. With everybody. Either Tommy Mallon was two people or the private person, out of some perverseness, had refused to grow up along with the professional man. "It's just a game," Jim Ambose had told his prize pupil, and the prize pupil had taken him at his word. While the game was on, he played his role as fearless defender as well as anyone could play it. Once the game was over, you had the feeling that the gamesman, Tommy Mallon himself, had been spectacularly uninvolved. It troubled Ambose. For Ambose "just a game" was the only game worth playing. Offstage as well as on.

10:30 A.M.

There were two long tables inside the Bar railing: the defense table on the left, the prosecution table on the right. Normally, they would have been flush against each other. For this hearing, however, a lectern had been set up between them. Behind each of the tables were three stiff-backed wooden chairs that were reserved for the investigators, witnesses or—although it was theoretically frowned upon —friends.

Behind the prosecution table, to Jim's surprise, sat the two arresting officers, Anderson and Schmidt. There was no more reason for them to be there for this kind of hearing than for twelve good men and true to have been sitting in the jury box. Especially since they had to come from way out at the very edge of the county.

The defendants, Garrett and Kehoe, were just being led—in handcuffs—to the defense table by two of Bob Stringfellow's deputies, which would only mean that the incomparable Peterson had called down to the feeding cage even before he had slipped in to help Judge Davies on with his robe. Mallon greeted his clients at the table, smiling and gesturing, while the cuffs were being taken off. You could see their comparative status as thieves just by looking at them. Garrett, slim and neat, scrupulously dressed—perhaps even too well dressed (look at that tie; Christ, stickpin and all). A distinguished graying along the temples. Sharp, fox-like features; sharp, fox-like eyes. There stood the professional bank robber, the aristocrat of the criminal world. In his younger days Garrett had served a term for bank robbery. He was, at the moment, out on bail while another conviction was being appealed in Wisconsin, and he was also out on bail from Massachusetts while awaiting trial.

It was bad enough that they let these thieves run loose even after they were caught; now they were granting bail even after they were convicted. More than anything else, it griped Ambose that he would not be allowed to tell the jury, when the case came to trial, that Garrett had any record at all. For all the jurors would know, he could have been an amateur trying to pull his first job. What griped him most of all was that he knew, as every law enforcement official, every judge, every parole board knew, that professional bank robbers never stopped, never reformed, never retired. If Garrett went to jail this time, he'd come out with a brand-new custom-made suit and a couple of brand-new, custom-planned jobs.

The other guy was . . . well, the other guy. Period. A nonentity, a guy who held a gun, an interchangeable part. The tie, obviously uncomfortable—no part of his image of himself—was loose around his neck. Mallon, still talking to Garrett, tightened it, jiggled the knot so that it lay dead center and straightened the tie all the way down the jacket. There was an aside to Garrett, a wink to Kehoe, laughter all around, and Kehoe, crouching low like a boxer, feinted a blow toward him. Kehoe was on bail from the Massachusetts job, too, and since the report that had come to Ambose from the district attorney in Wisconsin showed there had been a third man on that job who hadn't been caught, Ambose could be reasonably certain that Kehoe had been in on that one, too.

In the old days Ambose would have been able to sit, spraddle-legged, across from Kehoe—a heavy-fisted detective from Burglary Division at his side—and talk to Mr. Kehoe the way these characters had to be talked to. He may have had to leave the room a few times but, in the end, he would have convinced Kehoe that he'd be doing himself a favor by turning state's evidence in return for consideration on the local charge and a promise to do what he could for him in Massachusetts. He'd have kept his promise on the local case. The promise on Massachusetts would have been offered only to help Kehoe save face, and it would have been accepted in the same spirit. Yes, Ambose thought, in the old days Arthur Kehoe would have made an excellent stool pigeon, in prison or out.

You couldn't talk to them now unless their lawyers were present. A Garrett would always have a top lawyer, and a top lawyer would immediately understand that a Kehoe, while a weakness under the old system, was a strength under the new one. If Kehoe took the stand it would not be for the state but for Earl Garrett. If somebody had to take the fall, these days, you could be sure it would be a hood like Kehoe, not a businessman like Garrett.

It didn't matter as far as Kehoe was concerned. One way or the other, he'd be in and out of prisons for the rest of his life. With luck he wouldn't kill anyone in between.

Earl Garrett was the man who interested Ambose, though. As one pro looking at another, he could see that Garrett was a top man in his field. And still—just in case Kehoe was still under any delusion that luck doesn't run out—Garrett had been caught three times over a period of three years, a losing streak that once upon a time could have put him out of business. He had been caught this time on an absolute freak, of course, and there had undoubtedly been bad breaks, unforeseeable circumstances in Wisconsin and Massachusetts, too. But that was just the point. There were always bad breaks and unforeseeable circumstances to put these monkeys in the hands of the police. The sticking point was that the courts, under the tutelage of the Supreme Court—the goddamn Idiot Court—was turning them out as fast as the police could bring them in. Ambose could state with reasonable certitude that in those same three years Garrett and his partners had pulled a minimum of half a dozen jobs on which they had not been caught. Those were the jobs that were paying the lawyers in three different states. As a professional criminal, Garrett would follow every change in the criminal law as closely as any corporation head would follow the changes in the income-tax laws. Garrett would know that the top criminal lawyers had an excellent chance of springing you, one way or another. He would know that, at an absolute minimum, they would be able to use all their influence and their charm and their leverage (which could be nothing more than one judge's admiration for a brilliant criminal lawyer or another judge's fear that the top criminal lawyer would somehow make a fool of him) to put the case in front of the judge who would allow bail and to build in a series of appeals that could be stretched out into eternity.

But for first-class representation like that, a businessman knew he had to pay. And how did a bank robber pay his bills except by going out, while he was out on bail, and robbing a few more banks? He would also know that you never mentioned such things to a young hot-shot like Tommy Mallon. Mallon would ask him how much money he had and Garrett would give him a very accurate figure. If it wasn't enough Mallon would simply tell him how much more he thought the case was worth. Garrett would nod, slowly and meditatively, and promise that he would do his best to raise it. If, by some chance, Garrett was caught again and, by some miracle, Mallon was hauled before the Ethics Committee, he could tell them, with a clear conscience, that his client had led him to believe that he was going to borrow the money from friends.

But that was just the lawyer taking the elementary precaution of protecting himself at all times. From time to time the leaders of the Bar Association—unable to ignore the persistent rumors—might feel the need to investigate a criminal lawyer's fees. But that would be nothing more than the leaders of the Bar Association taking the elementary precaution of protecting themselves at all times. The investigation would almost never reach the level of a formal hearing, and never, never go the whole route into disbarment proceedings. The Bar Association was, after all, the lawyers' trade union. It was there to help lawyers collect their fees, not to hinder them.

Mollineaux had placed the Garrett–Kehoe file on the prosecution table. Since he had, from time to time, sat behind Ambose or some other assistant DA to observe the trying of a case, he automatically took the third chair alongside the two cops.

Chief Anderson, it developed, had received notification of the hearing and had assumed, not unnaturally, that he was being summoned to appear. That griped Ambose, too, since it left Haven Township with no professional police protection at all. To make it even worse, Anderson and Schmidt had arrived at the courthouse at nine o'clock and had been sitting around for an hour and a half waiting for someone to make an appearance.

But then, the capture of the bank robbers had undoubtedly been the great event of their careers. It was possible that it would have taken a direct order to have kept them away. As long as they were here, they told Ambose, they might as well stay until the lunch break.

Seated just behind them, on the other side of the railing, were the reporters from the morning and afternoon papers, a small open space between them. Ambose was disappointed to see that they were both second-string men. Disappointed but not surprised. Chobodian was sentencing the Principe brothers at 11:00 (they had chopped up the older brother's unfaithful girl friend with a set of carving knives), and the regular-beat men would be covering that. Still, it did reinforce that uneasy feeling—the unfailing instinct—that everything was somehow going to go wrong. Second-string men meant minimum coverage, and he had been counting upon the newspaper coverage to give Davies pause. He nodded to the two reporters to encourage them to come over and ask whatever questions might be on their minds. They merely nodded back and went back to doodling in their notebooks.

Ambose, returning to the table, patted the chair alongside him and told Mollineaux, not unkindly, "Come on in, Red, and join the team."

They had scarcely sat down when Peterson stepped into the courtroom from the corridor door and called out, "All stand, please." Judge Davies strode in, releasing them all with a negligent wave of the hand, as if to indicate that he was the last man in the world to put anyone to even that temporary inconvenience.

Seating himself, pulling his robes around him, he glanced rather peevishly at the clock behind him, as if he were just becoming aware that they were starting so late. In point of fact, Davies had an enviable reputation among his peers for starting late, finishing early and calling as many recesses as humanly possible in between. It was doubtful whether any court in the county, save for Chobodian's, opened on time more than one day out of ten. Elijah Chobodian was the appointment judge for the whole county, and when he said 9:30 he meant 9:30 on the tick. He meant that if you weren't there and you had co-counsel he'd start without you, and if you had no co-counsel you would be fined ten dollars for every minute you were late. Ambose, staring glumly at Harrison Davies, would have gladly paid the full fine to have had Chobodian sitting on this one.

12:22 P.M.

Judge Davies announced that he was taking Mallon's three motions under advisement. He wanted all briefs submitted to him by the end of the following week, he said, so that he could ruminate over the following weekend and, hopefully, deliver his decision by the end of the month.

As they walked out of the courtroom Mallon said, "The Honorable H.T. will be ruminating over the weekend, all right, and I can tell you what roommate he's gonna be ruminating with."

Peterson was waiting just inside his chambers to help Judge Davies off with his robe. "Hot in here, Judge," he said. "Something went wrong with the air conditioning, I think. I called maintenance."

"Well done, O good and faithful servant," Davies said. "That ought to ensure a steady flow of fresh cool ocean air sometime around November. If you think it's hot in here, Pete, you should have been out there."

"Ambose?" Peterson asked, sympathetically.

"Gentleman Jim, the friend of the judges and all other oppressed minorities." As he was speaking he heard Mrs. Coles, on her way to lunch, exchange greetings with someone in the corridor, but it was not until he recognized that the reply had come from the strong deep voice of Gentleman Jim himself that he picked the hanging exchange out of the air. If Ambose was coming the long way around to the front door of the judge's chambers when he could have just as easily strolled back through the side door with him, it could mean only that the well-known stickler for protocol wanted to make it clear that he was paying a professional call, not a social one.

Davies did not welcome a professional call. He did not want to be sounded out about this hearing, and he most particularly did not want to be sounded out by Jim Ambose.

He went back to the bathroom and, leaving the door open, splashed cold water over his face. He studied himself in the little medicine-cabinet mirror. He pulled down at the dark puffy ring underneath one of his eyes and stared at himself, eyeball to eyeball. God, he thought with pleasure, he looked terrible. Too much jazzing for a man his age. *Jazzing,* he thought, *that dates me, doesn't it?* Got to tell Marie to leave him alone. Got to tell her he needed a rest. *How had Ambose put it out there? First aid and re-sus-ci-tation.* A little giggle arose in his throat, startling him. "God, I'm beat," he called out quickly. "I don't know why. You sure did your best to keep me awake in there."

He grabbed a towel and came back out, wiping his face vigorously. "I didn't appreciate a lot of that, Jim. Goddamnit, one of these days I *am* going to send you to jail."

Ambose had settled comfortably onto the sofa. "I'll tell you, Harry, the way things are these days I could use the rest."

On the wall, just above Ambose, was the painting Marie had given him. An impressionistic painting: a splashing of color, mostly red. The more he looked at it, the more he liked it. Just like Marie had said, you've got to live with it awhile. He felt the picture gave his office class, especially when contrasted with all the obligatory diplomas, in the obligatory skinny black frames all along the other walls.

Especially, he thought now, in contrast to that hatchet man seated underneath it. Beauty and the Beast.

The judge didn't mind so much that Ambose frightened him. A lot of people frightened him. In the dark of night he knew damn well that the job frightened him. Especially these days when you had all these smart-ass young defense lawyers who were so much more interested in tipping you over upstairs than in winning their cases in front of the jury. What bothered him was that Ambose frightened him, night or day, awake or asleep. What bothered him was that he couldn't keep from showing Ambose that he was afraid of him. Well, just the look of the man with those little black eyes was enough to frighten a man of normal sensibilities. (Although Ambose's eyes were really of normal size, Davies never thought of them as anything except "little.") In the whole wide world who else had black eyes? And it wasn't only the eyes. There was a bony, grating look about him, all flint and sharp angles; a tall, lean man with big, swinging shoulders. There were the bony ridges up over his eyes that gave him the look of a fighter who had built up just about all the scar tissue he could use. And the high cheekbones. For as long as Davies could remember there had been some kind of talk that Ambose had Indian blood in him that he didn't want anyone to know about, which was ridiculous on the face of it since Ambose decorated his office walls with arrowheads. The truth of the matter, if you wanted to know what Harry Davies thought, was that Ambose *wanted* people to think he had Indian blood in him so they'd be afraid he would, for chrissake, scalp them if they didn't play ball with him.

Davies was a politician. If he knew nothing else, he knew, in his own little way, what the uses of power were. Ambose's power was that he had enough on everyone in the courthouse (or so everybody thought) that he could (and you knew *he would*) scalp you any time it suited his purpose. Judge Davies, who knew his own limitations as well as most men, flattered himself that he had got where he was because he didn't kid himself more often than was absolutely necessary to keep himself both ambulatory and sane. He feared Jim Ambose most of all, when it came right down to it, because he (like everybody else) didn't really know what Ambose might have on him, and he therefore assumed that what he did have on him was the worst damn thing he had ever done in his life—and who hadn't done enough in the past month alone to get themselves disbarred, thrown into jail and divorced?

Half of Hilliard Nevins' own power these days came out of the fact that everybody knew that Hilliard was the only man who had this crazy man under control. And if there was one thing Harrison Davies had no doubt about where Jim Ambose was concerned it was that he was crazy.

Like that performance in court today. A brilliant lawyer when he stuck to business, even Davies could appreciate that. They said he came into court on this kind of thing absolutely cold and just winged it, but Davies didn't believe that for a minute. That was just more of Ambose's propaganda. *Preparation* was the one thing all good lawyers had in common, everyone knew that.

But as brilliant as Ambose had been, he had squandered half the day making pointless attacks on Tommy Mallon, who was his greatest booster, and the Chief Justice and the Supreme Court itself, all of which would look great on the transcript if this ever went upstairs. What was the sense of it, except to see how far he could push Judge Davies, who could tell him he was out of order, who could tell him to get on with it—except that the more he told him, the more apparent it would become that Ambose was running right over him. That was going to look great in the transcript, too.

God, that had been a mess in there today. Another fiasco. He blushed for himself at the memory of it, even though—and the pride of that accomplishment wiped everything else away—he had protected himself against them all this time. Against the appeals courts, against Jim Ambose, against everybody.

Seated behind his desk, the judge, in a thoughtless, aimless movement of his hands, turned the picture frame of his wife and two children toward himself. You keep the picture of them as children, he thought, because they were more manage-able then and (looking at the pictures now with real affection) they left you with the illusion that life was still manageable, too. You kept the picture of them as children, he thought, shifting his attention to Eleanor, because it gave you the excuse for keeping the picture of your wife when she was younger, too, and visitors, in glancing down, could be tricked into observing what a young and pretty wife the judge had.

Oh hell, he thought, I keep those pictures on my desk because I put them there ten years ago when I took over this office and it's just too much of an effort to change them.

"Is this a social visit," he said, with his usual heartiness, "or is it going to end with me telling you to go to hell?"

"I thought it would be a good idea if we talked a little about this Garrett hearing," Ambose said as, damnit, Davies knew he was going to. Well, if he thought—

The phone rang and Davies, forgetting that Mrs. Coles was out to lunch, let it ring a few times while Ambose sat there waiting for him to pick it up. When he reached for it, finally, he knocked over the picture frame which, in turn, knocked the pen right out of the black onyx pen-and-pencil set on the other side of the phone.

Why did he let Ambose upset him like this? Why did he fall apart whenever he found himself alone with him? What did he expect Ambose to do, hit him? He was the judge here, by god. He, Harrison T. Davies, held all the cards in this case, as Jim Ambose, sitting there so cool and cocky, would soon enough find out.

Shaking himself out of what had been for him a long and unaccustomed bout of introspection, he became aware that it was Marie on the other end of the line, and that she had been telling him about an attack one of the Principe brothers had made on Judge Chobodian. What really jarred his mind loose was the news that Bob Stringfellow had made the judge cancel his calendar for the afternoon and sent him home, spluttering, under the protection of a couple of armed deputies.

The message she was really passing on, he knew well enough, was that if Chobodian was through for the day, so was she. The question she was putting to him was whether he could manage to shake himself free.

He placed his hand over the speaker. "It's Marie," he said. "Big excitement over at Chobodian's court." What the hell, everybody knew that he and Marie were shacking up these days, and Jim Ambose had probably known it before anybody else. The ugly bastard had probably known it before he slid the bolt behind them at the motel that first time.

"I'll tell you what, Marie," he said. "I'm in conference with Jimmy Ambose now. *(Jimmy? When had he ever called him Jimmy? What the hell was he trying to do, prove that he was his great and good buddy?)* I'll call you back later. But I think we can get that writ out for you."

Had he seen a curl on Ambose's lips when he said that about the writ? Was Ambose really tapping everybody's phone or was that just more of his propa-ganda?

"How do you like that!" Davies said, hanging up. "Those Principe brothers who were up for sentencing today. Chobodian gave the older brother the chair and he took it, Marie says, without batting an eye. Then he gives the younger brother the chair and the older one came after him. Christ, if they start going after

27

judges I'm going to find another line of work. Why can't these murderers just go to the chair like good boys?"

"Did he get to him? To Old Elijah?" It seemed to Davies that the little black eyes were glowing.

Now that the question had been put to him, it wasn't easy to admit that he hadn't been following Marie's story that carefully. Frowning in an effort of concentration, he said, "He probably would have if he hadn't bumped into her desk, she said. And then I think she said she bumped him over the head with her stenotype machine. And by that time that bailiff Moore—he used to be a special cop, didn't he?—was there. And someone else. I think, as a matter of fact, she said it was Pawley. Yes, Dee Pawley. Your Pawley. Jumped on him and bloodied him up some, Pawley did.

"But," he said more confidently, offering it almost as proof that he was not a total idiot, "she did say that this Patrice was screaming that Chobodian would be dead and in his grave before either of them, he or his brother both, were ever strapped in the chair."

Ambose gave a snort. "Hell, he could get a policy on that from Metropolitan Life." How old was Eli? Must be up in his 60s. Poor Dee. Ten years' worth of appeals coming up and all the crap that went with it. "But"—he grinned—"like Hilliard tells the voters every four years, that's what we get paid for."

He slapped his leg, in sheer delight. No wonder Pawley had gone after the guy. "He was probably trying to asphyxiate him right there. I'll just have to stop off and com-mis-er-ate with old Dee and hear him tell his wondrous tale of how he almost saved the state a lot of time and trouble."

But first, he said baldly, he wanted to find out something about this Garrett case. The thing about it, he said, was that he wanted to put this kid Mollineaux to work doing some preliminary study and research on it so that he could find out, once and for all, whether the kid had anything on the ball. And while he did not expect the judge to tell him what he had decided, or even if he had come to any firm conclusions one way or the other, he knew the judge wouldn't want the district attorney's office to waste the taxpayers' money if it couldn't be reasonably certain that there would *be* a trial. "So if you'll just tell me whether you'd advise me to start Mollineaux working, Judge, me and the taxpayers would be much obliged."

Although Harry Davies would have sworn that there was nothing Ambose could do at this stage of the game to surprise him, he was overtaken by the sheer gall of the man busting in there and trying to get him to commit himself. *You'll find out soon enough, you black-eyed bastard.*

"Well, I've taken it under advisement, Mr. District Attorney," he said coldly. "That means I'm going to examine the briefs, and do some research on my own on the indicated precedents as submitted by distinguished counsel on both sides."

"Aw, hell, Harry, come off that crap."

"Mr. Ambose. You understand this conversation is highly irregular and per-haps even unethical out of the presence of opposing counsel?"

"Yeah," Ambose said, "I realize that."

Davies started to rise. To his astonishment he was trembling. Visibly trembling. The word that kept buzzing around in his head was "affront." He had been coldly and deliberately affronted. Visibly affronted, he thought. He saw it as if it had been written in the Book of his Life. "His Honor arose, visibly affronted."

"Sit down, Harry," Ambose said. "I'm just trying to do you a favor. If you let these two bank robbers walk out of that courtroom, I'm going to put up a stink and Hilliard is going to put up a stink." And so would Bert Chester. In the same cool and measured tones he told Davies how Bert Chester had called to volunteer the information that if anything went wrong he'd be wanting to join in on any statement they chose to make. No matter how strong. "I don't want you to take my word for that, Harry. If I were you I'd call Bert and ask him myself."

He's bluffing, Davies thought. He felt a tremendous surge of relief. Of power. Ambose knew he couldn't call the U.S. Attorney about something like that. And if he was bluffing on Chester, he didn't have Hilliard either. If Ambose went after him, he'd have to go after him alone. And what would he have? He'd have nothing.

Ambose was taking out one of those little cigars he thought made him look tough. "Yes, Judge, I'd take a lot of time to think about this one if I were you. For your own good."

"I appreciate that, Jim. Sure do." He was in complete control of himself now. "And normally, you'd be right. But in this case the issues are so clear and the opposing attorneys have given me such a clear choice that it does seem to me that unless the briefs come up with something startling, my course of action is clearly indicated."

The hard eyes now. The hard voice. "Don't mess with me, Harry," the hard voice said. "You throw this one out," Ambose told him, "it's because you're so frightened about being reversed again the water's running down your leg. Well, I'm not taking any fall for any half-assed judges. You quash this indictment and I start screaming and Hilliard starts screaming, too. If a stand has got to be made, then this is as good a one as any we could hope to find."

"Why, Mr. Ambose," the judge said, "who said anything about throwing the case out? Who said anything about quashing any indictment?" The tone was just right. The reasonable man, fully in command, lecturing a slow student. "Who said anything about sending two criminals out to walk the streets? I would never dream of doing such a thing, Mr. Ambose. *You* may chose to do it, but I won't."

Ambose's bewilderment, his discomfort, was beautiful for Davies to behold. He couldn't have planned this better. What the hell, Ambose had to find out sooner or later; it was just as well to get it over with right now.

Ambose, saying nothing, was glaring at him with pure hatred, such pure hatred that Davies felt—as ridiculous as he knew it to be—in fear of his life. The man is crazy, he thought. He's a killer. We have to get Nevins to get rid of him. The Bar Association should do something . . .

"And how do you think you're going to throw out the evidence without throwing out the indictment? We can't very well put the policemen on to say they found the guns and the money if we don't have any guns or money to put into evidence."

"Of course you can, Mr. Ambose. You can do anything you want, that's *your* business. What the trial judge then chooses to do is *his* business." Should he spell it out for him a little more? *Why not?* "All I've been presented with are the grand jury proceedings. And since hearsay testimony is perfectly valid in the grand jury proceedings, the indictments are perfectly valid as far as I can see. It would never enter my mind to quash them."

Whatever reaction he had expected from Ambose was not the reaction he got. He saw that sly smile come over him again, and it made him wonder whether it hadn't been a mistake to tell him. *You always did have a big mouth, Harry.* But what harm could it do, unless—unless Ambose was bugged! He stared hard at the lapels of his jacket to see whether there might be a bulge there. He couldn't make out anything, but how could you tell? Everybody knew they were making those things so small these days that they could put them anywhere.

Well, just what had he said? He hadn't said that much. If there had been anything unethical it had been Ambose's bringing it up in the first place. He had only been trying to save the taxpayers some money, like Ambose himself had said. He was all right. *You've got a big mouth, Harry, but this time you're safe.*

"Well, Harry," Ambose said, "I got to congratulate you on figuring out the perfect fix."

Oh no you don't. Very quickly, in a loud and emphatic voice, Davies said, "Just so there will be no misunderstanding about this, my decision is being made on the facts of this case as I see them, presently see them, and is subject to change upon the reading of your brief. No final decision has as yet been made."

Ambose was patting one of the lapels. *The one on the left. His right, my left. I'll get him for that. He'll be disbarred for that.* Whoever heard of such a thing, a lawyer coming into a judge's chambers—an assistant district attorney at that, an employee of the government—wearing a bug, recording everything that was being said. Ambose was rising from the sofa, watching him closely, the little smile playing on his lips. His hands were clutching both of his lapels, he was pulling them both out, showing—

Jim Ambose stood up, pulled both lapels out and said, "Boo."

12:50 P.M.

As soon as Ambose cleared the door, Judge Davies returned the call to Marie Pappas. It just so happened, he was able to tell her, that he had put in such a strenuous morning wrapping up a very complicated hearing that he had been thinking of canceling the afternoon calendar himself.

"The writ lies?" she asked in that exciting, throaty voice she used when she knew they were on for the day.

"The writ lies," he said.

"Sweet man," she purred.

The judge sat back leisurely to give Marie a chance to get to the apartment and out of her dress. He smiled in sweet contemplation. Marie had a fifty-thousand-dollar home out in the deep suburbs where she lived with her mother, but she had also rented a rather expensive apartment closer downtown so that she could entertain Judge Davies. Goddamn, he had always known that court reporters made a lot of money but he had never dreamed how much they could make if they were really ambitious and could turn out the work like Marie.

The affair with Marie had lasted for almost a year now, which may very well have established a new record for a courthouse romance. The turnover, he thought to himself, is usually much quicker. Picking up the unintended double entendre, he had to chuckle. He'd pull that one on Marie. She liked that kind of talk, and she was, he had to admit, far better at it than he was.

The judge knew well enough that Marie had her hopes that his wife would give up and divorce him, which was hardly unreasonable since he was constantly assuring her that it was only his wife's stubbornness that kept him from marrying her. And, giving Marie her due, he had to admit that she was working like a little beaver.

Although the judge hadn't been without a courthouse lay very often during his ten years on the Criminal Court Bench, he had never come across anyone who knew how to dress it up like Marie. It tickled him to have her set it up like this just before the Bar Association dinner. It tickled him just to sit there and contemplate how he would arise from her bed and go home, as cool as you pleased, to pick up Eleanor and walk with her—the judge and his lady—to the dais to sit with the Chief Justice of the United States. Marie had a sense of the fitness of things.

She also had a sense of the dramatic. She would be waiting there when he walked into the apartment, with nothing on but a kimono or a shorty nightgown or what she called "my whore's nightgown" which he had sent her, as a joke, from New Orleans. Or maybe nothing at all. He had a hunch, by the way she had said she had to get out of her bloody dress, that she would be wearing nothing at all. She'd call him "sweet man" in that low, throaty voice, and she'd have some new delicacy to feed him when they were through.

God*damn*, Harry Davies, you're a gay dawg, he thought. He hugged himself as if he were under a cold shower and went *Brrrrr*. And he realized then that the air-conditioner had miraculously come back on.

12:53 P.M.

DeWitt Pawley, having had three stitches put in his forehead and a tetanus shot put into his arm, was lying on the sofa along the side wall of the district attorney's office, his head resting in the lap of Mrs. Corinne Zeigler, the curator of the law library. Hilliard Nevins was seated on the edge of his big, somewhat cluttered desk in the middle of his big, sunny office, one foot on the floor, the other on a chair. Between Nevins and the sofa were two other young ladies who had come up to look upon the wounded assistant DA. One of them was the secretary from the Mental Health Department and the other a clerk in Judge Rodgers' office. All eyes were turned toward Lenore Darringer, Nevins' secretary, who had just picked up the telephone. She put her hand over the speaker and whispered, "Ianello."

Nevins shook his head emphatically. "District Attorney Nevins is in conference," she said, in her professional secretary's voice. "Is there a number where you can be reached?"

"I hope everyone here realizes," Pawley said, "that a lesser man than I would now be lying in a hospital bed, moaning piteously."

Fingering the gauze bandage which was sitting rather rakishly upon the right side of his forehead, he let out a passingly piteous moan. "That was just an audition," he said, clearly dissatisfied. "If it weren't for this cut on my head I'd be able to do much better."

Mrs. Zeigler, a dark-haired, strikingly beautiful young woman, stroked his hair and cooed, "Poor sick man. Poor stricken hero."

From the outer office someone could be heard shouting, "Where is everybody around here?" Immediately, Bob Stringfellow's head popped through the door.

"I was wondering where everyone was," he said. "The place is like a morgue out there."

"You may talk about your inept choosers of words," Pawley said, "but I'll put Bob Stringfellow against anybody."

"Now, now," Mrs. Zeigler crooned, "don't you think you're overdoing it just a little."

The sheriff was a thin, dour-looking man, whom nobody could remember ever having seen without his brown felt hat. Although Stringfellow had been in office for just about as long as anyone could remember—predating any other elected official— he was a rather colorless figure, neither notably efficient nor notably inefficient. To anyone connected, however peripherally, with the law, he had become accepted as part of the civic landscape. To the voters, he was a name they saw occasionally in the papers, if, in fact, they noticed it at all. For although his name was on the voting machine in the county elections, generally unopposed, it would be fair to say that an independent poll would probably show that a remarkable number of the citizens of Brederton County would not have been able to tell you who their sheriff was or even be able to state, with any degree of certainty, whether the sheriff was an elected official.

Stringfellow was there to inform Pawley that he had already dispatched a squad car to park across from his house and that, like it or not, Pawley was also going to have a deputy sent home with him, and no lip about it. Upon being informed, in turn, that Pawley had got hit by Marie's stenotype machine, on the ricochet, before he'd as much as laid a hand on Principe, the sheriff seemed utterly bewildered. "Why doesn't anybody ever tell me anything?" he wanted to know. "What am I supposed to be around here, the guy nobody ever tells anything to!" All at once he became furious. Striding past Nevins, he picked the morning newspaper up from the desk and slammed it back down so that the picture of the Chief Justice being picketed was staring up at them. "Great bunch of lawyers we got in this town. They knew he was coming in for a month and nobody thought to ask for protection. A ladies' bingo club invites a television actor to an afternoon tea and they're calling me like every hour to find out why can't they have a parade down Main Street. Now, Hilliard, I call that criminal negligence on the part of the whole Bar Association."

"I guess they thought you'd read about it in the paper."

"Sure, I read about it in the paper. Don't you think I read the paper? *Today* is what it said, right? It said he was addressing the annual dinner of the Bar Association today. Where did anybody read anywhere that David Boone Wilcke would be arriving in the city last night? What am I supposed to do, call up Harry Brandt and say, 'Hey, Harry, do you want any protection today?' "

Nevins, seeing how agitated he was, assured him that nobody could expect him to do that.

"I thought, anyway, when nobody bothered to ask *me* for protection that the Secret Service or the FBI was going to meet him. Or, for all I knew, what about the police department? Who the hell has jurisdiction over the protection of the Chief Justice, anyway? Constitutionally, I mean."

This was one question, it seemed, that Stringfellow did want an answer to, and it occurred to Nevins that since he was the district attorney it was not unreasonable that Stringfellow might expect him to know. Not having the slightest idea, he kept quiet.

"Yeah," Pawley said, "and what does he think he's doing, traveling around free as you please, anyway."

"It's not funny," the sheriff said. He dented the newspaper with his finger. "That could have been a real incident except that the pickets were kind of peaceful. It wasn't anywhere near as bad as that picture looks."

Nevins restrained himself from asking how, since he hadn't been there, Stringfellow could possibly know that.

"The Chief Justice," said Pawley, "bows to no man in his espousal of the right to assemble peacefully for the purpose of petitioning for the redress of just grievances. I'm sure he viewed it as an inspiring tableau of democracy in action."

"Dee," Nevins said, "you can be a pain. Shut up."

The women, who had been looking uncomfortable anyway, now looked as if they would have given anything for an excuse to get out of there.

"Well, as it just so happens, the press of the nation doesn't agree with the Chief Justice." Folding his arms, Stringfellow leaned back defiantly to let the full impact of *that* sink in. "The press of the nation," he repeated. "That's right." The sheriff could tell them—and certainly would—that he had been getting phone calls all day from editors wanting to know exactly what had happened and why the Chief Justice had been attacked. He stabbed at the picture again. "This kind of thing doesn't do this city any good, and don't you think otherwise."

"Bob," Nevins said quietly, "don't you think you're just maybe making a little too much of this?" Something had happened, a minor incident, and his men had moved in quickly and established order. "They did what they were expected to do. All anybody *could* expect them to do. It seems to me that they acquitted themselves in the best tradition, and all that."

"You bet your sweet life they did! Those men are going to get a commendation in their jackets, I'm going to see to that personally. But all we get from the Fourth Estate is abuse about how we're laying down on the job."

It would be useless, Nevins could see, to tell him that nobody had abused his office in the newspapers or anywhere else. From Stringfellow's belligerence, he could only suppose that the sheriff had been taking a ribbing all day, first about the Chief Justice and now about the attack on Chobodian. Stringfellow himself may well have recognized that he was working himself up over nothing because without any warning his voice became strained and defensive. "You see? You still don't see what I'm talking about, do you? What I'm talking about is that nobody tells me anything. I had to come in here just now to find out—just by accident —that it was Marie Pappas who banged this Principe all up. Not Dave Moore. Not Pawley here. Marie."

There was a momentary silence as everybody wondered why in the world that was so important to him. "How would it look if on top of this . . . this incident with the Chief Justice, Dominic Principe's friends got ahold of Marie Pappas— *a woman*—while we were protecting everybody else? . . . Well," he said, glowering around the room. "It's possible."

Pawley rolled his eyes to the ceiling. "The press of the nation," he murmured, "would not take kindly to that at all."

1:04 P.M.

Jim Ambose avoided the courthouse cafeteria and went across to Dorri's, a small restaurant tucked behind the courthouse in a street so narrow that it was known around courthouse circles as "The Alley." The courthouse employees ate, for the most part, in the cafeteria in the basement. There was a sort of common understanding that the lawyers who were trying a case on any given day had preemptive rights at Dorri's.

The place was just beginning to clear out a little, and Jim very quickly sighted Tommy Mallon waving at him from a table down toward the rear. With him at the table were a couple of other lawyers, plus Caroline Beyner and Sam Tabor.

Caroline made a face at him. "That's the last time I trust an assistant district attorney," she said. "I thought you were going to buy me lunch."

"Fortunately," Mallon said, leering, "she fell into the hands of kind strangers."

The lawyer sitting alongside Mallon was a new kid from his office who had been working for the Attorney General in Washington. The other lawyer was Bo Gunderson, a heavyset man with a blond, almost white, bristling crewcut and skin that was so light and delicate that Ambose used to tell him that if he would just try a little harder he could become an albino easy.

Bo had been in the DA's office the same time as Mallon. He had left early for private practice, and while his practice was mostly in civil law, specializing in divorce, he took an occasional minor criminal case for fun whenever the spirit happened to move him. There was, speaking conservatively, nothing in the world Bo wouldn't do for fun.

They had all pretty well finished their meals and the table was a clutter of dishes, beer bottles and coffee. To make room for Ambose, Tabor scurried over to the next table, turning aside the suggestions, made purely for the sake of politeness, that they could easily squeeze in another chair. Another chair would have cramped them very badly, and Tabor—who had apparently come to Dorri's with Caroline—was known only vaguely to the others.

Gunderson, it became apparent, had been giving them an eyewitness report on the now famous battle that had bloodied DeWitt Pawley. Which figured. If there had been a shoot-out in a back alley at two o'clock in the morning, Bo would be telling about it at breakfast in undoubtedly colorful terms, and you would find out by lunch that he had, in fact, just happened to be cutting through the alley, that the bullets had, in fact, whizzed by him on both sides, nicking him on both earlobes, and that the whole unlikely tale he had told, making reasonable allowances for Bo's talent for embroidery, had been reasonably accurate.

Making reasonable allowances for Bo's talent for embroidery, he had been defending an itinerant stickup man who had won him over to his cause by having the colossal nerve to try to hold up a grocery store with a homemade gun and the even more colossal nerve to be named Duane. "Having taken the arresting officer severely to task for the casual mayhem he visited upon my bumbling but essentially good-hearted client," he said, in summation, "I begged the Court to permit me to cop a plea, made a genteel plea for mercy and, having polished off an honest day's work, thought it only fitting to reward myself by watching Chobodian sentence a couple of Ianello's clients to fry. I haven't seen Chobodian sentence anybody to fry for the good of all mankind for . . . oh, it must be a full fortnight by now, and here I had the opportunity of watching him dispose of two immortal souls in, as it were, a single breath." And then, of course, all hell had broken loose.

It didn't matter what Bo said, you knew that Tommy Mallon would laugh. From the next table, Sam Tabor was leaning in, chuckling appreciatively; happy enough, it could be seen, at being allowed to participate—and to be seen participating—in the conspicuous revelry. Ambose alone remained absolutely unamused. But, of course, he still had the Garrett case on his mind. "Don't stop laughing on my account, Tommy," he said. Grimly, he turned both thumbs downward. "That's my case on Garrett. The whole thing, damn near."

Any suspicions he might have had about Mallon were wiped away by the unmistakable shock of surprise, followed by a quick, suspicious shift of the eyes between Ambose and Gunderson to make sure it wasn't some kind of a gag they had cooked up between them.

"You're sure?" Tommy said. "How sure?"

"How sure do you want? You're not going to be able to trundle them over to the dais tonight to thank Wilcke for all he's done for them, if that's what you mean. But they'll be out in plenty of time to send him a Christmas card."

"Garrett?" Bo said. "Is that the bank robbery? The First National Bank? The guys they caught with the meat in their mouth over in Haven?" Ambose let his head fall heavily after each of the questions and Gunderson winced for him. "Oooooh," he said, holding his side. "That smarts. If I were you I wouldn't worry whether Tommy can bring his boys over there tonight. I'd see if I couldn't get Bob Stringfellow to give me the loan of the brothers Principe and their full service of carving knives for the evening."

Ambose lifted his eyes to him. Dumb as them dagos were, he said sourly, how was he supposed to work a deal for them to carve Wilcke up for him when they'd also be carving up their best hope for getting away with it. As the cold fury that had been building in him from the time Davies let him know what he was going to do broke through, he brought his fist down on the table so hard that every hand jumped out to steady the bottle or glass closest to it. "How it *griiiiinds* me," he rumbled through clenched teeth. How it grinded him that he had to go over there tonight and hear them tell that protector of thieves and pornographers what a great man he was. A taut, bony look had come over him, purposeful and deeply felt. "The greatest country in the world we had here before that miserable sonofa-bitch opened up the floodgates and let the shit come pouring through."

Bunny colored noticeably. The others shifted awkwardly and kind of averted their eyes. Everybody except Bo Gunderson, who was scrutinizing him with something that went beyond mere amusement. "If you can't swing the loan of brother Dominic and a carving knife," he said evenly, "maybe you can talk him out of a rusty penknife and a book of instructions." Their eyes locked, and in that long, long moment before they released each other, a soundless communication rode between them. "It's like my daddy used to say," Jim Ambose said, and if his eyes were thin and cold the man himself was cloaked in a serene, elusive menace. "If a job is worth the doing, you'd just better do it yourself and see that it gets done right."

2:30 P.M.

Booker Phillips, the chief deputy, used the public phone on the pressroom wall, just inside the alcove as you entered from the third-floor corridor of the Hilton Hotel, to call his boss, Bob Stringfellow. Phillips and his squad of six picked men had been assigned to report to the Chief Justice in the Presidential Suite and remain with him, as his bodyguards, until they saw him safely onto the plane.

Upon his arrival Booker had discovered that the Secret Service, FBI and city police had all assigned men to the hotel, too, creating such a royal screw-up that the Secret Service, taking charge, had ordered everybody out on the grounds that all those bodyguards hanging around would only make it easier for an outsider to slip in unnoticed.

To add to the confusion, the young publicity man at the hotel had sent word to the newspapers that the Chief Justice would be holding a press conference at 2:00, presumably to issue a statement on the incident at the airport, and the word had just come down that the Chief Justice, having awakened from a nap, had given notice that he would be staying in his room until he left the hotel at 3:30 to pay his respects to his old friend Mayor Karney. The word that had trickled down, off the record, from the Secret Service agent in charge was that Wilcke had informed him that he had called no damn press conference, never gave press conferences, never gave interviews to anybody on or off the record, and that it would, as any fool should know, be unethical, unpolitic and damn stupid for a Chief Justice to give interviews, and what the hell were they making so much out of nothing for anyway, he hadn't known anything had happened at the airport until he had been asked about it afterwards.

"This is a madhouse here now," Booker was telling Stringfellow. "There's nothing but cops and newspaper people, media people, stepping all over each other. They've even got TV trucks from all the stations parked outside. TV trucks. From what they tell me, they were supposed to put it on national television. The press conference. But what I called for, what I wanted to ask you, Sheriff, is do you want me to take all of the six men over to City Hall? I remember you were saying how you were stretched so thin on manpower and, I might as well tell you, I don't know how effective we're going to be. The Secret Service is going to let me ride in the first car behind the Chief Justice, but they said to keep the rest of our men the hell out of the way."

"Oh, they did, did they?" Sheriff Stringfellow paused, for the briefest of moments, for breath, and when his voice came through again with Booker's new instructions it was choked with the accumulated resentments of the past twenty-four hours.

3:50 *P.M.*

Judge Harrison Davies, well glutted for the afternoon, was lying on the thick, baby-soft, white-carpeted living-room floor, his knees drawn up, rubbing his bare belly. Marie was lying face down beside him, in a flimsy light blue chiffon nightgown, chin in hand, studying him. From time to time, she would take a cherry from the tray behind her, her eyes never leaving him, split it neatly between her teeth, and with her open mouth against his open mouth insert it slowly with her tongue.

"Debauchery," said the judge. "What this country needs is a little more of that medieval excess they keep telling me about."

Withdrawing her tongue, she said lazily, "Ready to file another writ, Judge."

"At my time of life, it takes at least two days just to draw a new writ up. And even that's when I'm bragging."

"Oh, oh, are you trying to warn me that you are not going to honor your contract with me for Wednesday. Your solemn promise. Certain commitments have been made. I'll sue you for nonperformance."

One of the advantages of shacking up with a woman employee of another court (it had been going on for so many years now—a healthy cross-fertilization, Marie called it) was that there was a long-standing agreement among the judges to recess early on Wednesday—it was known as "the Wednesday Custom" by most of the women and "Ass Wednesday" by most of the men—so that everybody could pair off according to the arrangements of the moment. The sheer convenience of it had made it almost mandatory for a man of Davies' nature to try out almost every-thing presentable on the payroll, and it was a matter of some puzzlement to him that it had taken him all these years to get around to Marie. Even Judge Chobodian, who rumor had it had never indulged in that kind of thing even when he was a young man, had always gone along with the Wednesday Custom, bowing in the name of judicial courtesy to what he would never have agreed to in principle.

"There is no thought here of breaking long-term commitments," Davies told her. "But the Court always reserves its prerogative of adjourning on short notice so that it may retire to its chambers for meditation, consultation and"—he smiled —"re-sus-ci-tation. Petitioner would do well to keep it in mind that the Court also reserves the prerogative of throwing the case out of court entirely. Quashing the indictment. Perhaps even declining jurisdiction."

She nuzzled him again. "In which case, I will always remember the pounding of the gavel most gratefully."

Goddamn, but that kind of talk excited him. He had wondered at first whether she had talked that way with the others, and she had sworn to him on her father's grave that she had not. "Only with you, Harry," she had said, titillating him further, "because nobody except you, Harry, has ever been able to bring out the cheap whore in me before."

"Marie," he said now, "did you ever shack up with Jim Ambose?"

"How romantic," she said, with a comic groan. "What a question to ask at a time like this." And then, as if she couldn't quite believe it. "Jim *Am*bose?" Harry Davies, groaning inwardly, couldn't quite believe he had asked it, either. Ohmy-god, he thought, she thinks I'm jealous. You let a slut like this think you're jealous and right away they think they have a hold on you. And then it's them holding out and trying to get you to coax *them,* to please *them,* to promise *them.* To make long-term commitments.

To break that kind of mood in a hurry, he rolled onto his feet and, with nothing else to do, went over to turn on the television set. For some reason, he glanced out the window. "Holy Mother of God," he said, with his hand still on the knob. "What in the name of holy hell is *that?*"

Coming quickly up behind him, Marie looked out upon a mob scene. There were reporters; there were all kinds of photographers; there was a battery of floodlights set up right across from the front door. There was even a TV truck at the curb and, just across the street, a marked squad car from the sheriff's office.

Seeing the sheriff's car, seeing Booker Phillips and Arch Merck in the front seat, she began—to Davies' vast displeasure—to laugh. "Either they have an advance tip that there's going to be a love nest murder, let us hope not in Apartment 5G, or good old Bob Stringfellow has decided to protect his favorite court reporter's life. And to hell with her reputation."

Poor Harry was pacing around the room in a panic, muttering to himself that he'd have to get out of there without having his picture taken, and making not the slightest move to get started. Suddenly suspicious, almost as an accusation, he croaked, "Did Bob Stringfellow say anything to you about sending Booker here? I swear to God, Marie, if you knew . . ."

"Oh, relax." Jesus, he was dumb. "The remedy," she said, holding up the phone, "is this close at hand." Before she had finished dialing, Davies was hovering at her elbow. As soon as he was satisfied that it was Stringfellow himself at the other end of the line he began to stroke his stomach, breathing freely again. "I know," she was saying. "And it was very thoughtful of you, Bob. You were wonderful to be that concerned about me. But really, Bob. I mean, what are the neighbors going to be thinking?"

"Tell him to get them out of here," Davies hissed. "Jesus—Jesus—Jesus, what are you waiting for?" She shook her head at him to show that she couldn't listen to both of them at the same time. Into the phone she said, "Well, that's just crazy, Bob. I don't think that's even in the realm of possibility . . ." She stuck out her tongue at Davies and made a funny face. "Well, let me put it this way. They'd be interviewed, photographed, put on television and told to bend over and cough before they got to the front door . . . That's right, Bob. Now you got it exactly. The whole Coxey's army." She gave Harry a quick look, and her eyes were bright and merry. "Well, I ain't saying he is and I ain't saying he ain't. All I'm saying is that you'd better call off your dawgs, sheriff, 'cause you done tree'd the wrong fox."

She hung up, laughing helplessly, though not so helplessly that she couldn't see the judge take a good long look at what was bouncing around under the chiffon before he went padding back to the window to make sure the call came through to the squad car. The judge, a man reprieved, began to pat her softly on the buttock as they watched the newspapermen climbing into the cars. When the TV men folded their floodlights and carried them to the truck, the sense of relief in him became visible, tangible. The hand, no longer patting, was cupping and grabbing and squeezing. *My god,* she thought, looking down at him. *There goes Wednesday!*

When the last of the cars had disappeared around the corner, he grabbed her by both shoulders and shoved her away from the window. Out into the middle of the room he pushed her, in a succession of quick, rough shoves, the violence she had occasionally seen in him never closer to the surface. One savage yank, and the gown was down to her waist. Instinctively, she tried to cover herself. Too late. He had already grasped the bunched material in one hand and was tightening it behind her. With his free hand he gave her a hard, free-swinging slap on the behind, so hard that the sound of it rang out like a shot. "Hey, Harry," she said, mildly alarmed. "That hurts!"

Breathing hard, a wild, manic glint in his eye, he kept tightening his hold, tighter and tighter until, for his delight and edification, Marie threw back her shoulders. "You can't have 'em, Judge," she said. "Jurisdiction has been declined, and petitioner refuses to resubmit her application." She let the tip of her tongue run around her lips. "You've had all you can handle for the day, honey. Come around again a week from Wednesday and we'll see if you've got anything to put where your brag is."

"You bitch," he said, clenching his teeth. Snorting. "You slut. You cheap, filthy whore." Pulling hard at the handful of gown in his hand, he spun her around and threw her, face down, upon the soft carpeting. She had a thought, as she was going down, of scrambling away so that he'd have to come chasing after her but before she could even begin to get her feet under her he had flung himself on top of her. The sonofagun had the bottom part of the gown now and she could feel him sliding it up and letting it fall over her head. "We'll see what fox is gonna get tree'd," he howled, his feet locked solidly inside hers. "We'll see what quick brown fox is gonna get jumped. Right—now!"

"My gawd, Harry," she shrieked, feeling a sharp, cutting pain. "You're in the wrong court!"

Jim Ambose's office was at the far end of the corridor, which meant that he had to pass Nevins' outer office and stroll on past the long line of offices occupied by the various assistant DA's and investigators. He could have had the big office right alongside the district attorney's for the asking, and while it wasn't as spacious as Nevins' own office it was plenty big enough, and full of windows and air and sunshine. But Ambose didn't want to be that close to Nevins, a sentiment Nevins undoubtedly shared. For if Jim did not always want Nevins to know what he was doing, Nevins didn't want to know, either.

There was an atrociously carved wooden head on the desk, complete with cigar and bowler and identified—for the skeptics—as Winston S. Churchill. There were some messages on his spike. Riffling through them, he saw that four were from lawyers, who probably wanted to talk to him about their cases. The other said that Caroline Beyner had called at 12:15.

The sixth message was on a piece of scrap paper that had been carefully torn to approximate the size of the other notes on the spike. Printed, in large, dark letters, was the message:

Harvey Leigh
4:00

He knew what that was. In the old days when he was first getting started Ambose had made it a practice to tour around with the squad cars. Watching the cops move in for an arrest, moving in with them himself, had been the most valuable experience any prosecutor could have. It had been important to him to hold onto those old friendships. Whenever he needed a special job done, off the record, he would send a message to one of the old crowd, like Harvey Leigh, leaving only his name and the time, and they would be waiting in a squad car at the warehouse loading platform just beyond the freight tracks. When they needed anything from him they would do the same. He could also guess what this was going to be about. Harv and his partner had shot three thieves in a fur loft a few nights back, and the way things were these days Ambose didn't have very much doubt that the first guy had gone for his gun and they hadn't been all that anxious to leave two live witnesses. The compulsion to confess, Ambose mused. Rosie O'Grady and the Colonel's lady, make way for the cops and the robbers. Harv would be able to unburden himself to the district attorney's office (after a fashion) and his old pal, Jimbo Ambose, would be able to tell him he had done right and to forget it.

From his own office Ambose could walk into a small, connected office that was officially known as the Evidence Room—although it had been understood for years that nobody except Ambose kept any evidence there—and unofficially known as "the Cave." Along the near wall as he entered was a solid block of old green file cabinets, set two deep and piled high with old file folders and a litter of paper bags and shoe boxes which held evidence on god only knew how many long-forgotten cases.

The litter was not what you noticed when you entered Jim Ambose's Cave for the first time, though. What you noticed, what you could not help but notice, was that the other three walls were decorated entirely by arrowheads, arranged in long parabolic sweeps from corner to corner so that you were left with the unmistakable impression of row upon row of sharks' teeth. Many a visitor to that office would tell you that, seated on the other side of Jim Ambose's desk, they had the weird impression—for the first few moments anyway—not so much of being under attack by a school of sharks as of sitting, like some modern-day Jonah, in a shark's belly.

There was, however, another entrance to Jim Ambose's Cave. Anyone who wanted to visit Ambose without having to set foot inside the district attorney's office had only to climb the staircase at the far end of the courthouse. Upon reaching the top he would find that a little corridor had been cut into the alcove, just large enough to accommodate the door that Ambose had been thoughtful enough to have built into the other side of the Evidence Room.

The room, being windowless, was brightened only by the dim light coming from Ambose's office. Ambose ignored the bright fluorescent overhead lighting and turned on the small goosenecked lamp on his desk. A brown suede jacket hung on the coat hanger in the corner. It had been left there years ago by a visitor who may well have left so hastily because the information he had come to hawk had not been very good. Jim still ran into the guy from time to time. The first time he ran into him, he had let him know that the jacket was there in his office whenever he wanted to come in and get it. That was all. Once was all that Ambose chose to tell these characters anything. That was one of his rules. Another of his rules was that when he did tell them something, whether it was a promise or a threat, they could make book on it. The suede jacket would therefore remain there on the hanger until the character either came for it or died.

Removing his own jacket, he threw it on top of the hanger. As soon as he sat down behind the desk, he opened the bottom left drawer and pulled out a holster, complete with a heavy police .45 pistol, and very carefully buckled it into place. Ambose was under strict orders from Nevins not to carry a gun, but here in his own private domain nobody gave Jim Ambose orders. Here in his own domain he felt more comfortable in harness; his mind worked better. In addition to which there could be little doubt that the exposed gun had a most salutary effect on the characters who came parading through from the stairway door to offer their little droppings of information. Or that it put him on more fraternal terms with the cops and detectives who came in here to pass on information or go over testimony. He wouldn't be taking it off when he walked out today, either; because Nevins or no, when Ambose rode the squad cars he packed a gun.

From the middle drawer he drew a compact four-speed tape recorder and, patting it affectionately, set it squarely in the middle of the desk. Still shrugging the holster into a more comfortable position, adjusting its set, he went over to the file cabinet and jockeyed the middle cabinet back and forth until he had worked it out far enough so that he could get to the cabinet behind it. Squeezing between them, he rummaged through one of the drawers until he found what he seemed to be looking for, an old, well-smudged routing envelope that was marked D1–D14.

Back at the desk, he turned the envelope over and let a pile of recording tapes spill out.

Working quickly and expertly now, he took one of the tapes out of its box, threaded it through the machine, dropped the speed button down into the 7–½ slot and pressed the playback keys. The quality of the tape was not good, which, considering its age, was to be expected. The recorders in those days did not approach the quality of recorders today. Neither, of course, did the phone taps.

Although it was impossible to catch the entire conversation, he could make out enough of it to lend some comfort. Amidst the static and the crackling, a distant voice was saying, "This one you got to throw out regardless because . . ." The voice faded away for a few seconds, and then the voice of Harrison Davies came crackling back, broken but intelligible. It was the voice of a much younger Harrison Davies, for it was Harrison Davies in his first year on the Bench, shortly after he had been appointed to the Municipal Court. Since Davies had been in the Criminal Court for ten years now, the conversation would have taken place up to twelve years ago. "I'm telling you," the young Davies said, "you got nothing to worry about. If I throw out the complaint on a technicality they can never file on him again."

The answer came back, but after the first couple of words it became completely unintelligible. And then Davies was on again. "Well, hell, of course not. It's the same difference. (indistinguishable phrase) Didn't I tell you not to worry? I can throw it out if I don't like the way it's typed, and there's no appeal. I can guarantee you that I'm not going to like the way it was typed. That good enough for you?"

It didn't seem to be. The man on the other side seemed to be saying that he didn't think it could be done that easily this time because there was some sort of citizens committee that was raising hell about their kids losing all their money.

"Well, if it gets too hot," Davies said, "we'll have to hold the runner for trial and your lawyer will ask for a postponement. At the very worst, if (indistinguishable) he'll get a six-month suspended sentence."

The other voice, sounding now as if it was coming from out of a tunnel, pointed out that with all the bookies being brought in on these raids, he couldn't keep disliking the typing. Davies suggested, rather abruptly, that he talk to his lawyer. The other voice, stiffening, said they were, by god, paying enough so that he had a right to know what was happening from the source.

"Well, you're not paying me," Davies said. (Ambose, remembering that part again, sighed sadly.) "I do what I'm told and you're not the guy who tells me. Your lawyer will know how to plead. He makes the pleas, I only rule on them. I don't know why you can't understand that." And then, typically, Davies' voice turned soft and wheedling, trying as always to please. "All he got to do is tell me that the middle name on the complaint isn't the name customarily used by his client. And if there is no middle name on it, that his client customarily uses one. Or the street address is wrong. Anything's good enough to throw it out on because once I throw it out they can't refile on it. Not unless I choose to allow it, and if there's one thing I don't appreciate it's sloppy police work."

Clicking the keys again, Ambose reversed the tape, put it back into the box and shoveled all the boxes back into the envelope. After returning the envelope to the file cabinet, he came back with another envelope, a clean and shiny one marked D&P. Although only about half as many of the boxes spilled out onto the desk this time, the tape itself proved to be much thinner. Mute testimony to the mighty advances that had been made by the recording industry.

Judge Davies had been quite right. It had been a good three or four years since

Jim Ambose had dared to tap a judge's phone. But when Marie Pappas rented her apartment, it had been no problem at all for Ambose to have one of his investigators rent an apartment in the same telephone exchange area and install a telephone. From there it had been a simple enough matter for him to inform the telephone company that he was going on vacation and arrange with Ambose's contact at the exchange to run a wire between Marie's lead and his own on the back of the frame in the exchange office itself.

What Jim Ambose now had, to all intents and purposes, was an extension on Marie Pappas' telephone.

Ambose, sitting there in his private cone of light, listened to the tape with obvious satisfaction.

3:55 P.M.

David Boone Wilcke was looking forward to his visit with Mayor Karney. The decision to accept the invitation of the Lowell Bar Association had been made on an impulse—he turned down half a dozen of these invitations every month—only because it would give him an opportunity to see Big Mike Karney one more time before the old boy died. There had been stories that the old boy was failing. He had read a news magazine article about the recall movement being organized within his own party after Big Mike had refused to move into the new, marbled City Hall. Big Mike was, unquestionably, the last of the old breed. An authentic bit of Americana. And then too, the invitation had come, by sheer coincidence, on the same day he had received a letter from an obituary writer on *The New York Times* asking whether it would be possible to set up an interview—preferably in person although a telephone interview would be acceptable—to discuss the part Karney had played in preventing him from getting the presidential nomination, a wholly inaccurate version of what had happened. Wilcke was used to that, though, and he did not discount the possibility that the reporter had deliberately approached him with an inaccuracy so that he would feel compelled to set the record straight. That approach had been tried before, too.

Unless Mike had gone senile he would know what was happening around the country. And if there was one thing you could count on, it was that Mike Karney would speak his mind, Chief Justice or no. Correction. Chief Justice especially. Wilcke hadn't been insulted to his face since he mounted the Bench, and if Mike Karney didn't rise to the occasion, nobody would.

Yes, he thought, as the limousine stopped in front of the old City Hall, the last of the old breed. The country was better for their going, of course, all the political scientists agreed on that. But in his secret heart Wilcke could not help but wonder whether we were so much better off now that the colorful rogues with their turkey dinners and their "honest graft" had been replaced by the stolid businessmen with their grudging welfare and bloodless dishonesties. Although he would never have admitted it publicly, in his secret heart the Chief Justice cast a rousing vote for the old bosses.

As the Chief Justice was walking up the high, broad steps to the rococo, columned City Hall building—and when had he last seen a public building with gables?—he could not help but reflect that the old City Hall, doomed as it seemed to be, was a most fitting monument to its final occupant.

Michael Timothy Karney had seldom felt worse, which considering his health chart over the last few years, was a very large statement. The old wit and warmth had turned to crabbiness and—worst of all—he knew it. There was a giant crab lying across his chest, scratching it raw, clutching at him. The morning (ahem) nip for which he had been so famous among his intimates no longer soothed him, no longer set him up for the day. The cigar, which had been his trademark for —what?—fifty years, had gone stale. *(Hail, Mary, full of grace . . .)* The flavor had gone out of life. *(. . . the Lord is with thee . . .)* He had lost his grip on the party. *(Blessed art thou . . .)* He did not understand the new politics. *(. . . and the fruit of thy womb, Jesus . . .)* He would not be allowed to run for another term. He doubted whether he'd live through this one. *(Ashes to ashes and dust to dust . . .)*

And they were right. His mind wandered. He forgot. He was old. He was cold. The mirror terrorized him. The eyebrows, which had never been a particularly prominent feature in the massive Karney head, now seemed to flourish while the rest of him was shrinking away. He was melting away like a damn icicle. If he didn't hurry up and die he'd end up looking like a dwarf peeking out of a bramble bush.

He selected the red smoking jacket from the closet rack, and while he was tying the sash into a knot took what pleasure he could at the thought of David Boone Wilcke's reaction when he led him into the receiving room. Cheered by the thought, he took a handful of cigars out of the can on his dresser while Madge Clougherty's boy looked on, hurt and disapproving. Oh, a bright boy that was. A truly promising young man. Brilliant career stretching out before him. He'd flunked the Pledge of Allegiance or something and they had to find him a job that would utilize his remaining talents to the utmost. That's what being Mike Karney's private secretary had come down to. To stand at his elbow so that he'd never forget for one minute that he couldn't do what he used to be able to do. Given his natural limitations, Madge Clougherty's boy performed those duties reasonably well.

Mayor Karney had lived too long to be surprised by anything—he had last been surprised, he would guess, when he was nine years old—let alone by anything in politics. But who would have thought that David Boone Wilcke would end up as Chief Justice of the United States, the darlin' boy of the pure of heart and the plumed knight of the professors. He could tell the professors something about David Wilcke back when their darlin' boy was the Boy Wonder of American politics, standing by the seashore with his little rubber duck in his hand, waiting for the wave—any wave—that could be ridden into the White House.

A cold stab at the heart! He stopped right where he was on the staircase and reached out to Madge Clougherty's boy's shoulder for support. Was it jealousy? Was he jealous because Wilcke had understood that the times were changing and that the professors were what counted now and to hell with the people. *Dear Mary, mother of Jesus, protect me from dying a crabbed and jealous old man. Protect me from dishonoring myself with the mortal sin of jealousy. Protect me from making a fool of myself, not for my sake but for the sake of our dear May who rests, if a heaven there be, in thy sweet bosom.*

"I am not an invalid," he barked at Madge Clougherty's boy. "Don't go giving me any help where it's neither asked for nor needed."

He could remember David Boone Wilcke when he was hustling delegates at presidential conventions, and Big Mike Karney—Governor Karney then—sat at the table with a solid delegation in the palm of his hands. Oh, the fabled memory had no trouble calling up the events, the dealings, the trivia of the grand old days. The only fault he could find with the fabled memory was that it couldn't tell him what had happened three seconds ago.

In those days you could do some dealing at the convention; the tight-suit boys hadn't sewed it up ahead of time. The damnable television screen, which they had originally thought was going to be his own great weapon, hadn't changed it all. Oh, it was going to be his great weapon, they had all assured him of that. And hadn't he been as sure as any of them? But not for long, not for long. He had seen himself the first time, and while they were all nodding and beaming and telling him how great he was, he—he alone—had looked at the man coldly—it was his saving grace that he had always been able to look at the politician coldly —and thought, Good Lord, the man is a clown, the great voice a burlesque, the great presence a harlequin. He had seen at that moment, for he was never a man to kid himself on the vote count, that the old order was passing.

Madge Clougherty's boy was at the door, talking to someone, telling him that the mayor was eagerly awaiting. . . . Mike hadn't heard any ringing, any knocking. He hadn't even been aware that the boy had left him. The mind was a sieve.

Wilcke didn't recognize him at first. He had taken the little old man in the red smoking jacket for one of Karney's staff members; he had, indeed, been thinking that Karney must have really lost all control if his people felt free to dress so informally. If the little old man hadn't stuck his hand out and thanked him for coming to see him, he would never for one moment have dreamed it was Big Mike. "Although my contact with the outside world is slight and chancy these days," the old man was saying, "I do manage to keep right on top of the amenities. There are, I am told by my keepers, many acceptable ways of greeting men of stature, such as Chief Justices, actors, bongo players, and even an occasional mayor taken out on a leash for airing. The most obsequious, and therefore my personal favorite, is to thank you for taking time out from your busy schedule."

"And well you should." Wilcke laughed. "I've been sleeping all day. I don't mind anyone taking me away from my schedule, but it's only for old friends that I get out of bed."

"Yes," Karney said. "Or, as a lady of my acquaintance was heard to say, vice versa."

The Chief Justice peered into the face, doing his darndest not to be rude, and he could not find, anywhere, the man he had known. It wasn't simply one of those cases where a man has lost so much weight that you had to look twice to find the substance of the old familiar features. Knowing it was Karney, there was still no way of reconciling this wizened old man with those bristling eyebrows with the powerful, big-chested man he had known for so many years. Even that business about "a lady of my acquaintance" seemed out of whack in those first disoriented moments because, as everyone in politics knew, Karney had always been scrupulously and even uniquely faithful to his wife. And yet in another way it was typical enough of the old Karney humor to relax Wilcke and, as ridiculous as he knew it to be, reassure him.

And then he accompanied his host into the reception room and his mind was reeling again. The room looked not so much like a museum as a warehouse for a museum. There were statues and there were bronzes and there were African masks and, in the corner, there was a huge wooden Indian standing in front of a pitched tent. Red velvet drapery hung everywhere. The windows, what he could see of them, were stained glass. Overhead were chandeliers with star-shaped bulbs. At the far end of the room a netting slanted down from the balcony to cover . . . well, whatever it was covering. Given the musty atmosphere of the room, it made you think of a giant cobweb. Given the somewhat sweet, somewhat sticky odor that seemed to seep into your pores after awhile, Wilcke had the impression that the mayor was raising rubber plants back there. No wonder the man from the city council had been so anxious to prepare him. No, Chief Justice Wilcke thought, Mike Karney was not exactly a public relation man's dream.

"A monstrosity, isn't it?" Karney said proudly, and since that happened to be exactly the word that had been rattling around in Wilcke's own head he found himself, for the third time running, sorely discomforted.

"Don't let it worry you," Karney said. "Everybody says it's a monstrosity." Had Wilcke detected a quick, measuring glance, as if Karney were checking his reaction? "Yes, the butcher, the baker and the candlestick man, they all have a way with the words these days."

He sank into an overstuffed, rather moldy-looking chair leaving his guest to sit—most gratefully—in the plain straight-backed chair alongside the table. "My May's sister came trottin' up from her retirement paradise in Florida, Thursday a week, to brighten my existence. The good woman couldn't enjoy herself knowing she was basking amidst all that luxury whilst I sat here alone, in the sunset of my life, pining after one last peek at her breathtaking beauty." He emitted a little cackle which turned at once into a phlegmy, ratchety cough and, finally, into a long drawn out wheeze. When his breath returned, he screwed up his features and spoke in a highfalutin voice that was apparently an imitation of his sister-in-law's. " 'What would May think of this monstrosity? That's just what she'd call it, I can tell you. A monstrosity.'

" 'You don't know your own sister, you great ugly loon,' I told her, it being a man's privilege to speak up in his own home, even to such a selfless benefactor as that. 'I can see my May coming into the room now,' says I, 'and she'd take one look and she'd say, "Blasphemy!" and walk out with never another word or look.'

"My May," he told David Wilcke, "was not a woman to follow the general tone of the time but she did have strong religious convictions."

His first impression had been right, Wilcke felt. The old man, for reasons that must seem sufficient to him, had been perpetrating a colossal hoax. The Chief Justice felt rather honored, against his better judgment, that Karney had chosen to let him in on it. Which brought up an interesting question. If a man sets out to convince everybody that he's crazy, does that mean he isn't crazy or that he has his own special brand of craziness?

To show Karney that he understood, perhaps even sympathized and certainly wasn't embarrassed, Wilcke described for the mayor how the city council had set their p.r. man on him so that he would not walk unprepared into all this grandeur. "Frankly, I'm a wee bit disappointed," Wilcke told him. "I always rather liked this style. What is it called again? Old American Storage?"

That did it. Howling in delight, the old man slapped at his thighs. "They can't wait to sweep me out of here and send in the exterminators, David! They send their scouts around every day to check up on my health. Oh yes, David, before I hit the floor the wrecker's ball will be swinging."

It was a scene that left the Chief Justice infinitely depressed. He had always been fond of Mike Karney; yes, even when Mike had been unable to see his way clear to supporting him for the presidency. And because he liked him, he began to urge him to come to the dinner with him as his personal guest. He could make a phone call right now, he suggested, and arrange for another seat to be set on the dais. It would do him good to get out. He was sure many of his old friends would be there. It would, he said as his clinching argument, show the city council that Mike Karney was still a man to contend with.

A little crooked smile, tired and weary, and the old man sank deeper into the chair. "As much as it grieves me to decline," Karney said, "the burdens of public office prohibit." The Chief Justice got the message, all right. "We had some grand times," Karney told him, "but it's all computers and polls now. Oh, those polls are terrible things, David. The thing that's so terrible is that they're always right."

When the cold wind blows, Karney thought, that's all there was. Memories of the grand old times. Wilcke had made the transition, or been lucky enough to fall into the right spot. No, it wasn't luck. Give the man his due. Don't be so afraid, Michael Karney, to give another man credit; it doesn't hurt that much. If Wilcke had remained in politics he'd have played it right, too. David Wilcke had a political balance wheel built into his head which would have turned him, unfailingly, in the right direction. Karney could understand that well enough, because time was when Mike Karney had that balance wheel too.

Oh yes, Karney understood Wilcke as only one dedicated politician could understand another. Far better, he would guess, than Wilcke understood himself. The only coin in politics was power. Once you hung your hat on that, my buckoes, you could never go wrong.

Social management—as a science and as a philosophy—had become the highway to power, and Wilcke had been quick to see it. Blocked off on the road to the White House, David Wilcke had had the foresight to make the deal that set him down in the other seat of high potential power, the Supreme Court. No, it wasn't luck. Wilcke had always been a grand opportunist. No slander in that; if you put all the opportunists in jail they'd have to put walls around the entire country. It was the mark of Wilcke's genius that he had always been able to mask his opportunism, the one neat little trick that had always been beyond Karney's capacity or—giving himself the best of it (and why not, who else was there to give him anything?)—his mischievous spirit and his honorable soul. As a young district attorney, Wilcke had been a hangman, a fact of history now well forgotten except by the old lawyers who had gone up against him. If you were a prosecutor, that's where the power lay. In getting the convictions. As a mayor, he had been a reformer, the only possible road from City Hall to national prominence. As a senator, he had become a moderate with liberal leanings, the road to power in both his state and the nation.

And then Chief Justice. As Chief Justice he had become a liberal interpreter of the Constitution, and there you had the greatest stroke of genius and the greatest opportunism of all. To interpret the Constitution conservatively meant that you followed the precedents, which meant that you sat there and nodded. There'd be security, yes. Prestige, yes. Honor, yes. But not much power. Ah, but to interpret the Constitution liberally gave you the right to rewrite it, and to be the most liberal interpreter of them all gave you the right to rewrite it like it had

46

never been rewritten before. By god, you could put yourself right up there with the Founding Fathers themselves. The marvel of the Court's great power, and Wilcke had very quickly seized upon it, was that it—it alone in the whole intricate system of checks and balances—had the power to grant itself whatever power it wanted.

But even that didn't show the full genius of the man. The one thing that could have stopped him was a massive outcry of public opinion, and he had been shrewd enough to use his power in the direction that was acceptable to the professors and the—the what?—the vague, swirling forces that controlled public opinion. He had moved with them and with the times into the open highway of social management. And if, in the moving, he had changed the social, political and legal structure of the country, what did he care? Denied the presidency, David Boone Wilcke had made himself more powerful than the President himself.

Oh, clever, clever, clever. The genius of geniuses. He'd give him a hip-hip-hooray if he didn't believe that if a man was nothing else, he should be loyal to his own self and his own philosophy and his own people.

Mike Karney could tell himself that he had always been loyal to what he was, and in a sudden explosion of pride he understood that he had, at least, gone down on his own terms. Loyalty was the cause of his downfall. Michael Timothy Karney, the more perceptive historians would say, had been done in by loyalty.

In the old days, before television, he had ended every campaign by returning to the old neighborhood on election eve, and he could see it now, how they'd be massed there in front of the hall, the old buckoes, to lift him onto their shoulders and carry him inside; into the choked and cheering aisle; down through the swirl and the shout, the clutch and the tingle—the human warmth, dear god, the hunger—of people wanting nothing more than to reach up and touch the arm of Mike Karney (he could see it again, the old wooden hall of the Bartenders Union, painted gray on the outside, with the old wooden benches inside). They'd deposit him on the stage and he'd stand there for a long minute—oh, the place would go quiet in the waiting for it—and then he'd shout, "I'm Michael Timothy Karney, and I know who I am and I know where I came from!" And how the drums would go bang and the cymbals would clang and the damn bagpipes would wheeze in his ears (Scotty Fergeson, he could see him now with the kilts and the bagpipes, he had never missed a rally in the old ward). And he'd shout above it all (dear god, he had the good lungs in those days), "I'm Michael Timothy Karney and I was born and dragged up in the Third Ward! I told you when I left that I'd always come back while there was life in the old body and, by the grace of God, here I've made it again."

The tears filled his eyes, and he didn't give a damn what Chief Justice David Boone Wilcke or the whole damn Supreme Court thought about it.

Oh, the grand times, he thought blowing his nose. They were his grand buckoes then, grand boys all, and who needed to spend their time in night clubs drawing up charts on the lady singers like he heard the Chief Justice did. The secret had been that while he was dishonest in all the small things, he had been honest in the things that really mattered. He had been what he was, and he had never pretended to be anything else. "You're a wicked man, Michael Timothy," May would say, but she had known that he was the man she had married.

Dishonest in all the small things and honest in all the big ones. He liked the sound of that. That was something for the gravestone, all right. Out of the habit of a lifetime, he was planning how to spread the word. When they came around on his next birthday, and they got to asking him whether there were still any ambitions, anything he was still looking forward to, he would answer lightly, "Just an old-fashioned wake and a sprinkling of lies and a fancy gravestone with a fine epigram."

"You want to know something, David," he said. "A monstrosity it is, but they'd love it, my people." He was rolling back and forth in the soft chair lazily, as if he were scratching his back. "Oh yes, the professors and the officers of the city council . . . and my pen pal from the editorial page come in, take one look around and they're running out into the street screaming to man the barricades, here come the barbarians again. My people would have come in here and they'd have thought, And isn't it marvelous that Big Mike lives in a fine palace that puts all the grandest emporiums of E. M. Loew to shame."

The sidelong, measuring glance again. A bird-like cocking of the head. "I was thinking of having them build in a sky on the ceiling with twinkly stars and the clouds circulating around like air conditioning. But then it came to me, dontcha know, it would be in bad taste." He sighed heavily. "There's much to be said, you know, for bad taste."

So that's what it was all about, Wilcke thought. He had been wrong about the old man. Whatever Big Mike was doing here at the end of his life, he saw it as a monument to himself and the people who had made him, and a final thumbing of the nose at all progress, all change, all the inexplicable forces that had brought him down.

"I'll tell you who to talk to tonight if it's a lively debate you're after," Karney said. "We have a lad named James Ambose in the district attorney's office, who would have a grand career in law enforcement in front of him if it wasn't that he gets so awful upset about it when they let murderers go trottin' off free. Tsk, tsk. Obviously a man of unsound mind and character. A psychological misfit. See if you can't find him. Big square-shouldered man. Wolfhound of a fellow with eyes that drill a hole in you. Oh, if it's a spirited debate you're after, Ambose, J., is your man."

"You sound as if you like him."

"Like him?" Karney snorted. "The fellow's too anxious to burn people for my taste. I never saw the good that came from that." *That surprises you, eh? Thought I was one of those hidebound old-timers who was all out of step with the modern new kiss-'em-on-the-cheek and pat-'em-on-the-head school of punishment.* "Jail does little enough good, as far as I could ever see, and I never found the man so evil that I'd want to be the one to say goodbye and good riddance and there goes nothing. If there's one thing I've noticed it's that if you wait long enough the good Lord will take care of that nasty job for you, which is the approach I have been urging upon the city council."

The quick switch had left the Chief Justice somewhat disoriented again. "Big bison of a fellow," Karney said, suddenly all business. "Stewing in his juices. Finger always twitchin' away like he's looking for a switch to pull. Poor loon comes to talk to me for an old man's wisdom and counsel. Thinks I'm gonna tap him on the shoulder and tell him, 'Don't worry about it 'cause I just made you district attorney.' Poor loon's got his ear so close to the ground he don't know I haven't got the power to fix a two-dollar ticket for spittin' on the sidewalk without consulting with the city council for their advice and consent." He smiled mirthlessly, a movement of the lips. "Hasn't got the sense to know the only thing we have in common is that I know the difference between the carpenter and the hammer and he doesn't."

The old man did wander, Wilcke thought. Still, he was more interested than Mike Karney knew in what he had been saying about this Ambose. It just so happened, he could assure him, that he believed in a strong adversary system, and what was most needed at the moment, to balance the stringent standards his Court had established for the protection of the defendant's rights, were some good, tough prosecutors who could represent the people's rights with equal vigor.

"I never could figure out these honest fellows," Karney said morosely. "I never could figure out what they want." In the wispy, faraway voice of the politician going off into a set little patter, he said, "When I went out into the world my father said to me, 'Son, I've got no money or earthly goods to bequeath to you. All I can give you is a word of advice. There are two kinds of men not to trust,' he said to me. 'Never trust a man with a deck of cards in his hand and never trust a man who's always trying to show you he's so much better than everybody else.' I've lived a long life, and I've had a degree of success. Enough success, at any rate, that it's given me the opportunity of talking to some of the wisest and most successful men in the world. My father was only a poor hod-carrier, but it still remains the best advice I've ever got."

4:40 P.M.

Through most of the conversation Mayor Karney had tried to steer clear of any talk about the Court, in part because he felt the Chief Justice would be reluctant to talk about it, and because he felt he probably heard the same complaints wherever he went. Some time had passed before he was made to understand that Wilcke was not only willing to talk about the workings of the Court, but rather anxious to sound Karney out. It amused Karney that he should ever have thought otherwise. Once a politician, always a politician. That was something you could hang your hat on.

"The burdens of office, as I don't have to tell you, are never what they seem to be," Wilcke was saying. "The most awkward part about donning our particular cloth and taking our particular vows is that you stop all conversation. A hush comes over every room you enter, and a guilty look comes onto every face. I always have the feeling that somebody has just stopped at the best part of a dirty joke."

"You should come around here more often," Karney said drily. "When a priest comes into the room I switch from the dirty jokes to politics, and when a judge comes in, I switch from politics to the dirty jokes."

The Chief Justice had a tumbler of whiskey in his hand, and he was leaning back, warm and mellow. He was enjoying Karney; he had come to the point where he was thinking what he would have to say about him on his next swing around the night clubs. "There's a body of opinion that holds Supreme Court Justices are not supposed to be concerned about what the latest poll says about our latest decision. Which is marvelous after a lifetime of wondering whether the hatters' industry will be sore at you if you go bareheaded, and the health addicts will be sore at you if you don't. I'll let you in on a trade secret. In the privacy of our chambers we call ourselves the Last Nine Virgins, which is, I can assure you, in one case at least, a wild and wanton misapplication."

He had been offered that tidbit, Karney could see, as one of those confidences passed between members of the same lodge, which was such an old political dodge

49

that Karney was annoyed with him again. Didn't Wilcke know that you can't con a con man? What had really offended Karney, though, was not the joke itself so much as the wholly gratuitous slur upon a colleague. With only eight other Justices to be loyal to, even David Wilcke shouldn't find it all that bothersome. More waspishly than he intended, Karney observed that perhaps that explained why that particular Justice had such a forgiving nature where the criminal law was concerned.

Oh, the Chief Justice would be ready enough to defend him on that score, you could be sure of that. Hadn't he started out as a prosecutor himself, and didn't he know how those fellows worked? "If I could get back at myself, ex post facto, I'd pick myself up by the seat of my pants and throw myself into jail. That goes back to the prehistoric era of American law, Mike. By today's standards, I'd guess that ninety percent of my convictions wouldn't stand up. I trust," he said complacently, "that the transcripts have all been destroyed."

The mayor didn't know how much of that to credit. The tone of self-satisfied self-reproach, the self-indulgent plaint about the terrible old times (really, of course, looked upon as the good old days), and, more self-serving still, the pit from which you had—through your own strength and courage—risen. The Chief Justice was the successful businessman saying, "We were so poor that . . . Yes, indeed. My father was only a poor hod-carrier, but, boy-oh-boy, look at me now!"

"Not prehistoric," Karney said. "Naive. We were naive, David. We respected our policemen and gave the prosecutors credit for doing a good job of it when they put the enemies of society in jail. There's the difference, if it's the difference you happen to be looking for. We believed lawbreakers belonged in jail and that we couldn't send them back to kindergarten to start all over. If they wanted to come join us when they got out, fine and dandy." If they didn't they'd soon enough land back where they belonged, because as long as they were safe in jail they weren't hitting anybody over the head with a lead pipe. "Dumb as we were in those prehistoric times, Mr. Chief Justice, we could walk the street at night without looking back over our shoulder. The one thing I have to give you and your boys credit for, though. You've brought new hope and prosperity to the lead pipe industry."

It was himself he was annoyed with now. Why had he had to add that? He had made a justifiable comment on the Wilcke Court. Why had he found it necessary to make it seem as if he hadn't really meant it? As if he were apologizing for it?

"We don't make the criminal law," the Chief Justice said, his eyes twinkling. "The Constitution makes it. It seemed to us, you see, that it was time the courts gave the defendants the rights the Constitution says are theirs. Nobody says the system is perfect. All we can say is that it's the best system ever devised by man."

It was the blanketing smugness of it that so offended Karney this time. "Well, now," he said. "I've always been a little confused on that, and it's pleased I am that you dropped by on such a fine afternoon to set me straight. The one leetle thing that keeps gnawing on my last functional brain cell is that if the system is all that good, how come you went ahead and changed it? How come nobody tumbled onto it that we were living in constitutional sin before you and your boys came along to sprinkle holy water on it? How did it come that the country got on so well from the time they cracked the bell in Philadelphia until you fellows come along, all full of hallelujah and the new catechism? How come all those other Supreme Courts never knew how to read the Constitution? Because if I remember my schooling aright, though my memory isn't what it used to be, they told us way back then that we had the most perfect system ever devised by the mind of man. And if I remember aright, the lawyers and the judges were telling us, seems like the day before yesterday, we had the best system ever devised by the mind of man. Was it that they were wrong or was it that they were lying to us? Or was it that . . . Now, you're not going to send an old man unhappy to his grave, David, by telling me that maybe the Frenchmen, Englishmen, Germans and Turks, that they're so backward as to think they have the best system ever devised by the mind of man, too?"

All right, he had shown him that he was a hidebound old-timer who didn't believe in the love-'em-until-they'll-be-good school of punishment. So what? At least he'd knocked that damn twinkle out of his eyes.

"I could be wrong, yes," Wilcke said. "I know I'm not lying. But don't ever completely eliminate the possibility that I'm only a poor loon who doesn't know any better. No, no, Mike," he said, seeing the distress come into the old man's eyes. "It's not such a bad idea to have somebody like you remind me of that from time to time. It's not a bad idea at all."

Mike Karney was completely disarmed. He could see now that Wilcke was a good man, and that he had been slandering him in his mind all day out of an old man's spitefulness. Ready for the ash can himself, he had been spitting on a better man. "What do we really know, Mike, except that you do your best, as you see it. Times change. Situations change. What looks right today, looks wrong tomorrow. I don't mind telling you—although I'm sure you envy me the freedom to move ahead without any thought to public opinion or the next election—that freedom is always an illusion. We are bound, although it may not seem so, by every decision every other Court has ever made. We are bound by every decision we make, even if—and I *do* mind saying this—what we say is not always what we meant to say. And if the Congress complains that we are not interpreting their laws the way they meant them to be interpreted, we can say that the courts below us—and that's who we are really setting the guidelines for—don't always interpret us the way we mean to be interpreted."

He sipped the whiskey meditatively and turned the tumbler around so that it reflected the light from the chandeliers. "I could name you a score of congressmen who have said to me, when the glasses had been drained and the night was growing long, 'Can't you fellows read simple English up there?' And I'd be very put out with them except that it might deprive me of the wonderful relief of being able to say, 'Can't those judges read simple English down there?' "

Madge Clougherty's boy had come silently into the room and he was standing behind Wilcke, clearing his throat. "Don't stand there like a lamp post, boy," Karney barked, "speak up."

Clougherty had come to remind the Chief Justice that it was almost five o'clock. There was also, it seemed, the matter of the press and television people collected on the steps outside. The press had asked him to find out whether the Chief Justice and the mayor would pose for pictures and exchange a few words before the television camera.

"Although this was primarily a social visit, a visit to an old friend," Wilcke said, rehearsing, "it would be permissible to say that we did have a most interesting and useful exchange of views." He winked at Karney. "Haven't had the opportunity to say that in fifteen years. Miss it. I'll tell you what let's do. Why don't I say a few nonpolitical, nonpartisan and nonsensical words, and then you can take over and perform your official duties as host."

"Well, what are you standing there for?" Karney snapped at Clougherty. "Didn't you hear what the Chief Justice said?"

5:03 P.M.

Jimmy Clougherty came outside to pass the word, most particularly to Josh Flowers, the prize-winning newsman from the local television station. It had become accepted practice for Josh to get first crack at any story he was covering, partly because everybody automatically went to the television camera anyway, and partly because Josh would hit them with the rough questions, the kind that only the best of them knew how to dance away from when the eye of the television camera was on them.

Josh Flowers and the newspapermen had already decided that if Wilcke came on camera, Josh would skip the demonstration at the airport, with its guaranteed "no comment," and use Wilcke's appearance at the Bar Association dinner as a lead-in for a question about the criticism being heard "in some quarters" about Supreme Court decisions. Wilcke wasn't going to say very much about anything, they had agreed, but it might be newsworthy to see what form his lack of comment on that question took.

"How's the old man feeling today?" one of the reporters asked Clougherty.

"He must be in a good mood," Clougherty said, with a grin. "He's been yelling at me louder than ever."

"Just between us girls, Jimmy," one of the photographers said, "is the old man's mind really failing?"

"Yeah," Clougherty said. "Just like a steel trap it's failing."

5:05 P.M.

The Chief Justice was feeling surprisingly frisky as he came out. He had been kicking himself all day for having subjected himself to this ridiculous trip to Lowell, and he was well satisfied now that it had been no mistake. The old man was indeed a monument worth viewing one last time. If he had any regret at all it was that the mayor's critique of the Court had come so late. Clougherty, who seemed like a bright enough young fellow, was introducing him to the television fellow, and with the cameramen already focusing all around them, the Chief Justice took Mayor Karney by the elbow and drew him gently up alongside him so the old man wouldn't find himself being cropped out of the pictures. A couple of the cameramen positioned along the stairs were calling for the Chief Justice to wave. The genius of America, the Chief Justice chuckled to himself, was that every man could rise as high as his talents could take him, and no matter how high he rose the photographers would treat him like a chorus girl. They wanted him to wave, huh? Out of his high spirits—and to his own astonishment—Wilcke stuck his thumbs in his ears and waved them like a donkey's. The sense of his own dignity returned just as quickly and, as he was pulling them out, the thought went flashing through his mind that he would do well to tell them that he hoped they didn't take that as a comment on their mentality because some of his best friends—

And that—right there—was where it ended.

The mayor had been momentarily blinded by the first flashbulb. The blindness had turned into a blur of red, which blended into a rapidly dissolving circle of light. It was in that dissolving circle of light that Mayor Karney saw and heard the shot.

It would not be inaccurate to say that Mayor Karney was the only man who actually did see Sam Tabor step out of the crowd at the bottom of the steps and shoot and kill David Boone Wilcke.

BOOK II

The Jugglers

"Truth, like your family doctor, doesn't pay house calls. On Wednesdays it isn't in at all."

—*Dr. Lennard Swann*

The press, which had been arriving in Lowell through the night and morning, was pressed into the hallway outside the district attorney's office. To see that they stayed out there, a policeman was stationed, straddle-legged, in front of the wide, glass double door.

Through the door they could see only Hilliard Nevins' secretary at her desk, striking poses of attractive contemplation. A sheet of paper was in her typewriter but she was paying very little attention to it. Although the extension buttons on her phone lit up constantly, she would let the console fill up almost completely before she made any attempt to dispose of them.

Lenore Darringer was a pretty brunette, pretty enough to get by on her features alone. Her best feature, however, was her trim figure, and it was being displayed to advantage by a royal blue sheath dress with a rather moderately cut cowl neckline. When, from time to time, she arose to walk rather purposefully into the law library, it could be seen that her heels were far more suited to evening dress than to the office. One could assume that Lenore, aware that the press of the nation would be observing her this day, had gone to some effort to look her very best.

She picked up the phone again and explained that District Attorney Nevins was in conference. No, he was giving no interviews. She was sorry but there were no exceptions. No, not for *any* newspapers or magazines. Well, she assumed that if he did have anything to say he would say it to the reporters who were already there. No, Mr. Nevins had no plans that she knew of to hold any press conference today.

There was a movement out in the hallway as someone new approached, and she could hear the guard calling out for the reporters to make way, to clear out, to open up a passageway. As the guard pushed the door open just a crack, she could hear the buzzing of the overlapping questions and then, as the visitor was identified, the note of uncertainty leaving their voices.

"Have you seen him, Doctor?"

"What did he say?"

"Does he admit he did it?"

"Do you think he's insane?"

"Jesus Horatio Christ!" a familiar voice rumbled. "I don't mind the rude jostling and the crude jests but hasn't anybody here ever heard of underarm deodorants!"

Lenore sighed heavily. It was bad enough that Lowell was getting such horrible publicity without Doc Swann having to come along to make a laughingstock out of himself and the city and, while he was about it, the district attorney's office, too. Knowing Doc Swann, she was hardly surprised that after having pushed his way through the mob—cursing, undoubtedly, as he came—he turned back, folded his arms behind him and announced, "While I am not a lawyer, gentlemen, I think I can state with some degree of confidence, in answer to one of the more cogent questions whispered into my ear, that the state may very well feel it can prove he did it. As to the state of his sanity, I can only pose to you the question that has agitated leading philosophers from Socrates to Albert Prengler. 'Which of us is sane?' Anybody here ever hear of Socrates? No? Too bad. Let me tell you something about Socrates. Socrates," he said, tapping his head, "had it up here. You take Albert Prengler and I'll take Socrates every time."

Doc Swann was, at best, a sweaty, unkempt man; a blocky man, built low to the ground and with no more neck than was absolutely essential. There was about him the compact look of whalebone and the acrid smell of nicotine, a combination that somehow seemed to belong together. He was, as always, wearing that grimy green shirt and —as usual—the collar wings had somehow managed to curl up above the jacket. His tie would be—yes—askew and, without looking, Lenore knew there would be some loose threads fuzzing out at the bottom.

With it all, Lenore liked Doc well enough. Where she might have been uneasy in the presence of a well-kempt, slicked-down psychiatrist who presumably knew her most shameful bedpan secrets and bedroom yearnings, Doc Swann left her with a feeling of womanly warmth and wisdom. She knew he was a widower, and what woman was able to withhold a fond, indulgent smile for a man who proved so graphically that even the most brilliant and educated of them were lost without the tender ministrations of a good woman? Without, in short, a wife to brush him off and feed him a good nourishing breakfast and send him out to meet the world on something approaching the world's own terms.

There was something different about him today, she saw, something in the glowing eyes and heavy breathing that went beyond the exertion of having pushed his way through the reporters. "Good fortune is smiling upon the beloved old doctor," he said, beaming. "Into my dusty, untidy laboratory has fallen the crime of the century, the murderer of the decade. The beloved old fraud has become the man of the hour. The first time I laid eyes on that Sam Tabor I knew he had good stuff in him."

"Mr. Nevins has been calling out to find out if you were here yet," she told him in a low, urgent voice that very clearly conveyed the message that for both of their sakes she did not want Nevins to hear them talking lest he get the impression that Dr. Swann was loitering in the outer office, wasting one of his interminable speeches on her.

She could also see that it was going to do no good at all. Doc Swann had taken his lecture stance, hands folded behind his back, stomach protruding. "No longer poor old Doctor Swann, the jailhouse psychiatrist, the longwinded bore, casting his babble before swine. Here in the Age of the Celebrity, I have through application, dedication and an uncanny devotion to scientific principle and the main chance heaved, in short asthmatic gasps, into the public domain." He pulled once . . . twice on his nose. "Pathé News is not completely out of the question."

She could not, for the life of her, understand why Hilliard Nevins prized Swann so highly. She had heard him say a dozen times, always in the same words, "The only genius I've ever met in my life. Smartest man I ever saw. If I was that smart, I'd *never* change my shirt. But I got to agree with you on one thing. The man sure can talk your ear off."

Forgetting for the moment that she was being observed by the flower of the nation's press, Lenore lifted her eyes to heaven and scowled at him most unattractively.

Hilliard Nevins was seated behind his desk in shirtsleeves, chewing on his cigar, one leg thrown negligently over the arm of his chair. For once the desk was cleared, except for the inevitable long yellow pad, already well turned and penciled. It was perfectly evident that the desk had been stripped for action.

Ambose and Pawley were both standing, and while it was perfectly possible that they had been pacing around the room Doc Swann had the distinct impression that having finished their legal discussions among themselves they had both just got up to stretch their legs.

"Well, Ambose," he said, "what are you going to do? Going to give the man a medal?"

"The man killed in cold blood," Ambose said. "If I have anything to say about it, we're going to burn the sonofabitch."

Stopping dead in his tracks, Doc Swann stared at him as if he couldn't quite believe that Jim Ambose of all people could possibly want to burn anybody.

Nevins was waving them all to their seats with the unlit, well-chewed cigar. "All right, Lennard," he said, "this is important now. How much did he talk to you?"

Swann settled himself into the most comfortable chair. "I was operating under some handicap," he said, in that vaguely combative way of his. "I was accompanied by one of your bright young attorneys who read him off a plenitude of legal mumbojumbo informing him of his rights, duties and legal redresses. I do declare your boys are outdoing our boys in mumbojumbo these days and I tell you we do not intend to take it lying down. I'm going to offer a resolution from the floor at the next convention of forensic—" He scowled around the room, pulling on his nose again. "My sensitive antenna has picked up violent streams of impatience emanating from at least three hot spots around this room. You want my report, Hilliard? You want the official word on Jim Ambose's friend, Sam Tabor, the best candidate for fried meat this country has ever produced? Now let me see, where shall I begin . . . Ah yes, I went over his day with him. From the time he got up to the time he found himself on the stairs of City Hall." He leaned back in the chair as if he had completed his report, and smiled around the room brightly.

"And he told you how he found himself on the stairs with that funny-looking black thing smoking in his hand?" Pawley said.

"Did he tell you why he did it?" Ambose wanted to know. "That's the thing."

"I didn't ask him. Didn't think you wanted me to ask him, Hilliard. Isn't good technique anyway. Let him talk about his day, see what he says, what associations he makes. I was there to determine whether or not he was suicidal, you will recall. So that I could advise his jailers whether he should be placed under a suicide watch." He winked broadly. They'd had him under a suicide watch anyway, of course—matter of routine—so the least said about that flimflam the better. "The facts are the facts. He will remember or not remember according to what his lawyers decide is best for him. Greatest system ever devised by the mind of man.

Will always be popular until someone devises a system that will give you a better chance of getting away with it."

"Lennard," Nevins said firmly, "just tell us what he said, what you think, what you might be able to testify to if it gets that far." That kind of thing. He knew what they were looking for. "The rest of it I'll be happy to listen to over the poker game tonight."

"A man less sure of his place in history would be miffed, as we medical people say, about being cut off in mid-sentence. Which reminds me, Hilliard. I've given the press my word that you can prove he did it. Laid my reputation smack dab on the line. So I do hope you'll be careful not to misplace those television films. Got them tucked away safely in a vault, I trust? Good thinking. Briefly, you say. Briefly, your celebrated prisoner is as full of self-approbation as a chimpanzee counting his toes."

Ambose had wandered to the back of the room and was leaning, half-seated, against the window sill with his hands shoved negligently into his pockets. "I thought," Nevins growled, turning to him, "that he was supposed to be full of remorse."

"He *is* full of remorse," Swann said. "Whenever he remembers he's supposed to be. He's really a conventional type, our Sam. He is also full of winsome smiles and modest disclaimers and bright hopes for the future. While he has not yet fully adjusted to his new station in life, I'm afraid the poor nut is beginning to get the idea he's a celebrity."

DeWitt Pawley gave a shudder. "Please do not use foul language in the presence of the prosecutors," he said delicately. "Now, this poor misguided sane man you were just talking to. Is he or is he not, in your opinion, legally sane?"

"Hey, what happened to you?" Swann asked. He had noticed the bandage on Pawley's head for the first time. "Cut your forehead shaving this morning?"

"God bless you, kind apothecary, you're the only person in the city who doesn't know."

"Or, for that matter, care." Doc Swann had pulled a handful of folded, wrinkled scraps of paper out of his pocket—some new, some old—and he was scrutinizing them from different angles and distances. "How the hell do I know whether he's legally sane or not," he said at last. "You think I work by divination or something?" Now, if they were asking him whether anyone who'd gun down the Chief Justice of the United States in broad daylight in front of fifty witnesses and a couple of television cameras was acting kind of peculiar, he'd have to say that in his offhand professional opinion Sam Tabor was as crazy as a bedbug. "If you are asking whether he is legally sane, that's another kettle of bug entirely. We are speaking, you understand, of that purely imaginary line that girdles the globe, separating the eccentric, the dotty and the nutso. Any *school*child could tell you that."

From the back of the room Ambose said, "Well, that's what we name our game, sir, That's what I'll be asking you on the stand. Did he or did he not, in your professional opinion, know the nature and quality of his act?"

"Well, I'll tell you, Big Fellow." His lips moved into the merest semblance of a smile. "Your good friend Sam Tabor asked me to say hello to you. If *you* had come along to stand there by my side, I have every reason to believe he'd have talked his fool head off and, with any luck at all, put himself right into the electric chair."

Oh no! Not if Nevins had anything to say about it. *Mister* Ambose wasn't going to talk to his friend *Mister* Tabor again until Mr. Tabor had an attorney at his side to advise him of his rights. "Isn't that right, *Mister* Ambose?"

"To advise him not to talk to you," Swann clucked. "Jesus Hernandez Christ, the way you people run your business these days, it's a wonder you ever get to burn anybody. If we had to tell our patients they had any rights, where would the American Psychiatric Association be today?"

While Swann had missed neither the note of censure on Nevins' side nor the ready acceptance of censure by Ambose—both patently absurd since Nevins himself had sent Swann to talk to Tabor only this morning—he felt no need to comment on it. Doc Swann knew, better than anybody else, what game they were playing and why they played it. Instead he said, "And don't go away thinking I missed the first passing reference to your visit to Tabor last night. The beloved old eavesdropper hears all. I was just wondering why Tabor didn't let me know he'd already talked to you."

"He didn't? Why would that be, sir? Why wouldn't he want you to know that?"

"Well, sir, I would hardly be in a position to answer that question unless I had an opportunity to examine at least two dozen of his childhood dreams. But as an educated guess, I'd say the poor fellow is suffering from the classic delusion that you fellows run this office well enough so that one cog knows what the other cog is doing."

Hilliard Nevins told the reporters that he had got the news from a perfect stranger on his way home. It wasn't that he wanted to lie, it was only that he didn't want history to record that he had heard about it in a dress shop, Mrs. Nevins having discovered that the formal dress she intended to wear to the Bar Association dinner had to be let out at the hips.

Lenore Darringer was just leaving the courthouse when she heard the squad car siren racing down Baltan street, on the far side of the courthouse, toward the courtyard entrance to the sheriff's office. A big open-faced kid whom she recognized from Brian McNamara's Young Adults Service was standing there in a red and white polo shirt, with a transistor radio held to his ear. Having no one else to talk to, he turned to Lenore and, grinning nervously, told her, "They must be bringing in whoever it was killed this guy Wilcke."

Lenore turned back into the courthouse to take the calls she knew would be pouring into the district attorney's office. She had just taken her cigarettes and cigarette lighter out of her pocketbook and placed them on her desk when the call came from Hilliard Nevins instructing her to have everybody from the office leave a number where they could be reached at all times. "And Lenore, if Dee has already gone home, tell him not to come back if his head is giving him any trouble. Tell him I said there's nothing we can't handle without him or, anyway, that can't wait until tomorrow. And Lenore, if anybody calls from Bert Chester's office tell them you're expecting me any minute. Got it?"

Tommy Mallon got the word from his answering service, which screened all calls to his home phone. "Sheriff Stringfellow wants you to call him immediately and urgently, Mr. Mallon," the girl said. And then, "Tommy, are you going to defend the man who killed Chief Justice Wilcke?"

"Give that to me once again, dear," Mallon said. "Give it to me slowly and e-nun-ci-ate distinctly. Now then. Defend the man who what?"

"Killed Chief Justice Wilcke. Didn't you hear? They say it was some deputy sheriff who went crazy."

June 15, Newport, N.J. (AP)—Famed Chicago attorney Norman Bannerman was holding a press conference in his hotel suite at the Continental Hotel when the news was brought about the assassination of Chief Justice David B. Wilcke. "Outrageous and incredible," Bannerman exclaimed. "This country is coming upon dark and foreboding times when the highest judicial figure in the land can be gunned down by a disgruntled police officer. I have every confidence that the American judiciary, from top to bottom, will have the courage and dedication to resist this blatant attempt at intimidation."

Mr. Bannerman arrived in this little town, without fanfare, two days ago to take over the defense of Alfred P. Harrenson, a 26-year-old illiterate Negro who is being tried for the rape-robbery of a 56-year-old white woman.

When he heard the news come over the car radio DeWitt Pawley made a quick and illegal U-turn and headed back to the office so that he could check with the Justice Department on which of them had jurisdiction. "Don't worry about a thing," he told the deputy seated alongside him. "I've got a lot of influence downtown. I'm a personal friend of Jim Ambose."

As he was entering the elevator he heard Corinne Zeigler calling out to him, and he reacted quickly enough so that he was able to hold the door while she came clicking over the marbled lobby floor. Corinne had also heard the news over her car radio and, anticipating that there might well be some poring-over of the law books that night, had driven right back.

No sooner had they pushed through the heavy glass doors than Lenore relayed Hilliard Nevins' obviously outdated message. "*Now* you tell me," Pawley groaned. "If I'd had the good sense to call ahead I'd now be resting in the bosom of my family, telling them all to shut up so that I could rest the wound in my headbone."

Lenore, who had been running her pencil down the long list of names and telephone numbers on her pad, explained rather wistfully that she had been trying to get Ambose at home and there had been no answer, and when Pawley disappeared into Nevins' office behind her without making any comment, she seemed to feel kind of left out of things. "Mr. Pawley," she called out hopefully. "Is there anyplace else you think I should try to get him?"

She reflected upon his unenthusiastic response to that one for a few seconds, tapping the eraser end of her pencil against the pad. "Well, if Mr. Ambose decides to call in," she said, raising her voice so that it would carry into the office, "do you have any message you want me to deliver to him?"

Pawley stuck his head back into the outer office. "You're damned right I do! You tell Mr. Ambose he's under strict orders to do exactly as he pleases. That way," he said, working his eyebrows up and down like Groucho, "we've got him right where we want him. Following orders to a T."

Squad Car 51 was cruising along Emerson Avenue, in the ghetto area of town, when the call came over for Cars 101 and 104 to proceed to the courthouse to help in traffic control. The monitoring corner of Ambose's brain in charge of protecting what belonged to him had homed in immediately on the word "court-house." Since he knew that Cars 101 and 104 carried the officers in charge of the Traffic Division, he assumed that an automobile accident had snarled the homegoing traffic.

And then, loud and clear, Unit 1 broke in: "This is Chief Wilson. For attention of all units: Chief Justice David Wilcke has been assassinated on the steps of the City Hall building. The perpetrator has been apprehended and is being taken to county jail in County Squad Number two. All units in vicinity of courthouse are to proceed to county jail to lend help in emergency traffic only. Repeat: Lend help in emergency traffic only. This is the sheriff's baby. Ten–four."

Jim Ambose and Sergeant Harvey Leigh had drawn closer to the radio as the report was coming over, as if they felt they could somehow find out more about it through sheer proximity. "Now isn't that too bad," Ambose smirked, leaning back. "I did so want to have a few words with the man tonight about crime in the streets."

As Squad Cars 31, 42 and 18 came in, in quick succession, to acknowledge that they were en route to Riverway and Baltan, Harv Leigh said with a grim satisfaction of his own, "Now maybe we'll get some cooperation on keeping these kooks and commies in some kind of law and order again. You see what happens! Didn't I say all along that something like this was bound to happen if they didn't put the authority back into the hands of the police where it belongs! Now maybe the next kook that gets up and says how they ought to put the poor disturbed boy in an asylum so they can study him will get a rap across the mouth!"

Ambose advised him not to hold his breath. The first thing they were going to have to find out was who had done the foul deed. After which, and he could make book on it, there would be a loud outcry by our more sensitive public figures not to desecrate the life work of the martyred Chief Justice by anything as ignoble as vengeance or punishment.

Everything about Sergeant Leigh announced that he was perfectly willing to bow to Ambose's superior knowledge on such matters. "Only damnit all, why did it have to happen in Lowell? You know who they're going to blame, don't you? The P.D. Whenever something like this happens they're always looking to put the blame on the P.D."

As they drove on toward the courthouse it became only too apparent that what was troubling Sergeant Leigh as much as the assassination itself was that they were taking the suspect to the county jail instead of the police station. Ambose could see what that meant, couldn't he? "It means that they've already begun the campaign of villification against the P.D." He shook his head in dismay. "I just hope they know what they're doing."

"Yeah," said Jim Ambose, dismayed not at all. "Wouldn't it be a shame if they had to let the guy go because they took him to the wrong jail?"

Ambose had not been aware that Leigh was so hipped on the subject ("campaign of villification" yet) and while he sympathized with him he could not help but be mildly amused at this latest example of how jealously each man guards his own small prerogatives. As far as Ambose was concerned, it was not at all surprising that the assassination of a Chief Justice should create its own rules.

Right from the beginning he had viewed the report from an entirely different perspective than Sergeant Leigh. He knew from experience that defense attorneys pounce upon any change in normal procedure to try to cloud the issue. If the defense went for a change of venue—and they had to go for it in any heavily publicized case if only to set up a basis for an appeal—the defense counsel would ask whoever had made that decision whether it was not true that feeling was running so high against his client in Lowell that the police had been afraid to risk the customary transfer between the police station and the county jail? Jim Ambose would then ask him whether it wasn't merely a reasonable precaution for a reasonable man to have taken, and that would be the end of that. It would amount to nothing, and Ambose didn't have the luxury of squandering his mind's time on nothing.

Thinking back over it later he would remember, not without satisfaction, that he had taken the news without any wasted emotion. For when David Wilcke became a victim, he had also become Jim Ambose's client. It would have been different, he was willing enough to concede, if it had happened anywhere else. But it had happened in his town, and if Harv was right about nothing else, he was right that nobody could take any pleasure in that. On the other hand, he was fully aware that if it had happened in any other town Jim Ambose would not be about to prosecute one of the great cases in legal history. The greatest case, quite possibly, anybody had ever prosecuted in this country.

Confident as he had always been that he could prosecute a case with anybody in the world, he had resigned himself—without really dwelling that much upon it—that he would leave office, when he did, unappreciated by anyone except his own boys and a few well-bloodied opponents. So OK. That was the way it was. As a realist, he had recognized very early that the glory always went to the defense attorney. He was the one who put on the show. He was the one who was pleading for men's lives or freedom, stripping souls bare, proclaiming innocence or beseeching mercy. For the prosecutor there was only the remorseless flow of evidence, the righteous stance, the pursuit of justice. For a prosecutor—for Jim Ambose, anyway—it was enough to know that he was doing a job for which society, if society had any sense at all, honored him.

In every trial there came the moment when his instinct told him to pick up the ball and make his run. As soon as he had absorbed the hard fact of the assassination itself, he recognized that unless the assassin turned out to be a raving maniac that moment had come in his career. James J. Ambose of Lowell was about to step onto a national stage. If everything went well—and he would see to it that it did—he would no longer need the support of Hilliard Nevins or anyone else.

With the radio crackling out nothing more than routine police calls, Ambose reached for the microphone. "This is Ambose in Squad 51," he said. "Assistant District Attorney James Ambose. If you have any information on the suspect, dispatcher, it's important that I know. Has any such information come over your hot line?"

The dispatcher gave him a negative about the hot line. "My information is that television has been broadcasting an unconfirmed report that the suspect is a deputy sheriff. I will repeat that the report is unconfirmed. And let's tighten up on procedure, all units, and stay with the CBC rules. These conversations are being monitored and taped."

"You see what I mean?" Harv said. Now the police were getting their information from television. "How do you think that's gonna look if anybody checks these calls and hears that?"

They being the conditions that prevailed, sound investigatory procedure dictated that they proceed with speed and dispatch to the nearest source of information. He had been meaning, said Ambose, to pay a friendly call on Muley, anyway.

Muley's was a small nondescript bar in a line of small nondescript marginal stores. Above the bar there had once been a gymnasium, long closed and still unoccupied. On one side was an old clothes store; on the other a radio–TV repair shop. Considering that it was the kind of working neighborhood where the men were in the habit of dropping in for a quick one on the way home, business didn't seem to be very good. Either Muley was losing his clientele, which Jim didn't like one bit, or—more likely—there had been a general impulse to rush home and talk about the assassination with family and neighbors. Muley was a big, heavy man, laboriously flat of foot. As soon as he saw Ambose come through the door, he drew a beer and moved along with him to the end of the bar. "Any day now, Mr. Ambose," Muley said, the soul of sincerity. "Look, don't I know who my friends are?"

Ambose, sipping without pleasure against the head of the beer, looked to the rather worn, fluttering television screen which sat atop a high wooden perch at the other end of the bar. Josh Flowers was saying that although the technical problems hadn't been worked out yet, they were going to rerun the film of the assassination.

"Hey, ain't that something about the Chief Justice," Muley said. "Was it really some poor off-duty deputy flipped his lid, Mr. Ambose? Boy, that don't do this city no good, does it?"

Halfway down the bar, a comparatively neatly-dressed, well-shaven little man muttered, "And now they're bringing murder right into your own living room. Sex and violence and dirty commercials, that's what's been the ruination of the youth of the country." His eyes had never left the screen. "And all of it coming right into your own living room."

There it was, indeed. David Boone Wilcke, big as life, coming into millions of living rooms. There he was, all right. David Wilcke coming out onto the portico, smiling. Karney's man, young Clougherty, introducing him to Flowers and then backing almost completely out of camera range.

"No sound," Muley said, as old Karney was being pulled into the foreground by Wilcke. "They been having some trouble with the sound there." Wilcke himself looked to be in great spirits. *(Great for the jury, the hearty, healthy man brought down in the prime of life.)* He was grinning even more broadly now at someone down the stairs, and then—astonishingly—his thumbs were in his ears and his hands were fanning out alongside his head and right there—all at once —the action stopped, freezing the Chief Justice in the attitude of one of those hallelujah dancers. Karney, having twisted his head around, was looking off beyond the camera, Flowers and Clougherty were both staring directly at Wilcke, and, in the background, like an undisciplined chorus, the newspapermen and lawmen were disported in every conceivable direction.

From the screen Josh Flowers was intoning that what they were seeing in the last second in the life of David Wilcke was a perfect example of the fun-loving, unpretentious attitude that had made the late Chief Justice so well loved by people from every walk of American life. *(Great for the jury, just great. "This most human and humane of men . . .")*

When the picture moved again Ambose had the feeling that they had taken out the key frame. The whole body seemed to snap back and lose focus, the victim and the camera both reeling with the impact of the shot, the upraised hands now leaving the distinct impression that he had been trying to fend off a silent attacker. In that vacuum of sound you were somehow left with the impression that the shadow of an eagle had darted across the right side of Wilcke's face, tearing it away.

Viewing it as a fellow human being, Jim Ambose couldn't help but wince. Viewing it as a prosecutor, he could not help but look with satisfaction upon such powerful and grisly evidence.

Up on the screen there was a sudden sense of vertigo as the camera, jolted by the surge of the crowd while it was being swung around toward the direction of the shot, swung instead to the sky (following, it seemed, the flight of the escaping eagle) and then, swooping down, focused into a mass of people struggling at the foot of the stairway. Immediately, the mass fragmented, breaking off at the fringes. "Look for the man with the drawn gun at the bottom of your screen," Flowers directed. "He has been identified as Booker Phillips, chief deputy sheriff, making the arrest on the alleged assassin."

Ambose had already recognized Booker Phillips pushing someone behind him as he retreated backwards toward the sidewalk, his gun drawn as if he were holding off the crowd. Although Booker's body was shielding his prisoner from the camera as well as from the crowd, there was something familiar about the build, the bearing, the total appearance. Just as Ambose recognized who it was, there was the dizzying shot of the sky again as the cameraman, trying to fight his way down through the crowd, was knocked completely off his feet.

Josh Flowers could only repeat that in addition to the unconfirmed report that the alleged assassin was a deputy sheriff, other reports were coming in from around the country that it was a right-wing plot and that to be on the safe side the eight other Justices were being provided with protection.

Returning to the squad car, Ambose gave Harvey Leigh a quick fill-in. "Alleged assassin." It was enough to make you cry. They had him with a moving-picture camera and they still thought they had to protect his rights by saying "alleged." "Alleged deputy" would be more like it. Half-assed deputy would be even better.

"The guy in Missing Persons?" Leigh was saying, in disbelief. "Sure. Kind of a balding dumpy guy." Back when he was in Theft and Burglary he'd had a couple of cases he'd checked out with him. After twenty-four years on the force Harv was not a man to be easily thrown but you could see that this had really thrown him. "Jesus Christ, Sam Tabor! You know him, Jim? You know anything at all about him?"

"Well, let's put it this way. I had lunch with him today."

"Sonofagun," Leigh said, brightening. "Sure. That explains it."

Now it was Ambose's turn to be thrown. Explained what?

"Why they took him to the courthouse," Harv said, his world now nicely back in order. "What is he, Jim, some kind of a commie or a kook or what?"

Three blocks from the courthouse they ran into such heavy traffic that Ambose jumped out of the squad car and walked the rest of the way. Which wasn't that much of an improvement. So many people had descended upon the courthouse on foot that the police had found it necessary to set up barricades. What these people, piling up behind the barricade, expected to see or hear was more than Ambose could fathom. They were just standing there, quiet and solemn, nothing at all like the usual gathering of curiosity seekers. Apparently they wanted nothing more than to stand there within sight of the building where the man who had killed the Chief Justice was being held. Jim Ambose could only conclude that they were stunned that such a direct assault could have been made upon the law itself. Stunned and frightened. And why not? If Ambose had found out nothing else in twelve years of law enforcement, it was that the great strength of the law rested in the wholly unwarranted faith the people had in it.

Hard upon the barricade, whimpering softly, was a middle-aged woman, a drab of a woman clutching a huge brown alligator purse to her. Her hair, almost completely gray, was uncombed. The thin shapeless sweater thrown over her housedress was far too flimsy now that the cool of the early evening was setting in. "What's to become of us?" she was whimpering over and over. "What's to become of us?"

Poor old lady. He saw them, poor old ladies, drifting in and out of the DA's office—it seemed like every other day—complaining about some imagined wrong or imaginary threat. The growing legion of nuts. And yet you could not discount them, in moments of crisis and disaster, as criers of the mass emotions. It was the nuts who were most sensitive to the throbs in the air, the adrenal stirrings. Being helpless to contend with themselves, knowing their helplessness, the law was the only protection they had, and when it was assaulted so directly they were confronted, head-on, with their own terrifying vulnerability. No, you could not discount them. The tune they chanted, however broken, was the tune that was on the tip of everybody else's tongue.

One of the traffic cops, spotting Ambose, came hurrying over to pull the wooden horse aside so that he could step through, and yet Jim paused there for a moment on the other side and, on some uncertain impulse, turned back and introduced himself, courteously and gravely, to the whimpering old woman. She looked at him without comprehension. He took out his wallet and handed her his card. "I want you to know that we're going to take care of whoever did this," he said, very distinctly. "You have my word on that personally."

"God bless you," she said. Uncertain. Hopeful. "God bless you."

"It will be perfectly all right for you to go home now if you want to. Nothing is going to happen. Nothing at all." He drew his arms into himself and shivered to show that he understood how cold she must be. "If you want to. Only if you want to."

"It's really all right?" she asked. Like a child. Poor, pitiful old woman. Frightened as a child. "Nothing's going to happen? I can go home?"

"That's right. You just go on home. And if there's anything you want, anything that's worrying you or any questions you want to ask, you just call me at that number, the number on the card, and I'll see that everything gets taken care of."

Her face opened up into a big craggy-toothed smile, beautiful with the trust and surrender of a child. In a slow and dreamy movement she enfolded the card between her hands and rested her cheek against it, like a baby showing her mother she knew how to go sleep-sleep. "That's a good girl," Ambose said. "You just make sure you don't lose that card, hear?"

He'd regret it, he knew. She'd be on the phone for the rest of her life, complaining about every man who came to her door. If he was lucky, he told himself, she'd lose the card on the way home.

Barricade or no, the television truck was parked like a brooding presence directly in front of the courthouse steps.

There were two ways to get to the sheriff's office. One was to go up those steps, through the front door and on past the Records Office. The other was to go all the way around to the courtyard on the far side and in through the jail office where the prisoners were brought in. That was the route Ambose would have taken if he had wanted to duck the press. He didn't.

Inside the lobby the reporters and photographers were milling around in force, sweaty and disgruntled, griping about the treatment they had been receiving all day and talking indignantly about the people's right to know. Rich Caples, who covered the courthouse for the *Morning Globe,* came hustling over to him immediately to plead on behalf of his soon-to-be-hungry children for anything he had on this deputy. Anything. His editors were screaming for information and Stringfellow had clammed up completely.

Walking on, carrying Caples along with him, Ambose said, "You didn't get this from me but there's a Sam Tabor works up in the courthouse in Missing Persons."

"That's great, Jim. My debt is eternal. What I got to know now, what my editor is screaming for, is whether charges are going to be filed tonight and what he's being charged with."

Sweeping the hall quickly, he saw that Caples' opposite number at the afternoon *News-Chronicle,* Conrad Rittenhouse, was backed up against the wall, talking to a couple of out-of-town writers. "I'll let you know what I can, *when* I can," Ambose said. "If I shake my head it means it doesn't look like anything's going to be filed tonight. If I nod it means he's been filed on, murder one." He couldn't really see how it could be anything but murder one, Ambose told him, but if he gave him any other sign Caples would just have to figure it out as best he could.

"More than that, old friend, I cannot ask."

Ambose had finally caught Rittenhouse's eye. "One thing," he said. "Tell Conrad." Telling Conrad would take not a thing away from Caples, because the afternoon paper had already blown its deadline. The *Globe* not only had the story all to itself for the rest of the night, the *Globe* also owned a radio and television station. Caples was losing nothing, Rittenhouse was being protected with his own editors and, most important of all, Jim Ambose was protecting himself with everybody.

There remained only one final detail to be taken care of. "I'm giving you this the same way I gave you the other," Ambose told him, beckoning him closer. "But from everything I hear there's a good chance this is part of a left-wing conspiracy."

Bob Stringfellow jumped up from behind his desk and came halfway out to the door to greet him. "Damnit, Jim," he growled. "Where you been? What's been keeping you? What do they say about the jurisdiction upstairs?"

When Ambose told him he didn't know what they were saying because he hadn't been up there yet, the sheriff turned his back on him in disgust. "They're supposed to be my lawyers," he told the room at large. "Huh! Some lawyers!"

The scene that Ambose had been prepared to walk into, a scene of high purpose and bustling activity, with phones ringing and people yelling and personnel—high-level and low—whipping in and out, was nowhere to be seen. Instead, there were only Red Torgeson, the special agent in charge of the Secret Service office, and Bernie Rogell of the FBI, both of them slouched, stolidly and lumpily, in their chairs; and, seated across from Stringfellow's clerk, Justice of the Peace Harold Morrison, who was one of Stringfellow's closer cronies. The whole atmosphere reminded him of a losing locker room after a particularly bad defeat; emotionally drained, physically spent, and yet somehow heavy with an overhanging sense of mutual blame and personal shame.

Morrison was from over in Harper, hardly the closest jurisdiction, which could only mean that Stringfellow was giving a friend the opportunity of affixing his name to whatever historical documents were going to be drawn up. Far from looking happy about it, Morrison was studiously avoiding Ambose's eye; looking right past him, in fact, as if he were studying the pictures on the wall. That was a laugh. The walls of Stringfellow's office—every spare inch—were covered with framed photographs of his deputies, either making arrests or receiving awards. The sheriff had a standing request with both newspapers to send him a glossy, suitable for framing, every time one of his men's pictures was taken. One of the great spectator sports around the courthouse was to watch the expression on the faces of Stringfellow's visitors turn from interest to bewilderment to dismay as they searched for *somebody* they could make some comment upon among what was known around the courthouse as "Stringfellow's Gallery of the Unknown, the Uncelebrated and the Unwashed."

Even Stringfellow's clerk, Dhalgren, looked whipped, and Dhalgren, a slim young guy with sharp features and silky blond hair, could usually be counted on for some kind of snotty greeting. Ambose had even had to slap him down a couple of times in the beginning to teach him some manners.

"If you're sending anybody out to his house with a search warrant," Ambose said, nodding toward Morrison, "I want to go along. But first I want to talk to Tabor."

Nobody was going nowhere, Stringfellow wanted him to understand, until he found out where his office stood. He turned his displeasure upon Torgeson and Rogell. "Let the Bureau go get a warrant if the Bureau's so interested."

When Rogell let it be known that the Bureau was also waiting to hear about the jurisdiction, Ambose wanted to know when had that ever stopped the FBI before? "Hell, I'll bet you've got three guys out there right now scooping everything that's good into their magic FBI Kits."

Ambose still couldn't understand why Stringfellow, who was, after all, only a jailer, was so concerned about the jurisdiction.

"Oh, you don't, don't you?" His face was set and stubborn. "Because this is my man who done it, and now I got him when I'm not supposed to. How would it look if I filed wrong on a deputy—which you know darn well, Jim, is what everybody thinks he is. Hah! *Some* deputy. It would look just great if we filed wrong and he got away with killing the Chief Justice, wouldn't it?"

"If you're asking me," Ambose said, "I think it would be a barrel of laughs." Now that he had the opportunity to let his mind linger over what it had been playing with ever since the news came over, the possibility that a man could kill the Chief Justice and get away with it because of the Chief Justice's own rulings struck him as being as close as we were likely to get to the ultimate justice.

"You're a barrel of laughs yourself," Rogell said, not happily. Very briefly, Ambose allowed his gaze to rest upon Rogell. As much as he would have enjoyed taking Rogell on, it was far more important at the moment to find out what was going on here. What was going on, he found out, was that Stringfellow was not about to let anybody question his prisoner until Tommy Mallon was at his side.

"You see the switch they got me in, don't you, Jim? If we don't question him, they'll say we're showing him favoritism. If we do question him, they'll say we violated his rights. That's the switch they got me in right there. When you're dealing with John Q. Public, you're—" He jerked his thumb toward Torgeson and Rogell, not paying them the respect of looking at them. "If these guys want to talk to him, all they got to do is take him away. No sweat. No trouble." Neither of them said a word. "Oh," he said, letting his eyes go to them now. "Don't want him, huh? Too bad."

While Ambose bowed to nobody in his delight over the discomfort of the FBI and the Secret Service, he had to tell Stringfellow that the law only said you had to tell the suspect he didn't have to talk to you; it didn't say that you couldn't ask him whether he wanted to.

Not on this one, Stringfellow said grimly. Not a chance. "I asked him did he want to talk to *me,* and he said he didn't want to talk to anybody until he'd talked with you and Tommy Mallon. And," he said, growing truculent again, "if you think that means *you're* going to talk to him until Mallon gets here, you'd just better . . . wash that idea out of your head in a hurry."

"Jim," Torgeson said quickly. "There's only one thing I got to know. Was he part of any plot? Is there anybody else in with him? Any accomplices? Did anybody know about it beforehand? You understand the importance of that. How vital it is that . . . how *essential* it is that if there is anybody else we find it out at once."

Ambose had intended to bull his way past Stringfellow anyway, and now that he knew Tabor had asked to see him, there was nobody on God's green earth who was going to keep him away. Not that he was anticipating any trouble. Despite what Stringfellow had said, if he had not wanted Jim to talk to Tabor he wouldn't have let him know, in that sly, indirect way, that Tabor had asked for him.

"I'll tell you what you'd just better do then," Ambose said. "You just better take up your problem with the dear departed's colleagues. They don't think it's all that essential at all. They say the prisoner's got to have his lawyer there. I mean, if there's eight other clerks out gunning for them, that's what's known in the Bill of Rights as tough titty." God, he thought, wouldn't it be great if it were true. From what he knew about Tabor, though, the idea that he was part of any cabal of assassins was too much to hope for. "Let's back up a little," he said. "Bob, if you don't want him all this bad, why have you got him?"

"Why have I got him?" The sheriff peered around the room, as if to satisfy himself that everybody had heard the question and been afforded the time to reflect upon its absurdity. "He wants to know why have I got him."

The sheriff was so agitated, the spare, bony face so strained, that Ambose was studying him almost clinically. It was clear enough that Stringfellow saw himself as a man unjustly beset by hostile forces. If it also seemed that he was cracking under pressure, then Ambose would have to find some way to prevent him from doing anything that might indeed jeopardize the whole case.

"Well, I will tell you why I got him. I have got him because Booker—*damn him to the eternal torture of eternal hell!*—took him from *that* one's Secret Service, which had the primary responsibility if you want to know what I think, and *that* one's FBI, which had the secondary responsibility and, for that matter, Phil Wilson's police department—where were they?—when every one of them, all of them, had an assigned force, a special detail . . ."

"You're acting like a damn fool, Bob," Torgeson said, mildly enough. "We didn't ask Booker to pull a gun on us. That was his own brilliant idea."

"Did I hear you say that Booker *took* him?" Ambose asked the sheriff. "Pulled a gun on *them?*" In the worst of clouds, it was plain, there was a silver lining. "Sheriff," he said, "give that man a raise."

Stringfellow gave him the look that said he was going to "give him" all right. But a look was all. The anger seemed to go right out of him, and in its place came the weary resignation of a man who knows that such things can only happen to him. "At gunpoint he took him. He took him at gunpoint because he was afraid, don't you see, that somebody else might get all the credit for letting the Chief Justice get assassinated. And he couldn't have that, could we?"

And why had Booker been that eager? "Because Booker took him there, that's why," the sheriff said. He was exquisitely patient now; he was a man who, having been tortured beyond all human endurance by the fools he had to contend with in the daily pursuit of his duties, had found it necessary to accommodate himself to their idiocies and incompetencies if only to preserve his own sanity. "Because Booker took him from this office, is that right, Dhalgren?" Oh, Dhalgren could tell him, all right. "From *this* office, in *our* car, so that he'd be sure to get him there in time to kill the Chief Justice, don't you see? I mean if you're going to take a man to kill somebody, it's only proper etiquette that you have to take him back again." The tone of patient suffering being hardly one a man of Sheriff Stringfellow's temperament was going to hold to indefinitely, he suddenly barked, "Door-to-door service, that's the way we do it around here, isn't it, Dhalgren!"

Dhalgren, flushing heavily, shuffled the papers in front of him. He chewed on the inside of his mouth. He said nothing.

"Nobody's blaming you," Torgeson said. "You're getting all excited over nothing."

"Like hell I am. It's our man done it and it's our man brought him there and it's our man arrested him. And that's all anybody knows or cares to know. Nobody's avoiding their responsibilities! Oh no! Well, all I got to say is this. If we're going to get crucified for a lamb, we might just as well get crucified for a . . . a . . . a fox. If the FBI wants to talk to him, the Justice Department can take him off our hands. If the Secret Service wants to talk to him, the Treasury Department can take him off our hands."

"You're talking like a damn fool," Rogell said. "I don't tell the Justice Department what to do. They tell me."

"Now you got it! And the Justice Department don't tell me. I tell them. Not in my jail, they don't. I say who gets to talk to people in my jail and I say who don't. I got to let him see his lawyers and his blood relatives. Anybody else, it's at my convenience and pleasure, and if there's no federal jurisdiction I don't see any com*pel*ling reason, if you please, why any federal agents need to talk to him."

Ambose could finally see what was really bothering the sheriff. And it wasn't jurisdiction. Jurisdiction, my eye. When Booker lugged Tabor back to the county jail, everybody else had become more than content to sit back and let the sheriff's office take the heat for the whole thing, including the breakdown in protection. Especially the breakdown in protection. Remembering the smugness in Chief Wilson's voice while he was telling his squad cars that this was the sheriff's baby, Ambose could only sympathize with him. Stringfellow, no damn fool at all, was letting them know that if there was any question about the jurisdiction, they had damn well better take the man out of his jail because as long as he remained there they weren't going to get to talk to him.

All right, then. Ambose was perfectly satisfied that Stringfellow wasn't panicking. The sheriff saw himself—not wholly without justification—as a man who was fighting to save the reputation of his department. Under those circumstances, the pictures on the wall took on a new and rather poignant flavor.

Ambose would do what he could for him. He would leak the real story to Rich Caples and, once it was in print, the other agencies would have to make some kind of statement, carefully guarded, mindful of their own image, but making it clear that they were magnanimously acknowledging their share of the blame. At the moment, though, the needs of the sheriff, however appealing, happened to be running contrary to his own. Maybe Stringfellow didn't want Tabor but, by god, Jim Ambose did.

Until he had walked into the sheriff's office it had never occurred to Ambose that the state might not have jurisdiction. "Bob," he said, "if there's no specific law that puts this under the federal code, it's our baby." And if there *was* a law, somebody in the Justice Department would certainly have come up with it by now. It was even remotely possible, he said, that somebody in the DA's office would have come up with it.

Stringfellow had already turned to his friend, Justice Morrison, by then and his friend was quite obviously concurring.

"I don't see any great problem here," Ambose said. He was on his feet now, moving smartly to get things rolling. As soon as Tommy got there, they'd charge Tabor with suspicion of murdering the Chief Justice, and Justice Morrison would be able to read him off the gospel in the strictest compliance with the most recent decrees of his victim. "If you want to, Bob, and I think you're right about that, we can have Justice Morrison arraign him before midnight, and history will record that you arrested, charged and filed on the man who killed the Chief Justice before the calendar day was over." He glanced down at his watch. "Always assuming his attorney gets here before the calendar day is over."

At a nod from Stringfellow, Morrison reached down for his briefcase and, holding it rather awkwardly in his lap, rummaged around until he came out with the form for a general affidavit. Jim Ambose watched over Morrison's shoulder while the justice of the peace filled in the date, and then, speaking slowly so that Morrison could stay with him, he dictated, "Did then and there, voluntarily and with malice aforethought, kill David Boone Wilcke, Chief Justice of the United States, by shooting him with a gun."

There remained, as always, the problem of his ticklish relationship with Hilliard Nevins. While Ambose didn't want to bypass Nevins, he didn't want to give him any chance of interfering with him, either. In addition to which he knew very well that Nevins didn't want to know what he was doing this early in the game. Nevins wanted him to get their case into motion, while retaining the right to second-guess him at his leisure.

"The only thing," he said, resting his hand on Justice Morrison's shoulder, "is that Nevins might want to sign this complaint himself, officially, it being a historical document and all that. Tell you what let's do. Let's throw in some surplusage so that he can be filed on again later, if the boss man wants to, without making him look like too much of a publicity hound."

With a quick side-glance at Torgeson and Rogell, he said, "How about, 'in furtherance of a left-wing plot to effect the liberation—I mean *liberalization*—of the Supreme Court, USA.' "

At the sound of the words "left-wing plot," Torgeson and Rogell had both come to their feet, shouting, "Hey . . ." And then realizing, sourly, that Jim Ambose was just playing one of Jim Ambose's little games with them they sank back, even more sourly, into their chairs.

"Just a thought, fellows. Just a suggestion." They were only putting it in, he reminded them with a wholly fraudulent innocence, so they would have something to take out. "I'll tell you, Judge. Maybe you'd just better add, 'on the staircase in front of City Hall' and let it go at that." That was ambiguous enough to be taken out and harmless enough to be left in. He repeated it more slowly, so that Morrison could write it down. "Good," he said, as he plucked the pen out of Morrison's hand. "I'll sign it for now, enjoy my moment in history's harsh glare and then fade away to be heard from nevermore."

Still blowing on his signature, he carried the affidavit over to Stringfellow, who had been sitting unhappily at his desk, his chin on his chest. "Don't make too much of this, Bob," Ambose told him, as the sheriff affixed his signature as the officer in charge. "From the little I know, it seems to me that Booker arrested the suspect within seconds after he committed the crime. I'd call that good police work." The only thing he wanted to know now was how come Booker had taken Tabor over there to begin with.

"Let Booker tell you." Stringfellow sighed, in a way that seemed to say that it would constitute cruel and unusual punishment to have to tell it himself this late in the day. "Just remember that I'm telling you ahead of time that you're not going to believe it."

Booker, it seemed, had been assigned to the Ready Room down in the basement where they had taken affidavits from the witnesses. There could not be too much doubt that making Booker listen to the story of the murder over and over *had* been designed as cruel and unusual punishment.

"If you don't mind," Ambose said, "I'd rather hear it from Tabor first."

That wasn't true. All things being equal, he'd much rather have started with Booker. But all things weren't equal. Time was passing, and he wanted to get a shot at Tabor before Mallon got there.

Stringfellow, giving up without a struggle, told Dhalgren to make him out a pass.

"He doesn't need a pass, Sheriff," Dhalgren said. "The prisoner hasn't been assigned to a cell yet. Remember?" The sulky, aggrieved tone told Jim Ambose that Dhalgren was not only showing that he was competent in his job but was making known, as best he dared, his justifiable complaint at the harsh words that had apparently been coming his way all day.

Stringfellow pushed his hat to the back of his head and stared at him in a sort of squintish disbelief. In the passing silence there was no doubt whatsoever that he was letting Dhalgren know, this one last time, that he didn't want any more trouble from *him*. At last he barked, sounding more like the man they knew, "Did I ask you what you thought, or did I tell you what to do?"

Dhalgren, flushing even redder, reached into his correspondence basket for the pad of passes. Stringfellow still wasn't through with him. "If you're unhappy in your work, Dhalgren, all you got to do is speak up and be heard. As difficult as it might be to get along without you, a man who uses his noodle the way you do, we might just be able to do that. I mean in a pinch."

Dhalgren made it out, silently and reluctantly. "What do you want me to put where it says 'cell?'" he asked Stringfellow.

"Well, where is he, you lunkhead!" Stringfellow roared.

Dhalgren, filling it in, muttered, "Never made out a pass to see a man in the Booking Room before in my life."

"That gives you and the late Chief Justice something in common," Ambose told him cheerfully. "The Chief Justice was never killed before in his life, either."

At the same moment that Ambose opened the staircase door to the Booking Room a prisoner was being brought in through the main entrance. A thin, sparrowy young man, olive-skinned, in high-heeled cowboy boots, dirty work pants and a smudged gray sweat-jacket. As each pair of eyes turned automatically to the other (Ambose's with no more than cursory interest), there arose in the young man's a fleeting, wholly unrealistic hope that perhaps from out of nowhere help had miraculously materialized. In the brief moment their eyes caught, he drew his hands into his chest and rubbed his left wrist tenderly and with that simple gesture was able to convey the message not that the wrist hurt but that the handcuffs were completely foreign to his experience and, therefore, to his nature. That he was a good kid really if only they could get to know him; that he hadn't meant it; that he would never, never do it again.

The deputy prodded him from behind with his nightstick, not gently but not urgently either. "Over there, Julio," he directed, steering him towards the fingerprint and mugging layout at the far end of the long room. Julio moved out with the stiff-legged, jerky step that sometimes took hold of them when they were so overwhelmed at having been caught up in the law, of actually being in jail, that they no longer had full control over their motor faculties. So caught up in his own minor calamity that he paid no further attention to the tall, big-shouldered man who was crossing behind him to the open doorway of the clean, white-walled dispensary where the other, considerably more celebrated prisoner was being held.

Sam Tabor was sitting on the examining table against the far wall, talking rather amiably to the two deputies guarding him. Stripped down to shorts, shoes and stockings, his bare legs (surprisingly pale and skinny) dangling a few inches from the floor, his hands entwined rather comfortably under his paunch. His clothes were hanging from a hook behind him. His effects—wallet, change, keys, a handkerchief and some letters—had been placed on top of the white metallic desk underneath the high cathedral-like window, the only window in the not very large room. One way or another, Ambose could mark, the routine would find a way to take over. For while the sheriff had undoubtedly left instructions that the prison doctor was not to be called, Ambose could guess that Herb Jacklin, the dayside first-aid attendant, had been there. The MD was charged with giving each new prisoner a routine physical to make sure he had no communicable disease and was in no danger of dropping dead on the spot, but since the doctor wasn't always around to examine them before they were taken to a cell, the first-aid attendant had the far more critical job of giving every new prisoner a rectal examination to make sure they weren't smuggling any drugs into the jail. The guards would say, "Nobody told me anything about not letting Jacklin go about his business," and Jacklin would say, "Listen, I don't ask what they're in for, I just bend 'em over and give 'em a high massage."

At the sight of Jim Ambose Tabor's face seemed to brighten—much as if Ambose were a friend who had come to visit him in his sickroom. "Geez, Jim," he said, "I was wondering when you'd be here."

Ambose had seen thousands of men soon enough after they had been brought in to know that arrest—meaning the loss of freedom—ranked right after death as the great equalizer and, in many ways, as the greatest of all indignities. He had seen them react in every conceivable way from paralyzing fear to high-strutting braggadocio. The note of mild reproach in Tabor's greeting was, he had to admit, something new. He recognized the echo of Stringfellow's greeting ("Damnit Jim, what's been keeping you?") but there was also a faint echo of something else—something not so readily identifiable and therefore far more disturbing—in the playful curl of the smile at the corner of the lips. Please God, he prayed, don't let this guy be insane.

Tabor had apparently picked up the note of reproach in his voice, too, because he added rather apologetically, "I hope I haven't ruined your night."

"Well, Sam, you know how it is in this business. If it isn't one thing it's sure to be another." And there, for chrissake, was an answer to match the greeting. *If you hadn't killed the Chief Justice of the United States, Sam, I might have been called upon to question some hillbilly who had broken into a liquor store.* It did serve to remind him where he would have been tonight short of anything except the murder of the guest of honor. "I'll tell you this, Sam. You sure as hell put a crimp in the Bar Association dinner."

The smile disappeared. "Gee," Tabor said, "I hope the boys aren't too sore at me."

Sitting there, plump, balding, eager to please, Sam Tabor was something of a disappointment to Ambose. The man who had handed him the file that morning had been nothing more than a high-class clerk; the man who had slipped so obligingly to the next table at lunch, an anonymous interloper. But Sam Tabor in captivity was the man who had assassinated the Chief Justice, a force—however minor—in history. A suitable arrogance had somehow been anticipated. Ambose was not asking for defiance; he wasn't even asking for a surly stare. He'd have been satisfied, when you came right down to the bare minimum of it, if Tabor had sucked in his gut and thrown back his shoulders.

Normally, Ambose preferred to interrogate a man while he was still stripped down, preferably to the buff. Nothing made a man feel quite so subhuman—and therefore helpless, vulnerable, alien—as to be stripped naked. Knowing that you could see the unclothed body, there was the corollary sense that you could see the unclothed mind, too. With Tabor, it seemed like such an excellent idea to play into this wholly unrealistic attitude that Ambose was a friend who had come, in this moment of his extremity, to pay him a social call, that Ambose demanded to know why he wasn't in prison whites. And when the younger of the guards, Johnny Gerard, answered that their orders were to issue no prison clothes until they got word from the sheriff, he barked, "Well, your orders now are to get him into a pair of whites."

Johnny Gerard was a big, square-jawed young man—so good-looking in a rough, rugged way that he would have looked exactly right on a recruiting poster. "I take my orders from the sheriff," he said in a flat, uncompromising voice that informed Ambose that Stringfellow was not alone in his feeling that it had become the sheriff's office against the world.

Johnny Gerard was Stringfellow's boy. More than his boy—his personal reclamation project. Johnny had never been a bad boy. Oh no! He had just run with a bad crowd. Oh yes! A very bad crowd, a crowd that had been hitting some of Felix McPhait's biggest card games. Anybody who was tough enough to crack McPhait's security would, Stringfellow had seen right away, make one helluva deputy. Even if it took a pardon from the governor to clear the way.

Loyalty being a fading virtue, Ambose was not at all displeased to find that Johnny was still so loyal to the sheriff. Especially since it would do Ambose no harm at all if he had to show Tabor how hard he was fighting for him.

"It's OK," the other guard said, "I'll get them." Dick Blasser, an older head, had apparently read Ambose perfectly, or if he hadn't, had at least been able to understand that if Jim Ambose, of all people, wanted a prisoner dressed, then Jim Ambose had his reasons.

"Sam," Ambose said, "there's something I want you to tell me."

"Anything you want, Jim. All you got to do is ask." As agreeable as he was —assentive, attentive, helpful—they might have been back in Tabor's office, with Ambose asking if he could see the complainant's questionnaire.

"I'm supposed to warn you that you don't have to talk to me without the presence of a lawyer, and to warn you that if you do talk to me anything you say can be used for you or against you. But there's one question I would personally appreciate for you to answer."

Tabor had been listening intently and nodding. "I understand all that. Hell, I'm not going to give you any trouble. I shot him all right."

"Well, I don't think we're going to have too much trouble proving that. You didn't exactly shoot him in a locked room in the dead of night, Sam. What I want to know is whether there was anybody else involved."

". . . involved." The head stopped going up and down and started going back and forth. "No, just me."

With the edge of his thumb Ambose pushed his hat back. "Sam, I want you to understand before you go any further that if your lawyer wants to fight this, about the only defense he has is insanity."

There was that crooked smile again, and Ambose realized now that what had disturbed him, what had been nudging at him from the beginning, was the hint of a chuckle in the center of mortal danger. "Hell, I'm not insane."

"Well, you see, there's a lot of talk. They're getting phone calls and they're printing in some of the papers the possibility that this was some kind of a conspiracy by right-wing extremists." He could see that Tabor couldn't believe it. "Because of all those Supreme Court decisions."

Blasser was coming back through the door, a pair of prison whites over his arm and a wooden hanger swinging from the bend of his elbow. "Oh no," Tabor said, shaking his head quickly. "Nothing like that."

"What organizations do you belong to, Sam? We'll find out anyway, but if you could help us . . ."

In trying to get into the one-piece prison uniform Tabor was having trouble pulling the pants leg over his shoe. He finally yanked the first leg over and, after a minimum of thought, bent over and took off the other shoe. "Well," he said, grunting, "I'm not really what you'd call a joiner." He had buttoned up the uniform and was smoothing down the collar. Considering that Tabor could hardly be an easy man to fit, it fit him very nicely. As his hand searched through the breast pocket, getting the feel and *dimension* of it, he looked quite comfortable and, for some inexplicable reason, not out of place wearing it. He lifted himself back onto the examining table, exactly as he had been when Ambose entered. "No," he grunted, as he laboriously crossed the leg so that he could tie the shoe. "You couldn't very well call me a joiner. I was never one for mixing and following the crowd, if you know what I mean. I always felt that a man should think for himself and go by himself and not conform to the general trend of popular thought."

Given the fix he was in, the stiff, artificial language would have been perfectly understandable if the tone hadn't been all wrong. It was the tone of a man who had been picked out to be asked the Question of the Day for the Man in the Street television program ("Do you believe in going along with the crowd?") and knows he is going to be seen and heard by all his friends and neighbors.

"You ever attend any meetings of, say, the Ku Klux Klan or anything like that? The Minutemen or the John Birch Society or that kind of group?"

Sam was shocked. Not so much on his own account, you could see, as on Ambose's. "I know you have to ask these questions," he said. "But I'm no nut, if that's what you mean."

"What about your wife? What was her opinion of Wilcke?"

Sam Tabor rubbed hard against the stubble of his beard. (It would be a long time, Ambose thought, before he'd be shaving himself again. Perhaps as long as never.) "I don't know. You can ask her. You can tell her I said that she should tell you whatever you want to know." (*Yes, what about his wife?* With luck, Nevins might have got to her. Fat chance! The FBI probably had her, he decided. That would explain why Rogell had been sitting so patiently in Stringfellow's office.)

"I mean, did you ever talk to her about Wilcke? About any of the Supreme Court decisions? Do you have any impression that she felt one way or another about him?"

Tabor's head gave a quick little jerk as if he were trying to flick away a fly. "Not that I can think of. I don't think we ever talked about that particular subject. But ask her, Jim. She'll tell you. She has an excellent memory."

Blasser had listed all of Tabor's effects on the property sheet and he had been waiting until Ambose completed his line of questioning before he asked Sam to check the list and sign it. Tabor, taking his word for it, signed without looking but Blasser read off each item anyway: the clothing, the contents of the wallet, each coin, plus the four keys and, finally, the three folded letters—an unpaid telephone bill, postmarked June 1; a stock market information sheet, postmarked May 12; and an envelope addressed to Resident containing some brightly-colored sheets of shopping coupons allowing the bearer up to fifteen cents off for an item. It was postmarked February 16.

Ambose, listening with half an ear, was wondering whether he could afford to question Tabor any further. And behind it always the nagging question: *Where was Tommy Mallon?*

Blasser affixed his own signature to the sheet, had Ambose sign as witness, and recited, "The property and effects as listed here and vouched for will *be* submitted to the property clerk and returned to you when you go free." Taking his leave he said, "I can't wish you good luck, Tabor, but I don't wish you any bad luck, either." Something about the way he said it made it clear to Ambose that Blasser wouldn't be returning unless Ambose wanted him there as a witness. He had a communication going with Blasser, Ambose recognized. Blasser had looked very good here. If he ever had to work with anyone from the sheriff's office, he knew exactly whom he was going to ask for.

Tabor was sitting patiently on the examining table, his hands clasped around one knee, waiting to be asked another question.

What the hell, Ambose thought, why not?

"Sam," he said, "are you willing to answer other questions? You will observe that there is no recording machine and that nobody is taking stenographic notes. I will probably make some sketchy notes after I leave, for my own benefit, but I won't be testifying because I'll be prosecuting and the court doesn't look kindly upon having a participating lawyer take the stand. But Johnny here might be called. Do you understand that?"

"I wouldn't try to hide behind any of those Supreme Court rules," Sam Tabor said. "You know me better than that, Jim."

As much as it angered Jim to have to give Sam all those warnings, it angered him even more that in this brave new world of criminal law he had to stand there, shifting from one foot to another like a goddamn fool, and decide how much he could afford to let Tabor tell him. If he had been getting this kind of cooperation in the good old days he would have tied this guy right to the polygraph and got the real story. The truth. Inadmissible as evidence, but the truth. He toyed briefly with the idea of proposing to Mallon that in a case of such overwhelming importance they owed it to the country to put Tabor on the machine anyway in order to get the true story settled once and for all. Reluctantly, he pushed it aside. The polygraph had become a trap. If the defendant came close to passing, the defense lawyer demanded his immediate release. If he flunked, his lawyer announced that the machine was full of faults, the test meaningless and the phrase "lie detector" a misnomer.

Guilt or innocence wasn't in question in this case, of course, but insanity was. If there was anything in the readings that would support a plea of insanity, Mallon would demand that it be submitted into evidence. If it indicated that Tabor knew what he was doing, that he was sane, that he had a motive, that he had planned it, the prosecution could take such confirmation that it was on the side of virtue as its own reward. It was heads you win and tails I lose, and there was no percentage in that.

There was yet another alternative, though, and it was this other alternative that Ambose was giving his longest thought. Ambose could call the Crime Lab and have Tabor put on the machine while Mallon wasn't around—and to hell with everybody. Mallon would scream to high heavens. Let him. He'd have to do all his screaming to the judge in closed session. He wouldn't be able to bring it up in the courtroom because, once he did, the jury would assume the worst. All Mallon would get out of it would be a basis for an appeal, and Ambose was perfectly willing to cross that bridge when he came to it.

Forget about it! He might be willing to cross that bridge but you could be damn sure that Nevins wasn't. What was the percentage of getting Nevins on his back and turning Chobodian sour when he had an open and shut case anyway.

Out of the hundreds of decisions that Ambose would make in the case of the People v. Sam Tabor that was the one decision he would regret for the rest of his life. Not blame himself for; just regret.

"Before you go not hiding behind anything," he warned Tabor, "you'd better talk to your lawyer. Tommy Mallon might not be so anxious to take your case after you've thrown away all your rights."

Tabor's eyes darted over Jim's shoulder to the door, as if he expected Mallon to materialize at the invocation of his name. "Well," he said, "I've been kind of hoping that Tommy would take the case because he's a friend of mine." Above the phantom smile the eyes turned wistful. "I guess you and Tommy are about the only friends I'll have left after this is over."

Ambose opened his mouth, and closed it. Although Tabor hadn't exactly been hiding that he looked upon him as a friend, hearing him say it flat out was something else again. Miscalculations as staggering as this one did not occur so often as to be passed over lightly. It could be said for Jim Ambose that he had the grace to reflect with an inner wince that with friends like him, Sam Tabor's prospects for living to a ripe old age were growing dimmer by the second. To keep himself from plunging in too deep, too soon, he took off his jacket, folded it neatly and laid it along the back quarter of the desk. Seated at the desk, Gerard had been doodling neat rows of perfect squares. And, Ambose could see, jotting down an occasional note.

Gerard, who may well have understood what was going through his mind, was quite still, avoiding Jim's eyes as scrupulously as Jim was avoiding his.

Reaching his decision, Ambose clamped his hand down over the back of the white metal chair at the side of the desk, spun it around so that its back was to Tabor and let himself settle down upon it, spraddle-legged.

"Well now, Sam," he said, "let's you and me have a little talk." Slowly and purposefully, he began to roll up his shirtsleeves, first one and then the other. Opposite him, like a mirror image, Tabor pulled up on the sleeves of his prison uniform. Slowly and purposefully. First one and then the other.

"Just so I know you understand this," Ambose said. "I'm not here as a friend. I'm here as the man who will be prosecuting you for murder. If I'm satisfied when I leave this room that you were in full possession of your faculties, by which I mean that you knew the nature and quality of your act, I am going to have to recommend that we ask for the death penalty. Do you understand that, Sam?"

Had he caught a little tremor at the word *death?* Had the full impact of the fix he was in struck home? If it had, it had been thrust away just as quickly. "Well, sure, Jim," he said. "I understand that. I mean, what else can you do? I mean, I'm not going to say I didn't do it when everyone knows I did. That would be crazy." A slight, self-deprecatory smirk pulled at his lips. "And I'm sure as hell not crazy."

That was a subject, thought Ambose, on which learned psychiatrists had been known to disagree. "If you want to get it off your chest, I'd like to find out what happened from the time you left the courthouse to the time of the shooting. Is that agreeable to you? Are you willing, of your own free will, to talk to me about it?"

Sam Tabor turned his palms up to show that he had nothing to hide. The fingers, while stubby, were delicate and quite white. "Fire away," he said.

"All right. You want to retrace your thinking for me from the time you got up this—strike that." Hell, with Mallon due in here any second, the thing to do was to hit him quick and watch him closely. "Sam, when did you first think of killing the Chief Justice?"

Something cloudy and opaque passed over Tabor's eyes. Not, as Ambose had hoped, the impact of the deed but, it seemed, a falling away from it. There was no wariness there; only a sort of drifting bewilderment. And then the small baffled smile with its annoying built-in chuckle. He nodded at Jim, as if to acknowledge the fairness of the question. At length, he came to his conclusion. "I never thought of it," he said.

In that moment Ambose identified the disquiet he had felt all along; the memory that had been jostling him without being able to identify itself from the moment he walked into the friendly greeting and the crooked smile. Ambose had seen wounded men in the army. He had been assigned to a field hospital when he first went overseas, and he had spent three months picking them up and lugging them in. There were those who had reacted with the same dazed amusement upon discovering they were unable to remember their name or their company. It seemed, to most of them, hilarious, a good joke on everybody, especially themselves. "Well, of course, I know my own name," they would sometimes say. "I'll think of it in a minute."

Later, after he had got himself sprung out of the hospital unit and into action, he had, on his own, hauled back a guy who had caught a hunk of shrapnel. He could remember how the poor bugger would put his hand to his head, study the bloody hand and chuckle with delight at the apparently remarkable joke on himself, and maybe the whole U.S. Army, that it could really be he who was bleeding to death.

He was astonished that he could see the whole scene—the man, the jeep, the road—so vividly. Astonished and pleased. But only with himself. The association of Tabor and a head wound did not please him at all. If it turned out that this guy had any brain damage, Tommy Mallon would try to show that the emotional pressure from something in Tabor's life had snapped something in the already weakened brain structure and rendered poor, sick Sam helpless; a walking automaton unable to recognize what he was doing, unable to control himself.

Tabor was in shock all right, Ambose decided. The shock of the deed. What had fooled him was that Sam, feeling as he did that he was among friends, had been talking with a relative lucidity that he could not possibly have managed if he had been talking to a stranger.

Following his instinct, for whatever it might be worth, Jim snapped, "What's your name?"

Sam let his knee slip out from between his hands and stared at him, wondering, you could see, whether Ambose had taken leave of his senses. So, for that matter, was Gerard.

"Your full name!" Ambose snapped. He snapped his fingers. "Quick!"

"Samuel DeMonteville Tabor," he said, reacting quickly enough to the command but still somewhat quizzically, as if he were not quite sure what game they were now playing but was willing to go along if it would make Ambose happy. "De what?"

"My mother was French, and that was her family's name in the sweet and olden days. I think it was some kind of royalty. You know . . . from way back."

Delusions of grandeur. The best clue yet.

"I don't ever use it," Sam said, with a throwaway shrug that seemed to announce that he wouldn't want anybody to think he would aspire to such heights. But it was his legal name all right.

"On your birth certificate?"

"On my birth certificate."

As unfortunate a juxtapositon as he knew it to be under the circumstances, Jim asked him whether he had ever suffered any serious head injuries. Tabor, taking it in good spirits, chuckled along with Gerard, both of them obviously taking it as a witty commentary upon his middle name. "Not that I know of, Jim," he said, gaily. "Not that anyone ever told me."

Thank god for small favors.

"What I'm trying to do, Sam, is to find out why you went out and killed Wilcke. There has got to be a time when you decided, and there has got to be a reason."

The quick little twitch of the head again. "There wasn't any time in particular, just—"

"In *particular*. What do you mean by that? If you can't remember the exact moment when you decided, when you thought to yourself, 'Yes, if I get a clear shot at him, I'm going to shoot him,' then there must have been some time before you got to City Hall when you made up your mind."

Tabor shook his head slowly. "Noooo. Never entered my mind."

"Did you think about it when you went to bed last night?"

". . . last night. Hell, Jim, I never even knew he was going to be in the city when I went to bed last night."

"When did you first learn he was in the city?"

". . . in the city. This morning. From the paper. The *Globe*. Riding in on the bus. They had that picture on the front page, don't you remember?"

"And did you think about it then, when you saw the picture?"

"No."

"When you read the story?"

"No."

"Were you incensed by the editorial asking for courtesy?"

"No. What editorial? I didn't read any editorial." You could see that he was surprised. You could see surprise turn into indignation. Had the *Globe* really asked for courtesy? After all the things they'd been saying about him? Gee, you couldn't believe anything you read any more, could you?

That sense of disquiet was nudging at Ambose again, that sinking feeling that there was something more here than met the eye. It was such a crazy thing to have said that Ambose could not help but wonder this time, not whether Sam might be insane but whether he might not be faking insanity. Tabor might not be anybody's prize specimen but he wasn't this dumb, either. He had been holding down a responsible job. He had been performing it to everybody's satisfaction for years.

But Tabor *wasn't* faking. Tabor wasn't sophisticated enough to fake it that well. Jim Ambose knew from long experience that a prisoner faking insanity could never resist the full award-winning performance, with the obligatory ranting and raving and hair-pulling, and maybe a little free and fancy wand-waving thrown in to convince the skeptics. They were like judges ruling on a fixed case —judges being somewhat weak on sophistication themselves. They couldn't just let the thief go, they had to call down the wrath of the gods upon the technicality of the law that was forcing them to free this scoundrel in the dock, and if the technicality or loophole was one that nobody had ever managed to find before, it didn't deter their hand or affect their performance one whit. As Nevins always said, "A righteous judge in a dismissal is as fixed as the stars. By which I mean, of course, that you can set your watch by him."

Nobody was going to fool around with this one, Ambose thought, letting his mind linger on that digression (which was not a digression at all but the central core to which all things flowed). Not Eli Chobodian. Not even Hilliard Nevins. This case belonged to Jim Ambose. Hilliard hadn't walked into a courtroom to try anything except sure things in years, and few enough of them, and while Hilliard would hate to let the glory slip away he would see very quickly that what he wanted, even more than personal publicity, was a clean trial and a neat conviction. And that meant Jim Ambose.

"When you got off the bus had you made up your mind to kill him?"

Tabor, still trying very hard to think each question through, shook his head. "No."

"By lunchtime had you made up your mind to kill him?"

"No."

"By the time you returned to your office had you made up your mind?"

"No."

"When you left work that night?"

The shake of the head, the "No."

Ho-Kay. We take the long way around.

Although he knew from Bob Stringfellow that Booker Phillips had driven Tabor to City Hall, he wanted that information to come from Tabor himself. There was something else he had wanted to clear up first, though. What was it? Damn. He had to let it go. Tommy Mallon would be barreling in here any minute *(where was Tommy?)* to aid the search for truth and justice by telling the only man who knew anything about the murder to shut up.

"Why did you go to City Hall to see him?"

Sam didn't seem to understand what he was trying to get at.

"Well, did you go to cheer him?"

He might just as well have accused him of having bad table manners. "You know me better than that, Jim."

Well, that gave him a new avenue of approach, anyway. He tipped the front legs of the chair toward Sam and gave him his best man-to-man approach. Confidentially, almost conspiratorially, he asked, "Sam, what did you have against Wilcke?"

Tabor leaned toward Ambose, his hands on his knees, his own voice lowering confidentially, almost conspiratorially, in return. "I didn't have anything against him, Jim. I never even met the man."

The chair rocked back again, and Ambose bounced to his feet. "But you were carrying a gun! Do you normally carry a gun?"

"What would I be doing carrying around a gun, Jim?" The gun, he explained, had been issued to him when he first came to work at the courthouse and was sworn in as a deputy.

"That was the gun? You've had that gun ever since then?"

"Not that gun, Jim."

"Then what gun? Didn't you just say—"

There had, it seemed, been a reissue a couple of years ago. So technically, if Jim wanted him to be technical and exact, it wasn't the same gun. They had issued him this gun when he brought the old one in for the semiannual inspection. "I have to get it checked every six months, see, to make sure it's in good maintenance and working order."

"OK. That I got. Now, do you carry the gun normally on your person when you go to and from work, or was this—strike that. Do you normally carry the gun?"

The quick flick of the head had begun to seem like a nervous twitch. "I told you that already. I never carry a gun. I keep the gun in my desk. Most of the time I don't hardly know it's there, if you want to know." Ambose waited, staring at him expectantly, attempting to create a vacuum of silence and tension into which Tabor would—hopefully—rush with whatever he was holding back. Tabor, filling the silence, said, "This was the first time I ever carried the gun out of this building in my life."

There it was, Ambose exulted. The one time he had carried a gun in his life, proof in itself of premeditation. *Sam, old buddy, you've just reserved yourself a ride on the electrodes.* There was, however, no outward change in Ambose's voice or manner. "And why did you carry it this time?"

"Well, I was trying to tell you. I have to get it checked every six months, on the fifteenth of June and the fifteenth of December."

"No. Why were you carrying it when you went to City Hall to see David Boone Wilcke?"

From off to the side Johnny Gerard said, "Jim, today is June fifteenth. We had our weapons checked out today, like he says." Or at least they had been supposed to, except that it got so busy that it had been put off for most of them until, he guessed, tomorrow. There was a fading away at the end which seemed to say that nobody was going to to be really that concerned about such things tomorrow.

Ambose leaned down heavily on the outer rim of the chair, tipping it back to him. His fingers began to slap rhythmically, both hands in unison, against the back slats, while he clucked out a counterpoint with his tongue. He could hear Stringfellow saying, "Just don't forget that I told you ahead of time that you're not going to believe it." He still had Tabor going to City Hall with the gun in his pocket, but he also had a very strong premonition that it was going to—had already—turned to nothing.

"The funny thing," Tabor said, "is that you reminded me of it." Worse than nothing. With a furtive glance toward Johnny Gerard and a momentary lowering of the voice, he recalled for Ambose the woman and the questionnaire. It had been only then, while Ambose was handing the questionnaire back to him, that he had realized what day it was. "That it was June fifteenth. I'd forgotten all about it, that it had come around time to have it checked again." Which was why he had told Ambose he was going to have to go down to the sheriff's office anyway, after Ambose had volunteered to drop it off for him.

Having disappointed him so catastrophically on the gun, Tabor was happy to be able to place the time almost to the second. He had waited until 4:30 on the dot, figuring that by that late in the day he could be checked out without getting in anybody else's way. "See, that way I don't lose any time and they don't down at the jail office."

"OK, who checked your gun? Inspected it?"

"Nobody."

"Damnit, Sam—"

"Well nobody did, Jim." Like Deputy Gerard had said, there was nobody there checking anymore. Morosely, his brows coming together, he said, "You'd have thought they'd have called me to let me know. How long would it have taken . . . five seconds? Although," he said, "I see now that they had other things to worry about. I suppose I should have figured it out for myself and called down first." There was a long, deep intake of breath. Yes, he supposed that was what he should have done.

Even with the quick recovery, Ambose had been able to catch the first glimpse of the sorehead in Tabor, not only in the complaint but in the hunched and brooding expression. Along with it had come the first suggestion that Tabor was grieving for himself. *For lack of a phone call, all this had happened.* That was more like it. He had to be sore about something to do what he had done. He should be grieving for himself, poor bugger. To Ambose, it was a sign that the shock was finally wearing off. He could feel the juices begin to stir in his body in the expectation that he might now begin to get a real look into the workings of Sam Tabor's mind.

Nobody had been in the sheriff's office except Stringfellow's clerk Dhalgren, and it was with the same pinched, complaining tone that he recounted how

Dhalgren had wanted to know what the hell he needed to have a gun inspected for, anyway; did he expect to go out and rob a bank or something? "You'd think a man who's supposed to uphold the law would have more regard for rules and regulations, wouldn't you? I mean there's a purpose to all the regulations even if it doesn't seem so at the time. Even if it's a . . . well, inconvenience for some people." He looked to Gerard, not wanting him to think he was being unfair to a colleague. "I guess he had a hard day, though. I wouldn't want to say anything against him on the stand."

"For all of me," Gerard told him, "I'd like to see that smart little bastard hanging by his thumbs."

By the balls, Ambose would have said if his mind hadn't gone elsewhere. Tabor's chances of ever being on the stand were so slight as to be nonexistent. If Tommy Mallon were dumb enough to let this poor fool take the stand, Ambose would tear him apart.

"So you didn't check out the gun. Where did you go from there?"

"Well, I didn't go anywhere."

"Of course you did." What might have irritated Ambose in private conversation bothered him very little here. Here, Jim Ambose was a professional, operating along a purely impersonal wire. "They arrested you at City Hall, didn't they?"

"Oh, I see what you mean. You mean how did I get over there, to the City Hall. I should have seen that right away." What he had meant to say was that he hadn't gone out right away. There was more to it than that. He shifted his position on the examining table, rocking down on his backside as if he were settling himself in so that he would be able to tell his story better. His hand moving comfortably within the narrow confines of the jacket pocket.

Just as Sam had been about to leave, Booker Phillips had come in with Arch Merck and Dhalgren had told him he didn't know where the sheriff was and that if he were Booker he wouldn't go looking for him. After a little while Booker had suggested to Arch that maybe they ought to go back to the City Hall and pick up the Chief Justice when he came out, and Arch had said, "Screw you, Jack. I already earned the Queen's shilling for the day." Something like that.

Sam's eyes had gone, uncertainly, to Ambose. "I wouldn't testify to his saying it that way. I'm just telling it to you here because I know you have to have all the details."

Nodding abruptly, Ambose motioned for him to keep going. "He seemed upset about something, Arch. Mad. He said, 'I'm getting the hell out of here before B.S. comes in and finds some other lovers for us to babysit for." That was exactly what he had said. Some other lovers. So Booker had said he'd better go himself then, because he didn't want to get himself reamed by the sheriff anymore, having already had all he could use for one day. Something like that. "And then," Tabor said, "he left."

"He left? I thought—" Ambose took a deep breath. "Look, Sam, I know you're trying to give me all the details, and I sure do appreciate it. But I'm not that interested in what Booker did. I'm interested in what you did. In how you got to City Hall."

"Well, that's why I'm telling you this. I wouldn't waste your time unless it had a bearing. Booker walked out, see, and in a couple of seconds, he stuck his head right back in and said, 'What do you say, Sam, how would you like a lift to the City Hall to see Chief Justice Wilcke?' And I said, 'Sure.' I could see he wanted company and the City Hall was on my way home, anyway. Not directly on my way, Jim, if you want me to be real technical, but in the same general direction."

Now that they had come around to it again, Ambose asked him whether he had intended to go anyway. If Booker hadn't asked him.

"Why would I want to do that? It isn't that much on my way, if you really want to know."

"What I mean is this," he said carefully. "Did you want to see him?"

"Why not?" Tabor said for the second time. "I didn't have anything against him."

Oddly enough it was Tabor's insistence upon saying *the* City Hall instead of just plain City Hall like everybody else that had begun to grate on Ambose's nerves. Or perhaps it was the thing on which his mind seized to draw off all the other irritations that were beginning to pile up.

What did he have so far? He had Sam Tabor, unable to say no to a casual acquaintance, accepting a ride to keep him company. That, at any rate, was Sam Tabor's story.

And now that Sam had come to the telling of it, he was talking freely, a timid pride breaking through, perhaps even a sudden exhilaration. "Just about when we got there, there was a lot of traffic. It was that time of day, see? But Booker had the squad car so we had no trouble parking. We parked right in front of the City Hall. Well, not right in front. On the corner in front. Meadows and Park, where the bank is. Behind a TV truck and a couple of, I guess, official cars."

Dutifully, of his own accord, he stopped to find out whether Ambose wanted to ask him anything.

"When you got out of the car, Sam, do you happen to remember what time it was then?"

"Gee, there'd be no way of my knowing that, Jim. I could place the time at my office exactly because of what I told you about going down to—" Oh, he could have looked at his watch, he could see that. But he hadn't. Had he known it would become important, you could see, he would have been only too happy to have. "But," he said brightening, "it was only a couple of minutes before the Chief Justice came out. Less than that. A minute maybe." Maybe even less.

Go figure Ambose had been building to the moment when Tabor would come face to face with Wilcke on the steps of the City Hall building, and Sam had jumped the question and come there of his own accord. And passed right over it without any visible sign that he recognized that the man was now dead because he, Sam Tabor, had killed him. That Ambose didn't like. If Sam had been approaching City Hall in the grip of the murder he intended to commit, he should be showing some physical signs that he was reliving it. A trembling of the hand, perhaps. A thickening of the voice. A few beads of sweat above the lip.

For the first time, Ambose became aware of the sound of traffic outside the window—quickly isolated to the harsh growl of a bad muffler above the general purr. OK. Bring him back down and run it over. His face felt stiff and tired. Out of the car, Booker on the street side, Sam on the curb side. "And you walked up the steps together?"

"Well, we had to walk down the sidewalk first. We were on the corner, remember? We walked along the sidewalk and when we got to the steps Booker went up and I sort of . . . well, I just stood there, I guess, and waited for them to come out, the Chief Justice and Mayor Karney. There were a lot of people up there, newspapermen and officers of the law and, you could tell, important people. I didn't want to get in the way."

"Oh, did you know the mayor was coming out with him?"

"Well, it was at the City Hall. The mayor was there, Jim."

"You said that you stood there *waiting* for them to come out. That would mean you knew they'd be coming out together."

"Oh, I see. You want to know what I knew at the time, not what I know now. *Before* they came out. I see that. I suppose I just guessed it. It was protocol." All at once, he straightened up, remembering something. "No, I heard someone say they were coming out together. One of the photographers was starting down the stairs and fiddling with the back of his camera the way they do. And he said it, this photographer. That they'd be out to say a few words. That's right. For the television. I remember that now."

"And that was when?"

"When I was on the stairs."

"I mean, when in relation to the time you got there? How long had you been standing there, waiting, before the photographer came down the steps toward where you were?"

"Oh, of course." There was a wrinkled, apologetic grimace at his stupidity. Booker had gone up, and Sam had stopped at the bottom of the crowd. "This photographer was just coming down. He was passing Booker. I didn't have to wait hardly at all."

When Ambose asked him to estimate exactly how long, just so he'd have an idea, Tabor gave it a great deal of thought. "Not more than a minute," he said finally. "Definitely not less than fifteen or maybe twenty seconds or more than a minute."

"And then he came out and what happened?"

Johnny Gerard, who had been making notes in his book, came to a stop, the pencil held in the air, immobile. Outside, a horn blew, harsh and insistent. "Well, that's when I shot him, Jim." Nothing. Absolutely nothing.

"I know that. We all know that, Sam." Patiently, patiently. The time had come for another go-around on the Big Question. Patiently, conversationally, Ambose asked, "How did it come about, Sam? Had you decided to shoot him when Booker invited you on the ride *(damn Booker to hell was right!)* or while you were driving up, or was it on the staircase when you heard the photographer say they'd be coming right out?"

"You asked three questions there, Jim. I don't want to get technical, but in a court of law . . ."

"That's right, Sam. You are absolutely right. Let's break it down. Was it when Booker first invited you?"

"No."

"Was it during the drive to City Hall, then?"

"No."

"Then it was there on the steps when you heard the photographer say they'd be coming right out."

"No, Jim. None of them times."

"Well, when did you decide, Sam? This is important for me to know."

"I know it is, Jim. Don't you think I'd know that?" There was the quick flick of the head again, once . . . twice . . . three times, the nervous, squinty tic. "Like I told you, Jim. I never did actually, what you could say, decide."

"You never did," Ambose repeated. His eyes narrowed. "You do remember shooting him, don't you?"

"Oh sure, I remember that. I'd never claim that about it going black. You know me better than that."

Ambose leaned back again, staring at him expectantly, waiting confidently for Tabor to finish the thought, giving him every opportunity to prove his good faith to his friend, Jim Ambose, by making a damning admission.

Tabor cocked his head sideways, not exactly sure what was expected of him. As if to break the silence, the sound of distant voices floated up the stairs. The door to Stringfellow's office had evidently been opened and then shut. Which could very well mean that Tommy Mallon would soon be on his way up.

Jim Ambose said, "If a man shoots somebody, Sam, he has to decide to shoot him. Usually it would be when he puts the gun in his pocket or when he's driving to where the man he's going to shoot is at—"

"In this case, the City Hall," Tabor said, nodding to show he understood.

"And there has to be a reason. Now maybe he hasn't formulated the reason in his mind completely during all those preliminary steps but when he's ready to do it, when he takes the gun out of his pocket"—he dropped a hand toward his hip as if he were reaching for the gun—"he had to give himself some reason, right? Or why—"

"Right."

"—else would he take the gun out at all? He has to be thinking, I'm taking out this gun because I am going to shoot him. Now he has the gun in his hand and he is pointing it and he has to be thinking, I am aiming this gun at him because I am going to shoot him." Tabor was staring at the "gun," fascinated. "And now, when he's about to pull the trigger, he has to be saying to himself, 'I am now going to shoot him.'" The middle finger, which had been half of the gun barrel, suddenly became the trigger. "Right?"

"Right. That's right, Jim. I can see that all right. I'd have to have decided before I did it. Absolutely."

Ambose waited. Gerard waited. Tabor, frowning heavily, said nothing. Darkness was falling outside. Weariness was setting in inside. Finally Jim Ambose said, "Well?"

"Well," Tabor said. "They came out and they were taking pictures. The flashlights popped, and I took the gun out and shot him. That's just the way it happened. I can remember it plain as day."

"But you said you decided. You said it was impossible not to have decided." To his own ears, it was the voice of a small boy complaining that his daddy had broken a solemn promise.

"I know it is," Tabor said. "I must have decided before I did it. I can see that. But the thing is, Jim, I don't remember deciding." The nervous twitch again. "All I can remember is how surprised I was." An extremely puzzled look passed over his face; a wrinkled, wondering look. "I'll bet I was as surprised as anybody there."

Not as surprised as Wilcke, Ambose thought. Not . . . by . . . half.

"I just took the gun and pointed it, just like you said, and pulled the trigger. That's exactly how it happened. I was surprised when it made that big a noise. I remember that. I didn't know a pistol had a kick like that." He looked down at Ambose, hopefully, as if to ask whether that last bit of information might not be of some help.

In a totally different voice, harsh and demanding, Ambose barked, "Don't give me that. You've fired that gun before!"

Tabor shook his head.

"Qualifying or something."

He hadn't had to qualify. "I don't know why I ever had to have a gun, if you want to know." They had just issued it to him along with the rules and regulations on a mimeographed paper. And one of the rules said he had to have it checked every six months. A little whine had crept into his voice. It was, as anybody should have been able to see, all their fault for giving him a gun.

"You never fired it? Not once? Never?"

"Never in my life, Jim."

Well, Ambose said, giving up—rising, flexing his back, twisting his torso, yawning—he'd sure as hell fired it now. Slowly, almost languidly, he wiped his face down from top to bottom, wiping the fatigue away.

"I meant *before*," Tabor was saying. "Yes, I shot it today. Of course. I thought you meant before today."

"He did," Johnny Gerard said. "That's what he did mean, Sam. Now, Sam, you're telling us you never shot a gun before. You know that you shot him right through the eye, don't you? Killed him instantly. Myself, I'd—"

Ambose, turning back—still yawning deeply—saw at once that Tabor hadn't known, was hearing it for the first time. A shudder had rippled over him, a trembling in the flesh. Within the ripple, the dark underside of the man could be seen, the shifting bottom at the base of the structure. What Jim Ambose saw— as he had seen so often—was not the face of the murderer but the face of the eternal victim, mortal man. The bullet through the eye, the empty hole in the skull, had brought home to Tabor that this was no social gathering in a neat white room, no coffee klatch with friends. He had committed an irreversible act for which he was irretrievably doomed. What he had done was unalterable, irrevocable, irretrievable. Nothing could change it nor anybody.

As much to himself as to Ambose, he whispered, "If they'd only let me know the inspection was off, I wouldn't be sitting here right now."

Moving quickly to plug into that circuit, Ambose said, "I hope you had a good reason, Sam. Because it's too late to say you really didn't mean it, and it won't do any good at all to say you're sorry."

It was already too late. The wind had died, the surface had smoothed, the compartment was self-sealing. The corner of the lips turned up again in the little crooked smile. "Through the eye," Tabor said, awed at his own marksmanship. "I'm glad he didn't suffer."

It would be back, Ambose knew. It would return again during the trial, and it would grow and grow until, if worst came to worst, he would walk to the electric chair either making the necessary accommodations to keep himself sane or finding his release in the total accommodation of a total retreat.

"Are you trying to tell us that you shot him. Just like that. Without thinking about it?"

"That's right, Jim. I guess I did." He looked reasonably ashamed of himself. The next thing he knew Booker was putting handcuffs on him and saying, "Sam, I could kill you for this."

"And what did you say to Booker?" Given the circumstances, this had become vitally important. What Sam had said in the moments immediately after the crime was res gestae ("things done" in the heat of the moment), the only statements of Tabor that would be admissible. If he had said anything that indicated any planning, any dislike for Wilcke, any delight at having pulled it off, it would go to show premeditation. And since Ambose seemed, at the moment, to be sorely lacking in that other essential element, motive, he had damn well better be able to show premeditation.

"Nothing," Tabor said. "No. I don't think so. Not that I can remember."

Perhaps Booker would remember. Booker or one of the witnesses.

"From the time he took the gun from you until the time you were put in the car, did you say anything?"

"No, I don't think so."

"You keep saying you don't think so. Are you sure? Think now."

"Not until I got into the car."

"What did you say in the car?"

"I said that I didn't know why in the world I'd done that."

"And what else!"

No good. Sam's head had snapped to at the crisp tone of command, but the eyes came up empty. "That's all, Jim. I didn't know why in the world I'd done that. I never had anything against Wilcke."

"Did you say that? 'I never had anything against Wilcke.' Or is that something you're telling me now?"

The nervous tic. He wasn't sure.

"All right. From the time you left with Booker. You're riding in the car, OK? On the way back here. Did you talk about Wilcke at all?"

"Not that I can think of. Just that it was a shame some of the rulings he'd been making to tie the hands of the police. You know. Just the kind of thing that's said every day."

Ambose's eyes went briefly to Gerard. Although the time element would be tight, he just might be able to jam that in under res gestae. It was, of course, the kind of thing a man in Tabor's position would very well say at a time like that to show that he was on the cops' side; in addition to which it was wholly in keeping with Tabor's personality. In a court of law, however—if it went in right —it could be made to mean something else entirely. With any kind of help from Booker, it could be made to sound as though he was explaining, in the heat of the deed, why he had done it. In short, motive.

Sam Tabor, a man who had worked around the courthouse for so long that he had come to identify with the law enforcement officials, had been growing increasingly restive at the limitations being placed on their effectiveness, had, in fact, been nursing a grievance. Through an accident in timing, he finds himself face to face with this man he has grown to hate, he has a gun in his pocket— *premeditation can be formed in the twinkle of an eye, ladies and gentlemen. . . .*

Placing himself in front of the jury box, hearing his argument come back to him, he made a small mouth of distaste. Tommy Mallon could take the same facts and hang enough light bulbs around them to show irresistible impulse.

It reminded him, at least, what he had been meaning to ask Tabor back in the first series of questions. "Let's go back to the office during the day," he said. Had he discussed Wilcke with anybody? Anything about his visit? Anything at all?

Tabor hesitated for a moment. "I didn't say anything to anybody, no." There was something in the hesitation, in the emphasis, that caused Jim to ask whether anybody had said anything to him.

"Just you," Tabor said.

"Me?"

"Sure, Jim, don't you remember? When you came into the office to ask about that questionnaire. Then at lunch, with you and Tommy Mallon and Bo Gunderson."

Johnny Gerard was grinning broadly from the desk alongside, and Jim couldn't say that he blamed him. He was not really sure what he had said to Tabor, but he was sure enough that this was one answer he would do just as well to forget.

The ringing of the phone on the desk cut so loudly into the room that all three of them gave a little jump. Reaching out quickly, Johnny Gerard grabbed the receiver, listened briefly, and handed it over to Ambose. "Stringfellow," he said. "The lawyer has a message for you."

It wasn't Stringfellow on the line, though. Nor was it Tommy Mallon. It was the reedy, imperious voice of Alfred Marma—"Li'l Alfie"—informing him that as the representative of the Civil Liberties Union he was advising Mr. Tabor to talk to no one. "All questioning," he told Ambose, "will now cease and desist."

Ambose permitted himself a faint smile into the receiver before he handed the phone back to Gerard. "Sam," he said, "you were saying that you must have had a reason. Now you're not like the usual run of prisoners we have up here. You're an intelligent man. An educated man. What do you think the reason *was?* . . . *Might* have been? We're not going to hold you to anything, but you must have some kind of an . . . inkling."

Sam started to say something, and stopped. His mouth moved as if it had gone dry. "I just don't know, Jim."

They could hear footsteps on the stairs. "Well," Gerard said, heaving himself up and heading out to the Booking Room. "I guess I'm appointed as a one-man welcoming committee."

For the first time Ambose and Tabor were alone. There was a brief, uncomfortable silence. Tabor stretched himself, yawning, and with his shoulders back and his arms outspread made a sad, resigned little gesture as if to say, "And who would have thought in my office this morning we were going to be here like this?"

For Jim Ambose time was running out. "A Civil Liberties lawyer is on his way up," he said, "and if Tommy Mallon isn't with him he'll be chugging right along. You'd better tell me anything that's on your mind, Sam. This may be your last chance."

What an odd thing to be saying, he thought. Even considering Tabor's anxiety to please. Odder still, he meant it. Something more than instinct, something very close to a premonition of disaster had informed him that poor Sam Tabor, sitting there so plump and vulnerable, was going to be ground up into little pieces if he went to trial with a story like this.

Instantly, he was annoyed with himself. What the hell did he care whether Tabor was chewed up. His *business* was to chew people up. If he was reaching the stage where he was confusing his own best interests with the best interests of the defendant, then the premonition of disaster would be well heeded. To compose himself, he took one long final look at Sam Tabor so that he would remember him not as the man for whom he had felt this unexpected surge of sympathy but as the man he was out to burn. Poor, vulnerable Tabor, my foot. When everything was said and done, poor vulnerable Tabor had sat there, smiling plumply, and told him nothing.

Studying Tabor that closely, he thought he caught something. What? An interior struggle? An internal qualm? Or was he—as he probably was—only imagining what he hoped he would find there. A twitch of the head and Tabor

90

was saying, open-faced and guilelessly, "Nothing I can think of right now, Jim. I guess I've told you just about everything."

The sound of voices had come into the Booking Room. Gerard was trooping back in with Stringfellow and Marma alongside him, and Blasser and Justice Morrison trailing behind. Marma, a very small, very black man, disengaged himself at the door and marched in, a full stride in front of the others, like a captain in front of his platoon. Crisply and efficiently, he announced that he was there on behalf of the Civil Liberties Union and Bar Association to ensure that Mr. Tabor's constitutional rights were not violated before the arrival of an attorney of his choice. Rocking on his toes, blowing out his lips, unable to resist letting Ambose know who he was talking about, he went on: "What will be done here will be closely observed by the entire world, Mr. Ambose, and we would not want the entire world to judge American justice by the overzealousness of a single, not necessarily representative official, would we?"

"Why, Alfred," Ambose said. "How nice of you to warn me." He had fallen quite naturally into the indulgent, patronizing tone he always took toward Alfred Marma. "I have been told that there are ye of little faith who cannot sleep at night you're so worried about what they'll think of us in France where a man is presumed guilty until he's proven innocent. To say nothing of the latest Gallup Poll in the Lower Antibes. On the other hand, there are those amongst us who don't give a piss in a whirlpool about the whole damn world and its immediate suburbs." But that was what makes this such a great and glorious country, wasn't it? The free and open exchange of conflicting opinions, which Mr. Marma and his organization were so fanatically dedicated to preserving that they didn't mind destroying anybody who disagreed with them.

Tabor, pushed into the background where he seemed to feel more comfortable, was grinning over their heads to Blasser and Gerard as though he were anxious to make it clear whose side he was on. Which didn't stop him from inquiring, however hesitantly, about Tommy Mallon.

"Sam," Ambose said, "be grateful for whatever aid Mr. Marma brings. That may look to you like a briefcase, but you can take my word for it, it's really the flaming sword of justice."

Marma, who reacted just as automatically to Ambose, made no effort whatsoever to disguise his loathing for him and everything he stood for. "The only trouble with you, Ambose, is that you have an incomplete and distorted understanding of the function of a prosecutor in a free democratic society."

Ambose looked down on him with real affection. "You know something, Alfred," he said. "I could become real fond of you if you'd only learn to say 'man' and 'down to the nitty-gritty' like a real nigger instead of trying to use all that highfalutin lawyer talk."

Doc Swann was snorting indignantly. "Aw come on, Ambose," he said. "When I nod wisely and say it's significant, you're to accept it on faith. It's significant because it's a defense. The human animal defends itself in ways too various to catalogue. How do we of the noble Profession contend with that, you may well ask." He peered around the room brightly. "We catalogue them anyway. No nut's gonna give us any trouble."

As difficult as Swann could be, Ambose could never remember him being quite this antagonistic before. He had in mind to ask him whether there was anything significant in his own attitude except that he was afraid he'd only be setting him off on another of those interminable stories about an imaginary patient. "That's just what I'm trying to find out, sir," he said. "Whether he just seems to cooperate while he's telling us as little as he can about himself without offending anybody. Or, like Dee says, is there any other possibility?"

"Probably no more than a hundred and twelve. Put your hand in the grab bag and come right on out with whatever's on your mind."

Ambose didn't have anything on his mind. That's why he was asking.

"Well, there's always the possibility that he could be stupid. But that would mean a GS-10 is stupid, which would reflect very badly upon the whole Civil Service System, and now that they're becoming unionized I wouldn't go messing around with them if I were you."

"You don't think he's stupid," Nevins said, putting an end to it. "You think that for one reason or another he's putting on an act."

"Who says I don't . . . ? No, not an act. The man is still shaken by his experience. As why shouldn't he be? It isn't every day a man shoots down a Chief Justice like a dog and becomes a footnote to history." His hand, which had gone to his nose, froze there. "It has become evident, has it not, that I view our assassin as little better than a dog." A guy who was around the courthouse, under foot. He was looking to Ambose and Ambose was nodding. "But not a mad dog." No, mad-dog murderer wasn't in his picture at all. "A mad-dog murderer might kill his master. Your ordinary, well-trained civil-service watchdog would only kill to please his master." He gave his characteristic snort. There was, of course, a third possibility. "If I weren't insulated by the sanctity of my calling, you might just say I didn't like the murdering sonofabitch."

The cranky expression under the sniffling nostrils became less belligerent, more thoughtful. For an anonymous man to become immortal he has to shake his universe up. If that's what Hilliard was getting at, that went without saying. "He has just committed a horrendous crime, and somewhere behind that wall of affability he has to be aware of it."

But wouldn't that assume he hadn't planned it, Nevins wanted to know. Wasn't Doc Swann describing the understandable reaction of an anonymous man catapulted into history by something that he hadn't planned? "I don't want to use the word 'stunned,' but . . . would you say he is still too stunned by what he did to have what we'd normally think of as a normal reaction? That he has retreated into some safe harbor of his personality until he can absorb what he has done?"

As always, Swann reacted altogether differently to Nevins than he had to Ambose. "Retreating into some safe harbor of his personality. I like that, Hilliard. He is a man who has come to understand that his ship has sailed, and that's the most unpredictable man of all. That's good because it brings us back to the essential part of his personality. When I was about to say 'anonymous' before, the word 'androgynous' came to my tongue. Don't laugh at that, Ambose," he said. "I believe all Freudian slips when they serve my purpose." Not androgynous in the sense of bisexual. Not a eunuch, either. But in the sense of neutral. "Did you feel that, Jim?"

Jim had. But when he also took care to caution him that he had never really known Tabor before, Swann dismissed it with the impatient gesture that is reserved for irrelevancies. "That's what I missed up there," he said. "The sign of the fanatic. A certain stridency of tone, a certain unhealthy sparkle of the eye." Doc Swann was becoming excited. "Where is it?" he wanted to know. "Where is the good old *sic semper tyrannis* we have come to expect in our better assassins? That's what I want to know!"

Nevins, who had been leaning back—his head resting on his hands, his glasses up on his forehead—agreed with him completely. The way he saw it, the unnatural calm was the one thing the defense had going for them. "The way things stand right now, they can make a helluva case for brain damage with only a very little help from an EEG."

"On the other hand," Ambose said quickly. "On the other hand, if he did what he set out to do, wouldn't there also be a calm? A sort of calm after the storm?"

"The passion spent," Swann jeered. "The life goal fulfilled." He snorted in disgust to show that he would have expected better from Ambose. "And he wouldn't want to brag about it?"

"Hold it right there," Nevins said before Ambose could say anything. "We're going to be running a trial here, not a pigsticking. So let's not be so gaw-damn eager to overlook the possibility that he *is* insane. Legally insane."

"The hell he is!" Ambose had come shooting up off the window sill so violently that for once he could not pretend to disregard what the others thought of him. "I don't say he isn't. He says he isn't."

"What the hell does he know about it?" Swann demanded. "He has neutralized the passions that led him to do what he did. He probably couldn't tell us why he did it even if he wanted to because he no longer knows. The moment he pulled the trigger he blotted out the reason."

Ambose, still furious, wanted to know why what Swann had just said was any different from what he had said about the calm after the storm.

"Because I have a license and you don't. Does that answer your question? Because *you* have the man sitting back exhausted after he's just ripped off a piece of ass and I'm saying that he blotted out the reason because it's too shameful for him to face."

"Then there was a reason," Nevins said quietly.

"Jesus Himalaya Christ, there's a reason for everything! Upon that rock the whole industry of psychiatry has been built. According to the latest census we now rank only slightly behind the automotive and entertainment industries in gross annual intake, buddy-boy. You don't think we're going to let a good thing like that go down the pipe?"

Out of their long association Hilliard Nevins knew that Doc had an idea percolating under his hood. And if it was a wild hunch, so much the better. Hadn't Nevins always said that he'd take one of Swann's hunches over a hundred facts gathered by a team of a hundred sociologists working a hundred days? And hadn't Ambose and Pawley both seen it happen often enough to have become believers?

"You take a man who's never carried a gun before," Doc said, thinking out loud. "We accept that he's telling the truth there, right? Come on there, Ambose, pay attention. I believed him and, what's more important, Jim here—a far tougher nut than I—believes him."

It was really more of a question put to Jim than a statement of fact. Ambose, eager for him to go on, said, "Absolutely."

Oh yeah? Why was he so sure?

"Doc," Nevins groaned, "please . . ."

"No, why are you so sure that Sam Tabor wouldn't lie to you? You're the man who's going to prosecute him if you have anything to say about it, aren't you?"

"Sir, you asked me a question. Did I believe him. Yes, I believe him. About the gun anyway."

"You believe him about everything, that's the fact of the matter, isn't it? He told you the truth as far as you can tell. You'd stake your life on it."

"As far as I can tell is one thing. That about staking my life you can forget about."

"And you're trained to know when a man lies to you. You can spot a lie as well as any of us here has ever seen."

He wasn't baiting Ambose this time, they could see. "He's carrying the gun when he leaves the office, when he walks down the hall, down the stairs and into the sheriff's office and is confronted by this clerk, the bright young fellow who so brilliantly advanced his career by telling him there's no maintenance going around here today, Sam. He is carrying the gun when Booker—what a name—Phillips sticks his head back in and says come ride with me in my county car to see the Chief Justice come out and take a bow. And now it changes. You see that, how it changes, don't you, Ambose?"

"Yeah," Ambose said. "I think I see what you mean."

"Anybody want to tell me?" Pawley said. "I don't see a damn thing."

"It wasn't a weapon up to then, and now it's a weapon. Is that what you mean, sir?"

"Don't ever let me underestimate you, Ambose," Swann said. "And don't ever let me do anything where I'd be at your mercy." That was precisely what he meant. What had been no more than an encumbrance, no more than a package he was delivering to the sheriff's office, to drop off and pick up again at his convenience, had taken on a shape and a function. "He has a gun in his pocket. A loaded gun. It is in his pocket as they drive to City Hall. How far would that be, half a mile or so?"

It was 1637 yards, Ambose told him. Almost as an aside to Pawley, he said, "Ike Weiland's boys in Intelligence measured it this morning."

"For a man not used to a gun, it would be a weight. He carried it in his jacket pocket, right? He would be aware of it at all times, even sitting down." It was, again, a question put to Ambose, and Ambose, remembering how his own gun had unbalanced him until he became accustomed to it, nodded.

"A forty-five weighs what?"

"Two pounds, thirteen ounces."

"Ike Weiland's boys were very busy this morning!"

"That I knew myself."

"I'll just bet you did." Despite himself, Ambose felt the blood rise. *Damnit!* . . .

"This is hot stuff for Sam Tabor. A man carrying a gun has a right to feel tough, a man to be reckoned with. If he'd missed Booker or vice versa, if he'd gone home, he'd have pulled up his collar and snarled into the mirror and given Jim Ambose twenty-four hours to get out of town . . ." He stopped to chuckle to himself, enjoying the scene.

"I get the picture," Nevins said. "But fill it in for me anyway, huh? I'm no GS-10. I'm just a dumb politician."

"It weighed on him. Two pounds thirteen ounces of power. What would a gun represent to a man not used to carrying one, let alone—" he sent an arid look over at Ambose—"a man who is used to it?" They had all heard men accustomed to carrying a gun say they felt naked without it. He turned toward Ambose with that wicked glint that warned Ambose another shaft was heading in his direction.

"Your friend told me how you got those mean old guards to give him a prison uniform. I took it as just another example of your basic humanitarianism. Haw!" He slapped his knee. "You had your man sized up pretty well, didn't you?"

"Sir," Ambose said, "I don't mind you getting on me if it gives you pleasure, but—"

"Come on, Lennard," Nevins said, drawling it dangerously. "You've got him in the squad car, feeling tough."

"It weighs on him. Taking him as we know him, a peaceful, an-onymous man." He grimaced, his whole face wrinkling. "Now why does the word 'androgynous' keep trying to slip in there?" Could they, he mused, have discarded the bisexual element too quickly? Not active, of course. Latent.

Unable to restrain himself any longer, Dee Pawley pushed forward in his chair. "The gun is the symbol of the sex drive for him. The missing, as we say colloquially, penis."

Doc Swann gave him a groaning look. "The subduing mortification," he said with a dramatic flourish, "becomes the avenging sword." He lowered his head modestly, holding up one hand to fend off applause. "It's easy if you're looking for it to begin with. Besides," he said, glaring balefully at Pawley, "I don't like it."

Ambose, hardly looking as if he were going to applaud, wanted to know if that was supposed to mean what he thought it did.

"It means that if you can't get it up, get a gun."

"Oh, shit!"

Doc Swann's sentiments exactly. Too obvious, he told Pawley. Too pat. "And yet," he said thoughtfully, "they do become pat by being repeated, don't they? By becoming part of the folklore. Sometimes even by being true."

"But you don't like it," Nevins said with an air of finality that expressed his own feelings exactly. "I can just see Ambose telling that to a jury." He allowed himself a bit of a smirk. "We'll have to decide whether we want women on the jury, Dee."

Dee Pawley wasn't ready to give up that easily. At least, he said, it gave them something to begin with. "If we can't get him for murder we can get him for indecent exposure on government property."

Swann seemed to have fallen into deep thought. "Not unless we find a history of sporadic violence," he said finally. "I don't mind telling you it would make a hell of a lot more sense. You listening, Ambose? In case you missed it, your boss just gave you the trial assignment. No, I can see you didn't. You don't miss much, do you?"

"Only an occasional penis here and there," Pawley said doggedly. Never mind. Taking him as they knew him. Anonymous, androgynous Sam. Somewhere on the drive, the thought enters his mind that he's got a gun. He's armed to kill. He can show them he's a man. Now, then, where were they going? Aha. They . . . were . . . going . . . to . . . see . . . David Wilcke. That alone would make him the likely target. He was, was he not, the *target* toward which they were speeding.

The noticeable lack of enthusiasm around the room discouraged Pawley not at all. "Speeding towards," he stressed. "That's power. He is in a squad car. Power! Booker was in a hurry, right, which means that the siren is probably going. They are even entitled to go through red lights and, man, that's *power*. Did they, Jim?"

"Did they what?"

"Bust any red lights? You talked to Booker. Did he bust any lights?"

"No," Ambose said. "They did not bust any lights."

Booker and Ambose had exchanged wan, meager smiles, the kind that said they both knew that the cops always got the dirty end of the stick. "Twenty-nine years in the department," Booker said, as if it were a joke which only members of the fraternity could understand, "and I offer a guy a ride . . ."

"If you feel bad about it," Ambose told him, "think how bad Wilcke feels." He gave him a congratulatory wink. "From what I hear, you managed to . . . uh, paralyze the other law enforcement agencies pretty good."

While the Ready Room wasn't a particularly big room, it was big enough to hold six desks and still allow enough space—just barely—for the deputies to move around in. Behind the desks, hung on the walls in no noticeable pattern, were clipboards thick with the accumulating shifts of assignment sheets. There was one small window, high in the back wall, just above street level, but if it had ever been opened—or, for that matter, cleaned—it had not been within the memory of anybody still in active service. It was, in fact, covered by a grill that seemed to make both of those matters highly academic. There was in the near corner of the room a not too large but remarkably powerful fan bolted to a pier-like stand, all enclosed in a heavy cage. Judging by the smell of stale smoke and old egg-salad sandwiches that hung heavy in the air, it didn't do all that much good.

With the whole room to choose from, Booker had chosen to seat himself, slumped and weary, at the corner desk. Indicating the stack of affidavits piled neatly on the desk, he passed on the news that none of the witnesses had noticed Tabor until after the shot was fired. "It doesn't seem possible," he said mournfully. "But there's not a soul there saw him draw the gun and, you know, take aim. It doesn't seem possible." His eyes met Ambose's, stolid and yet apologetic. "It just doesn't seem possible."

"Not my favorite kind of reading anyway," Ambose said, dismissing them. "I want to find out what you saw. From the beginning to—"

Booker had already reached inside his jacket and was holding his own affidavit out to him. Ambose could see, just from the small block of typewriting, that it wasn't going to tell him very much:

On June 15, at approximately 4:40 P.M., I returned to the sheriff's office in the county courthouse, Baltan and Riverway, from a stakeout with Arthur (Arch) Merck. Deputy Merck was going off duty. I reported back to Sheriff Stringfellow, but Sheriff Stringfellow being out of the office, I determined on my own authority to return to City Hall and proceeded thereto with Mr. Tabor, ariving at approximately 4:39 P.M. Upon my arival, much activity could be observed at the portico as Chief Justice Wilcke, Mayor Karney and others were being interviewed by the press and communication media. Leaving Mr. Tabor to watch from below, I proceeded up the stairs and was still just ariving at the portico when I heard the shot and saw Chief Justice Wilcke fall. I thereupon saw Sam Tabor standing several steps below with the gun in his hand and placed him under arrest.

That Booker had managed to leave out such an elementary detail as whether or not Sam Tabor had said anything when Booker grabbed him didn't particularly surprise Jim. It had always amazed him how cops, who were supposed to be so skilled in the art of interrogation, made out such lousy reports themselves. Not that he would have had it any different. The more they held themselves to the bare bones in their report, the more open they were to suggestion when it came to filling in the details.

While he was reading he had penciled in the second "r" on the misspellings of "arriving" and "arrival." "Swell," he said. "Now you say they were already out on the portico when you arrived." He looked down and read, "Upon my arrival, much activity could be observed at the portico . . ."

"That's right."

"You're sure."

"Sure I'm sure. You could see them there when I pulled up and parked, Karney and them. I was thinking that I just got there on time. A few minutes afterwards and maybe I'd have missed him . . ." He paused for one grim moment to think his own heavy thoughts about that. Still, there was something impersonal and professional about his delivery. He was accustomed to giving reports, he was an experienced witness. He could, even here, separate the man from the function. "I could see Wilcke coming out with Clougherty while we were walking toward the steps. Myself, I went up the steps and . . . well hell, Jim, I was still on my way up. I was maybe two steps from the top. I mean, of course they were out on the portico when I . . . we got there."

While he couldn't remember exactly how Tabor had put it, Ambose knew that Sam had left him with the distinct impression that Wilcke hadn't come out yet. A mild discrepancy which probably didn't mean anything. All it meant was that Tabor had been remarkably unobservant. It told you something about Tabor's state of mind, perhaps. What? That he was preoccupied? Why shouldn't he be? He had only been along for the ride. Or did it tell you, perhaps, that he was so terrified at the thought of what he was planning to do that his mind was in a whirl?

He tossed the affidavit back at Booker. "For a man who's always arriving someplace, you ought to learn how to spell it."

No, the weight of it was that Tabor could hardly have been planning to kill Wilcke if he hadn't noticed that his intended victim was standing there, exposed. Always assuming, of course, that Tabor had been telling the truth. But what did it matter? Tabor wouldn't be taking the stand to tell any story at all. Except, of course, that they could always get it in by having him testify through their psychiatrists.

"I'll tell you, Jim. It took me so long to learn to spell sheriff with only one 'r' that now it's got me all bollixed up putting two 'r's together for anything."

"When you went back down the stairs and collared him, how did he look?"

"Nothing, Jim. Nothing there. The crowd had kind of fallen back around him. I was almost ready to grab him before I saw—" He stopped, frowning. More slowly, he said, "Well, I was maybe halfway back down anyway before I saw that it was him."

"What did you think?"

"What did I think?" He might as well have said *What the hell do you think I thought?*

"Yeah. When you saw it was Tabor. The guy you had just left. What did you think?"

It had been a long day for Booker. He had been pulled and tugged, lifted and dropped so many times that he had passed beyond the normal threshold of weariness and reemerged at that state of idling reflexes, so well known to Ambose, where he had begun to feel indestructible. There was the illusion—if it was an illusion—that your mind was clicking along with a shimmering clarity. The only thing was that you found it an effort to bring the words up through the chest cavity; you spoke with a muted energy. "I saw the gun in his hand, and what I thought when I first saw him with the gun was that he had taken it away from the murderer. I was, you know, proud of him." He looked up at Ambose. "That was only for a second but, yeah, that's what I thought when I saw him."

"Just for a second, though?"

"You could see he was the one, all right. From the crowd, from the way he looked. Everything. You could tell it was Sam that had fired the shot."

"You knew he had a gun?"

"I never knew that. No. I never thought about that one way or the other."

"When you grabbed hold of him, did he say anything?"

"He didn't say anything or do anything. He came along, quiet as a babe."

Ambose went to the inside of his jacket for one of his little cigars. Booker accepted one out of powerlessness to resist. "These things of yours will either kill me or cure me, the way I feel right now. The way I feel right now I don't care that much which."

Squinting through the smoke, Ambose reminded him that he had just said that he could tell it was Sam Tabor almost immediately because, among other things, of the way he looked. "You said before that there was nothing in particular about the way he looked. Now, I know the guy had a gun in his hand, and that's a pretty good clue right there. But try to think. Was there anything else about him? Did he seem excited? Worked up? Or maybe satisfied, like he's done what he's come to do?"

Booker gave it a reasonable amount of consideration. "He was maybe a little dazed, glassy-eyed. But I tell you, Jim, I was probably a little glassy-eyed myself, I wouldn't tell you any different. I don't know. I just grabbed him. I was the jerk that brought the sonofabitch, I was damn well going to be the jerk that placed him under arrest." Whatever condemnation was in his description of himself had to be taken from the use of the word itself. Booker had not put any particular emphasis on it. At his level of muted energy, emphasis was too much work.

"You did all right," Ambose said sharply. "Did he say anything at all?"

"When I grabbed him? Not until we were in the car and driving back . . ." "Well . . ."

His breath seemed to be coming hard. Either this was the difficult part for him, or he was just about ready to collapse. "Well, I said something to him first, I guess. I jumped into the front seat, holding him by the elbow, I guess, and then I pulled him in behind me, and when we pulled away and I knew we were home free . . ." The big body sagged. You had the impression that a wave of nausea had passed over him. It was only for a moment, though, and then he was fine again. "I said, 'Sam, I could kill you for this.' Something like that. I said, 'What the hell did you do that for?' "

"And what did he say to that?"

"He said, as far as I could tell, 'Do you have to tell?' " He looked rather uncomfortable, as if the recollection brought a bad odor with it. "Well, that's what it sounded like to me, Jim."

"Do you have to tell? What's that supposed to mean?"

"Hell, I don't know. Myself, I thought it meant, you know, did I have to tell he was the one who did it. I know it sounds crazy but I just felt like that was what he was saying."

Do you have to tell? It sounded crazy sure enough, and crazy-sounding statements, res gestae, were exactly the kind of statements Ambose didn't need. *Do you have to tell? Do-you-have-to-tell? Doyouhavetotell?*

"Could it have been anything else? Maybe he said, 'You can go to hell.' That would have made more sense, wouldn't it?"

The expression in Booker's eyes answered that he was beyond the point where he expected anything to make sense anymore. Ambose stayed right on him, though, pointing out in three or four different ways that it made much more sense for a man who had just been told, "I could kill you for this," to answer, "You can go to hell."

"Jim," Booker said finally, "it could have been anything. It was pretty excitable in there."

"I'll bet. But that's just what I'm trying to find out, how sure you are."

"Jim, I'm not sure of anything anymore."

"Yeah. Then it probably was 'You can go to hell' all right." He nodded briskly, positively, wisely, to let Booker know he was well pleased with him, and moved on to the question of whether Tabor had said anything about how he felt about the Supreme Court decisions.

Booker looked a bit puzzled for a moment. "He was talking about that on the way *down.* I think. You know, I wasn't paying that much attention. We're talking about on the way down now, right? Yeah, I think he did. He's a kind of dull tool, Tabor. And I was thinking about . . . Well, between you and me, Jim"—he glanced toward the door to make sure nobody had come in—"I was kind of PO'd about the stakeout we'd been pulled off of, and my mind kept . . . like running back to that." His voice had begun to run down, and he seemed to stop to wind himself up. "To be perfectly honest, Jim, and I know you're going to ask me this, I don't know why I invited the guy along. I was already out in the courtyard, and for some reason—" Without moving, without any particular warning, he slammed his fist back against the wall so hard that the wall shook. "I . . . just . . . had . . . this . . . kind . . . of whim!"

He just let the arm hang there, not looking at the fist at all. It must have hurt like hell, but Booker was in a mood where he would welcome a reasonable amount of self-inflicted pain. Booker Phillips' mind had come back, Ambose could guess, to the philosophical point on which it had undoubtedly been chewing all evening. Booker would have been rerunning that scene over and over in his mind, wondering what dark Hand, out to destroy him, had bent him to its will. (No. Nothing as impersonal as a vagrant whim could have led him to this pass.) And, more frightening still, what sin he had committed to bring such dark and powerful forces down upon him.

"What's happened has happened," Ambose said. "You can't make it come out different so all you can do is forget it. Right?"

The fist, still hanging behind him, was opening and closing. "If you say so."

"There's one thing Sam told me," Ambose said, as if he were sorely puzzled. "He told me that he had said something about Wilcke getting what he deserved or something like that . . . Did you happen to hear that?"

"I don't remember." He shook his head. "I didn't hear that, Jim. I'm sorry."

"It's OK, Booker. You heard what you heard and that's all I'm interested in. None of your witnesses at the scene heard it either, huh?"

"At the *scene.* I thought—" He gave it another moment's thought. "Nothing like that, no. Nobody I talked to heard him say anything at all, for that matter. That was the first thing most of them told me. The man never—" All at once, Booker's eyes came boiling to life. The thrust of the question had finally penetrated through the personal misfortune on which his mind had been dwelling, and he saw what Ambose was trying to develop. They could have been Bernie Rogell's eyes saying: *What are you trying to do to me, Jim?*

Without taking his eyes off Ambose, he laid the cigar down on the ash tray. "He couldn't have planned it, Jim. I mean, there's no way. I'm going to have to testify that it was the sheerest . . . it was just an accident that he was there. A million-to-one shot. If we don't beat the red light at Landsdowne, Jim, we miss the whole thing."

"Well, like I say, just tell it the way it happened and you can't get into trouble."

Ambose was perfectly satisfied. The suggestion had been planted in Booker's mind, and if Booker decided it might be to his benefit to give Jim Ambose what Jim Ambose wanted, he very well might, on sober reflection, remember—truly remember—that he had heard Tabor say something about Wilcke getting what he deserved. It did not bother him one bit that Booker seemed to understand at this stage of the game exactly what Ambose was doing. Jim Ambose had come to recognize very early in his career that people came to truly believe what it was to their best advantage to believe. One of the first entries in his Journal read: "Just as nature has constructed the deer to run, the tiger to crouch and the snake to strike, it has constructed the human brain to throw off the dangerous memory and replace it with the safe. Man has the unique capacity to truly believe what it is to his best advantage to believe." Years later, leafing through, he had been impelled to add, on some inexplicable impulse—like Booker's inexplicable whim? —the perhaps conflicting parenthetical note: "Is it a quality that has helped man to survive, or is it a quality that will one day help to destroy him?"

In the meantime Booker would understand—was already beginning to understand—that it was far better for Sam Tabor to have told him "You can go to hell" than to have given him some crazy, undecipherable answer. It had been well worth getting to Booker this early just to have wiped that out of his mind. And he was perfectly satisfied that it had indeed, to all practical purposes, been wiped out of his mind.

Booker had turned his affidavit toward himself and was idly reading it over. "You know what I qualified at, on the range last time?" he said. "Ninety-nine. Number three man in the state."

"Go home and get some sleep," Ambose told him. "And Booker—don't talk to anybody. No newspapers. No television. No nothing."

Booker was still looking down at the affidavit. "I come to work here at the courthouse—it was the old courthouse then. Down on Court Street where the skating arena is now." He looked up at Ambose. "That's why it's called Court Street, did you ever know that? Harry Franchot was sheriff then." To Ambose, Harry Franchot was a dim name out of the distant past. "Sheriff Franchot gave me this job sweeping up. The numbers men and the dice men and the pimps and the prostitutes used to line up outside his office on Tuesday mornings and drop the payoff money into a wastebasket on his desk. That was one of my jobs, to make sure the wastebasket was cleaned out and on top of his desk. There's those I know make fun of Bob Stringfellow," he said, looking directly at Ambose. "Only they don't know what he did for this city, see? Bob Stringfellow may not have the sweetest temperament in the world but they don't know what he did for this whole damn county a long time before anybody ever heard of Hilliard Nevins or Jim Ambose."

Damn. Now that he'd told his story he seemed to have gotten a second wind. He seemed refreshed and eager to reminisce. Ambose was more than interested in hearing about how the sheriff's office was run in the old days, but he could pump Booker about that any time. For now, he had more important things on his mind. "I know," he said. "Booker. I mean talk to nobody. Nobody."

Booker shifted, heavily and laboriously, in his chair. "What about investigators? The FBI? Stringfellow says do what you say, it's your ball game now."

A grimly satisfied look came over Ambose as he was telling Booker to refer everybody to him. "For twelve years," he said, "our dealings with the FBI have been one way. We give and they take. Let's see how it plays the other way for a change."

"It's your ball game," Booker said. A warm little smile was on his lips, nothing at all like the foolish smile that had bothered Jim so much about Tabor. "I was eleven years old when I came to work at the courthouse, did I ever tell you that? My mother died of pneumonia and my father was already dead, and they were going to send us to the orphanage, me and my two sisters. I had two sisters, Jim. Jenny was a year older than me and Mady was, I think, five. Five years old. And we got together after they'd all gone, Jenny and me, and we said, no siree, we weren't going to let them break us up. And you know what we did? We took each other's hands across my mother's coffin, Jenny and me, and we took a vow on her dead body and immortal soul that we'd go get a room somewhere where they couldn't find us and I'd get a job and she'd keep the house and together we'd take care of the baby."

He was, Ambose could see, in the grip of an enormous emotion. "The first day, crack out of the barrel, I went down to the courthouse—we'd got a room around the corner, four–five blocks away—and the courthouse was the biggest building around, that's why I went in there first crack." He was nodding to himself firmly, remembering. "I walked in on Sheriff Franchot and his cronies—the Seven Thieves of Baghdad, they called them, I found that out later—and I told him I needed a job, and he gave me a broom and he said, 'You want to do nigger's work, boy? You need a job bad enough to take a starving nigger's job away from him?' And I looked down at my shoes and I said, 'Yes, sir.'

"I worked for Sheriff Franchot—from sweeper to elevator man to doorman— for seven years, and I never missed a day. And I never spent one minute of one day that I didn't hate that man from the top of his head to the bottom of his feet." Watching him, Ambose could see him come drifting back into focus. "There's those that call me a . . . that think I try to be maybe too nice to the colored people around here but it was a long time before I could go into a grocery store without thinking that there was a whole family of colored people starving somewhere in Lowell because of me. That's just what I did, Jim. I looked down at my shoes and I said, 'Yes, sir.' "

"Eleven years old," Jim said, just to say something. "Didn't anybody try to do anything, didn't anybody report it? What about school? Didn't they have truant officers or something then?"

"Who give a damn!" Booker said angrily. "You think it was then like now?"

All at once, his voice came unstrung and he was crying. "Eleven years old, and nobody cared . . ."

"Jesus God," Ambose said to himself. "How do I get out of this?"

Containing himself, pulling himself together by an effort of will, Booker said in a cramped, constricted voice, "When I was sixteen, I started to go to night school to learn to read and write so I could become a deputy, and the first time I applied for the exam, I misspelled 'sheriff' and that dirty bastard, Franchot, that fucken thief, he said, 'You got to learn how to spell it, Booker, before you can think about being it.' And he tore up my application and threw it in his money basket and I had to wait three more years before the exams came around again."

His throat had loosened up and he was talking free and natural again. Using his forefingers like windshield wipers, he squeezed them into his eyes and wiped the tears away. "God*damn,*" he said. "I don't know why I'm making you listen to all this. I'm sorry, Jim." He shook his head, smiling at him apologetically.

"It's all right. I can sure see why you're an admirer of Bob Stringfellow."

"Eleven years old," Booker said. He held up his hands, like two great claws, the fingers dug in toward himself. "And in all that time anything I got I had to dig for myself with my own two hands." Ambose was riveted upon the scraped skin and raw flesh where he had punched the wall. "When my own daughter got married, I had to sell my car to give her a wedding, and if next week's pay check don't come through, I don't know how we'd eat. See? And I got to cruise the town and hear these smart-ass college kids who never knew a hard time in their life tell me what thieves and grafters cops are."

"I know what you mean," Ambose said, starting to rise. "Listen, if you have any doubts about anything, call me. And if you can't get me, just leave a message and don't do anything until I get back to you. OK?"

Booker nodded absently. "I got a grandson thirteen years old now. I remember when he was eleven, at his birthday party, and I looked at him and I thought to myself, 'Dearly beloved Jesus, that's how old I was when I took on the work of a man.' " In a hushed, disbelieving voice he said, "I was looking at a baby, Jim. He was just a baby." The tears had begun to come again. "I was a baby when I became a family man." His throat was closing up on him again, and he was rushing to squeeze the words out. "One day I was a baby and the next day I was supporting a family." He buried his face in his hands, and through the sobbing he cried out. "I was never a child! I never had any childhood at all."

After an awful moment of silence Ambose said quietly, "That was the way it was in those days. I grew up on a farm, Booker. I know. Things are different now."

But Booker was straightening up in his chair. He was all right again. He was wiping his eyes with a handkerchief and blowing his nose. He was picking up the affidavit, folding it neatly and, with his elbow on the desk, he was leaning toward Jim and shaking it at him like a stick. "You see what I mean, Jim. What I mean is I'm chief of deputies for Robert S. Stringfellow, the best damn sheriff this county ever had, and maybe it isn't as bad as all that if I don't get to spell a word exactly right every now and then."

Pawley had called out to Lenore for four cups of "Rotten Coffee," his own brand name for the coffee dispensed by the vending machine one floor below. "I still say we're going to find some sexual hang-ups in Tabor," he said, smacking his lips. "Classic Freudian symbols everywhere you look."

"Classic Freudian symbols." Swann guffawed. "You wouldn't know a classic Freudian symbol if it crawled into bed with you and farted." All that crap about power sounded good, he said waspishly, but what did it mean. "In the good old days the man who killed the king became king. Is Sam Tabor going to become the new Chief Justice?"

No, but what Sam Tabor had done had changed the lives of some very powerful men, one of whom would become Chief Justice, another who would take the new Chief Justice's place and so on down the line. Ripples in the pond of history. It could change the whole drift of the Court, which meant that it could change the history of the country. Change the world. "Hey, Jim," he said, switching without warning from earnest advocacy to the sly dig. "Did you hear who's supposed to be the choice for Chief Justice?"

Ambose had heard. "That friggen fixer," he said. "The President's own fixer." All of a sudden, his eyes flew open. "Hey, maybe we can arrange to send Sam down to Washington to cover the swearing-in ceremony."

There was a wincing, accompanied by groaning all around the room, a common expression of incredulity and dismay that even Jim Ambose could have such a thought—and, having had such a thought, express it.

"Anyway," Pawley said, "you do see the thrust of my argument. If it's the result, why isn't it the reason? With or without the *sic semper tyrannis.*"

"Because, like Doc says, it's too easy. Because everybody wants power in their hearts, and only Sam Tabor chose to do it this way. In all the world, only Sam Tabor. You're not that much older than Tabor, Doc. Has your ship sailed?"

Swann's hand waved out beyond the window, toward some distant sea, wistfully bidding his ship *bon voyage.*

"You're damn right," Ambose said. "Everybody's ship sails. I still say that you're only defining what he did. We knew that anyway. We still haven't explained it."

Decisively, with the air of a man who was now stepping in to take over, Hilliard Nevins said, "Of course that's the motive." Part of it, anyway. The question was why Sam, and why now? "The question is did it have to be the Chief Justice or could it have been any prominent public official. Any prominent person at all." He looked to Doc Swann. "Why, at the age of fifty-two, did the man explode?"

"The dynamite had been tamped in the tubing waiting for some self-igniting fury to touch it off. That's the ticket, eh?" He closed his eyes and smiled. "Pretty good ticket."

In one quick, impatient movement Ambose pushed the cup of coffee away from him and came to his feet. "This is getting us nowhere fast," he announced. He peered into the coffee as if he had just made the obvious connection between it and the equally unrewarding conversation, and then strode over to the table so that he could plunk it down in front of Pawley. "You're talking about Sam as if he was subhuman and he isn't. He's an average guy."

Swann slapped both hands down on his thighs, hard. "Ambose, with that laser mind of his, has cut through the crap again. An average man who did a remarkable and frightening thing." He gave his shoulders a little shrug. "In a moment of inadvertency, Sam Tabor did shoot and kill the Chief Justice. As long as I'm here, why not shoot him?"

"Then that's it," Nevins said. He bit down hard on the cigar. "Either they find a hole in the guy's head or they're going to have to put on one whale of a medical case." And if the state wouldn't be able to keep their psychiatrists away from him, they could—he reminded them—put on a hell of a fight to keep them from putting him on the EEG, and even the serology and the rest of it, unless they had their own man there as an observer.

"If you're talking about me," Swann said, "I still like to look upon myself as my own man. A personal idiosyncrasy. A crotchet of old age."

"Hilliard," Pawley said. His glance encompassed the whole room. In a case of this importance, he said carefully, didn't he think they could get together with Tommy Mallon and Judge Chobodian and have a team of psychiatrists appointed by an impartial panel put him through the full battery of tests? "Make it a textbook case. We know Doc here wouldn't lean our way if it came to that kind of an agreement, and so does Tommy. If he says they've got enough to show insanity, we'll accept an insanity plea. If he says no, we go to court and they can still plead their case before a jury."

Nevins looked mildly interested but Ambose took violent exception. With all due respects to Doc Swann, Jim Ambose didn't believe the law was meant to be given over to the psychiatrists. "I think they come to the courtroom as expert witnesses, not as judges," he said, and Swann, hastening to agree, told Nevins quite frankly that it was not a responsibility he would welcome.

When Pawley tried to explain that it would still be the judge's decision to make, and then only after both the judge and the opposing attorneys had read the reports and, undoubtedly, examined the psychiatrists in chambers, Ambose objected that they were getting themselves involved in star chamber proceedings. "We're getting too much of that in this country already," he said virtuously. "And the Bar would be after all our asses. I think it's a lousy idea all around." Having wandered back toward the sofa, he plunked down into the corner, one arm flung over the side. If Mallon wanted to make Tabor a monkey in a cage, he said gloomily, let him come to the DA's office and make the proposition himself. "We've got the most open and shut case in the history of American jurisprudence, for chrissake. It's ridiculous to go to them looking for a deal."

So far, Pawley reminded him, they had a guy killing a man for no reason. And unless they came up with a reason, the defense could put on a good case of murder without premeditation. "Which is another way, in this one, of saying irresistible impulse."

Nevins didn't think a jury would look with any favor on an irresistible impulse that compelled anybody to kill a Chief Justice. "A jury is going to say that the gun is premeditation no matter how it got there," he said, "and the fact that he killed him shows there was a motive or he wouldn't have done it. Bad law," he said, turning to Swann, "but good logic. A jury, thank god, has more sense than the law, which may be the only reason this whole shooting match works." He looked down idly at his wristwatch and ostentatiously began to wind it, the sure sign that he was getting ready to break this thing up. "Ambose," he said, "you're on your way to see Tommy Mallon from here, aren't you?"

"The hell with all of you," Pawley said, rising on cue.

"There's a hell of a Freudian analysis can be made," Swann said before Ambose had unbent. "Damn right. The boys will be having fun with it for years." A soft, dreamy look came over him. "As a dear colleague of mine used to say, Freudian analysis is like playing poker with everything wild. No two players have the same hand but everybody is sure he won."

The words hung there for a moment. "Thanks for nothing," Pawley said. "Where were you, Doctor, when I needed you?"

"Wasn't such a dear colleague, after all, now that I think of it," Swann said. He pulled on his nose, snorting heavily. "Wasn't even smart. A dolt was what he was. Probably the only clever thing he ever said in his life. Don't know why

I bothered to give him credit when it would have been just as easy to pass it off as my own. You see, Ambose, I'm losing the killer instinct. The beloved old humbug is gone at the teeth."

Nevins was viewing him rather narrowly. "Damnit, Lennard," he said. "We've been sitting here all this time and you've been saying you didn't have the slightest idea. You've been saying . . ." He paused, trying to remember exactly what he had been saying.

"*What* have I been saying?" said Swann, triumphant. "The way you lawyers keep interrupting, nobody can get a word in edgewise."

Nevins bit off another chunk from the wet end of his cigar and spat it toward his wastebasket. "For instance?"

For perhaps ten seconds Swann examined the bottom end of his necktie with an attentive gravity. All right, he said, what did they know about Sam Tabor other than his age? He held up two fingers. Marital status: Married six years. He had told Doc he had met his wife at a dance. "Doesn't seem like the dance hall type to me, but what do I know? Haven't been in a dance hall for thirty years. Seen them in the movies, though. Gigolo types. Skinny, anyway. No pimples. Young."

Catching Nevins' eye, he very quickly held up a third finger. Parents dead. Older sister died when he was just a boy. Came from Appalachia somewhere.

According to Sam's civil service application, Ambose could tell him, he had been born in Twenty Hills, Maryland, and had graduated from a small, now defunct college with a B.S. in sociology. Seemed to be a two-year, not necessarily accredited, college run by the Children of the Redeemer, a regional religious cult.

Four fingers. Occupation: He worked, Swann said as if he were letting out a delicious secret, at the Bureau of Missing Persons. All five fingers. The Victim: He killed . . . the Chief Justice . . . of the United States. "From that data, Ambose, what do we conclude? From that data, Ambose, we conclude that his father deserted the family when he was a boy."

Nevins was standing at the side of his desk, following every word intently.

"How did we conclude that?" Ambose asked.

"He could have told us." He grinned at him mischievously. "But he didn't. But if he wants to cooperate with the classic profile, that's the way it's got to be. And if he won't cooperate," he said menacingly, "the hell with him. Who needs him? I'm doing the work of two men, as it is."

He snuffled some more while they waited for him to fill out the classic profile. "That job and—*ahhh!* that victim." He sat back in the sweet contemplation of it. "The gown-ed man. Yes, if Sam wants to be a good fellow, his father will definitely have flown the coop. When he was, oh, nine or ten. Preferably on his birthday." The head darted up and around again. "His father was a private detective. Part time. A bank dick. Part-time preacher, part-time bank guard. That's rendering unto Caesar to a fare-thee-well." The victim was the thing, though. My, yes. Just marvelous. "The Chief Justice himself," he said, chuckling to himself. "A veritable child's garden of symbolisms."

"Lennard," Nevins said, "you can be a damnably irritating man." He said it tonelessly but the underlay of muscle was so unmistakable, the displeasure of authority making itself seen, that Swann, suddenly subdued, protested that he could hardly be expected to draw a full-fleshed portrait when all he had been given was the canvas, not the paints. "It depends on what else we can find in his background. A patient comes in and says, 'I don't know what it is, Doc, but whenever I hear a toilet flush, I break out into this Irish clog dance. And I'm Hungarian. Is there anything wrong with me?' Well, yes, there is that possibility, Anton. But I've got to find out a few things about you first. Lie right there and show me your bankbook. Oh my, yes. Worst case of three-thousand-eight-hundred-and-seventy-six-dollar hydrophobia I ever saw! You understand, Hilliard? You and your sleuths are going to have to find me out a few things about Mr. Tabor." He closed his eyes, suffused once again in happy contemplation. "The gown-ed man. Yes, indeed. The thought does refuse to pass. Like a kidney stone in the old pisserarium."

Nevins wanted to know about *their* psychiatrists. Would *they* hit on the same thing?

Hit on it? Unless they hired a rank incompetent, of which the ranks were full, or a man so brilliant as to o'erleap the obvious, of whom, as Hilliard may have noticed, there were none, they couldn't miss it. But that wasn't the question. The question was whether any lawyer would, could or should submit a Freudian interpretation to cross-examination without being carted off to the booby-hatch himself. "Why," he said, lighting up lasciviously, "I can see James Ambose lighting up lasciviously at just the thought of it."

"Then it's true," Pawley said, almost in awe, semivindicated. "The Chief Justice did represent something to him, something out of his submerged subconscious. It wasn't Wilcke he was killing, it was what he repesented. The power of his office."

"True?" Swann's eyes opened wide. He bolted up straight in the chair. "How the hell do I know if it's true! I'm just the man comes in and paints the pretty pictures. You looking for truth, go to the—" For once in his life, Doc Swann was at a loss for words. If he was looking for truth, he said genuinely baffled, he didn't know where to send him. "Truth is like your family doctor. It doesn't pay house calls anymore. On Wednesdays, it's hardly in at all."

Nevins–Pawley–Swann minus Ambose had a tone and quality that were very different from when the four of them were together. A prime source of energy had been removed. The cohering tension had been sprung. There was a common understanding that a moment had to be taken while a realignment of relationships was taking place.

Hilliard Nevins was permitted one cigar a day, and he cheated by smoking the biggest cigar he could find. He had come to look forward to that moment in the day when he would open the drawer and gaze upon it, perched, as always, in the little curved pencil rack. It was his moment of self-indulgence and relaxation, his reward for enduring one more day's cares of office. He bit off the end carefully, lit it lovingly, and breathed out the first cloud of smoke. Then he leaned back in his chair, in that characteristic pose of his, glasses on forehead and hands locked behind his head.

"I know this sounds like I'm bucking," Pawley said suddenly, "but do you really think Jim can take an objective view of this case?"

"Yes and no." No, he didn't think Pawley was bucking. Yes, he did think Ambose could handle the case. Both of them, nevertheless, turned automatically to Doc Swann.

"He seems all right to me, if that's what you mean."

"No," Pawley said. Methodically, uncomfortable at having to put into words what they already knew, he explained that he was talking about the way Jim felt about Wilcke. Still felt about the Supreme Court. He wasn't saying that Jim would do anything deliberately. At least, he didn't think that was what he was saying. His fingers went to the bandage on his forehead. "I'm just wondering whether he might find himself so much in sympathy with Tabor that he'd . . . uh, perform with something less than his customary vigor."

"He damn well better perform with something less than his customary vigor or he'll hear from me!" Nevins removed the cigar from his mouth no more than was necessary to blow out a great cloud of smoke. "We're going to have the press of the world here for this and something tells me we don't smell sweet already." He was contemplating Pawley in amusement and disbelief, unable to understand how anybody could know Ambose that long and misjudge him so completely. Hadn't he seen how Ambose had reacted at the mere suggestion that the case be turned over to an impartial panel?

"I didn't say he didn't want a trial," Pawley said. He made a small, halfhearted gesture with his hand. "I'm just wondering what he might do in the trial. What he wants to use it for."

"I know what he wants to use it for," Nevins whooped. "He wants to burn Sam Tabor!" With a quick, expansive flick of the fingers Nevins sent the ashes in the general direction of the ash tray. Come on, now. With the Trial of the Century thrown into Jim Ambose's lap, did Pawley really think he could be toying around with the idea of throwing it? "Did you hear that, Lennard? And I thought we had a bright young feller here."

Still unconvinced, noticeably unhappy, Pawley threw a pleading look over to Swann and found nothing at all to comfort him. With anybody else he might very well have a valid point, Swann told him, and the attempt at kindness was so apparent as to have the opposite effect. But not Jim Ambose. "Jim Ambose is Jim Ambose is Jim Ambose." A hard, flinty point of light had appeared in Doc Swann's eyes. "When Jim Ambose begins to plan a case, the case takes over. And when Jim Ambose walks into a courtroom, the smell of burning flesh is already in his nostrils."

"Lennard," Nevins said, blowing an approving cloud of smoke at him, "you took the words right out of my mouth."

"On the other hand," said Lennard Swann, "if I were Sam Tabor I couldn't want a better man on my jury than James J. Ambose."

The one thing Ambose had never counted on was that Tommy Mallon wouldn't want the case. With clicking precision Tommy had run down everything that was wrong with it. They had Tabor on film, which went a far piece toward eliminating reasonable doubt. And also put him in a first-degree murder case without being able to give the jury another possible murderer to think about. He wouldn't even be able to show what bad guys cops were. That left him with two possible avenues of approach. He could try the victim, hereinafter known as "that depraved monster." Or he could go for an insanity plea, which would serve the dual purposes of enriching a clutch of worthy psychiatrists and giving the jury a chance of doing whatever it damn well wanted to do. Having already eliminated the possibility of giving the jury an opportunity to believe that his client, however misguided, had not done the world a bad turn by eliminating his victim, he was left with the prospect of finding something Wilcke or the Wilcke Court had done to drive Tabor to this desperate act, which, he would submit, ladies and gentle-men, could only have been the product of a diseased and disintegrating mind.

"He doesn't like the Law of the Land so he kills the umpire," Mallon said. "Collides head-on with the American tradition of fair play. Great case. I'll always be grateful to Sam for thinking of me."

"All you have to do is give him the best defense you can give him," Ambose said. "Nobody expects you to win. Only to fight."

Mallon looked at him sort of sideways. "For an appropriate fee I well might." He laughed shortly. "For an appropriate fee I would also befoul the memory of my sainted mother."

As it happened, to make this a real four-bagger, Tommy had received a call that morning from a Dr. Shtogren who, having identified himself as the official representative of Mrs. Tabor, had been good enough to inform him that Mrs. Tabor was being deluged with telegrams from all over the country from lawyers, otherwise identified only as distinguished, offering their services. "Our brothers at Bar seem quite concerned lest such a highly publicized murderer be deprived of due process. The operative word I need not stress was 'offered.'" He raised his glass, as if in toast. "I was pleased to hear that if I am as willing as my brothers to work for the glory of it all, I am still in the running."

Tommy was seated in the midst of the sunken-room splendor of his penthouse apartment, drink in hand. Beyond him, through the opening in the wall of drapery, you could look out over the skyline of the entire city. The full bottle was set on the low glass-topped table in front of him. From the look of him, as well as from the pale blue silken robe he was wearing, Ambose could see that he had been up all night. For all their friendship, Ambose had been in the apartment only once before. He had dropped by as a courtesy, for the grand-opening party. *You cannot run with the foxes and hunt with the hounds.* That was one of the sternest admonitions Ambose handed down to all his assistants. They could not go golfing with a criminal lawyer on Sunday, he warned them, and expect to treat him like any other lawyer when he came in on Monday looking for a deal. Jim Ambose, as anybody could tell you, did not say such things just to hear himself talk. Tommy Mallon was the only friend he had, really, in Lowell. He did not socialize with him.

"You've fixed the place up pretty good," he grunted.

"As long as they keep robbing banks." He raised his glass in salute. "And as long as they keep getting collared by an alert gendarmerie. You ought to come over to the sunny side of the rights, too, Jim." He gave him his boyishly appealing smile. "With any luck at all, I'm going to get to waste my substance in riotous living."

Ambose had picked up a heavy silver cigarette lighter, ornately brocaded at the belly and shaped to the genie of Aladdin's lamp. "Nice piece, this." Proffering it to him, he held Mallon, eye to eye. "You didn't know anything about this Shtogren until this morning. Why didn't you come down and at least talk to Tabor last night?"

The look Tommy gave him was wholly ambiguous. He twisted his body back and forth as if he were trying to work out a persistent stiffness. "Screw you, pal. I don't need it and, more germane to the issue pending, I don't want it."

"Ahhh, but he wants you. The worse the crime, the better the defense to which the suspect is entitled. Now where did I hear that before sometimes?"

Tommy stopped again, in mid-turn, the flat of his hand against the base of his spine. The painful wince had become a wince of disbelief. "I tell you, pal, the next time I am called upon to defend you to our brothers at the Bar I will no longer be able to say in all good conscience, 'Well, the one thing you got to give Jim Ambose, he's no damn hypocrite.' " He squinted at him, really puzzled. "What the hell is this? When did I become that easy? Or are you really that anxious to get back at me for Garrett?" A sour little laugh escaped from him. Someone he knew rather well, he reminded him, had once pointed out rather forcefully that if that line of reasoning were followed to its logical conclusion the worst criminals would always get off. He flashed the boyish grin at him again, asking to be liked, confident that he would be. "And, Jimbo, you and I both know that every once in a while they don't."

But Ambose was shaking his head at him, in a sort of sad disapproval at so weak an effort. "Not with me, you don't. I'm not pissin' on your leg, you're pissin' on mine. I'm going to be doing my damnedest to burn Sam Tabor. You're the one who's backing away from his sworn oath and stated principles, not me."

"My stated principles?" Since when? If some guy chopped his old lady's head off and hollered for the services of Thomas P. Mallon, did that mean Tommy had to take him on if he didn't have a mortgage he could turn over to him? Leaning toward Ambose, he whispered, "I wouldn't want to be quoted on this in the *Ladies' Home Journal,* but while I view the beheading of a spouse as one of the risks attendant upon the marriage contract, I look with no favor at all upon the assassination of a Chief Justice. There is a limit," he said, "to how much any legal system can stand. Even ours. If you want to know something, I'd give an eyetooth, the customary rate of exchange in these transactions, to be back in the office just long enough to help you put this silly psychopath into the hot squat."

Still, Ambose decided to give it one more try. With a smirking superiority calculated to infuriate, he allowed as how he had never expected to see Tommy Mallon so afraid of a case that he'd be mounting the soap box for the prosecution.

Look who was talking! "You've been doing p.r. for the fucking Civil Liberties Union from the time you walked in here." Mallon gave a dry little bark of laughter. "You know what you got here? You've got a temporary insanity case and you're not walking this guy out on any temporary insanity."

"That's your specialty, hot shot," Ambose said, grinning at him. "Who but you could have got that kid off in the Allenhoff killing?"

"Anybody," Tommy muttered. Allenhoff had been a dirty old rich man screwing around with the kid's wife. "The jury couldn't wait for me to sum up so they could let him go." The light that had been coming in through the opening of the drapery was fading away, and he was suddenly engulfed in shadow. "Geez," he said, more to himself than to Ambose. "That would be a bold defense. And nobody except Tommy Mallon . . ." He looked up and for just that moment he was the Tommy Mallon of the courtroom. "You're right about that, anyway."

Just as quickly the shadow passed and he was smiling at Ambose to let him know that whatever he had been mulling over in his head had been nothing more than an exercise in legal gymnastics. "A bold and brilliant defense," said Tommy Mallon, "which could very well ruin my reputation and, worse yet, my sex life." Because no matter what you did in this one, they were going to come back with first degree. "In the back of every juror's mind there will be the idea that there had to be something more to it than that and—we keep getting back to this— they're going to feel they have a patriotic duty to protect the high officials of this country." In addition to which, everybody would always believe that there was some hidden motive which the shifty defense lawyer had kept hidden from public view.

"The coward runneth away," Ambose said, "when no man runneth after."

That stopped Mallon in his tracks.

"I used to have a Sunday School teacher," Ambose explained, "whose favorite quotation that was."

To Mallon it sounded more like the football coach. "I keep meaning to become a biblical scholar some weekend," he muttered. "But what the hell is it supposed to mean?"

"It means that in our enlightened state the burden of proof in an insanity plea still lies with the prosecution."

Mallon let out a hoot of laughter. "Wise old heads like you and I know what a crock is there, don't we, old pal? Wise old heads like me and thee know that the jurors, being reasonable men all, will be looking at me and thinking, 'Hey, there, young fellow, *you* pleaded insanity and *you* brought in all those shrinks to stuff our neural passages with all that psychiatric crap. What do you mean, you slimy shyster, telling me now that you've got my head pounding that they've got to prove a negative—*viz.* and to wit, that Sam Tabor *isn't* insane?' "

He had been waving his arms so violently in the role of indignant juror that the robe had worked apart, exposing a massively hairy chest. Scratching his chest meditatively, he reminded Jim of a case when he had been an eager, apple-cheeked young assistant carrying the briefcase for him, where the high-priced attorney for the defense had, by doing exactly that, parlayed the ten-year sentence they had been willing to settle for into life. "And that was a straight insanity plea," he said triumphantly. "Never even tried to tell them that all of a sudden everything went green." He gave him his innocent smile from deep down underneath, the one Bo Gunderson used to call the-butter-wouldn't-melt-in-his-eyes smile. "I sure hope Sam Tabor doesn't get stuck with one of those fancy high-priced attorneys."

It had always been effective with juries, that smile, and, Ambose had to admit, with himself. But not this time. (For one thing, his mind was still brooding on the Proverb jury. He had never been so sure in his life that a jury was going to come back with death.) "That's what you want me to tell Tabor then," he said abruptly. "That you won't take his case!"

The contempt communicated itself. "Not at these prices," Tommy snapped back. "Tell him my charitable contributions are made to the Community Chest. Tell him I gave at the office." Ruffled now, he gave him his best apprentice-boy grin, trying to call up once again the easy-riding old days when he was Jim Ambose's pet protégé. "Honest, Jim," he said, "where does that leave Thomas P. Mallon, Esquire, star-studded lover, bust-out scholar and hot-shot KO artist of the local Bar, after they cart the guy off to Algonquin?" He wet his finger and pretended to make a note. "Star-studded lover," he sighed. "What a marvelous language we have fallen heir to."

It jarred Ambose again. It jarred him loose from whatever fixed relationship between them still existed. It was not the first time he had noticed that Tommy had a way of talking about himself as if he were still a bright young attorney, but where Ambose had always interpreted it kindly, as a form of self-deprecation (the dues friendship exacts), he could see now, viewing him afresh, that Tommy still saw himself, and probably always would, as the Boy Wonder of the Bar.

Viewing him afresh, from this new critical stance, Ambose could observe that the hair, dropping over his forehead, was already beginning to show signs of thinning. And, to jar him again, that the hand that poured the drink was trembling. Tommy Mallon had already come to the point where he needed that drink in midafternoon. Observing Tommy as he threw it down, he could see with a foretelling clarity that, small and stumpy as he was, Tommy was not going to age well.

His smallness was his weak point. Why hadn't he seen that before? Seeing the weakness, he was free to see the flaw. The same basic, underlying flaw that kept Tommy from jumping at this opportunity to grab the Trial of the Century had kept him from rising to Ambose's tauntings in the courtroom. Tommy Mallon was all brain and reflex, a walking, talking computer. He could have functioned just as well as the Boy Wonder of the Counting Room or Laboratory. Why hadn't he seen it before?

No, there must have been something more than that to the young man who had come to work for him. Ambose could not imagine that he would have lavished such training and—yes—affection on him otherwise.

Looking at Tommy Mallon, he experienced a vast, liberating pride in himself. If you were Jim Ambose, you took them as they came, day in and day out, the good ones and the bad. You put on your witnesses and you let them tell their stories, and if they turned out to be bad witnesses with bad stories, you swept your papers back into your briefcase and went back to the office to pick up the next case.

Let them change the law on you, buy the judges and suborn the witnesses, you fought them back as best you could and, win or lose, you went home and enjoyed your dinner and came back in the morning ready to take them on again.

To stand your ground was all that mattered. To fight the fight. The one thing he was sure of, at that moment, was that he would be losing few cases to Tommy Mallon from this day on. To make sure that Tommy understood it, too, he said, "How old are you, little man?"

Mallon's head came snapping up, stung. Stunned.

"Thirty yet?"

"That's right." Wary now. "Two months ago."

"Jesus Horatio Christ," Ambose said, smiling inwardly as he heard Doc Swann's favorite expletive on his lips. "Thirty years old and all that worrying."

AM PREPARED TO TAKE ON DEFENSE OF SAM TABOR AS PUBLIC SERVICE BELIEVE THIS TO BE LANDMARK CASE IN UNSHACKLING THE LAW FROM THE MEDIEVAL JUSTICE OF THE M'NAUGHTON RULE AND CATAPULTING AMERICAN JUSTICE INTO THE TWENTIETH CENTURY. WILL ARRIVE IN LOWELL ON AMERICAN AIRLINES FLIGHT #222. PLEASE HAVE ME PICKED UP. I WILL BE THE MAN IN THE MIDDLE SURROUNDED BY THE GENTLE-MEN OF THE PRESS. WE ARE EMBARKING UPON A GREAT ADVENTURE.

BANNERMAN

Dear Paul:

Herewith is the transcript of the Bannerman press conference, hot off the recording machine. If you want some background description, you know the Press Room at American Airlines. VIP stands on raised circular blue platform, the blue-white winged AA insignia behind him to see how much

111

free advertisement they can catch. You have a hundred pictures of it flying off behind somebody's left ear. The lights are 500-watt, one on each side and provided by the TV crew, altho the television interview came later. The reporters, there must have been two dozen, surround him on the outer rim (ground level) of the stand.

Noted Chicago attorney Norman Bannerman is a big one. Must go 6'3" or upwards. By my mostly intelligible notes I see he was dressed in a black silk suit of infinite weave, mit a white carnation in the lapel yet, and he was wearing a cummerbund—repeat, CUMMERBUND—which I put at wine-red (having asked a female researcher from *Time* Mag, who Bannerman was making goo-goo eyes at). If it helps in assessment of his overall competence, she put his eyes down as bedroom-blue. I always knew I went into the wrong profession. (Profession?)

The tenacious reporter who kept wanting to know how the hell he was hired was ye *Globe*'s own crack reporter, good old tenacious me. You will note the answer. It was also me who asked that last question about the M'Naughton Rule. It was not till I got to reading this over that I saw how nicely he swerved me. Which cud mean he not so sure which way he going to jump. Also means that good old untenacious me is (am? are?) even farther back on my heels than I thought. Can't imagine why that shud be, I had couple of hours' sleep three days ago.

"Noted Chicago attorney Norman Bannerman" handles himself well. (You will note the understatement for which I am noted.) I suspect that what's to be got out of this trial, he will get out of it. (You will note the suspicion of which I have been suspected.) As for me, Im going to go home and will return when you see me. Before my head hits the pillow and my eyelids slam shut, am going to drill following words, "Hello, my daddy isn't in," into the dutiful minds of my children, so if you don' want to lead preschoolers into sin, you will not—repeat, NOT—phone.

Rich

P.S. Suggest you leave Jim Ambose to me, but if you want to be a goddamn fool go ahead and send somebody else up there—maybe you can screw it up for all of us.

P.P.S. Paul, with all these reporters coming in, let's guard the morgue a little, huh? Let's be hospitable as befits but not be goddamn fools. What I mean is I don't mind them using the clips to their hearts' content but let's make sure they do not walk away with them.

P.P.P.S. What I really mean is if someone's going to be filing to the national magazines, why not us?

P.P.P.P.S. That was unworthy of me.

P.P.P.P.P.S. What *that* really means is that having made my point, I would now like the onus to be on you.

P.P.P.P.P.P.S. Zzzzzzzzzzzzzzzzzz

Q. Mr. Bannerman, have you definitely been retained to represent Sam Tabor?

A. I'm here. (Laughter) I'm here to discuss the matter of employment with Mr. Tabor and Mrs. Tabor.

Q. Have you talked to Mrs. Tabor? Would she be the one who hired you?

A. I trust I am being hired by them both, because I am a firm believer—if not necessarily an active participant—in marital accord. Especially if it should develop that they have a joint bank account. (Laughter) As always, I am in the hands of you gentle people of the Fourth Estate not to quote me out of context.

Q. Mr. Bannerman, why should Sam Tabor deserve the kind of a defense you can give him? He killed the Chief Justice, that's incontrovertible. Wouldn't it be better for somebody who might not be guilty to get the benefit of your talents?

A. You know something. That's the kind of question that frightens the beejeebers out of me. It is the duty of the attorney, under our system, to defend the indefensible, controvert the incontrovertible and bespeak the unspeakable. That is my quest and my mission. And, as for that young lady over there in the short skirt, that is my miss and she knows the question. (Laughter)

Q. Are you saying you can do that, controvert the incontrovertible?

A. I am saying that guilt is a legal judgment resulting from a finding of fact made by a jury or, if no jury is sitting, a judge. I am saying that the burden is on the state to prove that poor Sam is guilty and, if guilty, that he was sane.

Q. You're going to claim insanity, then? Is that what you're saying?

A. Claim? The poor boy is manifestly insane, as the millions of eyewitnesses who saw his insane act can testify.

Q. Mr. Bannerman, aren't you now trying the case in public? Aren't you making it difficult to get a jury, talking like this for publication.

A. Let me see if I understand the question. Are you asking me whether you boys and girls are enticing me into unethical behavior? (Laughter) Fair enough. I have never been in favor of any curtailment of the freedom of the press. The difficulty we are confronted with here is that everybody has already seen the shooting. That's a situation we have every intention of confronting head-on. In this country, thank god, a man is still innocent until he is proven guilty and I just don't happen to believe the Constitution was repealed when the Chief Justice fell dead. The jurors are supposed to take their seat in the jury box believing the man is innocent; or, in this case, not guilty by reason of insanity. If that were not true, the burden of proof would rest as heavily on the defense as on the prosecution.

Q. Do you intend to disqualify every prospective juror who can't swear that he thinks Sam Tabor is insane before the trial starts?

A. I didn't say that. You boys had better shape up. I said that if they *have* an opinion, and the opinion is that he is insane, they cannot be disqualified for cause. The prosecution will have to use one of its peremptory challenges. Got it now?

Q. I don't think so. I don't quite see the difference.

A. My course in semantics will begin in the courtroom. I do not hire out for private lessons. (Laughter) Except to those who can afford me. (Laughter)

Q. What *is* your fee, Mr. Bannerman?

A. To who?

Q. To me, say.

A. I can't answer that until I know your net worth. (Laughter)

Q. Mr. Bannerman, you seem to think it's possible to save Sam Tabor's life. How?

A. Awww, now you're trying to spoil all the fun. Let's just say this. I've made more new law than any other lawyer, firm or Xerox machine in this country, and it will not come as a complete surprise to me if I make some new law here.

Q. Mr. Bannerman, you ducked the question about whether you'd been contacted by Mrs. Tabor or someone representing her, or whether you inserted yourself into the case on your own.

A. I believe I said that I was here. How I got here is a privileged matter between attorney and client.

Q. Yeah, but is it a privileged matter with the Bar Association, though? Isn't there a serious matter of ethics involved?

A. Now there is an issue I am always happy to address myself to. The Canons of Ethics have grown rickety with time and, if I may be so impertinent as to say so, rusty with disuse. They are about as relevant to modern legal practice as the pernicious and archaic McNaughton Rule is to modern psychiatry.

Q. Then you're not worried that the Bar Association will take any action against you?

A. Worried? How can I be worried about the ABA when I never think of the ABA.

Q. From what you just said, would I be incorrect if I assumed that the new law you were going to make, that you were talking about making, was that you are going to try to upset the M'Naughton Rule in this case?

A. From the gingerly way you approached that, young man, you have a fine career ahead of you in the law. Let me take these last two questions together. We have emerging in this country a new type of lawyer, a circuit rider for justice. He doesn't arrive on a white charger in a cloud of dust, he comes jet-propelled, out of the sky, courtesy of the genius of modern aeronautical engineering. What do you think I got out of the Harrenson case? An exorbitant fee or no fee at all? When you promote that kind of hogwash, young man, you are playing the Establishment's game. Now, I was accused of inserting myself into the Harrenson case, too—and we all know what they were trying to do there, don't we? I entered that lawsuit—inserted myself into it, if you will—because I feel that the time has come when the progressive elements of the Bar—a category from which I specifically exclude the complacent hamfatters of the ABA—must rise up against the sleazy, shoddy and cut-rate justice meted out in this country to the poor and the black. Those cases, in sum, where the public clamor for vengeance is at its loudest. I can assure you that out of twelve similar cases, selected randomly, ten would expose the same legal anarchy, aided and abetted by an ambitious district attorney who, by some extraordinary moral exertion, has freed himself from the shackles of his oath of office.

Q. Are you seriously drawing a parallel between that case and this one?

A. What is the local district attorney's name again? Yes, Nevins. Thank you. The one who was all over the newspapers letting the voting public know that poor Sam Tabor would be wheeled off in a tumbrel without any indecent regard for due process. Well, gentlemen, I have "inserted" myself into the instant case to ensure that poor Sam Tabor will not be plumped into the electric chair according to the principles regnant in the customary district attorney's office in this country.

Q. Mr. Bannerman, I didn't quite catch it. What did you say your fee for this case was?

A. You're right. You didn't quite catch it. (Laughter)

The airlines public relations man had a taxi waiting. He had already sent the baggage on ahead. "I took the liberty," Harold Halpern told Bannerman, "of reserving a suite at the Coronet." He had deliberately not reserved a suite at the Hilton, he told him, because he thought it might be in bad taste for Bannerman to stay in the same hotel where his client's victim had been staying.

"The first thing I'll have to do with you," Bannerman said, "is to impress upon you the disutility of moral qualms." He was a big man with big features. Big mouth, big nose and those wide and incredibly blue eyes. Taken individually, each feature was a little outsized. Assembled in Norman Bannerman, they were in perfect proportion. "I take it," he said, "that you would have corrected me during that inquisition if I had been mistaken about where the burden of proof in an insanity plea lies in this state? Good. This is starting out most auspiciously, a bright young lawyer and a kind and understanding law. If we stick together, Harold, how can we fail but triumph?" Though the face was grave, the deep blue eyes were somehow merry. "Our client is, of course, insane, poor fellow."

Halpern liked him. He liked the way he had put him at ease. He liked the way he had included him in on the case. He was impressed by the intelligence that lay behind the rich blue eyes, full of vigor, full of life. He was delighted with this laughing interior dialogue Bannerman seemed to hold with himself, playing himself off against the clichés of his profession to show that he did not take himself too seriously.

Hal Halpern had heard about Norman Bannerman pretty nearly all of his life. They had talked about him in law school. This, he had thought, watching him come off the plane, was what a famous lawyer looked like. By a trick of the late-afternoon sun, the hair, low at the neck (but not too low), thick at the sides (but not too thick) seemed to be speckled with goldish-red sequins. It was only, later, in the pressroom that he saw that Bannerman's hair was an odd, kind of salmon color, with a light sprinkling of gray.

The way Bannerman had taken over the press had been particularly impressive; the beautiful rich voice, the carefully rationed eloquence, the skillful pauses for the expected laughs. He had been particularly impressed by the byplay on whether a prospective juror was entitled to hold a firm opinion on the innocence of the defendant. When you thought about it, why should it be disqualifying *per se* for a juror to believe what he was, in fact, charged with presuming; namely, that the defendant wasn't guilty? It would make an interesting test. You would have to lose, of course. Halpern wasn't sure why—the difference between belief and presumption, he supposed. But still, these were the kind of brilliant maneuvers, dancing the straddle-line of meaning, that you could expect from a top lawyer.

The way Bannerman got right down to business in the taxi was not unimpressive, either. He wanted to know, first of all, whether there was anything unusually distressing in the report of the arresting officer, and Halpern had to tell him that in this jurisdiction the defense didn't get to see a cop's report until he took the stand. "OK," Bannerman said briskly. "The first thing we do is goose 'em with a habeas corpus. That will make 'em either put their cop on the stand or give up Tabor on bail." He chuckled in anticipation, the blue eyes sparkling. "What's going to happen is we'll suck 'em into giving us the cop's testimony and then we'll get Sam sprung on temporary bail so that we can turn our headshrinkers loose on him. And while the headshrinkers are putting him through their wringer, we'll get to wring him out a little ourselves."

As delicately as possible Halpern explained that while the local lawyers did use a bond hearing to make the state put the arresting officer on the stand, they didn't seriously think they were going to get any judge to set bond in a capital case. In this state you had to convince the Court that a jury would not be likely to come back with a death sentence; that was the way the law read.

"And that," said Norman Bannerman, "is precisely what I intend to show."

"Well, yeah." He cleared his throat. "The trouble with that—and I'm only passing on what I've heard from the local lawyers, the better ones, and I've seen some when I was with the district attorney's office—not that I was involved in that many capital cases, I wouldn't want to give you that impression—the trouble, you see, the great difficulty, is that they feel they'd have to be giving the prosecution their own case instead of the other way around, giving away a heck of a sight more information than they got . . ." Good Lord, how he was rambling on. Taking himself in hand, he informed Bannerman in reasonably lucid syntax that nobody expected a judge was going to stick out his neck by prejudging a trial like that and, you know, letting an accused murderer walk loose. "Especially," he said, "in this one."

"You'd advise against filing a habeas?" Lifting an eyebrow, benign and amused, he begged Halpern to consider the possibility that there might be one or two other considerations that recommended themselves to seasoned counsel—and by rolling the word "recommend" off his lips as if it had at least six syllables managed, very artfully, to take the curse off whatever criticism might have been implied.

"First and foremost," Bannerman said, "and I hope the day will come when you can look upon this ride and say that this was the single most important thing you ever learned as a criminal lawyer. Because I promise you, Harold, if you learn this one thing and live by it, you can never be a bad one." The levity was gone from the voice and the twinkle was out of the eye. "If you were in jail, Harold, would you want to get out?" Fair enough. Was it not incumbent upon them, then, to do everything possible, within the bounds of legal ethics and human decency, to get their client out? They weren't talking about mere legalities or stratagems now. They weren't even talking about the lawyer-client relationship. They were talking about a relationship between human beings. "You and I," he said, with the quiet, beautifully controlled courtroom voice, "are the only force standing between our client and the electric chair." He was watching Halpern closely, letting the awful responsibility sink in. "Sam Tabor, lying in jail at this moment, has no rights except what we, as his attorneys, can plead for him"—the voice moved up a notch—"can assert for him"—the voice turned tough and raspy—"or can scratch out of the hard earth for him!"

Warmed as he most certainly was by the call to his humanity, Halpern was warmed even more by Bannerman's ready—and totally unexpected—acceptance of him as his associate in the case. He knew very well that he should let Bannerman know immediately that he was a most inexperienced lawyer, baby-sitting on the case overnight out of the sheer coincidence that he was the only lawyer at Stonebreaker, Knecht & Markham with any experience in criminal law. Fortunately, it was not a decision he had to make. Bannerman had already passed on, without a pause, to the strategic value of holding the bond hearing:

Everybody knew that poor Sam had killed Wilcke. Everybody had already decided that the case was hopeless. Harold himself had heard those reporters back there. Before that opinion became fixed, hardened into conviction, it was essential that they create a climate of insanity around him. "And that, dear boy, brings us to the second most valuable piece of advice you may ever receive." In any lawsuit you were trying three cases simultaneously. You were trying the case for the jury; you were trying the case for the transcript in the event, god forbid, the verdict went against you (his eyes rolled up to invoke divine intercession against such an injustice); and you were trying the case for public opinion. That third trial, he stressed, took place both inside and outside the courtroom and was at least as important as the others.

"To keep you happy," he said, lifting an eyebrow playfully, "we will give the district attorney no more than is necessary, consistent with the policy of giving the public the information to which it is entitled." He held out his hand. "Have we got ourselves a deal, pardner?"

Bannerman swept through the lobby of the Coronet like a sunburst of energy, joshing with the room clerk, winking at those guests who turned to stare at him, autographing a billiard ball (to attendant merriment) for a grandmotherly lady who for some imexplicable reason had a billiard ball in her purse and for some even more inexplicable reason wanted Norman Bannerman to write his name on it.

By the time they reached his suite he had discovered the bellboy's name was Charles but all his friends called him "the Count"; he had picked the Lowell ball club to pieces without quite convincing the Count that it had no chance at all to win the pennant; and he had listed the bartenders, the great and the near-great, whom he had known, loved and patronized through his long and distinguished career as a boozehound.

He tendered the bellboy a twenty-dollar bill, but as the Count reached, Bannerman pulled it back, hesitated, feinted, held it out again, pulled it back again . . . until they were both weaving and bobbing and jabbing like a pair of grinning boxers. At last, with a big sidewheeling swing of the arm he slapped the bill into the Count's hand and began to pump it vigorously, so that they were both standing there, shaking hands and laughing at each other. "I want you to know that this is not a tip," Bannerman told him. "It's a fee. A retainer. We're going to professionalize the bellboy racket. You are my man at the Coronet, Charles. When I want anything, I shall call for you." And when he wanted something, Bannerman emphasized, that meant he wanted it right now.

The bellboy folded the bill neatly in half and slipped it into his pocket. "You bet, Mr. Bannerman. You just ask for the Count." Although he didn't quite wink, there was something in his expression that said he knew very well what Bannerman would be calling for and that he was just the boy to get him the best in town.

For the moment, however, Bannerman was willing to settle for the names of the manager of the hotel and the owner. "Ten bucks a name. That isn't bad on today's market, is it?"

It sure wasn't. The manager's name was Victor Valentine ("Honest to god?" . . . "Honest to god!") and the hotel was part of a chain owned by an English syndicate headed by somebody named Theodore Lindfors. "And anything else you want, Norm, all you got to do is ask for the Count." This time he did wink. "They all know me by that here."

As soon as the bellboy had left, Bannerman picked up the phone and asked to be put through to Mr. Valentine. Bellboys, he told Hal, cradling the phone expertly against his shoulder, could be the most valuable of allies. If the district attorney's office bugged the room or monitored his calls, the Count would know about it instantly, and because of the warmth and depth of their friendship—and his confidence that there would be an extra twenty in it for him—Norman Bannerman would know about it ten minutes later.

"Mr. Valentine," he said into the phone, "this is attorney Norman Bannerman of Chicago in Rooms 520–522. Would you do me the honor of paying me a visit . . . No, nothing that can't be taken care of by your personal intercession. I always think it helpful for innkeepers to pay a courtesy call on their more distinguished guests, and what could be more delightful than to combine the social graces with the few modest requests I have in mind."

Victor Valentine turned out to be a thin, dark man who looked terribly weary, perhaps because he was, or perhaps because he was one of those men born with dark bags under his eyes. Bannerman greeted him with the same big, sidewheeling handshake and the same massive injection of instant charm. He thanked him for responding so promptly. He congratulated him on the fine little hotel he had there. The decor was congenial, the sanitary facilities quite good. The Van Gogh, delightfully unpretentious. "I don't suppose you have any Haut Brion 1929 on the premises? But of course not. How gauche of me to ask. You will forgive me, old chap, won't you?" The only thing that left him just a bit disappointed was the absence of all-night room service.

Having heard him out with the professional reserve of a man who was not in the habit of being summoned to his guests' rooms, Valentine informed him frostily that management had discovered through the years that the one o'clock cutoff time served the needs of their guests quite adequately. Bannerman nodded, cordial still. Anybody could see that he not only understood his problem but sympathized with him completely. For most of their guests, yes. The salesmen and electrical engineers and the occasional tourist who stumbled in, unawares, without an expense account. Not a bad idea to cut 'em off. If they wanted a little extra, let 'em transact their business with the bellboys. "But," he said, "I have a few eccentricities. I'm sure you won't find them so burdensome as to be unreasonable." He batted his eyes and gave a shy, ducking little shrug as a sort of apology that they were both stuck with his unfortunate idiosyncrasies.

When Valentine, still more correct than courteous, assured him that the whole staff was prepared to go to any reasonable length within the confines of established policy to make his stay in Lowell as pleasant as possible, Bannerman beamed at him so gratefully that it was perfectly evident whatever doubts he might have had about him had been dispelled. Since one good turn deserved another, he confided —as if it were a guilty secret—that he normally moved with the Hilton chain, which was by now so very well aware of his wants and needs, but that since Mr. Halpern of this city had been gracious enough to have reserved this suite he saw no reason to be so ungracious as to cancel out.

From there, it was a bravura performance, with Bannerman, by turns, syrupy and exuberant, chaste and impudent, but always, in that insinuating, mocking way of his, persistent; and the hotel manager, for his part, alternately stubborn and conciliatory, and never quite able to understand why the message he had meant to impart was not, somehow, the message Bannerman received.

Overwhelmed as much by the relentless good nature as by the shifting swirl of words, the hotel manager turned uncertainly to Halpern, and finding no help there, began to scratch at the bottom of one elbow. By that time Bannerman had begun to prowl the room, peering at the floorboards to satisfy himself there was an adequate supply of electrical outlets, since they would all want to cooperate —within *reason,* of course—with the television crews that would be slamming in and out of there night and day. Very good. He would let his longtime friend, Theo Lindfors, know how impressed he was with his Lowell operation. The Bannerman smile enveloped Valentine, warm and candid. He was sure Vic had heard that story about Theo and the Syndicate at last season's Ascot. Bannerman had got the story from the Count himself, he said, otherwise—the corners of his mouth drew down in otherwise disbelief. "But that's Theo all right," he said, brightening. "A man of unfailing courtesy." And Bannerman would let the man of unfailing courtesy know who was responsible for his patronage. Once the trial was under way, he would need perhaps a half dozen rooms, preferably contiguous, for his witnesses and investigators. "You take care of me, Vic, and I take care of you. That's show business."

"We do our best to provide VIP service," Vic offered, thawing somewhat. "Especially to the occupants of the suites."

Bannerman beamed on him, his faith in mankind and hotel managers restored. He would expect to pay for such courtesies, of course, he said, with a barely perceptible nod toward the keeper of his exchequer, Harold Halpern. "In a trial of this magnitude, where a man's life is hanging precariously in the balance, I will be working through the night, and while the justice of my cause will sustain the spirit, the body is sometimes in need of more protein sustenance." The benign, grateful look had suddenly become dedicated, intense. "God only knows, Vic, I wouldn't want you to go through life feeling that the poor sick boy went to the chair for the want of a chicken-salad sandwich at three o'clock in the morning."

Valentine took a full step backward, almost as if he had been hit. There was a visible shuffling of his feet as he dug in, ready to make his stand. If that was what he needed, there was an all-night restaurant only a couple of blocks down, on Sandiford, and he would be happy to send a boy down at any time of the night.

Bannerman was more grateful than ever. But alas— The big shoulders sagged, the expressive eyelids slanted to show how distressed he was that they still found themselves in this mutually unfortunate fix. What was needed was the full service of the Coronet's impressive menu. Yes, he hoped to be able to look upon the Coronet as his home away from home. He knew that Theo would be happy to hear that Vic was going to such heroic lengths to help a poor itinerant lawyer, even one who was in the city to represent a client who was perhaps not too popular with the civic and business leaders. The bantering tone had somehow become faintly menacing. Not, he said, that he blamed them. They were hardly to be condemned for having been brainwashed by the district attorney's office into believing that poor Sam Tabor, "this pitiful clerk," was a mad-dog killer. Nor that any highly-publicized out-of-town lawyer could only be coming to Lowell to launch an attack upon their stricken city.

To Halpern, who had watched the whole performance with a mixture of awe, amusement and sheer delight, the most incredible thing about it was that Bannerman had been able to put forth such outrageous demands with such merry posturing. There had never been a moment when you were not aware that he was giving a masterful performance and, more than that, that he was amusing himself and expecting Halpern to be equally amused.

Valentine opened his mouth and took a gulp of air. "It's not anything we've ever done before . . ."

". . . But there's a first time for everything," Bannerman said heartily, finishing it off for him. "I do hate to put you to all this trouble, and to make it up to you, I promise that when I return, limp and weary, from each day in court, we will sit together by the fireside, you and I, and while the hours away with talk of torts and corpora on the one side, and towels and silverware on the other." He had thrown an arm around Valentine's shoulder and was walking him to the door, thanking him profusely while making it perfectly obvious that now that he had capitulated so completely he was being dispensed with.

When the door slammed shut Bannerman threw a triumphant look across the room at Halpern, flung one arm above his head and snapped his fingers loudly. "Chalk up another Ho-lè," he trumpeted, "for the bull's side." He was standing on the upper alcove, legs apart, fist on hip, regarding him with humor and affection, a wonderfully practiced theatrical pose which only someone of Bannerman's size and presence could carry off.

"Those pompous peckersniffs with the flowers in their lapels," he crowed, as he came bouncing down toward Halpern. In a burst of sheer jubilation he swept the flower from his own lapel and flung it toward the ceiling. "When I hit 'em I'm striking a blow for all the little old couples from Des Moines and Sault Ste. Marie they've been pushing around all their lives." He dropped into the heavily upholstered chair, both legs extended, one arm hanging over the side, and there was a sort of wild animal vitality exuding from him, as from a racehorse snorting and steaming at the end of a winning race. When he looked up at Halpern, the deep blue eyes were shining. *"Are you with me, Harold?"*

"I'm with you, Mr. Bannerman."

Good. He brought his hands together with a loud clap and rubbed them together exuberantly. Tomorrow he would announce to the waiting world that Harold Halpern had been taken on as co-counsel. Sucking his cheeks in, he regarded him with a small, mischievous smile. "The first rule of criminal law is that you have to get your name in the paper. I hope that isn't going to be too distasteful to you."

"Distasteful?" Halpern was so elated that he had to choke back the impulse to say he'd probably remember it as the most valuable lesson in criminal law he'd ever had. Now was the time, he knew, when he had to throw back his shoulders, take a deep breath and lay his almost total lack of courtroom experience before him.

And it didn't turn out to be nearly as difficult as he had imagined. Considering his youthful gaiety and his smooth, unlined features—Bannerman smiled—he had not really looked upon Harold as a man of vast and varied experience. That wasn't the question. The question was whether he was going to enlist in the army of righteousness or serve with the peckersniff money-counters. "The time always comes, Harold," he said earnestly, "when you have to choose your side. Are you going to stand with the protectors of property or with the protectors of life and freedom?" He flattered him with a proselytizing smile. "The criminal law is the only branch worth practicing. Leave the defense of property to those who were born to it or who covet it unduly. For people like you and me, life and freedom are more precious by far."

"Good lord, Mr. Bannerman, I hope you don't think I need any pep talk." Good lord, he protested, he'd walk to the courtroom in his bare feet over broken glass for the opportunity to work with Norman Bannerman. He would, of course, have to pay his firm the courtesy of asking for permission and, to be practical about it, for a leave of absence. But that wouldn't be any problem. He twisted his lips in rueful modesty. "I somehow have the feeling they'll be able to get along without me quite nicely."

The boyish modesty seemed to have been lost on Bannerman, along with the rest of what he had been saying. "Yes," Bannerman said, more to himself than to Harold, "the time always comes and it's best when it comes early." A change had come over him. He was staring, in a heavily melancholy way, at the palm of his hand as if it were a lectern upon which some cryptic message had been written. Slowly, ever so slowly, the hand began to close over the air. "Once you let the smell of the counting room seep into your soul," he said, his attention never wavering, "the peckersniffs have . . . *got you.*" The trap had sprung shut. For a long moment his eyes remained riveted on the closed fist and then, with a wry little snort of laughter, the hand flew open again, flinging it away.

"Harold," he said, "it's never too early to start saving a man's life." He was crackling with energy again, and eager to seal their partnership with a drink. Halpern's first assignment in the service of Sam Tabor would therefore be to walk due north and turn east at the bedroom. There upon the bag stand or in the immediate vicinity thereof he would come across a large Gladstone bag wherein, wrapped in a face cloth, in the pocket under the flap, he would find a pint bottle of an amber-colored fluid bearing the proud imprimatur of one Jack Daniels, a former colleague of Theo's and himself.

The bottle wasn't in the Gladstone, as a matter of fact. Two other bags were standing right alongside, and underneath the stand a heavy briefcase bellowed out to fullness. On some uncertain impulse Halpern swung the briefcase up on the bureau, opened the clasp, and there it was. As he reached for the bottle, he caught his image looking back at him from the mirror, the image of Hal Halpern, the familiar image which he now found to be—no, not unfamiliar but somehow worthy of more than usual interest. The unwavering eyes held the unwavering eyes. Was this the same Hal Halpern who had awakened this morning to run his little errand? The sense of unreality that had been tugging at him all evening had finally taken hold. Who could have dreamed that he, Hal Halpern, would have become co-counsel with Norman Bannerman in the case that held the interest of the entire country? He, Hal Halpern—that image in the mirror—was about to become a footnote in history. And if he would be one of the most microscopic footnotes of all time, was that any reason to deprive himself of the full impact of his minuscule glory? A pleased, self-satisfied smile played at the corner of his lips. Today, a footnote; tomorrow, the world.

Bannerman insisted upon pouring the drinks himself, complimenting Halpern all the while upon his resourcefulness in having uncovered the fugitive bottle. "I can see that you have the true libertine's instinct for the finer things of life. I shall put you in charge of the vintage wines and the ballerinas." Before he put the bottle down he contemplated it with deep affection. "A friend for all seasons," he said in soft salute. "A shot of hormone injector, a faithful confessor, the silent companion of the long night. We have spent many a night together preparing our case, Harold, my faithful companion and I. Never complains, always encourages. Hail to thee, my warm and stalwart friend."

Lifting his voice, he raised his glass to Halpern. "Welcome aboard, pardner. We shall march into battle together, banners aloft, spirits high, secure in the ultimate triumph of our cause." He took one sip and studied the young lawyer over the rim of the glass. A faint smile came stealing over his features. "Woe unto the wicked," he intoned, the blue eyes dancing with his secret, inviolable joke.

Halpern, having taken much more than a sip, was enjoying the settling warmth, the spreading glow. "Woe unto the wicked, Norman," he toasted back. Oh, what a story he would have to tell Ruthie tonight.

BANNERMAN UNDER THE LIGHTS:

Norman Bannerman, bathed in the dim light from the floor lamp directly behind him, is seated, in vest and cummerbund, on the circular sofa at the far end of the sitting room. The jacket has been flung over the back of a chair. His hair is ruffled, his eyelids are becoming heavy, as of a man who has begun to fight off sleep.

Looking over suddenly, he says to Harold Halpern, "Did you ever meet Wilcke? I was very fond of him, you know. In his younger days we had some times in Chicago." A reminiscent warmth comes over him. "In his younger days the Chief Justice could move it pretty good. An engaging man and a great Chief Justice. We shall miss him. Yes, he shall be missed." He sighs heavily. "A terrible thing our psychopathic client did to the criminal law, Harold, when he knocked David Wilcke off. I wonder why he did it?" He passes a hand over his eyes. "Well, I'll see him tomorrow, Harold. I'll see him tomorrow."

Either the thought of Wilcke or the drink has suddenly depressed him. Probably, it is a combination of both. But what does it matter? He shifts in his seat, shaking himself out of his mood. He crosses his arms, hugging himself, shivering. He rubs his upper arms briskly, as if he is recharging himself for the long night ahead. He has paused to pay his last respects to his old friend; it is now time to get back to work. "You can start by giving me the lowdown on the district attorney. I take it your former boss is one of those clowns who couldn't go out and earn a living on his own . . ."

Harold Halpern ducked his head into the outer office and asked the trim dark-haired secretary whether Mr. Stonebreaker was still in conference.

"Indeed he is," she said, in a finely tuned, slightly chilled English accent. "You may rest assured I will send for you when he is free." One could see at a glance that she was one of those secretaries who identified herself so completely with the status of her boss that anything she took to be an affront to his position and dignity, she took as an affront to herself.

"Just asking, Miss Franz," he said, "just asking."

Inside the office Clifford Stonebreaker was in conference with a sculptured ivory chess set. The late morning sun shone through the curved, tinted window behind him and poured a gently subdued green wash over the morning newspaper, folded lengthwise to the morning chess exercise. It was Stonebreaker's pleasure to begin each day by recreating the game on his own board, always being careful to play the winning color from his own side and always picturing his opponent to be whatever judge or lawyer he might be contending with at the moment. There was nothing like a morning workout at the chess board, he would tell law students, to tune the mind to the complexities of the day.

Clifford S. Stonebreaker was a winner. A stranger walking into that office would know that he was a winner. It was announced by the carefully trimmed mustache, waxed at the ends; it was confirmed by the Italian silk suit, custom-made by Victor Santiangelo in a new color called, he had been told, *crème de menthe.* (Victor was under instructions to call him whenever a particularly intriguing bolt of material came off the boat.) Because of that mustache, he was known by his department heads as "the Secretary," as in Secretary of State. Stonebreaker liked that. He would have been happy if a set of circumstances could be developed where they would feel free to call him "Mr. Secretary" to his face —with, of course, the tacit understanding that it was a title he was permitting to be used in a spirit of affection on their side and avuncular good will on his.

Normally Clifford Stonebreaker was not a man to wear a new suit to the office, a lesson he had absorbed from Freeman Knecht. Old Money, Stonebreaker had observed—observing Knecht—had the confidence to appear unpressed. New Money thrust its weaves and patterns at you. He had been so taken by the aristocratic understatement—to quote Victor—of this new suit that upon seeing it hanging there in his wardrobe closet that morning he had, most uncharacteristically, given in to the whim to wear it.

In all truthfulness—and Clifford S. Stonebreaker had not got where he was by being anything but truthful with himself—it had occurred to him as he was being driven to the office that he might have been in particular need of something aristocratic and understated that morning to prove to himself that he had not let Norman Bannerman's entrance into the Tabor case disturb him. He had, it should be stated for the record, considered that possibility only briefly. There was, after all, much for him to congratulate himself on in his handling of the Sam Tabor file. He could not lose; he could only win. Oh yes, it was going to be another win for Stonebreaker, all right.

Clifford Stonebreaker was a master of the honeycomb alternative. Most men, being losers, came to believe that life was a matter of selecting the least bad alternative. Stonebreaker knew better. He had discovered very early that his taste and his talent lay in developing a situation to the critical point where the worst he could come out with was the least good alternative.

During his passage through law school he had very naturally fastened upon personal injury law as the field that a kindly benefactor had devised to fit his particular talents. Once you agreed to represent a badly injured client, it was not a question of winning or losing but only of the size of the judgment. And the size of the judgments, as anybody with an ounce of intelligence could see, was going up . . . up . . . and up.

In the beginning he had found it necessary to sell out a couple of clients for quick settlements, far less than any competent lawyer could have won in court and considerably less than the insurance companies should have offered. But his clients had been happy enough, especially after he explained to them how much better it had been to avoid the long delay and exorbitant court costs.

With his own share of those settlements, Stonebreaker had been able to rent the big office on the top floor of the National Bank Building and place himself within the plush surroundings that he knew—there was the instinct of a winner again—put the client in the proper frame of mind to pay the big fees. To speak to Clifford Stonebreaker cost money. The time of Clifford Stonebreaker was valuable. And it had all come, as he would readily admit to law students, from his readiness to take up the cudgels for a plumber whose back had been broken in a roof collapse, and a poor immigrant railroad worker who had lost a leg in a rail switch. No, no one could ever say that Clifford Stonebreaker, for all his aristocratic bearing, was a man to deny his humble beginnings.

From that base as a personal injury attorney he had quickly expanded, forming two very valuable partnerships. Freeman Knecht was the last withering leaf of an old aristocratic Lowell family, and what an inspiration he had been to an eager young attorney not too proud to watch and listen. Freeman Knecht, he had observed, was not aware that people deferred to him because they feared his power or coveted his money. How could he be? From the time he was a child he had been trained to accept all deference as the natural order of the universe.

The child, grown old, sat and listened with a thin smile on his lips, until the intruder on the other side of the desk, clattering away, began to raise his price (if the Old Man wanted raising) or lower it (if the Old Man wanted lowering). "I'll think about it," Knecht would say curtly, and make it sound as if he were doing the lump of clay across the table a favor by allocating whatever time the thinking might take.

Dean Markham was something else again. Markham was a political wheeler who had been admitted to partnership a few months after Knecht retired. With the Democrats taking the state over from the Republicans, a counterweight to Freeman Knecht had become advisable long before that, a cruel fact which Stonebreaker, out of his high regard for the Old Man, had been reluctant to pursue. Until, of course, that most unfortunate experience with that crook, Michael Timothy Karney, brought home the absolute necessity of having access to Democratic councils.

Cliff Stonebreaker could tell you, with justifiable pride, that Dean Markham had personally brought in many of the biggest of the companies doing business with the state and federal governments. His name alone brought in many others. It was astonishing how many fine, upstanding people were so ready to assume that if you hired Dean Markham's firm, you were fixing something with somebody, somewhere. And for a political fix, or the dream thereof, they were willing to pay enormous fees. It troubled Stonebreaker to find the average citizen so cynical about his own government. He found it truly disheartening. For while it was perfectly apparent that Markham was performing certain legal and lobbying services for his own clients—all perfectly in accord with the accepted practices —a man had to be crazy to think that the Stonebreaker firm would dream of doing anything unethical—i.e., anything that could easily be traced—for anybody walking in off the street.

Stonebreaker, Knecht & Markham had grown into the largest and, he could confidently state, most profitable law office in the state. The letterhead boasted a solid 142 associates with a limited partner heading up a division in every phase of civil law known to man. In the full flush of a successful career, Clifford Stonebreaker could be said to have only one deficiency—and that was a matter of almost no importance. He was, as the public thinks of such things, not a very good lawyer. But that was something neither he nor anyone else remembered since he had not been in a courtroom in more than thirty years. As far as Stonebreaker was concerned, trial lawyers were little more than the infantry troops who had to be sent into battle after the statesmen had failed. As for criminal lawyers . . . well, criminal law, as everyone knew, was the crummy side of the law. ("Criminal law wouldn't be so bad," he liked to say, given the right audience, "if the Mafia were made up of proper English gentlemen instead of olive-oil Sicilians.")

Let lesser men harangue juries. Clifford Stonebreaker had a far deeper understanding, a far more intimate knowledge of how the system really worked. Clifford Stonebreaker could be counted upon to place his finger, unerringly, upon the pulse of power. He knew when it was important to see the right person and he knew when it was more important to bring the right people together. He knew, in short, where every source of power lay, and he had an unfailing instinct for what was, inside that framework, negotiable.

Although his own specialty was rescuing lost causes for other firms, he liked to think of himself not as a romantic, not as a fighter for the underdog, but— and you could not help but admire the simple professional pride—as a "lawyer's lawyer." Other firms, with a bad case on their hands, would carry it hopefully to the green-tinted office and lay it upon Stonebreaker's desk to see what could be done with it. They didn't get an immediate answer, not did they expect one. Clifford Stonebreaker would say, like his mentor Freeman Knecht, "I'll think about it."

Unlike Freeman Knecht, however, Stonebreaker was a man of action. When one was approached for advice on a bad lawsuit, one sought out the club favored by the Superior Court judge who was presiding. During the course of the ensuing conversation one could hardly be faulted for saying, "Oh, by the way, I've been offered this ABC case. What do you think, sir, should I take it?" The initial approach was of vital importance, and Stonebreaker had refined it down to an exquisitely precise art. While it was essential to speak as a junior seeking the wisdom of age and experience, it was of equal importance to assert one's own position as a man of position and substance. The tone one reached for was the tone that said, See here, we both know we are too wealthy, too powerful, too heavy with honors to have to resort to anything improper, and so nothing said or done here could possibly be anything but proper.

The beautiful part of it was that it was true. A Superior Court judge was, by definition, beyond suspicion and above reproach. Stonebreaker himself was, as every member of the Bar would have been happy to attest, a man of unquestioned character and integrity, a man who had risen so high in the Bar Association hierarchy as to have a powerful voice in passing upon the qualifications of new judges.

It would be, as anyone could see, absurd to suggest that either of them could do anything dishonorable. That was important to Clifford Stonebreaker. The judiciary, as he never failed to point out in his speeches, was the last port of call in our system of government, which meant that it was the guardian of our whole way of life. "As long as our judiciary remains strong, independent and untainted by scandal or rumors of scandal," he would say in a peroration that never failed to bring a lump to his throat, "nothing can harm us. Should the judiciary ever become false to its trust, nothing can save us."

Among the least conspicuous clients in the office was Dr. Martin Shtogren, who had come to the firm as a speculator in real estate. Stonebreaker had made the mistake of sending a onetime mistress who was becoming a pest to Shtogren for treatment, and the even greater mistake of paying half the fee. As Stonebreaker would sometimes say, in an excess of self-reproach at his own good-heartedness, "I don't know, I guess I'm just a dumb hairpin that way."

And so, when Shtogren came crying to him after the assassination Stonebreaker had allowed himself—against his better judgment, as a matter of simple duty—to be talked into taking over the task of hiring a criminal lawyer.

The chess game had reached a critical point. Bannerman had shaken his rook free and with his bishops so nicely placed he was ready to rake him from all sides. But Bannerman had overlooked one thing, and it would, most assuredly, cost him the game.

Clifford Stonebreaker overlooked nothing. Once he had accepted the commission from Dr. Shtogren, his mind had moved in its customary crab-like way, setting out the priorities and alternatives that would leave him sitting pretty no matter what happened. And Harold Halpern had been the key to it all.

Halpern had served a multiplicity of purposes for Stonebreaker from the beginning. The first was in regard to his long-standing policy against hiring young men who had gained their trial experience in the district attorney's office. To Stonebreaker, the DA's office was even more tainted than the criminal lawyers on the other side of the rights. He disliked Hilliard Nevins (worse, he distrusted him) and he looked upon his hatchet man, Ambose, as a disgrace to the Bar. On the other hand, the Stonebreaker firm's lawyers had been getting themselves beaten by too many of Ambose's boys these past few years, and his department heads had been whining that they were falling under a competitive disadvantage.

Stonebreaker had also been under pressure from the Anti-Defamation League for what they took to be his reluctance to hire Jewish lawyers, a patently unfair, typically Yid tactic since he always tried to have two Jewish lawyers on the payroll. There was no way of explaining, Jews being so notoriously thin-skinned, that while he had nothing against Jews as Jews, he had simply found himself involved in personality clashes with the particular Jewish lawyers he had been exposed to—why, now that he thought about it, his favorite professor at law school, Professor Solomon Weintraub, had been a Jewish gentleman, a marvelous man; he had attended the services for him at the Orthodox Temple and been enormously moved by the solemnity of the ancient Hebraic rites.

As a final gesture of good will, he had promised to personally interview any bright young lawyers they might choose to send along, although he was sure they would not want him to hire a Jewish lawyer over a more qualified non-Jew.

It had become necessary to show his good will a great deal sooner than he had anticipated. Dean Markham had called him from the capital and, in his own gross way (Stonebreaker had always wondered whether Markham was his real name) had applied the pressure, too: "Hey," Markham had said, "the governor wants to know what the hell are our hiring policies down there, and when the governor wants to know, so do I. If you haven't got any Jews, get some. If we've got some, get some more. Jesus Christ, finding a Jewish lawyer in Lowell should be about as difficult as finding a whorehouse in Las Vegas."

And, finally, Halpern's application came across his desk shortly after he had heard that Sandford Wexler, that well-known leader in Jewish philanthropic circles (one thing you had to give the Jews, they certainly did take care of their own), was going to be nominated for the Court of Appeals, and Stonebreaker could not afford to have him feeling unkindly toward him. (Everybody knew how those Jews stuck together.) Any doubt that Halpern was the right man had been dissolved when he discovered during the interview that Halpern had worked with DeWitt Pawley in the Appeals section, which meant that he would come to them relatively uncontaminated by Jim Ambose and, more important still, that he could carry the briefcase into Wexler's court without making it too obvious. Stonebreaker's memo on the interview read: "Rather unaggressive, not too Jewish-looking type. Is still a little crude around the edges but after he has been exposed to our chaps we should be able to polish him up."

When the Tabor case fell into his lap he had recognized at once that Halpern was the answer to that one, too. With that DA's background, Halpern could be detached to hold Tabor's hand until Tommy Mallon was officially retained. If Stonebreaker then decided it would be worth his while to keep his foot in the door, a word to Mallon would be sufficient. The daily references to "co-counsel Harold Halpern, on temporary leave from the prestigious firm of Stonebreaker, Knecht & Markham," would be worth their weight in gold, the firm would have a couple of choice seats to pass out every day, and by instructing Halpern to report to the office every day for a debriefing he would always be in a position to drop a few remarks on the progress of the trial to his club members or his dinner companions. If, for any reason, the case turned sour he could extricate himself quite easily —and free himself of all responsibility for having hired the chief counsel—by pulling Halpern out. Should Halpern refuse to be yanked—and as a practical man, Stonebreaker could not blind himself to the possibility that a smart little Jewboy might not be willing to leave a case from which he would be reaping so much personal publicity—his resignation would be instantly accepted.

Yes, he had handled the ADL brilliantly from beginning to end. Nothing was more beautiful than a plan well hatched. He would have made a marvelous politician. Marvelous.

He saw himself in the . . .

Well hatched and perfectly executed; yes, the perfect symmetry of the egg.

Before his mind could clamp it off, he saw himself in the governor's mansion.

The square jaw clenched, the big vein in his neck began to throb. The face of Harold Halpern gave way to the face of that cheap, red-faced Irish smiling crook of a thieving bastard who had taken his money, assuring him he could get him the nomination, assuring him there were only a few of the boys to be paid off. Then a few more. And a few more. Twenty-five thousand to start with, then another twenty-five thousand, then the hundred thousand that would put it over. And all of it from the cash box and the masked account. Not a cent of it deductible. The chess piece was cutting into his hand. *(He had been such a . . .)*

The buzzer sounded on his desk. "I told you before," he barked into the phone, "no calls."

The lacquered English voice said, "I'm so sorry, Mr. Stonebreaker. Dr. Shtogren is on seventy-three, and I did think you might want to make an exception. I told him you were in conference but he did seem to be rather perturbed."

"Oh, he did, did he? Well, you just tell him I'm still in conference and while you're about it you can write yourself a memo that if I'm interrupted one more time you're going to see 'perturbed' like you've never seen it before!"

One damn thing after another. Nothing infuriated him more than when underlings failed to carry out his instructions. How could they expect him to function, to keep everything running smoothly, for them as much as for himself, if they couldn't get it through their thick skulls that the continued success of the firm depended upon their doing exactly as they were told? That was the trouble with this country. Nobody had any respect for designated authority anymore. Like that mountebank, Norman Bannerman. A terrible man; a wholly unprincipled man. The sheer gall of the man, moving unsolicited into the case like this. Wholly against the ethics of the profession. Sending a telegram for all the world to see. *Not even soliciting the case, but declaring himself in. (How could anybody be that . . .)*

Stonebreaker had met Bannerman from time to time at meetings of the Trial Lawyers Association—a fancy name, Bannerman had sneered, for personal injury lawyers. ("What are you ashamed of? We're all ambulance chasers here.") Leave it to Bannerman to declare himself in on that fat field, too. A thoroughly corrupt and obnoxious man. A shameless provocateur. The first meeting Stonebreaker attended, Bannerman had delivered a paper on the Necessity of the More Adequate Judgment. "Fellow Bloodsuckers," he had bellowed. "What the jugular is to the vampire, and the orphan to the probate lawyer, the cripple is to us—the fount of nourishment from which the good life flows." He had gone on, that slithering mountebank, to urge his colleagues to hammer the courts for larger judgments as the only way by which their clients could get what they deserved and still allow the attorneys to take their cut with a clear conscience. A scandalous misrepresentation, scandalously headlined, Bannerman having had the foresight to alert the press in advance. Oh, the man was shrewd. He had set himself up as the protector of helpless cripples—you couldn't deny the man his talent for self-advertisement—*when everybody knew that Norman Bannerman was the biggest bloodsucker of all.*

Still, Stonebreaker had recognized that there was no way of heading him off. He had been retained to get Tabor a top-flight attorney, and he could hardly claim that Bannerman wasn't top flight. The best thing to do at the moment was to drift with the tide. His day would come.

Taking comfort where comfort could be found, he could console himself with the prospect that if Bannerman was anywhere near as good as he was supposed to be, he would at least show Jim Ambose up as the overrated hoodlum that he was.

He let his mind slide off toward Harold Halpern, waiting so anxiously for an audience. Halpern had taken it upon himself to pick up Norman Bannerman last night, and if he was so anxious to talk to Stonebreaker this morning it was logical to assume that Bannerman had invited him into the case. Bannerman would need a member of the Lowell Bar to introduce him to the Court, and if that was all that was required of Halpern, Stonebreaker could hardly permit himself to refuse —although he would most certainly let Halpern know what a horse's ass he had made of himself running out half-cocked to the airport.

If, as he strongly suspected, Halpern was going to request permission to associate himself with Bannerman in the trial, that would be a horse of an entirely different color. Young Mr. Halpern had been engaged as a civil attorney, and Stonebreaker was not going to tolerate any ongoing association, in a criminal case, between Stonebreaker, Knecht & Markham and that unprincipled mountebank. Halpern would be given the alternative of withdrawing from the Tabor case or withdrawing from the firm, and it would be put to him with a bluntness that would make it very difficult for him to do anything but submit his resignation forthwith.

And that, dear hearts, would take care of the Anti-Defamation League once and for all. Hadn't he opened his heart and his home to Harold Halpern? Hadn't his own wife treated Mrs. Halpern like a daughter, introducing her to her friends, introducing her to the right dressmakers and hairdressers and salons so that she could acquire the polish, grooming and self-confidence that were so essential in the wife of a rising young attorney? Hadn't Marilyn become so fond of the little Yid that she had thrown one of her menopausal fits when he had crossed the Halperns from the list of guests they were having over to the Country Club for their anniversary?

Just thinking about that was enough to start the bile flowing. Marilyn had always been a damn fool, as he had damn well let her know, but how could even she have been that *dumb!* Michael Timothy Karney would enter the kingdom of heaven before a Jew set foot in *the* Country Club. To plan your life so carefully, allowing for all the exigencies of fate and genealogy, and then because of one youthful mistake . . . Oh, when Clifford Stonebreaker, like Fiorello LaGuardia, made a mistake, it was a beaut.

He himself, and he might as well face up to it, had been fond of Harold. There were lawyers in the office with far more seniority than Halpern who could have complained with perfect justification that favoritism was being shown. No, he would not be the least surprised if word had got to Judge Wexler that Halpern was Cliff Stonebreaker's fair-haired boy.

In his breast there arose the restorative rage of a trust betrayed. The one thing Stonebreaker could never abide was ingratitude. He would let it be leaked that it had been Halpern who had sought out Bannerman and offered him the case on condition that he, Halpern, be allowed to serve as co-counsel. And that Stonebreaker, appalled by such double-dealing, had fired him on the spot.

The chess board was laid out so nicely that he allowed himself a secret, fencing smile. He would let it be known in all the best clubs in town that despite this latest setback to his policy of integration and tolerance, he was, once again, setting about to quietly recruit another Jewish lawyer just so that he—he, Clifford Stonebreaker, who didn't have a prejudiced bone in his body!—could not be accused of discrimination. That would shut them up good. And *for* good. And it should give those japing monkeys over at the NAACP something to chew on, too. *(That was the trouble with this country . . .)*

He twirled the ends of his mustache. The Secretary of State had shown them once again that with patience and good will a man who keeps all possible options firmly in mind can, through strength of mind and character, protect himself against the deceitful and the envious. He smiled down at the chess board.

Nothing was left but the kill. Stonebreaker's queen came diagonally across the board to put the white king in check, and now that *he* had Bannerman on the run it was only going to be a matter of time.

Clifford Stonebreaker gazed across the table, as infuriatingly inscrutable as always. His smile was like a trigger being cocked. "Check and mate, Mr. Bannerman," he said quietly, the steady gaze telling Bannerman that both of them had known from the beginning that this was the way it had to end. Deliberately, devastatingly, in the tone of books, mahogany and brandy, he said, "After the bishop move I would have been willing to lay a considerable wager that it would be over in seven moves." Crisply now, putting the business to an end: "It took nine. My compliments, Mr. Bannerman."

Without taking his eyes off his crushed and humiliated foe he pressed the buzzer on his desk. "Vivian," he said, "you may tell Mr. Halpern that I will be ready to receive him in exactly five minutes."

Having heard the voices all the way down the hall, Halpern was hardly surprised to find the door of Bannerman's suite wide open. Having seen the TV truck outside the hotel it was no surprise to find Bannerman standing in a pool of light being interviewed by Josh Flowers. What did surprise him was that overnight the room had managed to take on such an untidy, lived-in look. Newspapers were scattered all around the floor and thrown helter-skelter on the chairs and table.

Seated off at the side of the room alongside the telephone was Hugh Fletcher, the investigator Hal had recommended to Bannerman. Not because he liked Fletcher, but because he was generally acknowledged to be the best private investigator in the city. Fletcher acknowledged Hal with a nod, and as he did the floodlights faded. The director stepped away from the camera, clipboard in hand, and said something about switching from the wide lens for some closeups. What he wanted them to do, he told Flowers, was to go over that business about the law on insanity again so they'd have it covered both ways.

Bannerman had closed his eyes to squeeze the light out of them. Opening them, he saw Hal in the doorway. "Come on in and join the party," he yelled. "The clan is beginning to gather."

Halpern's attention was fixed upon the floodlights set at either end of the camera. Having gone unnoticed while they were lighting up the scene, they had called attention to themselves by the loss of their function, and, perhaps because he had been up all night typing a brief for Bannerman on the laws and holding cases on murder and insanity, it seemed to him that there was some deep philosophical truth hidden there. Perhaps it was because of Fletcher that the thought occurred to him that they looked not so very different from the lamps that had been used in the photography class he had taken in college on somebody's suggestion that it would do no harm for a lawyer to know as much as possible about investigative tools and techniques. Which recalled to him how he had checked out a News Graphic over one weekend to take some pictures of Ruthie —it was their first home date, now that he thought of it. He had gone through all that business with the triangulation and light meters, and it wasn't until he was leaving, at the end of the night, that he realized (speaking of the loss of function) that he had forgotten to take the cap off the lens.

What a thing to . . . Where had the memory been for six or seven years—a small child's question—to be summoned from the briny deeps by a couple of dead-ass floodlights? By, to be precise, the withdrawal of light waves from the optic nerve.

A marvelous instrument, the brain. Separates the man from the dog. God's gift to the . . . Suddenly he saw the bullet splashing into Wilcke's exposed and pleated brain; through the optic nerve and into Wilcke's truly remarkable brain, wiping out all those memory banks, all that knowledge. Talk about the loss of function. Talk about the lights going out. "What about the victim?" Ambose always asked. Nobody gave a goddamn about the victim. The victim was dog-gone; a slab of dog meat on a hook.

Talk about a long night spent in the service of a murderer.

The director slapped his clipboard against his leg and signaled for the lights, and an instant transformation took place in both Bannerman and Flowers, a sort of stiffening of the spine that proclaimed the private men were changing into performers. The lights came on. The stage was formed. The puppets cranked themselves up and dangled themselves for display.

The Flowers puppet said that to its understanding the M'Naughton Rule held that a man was legally sane if he knew the nature and quality of his act at the time he did it. Said: "To most people that would seem fair and logical." Asked: "What would you substitute in its place?"

The Bannerman puppet expressed its disbelief that a diseased mind could know the nature and quality of anything it did. Asked: "If a man is intellectually aware, does that mean he is emotionally responsible?" Pointed out that M'Naughton predated Freud. Suggested that it be replaced by the Model Penal Code as written by the Law Institute. Said: "What a monument it would be to the life and career of David Boone Wilcke if out of this tragedy this entire regressive phase of the law were brought back into the mainstream of modern life and the witch hunters cast out into the darkness where they belong."

The director flicked his thumb across his throat. Director and cameraman moved off in opposite directions. The performers hung yet another second, caught between their two lives. It was as if a projector had slipped one notch in its spool, freezing them for just that split second in a transitional frame between fantasy and fact.

One more split second and the pool of light turned on its edge like a coin and was swallowed up. They closed their eyes and squeezed them tight, and when they opened them they were themselves again.

His incomparable self, Bannerman remained after the television people had gone. He was, in fact, full of himself, jumping around, rubbing his hands vigorously as of a job well done; a man in command of his world and impatient for new worlds to fall to him. "We've got it started," he said. Still rubbing his hands together, he turned to Halpern, "How did the Messieurs Ballbreaker, Knick-Knack and Mark-Up greet your association with the carpetbagger from Chicago? They did not, I can only hope, transmogrify on the carpet out of sheer joy."

"Let's put it this way. I'm not working for them anymore."

He had the satisfaction, for what it was worth, of seeing Bannerman's eyelids open wide. Apparently it was worth a great deal, for Halpern found himself even more eager to tell Bannerman about it than he had imagined. He told the story well. Not accurately but well. He had not really been so cool and disdainful in telling Stonebreaker that while there were those who still might believe that lawyers were supposed to be the protectors of privilege and property, the true calling of a lawyer was the protection of life and property. He had, in truth, been young and moralistic. In the green-tinted office, where Stonebreaker had been able to speak for himself, he had replied, drily amused, that perhaps Halpern had better wait until he got a little privilege and property under his belt before he came to any irrevocable decision. In the hotel suite, where the same words were spoken through Harold Halpern, he came out sounding like a pompous ass.

Bannerman was cackling with glee. "So C. S. Stonebreaker views my appearance on the scene with trepidation and alarm. Gawwwwwddamn! That's the best news I've had all day."

"I believe the word he used was mountebank."

"Mountebank?" He looked at the word as across a poker table, as if the stakes had just been raised. "You hear that, Fletch? I haven't heard anybody called a mountebank on this side of the Big Ditch since McKinley had that unfortunate encounter with his fan club in Buffalo. What did I tell you about those sonsa-bitches, Harold?"

Still glowing, he turned to Fletcher as if he were asking him what he thought of his boy now. "Chucked his job to carry the Old Mountebank's briefcase. Can't let that kind of a challenge to the home team go unanswered." Picking up the phone, he instructed the operator to get him C. S. Stonebreaker, attorney at large. "The fate of the nation may be hanging in the balance," he informed the operator. "But don't let that hurry you." While he was waiting he lifted his head back to Halpern, his brow suddenly wrinkled, his eyes gone flat. Here was a man sorely puzzled, sadly aggrieved. "I wouldn't mind if he called me a whoremaster, I know what that means. But mountebank, that sounds dirty."

The voice he turned upon Stonebreaker's secretary upon being told Stone-breaker was in conference was a fine, wooing instrument. *Miss* Franz, was it? How could it be possible that a young lady with her charming voice and obvious vocational advantages had not been lassoed and hogtied by one of our hornier American mountebanks? "That's cowboy talk, ma'am," he said, shifting to a chawing-tobacco drawl. "Where ah come from, a cute li'l filly like you wouldn't be left free to roam the prairie from one roundelay to the next. Would you be so good as to tell your employer, Cliff the Ballbreaker, that if he fails to return my call within ten minutes I shall schedule a press conference and pass on my message through the far-ranging channels of our communication media." His voice went flat but it was by no means unpleasant. "You can tell him the message has to do with his unconscionable attempt to intimidate my assistant, Harold Halpern."

If there was one thing he enjoyed more than depegging an old fogbound like Stonebreaker, he told them after he hung up, it was goosing an imported secretary with one of those phony High Street accents. "Mistuh Stewn-breakuh is in conference," he said, in a truly remarkable imitation of Vivian Franz's neat, wintry accent. "Mistuh Stewn-breakuh puts aside fif-teen minutes every forenoon to play with his gold-plated yo-yo."

Within ten minutes Fletcher was holding the receiver out to him with a little bow of congratulations. Bannerman scarcely looked up from his newspaper. "Tell him I'm taking a call from the Coast," he said, and (with Fletcher shaking his head in disbelief that anybody could be that childish) made Stonebreaker wait a full minute before he plucked the phone daintily out of his hands. "Clifford, old boy," he said heartily. "This is Norman. So good of you to hold on. I just happened to be in town and I would never have been able to forgive myself if I had left without telling you to go fuck yourself." It was said so naturally and pleasantly that a stranger walking into the room wouldn't have doubted for a second that he was passing the time of day with an old friend. "I have a young colleague here with me who would consider it an honor and a privilege to enjoin you toward the same exercise in a cappella endearment."

He started to hand the phone to Halpern, but then he winced, gave his head a shake and cleaned out his ear. "I do believe he hung up," he said. "No manners among the upper crust anymore. Where did it go, the old *noblesse oblige?*" The nose pointed to the air in horror, the lips tightened in disapproval. The tone, pitch and intonation became, once again, the tone, pitch and intonation of Vivian Franz. "I'm going to tell the *Queen* on him!"

It was Halpern he was performing for, of course. "Feels better already, doesn't it?" he said gently. "All right, that's something to remember. Any bridge worth jumping off is worth burning."

Hal did feel better. He could, in fact, see Stonebreaker sitting behind the big, solid desk quivering with rage. "Old Ballbreaker," he said gleefully, "must be dissolving into the floor like a man-of-war sinking slowly on the horizon."

Bannerman paused for a moment to consider that picture on his own account, and you could see that he found it good. "If this wasn't my busy season," he said, "I'd send over a fifty-piece band to play 'Nearer My God to Thee' or the traditional accompaniment of his choice." Unhappily, they seemed to be strapped for time. "You and I, Harold," he said, handing him his reward, "have a previous engagement with our client."

The Interviewing Room was an iron cell, black and spare. To demonstrate, Halpern suspected, that there was no place where a bug could be hidden. There was a metal table set in the exact center of the room. There was a light hanging down over the table from a narrow, tightly linked black chain. There were three straight-backed metal chairs, incongruously white. And that was all. When the door clanged shut behind them, the metallic ring reverberated like the final rivet being hammered in.

Although Halpern had been along while prisoners were being interviewed before, he had always come as part of the system. For the first time he knew what it felt like to be a prisoner, the fingered enemy of the great, vast, hitherto impersonal system. While outside . . .

He had the overwhelming impression that outside everyone was hurrying about their daily rounds, their routine, unthinking rounds, walking and driving, eating and shopping, entering and exiting, with never a thought for Sam Tabor.

Nobody except Norman Bannerman and Harold Halpern gave one damn about Sam Tabor, that's what it all came down to. Sam Tabor's life was in their hands. In that moment Halpern accepted him totally and without reservation as his client and, accepting him, he experienced a positive need to feel the tightness of the walls around him, taste the staleness of the air.

Sam himself didn't seem to realize who his friends were. Upon being introduced to Bannerman, there had been a rather oblique appraisal and a polite, obliging handshake. While Bannerman was clearing up the question of a possible conspiracy, he had sat, slouched and at ease, in perfect equilibrium—it would seem—with his surroundings. And yet there was something about that sly appraising squint that was disturbing. It was there in the way he shook his head when Bannerman offered him a cigarette, and in the ambiguous smile with which he said, "As long as I'm here, I might as well do something to work on my character."

And now Sam was saying, "Look, Mr. Bannerman. I'm an old courthouse hand myself. I shot him and if there is one thing I always believed, I have always been a firm believer in the . . . doctrine of personal responsibility."

Halpern was sitting off to the side of the cell as Bannerman had instructed. On his pad he printed: *Is he glad he did it???*

Norman Bannerman said, "I'm not here to tell you about your responsibilities, Sam, but about your rights. The law confers on you certain rights, which it is my duty, as your attorney, to explain to you."

Tabor's head had sunk to his chest. As he looked up at him his eyes were so narrow that they were almost closed. "I'm willing to be executed for what I done, if that's what the jury wants, but I wouldn't lie about it and I wouldn't want anybody to lie for me. And I don't want to hide under any so-called rights."

All out of context the picture came to Halpern of a little boy speaking up to the principal. *I cannot tell a lie. I'm the naughty boy who is proving that I am really a good boy by admitting how naughty I have been.* But then, just by looking at them he could see that it was more than that. A complete reversal had taken place. The plump little man with the narrow, scratchy eyes wasn't playing the expected role of the murderer wholly dependent upon the skill and good will of his famous lawyer. The famous lawyer had been placed in a position where he was wholly dependent upon the prisoner to permit him to try his case. With a dip of his head that was frankly conciliatory, Bannerman said, "All right. Just let me tell you what you should know about first-degree murder."

As it had turned out, Hal could have saved himself a sleepless night. A fully developed and annotated brief had been delivered to Bannerman's room that morning attached to a gleaming new mahogany clipboard. At the top of the clipboard, imprinted in gold leaf, were the words: This was Not Stolen from the Office of DeWitt Pawley. In the accompanying letter Pawley had informed Bannerman that while the brief was being sent as a professional courtesy, the clipboard was being offered as a memento of his high personal regard. Below his signature he had written in longhand: "If the investigatory operation in our office is up to par, you have Harold Halpern, ex of my division, working with you. To courtesy and regard, I add congratulations. H.H. carries my highest recommendation."

First-degree murder, Bannerman told Sam, meant that he had set out "with malice aforethought" to commit an act of murder. That was how the law was worded in this state, and he wanted Sam to understand exactly what "malice" meant. Malice was intent, not premeditation. The state didn't have to prove that he had been planning it for three months, three days or three seconds, but only that he had intended to do it when he did it. A fuzzy distinction in most cases, he conceded, but a perhaps vital one in this one. "Oh, it helps them if they can convince a jury that you planned it because in this state the jury sets all penalties." On a first-degree verdict, of course, they had only two options. Life or death. Life in prison or death in the electric chair. He took out a cigarette, puffed hard to get a light and, getting it, blew out a stream of smoke. "A jury tends to feel that nobody kills another man without a reason. We're off on a perimeter of the law here but as your attorney I feel I have an obligation to explain this to you. The jury *believes* that." He paused. "I believe it myself emotionally," he said. "Even though, intellectually, I know it isn't so."

"I don't blame anybody for that," Tabor said. "I believe it, too."

Second-degree meant there had been no malice. No intent. It was an act committed "under immediate influence of sudden passion, arising from adequate cause." Adequate cause. "Now you can understand why it was so important for me to know if you had any connection with David Wilcke." A wisp of a smile appeared on his lips. "If the adequate cause is adequate enough juries have been known to extend the limits of "sudden passion" over a truly remarkable span of time. It is considered good practice, therefore, by attorneys far more scholarly than I to give them something on which they can hang their hat." For second-degree the jury could come back with anything ranging from ten years to life. "In this case—and I'm speaking from extensive trial experience now—a jury coming back with a second-degree verdict would probably impose a sentence of somewhere between twenty and thirty years."

"Lowell juries aren't compromising juries, Mr. Bannerman," Tabor said. "They'll usually go high or low." Although the glance he sent to Halpern held only the trace of a smirk, it also contained an unmistakable home-town complicity. For all of Norman Bannerman's reputation, the small smirk said, they, as home-grown products, knew the terrain far better than he ever could.

There was also manslaughter, voluntary and involuntary, and Bannerman disposed of them quickly. For their purposes, manslaughter could be taken as a synonym for "accidental." It was voluntary if some negligence was involved and involuntary if there wasn't. If he had been cleaning a gun when the victim came into view and it had somehow gone off in his hands, that would be involuntary manslaughter.

It would also, Halpern jotted down on his pad for no particular reason, be farfetched. Sam, however, had no comment. He had drifted away from them. Drawn back to the central overpowering core to which, in him, all things repaired. Back, Halpern wondered, to the steps of City Hall? Bannerman ground his cigarette out under his heel, took the pack out of his pocket, looked at it in surprise and hastily put it back. "There is also," he said loudly, "not guilty by reason of insanity. In this country a man is not considered guilty if he has no control over what he is doing."

Sam Tabor pulled himself up straight in the chair, squinting at him intently.

In this state, Bannerman was saying, the M'Naughton Rule could be coupled with the doctrine of irresistible impulse. "With or without irresistible impulse, M'Naughton is an archaic rule. I have an hour speech on that subject, a half-hour speech, a ten-minute speech and a thirty-second station break. I will be making them all before I leave Lowell, but I will save them for where they will do you the most good."

"I'm not crazy," Sam Tabor said.

Nobody was saying he was. All he was doing, Bannerman reminded him, was explaining the law to him. For his own protection. As his right. "What it means is that if you knew what you were doing, you are guilty and they can put you to death. If you did not know what you were doing, you are not guilty." Without hurrying, never taking his eyes off him, he pushed himself back in his seat preparatory to standing up. "I did not say, you will notice, that you are 'guilty but insane.' I said you are not guilty . . . by reason of insanity."

"I have a right to . . . repudiate my rights, don't I?"

As a matter of fact, Bannerman told him, he didn't. He sent a pensive look over at Halpern, which the young lawyer couldn't interpret. But when he turned back to Sam his look was openly reproachful. "You're not a legal illiterate, Sam," he chided him. Old courthouse hand that he was, Sam Tabor would certainly know that he couldn't plead guilty to murder one. And murder one, he would know, was what the state would be going for.

In an odd, sulky voice, a kind of stubborn whine directed as much at Halpern as at Bannerman, Tabor said, "Well, that's the way I've always lived, and I'm too old to . . . alter my pattern of living now."

There was nothing ambiguous in the new look Bannerman sent to Halpern. Grimly, in the attitude of a man who was being pushed to a decision he had been hoping to avoid, Bannerman sat himself down across from Sam and adjusted his big body until he was comfortable. Sternly, in the tone of a man who was taking time to explain what should not be necessary to explain, he said, "When you were under Dr. Shtogren's care you didn't argue with him about the disciplines of his profession, did you? Any more than you'd argue with a surgeon about the best way to take out your appendix. You are under my legal care now and, in a legal sense, you are sick unto death. Murder one: unto death! You should live with that thought from this moment on." He gave him a good five seconds to start living with it, and then, with Sam beginning to look as if he were drifting away from him again, rapped heavily on the table. "What is the worst thing an enemy could do to you?" The worst thing an enemy could do, he said, was to kill you. "Or," he said, biting it off, "is it?" No, the worst thing he could do would be to set you out, naked against the winds, and stalk you through the forest so that he could hunt you down before he killed you. The big reddish head inched forward. "That is exactly what the state is setting out to do to you. You *know* that. That is what a murder one trial is. You *know* that." His voice had taken on an intense, persistent monotone, and Tabor was caught up in it, the tip of his tongue frozen between his lips. There was only one man who stood between the stalkers and their prey. Norman Bannerman. Every resource of Norman Bannerman's mind and energy was dedicated to stopping *them* and saving *him.* "I have unfurled my banner over your camp and I will fight to the end to save you. I am empowered by the law, by the Constitution and by my faith in you and your cause to do this." He bent to him, his ward and his brother, and spread his hands flat across the table. His voice became deep and, despite the ominous overtones, soothing. "The state knows I am its enemy. They will try to make you distrust me. They will tell you lies. They will feed on your suspicions. Do not believe them. Believe nobody except me." Tabor was nodding at each injunction, not quite transfixed, not completely convinced, but being pulled into Bannerman by the force of his will and personality. "They are your enemy. I am your friend. *They* are your enemy. *I* am your friend."

With Tabor held in almost hypnotic thrall, Bannerman let a few moments go by before he clapped his hands together lightly. "Now," he said. "At this time I am merely listing the possible verdicts and exploring their legal consequences. I will explain the law on temporary insanity to you, and then, I think, we'll have done it. Temporary insanity . . ." Having lifted his voice a notch to let the words ring out, it became necessary to refill his lungs while they hung there, vibrating. "Temporary insanity means that you were insane according to the legal definition of that term at the time you pulled the trigger, either because of a physical or mental stress, but that you are no longer insane as you sit in the courtroom."

He emphasized that they were talking about insanity as a legal term only, not as a medical one. He emphasized that temporary insanity carried the specific meaning that he was, just as he had said, not insane, legally or any other way, as he sat there right now. He also emphasized that the difference between insanity and temporary insanity, as a legal verdict, was that if Sam were found not guilty by reason of insanity, he would be sent to the state asylum at Algonquin where he would remain until three psychiatrists, two of whom would be employed by the state, certified that he had become sane. "Should the jury, on the other hand, find you not guilty by reason of temporary insanity, you would not only not be guilty, you would also be free. As . . . a . . . bird. You were insane then, legally speaking. You are not insane now."

"I know all about that," Sam said. "Like Jim Ambose says, the law is an ass."

To which Bannerman could not resist remarking that a backslid English court reporter named Dickens had beaten Ambose to it. Ass or not, the law was the framework within which they must work. "I don't know about you," Norman Bannerman said, "but I would rather ride to freedom on the back of an ass than be carried to heaven on the wings of Pegasus."

"Halpern," Tabor said, "do you think I'm crazy?"

And when Halpern, somewhat at a loss, reminded him that they weren't even talking about "crazy" that way, Tabor squinted at him with that sly, superior little smile. "That's all right, Halpern," he said. "You can lie to me if you have to."

And exactly what the hell, Halpern wondered, did he mean by that? Wondered then, and would wonder for the rest of his life.

As Bannerman had said, with the exploration of temporary insanity they had done it. Only then did he ask Tabor to take them through the whole story about how he had come to drive down to City Hall with a gun.

"I've told this so many times," Sam complained, almost before he had begun.

"I know. But not to anybody who was trying to help you."

And so, heavily and wearily, and yet with the resignation of a man who knows only too well that he has nowhere else to go, he told it again. When he came to the interview with Ambose, Bannerman looked as if he been stricken with an acute gastric spasm. "I want you to think carefully before you answer this," he cautioned him. "Did he inform you of your constitutional right to remain silent?"

Sure, Sam said. He must have told him that four or five times.

"Four or five times. It makes things so much easier to have a client with such total recall."

Which only succeeded in bringing them right back to where they had begun, with Sam stating, even more sharply, that he had already told Bannerman he wasn't going to lie. "I don't want a lot of them delays, either," he said. "I want to get this thing over and done with as quick as you can so that Vera can go on to picking up her life."

On that score, Bannerman could assure him, he had no need to worry. "You are not really," he said, rolling the "r," "inspiring me to make this case my lifetime work."

And oddly enough Bannerman's amiable irony, his automatic, unthinking response, had done what all the tricks of the trade had not been able to. Tabor chuckled, softly but quite audibly. They smiled across the table, understanding each other perfectly.

It was done. Halpern brought his chair back to the table and puffed gratefully on a cigarette. Sam, hunching over the table on both arms, said, "Mr. Bannerman, you don't really think there's any chance to. Everybody knows I killed him."

And while it may have been meant as nothing more than a casual disclaimer to show that Sam Tabor knew the score, it came out entirely different. The secret fear, known or unknown, had welled up from down under, turning it into a desperate question flung on the quivering air. Here, with the interview coming to an end, Halpern was looking upon the bare and defenseless prisoner he had expected to see from the beginning.

"There are many calls upon my services," Bannerman said. "I didn't come here to waste my time." And although there was nothing in Bannerman's voice or attitude to show it, a weight had shifted. The balance had been tipped. The attorney was back in command. "Of course, we still have to find our defense," he said lightly. "We'll talk some more about that the next time."

Halpern took a deep breath. "Are you glad you killed him, Sam?" He knew he was taking a lot upon himself, but damnit, it was the one thing Hal had to know. Sneaking a look out of the side of his eyes, he could see that while Bannerman's brows were knit into a rather quizzical frown he seemed more amused than annoyed. It was Tabor's reaction that was so unexpected. Leaning on his elbows, one hand wrapped over the other, Sam nibbled away at his knuckle. *He hadn't really thought about it before.*

"No," he said, discovering it as he was hearing it. "I'm not glad." He set his mouth solidly. "You don't think I like it here, do you?"

But that wasn't exactly what Halpern had in mind. Phrasing the question carefully, he said, "What I mean, Sam, is looking back on it now. Looking back. Do you think you did the country a service?"

That one really surprised Sam. His chin came up. An expression of mild shock and distaste played across his features. "Now what kind of a question is that? All I did that I can see is cause everybody a whole lot of trouble."

The first thing Hal had to understand, Bannerman told him, was that Tabor was not a professional criminal. He was a one-shot murderer, no pun intended. A good citizen in the toils of the law, the worst kind of client any lawyer could hope to have. As an amateur, Sam still had the wholly unrealistic dream that when he went into court, his friend, the arresting officer, would tell the judge that Sam Tabor had always been a good fellow and that he was real sorry for what he had done, whereupon the judge would tell him he had been a very bad boy indeed and send him home with the stern warning never to do it again.

What they hadn't seen, he wanted Hal to understand, was the Sam Tabor who had committed the murder. That Sam they were never going to see. Only for the briefest of moments had they caught a glimpse of the frightened man who would be walking into the courtroom. That Sam wasn't going to emerge, Bannerman informed him, until the end of Phase I—when his overwhelming sense of gratitude that they were treating a murderer like him so decently had passed.

When they were back in the hotel Hal said, "You asked me what I thought before. There's this. Tabor sometimes gives me the impression that . . . I don't exactly know how to put it, but that he thinks he's maybe just a little smarter than anybody else."

"That unfortunate squint." Bannerman had not only seen it—how could he miss it?—he was just as unhappy about it. "Most of the time he looks like such a happy, harmless fool, too. We'll have to do something about that, you're right."

Well, that wasn't exactly what Hal had meant.

"You think our client might be suffering from the fatal delusion that he's smarter than Norman Bannerman, is that it?" He turned to Halpern, in an easy swing of the eyes. "Or did I detect in your aggrieved tone the first faint gurgle that our psychotic client just might have thought he was the smartest man in the world when he shot David Wilcke?"

As soon as he heard the words spoken out loud Halpern knew that was exactly what he had been thinking. It was so absurd that he was left with a feeling of itchy disloyalty at ever having thought it.

Bannerman gave him another quick, appreciative look. "You ask the right questions," he said, "but you come up with the wrong answers. That's all right. Asking the right questions is what gives you the chips to sit in on the game."

Once Sam had emerged out of Phase I, Bannerman could tell him, Halpern could expect to see the whole syndrome of paranoia begin to develop. Except, he was at pains to point out, it would not be a psychosis. "They *are* out to kill him. 'They.' The state in all its power and majesty. Everybody and nobody. No matter how cleverly he tries to hide that from himself, he knows it. Because there's a bitch in the subconscious that always knows. That always knows and never goes. And sooner or later the bitch is going to reach up into the gullet and shake him by the eyeteeth, and when it does he will never be able to think of anything else." He nodded once to himself, confirming it. "Where Sam is at the moment," he said, "he has to feel that he can handle it or he'll fall apart. You noticed he's concen-

138

trating on not smoking? Typical." Transference of anxiety to a minor psychological discomfort he felt he could handle. Just the kind of thing he had brought Hal there to observe.

On his own behalf Hal was grateful. On behalf of his client he was deeply resentful. He resented having Sam Tabor talked about like some bug under a slide. From what he had seen, he told Bannerman, Sam looked as if he could handle his affairs pretty well. "It seemed to me," he said, with a maliciousness that surprised him, "he even had some definite ideas about what he did and did not want from his lawyers."

"I've been around a lot of courthouses in my time, Harold, and I can tell you that the will to live, however faintly it may flicker at times, governs all. Picture Sam Tabor right now, being led back to his cell and locked in. Picture him alone in his cell, day after day. His meals brought to him. His exercise taken only after the rest of the prison population is back in their cells. A man on trial for his life is a man on an island, bounded on all sides by the coming battle." The characteristic lift of the eyebrow served this time to call attention to his own high reputation. "And when you live on an island, Harold, the man who can swim is king."

Hal's reaction could not have been all Bannerman had hoped for. "Come on, now. I'm beginning to think you're losing confidence in me. By the time we go to trial Sam Tabor will bend over on command. And pucker. Harold, my boy, before this is over, he'll not only bend over and pucker, he'll be throwing in an extra twinkle or two on his own." He was smiling softly to himself. "Don't worry so much, Hal. I'm going to save Sam Tabor in spite of himself."

Ruthie Halpern was seated cross-legged on the parlor floor, the multicolored hostess pants tight across her thin shanks, totally engrossed in the biography of Norman Bannerman that occupied the entire front page of the feature section of the Sunday *Globe* and continued on to page sixteen. In the center of the page there were double-column cuts of Bannerman's first three wives. Bottom-right was an obviously posed picture of Norman Bannerman frolicking on the golf course with wife number four, a pretty, busty "model" who was wearing a tight jersey and short shorts and aiming what looked like a five-iron at his head.

In a box under the pictures of the wives was a brief résumé of his feuds with their respective lawyers. After divorce number one he had been accused of attempting to run down his wife's attorney as he was stepping off the courthouse curb. Lawyer number two had petitioned for an injunction (subsequently withdrawn) to require Norman Bannerman to cease and desist from phoning the lawyer's wife with wholly false and meretricious grounds for divorce and, it had been further alleged, guaranteeing to get a better settlement for her than her husband would be able to get for the second Mrs. Bannerman. The third lawyer, he had attempted to pay off in skunk pelts. "I sent the man the pelt I thought would be most congenial to his temperament and character," Bannerman had informed an indignant court. "It leaves me grieved and shocked to discover that he has taken my assessment of him to be seditious."

"Oooooh, I *love* him," Ruthie said, hugging the paper to her. "He's run through four wives and he's still so handsome and peppy and crooked. Tell him you have an intimate acquaintance who's willing to audition for number five."

Hal gave a grunt but contented himself with observing that from the look of the lady golfer he liked 'em a little heftier.

"Did he really do all these things?" she asked in panting admiration. "I never really thought they *let* you do those things in a courtroom, except in the movies or *Perry Mason*."

Unless the Associated Press had been taken in by falsehoods, he told her. "A prospect so unlikely as to be discounted completely."

"I like it when you talk like a lawyer." Her eyes lit up in a mixture of pride and greed. "I want that you should be brilliant and crooked and do terrible things that will make you famous and get my picture in the feature section of the Sunday *Globe*."

"Anything you say, dear. I suppose all famous crooked lawyers need a wife number one in their past." For the time being he was willing to make her a deal. If she would stop talking about Norman Bannerman for about ten minutes, he would tell her the brilliant idea he had developed for the defense of his—and Norman Bannerman's—famous client.

The traditional way of trying a murder case, he told her, was to humanize the defendant. The defendant comes into court day after day, and the jury gets to see him and, in a way, to know him. They hear all the details of his life. Defense counsel portrays him in the most sympathetic light possible. "And when the trial has come to an end, his lawyer looks into the eyes of the jurors and asks them, 'Do you want to have the death of this man on your conscience for the rest of your life?' " This case, he said, was different. It was unique. "In this one," he said, dropping his bombshell, "you don't want to humanize him. You want to dehumanize him."

Ruthie, who was listening with the concentrated, intensive stare of a wife who is resolved to keep up with her husband, signaled impatiently, eager for him to go on.

"No one knows why he did it, see? He doesn't know why he did it. We don't know why he did it. The jury won't know why he did it. He was like a robot impelled by some unseen, mysterious force. You know, *outside* himself." Since he had acted like a robot, they would let the jury see him as a robot. They would let Jim Ambose put on the prosecution case, and then all they would put on for the defense would be one psychiatrist who would say, yes, he was a robot. And then they'd rest. "The whole trial shouldn't take more than three days, and the jury sure isn't going to get to know much about him in three days."

"Your Honor," she cooed, "the defense rests. A hush falls over the courtroom."

The beauty of such a defense, he explained, was that the less the defense tried to show, the less the prosecution would be able to rebut. Which meant that the state's psychiatrist would be on and off the stand just as fast. "Faster. Because they can't have their psychiatrist examine him unless we agree, which we damn well won't. And," he continued triumphantly, "the burden of proof is on them."

It was a brilliant idea, she said, meaning it. But, she said, meaning it even more, Norman Bannerman of the four wives was never going to go for it. "Norman Bannerman of the wavy locks did not come flying halfway across the country to see how fast he could get the Trial of the Century over with. Norman Bannerman of the full-page spread is here to get his picture in all the papers like a . . ."

The ringing of the phone cut her off. "Damn," she said, "That's Mother . . ." Halfway there she brought herself to an abrupt stop and asked Hal to take it. Affecting her trilly, dumb-broad voice (she had played Billy Dawn in *Born Yesterday* for her amateur theatre group while they were courting), she said, "She's calling to ask how come your picture isn't in the paper, too."

Although Hal got up with great ill grace a delicious smile very soon came over his face. "It's Norman Bannerman," he whispered, "of the unexpected Sunday morning calls."

"I could have talked to him," Ruthie screamed. Her hands went to the top of her head. She pulled at her hair in theatrical excess. "I was halfway over there, and I . . . I always pick up the phone. I could have talked to him," she squealed, with a stamp of her little foot. "And won him with my wiles." She stopped stock-still, her knees buckled together, her eyes squeezed tight, her fists clenched alongside her head, her mouth straining in a soundless scream. "It isn't fair," she wailed, "it isn't fair."

"If it's important, Norman, it's important," Hal said. "I'll tell you, though. I've got to shave and get dressed, and if you'll do me the favor of explaining it to my wife, I'll get started." He stood there nevertheless while they were going through the preliminaries of introduction, the very picture of the indulgent husband.

"Mr. Bannerman," she said in a husky voice, "let's stop talking about my husband now, and let's talk about me. Have I told you that you're a spiffy dresser? Well, I'm a spiffy dresser, too."

Jim Ambose sat in his office, the Cave, waiting patiently for his visitor, his feet up on the old nicked desk, his hat tipped forward as if to shield his eyes. When Jim Ambose sent the word out, it would be a brave man who would not come running. The time had come for a debt to be paid, a neat and orderly balancing of the books, which Ambose found especially welcome after the inexhaustible coincidences of the past few days.

The decisive part sheer chance plays in life—that was something Ambose, with his compulsion for order and logic, had never felt called upon to examine so minutely before.

The moves in a chess game, however various, were limited by the game's interior rules and social order. A bishop could not become a castle, and not even a queen could behave like a knight. A pawn could be depended upon to hold within its narrow ambit, never aspiring to be more than a pawn. Until these last few days Jim Ambose would have said that life, for all its infinite variations, proceeded along a roughly similar logic of its own. You step off a curb and a truck hits you, that's understandable. Within the scheme of things a predictable insurance statistic.

This was different. Looking back on the day of June 15, Jim Ambose had the eerie feeling that the whole day had been wrenched out of the calendar, out of its chronological order. A tide had been missed. A circuit had been broken. A train had been derailed, and the passengers set loose from the normal restraints of space, character or time.

Consider the individual threads that had become so minutely interwoven. The Chief Justice, breaking a personal rule, accepts an invitation to speak in Lowell; a photographer is at the airport when he is attacked. A mad killer attacks an unflappable judge; a court reporter is given the afternoon off; the court reporter is playing games with another judge. And then: The Chief Justice has to be awakened from his nap to disclaim a press conference; the chief deputy has to make a phone call at a precise moment; the court reporter has to look out the window; the sheriff has to be there to take her call.

All these things have had to happen in precise military formation just to bring Booker Phillips into an empty sheriff's office at the precise moment in time. Pluck one thread from the tapestry and the whole vast pattern collapses. One minor collision at any of the thousands of intersections over the lives of each of the players, and David Boone Wilcke would be sitting at his dinner table or in one of his favorite night clubs, and anyone who suggested that he had been in mortal danger in Lowell would be shipped off to the funny farm.

What was the sense of it, Jim Ambose had to ask himself, if we were really such sports of chance? No. There must be a Hand somewhere weaving that tapestry, coordinating all those exits and entrances. All those roads could not have come to meet on the steps of City Hall, only to be dependent, at the end, on a lucky shot. David Wilcke had an appointment with Sam Tabor on the steps of City Hall on June 15, at 5:05 P.M., and nothing on earth could have kept them apart.

In such a scheme, did not the elevator door sliding silently shut behind him that day become the symbol of a restricting fate? Was Jim Ambose no more than that, a rat dropped into a predetermined alley of some vast, impersonal maze? His mind rejected that image out of hand. He could have waited for the elevator to return. He had chosen not to. Just as Sam Tabor could have resisted the temptation to reach for the gun. Man was, in the end, a reasoning animal. The final choice, and therefore the ultimate responsibility, was his.

It had been so quiet in the Cave that Ambose could well have been asleep. It was so quiet that you could, if you had listened, have heard the clock tick. But now a soft grunt emanated from beneath the hat. That was the solid core to hold onto. That was the logic that superimposed itself upon the seemingly random interplay of men and events. Once I show them the rainbow, he thought to himself, it should be easy enough to convince them that it had rained. That was for the Journal.

With a start of the mind he understood now what had been bothering him. His own life had been threaded into the tapestry, and the Ambose thread was still running. What had been set in motion could not come to an end until the foreman of the jury (moving now, unknown to himself, to his allotted role) arose on the order of the judge and read the verdict that would either allow Sam Tabor to live or send him to his death.

The sound of footsteps could be heard on the staircase. His visitor was arriving, right on cue.

Sam Tabor had kept his appointment with David Boone Wilcke; Jim Ambose was now rolling on toward his appointment with Norman Bannerman.

Behind him the door opened.

"I hear you want to see me, Jim."

Without moving, his hat still over his eyes, Ambose said, "Sure do, Hughie. Sure do. I had this funny feeling that maybe we can both do ourselves some good. I look good to my boss and you look good to yours." He heard the scraping of the chair as Hugh Fletcher settled himself on the other side of the desk.

"Ike Weiland says you were trying to do some good on the relevant police reports on Tabor. You should have known better than to try that on this one, Hugh. A cop does you a job here and there for fifty bucks, gets you a copy of a report for ten." He pushed the hat back just enough so that he could look at him in the semidarkness. "That still the going rate?"

"Depends on the market," Fletcher said at last. "Everything in this world is negotiable."

Ambose liked that word. Negotiable. It showed that Fletcher knew what he was here for.

They sat across from each other silently, Ambose looking as if he wasn't quite sure what to do with him, Fletcher never doubting that he was going to find out. "What you did, Hughie, it's attempted bribery of a police officer, huh? I don't know what else I could call it, Hughie." He was trying to be fair. "What would you call it?"

"I'd call it routine. I do my—"

"Do you want to try for 'dumb?' " Down came the feet. "You were *dumb,* Hughie!" And dumbest of all was that he had put Weiland in the spot of having to tell Ambose about it.

"I do my job," Fletcher said, his temper well in check. "My job is to hustle around for the lawyer who's paying my fee."

"Norman Bannerman?" Ambose was disappointed in him. Didn't he know that when this case was over, Norman Bannerman was going to pack his dirty little bags and fly away? "You now, Hughie. You're going to be dealing with Ike Weiland for a long time if you stay in this town. And," he said pointedly, "if you keep your license." Since, under the circumstances, Fletcher was showing no disposition to argue with him, Ambose contented himself with adding up the damage. "Let's see, attempted bribery on top of that little caper down in Lanning. Yup, that could very easy cost you your license, all right." He leaned back again and drew his lips across his teeth. "I wouldn't want to do you like that, Hugh. We've been friends too long. It's like you said, though. You got your job to do, I got mine."

Under the desk his right foot went unerringly to a button at the side of his desk, hidden away in the little notch just above the floor. The button activated the tape recorder in the bottom drawer. "Maybe," he said, "you can suggest a way out for us."

"You've been holding that ticket on me for Lanning for a long time now." Almost against his will a brooding, reproachful tone pushed its way into Fletcher's voice. "Just been waiting to cash it in, haven't you?"

Ingratitude! Five years ago, as a newly-licensed investigator, Fletcher had been called down to Lanning to tap a phone in a simple divorce case. The reason it had been considered prudent to call in an investigator from that far away was because the husband was a powerful behind-the-scenes political figure. Powerful enough, Fletcher was soon to discover, to have a pair of sheriff's deputies sitting watch on his telephone line. Poor Fletcher had been caught up on a pole, in a strange and lonely jurisdiction, with a plug in his ear.

For Fletcher's benefit, Ambose could now recall to him how he had come crawling practically on his hands and knees to do something for him. And how grateful he had been when good old Jim not only got the indefinite postponement but had arranged for it to be done in closed session so that Jesse Martin, Ambose's counterpart in Lanning, could hold onto the sheet. At the pleasure and convenience, need it be said, of James J. Ambose. And then lest Fletcher get any idea that Ambose had called him here to bargain with him. "When you were yelling for help you knew what I had to do. I had to tell Jesse you were doing your bit for me up here. He takes care of my stoolies on his turf and I take care of his on mine."

Never mind that Fletcher might very well suspect that Ambose would have had to tell Jesse no such thing. He was hardly in any position to argue the point with him. What Fletcher would be far more likely to recall was that in Jim Ambose's hard-riding early days he had been in the habit of stuffing the money into a stoolie's mouth.

Fletcher's cheekbones could be seen to stiffen. "I was never anybody's stoolie." He remembered all right.

"Well, hell, Hughie, *we* knew that." He leaned forward, his elbows on the desk. "Now is the time," he said deliberately, "for fulfilling the prophecy I made for you five years ago in Lanning."

The eyes were daggers! For just one second there, if looks could kill! Into those daggers Jim Ambose said, "You want to struggle with your finer instincts, make it quick. I haven't got all day."

And that was that. "I got to be careful, Jim, that's all." Most decorously. "I think I've got something for you," he said. The only thing, he said, was that he had wanted to understand in his own mind that he was going to get the ticket back. Ambose, who had hardly expected that Fletcher was going to have anything that good, this soon, sat back and pursed his lips and became a listener.

"Bannerman is sending me to Jefferson to see a shrink named Harmon Medellia. He's at the university there. I'm going down tomorrow when you have that get-together with Chobodian." The reason he thought this would be of particular interest to Ambose was that Bannerman had called the shrink at home from a phone booth and had him go out and call back from another phone booth. "One thing you've got to give this guy, Jim. He's all balls."

Now why, Ambose wondered, would the noted Chicago attorney want to go and put himself to all that inconvenience?

Fletcher remained studiously professional. His instructions were to take a room in the Holiday Inn at the Jefferson airport under a phony name and wait for Medellia to pick him up. While they were riding around Fletcher was to sound him out about accepting the assignment as Court-appointed psychiatrist on the Sam Tabor case. He was to tell him that the Court was going to appoint a psychiatrist acceptable to both sides, and that Medellia was already the number-one choice of both the court and the defense and was being looked upon with favor by Hilliard Nevins. "I'm supposed to find out is he interested before we go any farther. And before I leave I'm to drop it, like it's a suggestion, that it might be just as wise not to let anyone know the defense has been talking to him." Even here, Fletcher couldn't resist a little crooked smile to alert Ambose that he was about to give him something good. "Because Bannerman knows he's the best man for the job, see, and we wouldn't want him to get blown out of the tub just because Hilliard Nevins got any wrong ideas."

Chobodian and Bannerman, huh. "When the hell did they get together?"

"I didn't say they had. I didn't say Chobodian necessarily knows anything about it yet."

"That's very good, Hugh." He gave himself a little time to think about it. "What about Bannerman? Any plans for the Big Man to talk to him himself?"

Fletcher shook his head. Only if it looked like he was falling down drunk for it. If not, they were going to wait until Medellia came in for the bond hearing. Honored guest of all concerned. "He figures you'll go for Medellia, Bannerman does, because he's local. Past president of the Shrink Association, that kind of thing. And because he's stayed pretty much away from courtrooms."

Ambose was toying with a pencil. He brought the pencil up to eye-level, both thumbs pressed together at the bottom as if he were about to snap it in half. "That's why, huh?"

"They met once in Capri years ago—yeah, Capri—and had long, intimate talks about man's inhumanity to man." The only reason he happened to know about that, Fletcher was careful to add, was because Bannerman had happened to mention it during the phone call.

Ambose arose and switched on the lights. "Fletcher, how'd you like Booker Phillips' affidavit?"

Fletcher squinted against the sudden light. He held his expression, uncertainly. "I'd like to have my ticket punched, that's what I'd like."

"You've got that. Now how would you like Booker's affidavit?" To dispel any last lingering fears he stopped on his way out of the office to explain that now that they were square he figured he had better start doing him some favors. "If you're halfway as smart as I think you are"—he smiled—"you just might get to thinking that Bannermans come and Bannermans go but Jim Ambose is just liable to go on forever."

When he returned he also had a Xerox copy of the security report Booker had made out at Stringfellow's direction. "Hit Bannerman for a good bill on this," he advised him. "It will let him know you've got strong contacts. And that our police have their hands out." A dark cloud passed over his face. "Anything he wants," he said harshly. "All he's got to do is ask."

Still, now that it was over, the atmosphere had relaxed so completely that it was almost as if there was a bond between them. So much so that Ambose was willing to let him know, free of charge, that he had nothing to worry about as far as Ike Weiland was concerned, either. "If the truth were known, it was me that asked him to pass the word on. Some people might call it entrapment, except that as soon as you went to work for Bannerman you knew I'd be calling on you. Now, didn't you?"

"It's been so long, Jim, that I'd honest-to-god forgot. That's the truth. I thought we'd got to be friends."

"We are, Hughie. Hey. I think of you like a brother. But I told you at the time, 'You don't have to thank me,' I said, 'you'll get your chance to pay me back.' Don't you remember that?"

"I remember." He was remembering, you could see, to his sorrow. "You're a patient man, Jim. I could wish I had that much patience."

Not a patient man. A busy man. "A busy man seems like a patient man because he's got so much else on his mind. But he remembers. It's like a banker—a debt is a debt. The whole world is just one great big goddamn bank, Hughie. And the time always comes to square the accounts."

Jim Ambose sat there after Fletcher left, chewing on the stub of his little cigar. So Bannerman thought he was up against such yokels that he could walk in and plant his own psychiatrist on them. That told him something right there. It told him that, with all the publicity, Norman Bannerman had been going up against too many patsies lately. And if he'd been knocking over nothing but patsies, he'd be coming in soft and flabby.

The information about the bond hearing was well worth reflecting upon, too. It was, in fact, only after Fletcher had told him about the hearing that Ambose had decided he had not a thing to lose by letting him have Booker's affidavit. Which could have been exactly what Fletcher, nobody's fool, had been angling for when he had so matter-of-factly dropped that little nugget in there.

Rolling the cigar around on his tongue, his eyes narrowed to slits. What were the givens here? Not what did he *think*. What did he *know:*

For all his fame, Norman Bannerman had never had a case of such overpowering national interest. If, now that he had Booker's report, he went ahead with the hearing anyway, it could only mean that with the press of the nation waiting in the wings, Norman Bannerman could not bear to wait.

While Booker's testimony would be newsworthy, it would also be routine. The only way Bannerman could make the kind of splash he was after would be to put his own expert witness on the stand and give the public a quickie preview of the forces that had impelled Sam Tabor to commit the deed.

All right, then:

Bannerman would be viewing the bond hearing as nothing more than a showcase for himself. All the more so if he were encouraged to believe that he had succeeded in palming his own psychiatrist off on the Court for the main event. It was, therefore, Jim Ambose's clear duty to give the shithead every reason to think so.

No tests had been made on Tabor yet. Not even an EEG. And since it would be a waste of time to administer the tests until the Court-appointed psychiatrists had been named, Bannerman wouldn't push. His expert would be flying blind.

If Bannerman, as an experienced trial lawyer, was willing to take a chance like that it could only be because he was expecting the state to assume the conventional prosecution stance in a bond hearing. Purely defensive. Taking care to give away no more than was necessary to show the Court that they had a murderer on their hands.

A holy calm had settled over Jim Ambose. Jim Ambose did not have the slightest intention of playing it tight. Jim Ambose was confident that by the time Bannerman's expert left the stand, Bannerman's case would be considerably more limited than it had been when he mounted it.

He bit down hard into the cigar. There was nothing Ambose enjoyed more than to be playing with a stacked deck unless it was to restack a deck that his opponent thought he had stacked for himself.

The cigar had come apart in his mouth, and the wet tobacco was acrid on his tongue. Not really paying any attention, not really aware what he was doing, Jim Ambose expelled the tobacco flakes in a series of quick little spitting sounds. Jim Ambose was staring off into space. Jim Ambose was smiling.

He could hardly wait for the bond hearing to begin.

Halpern, suddenly realizing that Bannerman was looking at him expectantly, came to with a start.

"You block well," Bannerman said with approval. For a trial lawyer it was of the utmost importance to be able to climb inside himself for a private conference while all hell was breaking loose around him. "The only thing you'll have to be on guard against," he said, and there was something dark and bleak in the way he said it, "you'll have to be very, very careful not to climb in so deep some day that you'll never be able to find your way out."

Halpern gave a little shiver. "Sunday does depress you, doesn't it, Norm?"

It had been this muted, deeply introspective Norman Bannerman that Halpern had been confronted with from the moment he came into the hotel room to find him sitting, unshaven and lethargic, on the window seat. Hal's opening reference to the newspaper article had brought forth no more than a faint deprecatory smile. "Harold," he said, with the wisdom of age to youth, "don't believe everything you read in the penny press. The only lawyers who don't lose cases are the ones who never try them." And with a wave of the hand that seemed to take in the whole suite, "Work hard and get to be a noted criminal lawyer, quote–unquote, and if you're lucky you'll get to live in any number of fancy hotel rooms." Of course, it wasn't so bad when you were young. His first wife, Gwen, had liked to travel with him when he was a fledgling lawyer, it being her wistful theory that the first night in any hotel was like a honeymoon. "Ahhh, yes," he said. "Those halcyon days of yore. The best time in life, Harold, is the time you know you're going to make it big next week." He heaved himself a great philosophical sigh. "You want to know what's really the best advice I can give you? Don't be a howling success."

It was, in fact, while Halpern had been reflecting that this new Norman Bannerman was going to take some getting used to, that he had managed to block everything else out. "Yes," Bannerman agreed. "Sunday does depress me. So I'll depress you. Share and share alike. What I asked was how much do you know about psychomotor epilepsy?"

There had been a case . . . Damn. "There was a case where they used it as a defense the first year I was with Nevins. I remember it because it got laughed out of court. Guy shot a guy and—" As he was remembering the case a little more clearly, he was also reminding himself that Bannerman would not have asked about it unless he were considering it as a defense for Sam Tabor. "Charley Curran handled it for the state," he said. "Curran's good at the kind of a thing where you can ridicule something."

The attorney for the defense, Bannerman took it, *hadn't* been good at that kind of a thing. "The attorney for the defense in this one *is*." That sounded more like it. "We will lunch," he said, rather grandly. "If the service is up to its usual high standards it should be here in an hour." But, he said, what did it really matter, they weren't going anywhere, anyway, were they? It had taken that long for Hal to understand why Bannerman had got him over here. Not so much to go over the case as to have somebody around to talk to.

There was, nonetheless, the question of psychomotor epilepsy to be disposed of. Psychomotor epilepsy, Bannerman informed him, was—or at least came as the result of—a minor brain damage that brought on momentary seizure fits. The fits could last for as little as five seconds, during which time the victim had not the slightest control, medical authorities assured us, over what he was doing.

"Psychomotor epilepsy," Norman Bannerman said, with reverence, "may be regarded as the poor man's path to temporary insanity. And with temporary insanity one comes to the courtroom as to Lourdes, to be healed and to receive absolution."

BANNERMAN UNDER THE LIGHTS

Norman Bannerman, dressed, barbered and vaguely recovered in spirit, is making one small addendum to his earlier attack on hotel living. For all its deadening impact upon the soul, he is telling Halpern, it does have one great advantage:

"The circuit-riding defense attorney, having no home into whose bosom he can fly, works on his case at a fever pitch, while the prosecutors, being permanent cadre, drive home every night and relax in front of the TV set with the wife and kiddies."

Halpern has to tell him that however true he might have found that to be in other cities, he had better not count on having that kind of an advantage in Lowell. "Jim Ambose isn't married, and I'd be surprised if he owned a television set. Ambose has kind of a one-track mind. I don't know that he's interested in anything at all except his job."

Ambose, Ambose, Ambose, Bannerman cries. All he ever hears around this burg is Ambose. "If he's as good as everybody says he is, how come he hasn't left the DA's office by now and gone into business for himself?"

"Well," Halpern says, and there is something in his eyes that holds, inexplicably but visibly, the harsh reflection of Jim Ambose, "it's kind of a monopoly, you know. There just ain't no way for a lawyer to get to burn anybody if'n he goes into business for himself."

Elijah Chobodian, finishing his oatmeal, was trying to explain to Mrs. Chobodian why he had found it necessary to assign the Tabor trial to himself without making himself sound like an old fool with delusions of indispensability. Who else, he wanted her to tell him, was there? That great lovable boy, Harry Davies? Parks? Parks was a prosecution judge, and while Chobodian yielded to no man in his admiration for Hilliard Nevins, the prosecution wasn't really in any great need of a hanging judge on this one. "You are going to ask what's the matter with Johnny Rodgers. There is nothing the matter with Rodgers. With luck, he could get through the trial without reversible error." He glanced over at her briefly. "Without luck, he couldn't. You will have observed," he said, anticipating her, "that while Elijah Chobodian has no delusions of indispensability, only Elijah Chobodian happens to be qualified to sit on a case he wants to sit on. Why do you think I took this otherwise thankless job, anyway?"

He was, she should be able to see, in a happy, high-spirited mood. Full of energy and eager for the challenge of the day. There was, he was sure, no way for her to see the effort it cost him.

He had dressed with special care; the stiff high-necked collar he had worn from the beginning, and the gray pencil-line suit; the hair in its natural windswept coiffure. Chobodian had been born in Vermont and so it had been natural enough for the newspapers to have called him the Granite Judge. The joke around the courthouse used to be that he had a face like a Buffalo nickel: "No, not the Indian, the buffalo."

Hodapp was waiting out front in the limousine provided by a grateful county. Hodapp had been Chobodian's chauffeur for twenty-two years, and he was older than the judge himself. His eyesight was not all that it might have been, and neither were his reflexes. But how could you let a man go, Chobodian kept telling his wife, when you knew you would be putting him out to pasture?

"And you don't have the courage to look that old man in the eye and tell him that the time has come for him to retire."

"And I don't have the courage to look that old man in the eye and tell him the time has come for him to retire. And," he said, "because gray hair has earned a certain amount of respect. The older and grayer I get, the more wisdom I perceive in that simple old homily."

"There's no fool like an old fool," she said, "if it's the simple old homilies you're after."

"Well, since I am an old fool that means I'm no fool. A simple syllogism."

And what kind of logic, she asked scornfully, was that?

"That's lawyer logic. Devious and dishonest. That's the kind of thing they try to put over on me every day. And you think I'm sitting up there in my royal robes having myself a high old time. Just sentencing people to jail and warning those fortunate enough to have so far escaped my wrathful eye that they'd better watch out because I'm going to get them yet."

He was overdoing it, he knew. The effort to show no effort was showing through. There was that rawness in his chest again. He shouldn't have risked the coffee. With his corrosive, grainy voice, the constriction of his throat would not have been particularly noticeable to anyone except Katerine who, bless her dear solicitous heart, noticed everything when it came to the health, comfort and well-being of Eli Chobodian.

With Katerine watching him so closely, he pushed the cup away.

The amazing thing about her was that she looked so young to him, that was the wonder of it. Her skin seemed as smooth to him as the skin of a bride, although he was sure that to her grandchildren she must look like . . . well, like his grandmother had looked to him. If she never ceased to amaze him, it could well be because he had so thoroughly underestimated the girl he had married, in a match made by their fathers, during the early years of their marriage.

Mounting the Bench, he had found himself having second thoughts about arranged marriages. From the beginning he had seen them filing past, the victims of that flute song to spontaneous combustion. Where had it come from, he was soon asking himself, this heavily-merchandised fable that love descended upon you from the heavens with the blessings of a choir of angels upon it? More and more, they came parading through the courts these days, the shipwrecks around whom the vultures circled, the scuttled vessels upon whom the scavengers fed. In the long chronicle of mankind, had there ever before been a civilization that did not feel the necessity of guarding its nubile daughters? Had there ever before been a people, civilized or uncivilized, who did not recognize that a girl of a certain age was an emotional cripple, as needful of the protection of those who loved her as when she had first come to them as a helpless, squalling babe? The accumulated wisdom of the centuries had been cast aside and, for the life of him, Chobodian could not understand who had done it or why.

If Old Chobodian, drawing back to the root, had learned one thing in life it was that there was a natural law that you violated at your peril. The laws of man were arbitrary. They werè changed, equivocated, got around daily. The laws of nature and tribal experience were awesome and unchallengeable. Flout them and they exacted a terrible vengeance.

He made a face, pushing the old-man's thoughts away from him. He had been no better than they. He had been worse. He had let himself think about it and he had not thought enough of Katerine to take the trouble to keep her from seeing.

No fool like an old fool indeed.

She had caught him smiling at her. "Ah," she said, "I can read you like a book. You can't wait to get your hands on that Bannerman. All right, finish your breakfast and go."

"Don't need it. I'm full of vim and vinegar. Better watch yourself tonight, old girl."

"You're getting to be an old goat." She could still get flustered when he jollied her that way, and he still loved to see it—the quick surprised flush, the pleasure that he still wanted her—because it called to mind again the ungainly big-boned girl who could not believe that she could have the luck to be married to him, knowing that he would never have looked at her a second time if the choice had been his own. For the second time that morning Elijah felt the smart of tears in his eyes.

He'd have cast away this diamond to search for pearls.

"I don't like that man," she said.

He pointed out, sternly, that since she had only seen him on television, she was hardly a qualified witness.

"I'm qualified enough. I'm never wrong about people when I feel that strongly. There's something wrong with that man."

"You will see the logical absurdity there. Because you feel strongly, therefore you must be right."

"That isn't what I said. I detect something not quite right in the way he dresses, the way he talks, the way his lips move when he smiles, the way he combs his hair. He is the picture of a . . . what's that word, Eli? It means a clown dressed in a pattern of diamonds? Not harlot . . . harlequin. The man's a harlequin."

"My! I thought you'd be solidly in Bannerman's corner. Knowing the way you feel about Ambose."

"That Turk!"

"The Harlequin and the Turk. If your intuitions are to be trusted, this has all the makings of a historic battle."

Ha! She had been waiting for that. Whenever a man wanted to deride a woman and could not meet her on an intellectual level, he put on a superior smile and threw the word "intuition" at her.

Chobodian put on his best superior smile for her, and did not mention that if he had not answered on an intellectual level it could just have been because she had not set forth any intellectual premise.

"Ambose isn't so bad," he said mildly enough. "You just have to understand him."

"Why?" Her eyes grew cold. "I don't have to understand the man to know I despise what he does."

Ah, but did she understand what he does? "Jim Ambose has an obsession for justice. Don't laugh. What he sees as justice. He is an exceptional courtroom lawyer because he knows what he stands for. When you are living at a time, operating in a field, where, increasingly, nobody knows what they stand for, that can be a considerable asset."

"All tyrants know what they stand for. They stand for tyranny."

It delighted him that she could still become that passionate. But didn't she think she was doing Ambose too much honor? "A strong tide in a time of still waters, yes. But tyrant?" More thoughtfully he said, "An obsession such as his needs an equally strong obsession to combat it. In Norman Bannerman, I believe we may have exactly that. A strong tide running in the opposite direction. What, dear, do you get when two strong tides collide at the neck of a lagoon?"

She knew that it was a trap. "A tidal wave."

"No, a hell of a fight. A *hell* of a fight. Do you think I'd miss out on the chance of having a ringside seat?"

She poured herself a cup of coffee and sat down opposite him. "Not a tyrant, you're right. A bully. A bully who uses all the powers of his office, and yes, of *your* courtroom, to browbeat defenseless people."

He put on a show of horror that such an accusation could be leveled against his court. So it was all his fault, his expression said, was it?

"There is a law, as I understand it, that makes it an offense—I know you've explained the difference between a misdemeanor and a felony to me a thousand times but I don't see the difference and I don't want to anymore." Frowning, she patted the loose ends of her hair. "Now what was I saying . . .?"

"There is a law, as you understand it, that makes it an offense . . ."

"Yes. That makes it an offense for a professional boxer to hit somebody."

"Assault with a deadly weapon. Definitely a felony. Don't worry, I won't bother to tell you the difference."

"And yet you allow, you encourage, you honor a trained professional bully for assaulting an amateur with his voice. There's no other way to put it, dear. To assault him verbally. He is permitted to use his superior mental resources, his legal training and his professional experience on how people react to browbeat a defenseless witness."

He suspected that she was attacking his law, the discipline over which he was master, because she was angry that he had appointed himself to sit on the Tabor case. What did it matter? He liked to hear her talk like this over the breakfast table. He had recognized long ago that she had, unknown to herself, adopted his way of speaking; not so much his ideas or his vocabulary but the rhythm of his speech. Listening to her he could hear himself. Listening to her, he could hear the seasons of their life go rustling past.

He liked to argue with her, too, because it was always such an easy exercise in the triumph of male logic over female emotion: "Ah, you see where your argument fails. The trained brutes are on both sides. The battered amateur has a gladiator ready to ride to his aid in any emergency."

"Lot of good that does him. Picks him off the floor, patches him up and sends him a bill."

"If you sat where I sat," he said, "you would see how often the amateur confounds, fends off, the professional bully. As long as the witness sticks to the truth and can resist the temptation to embellish, to volunteer that least little crumb of self-justification—ah, that instinct for self-justification, that's what does them in. As long, I say, as he follows the instructions his own professional has given him, he has not a thing to fear."

He did not expect her to give in that easily. Not unexpectedly, she shifted her grounds. Into a wondrous tale about how she as an immigrant schoolgirl had been constantly punished for things that had been done by a little blonde witch who the teachers were convinced was a sweet little angel. It wasn't the punishment, she wanted him to understand. "It was the . . . the injustice that rankled."

"Injustice is the worst thing that can befall any man or woman," he said gently. "I'd be the last man in the world to deny that. That's why the law leans so heavily to the protection of the accused."

"And against the accuser. If it favors one side, it can't be very fair. Don't get me off on a tangent, Eli." The look of rebuke told him she knew very well how you lawyers work. "A good liar is always effective. If she's beautiful, so much the better. An ineffective person telling the truth will be ineffective, look guilty, be unconvincing, feel guilty . . . You see the weakness of *your* argument," she said

151

triumphantly. "The amateur cannot forswear, can always be counted upon to embellish, is in constant need of justifying himself."

She had come around to the right answer via the wrong route, something not uncommon to the pursuit of truth, either. Although he told her with his eyes that she had scored heavily, he was not quite ready to throw in his case. "The weakness of your argument, dear," he said, gathering his judicial authority around him, "is more fundamental. You were just attacking Jim Ambose for the vigor with which he does represent the accuser. The accuser being the state itself. I hate to alarm you, but Ambose would agree with every last word you have been saying."

"In which case I withdraw it. Every last word."

For shame, Elijah Chobodian! He had used the professional's tools against the amateur; pouncing upon the casual aside, wrenching it out of context and, through the gentle art of misdirection, taken her eye off what she had really said by flashing Jim Ambose in front of her.

A small victory at the breakfast table. He had proved her whole case while convincing her that he was disproving it. He *should* be ashamed of himself.

"But it happens, dear, that you're right. I was only engaging in the first rule of the trial lawyer, which is: 'When in trouble confuse the issue.' We do the best we can. We keep trying to do better. An ineffective person is ineffective. We cannot, by the act of putting him in the witness chair, turn him into anything else. It is part of the judge's duty, if he's any kind of a judge, to protect the ineffective witness as much as possible. You have my assurance that this judge does."

He had Ambose under control. Ambose was flint but Chobodian was granite. He had every confidence that he would be able to keep Bannerman under control, too. As his mind turned to the coming meeting in his chambers, Chobodian permitted himself a small complacent smile. Bannerman was a noted judge-baiter, and Chobodian welcomed the opportunity to test himself, one last time, against the best. "I was always a fighter, so one fight more, the best and the last." What was that from? It would be a fitting end to a long and distinguished career. At the end of the Tabor trial he was going to announce his retirement. He was saving that as a present for Katerine. His eyes went out the window, and to the problem that had been on his mind all morning. He owed it to Hodapp to prepare him. Would he have the courage to tell him today?

At the door, after the routine peck, Katerine threw herself on him and gave him a great big hug. "Take care of yourself, you old goat," she said.

At the end of the first hour Chobodian felt that it was going well. His wind was good. His voice was strong. And now that the early jockeying was done with, the look of bemusement had disappeared from Bannerman's face. Replaced by a measured apprehension. The only minor irritant was Ambose. Not because of anything Ambose had done or said, but because of everything Ambose had not been doing or saying.

During the preliminary formalities Ambose had remained very much in the background, just slouching around, his old bulging file folder under his arm, looking faintly shaggy and out of place while Nevins and Pawley took up the burden of their roles as hosts. Especially Pawley, who seemed to have something in common with Bannerman in relation to a clipboard. When they finally got around to settling themselves around the conference table in his big, well-lighted library, the judge opened the proceedings by announcing that they were there for a free and open exchange of views. "I propose," he said, "to have Miss Pappas take notes on any matter either party to this lawsuit deems suitable." His firm, controlled glance traveled around the table and came to rest on Bannerman. "Unless anybody here wishes to voice an objection."

Turning to look directly at Marie, Bannerman answered in his rich, rumbling boulevardier voice that he would insist upon having Miss Pappas there under whatever pretext could be conjured up "if only to lend some beauty to this otherwise drab and uninspiring tableau." Chobodian thought he heard somebody whisper, "well, la-de-da," and it could only have come from Ambose, seated halfway up the table with an empty chair between himself and Nevins.

And that had been the last that anybody had heard from Mr. Ambose. Bannerman, paying no mind to him at all, had leaped from his seat to set a chair for Marie at the corner of the table between himself and Chobodian. "The defense is always pleased to have a good understanding," he said, lingering a moment over her chair. "With or without notes. With or without beauty."

"That's what I always say, too, Judge," Nevins drawled. "A good understanding makes for good friends."

From Ambose, nothing.

"Let me be blunt, Mr. Bannerman," Chobodian said. The heavy tangle of eyebrows drew together. "Mr. Ambose and I have tangled before. He knows where I stand. You, Mr. Bannerman, have a reputation for engaging in courtroom histrionics . . ."

Once the rules of decorum to be observed in his courtroom had been laid down and Bannerman's objections dealt with, he read off his rules on publicity. There was to be no talking to the press by either side. "If there is any unattributed information that favors the prosecution," he said, "I am going to assume that it came from the district attorney's office."

"You know how them newspapermen are, Judge," Nevins said. "Sometimes they make good guesses."

Hilliard Nevins, he saw, was playing the bumpkin for Bannerman. Chobodian had always hated that in Hilliard. But that was not the business of the court; that was the business of the district attorney. Nevertheless, Chobodian throttled him with a look. "There will be no more good guesses coming out of this lawsuit."

"I read you, Judge," Nevins said, all rumpled amiability. "I read you good." And Ambose just sat there like a lump, his hands folded neatly on the table, the very picture of inoffensiveness. Could it really be possible that Ambose was overawed by Bannerman and Bannerman's reputation? The corners of Chobodian's lips moved ever so slightly. He'd have to tell Katerine about that.

At the moment he could only turn his attention to the other side of the table to inform Mr. Bannerman that he had had the pleasure for two nights running of watching him perform on the eleven o'clock news. He permitted himself to look faintly amused while he waited for Bannerman to produce a small acknowledging nod. "I have every confidence," he said, clipping the words short, "of being deprived of ever having that pleasure again."

"You have some fault to find with my behavior?" It was said softly, in the spirit of inquiry (if Chobodian chose to take it that way), in the spirit of advancing the good understanding they were all groping for (if Chobodian preferred to take it that way), but with a menacing ripple clearly audible under those serene waters (if Chobodian chose to take it *that* way).

The judge poured himself a glass of ice water, and with a sweeping glance around the table, inquired whether any of the others would care for a drink. When he got to Bannerman, he simply nodded and poured, as if Bannerman had been waiting for the water all along. The water pitcher had always been Chobodian's favorite prop. When you had a lawyer sitting on the fence like this, trying to decide which way he should jump, and how far, Chobodian had found that a small social amenity softened the atmosphere just enough to take much of the wind out of his sails. The pause itself broke into the lawyer's rhythm; the gesture of hospitality cast him in the role of guest in another man's castle. The water cooled.

Cooled and refreshed by his own small sip, the judge smacked his lips and drew a knuckle rather fastidiously over his lips. It had been with great pleasure, he said, that he had heard Bannerman tell the viewing audience that he intended to guard Mr. Tabor's rights with such scrupulous care. They were, he was pleased to be able to tell Bannerman, in complete agreement since the Court was jealous of its own duty in that regard. "If the Court took any inference that the attorney for the defense has been harboring any doubts about either its willingness or its ability to perform its duty I am sure it can be traced to the Court's wholly unwarranted sensitivity."

That brought from Bannerman a long, refreshed sigh and a dazzling smile. He spread his arms out, encompassing his good will. With that reddish hair and those shimmering teeth and those deep blue eyes, he must be something before a jury. Bannerman wanted to assure the Court that no such implication had been intended. Nor, for that matter, had such a thought ever been, no matter how casually, entertained.

Automatically again, beyond any conscious thought on his part, Chobodian had tensed himself to take the expected jolt from Ambose. With such an opening at other times, Ambose had been known to tell an opposing lawyer that he was full of shit. Beyond the empty chairs there was silence. Ambose was either overwhelmed or muzzled, that was clear enough. But instead of the expected sigh of relief at finding himself with a tame Ambose, Chobodian experienced a sense of annoyance, closely bordering on frustration. He hadn't really realized until this moment how much he had been looking forward to taking them both on at the same time.

Bannerman was running a finger along the inside corner of his eye as if he were wiping a speck of dirt away. His eyes were downcast. The impression he created was of a man who knew exactly what he was going to say but, out of deference to the Court, was making it seem as if he were giving it a great deal of thought. "Normally," he said, "I am an impassioned advocate of the civilities. But I must remind Your Honor that a judge is not a king and a courtesy is not a command." He glanced at Miss Pappas, directly alongside him, then pointed to her book to indicate that she was to take this. "I am charged with defending an unpopular client," he said. "I am therefore putting it into the record that I have been responding to the Court's threat that if I should introduce any innovating . . . precedent-shattering was the word used . . . motions in open court without prior consultation, this Court might feel impelled to rule against me as a matter, I take it, of personal privilege rather than as a matter of law. I am also suggesting herewith that Miss Pappas, whose charm illuminates this gathering, make a verbatim transcript of the rest of this meeting for the protection of everybody involved."

Judge Chobodian hadn't been challenged like that in years, and the first shock of outrage was very quickly replaced by a burst of energy, a sort of glandular explosion that rejuvenated and revitalized him. All it came down to, when all was said and done, was that Bannerman had been waiting to pounce on the first issue where he was clearly in the right so that he could force the Granite Judge to give ground. Well, if Mr. Bannerman thought the judge would now rush to place his defense of himself into the record, Mr. Bannerman had another thought coming. Norman Bannerman was about to be swerved.

"Let me be blunt and to the point," Chobodian said. "Every defendant is entitled to a vigorous defense." He let a beat go by. "Within the proper bounds of demeanor both in and out of the courtroom. I have every confidence in your ability to provide the former. I shall make it my business to provide whatever encouragement may become necessary to bring on the latter." He had already warned him that misbehavior in his courtroom was punishable by fines of up to a hundred dollars. He speared him now with his most ferocious look. "I have not found it necessary," he said sternly, "to jail a lawyer for contumacy in, it must be, ten years."

The clammy-sick taste rose to his throat. He saw the apprehension wash off Bannerman's face; he saw the forehead smooth, the bright eyes clear. Like Katerine's amateur he had gone one step too far, he had volunteered what need not have been volunteered. In a battle of wills one did not resort to idle threats, and everyone around this table knew that no lawyer was going to be sent to jail in this one. From the no-nonsense judge who ran a tight ship, he had become the tiresome old codger letting the world know what a man he had been when he had it.

Bury the dead. If he had lost something that might never be regained, he still had what he had. Power was in who told who what he had damn well better do. Judge Chobodian had been granted the trappings of power with his oath of office. He had earned it, as a right, by becoming skilled in its uses. Elijah Chobodian wielded every ounce of the power of his office because he took such great pleasure in wielding it.

The judge, having washed up, had come back looking considerably more relaxed. Now that he had established his authority, he had become reticent and almost benign. Content, as it were, to sit back and act as a sort of moderator between the lawyers.

Hilliard Nevins scratched his head and said, "Yeah, except that I don't see where we have any choice but to ask for the death penalty unless the pretrial examination shows there's something wrong with the man's brain. That's the only thing of it, Judge."

Ambose, having joined the party, was right there with an inimitable contribution of his own. "The whole country's seen the Chief Justice shot. We've got no choice but to go for the whole ball of wax."

"The whole ball of wax," Bannerman said. "What a charming way of putting it. Do you mind if I make a note of that for the next time I appear before the Supreme Court?"

To Bannerman's delight, Ambose's eyes flattened down into slits. Before he could come back with anything, though, Judge Chobodian was breaking in to complain that it was beyond him why they insisted upon misunderstanding him. "I am not asking for commitments," he said, letting his irritation show. "I am merely attempting to determine whether we should dismiss all other possibilities, here and now, and commit ourselves to the inevitability of a trial."

With the ball now so clearly in his court, Bannerman's strategy was to smilingly decline the opportunity to speak first. "I am as willing as the district attorney to genuflect in the direction of the Court," he said, inclining his head toward Nevins. "And as unwilling to take vows of conversion."

Jim Ambose was hunched forward, alongside Nevins, his forearms flat on the table. Where he had been completely removed from the scene before he now seemed to physically dominate it. "You see, Judge," he said looking directly at Bannerman. "The big lawyer from Chicago thinks he's going to get himself a lot of publicity for his scrapbook and he isn't about to let go now." Without moving his head, he let his eyes shift to the judge. "I'm just bouncing that along the table, Judge, because I want to follow your instructions of getting everything off our minds."

Nevins had placed a restraining hand on Ambose's elbow. "Jim has a way of talking before he thinks. He is speaking entirely for himself, and—"

"Oh?" Bannerman broke in coldly. "Then you dissociate yourself from his views?"

"Sure do," Nevins said. "Dissociate myself completely—"

"And disavow," Bannerman said.

"Disavow," Nevins said amiably. "Completely." As far as the district attorney's office of Brederton County was concerned, Mr. Bannerman, like all lawyers of good standing, was acting solely in the best interests of his client.

For just that one moment Bannerman couldn't help but wonder whether he wasn't being whipsawed. But then, thinking better of it, he could see that there was no way of getting around the fact that this Ambose was an odd duck. Nobody in Lowell seemed to be able to figure out whether he ran Nevins, or Nevins ran him, and Bannerman was beginning to see why. Nevins, as he had seen at once, was just another of those political clowns, and that meant he would have to step aside and permit Ambose to run the trials. Which also meant that he would have to assert himself in the pretrial planning to show everybody around the courthouse who was really boss. For Norman Bannerman, who was clearly going to have to isolate Ambose in order to plant Medellia on the others, that kind of setup was perfect.

"I can't tell you how refreshing it is to find a district attorney who gives his underlings such latitude for public disagreement," he said sardonically. "I hope to see much more of it in court."

"If Mr. Ambose keeps battling me in public," growled Nevins, "he won't necessarily be battling anybody in court."

Perfect. With a twinkle of a smile at Pawley, who was looking acutely embarrassed, Norman Bannerman readily conceded that if all the judge was asking for was a commitment to consider whether or not they wanted to make a commitment, he couldn't see how anybody would be able to quarrel with that.

Ambose's heavy voice came down like a hammer. "Why don't you cut out the bullshit, Bannerman!" This time he shook his elbow away from Nevins' restraining hand. "This guy ain't going to give up the chance of trying this case for anything in the world. Go ahead, Hilliard, offer him a twenty-year deal. That would get his man out in ten. Couldn't possibly get that from a jury." He was glaring fiercely across the table, his eyes smoky. "Go ahead, Nooorman. Tell 'em!"

You could not possibly have known from looking at Bannerman that underneath the cold, scornful exterior there ran a swift undercurrent of excitement. "To you, Mr. Ambose, I say nothing. You are in the position of a man offering to sell me a deed of trust to which you do not have title. That's known as fraud. Are you offering me that on your own behalf or on behalf of the district attorney?"

"Ain't offering nothing on my behalf," Nevins said.

"Mr. Ambose," said Pawley coldly, "speaks only for Mr. Ambose."

The moment had come for Bannerman. His sense of the rhythm of these meetings—the sudden weariness that had settled like a shadow over the conference room—told him that in another few seconds Chobodian would announce that they had covered just about everything he could think of and thank them all for their frankness.

"That's what I thought," he said. "You're not the deal-making man in that office, Ambose. If you were, you wouldn't be offering a thing." He patted Pawley's shoulder, as he moved to rise, to show that he was specifically excluding him from what he was about to say. "I know you, Ambose," he said. "I've seen you in every district attorney's office in the country." The distaste he felt for him and his ilk stood forth on every line of his face. "You haunt my days and occupy my nightmares. The lineal descendants of the hangman!"

A sick, oppressive weight bore down on Jim Ambose's chest as he saw Bannerman begin to rise. With a quick desperate movement beneath the table, he pressed his knee against Nevins.

"Damnit, Bannerman," Nevins said in his first show of anger, "you're forgetting this isn't any barroom brawl we're trying here. You're talking as though we're trying to burn a crazy man, and I don't mind telling you that *that* I resent."

"Where the hell does he get off being so high and mighty?" Jim Ambose wanted to know. "When it's him that's trying to get a murderer off? Insanity, my ass!" *(This is your opening, shithead. Do I see your eyes go clickety-click?)*

"Your argument would be salient, Mr. Ambose, if what you were saying happened to be true. It doesn't happen to be." He turned his attention to Nevins. "I had hoped to beat you in here this morning," he said quite steadily, "to suggest to Judge Chobodian that it might be worth considering the possibility of having Tabor studied by a Court-appointed psychiatrist before we cranked this case up." *(Oh, that was very good, Norman. Dropped the bird right into the oven.)* "It was just an idea that had occurred to me, Your Honor, but I saw nothing to be gained previously by throwing it onto the table until I had sounded you out."

"Well, you see . . ." Chobodian was practically aglow. "That's just the sort of thing I had in mind to explore. If you gentlemen will put your personal and professional animosities aside—there's nothing whatsoever to be gained in that sort of thing—we still might be able to accomplish something here."

"Hilliard," Bannerman said. "I am here to give my client the defense to which he is entitled. I am not here to go into court and make a damn fool of myself." There was in his voice a grudging note of weakness. "This is a capital case. I'm debarred from pleading my client guilty if we go to trial, and Mr. Ambose would try to debar me from offering the only defense that's left to me." He wasn't exactly a tyro at this, he wanted them to know. He was perfectly aware that the state couldn't entertain a plea without some independent testimony that the defendant was unbalanced.

Ambose let a mask of suspicion fall across his face. Turning his head away in disgust, he stared at the closed door that led back into the judge's chambers. *("I've got you, you sweet-talking fairy. Go on. Talk around me to the boss. You don't know how easy it's going to be.)*

"Ambose gets overexcited at times," Nevins said. "Pay no attention to him."

"I'll sure as hell get excited," Ambose said, snapping his head back, "if he comes in with some Court-appointed psychiatrist from Chicago." He was glaring straight at Bannerman to let him know he should live so long.

"If ever it should get to that point," said Bannerman, "I would be perfectly willing to accept any qualified psychiatrist we found mutually agreeable. I'm sure there is no shortage of highly qualified men in this state or"—pointedly—"in the forty-nine other, shall we say, neutral ones." *(Norman Bannerman, have I told you lately that I love you? Slipped the joker into the deck while they all had their eyes on Chicago.)* He should have brought young Halpern into this, Bannerman was beginning to think. It was a crime to have this masterpiece pass into history without anybody there to observe and admire . . .

"Shall we say forty-eight," Ambose hissed. "Just for the hell of it, I mean. I mean, just to humor me!"

Pawley and Nevins were exchanging openly inquisitive looks across the table, as of a question being asked and answered. Kneading his forehead, somewhat shamefacedly, Pawley was finally brought to admit that they had been discussing something of the same thing in their first meeting. "In all honesty," he said, "there were certain advantages we were able to espy and certain disadvantages. Jim here is a man with a very keen eye for the disadvantages."

Yeah, and Jim wanted them to know that he still didn't want any part of it. "If he can prove it in open court that Tabor didn't know the nature and quality, let him. Let him prove it in open court under the anvil of cross-examination. This way, for chrissake, the way you two are talking, it would be nothing but a showcase trial."

"The anvil of cross-examination," Bannerman said. "Such a felicitous expression. I'll have to engrave it in my memory book in enduring marble alongside the more eloquent dissents of Oliver Wendell Holmes." *(Look at Jocko burn. Oh, there's a man that can hate with the best of them. I'll give you reason, Jocko. Before I'm through with you, I'll . . .)*

A showcase trial, said Norman Bannerman in all sincerity, was not exactly what he had in mind either . . .

When they got back to Nevins' office they found Rich Caples waiting for them. "Eli's been reading Supreme Court decisions again," he moaned upon hearing of the news embargo. "Why don't he spend more time enjoying life . . . like the rest of our distinguished jurists?"

"No comment," Pawley said. "Except that they are all fine family men and a credit to the American judiciary."

Speaking of good family men, Caples wanted to know, all bullshit aside, what did Pawley think of Bannerman now that he'd had a chance to see him in action.

Pawley struck a reverent pose, his hand to his heart, and harkened to a distant sound. "He has a voice like the bells of St. Mary's summoning the faithful to their Eastertime devotions. And, for the love of the risen Jesus, don't quote me." His finger shot out to Ambose who had sprawled himself all over the sofa. "Quote *him!*"

Jim Ambose said, "Sounded more to me like Jinglebells on a dirty old sleigh sliding down a dirty old hill. You want to quote me, quote me. You don't know how to spell any of the words, ask."

Nevins looked up from his desk sourly. "Only if you want to lose Mr. Ambose his job. And yourself the best leak any courtroom reporter ever had." As the world's leading authority on Nevins' disciplinary glares, Jim Ambose rated this one as purely ceremonial.

Having spent the morning with Sam Tabor, Hal Halpern was waiting in Chobodian's office with the bailiff, Dave Moore, when the meeting broke up. Tabor had been upset that Bannerman hadn't been in to see him since that first day, and the information that Bannerman was closeted with the judge and the district attorney hadn't really placated him. Nor had the news that Bannerman was applying for a writ of habeas corpus so that they could get him out on bail. He was, in fact, even more upset that Bannerman was applying for the writ without consulting him about it. Not only wasn't there any chance of Chobodian setting bail in a murder case, he told Hal, but what was he going to do if he got out, anyway?

Tabor was not the same man Halpern had seen that first day. No longer did he give off the aura of a man who felt he was in control of himself. He was, it seemed to Hal, in a very low, very depressed mood. So depressed that Hal felt called upon to tell Bannerman that he owed it to Sam to see him immediately if only to calm him down and assure him that everything was moving along according to plan.

Bannerman agreed absolutely that Sam should be told constantly that every-thing was going along swimmingly. And, he said, throwing his arm around Halpern's shoulders in the gruffly affectionate way Hal was becoming used to, he expected Hal to keep right on doing it. Their agreement from the beginning, he reminded him, was that Hal was to keep Tabor reasonably happy, reasonably ambulatory and, above all else, reasonably out of Bannerman's hair. "I can either pat Sam on the head every time he feels like crying or I can prepare his case for him. I haven't time to do both." Now then. Sam Tabor's problem having been taken care of, he was beaming down on him. "You haven't asked me how went the historic meeting with my presumed peers in the chambers of the Honorable Elijah."

"How went the historic meeting?"

"Swimmingly. Swimmingly." Just thinking about it brought a warm chuckle to his throat. "Mr. Ambose will never admit it, but I can assure you that he learned a little about the practice of law in there this day." Rubbing his hands together, he chuckled some more.

"There's one thing I should have told you about Ambose. He'll try to get you mad."

"There's one other thing I can tell you about Mr. Ambose," Bannerman said. "He succeeds."

Most of the out-of-town press had gone home to await the first court session. Those who remained were waiting to descend upon Bannerman as soon as he stepped out of the elevator.

"I'll have to talk off the record, boys," Bannerman said, after he had explained Chobodian's edict to them. "I'll answer what I can generally, and trust you boys to protect me. Personally, I think *Sheppard* is being grossly overinterpreted by some of these local jurists but . . ." He made a motion with his hands to show there was nothing much that could be done about it.

Q. How about the merits of Judge Chobodian? Do you think he'd mind too much if you talked about that? (Laughter)

A. A most meritorious public servant. Mount Chobodian. The Granite Judge upon his granite throne.

Q. Does that mean he's solid or that he's tough?

A. Neither. From everything I've seen and heard about the Granite Judge, it seems that the milk of kindness flows. (Laughter) I understand he's four-square against mercy killing. . . . Not against the killing, you understand, against showing 'em any mercy. (Laughter)

Q. You think you've got a hanging judge there?

A. I don't want to be unduly harsh. The milk of human kindness, boys. In his heyday a judge sat in Criminal Court as a *grand seigneur,* meting out discipline to the unruly peasantry. They're beginning to install mandatory retirement in the more enlightened jurisdictions around the country, but we'll just have to confront the situation as we find it here.

Q. What about Nevins?

A. Who? Oh, *Nevins.* He didn't contribute much to the discussion once it got on the finer points of the law. But he was there, taking up space.

Q. Who did you hold the discussions with, Norm?

A. At times it seemed like the First Division of the United States Marines. They seem to come at you in waves.

Q. Was Jim Ambose there?

A. I can state with some authority that Mr. Ambose contributed to the noise. Yes. (Laughter) Now, now, boys. Mr. Ambose tries very hard. I don't think we should laugh at him because he doesn't quite make it.

Q. Ambose says he's going to burn Tabor. He told me that only yesterday.

A. Mr. Ambose is sometimes afflicted with hyperbole, a malady for which there is no known cure except a thumping acquittal. You may spread the word to Mr. Ambose's friends, if any, that he will be a healthier man upon Bannerman's departure than he was on Bannerman's arrival.

Q. Can you tell us something he said? That would give us the flavor?

A. (Long pause) I'm sorry, boys, but Mr. Ambose has a highly forgettable rhetoric. I understand the Lowell Bar Association has voted him its award, annually, over the last five years as the Man Who Has Done Most for Advancing the Batting Averages and Income of the Lowell Criminal Bar. (Loud laughter)

Q. You won't hear any of the Lowell lawyers saying that. The opinion around here is that Ambose is damn good. Vicious but good. He's been too tough for a lot of out-of-town lawyers before, I can tell you that.

A. What's your name, young man?

Q. Conrad Rittenhouse, *News–Chronicle.* I'm thirty-three, but thanks.

A. Yes, you do have that gaunt local look about you. No, he's tough all right. Still pining for the good old days before they outlawed the knout, the mace and the bastinado. But since local pride seems to be sitting up and begging for a bone, I am happy to inform you that I have already become a helpless admirer of DeWitt Pawley. Lowell can take pride in having attracted such a brilliant young attorney to their district attorney's office. And I won't mind one bit, young man, if you quote me on that for local consumption.

Q. What impressed you that much about him? Like something that came up where he did or said something that impressed you?

A. Well, I think I can tell you *this* without crumbling Mount Chobodian. There's going to be a habeas corpus hearing Wednesday morning and I hope to see you all there. (Laughter) Bye now.

Q. Hey! Mr. Bannerman! What's the hearing for again? What are you going to be doing?

A. (Surprised) Why, I'm going to spring Sam Tabor. You're all invited to the coming-out party.

Q. (All voices asking how and why and was he sure and was Hilliard Nevins agreeable.)

A. It isn't a question of whether Mr. Nevins is agreeable. It's a question of Mr. Tabor's constitutional rights. Sam Tabor is entitled to bond, there's no question about that. We've got them by the groin on this. No question about it.

"Listen, boys, you've already got more out of me than you were supposed to. Let us now seek a darkling enclave to which we can all repair for the pleasant tinkle of ice in glass, the gentle ripple of female laughter and a sporting run at *la dolce vita*. And if that isn't enough to entice you bums, I'm paying."

As soon as he had cleared the pebble road that led out of Professor Harmon Medellia's summer home alongside Lake Parridine, Bannerman gunned the rented red Mercedes into the interstate highway and, in what must have been world record time, pushed it up to 120 mph. It was just a kicking up of the heels, though. The gift he owed himself before he coasted back to a safe and sane 80. Once he was there he turned to Halpern with a deep muscular smirk that was not so much a smirk of triumph as of sturdy, solid-based, deeply felt satisfaction.

"And didn't he ramble?" he said softly "Didn't he ramble?"

"He's an idiot!" Halpern said.

Ah, but he was their idiot, Bannerman reminded him. And that made all the difference in the world. Nevertheless, he was observing Halpern very closely. "I have traveled up and down this cockeyed old world of ours," he said, deciding to pass it off with a joke, "and I have yet to see anybody stalk out of a room in a fit of anger because he thought he was being overpraised."

As soon as they were back in the hotel room, though, he picked it up again. "You are going to have to cultivate the habit, Harold, the discipline of mind, of breaking down everything, including men, into their component parts. That's all lawyering is. Isolating what is useful and discarding what is not." Bad men, he said, could do good work. Silly men, he said, indicating the manuscript that Hal now held in his hand, could do excellent work. And madmen, he said, turning to the Van Gogh on the wall, could do works of genius. The thin line. He stared at the Van Gogh intently, his arms folded behind his back. He continued to stare at it for a long, long time, so completely absorbed in it that he had, to all appearances, blocked everything else out. Hal had never seen a man who could

—what had Bannerman's expression been?—climb into himself the way Norman Bannerman could.

When at last he turned back to Halpern it was with a stiff, affirmatory little nod. "Sit down, Harold," he said. "If I'm going to be your daddy, I'm going to have to show you the dark and rheumy side of life." He rubbed his forehead, trying to decide where to begin.

All right. He made a reluctant little grimace, pulling down at the corner of his lips. "Let me suggest to you the first thing a criminal lawyer is not. He is not a patriot. He is not a good citizen. He is not driven by a passion for a just and orderly society." Again he made that curiously reluctant little gesture. "He is not —and this is what distinguishes him from his brothers at the Bar—he is not a joiner. He travels light and he camps alone. He wouldn't run for political office on a bet, and he wouldn't accept it on a platter . . ." A small private smile stole over him. "Unless, of course, he saw an opportunity to subvert the government from within." Because that was exactly what the criminal lawyer's job was. The criminal lawyer's job was to come riding into town on the day of the hanging, pluck the prisoner off the gallows and go riding out again, two jumps ahead of the posse.

The glow of the triumph and exertion of that day, never far from the surface, came rushing back into his face. "We're Saturday afternoon at the movies, that's the truth of it!" He slapped his thigh, gun high. "Beneath this velvet exterior, I'm all leather and buckskin."

Holding his hand right where it was, Norman Bannerman, gunslinger, peered down at Halpern. Crouched and ready. "Harold, do you have an itch?"

An itch? Like a trigger finger?

"An itch. Like you have to scratch."

Sometimes.

"When you scratch it, does it go away?"

Most of the time, he guessed. Sure.

Bannerman positively beamed at him, the joy of well-remembered pleasures crackling out of him. "Then you'll never be a first-class criminal lawyer. Sorry about that." He turned away from him, chuckling. The joke was on Hal. The best he could hope for was to be pretty good. "To be a great criminal lawyer"—he turned back and Hal could see that his eyes were shining more brilliantly, were more blue, than ever—"you have to have an itch that never goes away. Never. If you're on a hunting trip in Kansas and you wake up in the middle of the night you have to find that you're scratching . . . you understand? You have to jump out of bed, throw on your clothes and catch the night train to Omaha." He made a quick, impatient movement with his hand. "Too slow. Too slowwww. You're going to go running out to the airport and charter a plane. You understand?"

Hal wasn't sure that he did. Except that the itch was something far more than a mere craving for new and distant horizons.

After a tiny pause Bannerman thrust both hands under his shirtsleeves and began to scratch vigorously. He was here in Lowell, see, and that meant he was scratching. And when he boarded the plane to leave, if all went well, it would be with that indescribably marvelous feeling of relief and contentment that came when an itch was gone. "But by the time I land, Harold, god help me, the itch will be back and I'll have to start looking for another city where I can go to scratch it some more." He was no longer smiling. Because to have an itch and not be able to scratch . . . he shivered in the excruciating agony of it.

"It's an itch to get back into action," Halpern tried, knowing it was insufficient as he was saying it. "All the time." He could also see that Bannerman was becoming increasingly exasperated. Not with Hal but with himself. He massaged his forehead in those quick hard motions of his, determined not to let go of it until he had made himself clear.

"It's like sex!" Aha, he had it. The moment of conquest, the plunge of pleasure, the sigh of relief. "And then it's going to start again. In an hour, in a day, in a week. It's a discontent that . . ." He looked up, suddenly relieved. Now he really had it. "It's a terminal state of discontent."

Halpern, groaning quietly, pretended to rise. Terminal discontent wasn't quite what he had been looking for when he entered law school. Sorry about that.

It wasn't the ordinary sex drive he was comparing it to, Bannerman wanted him to understand, but with whatever it was that sent a rapist out into the streets in his pursuit after that more universal form of human endeavor. "It doesn't matter whether the woman is beautiful or ugly, young or old. When he needs it, he needs it. The itch is there. The itch is overpowering."

"Hell, you don't have an itch, Norm. You've got a hard-on for Jim Ambose."

An explosion of laughter! Norman Bannerman threw back his head and roared in delight. "Harold, my boy, there are times my hopes for you flag and flicker, but every now and again you come up with something that conclusively proves there's hope for you yet."

Hal felt himself go cold and rigid. "Hope for me for *what?* To become a rapist or a fixer?"

The end of laughter. "Oh? Do I detect the stirrings of mutiny in the ranks? You think you've got a complaint, spit it out."

"Yeah, I've got a complaint. That scene out there with that idiot. If I can't win according to the rules, maybe I don't want to win at all."

The scene, at the beginning, had been confusing. Bannerman had greeted Medellia as an old and treasured friend and after apologizing in a hearty, joking way about "all this gumshoeing," had launched right into an apparently accurate résumé of his rise through the worlds of academe and medicine. "You cannot imagine," he glowed, "what personal pleasure your success has given me."

And all the while that Bannerman was gushing on, cocking his head back and forth as if to find the most favorable angle from which to launch his admiration and affection, the professor, a thin man with a slightly fretful air about him, had been struggling manfully—Halpern could see—not to reveal that before a certain phone call he could not remember ever having talked to Norman Bannerman in his life. And the more he struggled to protect his slightly bewildered reserve against the onslaught, the more battalions Bannerman threw into action. He had particularly enjoyed his monograph on the compulsive lawbreaker, Bannerman told his dear friend, which he had found utterly engrossing, endlessly fascinating and—the pursed lips were prima facie evidence of the reluctance with which he was forced to admit it—highly instructive. To say nothing of the fluidity of the style. He sighed. His look became reverent. "One does not often come across literary talent in the field."

How Bannerman thought he could get away with piling it on that thick to a man of such undoubted stature was more than Halpern, walking alongside them to the house, was able to imagine until a quick sidelong glance at the professor's happily flushed face and diffidently averted eyes instructed him otherwise. "Yes," said the professor, with a limp, simpering smile, "I believe I can say that it has occasioned some little interest in the field." The eyes drifted off. "There are those," he said, his resistance crumbling completely, "who have been kind enough to have referred to it as one of those rare diagnostic breakthroughs."

The room to which he conducted them was highly polished and filled with mementos of the seas (which accounted for the way Medellia was dressed: white pants, hush puppies and a loose gray jacket with the zipper more down than up). A highly polished deck floor, highly polished mahogany walls and a highly polished steering wheel bolted to the floor. Unfortunately the room was so spare and uncluttered that there was only one chair, the swivel chair behind Medellia's desk—a problem their host solved very neatly by ignoring it. If standing there in the middle of the room wasn't enough to make Halpern uncomfortable, he had to endure a complete biography of himself as a product of the Lowell public schools (he had never heard it expressed quite that way before) and the district attorney's disillusioning postgraduate course on the law, who had joined "the old rapscallion lawyer" in the fight to eradicate the crime of capital punishment (the great cause, he now discovered, that bound Bannerman and Medellia together). "While you and I may not live long enough to see the day of ultimate triumph," Bannerman said, more unctuous, if possible, than ever, "we can solace ourselves in the certain knowledge that Harold will." Which left Harold standing there, shifting from foot to foot, while they both cast their envious blessings on him. The lucky young man who would be there on the day of the resurrection.

"Anything I can't tell you about Tabor," Bannerman said solemnly, "Harold, who visits him daily and has his complete confidence, can."

Immediately Medellia became alert and wary. There was no doubt about it, he had less ability to hide his feelings than anyone Halpern had ever seen. He was, he wanted to assure Bannerman, anxious to be of service where he could. "I told Mr. Fletcher that I'd be willing to examine your client and testify exactly how I found him." He forced a smile. A fixed bony smile, tense and sickly. If there was a word opposite to "poker face," that was the word for Harmon Medellia. "You understand, of course," he said, a slight quaver appearing in his voice, "that if as a result of my examination I became convinced that he had been legally sane at the time of the act, that would be the way I would have to testify."

"Harmon . . . !" Bannerman was hurt. If he had wanted it any other way would he have called upon him? "To me, it seems as if the poor boy is an automaton." He exchanged a confirmatory look with his nonconfirming co-counsel, which seemed to establish beyond doubt that they were in complete agreement on that crucial point. And yet, there were other times when he seemed quite normal. But that was wholly up to Medellia to decide. "With your expertise you might even bring him completely out of it which, in itself, would nullify the defense. But that's a risk I'll just have to take." Slowly he began to massage his jaw. More to himself than to Medellia, he murmured, "Wouldn't that be the ultimate irony? Wouldn't that be poetic?"

Drawing his head back to examine the man who had it in him to pull off this masterwork of poetic irony, he announced in a voice of sudden prophecy, "The examining psychiatrist sent to assess the degree of the client's sanity, in the very act of his examination alters the conditions, thereby changing the circumstances and course of the Trial of the Century and—to the consternation of the now rueful defense attorney—ascends to the stand and testifies to that effect."

Hands clasped behind his back, he strode to the window. Clearly, this whole concept was too powerful to be contained within the narrow confines of this room, this house. Norman Bannerman lifted his vision to the skies. "I don't suppose," he mused, "it would be easy to convince a jury of laymen that a man who was insane at the time of the act could have found his way back to sanity through the ministrations of a gifted man of science."

The gifted man of science had moved to Bannerman's shoulder, which was just as well because, behind them, Halpern winced quite openly. "It would be difficult," Medellia agreed. "You have raised some intriguing questions in my mind, I must admit."

Bannerman lay his hand on Medellia's shoulder and looked him squarely in the eye. When at last he spoke his voice was deep and soothing. "We can but make the try. Dare we do less?"

"Can he stand trial?" Medellia asked, rising to the challenge. "Is he competent?"

"Ah-*ha* . . ." Not to Bannerman's surprise, the professor had once again come right to the heart of the matter. That was the very question the Court would be asking. "In between his periods of noncommunication, he seems to be quite normal, quite . . . communicative. But . . ." He turned his palms up, a classic figure of bewilderment. Unwilling, anybody could see, to impose his layman's impressions upon the gifted psychiatrist.

On the purely legal issue, of course, he willingly confided that if he didn't think Tabor was both legally insane at the time of the killing and fully competent to both aid and advise his attorney in his own defense, he certainly wouldn't be submitting Tabor to the kind of racking trial that lay before him. "But," he said, cold and fierce, "what choice do I have? They'd kill that poor sick boy!"

Medellia looked back, utterly shocked. "No . . . my goodness."

"And yet . . ." The anger having melted, he was regarding Medellia with a fond, secret smile. In many ways a gentle and nostalgic smile. "Harmon," he said, "I have never forgotten our conversation in Crete. What you said that night made a very deep and lasting impression." To no small extent, you could see, the whole course of Bannerman's subsequent career had been influenced by it. He clasped his hands together. "That's why the incredible, palpitating rightness of this pleases me so. It's so incredible and *right*. Because it will establish your name throughout the field, nationally and worldwide." His jaws tightened as he contemplated the injustice that had heretofore deprived Medellia of the recognition that was his due; the skin, stretched taut across the cheekbones, rippled in anger at the insensitivity of an indifferent and perhaps unworthy nation and world. "I know it doens't mean anything to you, Harmon, but it does to me."

What Norman Bannerman envisioned, he could now reveal, was not so much a trial as a national seminar. Sam Tabor was going to become the instrument by which they would educate the public. By the time they were through, said Norman Bannerman, the trial of Sam Tabor would be embedded in the warp and woof of both their professions. He rubbed the end of his nose in hard, quick brush strokes. "This is most embarrassing but I feel I may impose upon an old friendship to speak with directness." He would have to insist that whoever accepted this commission agree to devote some time—a year or so—to lecturing and writing. He felt very strongly about that. "It may be selfish of me," he admitted, "but I do feel it to be of the utmost importance that a voice of reason, gentility and scholarship be added to the harsh national cacophony."

"Oh, that's out of the question." Harmon Medellia was already behind schedule on two National Grant projects that were occasioning great interest among his colleagues. It would be two years at the minimum before he would be free to take on anything of so grand a design.

As far as Halpern could see, Bannerman didn't so much as blink. Almost as an aside, more as if he were passing along some mutually distressing piece of news, Bannerman sighed that the legal process was, alas, so time-consuming that it would be a minimum of two years, more probably two and a half, before the appeals were out of the way and it would become possible for a man of conscience to discuss the case in public. "I know it's asking a lot of you," he said. "But I am hoping that your conscience will impel you to hit the lecture trail at that time and, time permitting, to write the definitive work on the compulsive murderer. The definitive biography of the most famous murderer of our time."

Even before they had come into the house Halpern had noticed that Medellia had a way of falling into the most awkward positions. Following the invocation of his busy schedule, he had crossed over to the open doorway and he was now leaning back against the jamb in precarious balance, with one foot on top of the other. "My goodness," he said. "I'm sure I'd find that most intriguing."

On the other hand, Bannerman wouldn't want to leave him with the impression that because he was being perhaps overly apologetic—since he did want him to appreciate the inherent risks and difficulties—that it would not be a most instructive professional experience for him. "This man Tabor is a whole Fourth of July of Freudian sparklers. He trails symbolic meaning in his wake." He had moved easily into his jury-box stance, one hand resting at his waistline just above the gold watch chain and the other free to gesture at will. "And that is why it must be you, or someone of similar character and stature, who gets to examine him before his symptoms become smeared over with the thumbprints of those of your colleagues who, though heavy in pedigree, are lacking—however loath, Harmon, you are to admit it—in that intuitive grasp that separates the truly gifted from the merely learned."

With Medellia willing to concede that the obligation was most certainly there, Bannerman was pleased to be able to tell him that this special appointment as the Court's expert did carry with it a special dignity. Norman Bannerman just didn't happen to think men who had become distinguished in their field should be asked to submit themselves to the heavy-handed badgering of some ten-thousand-dollar-a-year lawyer who had probably finished third from the bottom of his graduating class. "And," he said, "I can assure you that I have known lawyers who are not above resorting to such chicanery. Who . . ." For one fleeting moment, a covert smile flitted along the edges of his lips. And then his face turned stern. His voice even sterner. "Who attempt to crush truth on the anvil of cross-examination." Norman Bannerman could promise him that, as a neutral expert, the examination by both the defense and the prosecution would be respectful.

Oh-oh. As delicately as Bannerman had inserted it, the news that the Court's expert would be subject to cross-examination seemed to have given Medellia second thoughts. He was, at least, rolling his shoulders thoughtfully against the doorway, one foot digging into the other. When at last he pulled himself up, firm and erect, his face was every bit as stern as Bannerman's had been. There, for all the world to see, stood a man who had come to an inflexible decision.

"Fiddle-de-dee," he said.

Fiddle-de-dee?

"I have been on the witness stand before, Mr. Bannerman. I feel perfectly capable of taking care of myself."

FIDDLE-DE-DEE?

"Fine," Bannerman said. Now for the other disadvantages. "I know from what I've heard about you that you are going to refuse to accept any fee from the Court, save for expenses. I think you're right on that."

The strained, bony look had returned to Medellia's narrow features. His high brow wrinkled. Harmon Medellia, you could see, did not find anything so very admirable about turning down a fee.

"Now I want you to understand this exactly the way I mean it, and if it were meant any other way you could be sure I wouldn't have brought our young friend, Halpern, with me."

Well, now at least Halpern knew why he was there. As an offer of good faith.

Whatever Medellia's own wishes on the matter, Bannerman definitely did not see why he should suffer a personal loss. Especially since this could very well have a damaging effect on his future career. The lawyer in him turned grim, the lawyer's tone became faintly ominous. "I don't want to soft-pedal this, Harmon. You will be thrust, like it or not, into the cockpit of public controversy. The seclusion and anonymity so prized by the scholar will have to be forsworn. Because of all this," said Bannerman earnestly, "I would want to pay you my customary fee for a major case and there is no reason why the state has to know about it."

In the ensuing silence Halpern realized that it was the first time Bannerman had left himself with an open-ended question. A big, open-ended question that hung over the room. There was a scrambled smile on Medellia's face. More question than smile. More confusion than question.

"With the understanding," Bannerman said, "that you are in no way working for me or under any obligation."

The lines in Medellia's face were very slow in unscrambling. "Oh no, Norman. That wouldn't be right."

"It's only this. And I will of course respect your wishes on it. If you take a fee from the Court, most people will be inclined to discount your testimony." His voice was gentle and just a wee bit troubled. Sad though it was to say, most laymen believed that expert testimony was bought and paid for. That was the unhappy situation they had to contend with.

Turning his back on Medellia, he moved off in a wandering little circle, hands in pockets, slouching, clearly not wanting to push it, just trying to explain, hopeful that Medellia would understand the importance of this, confident that he would. By going on record that he was testifying without fee, Medellia would be placing the solid stamp of truth on what he was saying and, thereby, doing the greater cause incalculable good. Which was why it had become customary, Bannerman could tell him, for those experts who were most anxious to make their views salient to deliberately eschew their fee. By the time he was finished, his wanderings had taken him back to his original spot in front of the desk. "I've seen it happen again and again, Harmon, and I just don't think you should suffer twofold for your generous offer to contribute your expertise, any more than you should suffer from your devotion and your idealism."

Before Medellia was able to respond Bannerman flung his hands into the air in total surrender in the face of such unrepentent idealism. "All *right.* Let's just leave it at this. I'll see to it that you don't suffer financially."

He flashed his warmest smile, even to adding an extra little wrinkling of the nose. "Just as a matter of curiosity, Harmon, in the event the district attorney changes his mind and I do have to retain a psychiatrist, just what is your fee for testifying?"

Before his very eyes Harold Halpern saw a complete change come over Medellia. The thin, ascetic nostrils flared. His head came thrusting forward. To Halpern he was the image of a prowling fox; peering, sniffing, quickening. In Professor Medellia, transparent as always, you saw a man who did not want to set his price too low, with the resultant loss in both money and prestige, but did not want to go so high that he'd look ridiculous coming down. Halpern would not have been the least surprised to hear him say, "What are you offering?"

He didn't. While he hadn't testified *that* often, Medellia said at last, and never in what might be called a major case, he had heard that five hundred dollars a day was what the top men got.

Oh, Bannerman thought he should get more than that. "A thousand a day is more like it for a man of your eminence." (As casually as he had thrown it out, Bannerman's cadence had somehow buckled back on itself at the end so that the last two words came out as if he were bowing to "Your Eminence.") "But," he said quickly, "as you say, we perhaps shouldn't discuss it beforehand. I quite agree. Let's just leave it that I'll see to it that you're not the loser in the long run."

He smiled playfully. "And just between us girls, I'd be taking advantage of you at those prices. Men of your stature who testify for me in personal injury cases get considerably more." *Considerably* more. But of course good men were hard to find, in forensic psychiatry as in everything else. He shook his head rather wearily. "I do have such a large personal injury practice that when I find a top man who is available on more than a one-shot basis and is willing to travel . . ."

The slow intake of breath accompanied by the reminiscent weariness left little doubt that when he found a top man who was available for steady work the sky was the limit.

Harold Halpern had observed the entrapment of Harmon Medellia with all the fascination of a young doctor who had unexpectedly been given the opportunity to watch a great surgeon at work. Once he had begun to understand what was really going on, he had stood there on the sidelines, rooting for his side to win. When Bannerman pulled it off, he had been proud of him. And though it might now please him to express the doubts that had begun to assail him during the drive back in terms of morality and fair play, his reservations were primarily professional, too. Professional and, in the end, selfish. Of course it wasn't fair. It wasn't fair to the legal process and, most of all, it wasn't fair to Harold Halpern.

He had signed on with Bannerman to observe how a great lawyer conducted a major trial (at least, that's what Halpern now told himself and, at the moment of telling, came to believe) and he would now be watching something else. Why had he read all those cases, attended all those lectures, studied all those techniques —the rules of evidence, the art of cross-examination—learned so much about logic and speech and psychology if, in the end—in the biggest of the big cases, with the biggest of the big lawyers—it was only a matter of fixing a key witness.

The bastards had lied to him.

Even the trust implied by having him sit in on it was a lie. There was not a lawyer alive, himself included, who wouldn't look upon this as privileged information. Oh, if he had been asked in his orals whether he would instantly report such misconduct to the Bar Association, he would, of course, have unhesitatingly answered that he would. Which was like asking a prospective cop whether he'd give his wife a ticket if he caught her speeding. The cop would say yes—he had damn well better say yes—and both he and the examining board would know that he was lying in his teeth. The real question being asked was, "Would you, given this situation, *say* that you'd give her a ticket or are you one of those damn fools who's going to cause everybody a lot of trouble." The Bar Association itself, whatever its public pronouncements, would mark him lousy. He would never be hired by another lawyer—and who could blame them?—nor by any client who knew about his excessive concern for the niceties of ethics and fair play.

And who could blame them either?

Oh yes, Harold Halpern could, with every reason, give voice to the complaint that if he couldn't win according to the rules, maybe he didn't want to win at all. Just as Norman Bannerman could, with reason, nod several times in order to absorb it. And then say, in the parchest of tones, "Your scruples do you credit." And look at him with an aloof sourness, as if he were wondering how he could have been so dumb as to put so much faith in him. And inform him even more sourly that scruples were not exactly what their client had been looking for when he walked through the door. "I wouldn't be at all surprised," said Norman Bannerman, his eyes going wide and innocent, "if he was hoping we'd help him beat the rap."

Jesus Christ, the sight of all those scruples left Bannerman so shaken that he did something he may very well never have done before. He broke into the basket of fresh fruit the hotel management had been sending up daily and picked out an orange. "If I can't win within the rules," he snorted. "Tell that to Sam Tabor next time you see him. You've been telling me he's constipated, that ought to straighten him out in a hurry." He shook his head at Hal, his mouth all puckered. "I'll tell you what you do next time you visit him. Tell him that before they strap him in you'll come by and *moralize* to him for fifteen minutes. He's gonna love that!"

"Look," Halpern said. "I'm not one of your reporters. You can save your act, huh?"

"Just what the hell do you think we're talking about here," Bannerman shouted, "a bowling match? They've given us a license to ride in and snatch Sam Tabor off the gallows and, by god, that's what they expect us to do or get ourselves a very assful of shotgun pellets trying." He was examining Halpern critically now, and yet, somehow, not wholly with disfavor. Maybe, he suggested sweetly, Harold had better get into a line of work more suited to his less adventurous spirit. His mouth twisted violently to one side. "I do a lot of talking to taxi drivers," he barked in his tough-guy voice. "They tell me *hacking* isn't so bad now that they've got it unionized."

Harold started to open his mouth. As ridiculous as it was to drop a pun into the middle of an argument that went to the heart of any future participation he might have in the case, he couldn't resist it. "That," he muttered, "would only be trading one kind of 'terminal discontent' for another."

Bannerman managed to acknowledge it with an automatic wince without allowing it to intrude at any other level. Harold had been in the DA's office, he reminded him. Just how fastidious did he think Jim Ambose was going to be as he went about his gentle duty of disemboweling their mutual friend Sam Tabor?

Out of the side of his mouth again, he barked, "Choose one: Not very. Not much. Not at all."

When instead Hal shot back that he had not the slightest intention of apologizing for either Ambose or any defense attorneys who did things that were equally reprehensible, Bannerman didn't seem to have any idea what he was talking about. "You should be careful about making reckless charges." He was advancing toward Halpern, hand in pocket, a tinge of color high on his cheeks. "If you'd like to refresh your recollection . . ."

All at once Hal recognized a familiar scene. The man strolling toward him was the lawyer approaching the witness chair; the low resonant voice was the courtroom voice; the note of mild shock—most of all, it was the note of mild shock —was the purely professional shock of the lawyer letting the jury know he found it impossible to believe that such testimony could possibly be coming out of this witness. "You will remember," Bannerman was saying, "that if Professor Medellia takes the stand it will be because he was appointed by the Court after being recommended to the defense by the prosecution. Your objection would seem to have been out of order. Do you want to allow it to stand or withdraw it?"

Halpern could understand the high color now, too. Bannerman was still in a state of euphoria at having pulled it off, and nothing would give him greater pleasure than to show Harold Halpern, whose scruples did him credit, what it profited a man to have no scruples. The whole purpose of inviting him up here, he could now see, was to show off. Seeing that, Hal was free to see it all. The real reason Bannerman had taken him along to Parridine Lake was to have someone there who could appreciate the skill and adroitness with which he was handling Professor Medellia. The whole purpose of bringing him into the case in the first place, from the moment he had seen Hal watching (with undoubted awe and bug-eyed admiration) the performance at the airport, was to have a permanent audience. A permanent, portable audience, easy to carry around, always at his beck and call.

> Mirror, mirror, on the wall,
> Who is the smartest lawyer of all?

Not quite. His intention at the moment, it became clear soon enough, was to defend himself by drawing out from Halpern, in overlapping sequence, the advantages enjoyed by the state. He had found the tone he was after, too, and it was going to be persistent sarcasm. Placing one foot on the coffee table, his arms folded across his chest, he began by asking Hal how he had gone about getting an investigator when he was in the DA's office. Oh, *Ambose* had assigned him. How in the world did Ambose manage to do that? Oh, he called Jake Foxx, the *chief* investigator. That meant there had to be a pool of investigators for him to chief it over. Oh, maybe a dozen. How nice for them. *Plus* the whole police department?

"You might say that."

"If I might say it, I will say it. Whenever a witness says he 'might say that,' you know he's made what he considers to be a dangerous admission. Pursue it." *Plus* the state police while they were at it. *Plus* the sheriff's department. *Plus* the FBI, their brown-suited gumshoes and their gleaming laboratories. *Plus* a fleet of taxi drivers who were beholden to the police department for their hackie licenses. *Plus* most of the bellboys in town. *Certainly* every hotel manager. *Plus* an army of white-coated beauticians under whose metallic caps and besplattered fingers some incipient beauty had shot her mouth off.

Against the massed forces and bottomless treasury of the entire city, the defense had only Hugh Fletcher. And how had they got Fletcher? Norman Bannerman would give him a clue. He hadn't signed a voucher and sent it up through Finance. No, Norman Bannerman had paid Fletcher in good American cash money, out of his own pocket. Just as he was paying his occasionally helpful co-counsel from out of his own pocket. Just as, in most of his cases, he had to pay a photographer from out of his own pocket. Just as in most murder cases he had to hire his own specialists in the indicated fields of medicine from out of his own pocket; and even then they would only get to examine the remains or the autopsy report or whatever vital organs might have been pickled and preserved. To get those experts, or for that matter any other witnesses, the defense counsel had to find them, interview them and, if necessary, bring them in from out of town, paying their transportation, hotel bills and meals, all of which could come to a pretty penny.

Oh, it was getting better, of course. There were some states where they had to give you everything they had. But not this one. He had the arresting officer's report, he would now tell Halpern, but that was only because Fletcher had slipped an old police buddy a C-note. Scandalous! People with scruples didn't do things like that. But who, Norman Bannerman wanted to know, was more lacking in scruples? Norman Bannerman who had bribed a police official, or the state which had made it necessary for Norman Bannerman to shell out a hundred bucks for what they, with their bottomless pit, had for free?

"Look," Halpern said, "I'm not on the witness stand. OK?"

It was odd. Despite the crisp, goading way Bannerman had been rattling it off, Halpern had a distinct feeling that in some obscure way he was tuning in on something that was running far more strongly beneath the surface; something personal and bitter and, because it was so completely out of character, more revealing. Could it be that what Bannerman, in his role of Big Daddy, was passing on to him here was the sum of his own accumulated batterings when he himself had been young and innocent and—could it possibly be?—not without scruples?

Or was that only what he was supposed to be getting out of this? Having seen Bannerman play Medellia, could he doubt for one minute that he would hesitate to play him?

When the defense attorney was Norman Bannerman, he would be coming in cold, one lone man. That was why it was usually considered advisable for circuit riders like him to hire an old local hand to help him pick the jury. In a suddenly dry tone he said, "Whenever possible try to hire the sheriff's attorney. You'll find he's well connected politically and, just incidentally, he happens to be the guy who handles the jury list." He gave a sardonic bark of laughter. "When I hire him I'm buying the list. Nobody knows that, of course, except that everybody does. I have found sheriffs too numerous to mention, otherwise thoroughly uncooperative, who have, at first meeting, slipped me the word on who their attorney was and even, in a burst of good will and egalitarian fervor, pressed his telephone number into my hands." If he were not such a trusting sort, Bannerman might have suspected that they were splitting the fee. He had turned to Hal with a mildly challenging look, and when Hal remained silent he nodded to him politely, accepting his reluctance as not so completely unexpected after all. "Not in this county. First thing I asked Fletcher. Oh, you knew that?" Yes, in this county, the district attorney was himself the sheriff's attorney. Hilliard Nevins ran a very tight ship. On the day the veniremen were impaneled the defense would be given a list of names and addresses. Everything else they would have to find out for themselves. "Fletcher should be able to stay about five minutes ahead of me, provided I stall, shadowbox and hold in the clinches. So as much as I would enjoy having you warm my side at all times, Harold, you will quite probably have to dash out from time to time to lend a hand." He would find, alas, that the neighbors wouldn't respond to him as readily as they had responded to the prosecution. Especially in the case of Sam Tabor, who would not be looked upon, he was afraid, as a son who had brought any particular honor to the city.

Not that Nevins had struck Bannerman as a particularly bad sort. Nevins had, on the contrary, struck him as a genial politico, out to make all the friends he could. The dirty work would be shuffled over to Ambose. Bannerman's tongue lapped up over his upper lip. His eyebrows came up, watchful and sly. It seemed to Hal that he anticipated what Bannerman was going to say just a fraction of a second before he said it. "Ambose ever bug anybody while you were there?"

There had been talk.

"Yes," Bannerman said drily. "Scarcely a day goes by."

It might interest Hal to know that he'd had an electronic specialist in that morning to sweep the hotel suite. When the trial started he'd have to have it swept at least twice a week. Expenses, expenses. But it was really very exciting when they found something. As soon as they stopped ooohing and aaaahing they could all put their heads together and try to determine how much damage had been done.

They could, of course, complain to the police, who would launch a vigorous investigation, which would result in a report that would leave no doubt in the mind of any newspaper reader clever enough to follow the intricately woven plot of his favorite comic strip that it had probably been planted by the tricky out-of-town lawyer himself. And if the police did come to the incredible conclusion that he had not been bugging himself, and through some prodigy of police work traced the deed back to Jim Ambose, who was going to prosecute him? Himself?

"Nevins would. Like you say, he's a politician."

"Can't have any scandal in the DA's office without it rubbing off on the district attorney. Elementary politics. Like you say, Nevins is a politician."

And that reminded him. They would assume from the moment they went to trial that their phones were tapped. Hal's home phone included. He wasn't going to be so foolish as to instruct Hal not to tell his wife anything, or to think that a young wife in as publicized a case as this could or should be expected to keep her mouth shut. "I am only going to ask you to instruct your charming missus that she is never to discuss the case over the telephone, even unto its most minor ramifications, because you know as an absolute fact that it's tapped." His eyes sank into Halpern's. "Scare the pants off her, Hal. On that, I want your word." Getting it, his gaze turned affectionate and paternal. It shone, in fact, with that special benignity of a father who has confirmed the continuity of tribe and family by telling his son the facts of life and yet knows that the boy cannot really believe that mama and daddy could be doing such things. "Kind of a dirty ball game, huh?"

"Kind of a dirty ball game."

Against all the natural advantages accruing to the state, the law in its wisdom had given the defense one thing. It had cloaked the defendant with the presumption of innocence. The benefit of the doubt. "To introduce that element of doubt," said Bannerman, "there is nothing I will not do, and feel justified in doing, because they're trying to kill a human being and we're trying to save him." The quiet, measured cadence lent emphasis—gave credence—to what Bannerman was saying far beyond anything any explicit show of passion could have. "They're trying to kill Sam Tabor and we're trying to save him. I don't ever want you to forget that again."

For Harold Halpern, it had been a long, long day. His brain felt as if it had been put through a wringer and come out starched. And yet, he knew that if he did not carry this through to the end he would be right back where he had started, running errands and acting as the mirror through which Bannerman paid himself homage. The case Bannerman had made, though a strong one, had been the lawyer's trick of putting the victim on trial. The defense Norman Bannerman had entered for his client, Norman Bannerman, was that the other guy had made him do it. Self-defense. The specific argument that had been pitched to the personal prejudice of the juror was that as an attorney for the defense, he should be concerned exclusively with the interests of his client.

Harold Halpern shook his head. "You're not pleading to the indictment," he said. "You say reasonable doubt. All right, when you say that, you're talking about working within the process." What Halpern had seen had not been within the process. Was he really saying that there was nothing he would not feel justified in doing? *Nothing?* Would he fix a juror?

"You seem to be under some confusion," Bannerman said coldly. "What is this indictment? Just what do you think you saw me do?"

Hal hesitated for only a moment. "I saw you fix the key witness. I don't *think* I saw. I saw!"

"I could cross-examine you on that, but since you're so understandably sensitive about that, I won't. I'll just remind you what you did see. I paid a call upon the man I thought would be the best possible choice, by background and training, for this particular assignment. I advised him that he would personally come off better if he refused a fee from the Court, and I promised him—since I was the man suggesting it—that I would see that he was not the loser for it. In that regard money was never mentioned." He caught Halpern's raised eyebrows. "In *that* regard money was never mentioned. Money was mentioned only in the event that he became *my* expert, so sworn and so identified. It was specifically stated by both of us—he and I, H. Halpern witnessing—that he was to testify with complete honesty. If he, upon his examination, concluded that Sam Tabor was sane, he was to testify to that fact unhesitatingly. *You* were there. *You* saw. *You* heard."

"I'm not on the witness stand, remember. If I were, you might be able to make it seem that was the way it was. That would only prove you're one hell of a good lawyer, which we already know, and that I ought to find out more about that taxi union. For the record, I don't think you can. For the record, I know what I saw and you know what I saw, and, to quote a big-time Chicago lawyer I know, it's a dirty, dirty ball game."

"Well, Harold . . ." Bannerman spread out his hand quizzically, his jaw slack, his features unclouded. Wasn't that, he seemed to be asking, what he had been trying to tell him all along?

BANNERMAN UNDER THE LIGHTS

Norman Bannerman is sitting in his favorite chair in the hotel room, under the floor lamp. With him are Fletcher and Halpern. It is well past midnight, but they are still going over the transcript of his interview with Mrs. Tabor and, since Dr.

Shtogren had refused to be taped, the typed-up notes of the interview with him that had followed. Opening his eyes, he snorts, "Victorian attitude! Her rights as a woman!" He turns to them with one of those fastidiously disdainful looks that asks where in the bejeezus these guys pick up all that crap. "If we wanted testimony pursuant to woman's right to multiple orgasms, free and unfettered from Victorian stays, I wouldn't let that displaced rug peddler out of my sight."

"Sex should be free, free, free," Fletcher sings. The cigarette sticks to his lower lip as he speaks, the stain clearly visible every time his mouth comes open. "And maybe he should be getting some of that free stuff himself. Yeah."

Methinks I dislike thee, Mr. Fletcher. I don't know why, but methinks me thee dislikes. It is a refrain that runs through Bannerman's head effortlessly, calling for no thought, because it is the refrain that always runs through his head, coming from where he never knows, when the vibrations from the witness stand tell him to get rid of a witness or a prospective juror. "Of course he was screwing her," he says as if it is so obvious as to be unworthy of further discussion. "Where else in this benighted society can a woman go to tell a man she isn't getting what she's needing?"

"I don't think so," Halpern says, and Fletcher's eyes sweep lazily from Halpern to Bannerman and back to Halpern again, in a way which unmistakably says: Get *him* . . . ! While Fletcher and Halpern argue the matter back and forth, Bannerman retreats into a state of half-sleep which lasts until, lifting his head, he says, "Somewhere in the back of these fools' heads they have to know they're wrong. I have a half-assed theory that somewhere between the upper mandible and lower loin there glows a hard little knot of pure truth. Like a pilot light in a gas stove." He flits back into himself for a moment, considering his theory and finding it good. Finding it good, he becomes even angrier. "They *have* to know what a crock this shit about women's rights to free and equal screwing is. Women are made to bear the weight. That's why God drilled them a hollow crotch. You show me a woman who is plump, juicy and bruised and I'll show you a woman who sings at the washing machine."

Fletcher places a finger on his lips. "Don't stop them, Norm. When I was a kid we used to tell them that ourselves. You better do it for me, baby, or you'll get pimples all over your face. The kids today, they've got all the experts working for them, all them psychologists and psychiatrists and asshole professors. I'll give it to you straight, Norm. Nobody likes a big-shot lawyer who ruins a good thing."

Methinks I dislike thee, Mr. Fletcher. I don't know why, but methinks me thee dislikes. . . .

174

BOOK III

The Knife-Throwers

"Experts are a group of men, heavily diplomaed, who preside over the coming disaster."

—*DeWitt Pawley*

Surrounded by his three guards, Sam Tabor paused just inside the courtroom door and squinted at the packed courtroom; the lawyers and officials bustling around inside the rail, the deputies lined up along both walls. In many ways Sam Tabor had never looked better. His face, nicely scrubbed, shone; his sparse hair, freshly wet, glistened. He had lost enough weight so that his freshly pressed brown suit fit him for the first time in years.

Vera had brought the suit to the jail that morning, at Bannerman's direction, along with the new shirt, the freshly shined shoes and the new socks and underclothing. The necktie—rather sporty with its black and gold slashes—had been presented to Sam a day earlier by Bannerman himself when Bannerman had finally come to the jail to introduce Dr. Nicholas Zacharias to him.

Sam had paused in order to search the courtroom for Vera and, after her, any other face that might be familiar. But as the buzz of recognition arose in the courtroom and communicated itself to him, a quite perceptible change came over him; something in the deepening skin tone and in the shy flush of gratification that settled around his eyes. Was all this really for him, he seemed to be saying. You almost expected him to say, *Aw, you shouldn't have done it.*

Bannerman had been taken over to the jury box by Nevins to meet his wife. Mrs. Nevins, a guest in the jury box, was standing, and in an automatic wifely way, flicking the dandruff off Hilliard's shoulders. Lenore sat beside her. Off in the corner, two chairs away, Corinne, looking more stunning than ever, was talking to Marie Pappas. Alerted by the stir of excitement, they all looked to the doorway in time to see Sam being nudged by Johnny Gerard toward his seat at the defense table alongside Harold Halpern.

As Bannerman came bustling across to his client, it was as if a spotlight moved with him. In some inexplicable but bright and tangible way Bannerman managed to transmit the distinct impression that in his own mind the courtroom had become a camera lens focused entirely upon the scene of the famous attorney moving to greet his client, the frame always contracting to the distance between them until it locked on the closeup shot of Norman Bannerman dropping his arm around Sam Tabor's shoulder and whispering into his ear.

The three guards had taken their seats directly behind Sam, the chairs angled so that among them they could keep the entire area under surveillance at all times. Sheriff Stringfellow had followed them down the hallway and into the courtroom, watching their performance every step of the way. Catching Gerard's eye, he nodded in satisfaction.

177

All right, it was starting.

In the three front rows, set aside by Judge Chobodian for the press, the heads went up and down; looking, studying, then dropping back to their notebooks for some furious scribbling.

All right, it was only a habeas corpus hearing, as everyone kept telling everyone else, but the gears of justice had begun to grind. The first faint breeze had begun to blow. It was starting.

Bannerman had been asking Sam how it had gone with Dr. Zacharias that morning, the psychiatrist having returned to the jail to complete his examination. With a final encouraging pat, he transferred his attention to the guards and . . .

. . . the camera lens fastened upon Bannerman full-face, bright-eyed, smiling, shaking hands all around as he told them, with some joviality (democratic sentiments could glow along with him) how pleased he was to have such dedicated officers looking after the safety and well-being of his client. The audience, become a single camera lens, could watch him straighten Johnny Gerard's tie and adjust the set of Blasser's lapels and fuss over the way the suit of the third deputy, Clyde Rainey, hung across his shoulders (democratic sentiment sometimes reducing the object of its concern to unresisting, foolishly delighted props).

And yet, the moment Bannerman turned toward the prosecution table to resume his conversation with Nevins, the spotlight faded and the camera eye unclenched into a thousand separate, sovereign eyes. Some common instinct in the natural-born, well-trained audience had signaled that the performance was over. The Bar rail rose back up between them. Whatever was being said at the prosecution table was, they somehow knew, lawyer business.

Seeing Bannerman and Nevins together, gesturing and explaining, laughing and frowning, expressive and attentive, you were struck with the sudden knowledge that these two adversaries, out of nothing more than the bond of their common profession—with all its mystical ties, its unspoken rules, its perquisites and powers—would always be closer to each other than Norman Bannerman, with the best will in the world, could ever be to his client.

Jim Ambose came into the courtroom last; in long, hurried strides, just a little out of breath, one of the strings on the scuffed old folder flapping. Sam had looked up sharply as he saw him come through the door. He turned to him again, rather wistfully, as Ambose settled into his seat and began to pull some papers out of the folder. Neither Bannerman nor Nevins, sitting right alongside, paid the slightest attention to him. Ambose paid not the slightest attention to them.

"Hal," Tabor said plaintively, "what were all those tests he gave me, that doctor? All those questions? What's that for? What's the sense of all that?"

Hal was explaining that it was all for his own good, that he could trust Mr. Bannerman to do what was right for him, when Furness, the bailiff, who was suddenly at the corner of the inner rail, sang out in a remarkably musical voice, "All stand. Judge Elijah Chobodian is about to enter the courtroom. This Court is herewith in session."

Chobodian looked the crowded courtroom over with no particular pleasure before he told them they might be seated. Amidst the shuffling of feet and scraping of chairs Sam caught Ambose's wandering eyes. Not really looking at him, Ambose nodded, short and snappy. Before Sam could nod back, Ambose had turned away, leaving him, half-standing, both hands flat on the table, the beginning of a smile left abandoned on his face.

"Gentlemen," Chobodian said briskly. "The matter before the Court this morning is the application for a writ of habeas corpus, the relator being Samuel Tabor, filed against Robert S. Stringfellow, sheriff of Brederton County. What say the state?"

Halpern and Bannerman both came to their feet, but Nevins had turned around to whisper something to his chief investigator, Jake Foxx, a large, fat man sitting directly behind him against the back of the Bar rail. He turned back, in his own good time, and came to his feet, scratching his nose. Ambose slid some papers in front of him. "The state stands ready, Your Honor."

Hal Halpern's moment had come and, thank god, his voice was strong and clear as he introduced the Honorable Norman Bannerman of the Chicago Bar and moved for his admission to practice before this Court "in this matter and all subsequent proceedings as chief counsel for Samuel Tabor."

With a mechanical smile Chobodian welcomed Bannerman to his courtroom "for the purposes of the matter now before it." The formal application, he told Halpern, could wait until the opening of the trial.

Just loud enough to be heard at the defense table, Jim Ambose said, "Tough, Norm."

While Nevins was putting in the exhibits attendant to any habeas corpus proceedings Bannerman asked Halpern whether he had heard anything about Pawley. It was not until that moment that Hal realized Pawley's chair was still empty. Frowning at the unoccupied chair, Bannerman said, "Keep your ears open."

Marie marked Exhibit 5, the sheriff's response to the writ, and handed it back to Nevins. Nevins deposited it on the "exhibit table," a low, shelf-like protruberance from the front of the Bench, and said, quite casually, "The state will call its first and only witness, Chief Deputy Booker Phillips."

Stringfellow, who had been holding Booker at the door, gave him a little push toward the stand, not unlike a football coach sending a player into the game. Judge Chobodian sent a mild look of warning out into the stirring courtroom. He tapped his gavel lightly. After a small pause he decided it would be as good a time as any to instruct the spectators as to their rights and duties. They were in the courtroom, he told them, because the relator had the constitutional right to have them there as guarantors of an open trial. "The Court," he said, "expects each of you to be the kind of fair and wholly observant spectator you would hope to have under the same circumstances." He turned to Furness. "Bailiff, will you swear the witness."

Ambose leaned forward in anticipation of rising. Alongside him, he heard Hilliard Nevins say, "I'll take him, Jim."

Typical! He should have known! With so much press here he should have known that Nevins would not be able to resist taking the first witness over. Knowing that, Ambose was kicking himself for not having made certain that Nevins was prepared. The rule of the jurisdiction was one lawyer to a customer, which meant that while Ambose could feed Nevins questions, the Great White Father would have to ask them.

And there went the chance of getting the "You can go to hell" answer he had planted on Booker into the record. For while there was no doubt in his mind that Booker would give that answer to Jim Ambose, he had little confidence that he would give it to Hilliard Nevins.

Leaning back comfortably, with one hand draped over the side of the chair,

Nevins carried the witness from the point where he had heard a shot, seen the Chief Justice fall and spotted Sam Tabor at the bottom of the crowd with a gun in his hand.

Q. You say—Tell me . . . tell the Court, do you see Sam Tabor here in this courtroom?
A. Yes, I do.
Q. For the purposes of the record would you be so good as to point him out?

Booker, who had already turned in his seat to look at Tabor, inclined his head toward him. "He's the man in the brown suit seated at the defense table between the two attorneys."

Nevins was identifying the two attorneys by name when Bannerman arose to announce that he would stipulate the identification.

Booker's identification had been routine and impersonal, the purely professional identification of an experienced witness. It was Tabor who became flustered. Halpern could see the pained, shriveled glance he sent back to Booker in what seemed to be a rather abject apology at having done such harm to his career.

From the stand Booker saw it, too. He felt a surge of pity for Tabor, an emotion so uncalled for, considering who had done what to whom, that it left him oddly unsettled. For Booker had seen something entirely different from what Halpern had seen. The pain he saw in Tabor's eyes was a sympathetic pain flowing back to him; the apology was a sympathetic apology at having put Booker in the uncomfortable position of having to take the stand and identify him, a friend, as a murderer.

While Booker was not a man who was able to analyze what he felt, he was a man who had been trained to see what he saw. The words "disoriented as to . . .", words that attached themselves so naturally to this stand, floated through his mind.

"What," asked Nevins, "did you do then?"

Booker described the arrest. He was not asked whether he had drawn his gun. He was not asked why he had taken it upon himself to make the arrest.

Ambose had slid a glossy photograph over to Nevins. Picking it up without looking at it, Nevins strolled to the witness stand so that Booker could identify it as a true and accurate representation of the arrest, waited for Marie to mark it as State Exhibit Number 6 and then handed it over to Ambose to be passed, in turn, to Bannerman.

"Yes," Bannerman said, examining it. "It seems to me I've seen it before." Since it was a picture that had been on the front page of every newspaper in the United States, there was a little rise of laughter. It died instantly. The spectators were still obviously mindful of the judge's admonition.

The judge had motioned Furness up behind the Bench to instruct him to get him one of the orange pills he would find in the top drawer of his desk. (Chobodian had a tacit understanding with Moore that the pills were to settle his stomach; he wondered whether Furness would recognize that they were amphetamines. Katerine would have a fit if she knew about them.) As Ambose took the photograph back from Bannerman, he glanced surreptitiously toward the inattentive judge and made a quick furtive motion across the lower part of the photograph before he leaned over the table to hand it back to Nevins.

"Hey!" Bannerman, who had caught both the guilty look and the masked motion in his peripheral vision, leaped to his feet and came racing out into the well of the Bar. "Let me see that!" he shouted. "Your Honor . . .!" As Judge Chobodian turned back to find out what all the commotion was about, he was presented with a strange and confusing tableau: Nevins, with his hand outstretched toward Ambose and his head turned sideways toward Bannerman; Bannerman pointing an accusing finger at Ambose and shouting, "I want that back!" Ambose looking startled and holding the photograph behind him, as far away from Bannerman as possible.

"Your Honor," Bannerman thundered. "He did something to that picture!"

Ambose was all meekness and innocence. "What's he talking about?" he asked, in a small bewildered voice. He turned to, of all people, Marie. "Do you know what he's talking about?"

"He defaced that picture," Bannerman declared with grim conviction. He held his hand out. "Your Honor, I want that picture."

Reluctantly, like a small boy caught in the act, Ambose brought the photograph out for everybody to see. "All I did was pull the caption off."

"All you did was deface evidence that had been identified by the witness and thereby became an integral part of these proceedings. What you did was—"

Bannerman saw the contemptuous little smile curl Ambose's lips no more than one second before Ambose saw the look of utter dismay come into Bannerman's eyes. "I didn't know the caption from the *Morning Globe* was all that fascinating to Mr. Bannerman, Your Honor. I was brought up to think that captions were hearsay evidence, and inadmissible." Unclenching his hand, he revealed the crumpled ribbon of paper. "You want to reattach it," he said, leering his shark's grin. "The state will be happy to lend you some stickum."

"No," Bannerman said, trying desperately to preserve some scrap of dignity. "I want to offer it into evidence as Exhibit Number One for the defense to demonstrate that the state has placed a defaced photograph into evidence."

Having finally succeeded in placing the photograph on the evidence table, Nevins sent a chill running down Ambose's back by asking first crack out of the barrel whether there had been any conversation during the drive back to the jail.

"There were a few words exchanged," Booker said.

"Did he seem in control of himself?"

"Yes, sir."

"By which do you understand as a long-time officer of the law, a man versed in lawyer language, that he was oriented as to time and space?"

Bannerman objected that the district attorney was putting words in the witness's mouth.

"On those grounds," Chobodian said, "the objection is overruled." He was looking at Bannerman expectantly. So was Hilliard Nevins. Bannerman continued to look straight at the witness. "Go ahead," Chobodian told the witness, "you may answer the question."

"Yes, sir. He seemed that way to me."

"Knew right where he was at, did he?"

"Yes, sir. As far as I could see."

"Didn't throw any fit or anything like that?" (No, sir)

"No frothing at the mouth?" (No, sir)

"Nothing like that at all?"

That last question was so vague that Booker himself automatically waited for the objection. When none was forthcoming, he said, "I'm not sure exactly what you mean by that, Mr. Nevins."

"I'll withdraw it then. That's all." Tilting his head back, he called across the backs of the chairs between then, "Your witness, Mr. Bannerman."

As Bannerman rose, a rustle of excitement swept through the courtroom, an electric tingle that could be felt in the air.

"Deputy Phillips," he said, "my name is Norman Bannerman. The young gentleman seated at the end of the table alongside Sam is Harold Halpern." He motioned for Hal to stand up. "You may know him from his service in the district attorney's office where he worked alongside Mr. Ambose under the direction of Mr. Nevins."

Everything about him was perfectly open and friendly. "Now, then. Did I understand you to say, Booker . . . may I call you Booker?"

"You may call him Deputy Phillips." Ambose scowled.

Judge Chobodian patted his fingertips together, slowly and meditatively, before he leaned across the Bench to express his confidence that both the traditional relationship between witness and attorney and the amenities between counsel were going to be observed. And if there emanated from him the sense of a tightly held, barely contained wrath, that was exactly the impression he was attempting to convey. The pill was beginning to take effect; he felt much better.

Fortunately.

After Bannerman had led Booker to the point in time where he had heard the shot and turned down the staircase to see Sam Tabor with a gun in his hand, he asked whether Sam had made any attempt whatsoever to escape before he had been engulfed by the crowd.

Before Booker was able to answer Ambose shot forward, his hand cupped around his ear. "I didn't get that last phrase. Before he was what? Would the reporter be good enough to read that back, please?"

"Engulfed by the crowd," he repeated, nodding as if he had found some ancient Oriental wisdom in there.

Normally, a jury not sitting, Judge Chobodian would have been quick to inform him, in the most acrid tones he could muster, that the Court had heard the significant phrase the first time around and had no need of being clubbed over the head with it. But since Bannerman had himself just done a complete vaudeville turn, pantomiming Booker's climb up the stairs and subsequent shock of surprise upon hearing the shot, he settled for a stern and hopefully intimidating stare that fixed Ambose into his chair with the sulky expression Chobodian knew so well. With luck, he'd stay put for a while. (Today, he somehow knew, was not going to be his lucky day. Not with these two.)

A few minutes later, to nobody's surprise at all, Bannerman had drawn himself to his full impressive height and was casting great streams of theatrical amusement around the courtroom. "It would appear, Your Honor, that the state is now fully cognizant of the imprudence, the sheer recklessness of Mr. Nevins' question. Unfortunately, however, the state did ask the question, and when it got its answer it opened the door." If Mr. Nevins and his assistant were now arguing that it was unsportsmanlike of him not to have shut it for them, that was an argument Norman Bannerman was repudiating and rejecting. "Your Honor," he said, like the simple, honest man that he was, "I'd like an answer to my question."

"He's asking him to testify on another man's state of mind, that's what he's doing," said Hilliard Nevins, coming up with yet another objection. "Not even a qualified *psy*-chiatrist could do that." The district attorney's voice was so full of scorn that you would hardly have suspected that no more than a few minutes earlier he himself had asked the very same witness to do precisely the same thing —describe how Sam Tabor had looked to him.

All Bannerman had done to bring on such unwarranted abuse was to inquire of the witness what emotions had been playing across Sam's face as it had been first exposed to him and—having graciously withdrawn that question with a little bow and winning chuckle after Ambose had pointed out that it was vague and general and all-encompassing—asked, as any honest man would, "He just had the gun in his hand and looked dazed?"

Nevins had immediately objected that he was putting words into the witness's mouth. Ambose, clattering to his feet as Nevins was on the way down, added that the witness had already answered that question. "He said he couldn't say. That's his answer. Period."

"And I'm trying to qualify his answer," Bannerman said, just as sharply. "This is cross-examination. I'm not going to have to send you back to law school, am I? Question mark!"

It got Bannerman the first real laugh of the day. It also won for the audience its first gavel-and-glare from the Court.

The barrage had followed. Nevins bawled that Bannerman was seeking an expert psychiatric opinion from a police officer; whereupon Bannerman reminded the Court that in asking the witness whether his client was oriented as to time and space, the district attorney had put the legal question for competency to him; whereupon Ambose reminded the Court that the state's questions had been narrowly limited to the kind of thing, like foaming at the mouth, that was readily observed by any layman. "So what did I ask him?" Bannerman wanted to know. "His rate of breathing? His blood pressure? His skin temperature?" On and on it went, until finally Bannerman assumed the kind of lofty stance that only he could have pulled off and announced, "Despite his assistant's loyal representation to the contrary, it was the district attorney who clothed this witness in the garb of the expert, not I. Where he leads I may follow."

And not a word of it mattered. The objections had been purely tactical. A scouting expedition. Nevins and Ambose were out to find out how the big-shot Chicago lawyer handled himself when he found himself being hammered from both sides while he was trying to zero in on his target. They had discovered that he handled himself very well. Which didn't mean that Ambose wasn't going to let him go without one last shot. Just because the defense attorney had chosen not to assert his client's rights under the rules of evidence, he said, letting a mocking little glance go over to Bannerman—and whether it had been a deliberate choice or a careless oversight, he did not feel was germane here—did not mean that he had forfeited the state's rights for them, too.

Judge Chobodian, who had been sitting back grumpily while Ambose and Nevins were jumping up and down, suddenly leaned forward, his hawk's nose flaring. Was he to understand, he asked Ambose icily, that the state's encyclopedia of objections had achieved some kind of a grand finale and they were actually coming to the Court for a ruling? That being the case, his ruling was that it did not require a degree in psychiatry to read the surface, everyday emotions. "The witness is fully capable of telling us what he saw the way he saw it. The Court is capable of drawing its own conclusions therefrom."

Nor was it lost on Ambose how neatly the judge had sidestepped the whole issue of whether the state had opened any door. You didn't fence old Chobodian in. The old boy was letting the lawyers know that he was going to decide exactly how far he was going to permit Bannerman to go, question by question.

Q. How would you say he looked, Mr. Phillips? Dazed? Surprised?
A. I couldn't say.

A groan went through the courtroom, followed by nervous laughter and then a rising good-natured exchange. Bannerman played it perfectly, dropping his head and smiling ruefully. He was, as anyone could see, a good sport—a man who, despite the serious work in which he was engaged, did not take himself too seriously.

It also happened to be, as they would eventually see, exactly the kind of answer he was looking for. After he had gotten the same kind of answers to a series of similar questions, he toted up for Booker's benefit all the things he hadn't seen. Sam hadn't looked dazed, surprised, exultant or conscience-stricken. He had seen no look at all on his face, nothing at all stirring in his eyes. Where Bannerman's approach to the witness had been rather deferential, rather flattering, his voice now became soft and insinuating. "He had a gun in his hand. He had just fired. For those two brief seconds before the crowd engulfed him, the face of the murderer was exposed to you." (There was a gasp of surprise from the courtroom that Bannerman had come right out and called his client a murderer, since the newspapers had been warning the city that murder was something the state would have to prove.) "I am suggesting that if you, a veteran of twenty-nine years of service, saw nothing it could only be because there was nothing to see. I am suggesting that if you did not feel any fear it was because you could see very clearly, by his demeanor, by his calmness, that there was nothing to fear."

At the word "calmness" Nevins pressed his knee against Ambose's. Calmness suggested psychomotor epilepsy. Score one for Hilliard. Without moving his head, scarcely moving his lips, Nevins said, "Let's give him his head and see where he runs off to. Booker doesn't look like he needs too much help."

Normally Ambose would have said the same thing. Booker's story was Booker's story. After you had jacked it around and turned it inside out and grown hair on it, what had you done? The state would get him back on redirect and straighten it all out in three–four questions. Unless, of course, they happened to get around to talking about the conversation in the car.

With Booker telling how he had responded as quickly as possible after hearing the shot, the first hurdle was not long in coming up. "Good enough," Bannerman said. "To the best of your memory, that's all the defendant is asking of you, sir. We'll get along fine if they'll just leave us alone." And what, he asked, had Tabor said at the time of the arrest?

"Nothing that I could make out. I was trying to peel people off of him."

"Perfectly understandable." The warm, pleasant smile again. "You were far too busy to worry about that. You had other things on your mind."

And so did Bannerman. By the time he got to the conversation in the car he was concentrating entirely upon showing that Sam had been calm, hence normal; and that, under those circumstances, normal behavior constituted "an unnatural calmness." By then it had been determined that Booker hadn't thought it necessary to cuff him, even though he was driving and therefore practically helpless. "You weren't driving with one hand on the wheel and the other covering Sam with your gun, were you?" (No, sir)

"But you had drawn the gun before you got into the car?" (Yes, sir)

"Yes, I thought I remembered some pictures of you with your gun drawn, holding off the crowd. That would seem to suggest that you put the gun away after you got into the car, wouldn't it? Or was it before you got into the car?"

"After. I had to start up the car."

"Oh, *immediately* after. Let's see if we can't narrow the time element down even further. You had drawn the gun to hold off the crowd . . . is that right?" (Yes, sir)

"Then you collared him—is that the colloquialism?—before you drew your gun?"

"That's right. He was in no position to fight back."

"Whether he was or was not in a position is a matter of conjecture. We are trying to deal in fact now, and the fact in this instance is that the moment you were alone in the car with him, safe from the crowd, you put your gun away?" (Yes, sir)

And he had put the gun where?

"In my belt. Tucked inside my belt."

"Is that where you usually carry it?" (Yes, sir)

"Then you didn't take any special precautions due to the fact that you were alone with a murderer?"

"Not that way." But he had been alert. Ready to react in case anything happened.

"But you weren't expecting anything to happen, were you? I mean, seeing that you put your gun away and didn't bother to handcuff him."

Booker wiped his hand across his forehead.

"That's all right, Mr. Phillips. If I'm going too fast for you I'll slow down. You could have stopped the car at any time and put the cuffs on him, couldn't you?" (Yes, sir)

"And if you were in any fear of your life or safety you most assuredly would have?" (Yes, sir)

Now then, he had told the district attorney during direct examination that some words had been exchanged in the car during the drive back to the jail. "I take it they were not of a character and quality to cause you any concern, either?"

"I wasn't paying that much attention, Mr. Bannerman. I was just trying to get him back in a single piece."

"Of course you were. But since you were also alert, just in case anything happened, you would have been particularly sensitive to anything out of the ordinary. Any increase in the volume of his voice, any pitch of excitement, any distraught tremor or emotional outburst?"

"I suppose I would have. I was alert for that kind of thing, yes."

"Whatever words were exchanged, then, were exchanged in a perfectly normal voice? From Sam's side of the car anyway?"

"I don't know what you mean by normal, Mr. Bannerman. What's normal?"

"For most people I'd say the normal tone of voice would be calm and steady. What would you say?"

"For most people. After a murder, you'd make allowances."

"Are you now telling me that you made allowances for Sam? That his voice wasn't normal by ordinary standards?"

"I'm saying I don't know whether I did or I didn't. I'm just not sure."

"Because you were watching the road?" (Yes, sir)

"And not even paying any particular attention to Sam. Considering the gravity of his offense, if you had noticed—he was right alongside you, wasn't he? In the front seat?" (Yes, sir)

"Now, think back, Mr. Phillips, if Sam had been excited, distraught, emotionally agitated . . . *dangerous,* you would most certainly have thought it necessary to put him under some restraint, isn't that right? If only to ensure that you delivered your prisoner intact? In a single piece?"

"Yes, sir." Booker continued to look at him intently, unhappily. "If I thought he was dangerous."

"But you didn't?" (No, sir)

"Because you could see he was calm enough to pose no threat to you?"

"Well, Mr. Bannerman, here's the trouble I'm having here with this. It's what you mean by was he calm. There's was he calm and there's was he not so calm that he was dangerous. You understand? That's the trouble I'm having."

"Very good. I do understand. All things are comparative. Let's say as calm as he is sitting here right now . . . Go ahead, Booker, you can look at him."

"Well," Booker said, looking at him, "that's a very hard thing to say."

"All right then. Let's try it this way: In your best judgment, to the best of your recollection, would you say he was as calm, more calm or less calm, than he is right now . . . That's all right, take your time."

Under Booker's close scrutiny Tabor had, in fact, become rather flushed and flustered. Not very calm at all. Booker was at such a complete loss that Ambose pressed his knee against Nevins'. Without looking at him Nevins shook his head.

"Just about the same," Booker said finally. "More or less."

A roar went up in the courtroom, and although Judge Chobodian banged his gravel angrily he couldn't quite constrain himself from frowning down at Booker and saying, "Mr. Phillips, in my long career as a handmaiden to the law I have had the opportunity of observing all kinds of witnesses in all manner of circumstances. But I have never before had the privilege of hearing any witness, given the choice of three alternatives, cover them all so completely in so few words. Now will you plumb your memory and see whether you might not be able to find something there that would permit you to give this Court a somewhat more helpful answer?"

Booker, really floundering now, took another long unhappy look at Sam Tabor. This time Tabor was smiling along with everyone else inside the Bar rail. Everybody, that is, except Jim Ambose, who was glowering.

"Just about the same," Booker said, surrendering. "As far as I can remember."

"And you found that strange?" Bannerman asked.

"Sir?"

"I am asking whether you found it strange that a man who had just assassinated the Chief Justice of the United States could be that calm. As calm as he is right now sitting in this courtroom." There was nothing warm or friendly about Bannerman anymore. A slight note of irritation had crept into his voice. "That's all right, Mr. Phillips, take all the time you need to think about that, too. No, you don't have to look to Mr. Ambose. He doesn't want to help you. He only wants you to follow Judge Chobodian's instructions to testify to the best of your ability."

A cold fury came over Ambose. The kind of fury that left him clearheaded and poised to strike—and impervious to anything or anybody else. Rising slowly to his feet, he said, "Mr. Ambose wants it on the record that the witness did not look to the prosecution for help, and that the prosecution offered none. Mr.

Ambose wants it on the record that the statement was a figment of the defense attorney's imagination."

"That's all, gentlemen," Chobodian said. "I want no more of that."

"Mr. Ambose also wants it on the record"—he pulled his elbow away from Nevins, and it was no act this time—"that there is nothing in the record to say just how calm Mr. Tabor does look at this moment. He doesn't look very calm to me, seeing that he's on trial here for his life."

With a tight, menacing calm of his own, Chobodian peered down over his glasses and said, "Your observation is in the record. And you will now take your seat."

Nothing was going right for Chobodian, nothing. Here was Ambose offering him this golden opportunity to slap him with a fine—and Chobodian was under no illusion that he wasn't going to have to slap a fine on Ambose sooner or later to bring him under control—and he was going to have to let him get away with it again. Having watched Booker very closely through his struggles, the judge knew that Booker had not made the slightest effort to look to the prosecution table.

Things had started to go wrong from the beginning of the day when Dave Moore had called in sick again and he'd had to start this case with a strange bailiff. That thought, held back all morning, jarred him. It was ridiculous. But ridiculous or not, it was true. The absence of the familiar figure unsettled him. There it was. It was only, he knew, because he was so anxious for this one—the last one—to go well, but still . . . yes, it was time for him to go back to the barn all right.

Norman Bannerman, in that too smooth, too mellow voice, was pointing out for the record that Sam Tabor was not on trial for his life here. That, quite the contrary, he was in the courtroom to petition that bond be set so that he could have his freedom.

"You can sit down, too, Mr. Bannerman," Chobodian growled. "And you can ask the rest of your questions from your seat."

Bannerman, sitting down as ordered, leaned across Sam Tabor to say something to that kid, Halpern. A lot of help he was going to be. Halpern was shaking his head, shrugging. If Bannerman had asked him whether the judge had a right to forbid a lawyer from standing in this jurisdiction, then Halpern was giving him the right answer. Well, he didn't suppose the Supreme Court was going to start overturning verdicts because a trial judge made a lawyer sit down in a bond hearing. To hell with them, anyway. He'd show them who was in charge here. Testily, not looking at anybody, Judge Chobodian directed the reporter to read back the last question.

"Well," Booker said uncertainly, "when you say did I find it strange, I'm trying to decide in my own mind what you mean. I've arrested a lot of people in my time, like you say, and some of them have acted mighty strange."

Ambose, who would have cut an arm off before he would let anybody see that Bannerman had scored, winced visibly.

"Much stranger than Sam?" Bannerman suggested.

"Yes, sir."

"In fact, from everything you've said, Sam didn't act strangely at all. Would you agree with that?

"That's right, sir."

Bannerman was all aglow. "Thank you, Mr. Phillips, that will do very nicely. You've been most helpful."

Halpern was sure that the cross-examination had come to an end right there. A perfect ending to a perfect cross-examination. "Just one more moment, Mr. Phillips," Bannerman said, "and we'll be through. Let's see if we can recapitulate what you have testified to here: As you turned, no more than two seconds after the shot, you saw Sam Tabor, strangely calm and unemotional, and making no attempt to escape. When you reached him and took him from the crowd he was still calm and unresisting but babbling incoherently. Even in the car, he remained so calm that you tucked your gun back into your belt and didn't bother to handcuff him. He remained so calm throughout the drive back to the jail that he engaged in ordinary conversation with you in a normal tone of voice, just about the way we are speaking now."

Ambose had come to his feet halfway through the summation and waited patiently, his arms folded, for the question to be completed so that he could enter his objection.

"In the first place," Ambose said, "the question is obviously mutifarious, about six questions in one. And in the second place, he's citing facts that are not in evidence, and are contrary to the evidence."

Somewhat mischievously, Bannerman asked if he might stand to respond to the objection. Permission being granted, he came skittering to his feet, as if he feared the judge might change his mind. "As much as it pains me to disagree with my revered brother," he said airily, "there were only three questions, not six. I will ask them separately." He was enjoying himself, Halpern could see, and yet there was that little giggle in his voice, a disturbing little giggle that underlay all.

Answering the questions separately, Booker denied he had testified that Sam was either strangely calm or babbling incoherently.

The little smile never left Bannerman's lips. "But you did say, did you not, that you thought it strange that he seemed so calm?"

Ambose was still standing, his arms crossed across his chest. "Now, Your Honor, to draw that conclusion from what we all just heard this witness say would be like saying that if I thought it queer that Mr. Bannerman dresses so fancy, that means I think he dresses like a queer."

Chobodian was utterly aghast. His nose wrinkled up as if he smelled something bad. Leave it to Ambose to go beyond the bounds, and, yes, leave it to be done, the way things were going today, in a way so that Chobodian could not quite pin him down to it. "Mr. Ambose," he said, seizing upon the only available grounds for censuring him, "you will not conduct a reexamination under the guise of an objection. Not in my courtroom, you won't! I will not tell you that again!"

Stunned to speechlessness, in an absolute stupor of outrage, Norman Bannerman still hadn't moved. After the first small, embarrassed laughter, a strained, heavy silence had fallen over the courtroom. When, at last, Bannerman did turn to Ambose, his shoulders were heaving. He took two quick steps toward him, his fists clenched, and stopped. In a low, strangled voice he said, "If you are making any invidious . . ."

"Oh, relax," Ambose said. "You know very well I did exactly the opposite. I was trying to give an example that anyone in his right mind would know wasn't true. That was the whole purpose of it."

The judge was still looking down at Ambose as if he were a freak. The district attorney had swung around in his chair so that he was leaning on his chin, with his back to Ambose and his eyes riveted to the wall behind the jury box.

"Mr. Ambose," Chobodian said at last, "you will apologize to Mr. Bannerman for any misunderstanding, any momentary embarrassment you might have caused him by your ill-chosen and wholly despicable choice of words."

"Why sure, Judge. Glad to."

Bannerman returned to his chair and dropped down, still breathing heavily. The judge had to ask him whether he was finished with his cross-examination. "Yes," Bannerman said woodenly. "We pass the witness back."

As the attention of the courtroom swung back to Hilliard Nevins, Bannerman turned his head very slightly toward Halpern. There was a dull film over his eyes, his lips were very dry. "OK," he said, "now I *am* going to pin that fascist hangman's ears to the rack."

REDIRECT BY MR. NEVINS

Q. How much time was there between the shot and the time you were on him?

A. Seconds. I'd like to think two or three seconds.

Q. Did he have time to turn and run?

A. Very little.

Q. If he wanted to make sure his shot had struck home, that another shot wasn't necessary, would he have had time to turn and run? (No, sir)

Q. When he was on the ground and you were peeling all those folks off him. Did you hear him say anything? (No, sir)

Q. Have you any reason to think he said anything? (No, sir)

Q. Anybody near him, on the scene, did they hear him say anything?

BANNERMAN: Object. Hearsay.

NEVINS: It was this man's job to question them, Your Honor. He did most of the interviewing, taking the depositions, the affidavits and all.

BANNERMAN: And it was the district attorney's job if he wanted that in to bring it in on direct examination. This is redirect.

NEVINS: Withdraw the question.

As Nevins started to pass the witness back, Ambose leaned over his shoulder and whispered something in his ear.

Q. Booker, did you see anything on Tabor's face one way or the other in those two or three seconds you were jumping down the stairs after him? (No)

Q. Do you know how he looked? Calm or agitated or whatever?

A. No, sir. I couldn't say that.

Q. Just the way a man looks who's shot another man?

BANNERMAN: Now of course I object to that.

THE COURT: Sustain the objection.

Ambose whispered something else into Nevins' ear.

Q. Was there a lot of action in the crowd?

A. Yes, there was.

Q. Was Tabor struggling with the crowd or was the crowd struggling with him?

A. Well, it could have been either way.

Q. Could have been either way, huh? No way a man could tell.

RECROSS-EXAMINATION BY MR. BANNERMAN
Q. There was one shot? (Yes, sir)
Q. How many bullets in the gun?
A. Five more. Six altogether.
Q. Is that the same gun you normally carry? Issued by the sheriff's department? (Yes, sir)
Q. So you're quite familiar with it? (Yes, sir)
Q. How fast does it shoot?
A. Well, in exhibition shooting—shooting at a narrow target area—you're supposed to squeeze off five shots inside a second. If that answers it, Mr. Bannerman.
Q. Was there any indication by any movement of Sam's hand or body that he had any intention of shooting again? (No, sir)
Q. As you came down the staircase toward him, were his eyes focused beyond you, as if he were ready, if necessary, to squeeze off another shot? (No, sir)
Q. Did he make any attempt to fire the gun again that you could see?
A. No.
BANNERMAN: That's all we have here, Your Honor.

RE-REDIRECT EXAMINATION BY MR. NEVINS
Q. Did he have a clear shot to get off a second shot?
A. I don't really know. Everything happened awfully fast, Mr. Nevins.
Q. Who got to Tabor first, the crowd or you?
A. The crowd.
Q. Then if he had been about to shoot again, the crowd would have stopped him before you got a chance to?

Bannerman objected on the grounds that it was a leading question, called for a conclusion and that the witness had already testified that Sam was not trying to shoot again.

"We'll withdraw it, Judge," Nevins said with a bored air, as if it were too picayune a point to argue about this late in the day. "The state rests."

With the state's proof of the murder in, Bannerman made the automatic motion for bail to be granted on the grounds that the state had not made the necessary prima facie case that a fair-minded jury would "in all probability" return a death sentence.

But instead of waiting for the judge's automatic denial of the motion he requested permission to make an argument that, should the motion be denied, would serve the additional purpose of constituting his opening remarks for petitioner's case. To Halpern's utter amazement, he then proceeded to cite *Geneen,* the least relevant of the four precedents he had drawn up for him.

For the purposes of this hearing, Bannerman told the Court, he was quite willing to concede that Sam Tabor had shot and killed Wilcke. The only question was whether it had been done by a sedate, formed mind, and by deliberate design. "If both were not present then no expressed malice was present, and under the laws of this state if no malice is present the death penalty is out and petitioner is entitled to bail." It eluded Norman Bannerman quite clearly how the state had shown either.

Geneen, as Ambose now informed the Court, had been cited frequently in bond hearings during his early years in the district attorney's office without having once been ruled upon favorably. "It is, I believe I may say, one of those freak decisions that everyone would like to see go away." The day after George Geneen had returned from the Army, he had walked into the victim's office in the Mercantile Building, emptied a shotgun into him and said, "You will never force your attentions upon my wife again."

Bail had been granted by a perhaps overlenient Court, understandably patriotic during a time of war and understandably sympathetic toward a wronged serviceman. "There is evidence in the present case," the decision had read, "that the mind of the relator became inflamed with passion by the reports of his relatives that his wife had, in his absence, cohabited with her employer."

Ambose pursed his lips and rocked back and forth on his heels, letting his gaze wander to a spot far above the judge's head. "It is perhaps of only the smallest interest that the victim, the cohabiting employer, was a lawyer."

There was laughter from all the lawyers and the lawyers' female employees, who by now filled the jury box and sat in chairs along the wall. Judge Chobodian's nose wrinkled up again. "All right, Mr. Ambose," he said. "Move on."

Ambose rattled the papers up toward the Bench before he dropped them back on the table. "Before Mr. Bannerman could even begin to draw a parallel, Your Honor, he would have to show that his client had a justifiable grievance against the late Chief Justice Wilcke which had left his mind inflamed. With all respect to Mr. Bannerman, what he seems to be trying to show is that all the lights had gone out—for reasons known not to him or me or mortal man, let alone to this Court."

The tight little smile was on Bannerman's lips. "If Mr. Ambose will exercise a minimum of patience and restraint, it is the intention of the petitioner to do exactly that." Bannerman was now rocking back and forth on his heels himself, looking not at all displeased with the way things were going. "While it has been our intention to build our case, block by block, with all deliberate speed, I am quite willing to bow to my friend's importunities and hasten the process by demonstrating exactly who did inflame the mind of the relator, Samuel Tabor, against the Chief Justice of the United States, and why. I call to the stand Assistant District Attorney James Ambose."

Judge Elijah Chobodian's gavel reverberated through the courtroom all the way up to his elbow. "This court will stand in recess for fifteen minutes," he proclaimed. "All lawyers in these proceedings will meet immediately in my chambers."

Without so much as a glance at the reporters who had launched a wild charge toward the door, Chobodian stalked down from the Bench and out the door. It was left to Furness, Stringfellow and the deputies to cut the reporters off in the aisle and warn them that they were to remain right where they were until both the judge and Sam Tabor were out of the courtroom.

Judge Chobodian, seated like the wrath of God behind his desk, made it known to Norman Bannerman that he frowned upon lawyers calling other lawyers to the stand. "It has the smell of cheap dramatics about it and the even more noxious odor of malevolence. I won't stand for that, Mr. Bannerman! Not in my courtroom, sir!" When a lawyer became a witness in Chobodian's courtroom, he was no longer permitted to participate in the trial.

Biting down on his pipe, sending forth short, angry puffs of smoke, he gave

Bannerman the choice of two alternatives. If he should insist upon calling Mr. Ambose to the stand, the Court could not gainsay him. Mr. Ambose would be sworn and Bannerman would be allowed to examine him to his heart's content. And if he could substantiate the claim he had just made . . . All at once, the whole face wrinkled up as if he had come upon something unbelievably loathsome. "If you can substantiate what you have said, Mr. Ambose is off this case and I will do my very best to have him removed from the district attorney's office." If he couldn't substantiate it . . . He leaned back in the chair and examined him tightly. If this proved to be no more than a petty rejoinder in a petty feud, he would remove Bannerman from any further participation in the trial—need he remind him that he had not yet been admitted to practice before his court?—and use whatever powers were resident in this office to have the Illinois Bar Association take action against him.

Now, then. There was still that other alternative. If he chose not to call Mr. Ambose, he was to inform the press that calling Ambose to the stand had been a purely legalistic maneuver that had been settled to his satisfaction in chambers.

Abruptly the pipe went skidding across the desk. "Now then, Mr. Bannerman. You think it over. When we return to the courtroom you will have decided what your course is to be." He looked down at his watch. "We will be returning promptly. In my courtroom, Mr. Bannerman, a fifteen-minute recess means fifteen minutes."

"For the time being," said Bannerman, not in the least perturbed, "I'm withdrawing any intention of calling Mr. Ambose." Looking directly at Ambose, he said brightly, "Why, I wouldn't dream of having Mr. Ambose removed from this lawsuit. I want him on this case. Always reserving the right, Your Honor, to call him to the stand during the course of the trial should the best interests of my client so dictate."

Ambose just laughed at him. "Any time you want me, Norman. I show up in court every day."

Bannerman's first witness, there under subpoena, was Dr. Lennard Swann, and Doc had honored the occasion with a shave. Otherwise he looked exactly like . . . well, like the Doc Swann who had been described by Jim Ambose on one notable occasion as "looking like a scrambled egg made by an eight-year-old girl on Mother's Day so that mama wouldn't have to get out of bed."

In being sworn in he somehow managed to intone the simple words "I do" so that they were in perfect harmony with Furness' lyrical chant. Taken altogether, Doc Swann wrought a change in the quality and mood of the courtroom as completely as if the tumblers and jugglers had come rolling onstage.

After Bannerman had led him through his background and into his current occupation as director of the Lennard Swann Children's Home, he moved into the visit he had paid Sam Tabor on the morning of June 16. "Didn't take you long to get at him, did it?"

"Not much longer than it has taken you to get at me," Swann answered with the relish of a disputatious man who didn't care who knew it.

While the Court was rebuking the witness, not entirely without affection, Bannerman went skittering back to the rail and out beyond the guards so that he could take a clearer look at this droll local character. "What do you say," he asked, suing for surrender. "Shall we start fresh?"

"Would that we could," Swann sighed. "We and all mankind. Fire away."

"Here goes! What was your purpose in examining Sam Tabor?"

Ambose shifted forward in his seat, prepared to cut this off the moment Bannerman got to the examination itself.

And what, Bannerman asked, had Dr. Swann recommended to Sheriff Stringfellow?

"That he was not suicidal." Tapping wood on the arm of the witness chair, Doc Swann swung a quick little beam of gratification toward Sam, his heartfelt thanks for coming through for him so magnificently.

Judge Chobodian observed the little byplay with a heavy sense of unease. Lennard was becoming more erratic by the day.

Almost directly in front of him Norman Bannerman threw back his broad shoulders, bracing himself (and alerting the audience behind him) for the question he had been leading up to: "I now ask you, Doctor, to tell the Court what else you found?"

"Now, Your Honor . . ." Jim Ambose very carefully set his chair aside and moved away from the table. "I am going to object to Mr. Bannerman asking any further questions of this witness at this time for the reason that Dr. Swann is an expert witness employed by the state in this case. Whatever findings he has made and whatever opinions he may hold are his work product and ours." Bending his narrow eyes to Bannerman, he said, "Neither the federal nor the state constitution authorizes the usurpation of his work product under the guise of pretrial discovery."

Bannerman literally—quite literally—smacked his lips as he reminded his learned colleague that the Supreme Court had recently ruled in *Stanton* that the state was not permitted to withhold any evidence that would tend to show the insanity of a defendant. He wasn't claiming that the state was deliberately attempting to withhold such evidence, he told the Court in a tone that indicated he was doing exactly that. The relator's position was that it was entirely possible that in his first, fresh interview Tabor had confided some small fact or some casual passage that, while not considered significant by the state's psychiatrist, as talented as he undoubtedly was, would provide the distinguished array of psychiatrists and psychologists that the defense would be producing with the vital clue to illuminate an otherwise confused and patchy pattern. Just as, he said—his voice hushed and throbbing with the sweet mystery of it all—one drop of the precipitating chemical introduced into a previously muddied solution would turn the liquid, as if by magic, clear and transparent. "How do we know what is in the bottle," Norman Bannerman cried, "unless we are permitted to drink the draught?"

The citing of this most recent of Supreme Court rulings hardly seemed to have sent Ambose into panic. With that lazy, curling smile that always reminded Chobodian of a great hound dog warning you that you were entering his domain, at your peril, Ambose assured the Court that Dr. Swann would be testifying fully at the trial, at which time Mr. Bannerman would be free to cross-examine him to his heart's content. "What we have here is a bond hearing, and there is nothing in the Supreme Court's decision—we read them here too, Your Honor—that gives him any right to use it for a fishing expedition." Ambose was sprawled back against the rail, his hands stuffed into his pockets, his feet splayed out in front of him. "Mr. Bannerman is opening doors and magic boxes and perfume bottles all over this courtroom, Judge, but here where I'm standing all I can smell is fish. That's all in the world it amounts to, Judge."

Bannerman came bounding forward, his arm flung out toward the witness.

"No, what we have netted here," he said, "is a living, breathing medical man who is in the unique position of having questioned Sam Tabor within twenty-four hours of his deed. I would urge upon this Court most strenuously that such information belongs, by its intimate and confidential nature, not to the state but to Sam Tabor himself." Having extended the Supreme Court decision so drastically, even Bannerman looked to be in awe of himself. So, what the hell, he decided to extend it even further. "The privilege of silence, wherever it may exist, belongs not to the state but to the defendant."

Nevins: "Judge, Dr. Swann is sitting there as his witness. He brought him here under subpoena. Is he now telling this Court he has a right to use his work product, obtained by and paid for by the state, when, where and if he wants to, but we won't be able to get the same information at the trial when we put him on? I don't know that I heard him right."

Chobodian asked Bannerman if that *was* what he was saying. "Because if it is, I must say that it is a most novel concept of the law."

What the Court had meant as a mild rebuke Bannerman was quite happy to accept as a compliment. Looking rather owlish about it, he slipped through the opening between the defense table and the prosecution table and out into the well of the Court. "If this Court will permit me to call Dr. Swann as an expert witness for the defense, I personally stand ready to make the necessary financial arrangements to compensate him handsomely for his time." Not only for the time spent here in this courtroom but the time already spent with Mr. Tabor in the jailhouse and making out his report. Flatly and firmly the Court informed him that it did not serve as a broker between lawyers and witnesses. "And unless you have a good reason for approaching this witness, Mr. Bannerman, I suggest that you return to your seat."

Instead, to the astonishment of everybody in the courtroom, Bannerman pressed forward to the witness stand, his hand extended confidently. "You made out a report, didn't you, Doctor?" he asked pleasantly. "Would you hand it over to me, please?"

"No," Swann said. "I didn't make out any report."

Having advanced to the bottom step of the witness chair, Bannerman stumbled a full three steps backward. "You didn't?" he gasped. From the courtroom—from the press rows at any rate—it had every appearance of a dreadfully hammed-up act, wretchedly performed. Seated right above him as he was, Judge Chobodian could see that it was no act at all.

He could also understand why. While the state had been quite correct in arguing that Bannerman was not entitled to call Dr. Swann in a bond hearing for the purpose of eliciting his expert testimony, Bannerman had been every bit as correct in believing that the one thing the defense would be indisputably entitled to under *Stanton* was the report itself. And if a lawyer as experienced as Bannerman could hardly have expected Swann to have been so obliging as to bring the report into the courtroom with him, he could, with reason, have expected to force him to turn it over to him eventually either by direct order of the Court or by serving a subpoena on Swann where he sat.

Owlish no more, Bannerman was demanding that the witness tell him who had told him not to make out a report. Ambose? Nevins? Who and where and why!

"Mr. Bannerman," Doc Swann said at last. "Your needle is stuck on a dead end. Nobody gave me any instructions. I just don't bother to make out that kind of a report."

"You mean you don't make out that kind of report *no more,* isn't that what you're telling us?" He turned stiffly to the prosecution table. "Yes, Mr. Ambose. I can see that you do read Supreme Court decisions here."

As harshly and insultingly as possible, Hilliard Nevins brayed, "He hasn't got any report to give you, Bannerman! You heard him! Now sit down! He knows the rules, Judge!"

Instead—once again—Bannerman wheeled around and planted his foot on the step of the witness chair. His mouth twisted violently. "You made notes, didn't you, Doctor?"

Elijah Chobodian felt a thrill of excitement flow through him. For once a lawyer was coming to town who was everything he was cracked up to be. A match for Nevins & Company, and more. Bannerman was fast on his feet all right, but that wasn't all. You didn't get to the top of this scrap heap unless you had the iron in you. Oh, this was going to be a trial to remember. This was going to be a brightly painted battle wagon to take back to the barn with him.

Not, of course, that Bannerman thought he was entitled to the notes. Chobodian could have written the script from there himself. Lennard would testify that he didn't believe in making notes in the presence of the prisoner but that he had jotted down the important data as soon as he got outside. Bannerman would ask him to hand him the notes, and Ambose would be careful to let Lennard answer that he didn't have them with him before he rose to his feet to shout that the notes were the doctor's personal property, belonging to nobody but himself.

By that time Bannerman had become a big, bashful boy. "Your Honor," he said, folding his hands across his stomach. "As chief counsel for the defense, I must confess to finding myself in a most difficult and embarrassing position." In bringing this witness into the courtroom and putting him on the stand, you see, he had been vouching for his character, integrity and professional competency. He did not have any basis in fact, he now found it necessary to confess, for making that kind of representation. "I believe," he said, with the utmost of gravity, "that this Honorable Court is entitled to have me read Dr. Swann's notes to aid me in arriving at those judgments before I impose him upon these proceedings any further."

"That's all right." Nevins guffawed. "If it will make him any happier, Judge, we'll just stipulate to his witness's competency.'

It seemed to Judge Chobodian that a feeling of good will had suddenly invaded the courtroom, if only in tribute to Bannerman's unlimited imagination and unmitigated gall. It lasted for about a second and a half.

"We are examining Dr. Swann as an adverse witness," Bannerman said, turning back to the witness chair. "I will now ask you, sir, what—"

"He's an adverse witness now?" Ambose yelped, his voice climbing up above five octaves. "It's *his* witness! He's been arguing for ten minutes now that everything he's got belongs to him."

And the state, Bannerman said sweetly, had been arguing with equal force and considerably more success that it didn't. "This is not a defense witness. We had to subpoena him to get him here. The state is now guaranteeing his competency. We most definitely are not. Your Honor, we are invoking the adverse witness rule."

"So what?" Ambose's voice was still in the upper registers. "You can invoke the Holy Bible or . . . or Snow White and the Seven Dwarfs for all I care and that still won't change the fact that you are not entitled to his work product. And," he said, "will you tell him to sit *down,* Judge!"

Chobodian chose not to hear that last part. As nonavailing as it was going to be, Bannerman had earned the right to make his final argument on his feet before the Bench. Stubbornly, holding his ground, Bannerman put forth his contention that an intolerable burden would be placed upon his client's constitutional rights if he were to be denied access to the witness's unique knowledge at the present time.

"Ah yes." Ambose sneered. "I've been wondering when Mr. Bannerman was going to get around to that."

"Ah, yes, those cranky constitutional freedoms, how they do offend thee, Mr. Ambose."

Well put, Bannerman, Judge Chobodian thought while he was frowning his judicial displeasure at them both. "I'll just stop this high-level debate on constitutional law between you two scholars right now by sustaining the objection. You may take your exception, Mr. Bannerman, and pursue the matter in a higher court." More kindly he said, "And I am afraid I will have to ask you to return to your seat, sir."

He watched Bannerman's broad back recede, saw him rap the table reflectively as he squeezed back through the narrow opening between the two tables. For such a big man, he thought as he was reaching for his gavel, he was surprisingly graceful. He nodded to Lennard to let him know he was being dismissed. With any luck at all, they'd all feel better after lunch.

"Just one moment, Doctor," Bannerman said. "If you please, sir."

Doc Swann stopped where he was and turned an inquisitive face to him.

The judge's gavel hung where it was, above the gavel stop.

In his cool, clear clarion voice Bannerman said, "Your Honor, I am withdrawing the subpoena and recalling Dr. Swann to the witness stand as a recording lay witness."

Ambose's head snapped completely around. "As a what?"

Swann, looking up to the judge for instructions, saw the judge looking, somewhat befuddled, down at Bannerman.

"I am calling him not in his professional capacity as examining psychiatrist," Bannerman explained, "but as a witness to the conversation that took place between himself and Mr. Tabor."

"What the hell is he talking about?" Nevins grunted, loud enough to be heard in the front rows behind him.

"Talk," Ambose said. "That's all it is, more of his talk."

Looking to the Bench, however, Ambose could see that Chobodian was smiling down on Bannerman as if he had just found grace in the Court's sight. To Ambose's immeasurable disgust, Chobodian instructed Swann to make himself comfortable while the lawyers were approaching the Bench. Marie joined them to take down what was being said.

Was he to understand, Judge Chobodian asked, that Bannerman wanted to question Dr. Swann not as an expert witness but as a sort of recording secretary to his own conversation?

"That expresses it quite concisely, sir. An analogy might be if I were to ask a doctor who had been driving the car to describe an accident, not as a medical man diagnosing the injuries but for an eyewitness report on what he had seen and heard."

Now that would be treading on very dangerous grounds, Nevins protested. A doctor could very easily testify that somebody's arm was broken and there was a lot of blood around without making a professional judgment. "But how are you going to separate the lay witness hearing the questions from the psychiatrist who asked them when they're one and the same person?"

From the gleam in the judge's eyes, however, it came as no surprise when he informed Bannerman that he was disposed to give him his chance to demonstrate how it was possible to slice a witness in half. "Have you ever done this before?" he asked him. "Can you cite me a precedent that might ease my burden?"

Bannerman was afraid that he couldn't. "It came to me," he chuckled, "in one great rocket-burst." He folded his arms across the Bench and pushed in closer to the judge. "I warned you," he whispered, "I might have you plowing new legal ground before we were through."

On the understanding that Bannerman would steer clear of professional opinion Chobodian gave him permission to proceed. His eyes crinkled, warmly but warningly. "But gingerly, Mr. Bannerman. Gingerly."

It was not, he could reflect at leisure, the wisest decision any wise old jurist had ever made. Gingerly, but always extending the boundaries, Bannerman led the witness through his conversation with his client.

They were not more than a few minutes into the interrogation before Bannerman asked whether Sam had talked about his wife.

A. He did. He said he was glad she'd had the good sense to stay away from the jail. (He was about to say something more, but stopped, suddenly mindful that he was testifying only as to fact, not opinion.)

Q. What else?

A. He talked about how much he enjoyed his job. How good it made him feel to know that he could help some unhappy woman get back her husband. He indicated that he didn't have many close friends. *Any* close friends. He said that he occasionally got depressed, and then he said, "Doesn't everybody?"

Q. Well, Doctor, does everybody? Or would that be an invasion upon your professional opinion?

A. Yes, Mr. Bannerman. Everybody does. Hence the universal plaint: Blue Monday. Hence the rising profits of the drug industry.

Q. Did you find him difficult to talk to? If you can answer that as a layman, doctor. (Laughter) What you observed rather than what you concluded. I appreciate that's cutting it rather thin.

A. Ostensibly, he was open. In reality, he told me as little as he could without incurring my anger.

Bannerman couldn't resist a smile. "Thank you for the diagnosis, doctor. I'd really love to know what you concluded from that. But . . ." He outspread his hands.

Nevins said, "Go ahead. We'd all like to know now."

Ten minutes in, Swann was explaining that during the course of any conversation the psychiatrist would be making scientific assessments as to the values the patient was floating out before him, and while he might discount some of them he would not, unless he was a fool, discount them all. "I am also listening for many other things which I don't know whether Mr. Nevins wants me to go into."

NEVINS: He doesn't.

Q. Would Mr. Nevins object to you telling whether you would call Sam an emotional person? (Pause) Go ahead, Doctor, it appears as though you may answer.

A. Not by the accepted definition.

Q. Well, I guess I'd better not ask you what you mean by that. Did you find him an unstable person?

A. Yes, I'd say he was unstable.

Q. Now let's see if we can extend that one tiny step further. Will you accept the word "irrational?"

Ambose objected rather routinely that with the word "irrational" Bannerman was deliberately and in direct disobedience to his agreement with the Court moving into the professional jargon. And then he decided to stick it to him. "A tactic," he said, "which I, as a layman, find unstable though not necessarily irrational."

Twenty minutes in, with Chobodian looking about as displeased with one of them as the other, a sporadic rattle of coughing was touched off in the audience. Hilliard Nevins turned his yellow pad toward Ambose. On it he had written: "Sit still from here. If he dumb enuf to spit in Eli's face let him."

Jim Ambose sat back, prepared to give Bannerman all the latitude he needed.

Q. Did it surprise you that he didn't seem more agitated?

A. As a layman, of course? A little.

Q. It did surprise you a little? The unnatural calm you encountered did surprise you?

A. My testimony was that Mr. Tabor didn't seem particularly agitated to the naked eye. I did come to certain conclusions as to his mental state.

Q. Which you don't want to tell us?

A. I'll tell you anything the Court wants me to tell you.

But Bannerman just smiled at him and said that he thought they had better leave that subject.

Q. Did he tell you about his blackouts?

A. No.

Q. Did he tell you of any periods of unconsciousness?

A. No, he did not.

Q. Did he tell you about any history of head injuries?

A. No, he did not.

Q. Did you ask him about the shooting?

A. No, I didn't ask him about that.

Q. Did you ask him any questions that would indicate to you whether he was aware what had happened on the stairs of City Hall?

A. I believe I've already told you that I didn't go into the murder, Mr. Bannerman.

Q. I know, but that isn't what I just asked. Listen a little closer, will ya? Did you ask him any questions that would indicate to you whether he was reconstructing what had happened in his own mind, filling in a vacuum of time, or even whether he knew what had happened at all? Were any of your questions directed to that end? I'm not asking for the methodology, you understand. I'm not asking for your analysis or conclusions. (He glanced quickly to the Bench.) I am merely directing your attention toward certain unspecified areas of your conversation.

Swann had begun to study Bannerman with an almost professional curiosity, his brows knit, his head cocked. "Methodology— a word I avoid like a plague —is what you *are* getting into, Mr. Bannerman. Unlike a lawyer, a psychiatrist does not ask direct questions very often in his search for answers."

Bannerman lowered his head. A sweet and rather reluctant smile played across his lips. "If I may make an observation on your observation, Doctor. We can ask them but we don't always get them answered."

"Now, Mr. Bannerman . . ." Swann said, chiding him.

But Bannerman merely widened his smile in admission that the rebuke had been richly deserved.

It couldn't last, of course. Not ten minutes later Chobodian was contemplating Bannerman in a curiously forbidding way, as if he were both relishing and deploring whatever head-to-head confrontation might be in store. "I assumed your good faith, sir," he rumbled. "Don't trifle with me again."

Bannerman apologized profusely and then went right back into the sensitive area of psychological testing that had brought on the warning. Since Dr. Swann had requested permission to interview Tabor again for the purpose of running some tests, perhaps he would be willing to help this Court, with the Court's permission, by listing the tests he had planned to give and would therefore recommend to any qualified psychiatrist who might, at some future time, be appointed by the Court. "Assuming always that you do believe that psychological testing is of scientific value in reaching a differential diagnosis of a psychotic state."

"By god, Norman," Ambose whispered across to him, "you speak the language like a native."

Swann, who had granted rather grudgingly a few minutes earlier that testing could be a useful diagnostic tool if you didn't go overboard on it, reeled off a long list of the generally accepted tests. He shrugged. "And there are half a dozen others that are useful to varying degrees if it's a rainy day and you haven't anything much better to do."

"Weather permitting, Doctor, did you also plan to do any neurological testing?" There was a snap to the question that immediately alerted the prosecution table that he was zeroing in on psychomotor epilepsy again.

"No. I would assume they'd get a neurologist to do that."

Bannerman appeared to be stunned. "You mean you've never done any neurological testing of a prisoner . . . *Doctor*? Not once in your long career as Mr. Nevins' trusted jailhouse psychiatrist?"

Ambose came exploding out of his chair: "We object to this Chicago clothes-horse coming into this Court and casting aspersions on us folks here! We want it stopped right now!"

Chobodian gaveled hard twice, glared at him harder and announced, "That outburst will cost you one hundred dollars, Mr. Ambose."

Bannerman didn't even wait for the courtroom to quiet down. Never looking at Ambose, never turning his head, he said, "Now, Doctor, would you call that outburst by the assistant district attorney unstable or irrational? So there will be no misunderstanding about this, I am calling for a professional opinion here."

"And that," Chobodian said grimly, "will cost you a hundred dollars, Mr.

Bannerman. You may follow Mr. Ambose to the cashier's window. He knows the way."

Down came the gavel. "It is now eight minutes to one. We will reconvene at two o'clock sharp."

With Bannerman going off to the park with a crew of writers, looking for all the world like a luxury liner being escorted to sea by an honor guard of tugs, it fell to Halpern to entertain a most unhappy Dr. Nicholas Zacharias. Halpern could commiserate with him. He had been in and out of the hotel suite for the past two days himself without being able to get Bannerman's ear either.

Zacharias' complaint, he wanted Halpern to understand, had nothing to do with being deprived of the sparkle of Bannerman's company. What had Bannerman's expert witness so upset—and gave Halpern something to think about—was that he had only the vaguest idea of what he was going to be asked when he took the stand. All Bannerman had told him before he had been enveloped by the press was that they were out to show the world that Sam had been impelled by forces beyond his conscious control.

Dr. Zacharias was a tall man, thin but big-boned. His hairline rose in a high bell-shaped arc exposing a mass of large freckles. But his dominant feature after Halpern had talked to him awhile over a bowl of chili at Dorri's proved to be the huge hands with which he gestured incessantly, hands so huge and knobby that they seemed rather like a cop-out for a psychiatrist.

"He's throwing my testimony away, you know," he said, looking up suddenly as he was reaching for a roll. "He didn't tell me when he called me down here to examine his client that I was going to be testifying in any hearing." From his obviously low opinion of hearings and the swift, appraising look that accompanied it, it came to Hal that his luncheon companion was out to pump him. It also came to him that if the doctor had the feeling he was being used as a decoy, the doctor had to be rated as a pretty shrewd cookie. Forgetting Medellia for the moment, unless the EEG tracings came out with scarcely an aberrant wiggle, the defense was very definitely going to be psychomotor epilepsy.

Just between the two of them, and strictly confidentially, Hal confided to Zack —after Zack had asked who Bannerman had lined up to headline his medical defense in the trial—it looked pretty much like both sides were going to settle for a Court-appointed psychiatrist. He supposed, he said, happy to be the bearer of such good news, that was why Norman wanted to get his testimony in now. Just in case, you know, there was no trial.

Zacharias screwed his face up at him. "If you think that," he said, "you don't know Norman like I know Norman." Out of his mouth came the dry powdery sound of laughter. "There'll be a trial." The long, lean face grew more morose than ever as he scooped the roll around the bottom of the bowl to sop up what was left of the chili. "All right," he said, giving them all fair warning. "If he wants my testimony now they're going to be ready for me at the trial."

DeWitt Pawley was sitting in Nevins' office, behind Nevins' desk, chewing on a sandwich which, from the looks of the waxed paper underneath it, had been brought from home. He stared accusingly at his wristwatch as they came in. "That Judge Chobodian runs an intolerably long morning session. Didn't any of you lawyers *tell* him I was up here skulking in my cell." He took a swig of coffee from the paper cup.

"I always said you were better than an empty chair," Ambose said. "Didn't I, Hilliard?" He heaved his shoulders in a great shrug. "But listen, I've been wrong before." Unable to restrain himself any longer, he slapped his thighs in wicked glee. "Don't worry. I had Jinglebells bleeding from all pores. Tell him, Hilliard . . ."

Pawley held what was left of his sandwich out in front of him, contemplating it earnestly. "And that's all the thanks I get," he said, speaking directly to the sandwich, "after my supreme sacrifice." He took another bite. "My sources tell me you may have bit off a little more than you can chew this morning, James A."

"Bannerman?" Ambose scowled. "Shiiiiit. I ate more than that for breakfast." Happily indignant, he plumped himself down in the square-backed chair behind the coffee table. "From all pores, Dee . . ." He looked again to Nevins for support. "I thought he was gonna bust an a-orta all over his fancy vest. I thought they was gonna have to bring in the dog to lick up the blood."

Halpern and Zacharias found Bannerman seated on the courthouse steps surrounded by reporters and photographers. Stretched out alongside the building, guarded by a pair of deputies and set off behind rope, the long line of spectators, still hoping to get into the afternoon session, watched every move Bannerman made.

Zacharias wasn't able to get him alone until they were entering the courtroom to wait for Sam and his guards. "All we need," Bannerman told him soothingly, "is something to set the public mind that there's something odd about this guy. A screw turned wrong." Without, of course, he hastened to add, blowing too much of his testimony for the trial.

The more dubious Zack looked about it, the merrier Bannerman became. "Just leave it to me to set the limits, Zack. Trust me. You can do it sitting down."

Dr. Zacharias on the witness stand was perfectly composed, completely self-possessed. His voice was clear and confident, his manner that of a man who was there to impart his special knowledge.

Bannerman had begun by qualifying Zacharias as both a clinical psychologist and a psychiatrist. He led him through his education, background, his experience in the Army, the boards on which he was a diplomate, his teaching experience, the books and technical articles he had written.

When he said his main interest was in the emotional stresses that brought about and, in some cases, impelled the man to the crime "as an arrow is impelled toward its destination by the release of the bow," Ambose wrote down, "Bet you a Coke that came right out of the book," and slid the pad over to Red Mollineaux who had slipped into the empty seat alongside him. Mollineaux wrote back: "You got a winner."

Dr. Zacharias had not been mistaken in warning Halpern that the DA's office would be ready for him when the trial came around. He had simply underestimated the reach of the informal information-gathering network Jim Ambose had laid over the city. But how could Zacharias have known that the taxi driver who had picked him and Fletcher up at the airport had overheard enough of their conversation to come to the conclusion that he might have something worth passing on to Ambose.

Ambose had immediately called Chicago to talk to Paul Fleigler, an assitant DA with whom he had exchanged a great deal of useful information over the years. "Ring-wise" was the term Fleigler had used for Dr. Zacharias over and over. Fleigler had gone up against him a couple of times himself and he could tell Ambose that he would make every admission he had to make right up to the point where you thought you had him set up for the key question, and then Ambose would find that he couldn't touch him. "A real good witness," Fleigler had said. Why else would Bannerman use him? Within the hour he had called back with their full file on the books and professional articles Zacharias had published, including one book *Born to Kill?* that should be available at any good library.

Mollineaux, who had been set to the task of reading, marking and excerpting the book, was there at the table not because Ambose had any intention of blowing any of that ammunition in a bond hearing but only because Ambose wanted to give him a chance to see his man in action.

Up on the witness stand Zacharias was testifying that in his first meeting with Tabor they had talked for two and a half hours on his personal history, his sexual life, his emotional life, his industrial life and his school life. Returning to the jailhouse early this morning, he had given Tabor two hours' worth of psychological tests. "And, of course," he said, "I also talked at some length with Mrs. Tabor."

"Incidentally, Doctor," Bannerman asked, "in your expert medical opinion, would you recommend that Sam be given a complete neurological workup?"

While Zacharias was running down the list of tests that should be given, Bannerman raised himself to his feet. The litany over, he studied the witness carefully, as if what was coming was of paramount importance, and finally asked him whether he would be willing to serve the Court in that capacity.

If he were asked, said Zacharias, he would be happy to.

"Oh come on, Bannerman," Ambose hooted, "you've already introduced him as your own paid psychiatrist."

"Am I paying you, Doctor?" Bannerman asked, smiling at him.

"I hope so, Mr. Bannerman," the doctor said, smiling back.

Ambose made a small, involuntary movement of his mouth. As usual, Fleigler's information was good. This was a ring-wise witness, all right. And he worked very nicely with Bannerman. Ambose would have to make sure they got no more of those cheap shots off him.

"And did I understand you to say that you'd be willing to serve this Court without fee?"

"If I were asked."

Ambose sat, very still and unhappy. If he objected that this was all selfserving, he would only be giving Bannerman the opportunity to challenge him to take the doctor up on it.

"But you're not volunteering?" Bannerman asked. If he couldn't go one way he could always go the other.

"No, sir." He sucked his cheeks in and stared off into space. "I had the impression you were volunteering me."

As the laughter came at them from the audience, Bannerman lowered his eyes primly to let everyone see that his own man had scored off him. Even Chobodian looked down at the witness from over his glasses and said most pleasantly that while there remained some doubt whether the offer of aid had been volunteered or conscripted, the Court would acknowledge it for the record.

Ambose sank deeper and deeper into his chair.

Having been so nicely established as a man of utter candor and playful wit, Dr. Zacharias was launched into his diagnosis:

Sam Tabor, he said, was suffering from what was commonly called a passive character disorder, which speaking grossly was a form of schizophrenia with paranoid features.

"And now that we have the label and category," said Bannerman quietly, "would you be good enough to describe the symptoms?" Having asked the question, Bannerman settled himself into his chair in an attitude of deep and appreciative concentration, creating the distinct impression that he was turning the ring over to the champ.

Along with the rest of the audience Sam Tabor learned that a person suffering from a passive character disorder saw himself basically—psychologically—as a perpetual victim. He was overwhelmed by the world. Being overwhelmed, the environment around him shaped everything he did. He followed orders because he was too fearful not to. He followed whims because he had no firm life-plan or life-style of his own. "He has a whole complicated system for justifying his own activities, failures and ineptitudes. It's always outside him, don't you see? It's never anything he did, it's something that happened to him, that was done to him. Next time, he keeps telling himself, he'll know better."

Feeling psychologically so weak and helpless, so persecuted by unknown, vaguely hostile forces, he wooed the oppressor by becoming completely passive. By presenting himself as a child, really. A child who should be loved and protected.

Unlike Dr. Swann, he had been speaking with a sense of detachment that was at the same time quite dignified and quite effective. All at once, the tone changed, taking on a heavier, more somber grain. "But underneath it all, there is a burning anger at his own weakness and his inability to cope. There is a secret rage which, when it surfaces, is very easily projected onto those who have made him, he believes, the pitiful creature he secretly knows himself to be."

Sam Tabor had a strained, puzzled look about him as he listened; a trapped, bird-like quality. He was still just plump enough so that, freshly shaven as he was, he looked like a turkey who had been fattened for the axe.

In the field, said Zacharias, they were frequently referred to as the Veterans Administration type, for although their military careers were uniformly unhappy, they settled very naturally into the civil service where they got points for being passive. "Under such conditions," he said, pleased at nature's clever way of righting the balance, "they are able to exist quite comfortably as dependent hacks within a system they could not otherwise tolerate."

Tabor had cocked his head to the side, his mouth slightly open. He seemed to be having trouble breathing.

Bannerman uncrossed his knees and straightened his shoulders. "Now just a minute, Doctor. You're going too fast for me." The question that had occurred to Bannerman was how it was possible for such a man to exist in such a regimented system without his superiors or co-workers seeing that there was something wrong with him.

"Not at all. He is well compensated." The witness had entwined his fingers into a sort of cradle and he was flexing them up and down as if he were cracking his knuckles. "If you remember, Mr. Bannerman, this type is characterized by an ability to blend into the surroundings." He was a meticulous worker. He never missed a day. He was never late. "Because he is afraid, don't you see—even in such a protective, well-ordered environment—that somebody in authority will become angry with him." His smile was automatic and mechanical. "No, if his co-workers think of him at all, it would be to say that he was a real nice guy."

Tabor tugged lightly at Bannerman's elbow. Getting his attention, he hissed, "What's he doing to me? You told me to talk to him. I only talked to him because you told me." Bannerman gave him a quick headshake and a reassuring *shussshhh,* as if he were indeed dealing with a well-loved child, very much in need of protection.

In his professional, matter-of-fact, systematic way Zacharias had been adding that even in that highly protective environment, where promotion—as a symbol of worth—came routinely, such people's need for a protector was so great that they would frequently attach themselves to some superior and identify with him so completely that their own career became, in their fantasy life, inextricably interwoven with his. "We find that the breaking point comes in a significant number of cases when this source of strength seems in danger—or, for all that, is quite legitimately in danger—because the patient feels, don't you see, that with the destruction of his protector he and his whole world will be destroyed, too." He gestured toward the defense attorney to make his point emphatic, the big hands extending far out of the jacket, and for the first time Halpern was able to see him as the man who had sat across from him at lunch. "And that," Zacharias said, "is when he blows sky high."

"You're speaking only in theory, of course? You are aware from the history you took that Sam had no visible superior?"

Dr. Zacharias could not quite contain a superior smile while he was reminding Bannerman that nowhere had he said that there was anything realistic about the attachment. It was *highly* unrealistic. The protector, in most instances, would scarcely be aware of his existence. A certain amount of distance, he added thoughtfully, might even be desirable. "What he represents to him, don't you see, is protection against the hostile forces of the total environment."

He touched the side of his nose lightly, as if he were not quite sure whether to take this phase of it any further. The Chief Justice himself, he said, had been such a figure for thousands of persons all over the country, many of them quite able to function on a daily basis. The polished professional delivery had been replaced by something more casual and intimate—gossipy even. What he was imparting to them now was not mere theory but good, solid inside information. The assassination of the Chief Justice, the very embodiment of protective power, could—and he could tell them from his own experience, *did*—present just such a crisis situation for inmates of mental hospitals all over the country.

Bannerman tapped his fingers a couple of times thoughtfully, and then, quite abruptly, changed the subject. The witness had testified that these people saw themselves as perpetual victims. Was he speaking generally there, too, or could he relate that specifically to Sam?

You could see right away that he could. Yes, fortunately, Zacharias could give him a perfect example. When they had been talking about Sam's failure to take his Librium pill that morning and how that usually left him irritable and jumpy, he could see that Sam's mind, working in concert with his own, had leaped ahead to the obvious conclusion. An expression of tolerant amusement slipped over Zacharias, his voice turned reedy and faintly querulous. "And I could detect the attitude of, 'Now isn't that just my luck. They give me this thing so that I can live in this world, and it becomes the very thing that destroyed me. Can you imagine anybody else in the world having that kind of luck but me?' "

In answer to Bannerman's next question he described Librium as a standard self-administered drug for middle-age depression. "It's excellent for this kind of depression. He gets the blues any time of the day and all he has to do is pop one into his mouth." Smiling broadly, he went through the motion of popping a pill into his mouth. "Beautiful!"

The sheer unguarded joy of it was so discordant—so much admiration for the chemists, so much relish for his own role as witness, and so little feeling for the man he was talking about—that Sam Tabor looked more wounded than ever. This man had come to him as a friend and there he was, up there before the whole world, gleefully *ratting* on him.

Norman Bannerman said, "And so we come at last to the moment of eruption, don't we, Doctor?" He had no difficulty at all in sustaining a dramatic pause. "While I am aware that your examination is as yet too cursory to provide us with a complete emotional workup, could you, at this time, make an attempt, a preliminary stab, at relating the man to the moment?"

Harold Halpern could look at that question and, like Zacharias, exclaim, "Beautiful!" With his opening Bannerman had warned his witness that he did not want him to go any further into Sam's background. With the ending he had cut himself an escape route if he should want Medellia to ignore everything Zacharias was about to testify to.

And yet, on another level, it was a question that posed a question of its own: If his entire testimony was so discardable, what was the necessity of causing Tabor all this pain? The climate of public opinion, Bannerman had said. Could the climate of public opinion really be that important?

That, as even Halpern could see, was irrevelant, immaterial and out of order. If Sam Tabor didn't want to be hurt, Sam Tabor shouldn't have gone out and killed anybody.

Zacharias, picking up the signal perfectly, cautioned Bannerman right back that they were moving into a highly complicated situation. "I can give you one facet of it, which I am doing on the assumption that you wish, for this session, to speculate on the reason why Mr. Tabor directed his murderous impulse at the Chief Justice of the United States, a perfect stranger."

"We're just going to have to object to that, Your Honor," Nevins said. "He's testifying there to a fact not in evidence, and for which no foundation has been laid." With Bannerman—and everyone else—looking to him in various degrees of bewilderment, Hilliard Nevins said, "There's no evidence been introduced in this courtroom that Wilcke was any perfect stranger. Or anywhere else for that matter."

Bannerman gave a surprised little grunt but, recognizing the technical validity of it, asked whether the district attorney wouldn't be generous enough to reassure the people who had elected him that there was no conspiracy afoot against their physical and mental well-being by stipulating that David Wilcke was a stranger to Sam Tabor.

"We're not here to stipulate *anything,*" Nevins growled. "You filed for this hearing because you want to show something. Well, go ahead and show it!"

"In my own good time, Mr. Nevins." He executed one of his more gracious bows. "In my own good way." Moving behind Tabor's chair he placed his hands on Sam's shoulders. "Doctor," he asked, "did Sam here tell you whether he had ever seen Chief Justice Wilcke before? In the flesh?"

Ambose had barely got out his objection that anything Tabor had told him on that score was obviously self-serving before Nevins yanked him back down into his chair and said rather blandly to Bannerman, "We have no objection whatsoever to hearing what the witness has to say to the Court, just so long as we know where the information came from and the Court wants to hear it."

The ruling of the Court, accentuated with an auctioneer-like bang of the gavel, was that the witness might testify to what he had been told, with the understanding that he would be repeating only that portion of any conversation that had led him directly to his conclusion.

Sleek and imperturbable, Bannerman stood behind his client, both hands on the back of his chair. "Let me see if I can't help to cut through this thorny thicket, Doctor. Was there any reason why he picked the Chief Justice as his victim?"

"One of the reasons, needless to say," Zacharias said at once, "was because the Chief Justice was in town." Ring-wise was the word for this guy all right. He had just pulled the teeth out of the question Ambose had been ready to hit him with on cross-examination. "I think we can all see," he continued, "that the Chief Justice could represent many things symbolically." As the final authority on the law, he could represent the stern father or the forgiving father. As a figure who wore a robe, he could represent either the good mother or the cruel mother, depending upon the subject's view of the Supreme Court and of his own mother. He laced his fingers together and held them up so that everyone could see. "Putting them together, he could represent the total parental figure, overly punitive or overly permissive, depending once again upon his personal view. He could also represent the high priest, a link with an even Higher Authority, or the parish priest, a link with the Ultimate. Death."

Despite his best intentions a faint but unmistakable overlay of superiority had settled over him. Having made those introductory remarks, he would now be more specific. "I think you can see, without any great difficulty, how the Chief Justice could become the symbolic representation of the superego, which we can define very loosely here as the conscience, the controller of the ego. Now, Mr. Tabor has a very weak ego, which is always the result of an imperfect transition from the Oedipal period to adolescence." Dr. Zacharias looked first to the Bench and then to Bannerman. "Shall I expand on that for the Court, Mr. Bannerman?"

When Bannerman was rather slow to answer, Ambose called out, "Expand on it for me, Doctor. You've got me all puckered up." He leaned back in his chair just enough so that he could watch how Tabor was taking this.

As Zacharias proceeded through the conventional Freudian explanation of the boy wishing to sleep with his mother, Sam pushed his head forward, his hands clasped against his chest. As Zacharias went on about how the boy, fearing that his father was going to find out and castrate him, abdicated his impulses toward his mother and transferred his identification to his father, Sam gave a little shake of the head that had all the appearance of the blink of a man trying to shake the sleep out of his eyes. He was having difficulty with his breathing again.

"If, for one reason or another, the transference does not take place, the result can run the full range from habitual criminality to homosexuality. With Sam Tabor having a sometimes absentee father, the transition was much more difficult and, at best, imperfectly made."

He flexed his interlocked fingers again in a couple of quick, reflective snaps. "You can see," he said, "how this meshes into the passive character disorder. Once a source of strength has come into the picture, you are already talking about the homosexual relationship."

Chobodian was all puffed up and glaring at Bannerman, not the least bit happy about having this kind of thing flung at the defendant. As for Tabor, his soft, round face had drained and retreated as if it were being jolted by every word. His mouth worked once or twice before he managed to say, in a shaky voice, "What's he doing to me, Hal? Why is he saying that kind of thing?" His eyes flicked over toward Bannerman, with a sort of guarded suspicion, and for a moment Halpern was sure Sam was going to ask how this kind of thing was going to help him. He opened his mouth. He licked his lips. But all he managed to say was, "For crying out loud . . ."

Hal pressed his hand down reassuringly on Tabor's knee, but Tabor, looking up, had caught Chobodian's eyes on him and since what he saw there was not the old man's sympathy and discomfort but the exterior set of judicial displeasure, the warning signal that had been for Bannerman, he folded his hands and shriveled back into himself.

The rest of the examination went off coolly enough, the original sweaty interest in the courtroom diminishing steadily as the spectators came to understand that they were not going to find out as much about Sam Tabor *qua* Sam Tabor as they had initially thought.

Ambose's first question, snapped out bluntly, was, "Are you saying it was a whim?"

With Dr. Zacharias showing that he didn't understand what in the world Ambose was talking about, Ambose scowled. "Well, you said about ten minutes ago that these people in this passive disorder thing were always following *whims.* Isn't that what you said? If you've fogotten already, we can have it read back for you."

The witness moved his shoulders disparagingly to let everybody know that as a man experienced in the ways of prosecutors he was letting this kind of thing roll right off of him. He had cited the tendency to follow whims as one of the symptoms in an overall syndrome, that was all. Not even a symptom really, a characteristic.

"Why did he kill him then?"

"To answer that, sir, I would have to examine Mr. Tabor far, far more extensively than I have been able to in the limited time that has been afforded to me."

"You don't know, is that what you're telling us?" Ambose raised his eyes triumphantly to the Bench, and then twisted his head around to afford the whole courtroom the full impact of his profile.

Patiently and with quiet dignity, Dr. Zacharias said, "I don't know enough at this stage to go any further than I have gone." The doctor's eyes were large and sorrowful, and through some miracle of chemistry they managed to inform his audience that he was saddest of all for the prosecutor for not having the wit to comprehend that Dr. Zacharias was, despite his professional caution, at the very brink of discovery.

It told Ambose, once again, that it was no second-stringer he was up against here. And how it galled him. He had read Bannerman right on his purposes for wanting the hearing. Off that same reading, he should have known he would be bringing in a top man and that they would be keeping his testimony as general as possible. And yet, on that crucial point, he must now admit, he had allowed wishful thinking to take over. It was almost enough to convince him that the best thing to do, now that he had put the testimony into its proper perspective, was to sit down and let Bannerman and the boss-man fight to see who'd get to make the motion to dismiss the writ first.

Almost. Something stirring just outside the membrane told him he knew something he didn't know he knew yet. "Come on, Ambose," it urged. "Go on with it." He glanced down at his pad, hoping to find a clue. The only note he had made to himself was: Schitzo w/paranoid.

Well, all he could do was get up on his feet and keep talking, bobbing and weaving like a lawyer in a strange jurisdiction until he got the feel of the ground under his feet. "All right, Doctor. Now, I'm not sure about this connection you've made between murder and homosexuality. You want to clear it up for me?"

"Shooting can be a homosexual act. Symbolically. Any violent attack can be." Put simply, there were two kinds of impulses that could be overwhelming. Sexual and aggressive. "Where a sexual block exists," he said, "the sexual impulse can come out in aggression."

Ambose was in the difficult position where he had to conduct his examination with one part of his mind while his other mind—more active, more lucid—was chasing after a fluttering of wings. To relieve himself of the necessity for coming up with a series of questions, he turned a puzzled countenance to the witness and asked him to explain, as fully as possible, why Tabor had waited until he was fifty-two to do what he had done.

As Zacharias explained how the sight of the Chief Justice, with all those highly charged symbolic meanings, had been the final link in an infinitely drawn series of events extending over a lifetime, Ambose was listening for another answer, with another ear. As eager as the witness was to be helpful, a bored, repetitive note had come into his voice. "The sight of the Chief Justice impinged upon . . . his current mental, physical and emotional difficulties . . . a combination of sheer accidents which ignited the fuse that . . ."

That shot the arrow in the air that fell to earth you know not where. As the refrain ran through Ambose's mind, he saw a flash image of an arrow sticking into Tabor's forehead.

Still stalling, he picked up Zacharias' words and asked him if he wanted to tell them exactly what Tabor's current physical and emotional difﬁculties were.

"His most pressing current difficulty," answered the witness, "is that he's in jail on a murder charge."

Ambose pulled his head back and grinned at him, enormously gratified, it could be seen, to find such common sense coming from, of all people, a psychiatrist for the defense. (It was never too early to let the witness see that you really liked and appreciated him for his finer qualities. If the time ever came for it, he'd have to have the cagey bastard relaxed and ready.)

"Just thought I'd ask," he said in rueful surrender. While he was about it, he might as well ask whether it could have been anybody else, like the President or some other high official, who could have set Tabor off? You know, ignited the fuse?

The witness's opinion "at the moment" was that the situation was so polarized that all of Mr. Tabor's pathological energies had coalesced in that one figure, at that one time.

Ambose went on to run down all the other possibilities. What if it was the same man but a different setting? Did the steps have any symbolic meaning? The time of day? The trip in the car? City Hall itself? The television cameras?

The witness could only answer variously that it was possible; that he couldn't say; and that it was a useful area for future exploration.

He was boring the hell out of everybody, Ambose knew, and yet he stayed with it doggedly, like a man casting for trout, because a third area of concern had invaded his mind. Fishing around for questions to ask while being faced with all these uncertainties, he had become struck once again with the impossibility of reconciling the neat, retroactively predictable universe of the psychiatrist with the chance-filled world of random collisions, the world of a thousand weaves he had pondered while he was waiting for Fletcher. The wings fluttered, the feather rustled. If this had invaded his surface mind, at this time, under these circumstances, it could only be that the other mind had been drawn back to the meeting with Fletcher. What had Fletcher come to tell him? He had come to tell him that Medellia . . .

"Mr. Ambose," Chobodian said, "this line of questioning is highly problematic. I don't think it's going to get you anywhere."

"Yes, sir," Ambose said, trying to hold onto it. "Leaving the problematic, Doctor. What you are saying is that it was an accident of timing." He ticked them off: "The lone man, the critical moment, the fateful meeting."

This time the reply did not come so quickly. Zacharias blew into his loosely held fist like a man who was trying to warm his hands. Ambose had moved to make the witness commit himself completely, and the witness, knowing that this was the answer from which there could be no retreat, was scanning the question carefully before the commitment was given. "That's my hypothesis," he said carefully. "At the present level of development."

"Hypothesis? That means guess."

"I prefer to believe it means a scientific appraisal based upon thirty years of experience."

"A well-seasoned guess?" Ambose offered, willing to strike a bargain.

"I'll accept that."

They were smiling at each other again. Ambose was beginning to feel that he had already used up about six months' worth of charm on this cagey bastard. He was also beginning to feel that he had better not strain himself by opening up a whole new line of questioning. "Are you under the impression that the Chief Justice was gowned when he was shot?"

"No. I've seen the pictures."

"Are you suggesting that it was just as well he wasn't gowned?"

Zacharias came forward in the chair, as if he were studying Ambose professionally, exactly the same gambit Swann had pulled on Bannerman, with far less reason, in the morning session. Judge Chobodian, having reached the limits of his patience, said, "Mr. Ambose, see whether you can't ask a question that can be answered. It would be a most refreshing change." From right alongside him Nevins rasped, "Finish it off. You're making a damn fool of yourself."

"One more minute," Ambose muttered. His eyes went to his pad as if he were in deep and profound thought. It was not beyond Hilliard, he knew, to get up on him and rest the state's case himself. He lifted the top sheet and dropped it. Out of everything that had been said on direct examination, why had he bothered to make, write down, doodle this one note on the most common form of mental disease heard in the courtroom.

"You say schizophrenic with paranoid features . . ." He pronounced it as if it were a mythical bird that had disappeared, if ever it had existed, somewhere around the Ice Age. ". . . all freckled over with homosexuality?"

In a high, angry voice Harold Halpern said, "I object to that!" Halpern was leaning in a half-crouch over the table. "Mr. Ambose is deliberately misinterpreting what the witness has testified to in that regard, and I ask the Court to direct him to stop."

For several seconds Chobodian continued to stare at him, speechless. If the chair itself had heaved up on its hind legs to enter an objection, he could not have been more surprised. A soft, indulgent smile was playing across Norman Bannerman's lips. Sam Tabor, however, had turned his face up to him in undying gratitude. "Your objection is well taken, Mr. Halpern," Chobodian said, with a bit too much admiration. "You will take leave of that line, Mr. Ambose. Permanently."

Well taken was right. It had given Jim Ambose time to think. Medellia was the key here. The defense that Bannerman had been planting.

Just outside the membrane a cool breeze blew. He had been right about this all along.

In front of him the judge and the witness were waiting.

"Tell you what let's us do, Doctor," Jim Ambose said. "I'll ask you whether you came to your conclusion as a result of your tests." (The breeze blew stronger, rustling the leaves . . .) He asked the witness whether he could tell the Court, briefly, how he had used those tests to arrive at his opinion. "One example, say."

Zacharias went into a delightfully long description of the Immediate and Delayed Story Recall subtests of the Babcock Test of Mental Efficiency. He reeled off a story about a flood and explained that while Tabor's recall had been fully consonant with his IQ, he had changed two significant details. Where the story had said fourteen were drowned and six hundred caught cold, Tabor had said six hundred persons had drowned. And where the test story had said, "In saving a boy who was caught under a bridge, a man cut his hands," Tabor had said, "In trying to save himself by grabbing hold of something under the bridge, a poor old man cut his wrist and bled to death."

Tabor had perked up for a moment, listening, but very quickly seemed to lose interest. Nevins had turned away, toward the jury box, his legs crossed over the side of his chair. Even Mollineaux had become less than enchanted.

Jim Ambose hadn't even been listening. Halfway through, his knee began to jump. A cool, liquid thrill ran down his back and spread out, radiating through his loins and thighs like sparkling ice water.

He had it! The arrow was quivering in Sam Tabor's head. Not sticking out. Pointing in.

"Now these tests you gave. Did you give them as a clinical psychologist or a psychiatrist? In which capacity?"

"That's an excellent question," Zacharias said, and you could tell by the way he gathered himself together that he was not going to be at all displeased to let everybody know why. The tests could be given by a clinical psychologist, he said, and even interpreted by a clinical psychologist. But only as a preliminary diagnosis. Just as, if Ambose would like an analogy which Dr. Zacharias believed he would find more exact than most, a medical doctor might examine a patient and, finding no organic disease, diagnose the condition as psychosomatic and also refer him to a psychiatrist. "The answer to your question, then, is that I gave the tests as a clinical psychologist and interpreted them as a psychiatrist."

Perfect. He had him talking free and easy. Relaxed, confident and on his home grounds. Timing was going to be everything in this.

"I think I've finally got it," he said, dawn breaking across his craggy features. It was clear that he had been struggling with that knotty problem through his entire tenure in the prosecutor's office, and now this witness through his genius for simple analogy had finally set him straight.

But wait . . . one last little breeze of curiosity could be seen to rustle across his brow. What he still couldn't see was how Dr. Zacharias could be so sure it was a mental illness. "Wouldn't that be exactly the same as if you examined a patient as a psychiatrist without even bothering to give him the medical examination?" A softly plaintive note ran through the question, as if he were asking him whether out of their new-found friendship he didn't want to come clean with him. "Now, don't you really have to put the man on the EEG machine before you can make that kind of a determination? Isn't that the absolute truth of it?"

"No." A tolerant smile was on the doctor's face as he slowly and emphatically shook his head. There sat the doctor, an impregnable fortress, letting the whole world see that he knew exactly what game Ambose was playing.

Ambose was disappointed. "Couldn't be, huh?" And a little querulous. "Are you really telling me that if this man had brain damage, an organic defect, you'd have been able to find out just by telling those bedtime stories back and forth?"

Bannerman said, quite loudly, "I'll have to object to that!" Noisily, and with unusual deliberation, he came lumbering to his feet. "While I assure the Court that we have no wish to hold back anything that might appear to be helpful, I must point out that we did not touch upon the subject of brain damage in direct imagination."

Ambose had come to his feet one second behind Bannerman. Although his question had been a perfectly good one, an objection of some kind from Bannerman had been fully expected. But Holy Toledo, the man was fast on his feet, throwing in "imagination" instead of "examination" like that to signal his witness to start thinking; to warn him that something was wrong. (Instantly, Ambose decided it was a little too clever. He had caught it himself only because his ears had been straining for signals. Everybody else, he suspected, would hear what they were accustomed to hearing.)

With a humility at least the equal of Bannerman's and a lack of urgency at least as persuasive, he said, "Well, he did bring up this business about the tests, Judge, and the witness did testify that his opinion was the result of these tests, so I don't see any reason not to go into it a little." He had picked up the yellow writing pad and he was tapping it rhythmically on the table in front of him to hold Zacharias' eye. He shrugged rather wistfully, with a small accompanying half-smile of chagrin, to let the doctor know that this was a matter of small import because Jim Ambose knew as well as he did that he was barking up the wrong tree.

Less than fifteen feet away Bannerman moved his shoulders in a much broader, more expansive shrug as his objection was overruled. He sat down very slowly, scraping his chair forward and setting it down noisily as he settled himself back into place. From first to last his eyes bore in on Zacharias, attempting to draw his attention away from Jim Ambose through the sheer magnetic pull of his own powerful will.

But Ambose, standing dead ahead of the witness chair, had position on him and he never let go. Now where were they? Oh yes. "On my brain damage hypothesis. Why not, Doctor? How come my hypothesis isn't as good as yours?"

"Because the tests didn't show it. I don't want to get too technical, as you have directed me, Mr. Ambose, but the responses would have been entirely different."

"Well, don't get any more technical than you have to, how's that?" They had another good chuckle between them.

On brain damage, Zacharias said, becoming serious, the patient tended to persevere; to hold on to the subject and become repetitious. He also, as contradictory as he knew it sounded, wandered. His speech became prolix and was inclined to become disjointed. "I could go into it in more detail if you'd like, but none of this was evident in Mr. Tabor's responses."

"It wasn't?" Weakly.

"No, sir."

"None of it?" Resigned.

"None of it."

Jim Ambose clucked his tongue loudly against the roof of his mouth, as if to say, "There goes the ball game."

"Not even prolix, huh?"

"No, sir."

Ambose's face seemed a thousand miles away from him. Inside, there was a vast, cathedral calm. ("The lord shall commend the blessing upon thee in all that thou settest thine hand unto . . .") He could win it here. When he walked out of this courtroom, not only wouldn't Bannerman have Medellia, he'd have blown the whole defense he had prepared.

Impassively, without a change of expression, he moved to cut the legs out from under whatever chance Bannerman still might have to recapture any of the lost ground when he got the witness back.

"Those tests of yours must be heap powerful medicine," he grunted. Nevertheless . . . Dr. Zacharias did have to admit, didn't he, that if the EEG tracings showed that brain damage was there, his own tests would be no good? A certain sharpness came into his voice. "Or would you still hold your tests to be superior to the machine's?"

"Well, by the way you have worded it, of course they wouldn't."

"Then you admit the possibility that it could turn out to be brain damage?"

Bannerman gave it another try. Without moving from his seat, he called out in a resigned, barely audible voice that Ambose was badgering the witness.

No good. This witness actually held up his hand to let Bannerman know that he had everything under control. "Now, Mr. Ambose . . . you put a hypothetical question to me, and based on that hypothesis I gave you my answer. In answer to the nonhypothetical question on what the tests did show, I gave you a nonhypothetical answer. The tests just don't show it."

And right there was where Ambose could see it hit him. As sooner or later it had to. Across the narrow corridor of space that separated them, he saw the sinking haze drop over Zacharias' eyes as he realized how strongly he had committed himself and began to backtrack, too late, to find out exactly what he had committed himself to and ask himself how he could have been brought to commit himself so completely without taking that precautionary scan.

Dr. Zacharias drew his fingers across his chest and coughed twice into his fist. Struggling not to look toward Bannerman and finding it impossible to look directly at Ambose. "When you say possibility, Mr. Ambose. I want to be particularly cautious at this juncture. I should point out, I think, in that respect —you were asking about the possibilities—that the electroencephalograph is a notoriously imprecise instrument." His voice, like his gaze, had an aimless drift to it. "There have been many borderline diagnoses, both by myself and other qualified psychiatrists, where a difference of opinion has occurred."

That ain't gonna do it, Doctor. "So that if your tests said one thing, and the EEG tracings said another, the machine would probably be wrong?"

"Well . . ." His fingers brushed lightly across his chest again. "There'd probably be a difference of opinion there between the disciples of psychological testing and the disciples of electroencephalography on that one, too."

"Your modesty becomes you, Doctor." And modesty was one virtue Jim Ambose wasn't going to let him get away with. Rising to the occasion, Ambose expressed every confidence that as one of that distinguished array of psychiatrists Mr. Bannerman had promised them, Dr. Zacharias had not often been proved wrong when he found himself in disagreement with a machine that was so notoriously imprecise.

The eye-to-eye contact was impossible to reestablish. "With one reservation, Mr. Ambose. You understand, of course, there can be borderline diagnoses and borderline tracings." He tried to smile, and it didn't come off well. "And then it's one man's opinion is as good as another's."

Ambose's smile was perfectly ghastly. "Well, aren't we lucky that we don't have a borderline diagnosis here?"

Bannerman tried to recapture some small beachhead by asking if he had understood Dr. Zacharias' testimony to have been that there were occasional differences of opinion among experts? And that other qualified experts, in both disciplines, had even been foolhardy enough to dispute Dr. Zacharias' diagnoses from time to time? And that as earnestly and energetically as the best scientific minds of our times had labored to perfect their highly specialized batteries of tests, did he understand Dr. Zacharias to have said that there were men of high caliber and unquestioned integrity who still looked upon the machine as the final arbiter?

The witness responded with increasing vigor that all of these things were true.

Ambose put an end to it right there. Shambling to his feet, scratching his head in his best country-boy style, he interposed himself, with obvious reluctance, to suggest that the distinguished attorney for the defense was leading his witness. "I don't quite understand this, Your Honor. I didn't understand the witness to say the machine was infallible. The way I understood it, it's maybe the sloppiest machine ever made. I thought he was saying that if it came to a shoot-out between the machine and his tests you could sell the machine for scrap iron. Is Mr. Bannerman trying to impeach his own witness now?"

Judge Chobodian, who had been wondering the same thing himself, passed the question on to Bannerman. "Are you trying to impeach your witness, sir?"

Bannerman considered his course so briefly that it could have been noticeable to no one except Ambose. All he had been attempting to do, he said amidst a flashing of teeth, had been to clarify that phase of the testimony before he rested his case so that it would be clear, beyond peradventure, to the Court. "Apparently," he chuckled, in the manner of a man who knows any protestations of failure coming from him are not to be taken seriously, "my mission has not met with unqualified success."

He bounced right back up again. "If the Court has any further questions to put to this distinguished witness, I know he would be delighted to be of assistance."

Judge Chobodian had no questions.

There was a flurry of activity at both tables. On the defense side Bannerman leaned across Tabor, his arm draped loosely over Sam's shoulder, to instruct Halpern to wake up the bailiff and ask him could they kindly have their application for the writ back. He gave Sam's neck an encouraging squeeze. "Stay loose, Sam," he said. "Pluck and fortitude will win in the end." He rubbed his hands together as if the real activity of the day was just about to begin. OK, so he had lost brain damage on a borderline tracing—he'd have to live with that from now on—but as long as he had Medellia as the Court-appointed psychiatrist one defense was as good as another. (Speaking of luck, students. Oh, what a tale I have ye to tell.) The Ape First Class (speaking of vestigial tails . . .) had bumbled around, showing everybody how not to conduct a cross-examination, and all of a sudden he had stumbled right into it.

But it was all to the good. (Luck, like any well-wrought candle, students, can burn at both ends.) Ambose was the only man who might have gummed up the works on Medellia, and Ambose would be so cocky right about now that he would no longer be watching Bannerman with those steely eagle eyes.

Bannerman's own eyes, following Furness to the exhibit table, caught Marie's. There was a whiff of the haystack there; he was never wrong about that kind of thing. He winked at her roguishly, his thoughts turning to the more genial sins.

As soon as Ambose saw Furness pick up the writ he put his head alongside Mollineaux' and told him, "In a couple of seconds that shithead over there is gonna pick himself up and make a speech that will sound like the raising of the flag over Pearl Harbor. When he gets to the part where he says the words, 'Withdraw the writ' I want you to go back and sit next to Jake. 'Withdraw the writ,' right? Atta boy." He sniffed a couple of times, his eyes ranging around the courtroom. "And Red . . . if I were you I'd take the far seat because the shit is about to hit the fan."

Bannerman set everything neatly in front of him, squaring the writing pad off with his briefcase, and laying his pen flush against the pad. The gold pen given to him by his first wife twenty-two years ago.

"Mr. Bannerman," the judge said, "do you wish to rise to the motion?"

Bannerman squared his cuffs off, wondering whether there was enough sunlight left to strike a few sparks from the diamonds on the cuff links. Who could have dreamed the dumb ape would go fishing around like that? Luck, sheer luck. Well, a slight change of plans was definitely called for. He'd have to hit it head-on. And that was all to the good, too. He reached for the writ. No, he couldn't have planned it better if he had tried.

"Your Honor," he said.

Pushing himself up quickly and purposefully, Norman Bannerman strode to the corner of the Bar, the farthest possible point from the Bench. Every head in the courtroom turned with him. "As Your Honor well knows," Norman Bannerman began, "counsel for defense had a dual purpose in filing this application for a writ of habeas corpus." By the dip in his voice and the set of his stance you could tell that he was about to change the pace and purpose of the courtroom.

"While we have been petitioning for bail in all good faith, Your Honor, our purpose was to have the body of the petitioner, Samuel Tabor, so that we might submit him to the full battery of neurological and psychiatric examinations amidst more congenial surroundings."

He reminded the Court that in response to a question from Mr. Ambose, the last witness had answered, in all candor, that the very fact of the petitioner's environment was indeed one of the variables that had to be accounted for in interpreting his responses.

With a quick twist of the wrists—as if he were twisting the neck of a chicken —he rolled the writ even tighter and slapped the ends, top and bottom, against the palm of his hand. Those quick nervous movements, together with the high, straddling posture and a richer, more lyric resonance announced that he was swinging into stride:

"It is, and has been, our contention that the greater interests of American justice invite us to *subdue* the vigilante impulses that cry desolation and havoc and *remove* the petitioner from the reinforced concrete and tempered steel out into the white-walled, test-tube solitude of the laboratory . . ." The lofty voice hovered over its prey like a great bird, ready to swoop or ready to soar. Down it swooped: "For we have before us an opportunity, unexampled in the history of American jurisprudence, to set forth on a journey of discovery through the dark, uncharted interior of a murderer's subconscious." Up he soared: "As St. Augustine has so truly said, man wonders over the restless sea, the flowing waters, the sight of the sky and forgets that of all the wonders of the universe, the greatest adventure of all remains the journey into man's mind."

Abruptly, without pause, he came back to earth to express his pleasure that through the enlightened attitude of the district attorney and the good offices of His Honor, an agreement had been achieved whereby the prisoner would be removed to the Phillips Brook Hospital, there to be examined by a team of neurologists and a disinterested psychiatrist appointed by the Court.

A lilt came into Bannerman's voice that was damn near incantational as he likened this agreement to a freshening spirit implanted between defense and prosecution "which we may yet live to see sprout and flourish toward the end that Truth, whose pursuit is the glory of American justice, will become the paramount and overriding concern wherever a psychiatric defense is raised in an American courtroom."

He would be in default of the elementary obligations and courtesies, said Norman Bannerman—soaring still—if he did not engrave upon the record, for all men to see, that this progressive and far-reaching agreement was one for which the Court deserved primary credit.

He also paid his respects to the district attorney. "For who cannot rejoice," cried Norman Bannerman, in full throat and throttle, "when a prosecutor empties his sword and takes up the shield? Who would be so *pinched* as to fail to pay him full honor?"

It was remarkable. Perhaps it was only a trick of the feeble afternoon sunlight, but as Norman Bannerman held the writ aloft, curled like a baton in his hand, a phosphorescent glow seemed to radiate from him. "I therefore beg to move," he said, slapping the writ into the palm of his hand, "that our application for a writ of habeas corpus be dismissed, without prejudice, and the prisoner remanded to Sheriff Stringfellow along with the instructions to remove him, posthaste, to an assigned room at the Phillips Brook Hospital."

The performance over, he waited a long moment to cast off the hypnotic spell he had spun upon himself before he went gliding back to his seat—scarcely noticing that the younger, smaller redhead had slipped out of his seat at the prosecutor's table.

Standing by his chair, Bannerman advised Judge Chobodian, in his most engaging manner, that he thought he might be able to rearrange his calendar should His Honor wish to invite him to his chambers to discuss the details with his good friends from the district attorney's office.

Chobodian declared that since the writ had been withdrawn the hearing would seem to have come to an end. Should the attorneys wish to consult with him, he said, throwing the initiative back to them, he would be at their disposal for the rest of the afternoon. He tore off the top sheet on his note pad, on which several words had been scrawled and crossed out, crumpled it in his hand, and as he began to rise dropped it into the wastebasket under the Bench.

The guards moved to take possession of Sam Tabor.

The newsmen started to move out from the press rows, causing Stringfellow to take two quick steps toward them and fix them to their spots with a rigidly pointed finger and a stern warning glare.

The audience shifted, scraped, shuffled and sent out a rising buzz, causing Chobodian to turn back in disapproval and Furness to call out that the Court was still in session until Judge Chobodian had left the room.

Through the hubbub cut the rumbling, doomsday voice of Hilliard Nevins.

"Your Honor," said Hilliard Nevins, "I don't know what in the world Mr. Bannerman is talking about."

The district attorney had not so much as shifted in his chair. One of his legs was still crossed indolently over the other, one arm hung loosely over the back of the chair. Between him and Bannerman Ambose was sitting perfectly still, his elbows resting on the table, his chin resting on his hands. "Now, Your Honor," Nevins said, "the state has agreed that Mr. Tabor should be removed to Phillips Brook for the medical examination, the serology and all of that. The brain waves, if that's what they want, too. But on that other thing, Judge, we didn't make any final agreement on any single Court-appointed psy-chi-atrist. All we ever agreed to was to try to find somebody we could agree to, all of us. The prosecution, the defense and the Court."

Bannerman had turned toward the prosecution table, his big body sagging.

Nevins, continuing to address the Court, never looked at him. "If we can't agree on any one man," he said, "we're going to see if we can't agree on a three-man board. That's the way I understood it."

Bannerman was staring dully at Pawley's empty chair, as if he were trying to remember who had been seated there only a few moments ago.

Either way, Nevins said, the state was going to agree that Mr. Tabor should be examined in that test-tube world Mr. Bannerman wanted. "We've got no fault to find with that part of it, Your Honor. But I just thought I ought to clear that up about the psychiatrist before Mr. Bannerman went ahead and withdrew that writ of his. That's the agreement we had, isn't it, Judge?"

Chobodian, having turned back, was still trying to get his bearings. "Yes, yes," he said irritably. "That's the agreement." He squinted down at Bannerman. "Mr. Bannerman?"

Bannerman's entire range of vision had been narrowed down to a lineup of chairs. First chair, empty; second chair, Ambose's upturned face; third chair,

Hilliard Nevins slouched back in total unconcern. As in a dream, he was outside the scene as well as inside. As in a dream, he didn't have to look at them to see himself being looked at.

The range of vision tightened down to one man. Down to one slit. Down to Jim Ambose's flat and filmy eyes. In that instant Halpern could feel Bannerman drawing vigor from himself, out of his need. The fiber stiffened, the syrup flowed. The mind broke free.

"Why yes, Your Honor," Bannerman said heartily. "That's the agreement as I understand it."

Considering everything that had happened, Harold Halpern had to marvel at his self-control. As soon as the judge was out of the courtroom, Bannerman turned to the press row, chipper as ever, grinning and nodding to those of the newsmen who were signaling that they wanted to talk to him outside. There was no way of knowing, if you had not known, that Norman Bannerman had just had his defense blown out from under him.

As Sam Tabor was being moved, Johnny Gerard, lagging just behind the others, held out his hand, low, to Halpern as if he wanted to shake his hand. Halpern, reaching out automatically, found himself holding a folded-over piece of white notebook paper, complete with marginal holes. On the outer fold, in neat blue ink, was written: *Sam gave this to me on the way down after lunch, he wants I should give it to Ambose.*

Unfolding it, Hal found a neatly printed pencil note:

Dear Jim:

I didn't have anything to do with Bannerman saying you put me up to anything this morning. I would not want you to think it was me. I am going to instruct him not to do that anymore.

As ever,
Sam T.

Jim Ambose came out of the judge's chambers first, Hilliard Nevins having sent him in alone to discuss the practicality of pursuing the search for a three-man panel of experts. An inordinate amount of work had piled up on the district attorney's desk during the day, it seemed, forcing him to assign Ambose to work with Bannerman "until Pawley gets over his indisposition."

Surrounded by a dozen or so waiting newsmen at the end of the corridor, he had very little to say, mostly because he had been instructed by Nevins that he was to do nothing that would upset Chobodian. To be precise, Nevins had said, "Now don't go calling him shithead in front of Eli, huh? Little things like that can get the old boy upset at his time of life."

Asked what the state intended to do from here, Ambose said, "We intend to show up. We're not fancy but we're there." All he could tell them was that they would reconvene after the Fourth of July weekend, at which point he took it that Bannerman was going to move for a change of venue.

When one of the writers asked why, Ambose stared at him blankly. But instead of saying, "Because that's the way the game is played," he said, "You better ask him. Maybe he don't like us."

Did he think Bannerman could show that Tabor was insane?

"That would be prejudging the case. I'll say this, though." He pinched his lips hard enough to serve notice that he was choosing his words with exquisite care. "If we didn't think we could show he wasn't, we wouldn't be going to trial."

Yeah, but did he think the passive character disorder–Oedipal kind of thing was what Bannerman was really going to go to trial with, or was he expecting him to come up with something else?

"I wouldn't know anything about that. I'm just a guy that works around the courthouse." Nevins or not, a faint elfish smile perched upon his inhospitable features. "These fancy lawyers with all their fancy talk, huh?" He shook his head to show it was all too much for a poor working stiff like him. "That Bannerman sure is one talking piece of machinery, ain't he?"

When Bannerman emerged with Halpern about fifteen minutes later he was considerably more expansive. The purpose of the writ, he said, in explaining why it had been withdrawn, had been to get poor Sam to a hospital. "Once they folded on that, there was no need to go on. We'd already won." When it came to the question of whether there was going to be a three-man board, he pleaded that since the issue was still under active discussion he'd have to refrain from comment. And then he threw them a broad, strutting wink that brought on a whole gaggle of questions about whether there was going to be any board at all.

"I guess you got me." He laughed. "Just between us, I had to make them think I'd be giving them that in order to get them to spring Sam so we could put him under psychiatric care before it was too late. With this medieval system they have here, there wasn't a snowball's chance of getting them to let him go unless I could make them think one of their own headshrinkers was going to get a shot at him."

"That's right," said Harold Halpern, responding promptly.

Having just discovered that the way to handle a crushing defeat was to hail it as a glorious victory, Halpern was about to discover how magnanimous Bannerman could be in victory. "I like this judge," he said, unwilling to brook any criticism of him. "He gives you a bedrock to work off." Very important in trial work, he assured them. "You get one of these judges who gives you no bottom, and you flail around until you're mired down to the knees." The only fault he could find with this judge, he said frowning slightly, was that he was too damn honest and trusting for his own good. But that was something he would worry about later. "The important thing is that Sam is in the hospital. And they can't rescind that order now. What we're going to have to do from here is see to it that he remains in the hospital where he belongs until the trial starts."

Ah, that looked more promising. Did he think he was going to be able to? Norman Bannerman smiled. "All I can say in answer to that, gentlemen, is what would you have given for my chances of getting him out of that cell two days ago?"

While it was impossible for Halpern to be impressed by the irrepressible humor and unquenchable vigor with which Bannerman had kept bouncing back all day, the ineradicable optimism was beginning to wear. Once they were alone in the taxi Halpern told Bannerman he had just learned something of value back there and hoped to learn something of even more value in here. "How bad," he said, pronouncing each word separately, "is it?"

"Good question." Bannerman settled himself into the corner, his mind, to all appearances, racing. From time to time he touched his fingers to his temples, massaging them lightly. Occasionally, he gave a little, barely audible snort, a small grimace, or a willful, barely perceptible smile. When at last he turned to Halpern his first words were: "Harold, I have a guardian angel who watches over me . . ."

Oh, god! Norman Bannerman, having settled himself in the corner, had touched his fingers to his temples, and massaged them lightly. There was nothing for it now but to tot up the damage. In losing the marginal EEGs, exactly what had been lost? If the EEGs showed Sam had a hole in his head, it would be off to the nuthouse and it wouldn't matter what Zack or anybody else had said. (The tracings wouldn't come back that bad, though. Rushed though Zack had been, his tests were never that far off.) And if they came back routinely abnormal tracings, so what? Routinely abnormal tracings might go over great in personal injury cases where everybody knew the plaintiff had been injured and—even though it couldn't be said openly in the courtroom—that the insurance company was going to be picking up the tab. They might even be good enough in a minor-league killing. But, by god, they weren't going to be good enough to explain away the murder of a Chief Justice. *It had been a mistake from the beginning to try to build this case from the EEGs up.* Every man-jack of 'em in the jury had got hit in the head sometime or other in their life, and they knew damn well *they* weren't crazy. In losing psychomotor epilepsy, he had lost nothing!

With psychomotor epilepsy he'd have had to convince the jury that Sam had suffered a sudden attack at the most inopportune possible moment, and how in the bejeesuz could you get twelve subway jockstraps to believe that?

"I have a guardian angel who watches over me, Hal," he said, "to protect me when my feet get too close to the fire. Did I tell you that I was a religious man?" It was perhaps a testimonial to his charm that he managed to make it sound as if he were doing the Deity a favor by believing in Him. The best thing that could have come out of the hearing, Bannerman was explaining, was getting all that garbage about brain damage cleared out of the way. "We couldn't get temporary insanity on any kind of epilepsy—no way, no how—because if Sam flipped under pressure once he could always do it again. Even those twelve dolts would pick that up."

Already he had worked himself up to a nice pitch of excitement. Any briefcase carrier from a municipal pool knew how to yell brain injury. Norman Bannerman, in a case of this weight and trajectory, should—and would—put together a Freudian mosaic of such sweep and artistry that they'll be letting the children out of school to watch. "A psychiatric case is a hell of a lot more fun to try," he said, giving Halpern a rah-rah punch on his forearm. "Yessireebob, they'll be studying this trial in your better law schools after both of us are rolling in the dust."

A tight smile was on his face as he sat back to think about it. That was exactly the way to do it. Oh, he'd make this lawsuit sing. The whole psychiatric world would be with him on this one, eager as ever to push their pet theories (it was simply amazing how consistently they found in favor of themselves) and even more eager (as who knew better than Bannerman) to assert their jurisdiction over mental illness wherever it might be found.

"Do you know what we're going to do, Harold?" Although his voice was hushed and reverent, his eyes were round and merry. "We are going to impanel the most brilliant jury ever to grace an American courtroom. We are going to requisition jurors of education and compassion and sensitivity, men whose minds are open to fresh winds and new concepts. How does that strike you, Harold?"

It struck Harold that he would have felt a heck of a sight better about it if Bannerman had been able to bring himself to give some small indication that he had some slight understanding of what had happened to him.

He could feel Tabor's note crinkling in his pocket, raw and squiggly, and all at once he realized that he was not going to turn it over to Bannerman. He realized, sitting there, that for some reason he was not quite able to understand, he had never had any intention of giving it to him.

"I don't know," Hal told him. "But don't go by me. I was never one to see how you could win by losing."

Except for one loud grunt Bannerman gave no indication he had heard him. Oh, they had their work cut out for them if they were going to be ready for trial by a week after the Fourth, and Bannerman was already setting to work. They would be expecting Bannerman to hit the city hard on the change of venue, attacking everything except their parks department and sewer system. But Norman Bannerman would fool them. He would put in no more than was necessary to keep the issue viable for his appeal.

That would set up a friendly climate for a friendly jury, boys and girls, would it not? God forbid that the trial be moved out of Lowell. If it went out of Lowell he might never get a chance at a return go with Ambose, and he wanted Ambose so bad he could taste it. The thing to keep in mind was that anything less than the chair was a win for Norman Bannerman, and Norman Bannerman hadn't lost a man to the chair since his first year in practice.

Nick Zacharias rather sluggishly dealt out two hands of gin rummy, and just as sluggishly Halpern picked the cards up. Neither of them saying a word, each of them avoiding the other's eyes as if they shared a guilty secret. The secret being that both of them knew that neither of them quite dared to say what he was thinking. From the bathroom came the sound of running water.

"Are we playing that you can knock," Halpern said, "or do we have to go for gin?"

Why wasn't Bannerman able to admit that Ambose had very brilliantly—if it made him feel better let him say shrewdly—seen his chance to get Zack to eliminate one possible defense and, through sheer luck, it had been the defense Bannerman had intended to use? It was no disgrace to be outlucked. It wasn't even a disgrace to be beaten.

"Make it easy on yourself," Zack said.

It had been a disgrace in there, though, hadn't it? Who the hell ever heard of putting an expert witness on the stand without knowing what he was going to say? If Chobodian ever found out what had happened he'd throw—

The note in Hal's pocket had come alive again. Why had Johnny Gerard slipped the note to him and not to Bannerman? No, Ambose first. Why hadn't he given it to Ambose like he was supposed to? Guards weren't supposed to pass messages for prisoners, of course. Their orders were undoubtedly to bring them to the sheriff. Everybody knew that Johnny Gerard was Stringfellow's pride and joy. So why would he take the chance of getting in trouble with the sheriff, who —loyalty aside—held his future in his hands, and with Jim Ambose, who never forgot or forgave?

Why would Johnny Gerard be more concerned about protecting Tabor than protecting himself? That's what had been bothering him, Hal suddenly realized, from the beginning.

"I'll make it easy on myself, then," Zack said. "With this hand we'll go for gin."

Protecting Tabor was exactly what Gerard was doing. If Ambose ever found out that Tabor, that poor sad bastard ("Poor Sam" was right) was more worried about staying in his good graces than letting his own lawyer defend him—Ambose would rip him apart. It seemed to Hal that he had heard somewhere that a prison guard develops an identification with his prisoner at some lower animal level (having something or other to do with his own inevitable death) that can become sensitized to the point where he can smell death on the prisoner.

But that still didn't explain why Gerard had given the note to Halpern instead of Bannerman. His hand went to the deck to pick another card. Who was Johnny Gerard protecting Tabor from? Had Gerard smelled what Halpern thought he had smelled? A momentary nausea swept over him. Holding his hand where it was, he turned his eyes to the bathroom door.

Norman Bannerman, having hung his jacket over the hook on the door, had washed his face, wet down his hair and very carefully and methodically combed it. Watching himself in the mirror, without expression, he brushed both sides smooth with the flat of his hands, over and over and over. Faster and faster and faster.

It was Fletcher, of course. The only other person who knew about Medellia was Halpern, and Halpern was the one person in Lowell he could trust. In all the city, only Halpern. So be it. Norman Bannerman was not a man, they would find, to forget a friend or forgive an enemy. He would reward Halpern royally by making a trial lawyer out of him. He would leave Halpern behind as a scourge upon the district attorney's office and a monument to himself. The bastards would pay for this. One way or another, he always paid the bastards off.

What troubled him so deeply was that he had not picked up the emanations of danger coming from Fletcher. Except faintly, that one time, after the interview with Shtogren. What had happened to his screen? Where had it failed him? No, the screen was all right. It had picked up the signals from Shtogren before Shtogren had even begun to speak. It had warned him about Ambose. If there had been anything wrong about Fletcher before he sent him to sound out Medellia, it would have picked that up, too. The screws had been put on him later, and once it had been done there would have been nothing to pick up except some feeble residual guilt.

The eyes in the mirror stirred so briefly that it was no more than a glint of movement. What would be done about Fletcher could wait for another time. He might still be of use. Knowingly or unknowingly, Fletcher could be turned into a double agent. There was one little beauty he had been toying with for a long time.

Now comes to the bar of justice DeWitt Pawley. Had Pawley been in on it? As difficult as he found it to believe that he wouldn't have picked up the danger signals, he found it even more difficult to believe that Pawley could have been kept in the dark. Better not go overboard. There were still a few honest prosecutors left, and Pawley had certainly been impressed with him. As treacherous as those bastards had been, it didn't pay to become too cynical if Pawley could still be of use. All that static he had been picking up about a fight between Ambose and Pawley couldn't be totally wrong. What had probably happened was that Pawley, finding out what the plan was and thinking too highly of Bannerman to become a party to it, had taken himself out of the hearing. Enlightened self-interest was permissible. With Pawley, we would see what we would see.

Studying himself, his eyes expressionless, he brought his hands down to the top of his gleaming white silk shirt, clutching it at the neckline. He studied himself, his eyes expressionless, and with a sudden violent motion . . . *rrrrrripped* the shirt completely down the front. Without any change of expression, his gaze steady on the mirror, he pulled himself free from both sleeves and threw the shirt into the tub.

Solemnly, without any real expression, he dug the fingernails of his left hand into the mat of fine, silky red hair on his chest (redder and grayer than the hair on his head). There was a slow intake of breath. Without moving his head, never taking his eyes off the mirror, he *rrrrraked* his fingernails down the full length of his chest and stomach.

Breathing heavily, but still without any . . . no, a faint strain of interest had come into play as, straightening his shoulders, he watched the four red welts come up in four gently banked curves—the pattern and symmetry were perfect. He studied the mirror, observing carefully, as the scattered dark red beads pushed up under the skin.

A faint smile came through; deeply satisfied. He nodded to himself in one short, assentive flip of the head, like a man who had carried a heartfelt plan through to a successful conclusion.

Humming a tuneless little song, he reached up above for a bath towel and draped it around his neck, arranging it so that it would cover the welts. He stepped back for one final little jaunty look at himself. At the door, he took a deep breath, composing himself. Smiling broadly, holding tightly onto both ends of the towel, he threw back his head and shouted, "It's party time! Let us pamper the palate with gluttony and booze."

Halpern and Zacharias, looking up from the cards, saw Norman Bannerman come stepping out into the room, a white towel held sportily in place like a scarf with one hand, his jacket hooked over the shoulder with the other. Leaning with debonair ease against the jamb of the door, he snapped out orders for calling down to room service ("mention my name") for the food and drink. "Having gobbled and tippled, Zachary my man, we shall send my friend, the Count of a Thousand Pleasures, to fetch us a brace of well-matched, high-nippled ballerinas, suitable for an evening's diddling."

He turned his humorous heavy-lidded eyes on Halpern to let him know that he was not being completely ignored. That crew-cut fellow asking the snotty questions back there, that was Caples, wasn't it? The eager-beaver from the *Globe* who'd been getting all those leaks from the DA's office? "This Conrad fellow can't be too happy about having everything fed to the morning paper. Why don't you be a good fellow and cheer him by telling him how he's going to be slipped the report on Zack's tests as soon as they're typed up." Out of the side of his mouth he barked, "And let him know there's more where that comes from. It's about time we took the gloves off and made ourselves a few friends in this burg."

BOOK IV

The Mind Readers

"God, in His infinite power, created man; and then in His infinite wisdom and compassion fashioned woman from his rib to give him someone to blame."

—Dr. Lennard Swann

There had been something about Julie from the beginning. Perhaps because she was the first thing Halpern saw, dead ahead, when he came into the motel room —the long line of her crossed legs, the spiked heel dangling. Since she was writing in a notebook his first impression was that she was Lionel Allbright's secretary, Allbright being the kind of man who might easily decide to fly a secretary in.

Hal had known all three defense psychiatrists were going to be with Bannerman at the Executive Suite Motel. He had not expected to find a woman with them. Least of all a woman with the fine, enameled look of a model. Or—still another new face—the thin young man sitting on top of the bureau with a drink in his hand. "Frank Cowhig," Bannerman boomed, waving his own glass toward him. "Investigator *extraordinaire,* beyond compare." The investigator's face was scarred by old acne and he had a leathery skin that somehow brought to mind too many X-ray treatments. He also had the kind of exceedingly open, frankly approving smile that informed Hal he had been hearing good things about him.

"And Julie." Bannerman himself was seated, placid and wide-legged, in the corner, facing out to the room. He had put on weight. A lot of weight. "Julie is our lady of all purposes. Secretary, investigator, femme fatale and, hardly the least of her duties, keeper of the full glass."

Acknowledging him with vast disinterest, she rose to get the bottle, the lone bottle, from the bureau. "You've got a wide choice, Harold," she said. "Scotch to name but a few." Her voice was deep and cozy. "Catch water? Catch ice?"

He told her he'd take ice.

"Horny," she said.

Suddenly rattled, he looked around the room for a place to sit.

Lionel Alexander Allbright was seated against the wall, on the other side of the door from Bannerman, a mastiff of an old man with big features and a great shock of shining white hair that fell, more or less uncombed, straight down over his forehead. Harmon Medellia was stretched out on the far bed, in a corduroy smoking jacket and his gray hush puppies, staring straight up at the ceiling. Nick Zacharias, who had been standing when Hal entered, settled down on the edge of the same bed, leaving Hal with little choice except to seat himself at the end of the first bed, across from Allbright. So close that Allbright was able to lean forward and pat him on the shoulder in a warm paternal greeting that pleased Halpern more than he would have cared to admit. An imposing man, he had thought upon picking Allbright up at the airport two weeks earlier. *An imposing man,* he thought again.

"We've got our heavyweight!" Bannerman had shouted over the phone, and since Hal had heard about Lionel Allbright and the Allbright Institute just about all of his life his own pulse had quickened. Bannerman had been calling from some place in Colorado to tell Hal to let Stringfellow know that Allbright would be wanting to interview Sam in the hospital. "And Hal, I won't be mad if you wait until morning, huh? Call him now and the *Globe* will have it five minutes later. You can't trust any of these fellows." The familiar Bannerman chuckle had floated, warm and welcome, into his ear. "And don't forget to give my regards to Conrad."

Once the first excitement had worn off, however, Hal hadn't been so sure that Sam would open up to another psychiatrist. Not even Lionel Allbright. The massive depression of the prehearing days had been replaced by a deepening, and even more worrisome, state of listlessness. The depression had been understandable; if Bannerman was to believed, even natural. But there was something pale and pasty about this new thing that left Hal with the feeling that Sam had not so much resigned himself to his fate as that he was already dead and gone and grieving.

He had forgotten, however, that Sam Tabor was a sociologist of sorts. (He had forgotten—if he wanted to be honest about it—that Sam was a human being.) The news that Lionel Allbright was coming in to see him and was actually going to be testifying for him had snapped Sam out of it so completely that he was telling Hal, before Hal had a chance to tell him, that while Allbright had occasionally served as a special consultant to the court, this would be the first time he had ever consented to testify in an adversary proceeding.

Julie handed Hal his drink without particularly looking at him and strolled in an easy, negligent way back to her chair beyond the bureau, her dark hair falling and curling back at the neck like a thousand strokes before the mirror. She reached for the notebook and pencil and crossed her legs again. (Behind her was the television set; behind that the clothes rack aglitter with Bannerman's suits.) Since the psychiatrists had never stopped talking, note-taking was clearly not her main function here.

Picking up the conversation in midstream, Hal had been able to see that while Allbright had every confidence that a valid "overwhelming impulse" case existed for Sam Tabor, he still had his reservations about whether it was a case that could be presented in an American courtroom. Psychiatry, he said, speaking directly to Halpern, was simply too delicate a bird to withstand the heavy handling of the adversary system. "Which is why, as I have told Norman, I have always insisted, as a matter of principle and perhaps self-indulgence, upon preserving my own pet owl from both the taxidermist and the embalming fluid." There was a gentle, playful quality about him—Halpern had already been exposed to his delightful, self-deprecatory wit—which conceded that he had also agreed to allow Bannerman to decide how it was going to be mounted in the courtroom setting. "My peculiar value in this case, I take it, is that a clever lawyer might hope to induce a jury to accept the splendor of my name and accomplishments no matter what kind of mincemeat the district attorney makes of my testimony."

"The adversary system," Julie said archly. "That's men against women, isn't it? I knew all about that when I was nine."

Allbright was delighted. "Now that happens to be truer than you know, Julie.

You just may have given the best thumbnail description of courtship among the American natives that I have ever heard."

She lowered her eyes at him. Her voice, too. "I also know that you're presumed innocent until caught. In which event, you had better get yourself, flying, to a lawyer or an abortionist."

Allbright's lusty, robust laughter boomed through the room. The look he sent to Bannerman told him that he approved of his young lady. Everybody was laughing except Halpern. Out of the corner of his eye, Hal could see Julie watching him not laugh.

The laughter tailed off into silence. The silence turned thoughtful, became heavy, thickened into guilt. Halpern, sipping on his drink, became acutely sensitive to the dank motel odor emanating from the drapes behind Allbright.

While nobody was looking, Sam Tabor had slipped back into the room.

"You have a strong case, all right," Allbright said, "and this new information fits in nicely." He made a pass at brushing the hair off his forehead. "But . . ."

From what Hal could gather, Hugh Fletcher had dug up a medical record showing that Tabor had been circumcised at the St. Cecilia Clinic when he first came to Lowell, a minor operation that seemed to hold vast psychological implications for the assembled psychiatrists. There was general agreement that given Sam's age, background and the change of environment, the operation had quite probably followed his first sexual experience.

"My bet," Allbright said, "is a prostitute. The act itself being unclean, the operation becomes an act of contrition. He punishes himself by inflicting a wound upon the offending member—'If thine eye offends thee pluck it out,' let's not lose sight of that religious upbringing—with the additional and most desirable effect of rendering himself *hors de combat.*"

Zacharias' interpretation, interposed with great respect, was that Sam's motivation would have run far deeper than the merely punitive. The thing to remember, he said for the benefit of the civilians, was that an event had to be interpreted in terms of the major challenges of your life at any given stage of your life. "The adolescent is coming to terms with the adequacy of his body, so it has a meaning altogether different than if . . . let's take damage at fifty. At fifty, he's struggling with the emotional depletion of his resources anyway, and any damage triggers off the feeling of 'I am totally depleted now—' "

"Which is not quite the same thing as the adequacy of his organic function," Medellia said loudly. "Not the same thing by any means."

Zacharias didn't appreciate the interruption at all. "When you're talking about circumcision after twenty-one," he said, squeezing his temper tightly, "eighteen even, it's self-destruction of one kind or another. I'm sure," he said, without looking at Medellia, "we can all agree on that, anyway."

What Julie wanted to know was how they could be so sure it wasn't necessary. "What if, the opposite, he picked himself up a flying chick at the bus station and he was having trouble with his foreskin, the cheese or whatever. That can hurt like hell, too, Nick. I got it straight from the Mafia."

Zack was willing to guarantee that as a purely medical procedure it could have been taken care of by hygienic measures far less drastic than circumcision. And that Sam's history quite effectively ruled out any likelihood of a girl friend, flying or otherwise.

"If not before," she said agreeably, "he was a clear lonesome little feller after."

Medellia was staring up at the ceiling again. "You're wrong, young lady. The theoretic infection, bacterial infection, was only the excuse, masking tremendous anger. I wouldn't dismiss this incident lightly, Norman. We have here a man leaving a tight, inbred society—sect would be the appropriate term—and moving into a cosmopolitan social situation in which all his values, deeply ingrained values, were being threatened."

When Allbright frowned, deep creases formed along the corners of his lips and the heavy mastiff look became even more striking. He had been listening politely, willing to hear them out, but always ready to step in and restore order. As an isolated incident, he explained for Bannerman's benefit, it would be of very little interest. He himself had known cases where the husband in a barren marriage had found superficially valid reasons for being circumcised late in life. Obviously, then, he was about to explain why it was more than an isolated incident. "You know what was happening there as well as I do, Halpern," he said, bringing him into it. The old Japanese pattern of shame followed by guilt followed by aggression. In this case, turned inward. The only question that concerned them, therefore, was whether Sam's circumcision could be fitted into a recognizable pattern of behavior. "Repetition of behavior," he stressed, "being the key to what we may call, for legal purposes, irresistible impulse, and more accurately, from ours, overwhelming impulse." He let his gaze roam ponderously from Julie to Cowhig to Halpern and back to Bannerman. Given a certain stimulus, would Sam Tabor always react in a predetermined way? Even when—especially when—it seemed to be against his best interests? "Because if we are able to show that, Mr. Bannerman, we will be demonstrating that these acts are compulsive and, by definition, beyond conscious control."

At the moment they had four parts to the pattern. To begin with, they had a working knowledge of his unhappy family background. They had to show—it was essential it be shown—that Sam Tabor, given the appropriate stimulus, had been programed for murder in his childhood. "If we are speaking of compulsion, we are saying that a central nerve in his emotional ganglia—*the* central nerve—was left twitching with unconscious shame and guilt. And that when that raw, sensitive nerve is irritated to the point where it becomes inflamed, he explodes into apparently irrational behavior."

Medellia, looking at the ceiling, said, "Especially with his weakened brain."

Sonofabitch! So that was what the strain between Zack and Medellia was all about! Medellia had found something in the tracings. Enough, he obviously felt, to have made some kind of a case for organic damage if Bannerman—you could hardly blame Zack—hadn't blown it in the hearing.

They could also show, Allbright was saying, that upon leaving his native surroundings, Tabor had removed the temptation of sin by removing the organ of sin (circumcision at the age of thirty amounting to temporary castration). And that upon being married he had developed "an infantile and therefore castrating" pattern of sleeping with his wife. "All of which is purely clinical data, interesting of itself but not particularly persuasive to the defense of Sam Tabor unless we can make the crucial leap to the killing of the Chief Justice as the most recent response to the same overwhelming impulse."

On that he and Bannerman were in total agreement.

"Before you do . . ." Frank Cowhig had hunched forward on his bureau perch, kicking his heels back and forth lightly like a kid. (Although on closer look he didn't look so young at all, he looked more like a fortyish man with perpetually youthful features.) "I'm one of those stubborn cusses got to be shown. You're saying castrating. Infantile, all right if you want to. I'll buy that. But even she says maybe about once in a month in the tape." His eyes widened, but only slightly. So all right. Maybe that didn't make Sam the answer to a young girl's prayers, but it didn't make him a eunuch either.

Jake Foxx was squinting at the bottom of the memo sheet where Ambose had written in his neat, tight hand: *Lew Brahms—#118 arr. 12:15.*

"Well, God bless . . ." Lew Brahms was a Chicago-based wiretapper. More than that, Lew Brahms was probably the best-known wiretapper in the world if only because he was the one wiretapper who couldn't resist going on television interview shows to talk about it.

"I've got a friend in Chicago, too," Ambose smirked. "Called me no more than an hour before you got here to tell me Lulu Brahms has taken a reservation to fly to our fair city tomorrow. The first team is coming in, Jake. Allbright, Cowhig and now Brahms."

"I'll put a tail on him."

"You don't have to play it that cute!" He spat the words out. "Not with this guy you don't!" Pulling the cigar out of his mouth, stabbing with his finger, he barked out his orders. What he wanted Foxx to do was have his friend at the phone company clear the lines of the top echelon at the DA's office—home and office both—just in case Brahms had already been in and out of Lowell. Ambose himself was having Harvey Leigh detached to the office, special detail, for the duration. Harv and one of Weiland's men were going to introduce themselves to Mr. Brahms as he came off the airplane, and to make sure he didn't become lonesome during his stay in their fair city they would march with him, shoulder to shoulder, all the time he was in town. "You, Jake, are going to have two men at the hotel to camp by his door and make sure he doesn't do any sleep-walking after he's gone beddy-by."

Jim Ambose ground the cigar out viciously in the ash tray. "I don't want him tailed. I want him out! Got it?"

From their long association together, Foxx knew exactly the answer Ambose wanted from him. "I'll do better than that, Jimbo," he said. "I'll attend to it personal."

After Foxx left, Jim Ambose put out the lights and sat in the semidarkness totting it up:

Norman Bannerman wasn't any magician in the courtroom, he was just a guy who reported for duty like everybody else. From the moment he found out about Medellia, he had been sure of it. Like most of these hot-shots with their fancy suits and their fancy reputations, Norman Bannerman was a fixer. Jim Ambose had turned the fix upside down on him in the hearing. And now Jim Ambose had his wiretapper pegged and bracketed. The apparatus was clicking right along, and Jim Ambose was firmly at the controls. Norman Bannerman was going to be no sweat at all.

And neither was Lionel Allbright. Lionel Allbright's willingness to break a rule of a lifetime was, Ambose had to concede, a public relations score for the defense. But since the victory would be temporary, it bothered him not at all. If Lionel Allbright had never testified in adversary proceedings before, it followed that he had never undergone cross-examination before. Fresh meat for Jim Ambose. The more they built him up, the better Jim Ambose was going to look when he flat ate the world-famous Lionel Allbright's lunch as a fitting climax to the Trial of the Century.

Jim Ambose, sitting motionless in the growing darkness, was, for one of the rare times in his life, wholly content with the state of the universe.

There was in Lionel Allbright as he spoke the authority a man who had devoted his life to dispelling doubts, not to accumulating them. Unpretentious he might be but he sat on a mountaintop, and what he knew, he knew. Lionel Allbright would, Halpern thought, forgetting Julie for the moment, make one hell of a witness.

"I'm betting that at the critical moment she pushed him away," Allbright had been saying, "leaving him with deep feelings of rejection. How the hell can you please a woman like that? he asks himself. Aha, he can't. Only his father can. What's missing is something only his father can supply, something his father has which is crucial to her existence. He is convinced ultimately that she is getting something from the father that is really her source of strength. And since Sam, like any other young boy, needs his father's strength, too, he identifies completely with the mother."

For the first time since Halpern had come into the motel room Allbright picked up his drink from the floor, smacking his lips; there was a sense that what he was enjoying so much was not the drink or even the interlude of heightened drama but the play of his mind against the problem.

"The anger at the absent father is twofold. One is that he's not protecting him. The other is that he's withholding the power from him. And there's the homosexual *stance*. Because if only he would *give* me this mysterious thing he has, this mysterious thing that he's giving this woman—who anyone can see doesn't appreciate it and is really driving him away—then I would be strong. And once I was strong I would be a better person for him than this woman and he wouldn't have to go away anymore. And there's the homosexual *dilemma*. Identifying with his mother and hating her; longing to identify with his father and not being allowed to." Zack, he said, happy to give credit where credit was due, had been dead on the mark in seeing this through an Oedipal lens.

Being no fool, Zack was also able to guess what all the civilians would be wondering. "Whether the penis becomes what he gives or anything else," he hastened to explain, "it's all wrapped up pretty much in that bag. The wish for his father's love and affection and whatever nourishment the father can give, that's really the controlling factor."

Allbright's bet was that there was a traumatic incident where the mother caught Sam playing with the gun, the way boys will and, more crucial here, as a way of imitating the father. Much the same as if he had dressed up in his father's clothes. "And boy," Allbright chuckled, giving the air a good workout with his arms, "he caught it then." The gun was evil and anti-God and therefore Sam, like his father, was evil and anti-God and worthless, too.

Nor did he think they should dismiss the probability that Sam's father returned home one day and, finding him playing with the gun, had given him a good beating; possibly because he was mindful of the danger to his son, possibly as a conciliatory gesture toward his wife, or, well . . . simply because he was the kind of man who didn't mind belting people around. "And boy," Allbright said, sad and solemn this time, "that really cuts his balls off. That'll do it like nothing else.

And if he kicked him . . . ? Well, is there anything that can make you feel more like a dog than being kicked?"

"The poor little kid," Julie said. "No wonder he couldn't wait to grow up and kill Wilcke."

As always, Allbright accepted criticism with such good nature, even to enjoying the joke on himself, that his very amiability became an admonishment to patience. "What happens to a kid whose father is missing, emotionally and physically?" he asked Julie. Compressing his lips, he looked around the room, inviting an answer. Getting none, he announced, "He is always looking for the missing person to come and rescue him."

The room stiffened to attention, eyes widening and narrowing. Bannerman grunted. "Yes," Allbright said, well satisfied with the reaction. "Jobwise, he finds himself in—these things are never completely accidental, you know. Fortuitous, yes. Accidental, no. People gravitate to certain professions to satisfy certain needs." His own embattled profession, for instance. The belief that psychiatrists were crazy people seeking out the dirty secrets of their own lives in the dirty secrets of other people's lives had become so widespread as to have achieved the status of a cultural joke. He spread his hands in what started out to be an elaborate show of bewilderment and very quickly turned into something else. "Never underestimate," he said, suddenly quite serious, "the shrewd wisdom of folk humor."

"Thank god us investigators are looking only for the good, the true, and the beautiful," Cowhig murmured. And even as he was saying it, the truth of that other folk belief could be seen stirring in him; and in Halpern and perhaps even Julie. The psychiatrist seen as witch doctor, the man who knows the secret answers. Allbright must have seen the same desperate question rippling through the air of every room he entered. What does it mean, Doctor, if . . .

Out of politeness as much as anything else he said, "All of us have our deficit. The frayed lining. The damage done." He held his glass up to the light. Drink was a supporting prop for most people at some time, he reminded them, bringing forth the self-conscious smiles. "If the deficit is too great—this is a very poor illustration because alcoholism is such a complicated business—the support only serves to make the deficit visible and compound the damage."

On the other hand . . . Ah, on the other hand, there were those for whom the support was so powerful as to obliterate the deficit. He sent a small, genial glance toward Bannerman. "For the lawyer, like the psychiatrist, the business tycoon, the comedian, the deformity can be the driving force that makes it impossible to settle for success at a less than conspicuous level. You show me the man who would be downright psychotic without his professional triumphs and I'll show you the top men in every profession. Present company," he said, with the obligatory bow, "always excepted."

They smiled across at each other, in mutual understanding and appreciation, these two men, otherwise so different, who shared the one thing that counted: they were the best at what they did. Nobody in the room could have failed to see the message that passed through the rarefied air above them and they felt the poorer for having seen it. It occurred to Halpern that if Ambose and Bannerman had met under other circumstances that same swift look of recognition —the pride of the lonely hunter—would have passed, sooner or later, between them.

"I've come clean, Norman." The questioning lift of Allbright's eyebrows, the challenging lift in his voice, said that now it was his turn. "Why do people become lawyers?"

A single beat passed. No more. "Same reason." The lifted glass, the obligatory bow were returned. "So we can ask questions like that instead of answering them."

For Halpern, who had anticipated that he was about to learn something more about the Bannerman itch, that was no answer at all. To Allbright, it was. "Quite right," he said, "We are both *voyeurs.*" An entirely different, and far more ambiguous look passed between them. "But," Allbright asked, getting back to business, "what happens if the thing—the impulse—boils up and becomes overwhelming and *breaks* beyond the bounds of the control and you find yourself . . . you've found you've done the dirty thing yourself, either as a thought-crime or a crime in fact? Then you've got to want to destroy the guy you think should have given you the strength to stay out of it." He could see that the others were straining for his meaning. "Look. It's not *your* fault that you have these evil impulses. That's the kind of guy you are. If you've done the dirty thing it's somebody else's fault for not stopping you!"

There was utter silence in the room. Medellia had come up on his elbow. Halpern was completely lost. He was going to show them how it was all David Boone Wilcke's fault? "They say the mind's a poet." Clapping his hands together, Allbright sat back and laughed in sheer exultation and delight. "The newspapers now . . . they're calling this the Trial of the Century, and they have no idea how right they are." He gave his head a little shake, smiling to himself. "The Trial of the Century must follow the Crime of the Century. You see? And what is the crime of the century?"

Zacharias and Medellia nodded in unison. Seeing all.

Allbright placed one hand on his chest. He threw back his head. And in a low and rumbling voice, he intoned, "Forgotten by the womb, the womb he cannot forget."

Flushed and breathless, Dr. Lionel Allbright, no longer imposing, looked haltingly and timidly around the room, his wish for approval hanging out. Clearing his throat and looking off in the general direction of the clothes rack, he said, "I wrote a poem about that once. When I was interning. Just happened to pop into my mind."

Cowhig had a quiet and easy authority about him. The trouble with all this from an investigative point of view, he told Bannerman, was that with all due respects to the experts, everything they had on Sam's history had come from Sam or his wife.

"Brilliant minds," said Bannerman, as he began to hand out assignments, "follow similar paths." Julie would head out for Cumberland immediately. As soon as the meeting broke up. Frank, of course, had his work cut out for him in Lowell. The drink resting lightly on the arm of his chair began to tap while he studied Hal as if he had something special in store for him, something full of merriment and promised pleasure, and was wondering whether he could handle it. "Harold will join Julie in a day or two," he said, watching him so closely, his eyes so agurgle with his secret joke that Hal couldn't help but see that his reaction was being carefully noted and openly enjoyed. Julie wasn't paying any attention at all. At the first word from Bannerman, she had headed for the telephone and, efficient as always, was making her reservations for a flight to Baltimore and a rented car.

"What do you think, Frank?" Bannerman asked, looking mischievous. "Don't you think Hal and Julie are gonna make a tip-top team?"

There had never been a moment when Hal had not been conscious, somewhere along the filament, of her presence, but now the consciousness of her enveloped him, calling up all the questions that had been on his mind from the beginning: How long had she worked for Bannerman? Was she a professional investigator? Or was it Cowhig she was working for? If it was, was she sleeping with him? Or with Bannerman?

As Allbright took the center of the stage again and began to tie Sam's marriage into the pattern, a couple could be heard walking from the office toward their room and past it and up the staircase, the woman's heels at a crisp, imperious click . . . click . . . click above the man's muffled tread. Harold heard Allbright's words without quite being able to follow the meaning. The marriage was not a sign of health but of retrogression . . . (how could that be?) . . . Not a weak woman in Sam's view, a strong woman . . . (Vera Tabor?) . . . Draw-a-Man Rorschach . . . (Where did they come from?) . . . Reverting to infancy, he relives his . . . (Huh?) . . . I'm betting their frequency of coitus was . . . (Hey, listen to this. Concentrate.)

"And now that the feeling he's being taken care of no longer wells up in him, he's in trouble. Alone in his bed, he had nothing to hang onto. I'd like to see his dreams." Dr. Allbright laughed shortly. "Nightmares would be more like it."

Oh, oh, Julie had caught him looking. So what? She thinks he wants his glass filled, that's all. Bannerman's, too. And just what the hell does Bannerman think he's grinning about?

"Say when, partner," Julie said.

Willfully, with increasing belligerence, he began to challenge everything Dr. Allbright said. Casting himself as a member of the jury he demanded to know whether if Allbright had had all this information on June 14, he would have been able to predict that Tabor was going to murder anybody. And got the surprise of his life. Knowing no more about Sam Tabor the day before the murder than he knew now, Allbright suspected that he would have prognosed the potentiality of murder. Anything more than potentiality, he would not presume to prognose. *Knowing what he knew now,* it was his bet that if the Chief Justice hadn't happened along, Mrs. Tabor would have been his victim. He was also willing to hazard the guess that he would have used a knife. Several knives. And that by the number of knives they would have learned how many people he was eliminating from his life and how many lovers he thought his wife had. "There's not the slightest doubt that he thought Dr. Shtogren was her lover, on both conscious and unconscious levels. That's not guess work, Halpern, the tests show it."

Now that he was there, he stayed with Dr. Shtogren. "A doctor is thought of as a man who wears a gown, too, you know." Doctor, mother, wife, judge. This doctor, to add another layer of association, was also cast in the role of a judging person. "He keeps tally on the marriage, tells them who is at fault and, in a very real sense here, metes out punishments and rewards." Rubbing his face, he squeezed his eyes shut as if suddenly weary. "A gun murders. It puts people to death. So do judges, and so do doctors." So, in a more symbolic way for men like Tabor, did mothers and wives. He spread out his hands. "I could go on, but I think you can see that the supporting subterranean stream can be adequately established."

"I follow you perfectly, Alex," Bannerman said. "But you've been shuffling levels of consciousness a bit too fast for me. Where does the emerging incestuous impulse tie in with the assassination?"

It came in with a twist that Halpern had never expected, and yet it sounded right, it sounded irrefutable and, taken together with Allbright's overmastering personality and reputation, well . . . downright brilliant. Jesus, the way these guys thought. The only objection he could have made to it, if he hadn't already objected himself out, was that he didn't believe a word of it, and even if he had, he couldn't for the life of him see how it could be used in a courtroom.

Bannerman had been sitting lumpily in his corner, his eyes closed. Except for the thoughtful set of his mouth, you would hardly have known he was listening. Allbright said, "When Sam said he didn't know why he did it, he was telling the truth. On a conscious level, if there *was* anything resembling a conscious level, Sam killed the Chief Justice for exactly the reason I have stated, because, you understand, it made him feel threatened. Never dreaming that the real reason, the compelling force, the unknown—"

"*If* there was any conscious knowledge, Alex?" Bannerman asked quietly, and the very mildness of the inquiry was the most effective expression of his concern. The lawyer in Norman Bannerman had smelled something out. The lawyer in Harold Halpern picked it up on the rebound, in the refinement of language. Allbright had said *conscious level.* Bannerman had asked *conscious knowledge?*

Coloring slightly, Allbright said, "Well, he did know he had the gun in his pocket, didn't he? He was going to have to come back the next day to have it checked out, anyway, so—" He shrugged expressively. "Why not just leave it there?"

And that was how Norman Bannerman discovered, on the day before the trial was to begin, that Sam had laid the gun on the counter when he came into the sheriff's office and was literally halfway out the door before he came back to get it. Once he had determined that Allbright knew about it because he had asked Sam, and Sam had told him, he let out a groan that was almost comical. "That's one question you can be sure I won't be asking you, Alex." There was, it could be seen at once, nothing comical about it.

"I won't be *volunteering* an answer," Allbright said, and then, to make sure Bannerman understood exactly what he was saying, made it explicit that he would not be so lacking in sound professional and discretionary practices as not to answer the question, directly and truthfully, if it were put to him by the district attorney. Picking at his lower lip as if at a scab, he explained that if he were permitting himself to testify this one time to something less than the full fact, it was only because of the peculiar difficulty of explaining such things to a jury of laymen. There were times, as they all knew, when a small evasion best served the cause of ultimate truth, just as there were times when full disclosure frustrated the pursuit of the greater truth.

There are times, Halpern thought, *when the frayed lining shows through. The damage done.* "Then you are saying that Sam didn't know what he was going to do?" Halpern asked.

"Well, Hal, I wonder if you've been listening. There are things we know that we don't know we know. Which is really what my business is all about, isn't it?"

"It all fits together very nicely," Bannerman said crisply. "Alex, you've given me plenty to move with. Let's both of us put it on the back burner and let it bubble." Bannerman had risen abruptly, the personification of the top-rank executive who saved everybody time by hanging up when the conversation was over. To get them moving he began to bark out marching orders. The medicos would now race headlong to the airport where they would return Julie's car to Mr. Hertz and catch the six o'clock bird to Chicago. The night on the town, he said, with his slyest wink, was on the defense. Frank and Harold were to remain loyally at his side until the more pressing matters at hand had been disposed of. Julie-girl would return to her cabin by the side of the Coke machine to pack and, at the appointed time, Harold would drive her to the airport, during which journey, they might, if they wished, stop at Phillips Brook to discuss in whatever lyric tones seemed suitable, the scenic beauties and other vital data of Cumberland.

After Julie had turned the keys to her rented car over to Zacharias she returned to Bannerman's room, plumped herself down and told him, in tones uncivil, that she needed no time to pack since she hadn't been there long enough to unpack. "My bed remains unslept in," she said to Cowhig. "For which wastage blame the Jolly Red Giant. All right, Harold, deliver me the data."

Hal could begin by telling her that Sam hadn't really lived in Cumberland; he came from a little town called Twenty Hills about twenty-five miles west of there. The leading industries, from what Sam had said, were the chapel and a sanitarium, both belonging to the Children of the Redemption.

"Sounds horny. The pure-as-driven body is frosting for redemption. If I have to play a hootchie-kootchie under the moon with a snake bite, chief, it's going to cost you."

The Children were an extremely close-knit and secretive sect, Bannerman informed her. The press hadn't been able to get close, and unless the FBI was lying they hadn't done much better. "It does my heart good to believe the FBI struck out," he said. "So I'll believe it. You're working virgin territory."

"The hell you say!"

With the psychiatrists gone, the atmosphere had changed completely. This was the stripped-for-action core of the defense team, and it had the *esprit* of a picked group of fighting men. There was, therefore, no sense whatsoever that Halpern was a temporary member and they were permanent party. He had his part to play in this, and they were accepting him without reservation. He was an outsider only in the sense that a long-ongoing and intricately involved relationship existed between the others. A cross-patch of memories and resentments that came out not so much in words and reminiscence as in the ability to communicate without words or reminiscence.

"Don't worry about Julie," Cowhig said after Halpern had warned her to expect some difficulty in finding accommodations in Twenty Hills.

"No, don't worry about Julie," she said, glaring at him. "I've seen me a lot of towns, big and small, and heard me a lot of talk, sweet and sour. And all I've ever learned is that from up on top it's all grunt and muscle."

Cowhig threw up his hands and said, "Pardon me!" And with those two words, he was saying that he had meant it as a compliment but forget it; that he knew better than to come close to her when she was like this; that he was getting pretty sick of it; and that he didn't really mean any of it. And who knew how much more?

The strain that existed between Cowhig and Bannerman came out, most unexpectedly, after Halpern had suggested that he knew Caroline Beyner and the courthouse people well enough so that he thought he and Fletcher would be able to handle the Lowell end of the investigation without any trouble if Bannerman wanted to send Cowhig to Cumberland with Julie. "Ye gods!" Bannerman roared, in full quiver and outrage. "I had not been hitherto aware that I have placed the conduct of my investigation up for public debate. I would take it as a vote of confidence if it were removed from the agenda pronto."

"Norm can tell you all about investigators," Cowhig said in a voice that was full of meaning. "If the investigator's good enough, any lawyer will do. That's what he keeps telling me, and I want to believe it so I will." He could also tell Hal while he was about it that there was only one thing he had to remember when he got to where he was hiring investigators himself. "Money and a pat on the head will get you everywhere. As long as they come in that order." And if it could be seen that there was something between them, it could also be seen which of them had a leg up at the moment.

Moments later it turned around completely. Bannerman hopped up on the bureau and was taking a hard-headed look at what had transpired with Allbright. They had learned a great deal about what they could expect from their heavyweight, he said, casting an approving eye on Halpern, and some of it was fraught with danger. And no, it wasn't the gun he was talking about, either.

There was only one other thing Halpern could think of. "I wouldn't be in any hurry to ask him whether he could have prognosed murder the day before."

Right on the button. Medellia and Zack were prepared to testify that they would have prognosed potentiality for murder and hold to that opinion under strenuous cross-examination. "And then up steps our heavyweight, for whom they are only window-dressing, to say no, he personally couldn't have because it is his opinion that nobody could." Bannerman's expression let them know that would never do. "Our heavyweight has questioned the validity of their professional opinion—if he doesn't know, who does?—and all that means is he's impeached their entire testimony. If I'm on the jury, I've got to be thinking that if they've put on two out of three that are impeachable, their case must be pretty sick."

"Good old Alex," Julie said. "He's wiped us out."

Bannerman looked from face to face, open for suggestions, and yet . . . Despite everything he had said could be seen that he was conspicuously unworried.

"Oh no." As Cowhig began to shake his head, Bannerman's smile grew broader and broader. "If you think you can geek him," Cowhig said, "you're a schmuck, schmuck."

"No, huh? As my sainted old mother used to say, does anybody around here want to put his money where his mouth is?" He was going to let him off easy. "Ten dollars American, sucker."

Cowhig, looking less and less confident, said, "You've got it, schmuck."

"Because I'm such a dumb gumshoe," Cowhig was saying, "I can tell you everything you have to know about Sam Tabor. You take women now. There's some guys they have to keep them rationed, and there's some they know they have to produce on demand. That's maybe the first thing they figure out about you. Sam's wife probably went to the shrink to keep him in line. That's what I'm going to find out after I've been batted back and forth by all his friends. None of which, by the by, he seems to have."

"As a psychiatrist," Bannerman told him, "you make a great investigator."

Cowhig answered with a shrugging expression that disclaimed both the need and desire to be anything else. "I've followed these guys by the hundreds where their wife thinks they're cheating, and the guy wouldn't know how to move it if it was laid in his lap. If they happen, about once in a blue moon, to get lucky and land in a motel, they end up showing her the wallet pictures of the wife and kiddies. I talked to your fellow this morning, Norm, and I'm telling you. How many psychiatrists you think have spent the best hours of their lives watching the wandering lover-boy drinking by himself in a corner? I know these guys!"

"Frank's right," Julie said. "Sam's the kind rides around the motel three times and tells her he can't find a parking space."

But Bannerman is no longer listening. From one second to the next the current has shut off as all of them have seen it shut off before. Sitting there on the bureau, with the light reflecting off the mirror on him, Norman Bannerman is thinking that Lionel Allbright isn't going to be taking the witness stand so that some loutish assistant district attorney nobody heard of can make him look like a fool. Once he was on the witness stand, with the glare of publicity on him, Allbright was going to discover that he was in a mortal struggle for the meaning of his life. If winning meant going the last gasp of the road for the defense, Allbright would go it. What the hell difference did a little thing like that make when it was, like Cowhig had said, about fifty percent bullshit, anyway?

She had room number six, just on the other side of the Coke machine. When he entered she was painting her lips. Looking back into the mirror, she went *"Twaaaang"* with a lack of expression that very clearly communicated her satisfaction at having laid on an entirely new face and her unhappiness that it was necessary. She continued to stare at herself, not with the quick, hard-eyed last look of most women, this way and that, but with a long, melancholy look of deep and abiding dissatisfaction.

"Looks good to me," he said.

"You don't see what I see."

Still staring, pronouncing each word as if it were a separate block of cement, she said, "I am looking at the face I had before the world was made."

What was he supposed to say to that?

"Me and Alex," she said. "Scratch a little and you'll find a poet every time." She shook her eyes away from the mirror. "Me and Alex. I put myself in pretty classy company, hey?"

Her valise lay open on the bed, the baby blue frilly lining showing. Alongside it there lay, to his astonishment, a stewardess's uniform. Following his eyes, she said, "You know the joke. What has two thousand legs and one cherry? You don't? I'll deliver you a clue. Somewhere in a lonely apartment there sits an American Airlines stewardess who will be ineligible to serve on the Sam Tabor jury."

She walked back to the bed to drop the lipstick and compact into the pocket of the valise. "I never said that. If the jury can be instructed not to hear what they just heard, so can you. Though not on duty, I have all good intentions of traveling American Airlines and one should not speak ill of the employes of an employer who permits you to travel free, space available." She folded the uniform into the valise, tucking it in with great care at the sides, chattering away all the while. Her agreement with her temporary employers, Norman Bannerman to name but a few, allowed her to list transportation, full charge, tax included, on her expense account. "Perfectly honest and aboveboard," she said, wide-eyed and innocent, "because I need the money more than he does." She snapped her fingers sharply and rhythmically, her shoulders rolling. "Vacation time with Bannerman. Catch money. Catch excitement. Catch let-the-good-times-roll."

"Well anyway, I'm glad you're not in uniform now. Because I like that dress."

She had that way of sucking in on her lower lip. She had that long, low look. After a moment, she ran her hands down the side of the dress, turning slowly to model it for him. "Just a little old thing I wear for traveling. Cost next to nothing." She looked back at him over her shoulder, naughty and inviting. "But I'm glad you're looking."

They had stayed so much longer at the hospital than they should have that he had to make time.

"Sam looked pretty good," he said, "don't you think?"

And no wonder. Julie had brought such life and freshness into the hospital room that she'd had Sam sitting up and cooing. And also writing letters of introduction to his minister, to the man who ran the newspaper in Cumberland and to the superintendent in charge of the sanitarium.

She had handled the two deputies on duty with ease, too. Their orders were that nobody was to talk to Sam in private except on direct orders from Stringfellow, an impasse she overcame by a flaunting of her sexuality that was so flagrant as to amount to a sporting proposition and so shameless as to be admirable. Not a thing to worry about, she told them, sitting herself down on Sam's bed. "This time it's only a trial run. Next time, I come with the bust-out kit."

"I'd better remember to frisk you, then," the corporal in charge leered, and you could see that while he knew damn well what she was doing, he was also wondering if he could get lucky and knowing all the while that it was out of his class.

"You damn well better," she said. "That's what the bust-out kit is. While you're gang-frisking me in the closet, Sam busts out."

Once she had them drooling it had been no problem at all to get them to step outside so she could have a word with Sam in confidence. "You're just the kind of a horny guy," she told the corporal, pouting her prettiest, "who'd promise a poor girl anything and then remember the call of duty and go back to your boss with all the goodies."

Back in the car she had slumped into the seat, silent and rather moody. Instead of answering Hal's question directly she said, "You think he's nuts?"

"Sam?" He wasn't sure why the question should have surprised him except that it seemed so out of character.

"No, Adlai Stevenson. Norman Bannerman now, I *know* he's nuts."

As perfect an opening as that was for asking her how she'd met Bannerman, he somehow had the feeling that it would sound like an accusation. "You want the truth?"

"No. I want a stock tip direct from the Mafia. You're a barrel of information, Harold."

"To be perfectly honest with you, Julie, I don't. Not legally. And not any other way, either."

"How do you know?" She sounded angry. "Do you think you can just look at someone and tell whether they're leafy? I'll bet you pass a hundred people in the street every day, and they've just climbed down from the tree house and you don't even know it." She bent toward him so that her fingers rested on his arm. "You're a dumbbell, Harold Halpern."

She disturbed him. He was not so dumb that he didn't know it. Neither, he could be sure, was she.

"Oh, I don't know about that. If they're out, that means they've shed their leaves. The weight of the entire medical profession is with me."

"Ehhhh, you can buy them all. Alex Allbright with the rest of them. I could tell you stories." Could she tell him stories! "Everybody's leafy. The nuts just got themselves looked at full in the face before the leaves began to fall."

"Presumed sane until caught," he said. "Is that it? And then you consult a lawyer."

"Yeah. Or a gynecologist."

She shifted her attention back to the parkway, her hands dug into her coat pockets as if she were chilled. "Bannerman's all right," she said suddenly. "A little leafy, that's all." She touched his arm again. "Harold, I want you to do me a favor. Whenever I say anything against the Jolly Red . . . if it's clear mean . . . you've got to defend him with all your might and main. Will you do that for me because I'm so pretty?" There was an odd little smile on her face, so bleak and fragile that he couldn't imagine how he had ever thought of her as being cool and mannered. "And if you're not of a mood to defend him, you can belt me like right in the mouth. I'm signing over my power of attorney."

Given an opening like that, it was in his mind to tell her he was willing to do just about anything in the world for her except belt her in the mouth. In his mind and on his lips. He said, "I'm sorry about Frank. That you'll be working with me there instead of him. He seems like one hell of a nice guy."

Julie sucked her lower lip all the way in, unable to make him out at all. "Frank?" she said, as if she couldn't understand how he could possibly think Frank meant anything to her.

"No, Adlai Stevenson."

"Frank's the salt of the earth. I'd walk through walls." She slid herself toward him and whispered hoarsely, "I try to make him feel good because he likes to think he has charisma."

Charisma? They grinned at each other in a delight of surprise. She as much as him. The word was so wildly out of context—making such a joke of it and her and him and them—that it was as if she had whispered something special about herself. "Tell me about yourself, Harold. You faithful to your wife, you chase or are you still trying to make up your mind?" She gave him an oblique look. "That's the first thing a woman wants to know. The second is whether . . . what Frank said back there."

Up ahead a plane was making its approach, the landing lights flashing in the dusk. The Municipal Airport Hotel had come into view across the marshland. In the distance the lights of the control tower could be made out dimly. He had better stay alert; the turn-off could be tricky. That was the way he affected women, all right. Put him next to the world's leading swinger and he'd have her watching her language before he could make up his mind whether he wanted to be faithful to his wife or—

"When I make up my mind," he said, peering through the windshield, "you'll be the first to know." Hoo-boy, there was a snappy comeback. She'd practically propositioned him for— Or had she? And he'd practically told her— Or had he?

At the airline counter she showed the clerk her vacation pass and was placed on stand-by. That's when he discovered that her full name was Julie Elkins.

And then she really surprised him. After all their rushing, the departure time for her flight had been pushed back twenty minutes. The ticket clerk had assured her there was plenty of space but as the departure time kept being pushed back ten minutes at a time, Julie became increasingly anxious and then utterly certain that the flight was going to fill up. By the time the third delay went up on the board, she had become a bundle of nerves, jumping up and down and pacing back and forth, her eyes going constantly to the lines at the ticket counters. When she had worked herself up to such a panic that she was ready to buy a ticket to protect herself and Bannerman, Hal took her firmly by the elbow, pulled her into the coffee shop and set her to picking at some blueberry pie and coffee until her flight was announced.

By the time she was ready to board she was her old self again. Tilting her head, she tapped her cheek alongside her lips and commanded, "If it's pretty, kiss it."

He watched after her, pleased and speechless, while she disappeared down the concourse—her heels going click . . . click . . . click—trying to decide, all the while, whether the look she had slanted at him had been warm or merely amused or, just possibly, mocking.

BOOK V

Audience Participation

"A trial is a tiny Island around which the whole Ocean flows."

—Norman Bannerman

While not normally a flusterable type, Marie was visibly flustered to find Norman Bannerman come glittering through the door, leaving his train of reporters out in the hallway. It was not that she was particularly overcome by the splendor of his masculine presence, what flustered her was that she was right in the middle of a conversation about him with Judge Davies. She had called Davies the moment she returned from the courtroom to pass on the bad news that Bannerman had trotted out the constitutional right to a speedy trial to insist that they go right into the voir dire, and there went Ass Wednesday again.

After he had groused a little about how the Founding Fathers would have been considerably less zealous had they been fully cognizant of the strain they were placing upon Harrison T. Davies' love life, she was able to bring him to a more practical understanding of where the real constitutional crisis lay. If tomorrow was out, today was the last time they'd be able to sneak in an afternoon session until the trial was over.

She had begun to tell him that the high point of the day had come when Bannerman proposed that the defense be allowed to give Tabor a lie detector test and a truth serum test and put him under hypnosis to see whether they could establish a "consciousness of innocence," his argument being that it was a long overdue counterweight to the prosecution's right to cite "flight" as evidence of "consciousness of guilt." It was at this point that she straightened up in her chair, and in a brisk, cool-of-the-evening voice, said, "Thank you, Phyllis, I'll call you back about it."

She had seen Bannerman too late, though. From the finger-licking preening air with which he approached her—he reminded her of a big, well-fed cat—it was evident that he had overheard enough to know who and what they had been talking about. "I hope," he said, "you told Phyllis I'm sure to win that one on appeal."

"Well, not exactly. I told her you were a great kidder." Pretending to look startled she said, "You *were* only kidding, weren't you?"

"Never more serious. Unlimited imagination and infinite recourse to gall are the prime requisites for scaling the heights of the legal profession."

Although he was there to pay a courtesy call on the judge, he said, in a low conspiratorial whisper, he had really come to do her a favor. The press, no less than her friend Phyllis, was hungering for the exact wording of the arguments on his eight pretrial motions and if Marie wanted to type them up and run off a dozen or so Xerox copies, she could pick herself up a fortune in money. For himself, he would be hopelessly and eternally in her debt if she would but read him the blow-by-blow account on the "consciousness of innocence" argument that seemed to have everyone so intrigued.

It was no trouble at all for Marie to find it. She had taken the proceedings down in shorthand, which she found easier and more accurate than the machine, starting each new motion on a new page along with an identifying notation in green pencil. Bannerman, having settled himself across the desk while she was thumbing through the pages, listened with a giddiness of admiration as his words came back at him, nodding his head from time to time and breathing, "Beautiful. Beautiful."

As an exercise in autoeroticism, it was so striking that an hour or so later Marie was telling Davies, "I tell you, Harry, I thought he was going to come. It's the closest I ever hope to come to watching a man masturbate. With his clothes on, anyway."

The judge, always interested in anything about Bannerman, had stopped to listen, squinting with a sort of dogged effort of concentration. Making no comment at all, he resumed his pacing—and his complaining—his hand running constantly over his hair.

"Marie," he said. "There's something I want to ask you. And if you want time to think about it, that's all right."

She forgot all about Bannerman. She forgot all about breathing.

"Marie, have you got five thousand dollars you can spare? For a little while?"

If she'd had any self-respect left, she would have blushed for herself. If there was anything saveworthy still crawling around in her, it should have died right there. "We know what you are," she murmured, absorbing this new insult with no difficulty at all. "All we're doing now is haggling over the price." With Harry pretending not to understand, she looked him in the eye and said, "What's that, dear, your stud fee?"

Oh my, he was hurt. The pained mouth let her know—let the whole world know—how sorely he had been misunderstood, how grievously he had been wounded. She didn't think he enjoyed asking her, *her* of all people, did she? And for just that reason! Did she think he would even think of asking her if it wasn't a matter of life and death? "All right," he grumbled, seeing that she was unmoved. "You've entitled to know." He took a deep breath. "I'm in hock to Felix McPhait. Up to my hamhocks." The reproving look, sullen and in a laughable way, vindicated, said, *You had to know didn't you?* and *You didn't believe I was in that much trouble, huh?* and *Now are you satisfied?*

"Oh, Harry," she said, and could have kicked herself for the tone of maternal disapproval. The damn fool, he should have his ears boxed. Just to get involved with McPhait was bad enough, but to let himself get in hock to him . . . ?

"Tell me more," she said. "I love compliments."

There wasn't very much more to tell. Five thousand would settle it for now. McPhait would be willing to wait for the rest.

He looked at her pleadingly. The big bluff face was flushed, and there were beads of sweat across his upper lip, and yet the little boy's lips puckered winsomely. It was remarkable how naturally he had settled into the role of the naughty child to whom everything would be forgiven because—come on now—wasn't he also the charming boy whom everybody loved? "A real boy," as his parents had undoubtedly told their friends while they were getting him out of his latest mess.

"Just like a boy," the friends would undoubtedly have agreed.

She couldn't help but wonder whether he fell into the same pose of endearing helplessness, the little smile waiting behind the eyes for permission to come out, when he talked to Eleanor about the divorce. About *her*. What did Eleanor call her—*that tart of yours?* "Have you still got that tart of yours in the courtroom?" she heard Eleanor saying.

She also discovered, soon enough, that anybody who said Harrison T. Davies was beyond shock was a liar. All she'd had to do to prove it was suggest that he might be making too much of this since McPhait, for all his political influence, wouldn't dare do anything to a judge and what would it profit him to let anybody know that Harry had been gambling with him? A gambling debt, said the shocked Judge Davies, was a debt of honor. The fact that it couldn't be collected in a court of law had nothing to do with it. Didn't she understand that his reputation would be ruined if he welshed on a gambling debt? "A judge's reputation is—when you lose your reputation you might as well retire from the Bench."

Just like a man, she thought, and was immediately struck by the world of difference that lay between the mother's "just like a boy" and the woman's "just like a man." A man's honor demanded that a gambling debt be paid to a law-breaker who, for all he knew, had cheated him. Well, Marie Pappas held a promissory note too, which while not enforceable in a court of law was also not enforceable under any code of masculine honor. Redress was demanded. She had been faithful to Harry ever since they began to sleep together. Perhaps she should think more seriously about that.

"What's so funny?" Davies asked, ready to have his tender male ego bruised at a moment's notice.

She hadn't realized that she had laughed. She had laughed because having made the decision to go to bed with Bannerman, she understood that she had found an excuse to do what she had wanted to do all along. Already she was wondering how she could manage it without Harry getting wind of it. Taking it one step further she wondered whether it might not be just as well if Harry did get wind of it.

Marie had enough money, as he damn well knew, so that five thousand dollars wasn't going to kill her. The trouble was that she had spent so much in the pursuit of him that she was not able to bring herself to even consider giving it to him, an irony that, to give him his due, might not be entirely lost on him. There was something else that had better be considered, too. (Unknown to herself, she had been considering it from the beginning, much in the same way that mothers, in their sleep, are tuned to the cry of their babies.) If Harry was in such terrible financial condition that he didn't have five thousand dollars, he could not possibly make the kind of settlement that would encourage Eleanor to give him the divorce.

"Harry, she said, watching him pace, "you keep doing that and you're going to pull out all your hair."

He didn't have the slightest idea what she was talking about, but in his befuddlement he removed his hand from his hair anyway. "If only I could get a big case," he said, clenching his fists. "Ha! Can you imagine me getting a break like that?" With everything about him discounting any such possibility, he immediately assumed that he could. If he had the Tabor case, for instance, he'd be instantly famous, and once the trial was over he'd be in demand on the lecture circuit. There was big money there, he told her sagely. One speech was all you needed and you could deliver it over and over at twenty-five hundred a crack. He had a dozen of them, all of them informative and full of his distinctive wit and humor, and he'd been giving them away at luncheons for years.

He had already figured it out. If he held his lectures down to only one a week, that would be ten thousand a month, or a hundred and twenty thousand a year. That was less the agent's cut, she was to understand; apparently he didn't want her to go getting any ideas. "They take a third in this business, but eighty thousand a year, do you think that's so bad?" He came very close to laughing. "You bet it ain't."

It was ethical, too, he told her virtuously. They had Supreme Court Justices making the rounds regularly.

She searched his face, the big handsome face untouched so far by scandal, disgrace or brains. "Harry," she said, "I should be able to do all right during the trial." That money he could have, she said, letting him see that was as far as she would go. She had responsibilities, too. She had a mother to take care of. And herself. "Until someone can offer me some security, I just can't see my way clear to dip into capital."

"Security?"

"That means marriage, Harry. A husband to have and to hold. That means speak now or forever hold your peace."

"Marie . . . !" Harrison T. Davies—God bless him—was stricken. She didn't for one second think he was handing her a line, did she? "Aw honey. Why, if I could get Eleanor to . . . In a minute, honey. Tomorrow!"

She signaled him with a wave of the hand not to bother. When the papers were filed, and the break was complete, he could have access to her bank account. Her steady, stubborn gaze said: Not until.

She didn't tell herself that it was over. She didn't tell herself that now was the time to get out. It wasn't love anymore. Or security. It wasn't even protecting her investment. It was an even more overpowering bitch-female excretion handed down from the Mother of Them All. Curiosity. Having worked so long and planned so hard, she would never forgive herself if she didn't hang around long enough to find out how it was going to come out.

She knew, though. If she didn't know that it was over, she knew that the time would come when she would look back on this moment, in this apartment, with Harry standing over there and her standing over here, and she would say, I *knew* I should have got out then, I *knew* it!

All she knew for certain at the moment was that if she was the only hope he had, she had him in a mood where he would aim to please. The bitch-female in her, having been roused, would now proceed to put him through the jumps in the bitch-female's time-honored way. She turned her back and, raising her arms languidly, asked him to unbutton her. Seeing his surprise, she said, "Well, honey, I didn't say until then, nothing doing."

Framed on the wall behind Pawley's desk was his personal motto:

The Law of the Day
Everybody gets Everything Wrong

All the time or Does it for the
Wrong Reason and it comes out
Opposite from the Way it was
Supposed to, anyway.
But Don't Worry, I've got
Everything under Control.

DeWitt Pawley, even more immaculate than usual, was saying, "Having enjoined the press from accepting jurisdiction over this case under the cover of some presumed rights of a free press—what do you think this is, a free country or something?—having forbidden you gentlemen of the Fourth Estate from interviewing any of the participants lest the prospective jurors become contaminated with any truth we do not wish to burden them with . . ." He was trying very hard to remain solemn. "I don't see how it would have been possible to get Bannerman to talk anyway. Ambose's spies tell me he sneaks into the courtroom under cover of darkness . . . having, as I say, stifled a compliant press, the lawyers for the people and for the defendant will now attempt to pick a jury as prejudiced to its own side as possible by reason of age, temperament, background, experience, race, religion, nationality, geographic origin, occupation, economic and marital status and, if we're really up against the wall, intelligence. When such a juror falls to us we will fight like tigers to keep him. When the other side gets such a juror we will fight like tigers to disqualify him. This is known as the pursuit for truth. For further detail, I will refer you to James Ambose, assistant district attorney, Brederton County."

"Come on," Caples said. "You can get a little more specific than that. Just what kind of a juror are you guys going to be shooting for?"

"For publication? For publication you may say that the state seeks nothing more than twelve impartial jurors who will listen with open minds to the prosecution and defense alike." Lowering his voice, he said, "Between you and me, Rich, we'll take all the psychopathic killers we can get. Just offhand, I'd say the ideal prosecution juror for the Sam Tabor trial would be Sam Tabor. Bring your friends around to see Bob Stringfellow, Corinne," he said, raising his voice and looking past Caples to the door. "But I'd get them there early if I were you. Chobodian ain't gonna let nobody, but nobody, sit in the jury box."

Corinne told him, most gratefully, that was all anybody could ask for and declined his invitation, most ungratefully, to come on in and listen to his lecture on the selection of jurors.

"That's too bad." He sighed. "It's really worth traveling miles to hear. I myself am learning new things just by listening to myself."

Caples was glad one of them was.

"There are those attorneys who will tell you that picking juries is an art, and that being an art, it can be mastered. I'd be the last person in the world to tell you they'd be kidding you, since it's always possible that they're kidding themsleves." The first case Pawley had prosecuted had involved an insanity plea and he had studied up on schizophrenia until it was running out of his ears. After the jury came back with a death verdict, he had set out, with the energy and ambition of the young, to interview all twelve jurors so that he could find out which part of his brilliant presentation had been most convincing. "The first one told me he had noticed that every time the judge came into the room, the bailiff told everybody to rise and put out all cigarettes, and the defendant would immediately rise and put out his cigarette, and so how crazy could he be?" The second one had carefully noted that the defendant's girl friend was a very pretty, obviously sane young lady, and a girl like that wouldn't have been going around with any nut, would she? "My tender ego rose up at that point to enjoin me from further investigation."

Caples gave it a little thought. "Are you saying that insanity pleas should be heard by a panel of experts, then?"

"I don't know what I'm saying. Maybe I'm saying the jurors know more than we do." He stubbed his cigarette out in the ash tray. "No, let's keep decision-making policy out of the hands of the experts. Experts are a group of men, heavily diplomaed, who preside over the coming disaster." His lip puckered impishly. "Hey, I've finally given you something you can quote me on. Here's something else. DeWitt Pawley, handsome and popular assistant district attorney, observed humorously that the women, almost to a man, would take the capital-punishment out."

Caples, doodling around in his notebook, said, "Just for future reference, Dee, are you a candidate for district attorney if Nevins gets his judgeship?"

Pawley threw back his head and laughed. "Speaking of experts, what will be my own modest contribution to the chaos of our times, huh?" He put on his best politician face, grave and pompous. "You may say, for the record, that I have no ambition save to spend the rest of my days as an assistant to that gre-e-e-at public servant, Hilliard Nevins. You may say, furthermore, that while it would be presumptuous of me to decline a position that is not available and has not been offered . . ."

"But if Hilliard Nevins should go on to higher office . . ." Caples prompted, falling into the same playful spirit. He had taken his shot and either he had been wrong or Pawley had snapped to, faster than the eye could follow, and realized that the man across the desk, a friend in all other regards, was no friend here. Not where a story was concerned. Having been brought up in the adversary system, Pawley's bones would understand that.

"That'll do it." Caples slapped the notebook shut. "I can fill in the rest of it from memory. Humility and all."

Ambose had a *Washington Post* writer in interviewing him for a Sunday piece on the difficulties of picking a jury in an insanity trial, the first out-of-town writer to seek him out since the proceedings had got under way. He was a short man with rimless glasses, probably in his forties, extremely soft-spoken and obviously quite capable. His article, he had been telling Ambose, would appear in both the *Washington Post* and the *Los Angeles Times* and would also be put on the syndicate wire to be picked up by any of the subscribers, including the *New York Post*. "Be happy to talk to you anyway, Larry," Ambose said. "We wouldn't want you to think Bannerman was the only publicity hound in town."

The man from the *Washington Post* didn't react one way or the other, which Ambose took to be his way of showing that he wasn't going to be jollied into taking sides. That told Ambose all he had to know. The man from Washington would be an Eastern liberal and therefore against capital punishment, all for rehabilitation (whether he could tell you what it meant or not), automatically on the side of the defense and therefore incapable of watching the trial with any objectivity, and would consider himself, on all things, on the side of the angels. A typical newspaperman. Ambose would answer his questions to the best of his ability anyway in the hope of getting some part of the prosecution story into the papers. In addition to which, it would do him no harm at all to get his name into the papers in Washington, Los Angeles, New York and all those other places. (There was another reason Ambose would answer all questions honestly, but that was a reason Ambose couldn't possibly be aware of. Jim Ambose didn't really know how to lie when he was asked for his opinions, a defect of character that kept him shuttling in and out of Nevins' dog house for years.)

In honor of the first question, the man from Washington raised his voice so that Ambose didn't have to strain to hear him. Bannerman was saying it was going to be impossible to pick an impartial jury in Lowell. How long did Ambose think it would take?

"Just when you think we'll never pick one, Bannerman will run out of his peremptories, or he'll decide, what the hell, he's got to put a jury in the box, the law says so. And all of a sudden it will be over. If he wants to run out all his peremptories—he has twelve, we have nine—before he puts one in the box, that's just fine with us. All he's doing there is letting us pick the whole jury."

"Which do you think he'll do?"

"He's made a lot of noise to you newspaper people about running them out, so my guess is he won't take anybody the first day. The first good-looking juror he runs across the second day, he'll grab him. You've covered trials before, haven't you, Larry? Then you know that a trial has a life all its own. What he says outside the courtroom and what he does inside are two different things. What he thinks he's going to do and what he finds himself doing could be two different things, too." He caught just enough of a smirk to admit, "I say 'he.' I mean all of us."

"I can see you take a very practical view of these things. If you had to bet right now, practically speaking, what the verdict is going to be . . . what would your bet be?"

"Life or death," Ambose said immediately. "First degree either way. You want a straight answer: Death. Maybe one chance out of fifty they'll find some reason to let him off with life."

What about insanity, Larry wanted to know. Was he really, as a practical man, discounting the actual plea before the trial began? Or was he perhaps discounting it for public consumption only?

An insanity plea, Ambose told him gently, was just a way of giving the jury a chance to do whatever it wanted to do. That was his one chance in fifty. "Temporary insanity now, that's something else altogether. Temporary insanity is really a way of pleading justifiable homicide. Usually—if you were there at the bond hearing—it's a way of giving the jury a legal way to find for the unwritten law."

Ambose wanted to ask the reporter a question now. In all his career as a journalist, how many insanity verdicts had he come across? In big publicized cases especially? When the man from Washington couldn't think of any offhand, Ambose nodded in satisfaction. Where his answers had been quick and measured —rapid-fire answers reeled off upon request—he now leaned forward, resting lightly on his elbows, and began to talk in a far more relaxed conversational tone. "In an insanity case the jury's sitting there not wanting to be fooled by all those highfalutin professors. The jury hears the evidence, and then the folks bring in the verdict. Understand what I'm telling you? It's a plea where the lawyer can't lose and the client can't win. Now you're wondering why I say that?"

Before he could tell him why, an inner glow of recognition, well pleased with itself, arose in Larry's eyes. "Leopold–Loeb," he said. "Of course, I know that's going a long way back."

He'd gone all that way, Ambose told him, for nothing. "Leopold–Loeb was heard before a judge, no jury sitting. Darrow was no fool. He didn't plead them insane, he pleaded them guilty on murder one, with mitigating circumstances. The mitigating circumstances being they were so rich there had to be something wrong with them or they wouldn't have done anything that dumb, and if there's something wrong with them . . . well, that's a mental disease, isn't it? The judge sentenced them to life for murder plus ninety-nine years for kidnapping, on His Honor's honor, cross my heart and hope to die, no parole. You ought to read up on that case sometimes if you got a stomach for bullshit."

As the man from the *Washington Post* looked on, fascinated, the same smoldering anger that he must have felt when he himself had first "read up" on that case came over Ambose. "What that smart bastard did was to hang an insanity case in front of that senile old judge to give him something to hang his hat on. But when it came down to the money," he said, with a thin, mirthless smile, "you can bet he wasn't pleading insanity. What he did, the slippery bastard, was to turn it into a plea for mercy because of their youth."

The anger, spent, curled comfortably into contempt. "Hell," he said, biting off the end of a cigar and spitting it out. "Two-bit lawyers do that in Juvenile Court every day without bothering to run their pet psychiatrists in and out of the chute."

Before the *Washington Post* man's startled eyes Jim Ambose's craggy features became prim and in a pinched falsetto he was pleading, "Mercy, judge! Oh, please have mercy, mercy and more mercy on these poor unfortunate lads." A moment later and Ambose was sitting back, smiling at him, the little cigar clenched dead-center between his teeth. "Does Bannerman strike you as a man who's going to stand up before the world and plead for mercy?"

It seemed to Ambose that the man from Washington was looking back at him with an air of discovery. Which probably meant that he had come to understand that he had finally run across the one lawyer in this case who would give it to him straight, without the bullshit. "I'm going to write this, you know," Larry warned him. "And that means Bannerman will be reading it."

Ambose's smile became even broader. "Good," he said. "That's all the more reason why he won't."

As his final question, the man from Washington wanted to know whether Ambose, out of his considerable experience, agreed with those elements of the Bar, generally considered progressive, who believed that insanity pleas should be submitted to a board of qualified experts instead of to a jury of laymen. "From what you've said about juries being so predisposed against psychiatric evidence," he said helpfully, "I'd suppose you would."

It was only then that Ambose realized, as he should have known all along, that they had been operating on completely different wavelengths from the beginning. This guy, no fool, had heard all the words and played them back to his own music. The only thing that surprised Ambose was that, after all this time, he should have been surprised. Temptation was running strong in him to save what he could for himself by turning the question away with a soft answer and then going back to clarify a few meanings. It wouldn't have cost him very much because he rather liked this guy, if only for having had the editorial enterprise to seek him out. And then he thought, To hell with it. That's all, just to hell with it.

"Them shitheads!" he said, riding free. "Them shitheads, they're just as like to get all mixed up and decide the defense lawyers were the crazy ones. In this one they might be right."

Larry was writing it down word for word, cleaning the inside of one of his lenses with one hand without stopping the movement of his pencil for a second. Nevins was sure going to love this.

"I was going to ask you," the man from Washington said, rising, "can we send a photographer around to take your picture?"

"Is the Pope a Catholic?" answered Smiling Jim Ambose, with the freedom that can only come to a man who knows he has returned to himself.

On his way to the courtroom Ambose stuck his head into Nevins' office. "You hear what that shithead's gone and done? He's hired my li'l friend, Alfred Marma, for the voir dire. You don't suppose he'll be crazy enough to have him sit there through the trial, do you? The jury would just have to look at Alfred, and Wilcke would never be out of the courtroom."

Nevins was working in his shirtsleeves, chewing down on an unlit cigar, the surest sign that he was beginning to feel the pressure. He scowled at Ambose, grunted, and turned his attention back to his papers. But as soon as Ambose turned to leave, his head shot back up and he growled, "Let's just see if you can get a couple of your friends from the Birch Society in the box. I'll like that even better."

Between the courtroom and the outer corridor there was a small square room, usually called the Judge's Cloakroom, which had been drawn into the original blueprints as a sort of temporary chambers or general utility room. Since Chobodian had never bothered with it, it had come to be used as a place where the lawyers could meet with their clients before the court was called into session. The furnishings were spare and utilitarian. Nothing more than an old bare wooden table, upon which Norman Bannerman was sitting, and a couple of wooden chairs. (There was also an old battered coffeepot sitting in the chipped enamel sink.)

Cowhig was seated in one of the chairs, his legs crossed comfortably, ready to take notes. Halpern, Marma and Bo Gunderson were gathered around Bannerman for a final discussion on the voir dire. Gunderson had been hired on a strictly hourly basis (one hundred dollars per), having offered his services to Bannerman while he was being interviewed about the luncheon with Tabor.

Bannerman had got rid of Hugh Fletcher by sending him off to set up a "command post" in the fourth-floor office Chobodian had assigned to the defense. After the veniremen were impaneled and Chobodian had shuffled the cards, Stringfellow was going to have the entire list typed up and mimeographed for the lawyers and the press and he had promised that he would also send a copy up to Fletcher. To give Fletcher some elbow room Bannerman had told him to ignore the first fifteen, since he was going to strike them anyway. Picking up on number sixteen, Fletcher and two of his men would interview the prospective juror's neighbors and employer and the people he worked with. Cowhig would be a swing man, filling in or manning the phone as the need arose.

Gunderson, who had never seen such a well-organized operation before, was visibly impressed. He himself had solved the problem, he told Bannerman, by relying upon the good will of his friends, the avarice of tipsters and—his tongue was in his cheek—the essential honesty of his fellow man. "I don't win many cases that way, but I sure save a lot of money."

"What you mean," Alfred Marma said, in his high, reedy voice, "is that you've kept up your connections in the DA's office."

You could see Bo's mind turn over and come to the decision that there was fun to be had here. "It is perhaps true they have come to look upon me as a friendly sort," he said, affecting a small voice and a ragamuffin innocence. "I mean no harm to anybody." But if it was connections Marma wanted to talk about, he said, in a hopefully devastating change of pace, he wouldn't dream of putting himself in a class with the Lowell Civil Liberties Union.

Getting down to the business at hand, Gunderson had found farmers on the outskirts of the county to be a generally conservative, religious lot, hard-headed and hard to fool. "You'll try to razzle-dazzle them and they'll sit there, without blinking an eye, and go back upstairs and kill you." Marma was not so pessimistic. He had found them generally sympathetic on his type of cases. "Not predictable. Just sympathetic."

What Bannerman had to watch out for particularly, Gunderson said, were the hillbillies who had been migrating into the city. They lived mostly in South Section, in an area called Paynter's Corner, and were beginning to spill over into the black section. "Some of 'em are good, but . . . " He turned both thumbs down. Emphatically. "Nine times out of ten they're conviction people. Don't ask me why, they're treated like hell. Must be they're still Christers."

When Marma told him that the question of black jurors was moot because Nevins wasn't going to take any of the brothers, Bannerman snapped back, with approval, that maybe he wouldn't have any choice. "If he dumps 'em all, we get ourselves another ground for appeal. Nonrepresentative jury." Marma couldn't see how he was going to get away with that when it wasn't a black man on trial. "Part of the pattern of exclusion," Bannerman said airily. "I don't imagine we're going to get too many of 'em on the panel to begin with."

Halpern wasn't as sure as Marma that Nevins would want to exclude blacks. It seemed to him that with Wilcke as the victim blacks would be good prosecution jurors. But Marma only looked at him with a sort of curdled tolerance. Nobody, he informed him, was going to be choosing up sides between Wilcke and Tabor. "It's the authorities against a man who attacked the power structure in a rage, and in case the word hasn't gotten to you, the authorities ain't loved down where I come from."

"Ambose," Bannerman said. "I can well understand."

Ambose? Hell, Ambose wan't the problem. With Ambose you always knew where you stood. Alfred Marma rocked up on his tippy-toes, smiling to himself in a dreamy, faraway sort of way as if something had suddenly tickled him. "Nobody ever called Ambose a middle-class liberal, man. Ambose don't give you no sweet cream but he don't tell you no sweet lies either."

An even more basic disagreement was exposed on where the sympathies of the working man might be presumed to lie. There had been a lot of union trouble in town over the past couple of years, particularly in the building trades with all the new buildings going up, and with most of the building unions having been hit with court injunctions and fined pretty heavily Gunderson saw no reason for them to like the authorities at the moment, and especially the judges.

On the other hand, Cowhig said, they were law and order men, great for the prosecution.

On still the other hand, said Halpern, holding to his own view of the priorities, being law and order men they had little use for Wilcke.

Sure, Marma said, but they were racists. "For what it's worth, Bannerman, I get rid of them quick."

"In your civil rights cases," Bannerman said.

Alfred boggled at him again. "Civil rights, civil shit," he squealed. "There's some of them fuckers so prejudiced they'll look right at me and think I'm black."

The rest of it was pretty routine, Gunderson told him. Except that there had been a big thing on about auxiliary police in some of the city neighborhoods, so Norman had better make sure they didn't slip an auxiliary cop in on him. As to the ethnic groups, he didn't really think Bannerman wanted to be burdened with his own pet theories, that being a free form of expression, like nonobjective art, where it was every man for himself. "Now, most lawyers say cold-weather countries make for cold-blooded jurors. But somehow," he said, pulling at his ear and smiling crookedly, "I find Norwegians and Swedes just kind of take to me."

He squinted at his notes again, bringing the paper up close to his eyes and then drawing it away. "I hope my eyesight is failing," he said, "because if it ain't I've got lousy handwriting. Ah yes, the Italian factor." An Italian colleague, Ianello by name, had warned him never to take Italians on a murder jury unless they were second-generation college graduates or they had the fruit-peddler laugh in them. "I asked him, as you are about to ask me, how you can spot the fruit-peddler laugh, and he said you couldn't unless you're Italian yourself. After giving it reasonable consideration I decided the inducement to be insufficient." Italians were bastards, his Italian colleague had advised him, because they had been brought up in the tradition of vendetta. "You do something to them or theirs and they have the curious notion that they're supposed to go out and do something back to you. No regard whatsoever for such legal niceties as due process and lawyer's fees." In a rape case, according to Ianello, they would vote conviction without leaving the box, and if the lawyer had been too rough on the lady they just might jump the rail and execute a little summary justice on him.

There was in the air the feeling of a beat being skipped, lasting just long enough to take one long deep breath, while Bo, having moved from advisor to raconteur, slipped back a notch into an intermediate gear. "Ianello's bona fides in this regard are to be respected. He's had the lock on the lucrative rape business ever since Sandor Zabilski got his head kicked in in an alley behind the Red Devil Tavern. Zabilski, as you have probably gathered, was an earlier specialist in browbeating the unfortuante maid who had loved not unwisely but unwillingly." With precise and elaborate care, almost as if he were following stage directions, Bo sat himself down in the empty chair, turned to Bannerman and said, "There's some who think Jim Ambose did the kicking."

Bannerman's mouth opened and, for one split-second, as Halpern thought he heard the hiss of breath being expelled and saw Bannerman's head cock and his forehead wrinkle, he was reminded of Sam Tabor. Just as quickly, the image dissolved and there was nothing to be seen on Bannerman's face except an expression of mild annoyance that Bo should have gone to all that trouble just so that he could bring in that zinger from out of left field.

"All he means," Marma told Bannerman, with a sidelong glance of rebuke at Bo, "is that Ambose was on the other side." Marma's version, which must have been a mixture of what he had heard and what he had read, was that Zabilski had got the poor girl so hysterical that her family had withdrawn charges rather than let her go back on the stand. A couple of nights later Zabilski was found in the alley and his client was picked up away over in another part of town with his neck slit and an essential portion of his anatomy missing. Since the girl had six brothers, there wasn't that much doubt who had done it, even though by one of those fortunate coincidences all six happened to have convenient alibis. Each other. "That doesn't mean Ambose wouldn't pass the word around that it was him if he thinks it's gonna scare you. You let him think for one minute he can scare you and he's all over you like white on rice." In a suddenly dry tone that had to be shoehorned into his meager voice, he told Bannerman, "In case you don't already know it, he plays rough."

"In case he don't already know it," Bannerman said pleasantly, "so do I. I think we've done it, gentlemen. Shall we go out and count the house?"

Having determined that the courtroom was already filled, Bannerman hung back in the well area of the bar with Gunderson to settle their account. Bannerman proposed that they call it a flat hour and, to sweeten the pot a little, he'd throw in some free advice. "That Italian Factor," he said. "You never did mention whether your friend Ianello ever wins a murder case." He shook his head in sad disapproval. "Italians are the best murder jurors you can find anywhere. I'd be happy to tell you why, except that I know you look upon it as a personal challenge to figure it out for yourself."

Bo was smiling past Bannerman to some friends who were waving to him from their courtroom seats. Like he had said, that kind of thing was a matter of taste, personality and trial-and-error. "Jim Ambose calls it a crap game, although I'm not sure exactly how he means that. Just as an example, Norman. You've made one bad mistake already. You should have gone all out in the change-of-venue and I *know* it didn't make a damn's worth of difference to you whether you got out of town." Bo placed his hand on Bannerman's shoulder. "But there wasn't any way for you to have known about it. There isn't any way for anybody to know about it except me." Just, he said, doing his best to look terribly sincere, as there wasn't anybody else who could have known that it would have been impossible for Ambose to have done the job on Zabilski because, by another of those fortunate coincidences, Ambose had been inside the Red Devil at the time drinking with Bo. "The only reason I happen to remember it so distinctly," he said, "is that Nevins took such particular care about having me set it down in writing that Ambose never left my sight that night."

Lowell, July 12 (AP)—The first juror, a 58-year-old printer, was seated in the trial of Samuel Tabor today, in a tense and dissension-wracked opening session which started with famed defense attorney Norman Bannerman and Asst. District Attorney James Ambose being hit with $50 fines and ended with the startling indication that the alleged assassin of Chief Justice David Boone Wilcke would take the witness stand and testify in his own behalf. The fireworks began when the silver-tongued Chicago attorney Norman Bannerman challenged the entire Grand Jury system of Brederton County and hence the legality of the murder indictment itself by contending that these jurors did not sufficiently represent the poor, uneducated and unpropertied. Grand Jurors are nominated by a Superior Judicial Panel here, and Mr. Bannerman was able to submit affidavits from two of the three panel members describing the process of selection.

By the time the afternoon session was an hour old, Mr. Bannerman had also entered a sweeping challenge against the whole system whereby those who express a moral compulsion against capital punishment are excluded from serving on American juries. In compliance with a recent Supreme Court decision, Judge Elijah Chobodian, the rock-faced presiding jurist, had already asked Mrs. Lois Hawkins, an obviously nervous 33-year-old housewife, whether there were any circumstances under which she might be induced to lay her scruples aside and return a death penalty. It was not a matter of laying anything aside, the young matron replied firmly, it was a matter of principle. "The cream of the panel is being skimmed right off the top," Mr. Bannerman declared, in objecting to Mrs. Hawkins' exclusion. "By the very act of asking for the death penalty, Mr. Nevins is being permitted to harden the face of the jury."

The most dramatic and explosive outburst of the day, however, came hard on the heels of the defense attorney's two-and-a-half-hour interrogation of the first venireman, John Lahrke, an interrogation so intensive that it took up the entire morning session. Like all but one of the ten veniremen questioned, Mr. Lahrke, a 34-year-old camera store manager, admitted to having seen the television pictures of the murder of the late Chief Justice. Mr. Bannerman, whose courtroom theatrics have become legendary, threw the courtroom into bedlam and enraged District Attorney Hilliard Nevins as well as the gray-haired, normally unflappable presiding jurist by . . .

The man who got in the first dirty blow was neither Ambose nor Bannerman. It was Hilliard Nevins. As soon as the first venireman was sworn, Nevins introduced himself and his assistants and asked whether he knew them or anyone else connected with the district attorney's office. In the same folksy way he said, "Over there at the defense table, there's Norman Bannerman of Chicago. He's well thought of up there. They say he's one of the best six or seven lawyers they have."

Chobodian was already banging his gavel before Bannerman, who had been paying very little attention to the routine introductions, jerked his head around and shot him a look of profound contempt. By then, Nevins was already telling the juror that he'd probably heard more about Mr. Bannerman's associates. "They're local people Mr. Bannerman hired to bring him up to snuff on our local laws. On Mr. Tabor's right, closest to us, is Alfred Marma of this city and on the far left, that's Harold Halpern, a former member of my own staff . . ."

Lahrke was a youngish-looking man with sideburns. Looking down from the Bench, Chobodian could see that his suit was a little loose, leaving the judge with the impression of a man in a constant battle with his weight, and because the suit was clearly an expensive one, it was reasonable to assume that he was in his best condition in years. All in all, here was the kind of man who would probably have been able to duck jury duty if he had wanted to. He had stayed on, it could be surmised, hoping that he'd hit the Tabor trial, and first name out, had hit the jackpot. Which meant, little did he know, that he had no chance at all of being accepted.

If Nevins' introductions had annoyed Bannerman, his opening statement destroyed Sam Tabor.

"The duty of a juror, as I expect you know, is to determine guilt or innocence and then to assess punishment. The defendant, Sam Tabor," he said in his casual, folksy way, "is charged with first-degree murder. The maximum penalty on that charge in this state is death in the electric chair, and I will now inform you that we will be asking you and the other jurors to return the maximum verdict. Death in the electric chair."

Tabor's head snapped back as if he had been hit right between the eyes. What he had known all along had not become real, apparently, until he had heard it spoken aloud in open court. *They really mean it!* Hilliard Nevins, whom he had seen around the courthouse for years, whom he had said hello to a hundred times, *whom he had smiled at and who had smiled back at him,* was really asking this complete stranger if it was all right with him if they killed Sam Tabor. They were *(dear Jesus, I love you)* out to take his life away from him.

A glaze came over Tabor's eyes at that moment, and his face seemed to stiffen. It would continue to stiffen, day by day, as if he were slowly and very carefully building a protective fiber network around himself.

Nevins was asking the stranger whether he had any religious or conscientious scruples against capital punishment. "The only thing I'm asking you, in the roundabout way we lawyers do these things, is do you believe in capital punishment?"

Bannerman had instructed Halpern to always watch a prospective juror's hands and legs when the capital punishment question was put to him, because if he crossed (or uncrossed) his legs it meant he was lying, and if he jerked his thumb . . . well, Halpern could be sure that he not only believed in capital punishment but was so eager to get the job done that he was throwing the switch himself. Lahrke's hands remained folded in his lap as he answered that he did, and he even felt constrained to add, perhaps too virtuously, "If the circumstances warrant." Bannerman, who had been watching him like a hawk, jabbed his elbow into Halpern and hissed, "Did you see his lips? Did you catch that twitch? It's gonna turn out this guy was in the infantry and he was biting off a grenade. Oh, we've got a real killer sitting up there. Just wait till I get my mitts on this guy."

Nevins' style, it became apparent soon enough, was not so much to ask questions as to assure the prospective juror that he, as his duly elected law enforcement officer, was confident that he would do the right thing.

"Now you don't know anything about this case from your own knowledge, do you?"

"You're not the type of man who'd try someone because of what he's read or heard or seen? You'd want it proved all the way up, to your own satisfaction?"

"You could serve on this jury with an open mind and find according to the testimony, as it was presented, giving a fair and equal hearing to the defense and the state alike, is that about the size of it?"

"Now, there've been indications that the defense is going to be based on an insanity plea. You probably know what that means anyway, but the law says I have to explain it to you so that's what I'm gonna do. The law presumes a man's innocence but it doesn't, in this state, presume his sanity. That puts the burden of proof on the prosecution. That's us. That's all right with you, isn't it?"

Bannerman, making his only objection, said rather dourly that the question would be all right with the defense if Mr. Nevins would make it just a wee bit clearer that "us" did not include the man in the witness chair.

Nevins had been leaning forward, gesturing with his hands. Before he turned the prospective juror over to Bannerman, he settled back, took a hitch on his pants, and in a voice that showed he was drawing the only possible conclusion he asked, "If you were satisfied he was guilty then, you'd vote guilty, and if you were satisfied he was sane, you'd vote he was sane?"

Bannerman arose with alacrity but his voice was so soft that the audience had to strain to hear him. "Mr. Lahrke, I believe we have already been introduced. I'm that fellow from Chicago you've been hearing about. It is my duty to examine your feelings, your opinions, the state of your mind, to comb through your conscience for any prejudices that might be lying around loose. You understand that, I hope? No offense will be taken?"

"Of course not, Mr. Bannerman."

Bannerman smiled at the witness, no less pleased with him, it appeared, than Nevins had been. Lifting his voice a couple of notches, he said, "So you're all for capital punishment, are you?"

"In a fit case."

Bannerman brought his hands up in the gentle attitude of a Buddhist priest and lowered his eyes. "Let us pray."

"All right, Mr. Bannerman," Chobodian said. "Let's understand each other!"

"I'm interested, Mr. Lahrke, in knowing what you've read about the murder of Chief Justice Wilcke that you don't believe."

With Lahrke insisting that he couldn't remember exactly what he had read about it one way or the other, Pawley arose to object in loud and scornful tones that while the state had no fault to find with Mr. Bannerman's line of questioning there was a right and a wrong way to go about it, and the right way was not to throw out a net and see what he might be able to drag in.

"Well, let's find out just how much you do know, then. Do you know that David Wilcke is dead?"

"I know that."

"The word got to you, huh? Have any idea who did it?"

"No, sir. Well, not for sure I don't."

"Let me see if I can be of any help in piercing this veil of mystery. Do you have a sneaking suspicion that it might be this gentleman, Sam Tabor, seated beside me? Stand up, Sam." With a helping hand from Bannerman, Tabor came, somewhat dazed, to his feet.

"I know he's accused of it."

"Now, Mr. Lahrke," he said, and he might as well have been admonishing a small boy for telling a foolish lie. "You saw him do it on television. Now, didn't you?"

"I saw something on television. A rerun is what it was. A couple of days afterwards."

"How did you hear about the assassination? You never did get around to telling me that."

"I believe it was at work. Just before leaving."

"And you didn't rush home and turn on the news to watch it?"

"No, sir."

"Not that night or the next?"

"No, sir."

"Just wasn't interested?"

Nevins said, "He said he didn't see it until then, Judge."

"That isn't what I'm asking now," Bannerman said, trying to hold his rhythm. "How many television sets do you have in the house, sir?"

The man in the witness box hesitated. "Two."

By actual computation, Bannerman informed him, the film had been shown on the various Lowell stations seventeen times in those two days. He could hardly have turned on the set and avoided it.

Nevins said, "He said he saw it two nights later, Judge."

"Could it have been one night later, Mr. Lahrke?"

Lahrke took a deep breath. "It could have been, Mr. Bannerman, it could have. It seems to me it was two nights later but I wasn't keeping count that much."

"Of course not. I didn't ask you, sir. Which of the papers do you get delivered?"

He hesitated just a little too long to be able to say he didn't get either of them. "The *Globe.*"

"That's all right, Mr. Lahrke, you're doing just fine. You just get it delivered to your doorstep so that you can look at the camera ads, right?"

Before Nevins could object, Chobodian was instructing Bannerman to rephrase the question.

"Why bother? Would you tell me, sir, just what you saw on the rerun a couple of days afterwards?"

Having been brought by degrees to admit that he had seen the Chief Justice fall and a lot of people milling around on the stairs, Lahrke not only was looking tired, he was looking as if he wished he were any place in the world except where he was.

"You saw Sam shooting then," Bannerman snapped. "Right?"

"I don't know who was shooting. It didn't show the shooting."

It was Bannerman who let the air go quiet then, and since he had been firing his questions off so rapidly the next few seconds seemed considerably longer. "You see, Mr. Lahrke, how badly you have been underestimating your powers of observation?" They would now test Mr. Lahrke's powers of deduction, and Bannerman hoped he wouldn't be excessively modest. "Why do you think Sam is sitting here in this courtroom if he wasn't the man who did the shooting?"

"Arrested's one thing, shooting's another."

"Fair enough. I can see that you subscribe to the romantic notion that a man is presumed innocent until proven guilty. Sam Tabor sits beside me as innocent of the murder of David Wilcke as you or I or anyone in this courtroom until the state proves its case." His voice cracked like a whip: "Right?"

A wary look stole over Lahrke's face. Everybody in the courtroom could see that he was wondering what new trap was being set to make him look ridiculous before the world. "Yes, sir. That's the American way of justice."

"You heard it was Sam did the shooting, though?"

"I don't believe everything I hear."

"You're a delightfully skeptical man, Mr. Lahrke. But I don't suppose you can trust anybody in the camera game, can you? Suppose I tell you—"

Chobodian, looking very stern, said, "Suppose I tell you that we will do without the personal asides, Mr. Bannerman."

By absorbing the judge's warning into his own rhythm, Bannerman was able to use it to build the tension. He studied the witness, rubbing his chin. "If I now tell you it was Sam Tabor who shot him, and that's why they nabbed him and he hired me, would you believe me?"

"I'd believe you."

"Well, we're finally making a dent in the old noggin." He folded his arms and crossed his knees. "So now you know that Sam Tabor killed David Wilcke?"

"Not until a jury says so."

"If a jury says he didn't kill him, you'd believe it?"

"I'd accept what the jury said," Lahrke said stiffly. "That's what I said." There was a stubborn set to his lips and a glare of hatred toward the lawyer who was twisting around everything he said.

"You'd *accept* it, as a citizen who believes in our system of justice. But you wouldn't believe it?"

Nevins had started to say, "That's all he—" but the witness had already snapped back, "I'd accept it and I'd believe it."

"If a jury finds my hair is purple, will you believe that, too?"

"That's different."

"Well, we have finally found the departure point of your credulity."

Norman Bannerman stood up, faced the Bench and asked that the venireman be dismissed for cause on the ground that he was so transparently and cynically attempting to hide his full knowledge and true opinions in a flagrant effort to qualify himself as a juror. "It is the contention of the defense further," Bannerman said, "that this juror's eagerness to serve can only be accounted for by a vindictive desire, arising from both the conscious and the unconscious, to execute Sam Tabor for bringing such shame and notoriety to the fair city of Lowell. With this in mind, Your Honor, I am at this time renewing my motion for a change of venue. I urge this Court, sincerely and prayerfully, to reconsider its earlier ruling."

From high on his eagle's perch Eli Chobodian had been observing the witness's squirmings with considerable discomfort of his own. How many of them had he seen climb into that chair and proceed to dig their own graves with the first hesitant little lie that was not really a lie to their own way of thinking so much as an honest disclaimer of personal prejudice. Judge Chobodian was convinced —an impression built up over so many years had to be heeded—that since they knew in their hearts that they could come to a verdict based solely on the evidence as it was presented to them in court, they felt they would be doing themselves an injustice if they allowed themselves to be marked on some enduring record sheet as biased men and flawed jurors.

Of course men like John Lahrke wanted a front-row seat to the coming spectacle. Of course they saw themselves acquiring a new weight in the eyes of their friends. But they were also full of the awe of their assignment, and whatever the personal cost or inconvenience they stood ready to do their duty as citizens.

The ones he despised were the pink-livered ones who took the capital punishment out, letting their spiritual superiority shine forth for all men to see while Chobodian was sensing, out of some instinct of long service, their base inner tremblings at the prospect of having to pass judgment upon one of their fellow men.

The delicate calibrations of the conscience, he thought (not for the first time), how did one measure them?

The infinite cross-patchery of the mind, he thought (not for the first time), how did one hope to slice through it?

You did your best, by god! That's what you did.

Pondering John Lahrke's problem, sympathizing with him as he did, Judge Chobodian had never for one moment been unmindful of the other, greater problem—his own problem as the presiding judge. Looking to the future, Judge Chobodian could assume that every venireman who climbed into that chair would have seen the film and read the newspapers. With Bannerman looking as if he might be serious about proving the impossibility of impaneling a jury in Lowell, Judge Chobodian was going to have to establish a formula that would give the state every chance to save those jurors who could lay that knowledge aside. Otherwise, they could be here until fall.

For very practical reasons, therefore, the Court would be establishing a very bad precedent if it let Mr. Lahrke go this early. Chobodian would protect him as best he could, but Mr. John Lahrke, summoned from his home by the power of his government to be insulted and made a fool of, was going to have to suffer for awhile more yet.

Amidst the general shifting and scraping of chairs at both tables Bannerman was brushing the sides of his hair back vigorously over and over and over. If he couldn't go one way, he would have to go the other. "All right, Mr. Lahrke, we have established that you haven't read anything about it, and that it took you forty-eight hours to get around to looking at it on television." His manner had changed abruptly. Where the corners of his questions had previously curled with scorn and disbelief, there was now a hard edge of hostility. "What you are telling us is that you tried to put all thoughts of that gruesome murder completely out of your mind because it was just too terrible to think about, isn't that right?"

By the time Bannerman finally got around to asking the question he had been spending an hour and a half leading up to, it really didn't seem to amount to very much. The question was: "You have a fixed opinion that Sam Tabor was the murderer of David Wilcke?"

"I have a lingering impression," Lahrke answered, willing enough to be reasonable about it.

"Of course you do. I will now ask you whether you can ever forget the lingering horror at the sight you saw on the television screen? It will haunt you the rest of your life, won't it?"

That was it. "The law doesn't say he has to forget it," Pawley said. "All the law says is that he has to be able to lay it aside."

With Pawley remaining on his feet, Bannerman stood up, too. "Mr. Lahrke, I ask you now to think very carefully before you answer. You told this Court that you know Sam Tabor killed David Wilcke, is that not so?"

Ambose had carved that one out for himself from the time it had come up. "He told him that himself, Your Honor. And then he asked him whether he believed it. The record will show that this venireman immediately and without hesitation thereupon indicated a willingness and an ability to lay what he had been told aside. And even to turn it around if that's what the jury decided. You'll remember that, Your Honor."

Ignoring them, drawing to his full imperious height, Bannerman called for an answer. Getting it, he moved that the venireman be dismissed for cause "as being tainted with the full knowledge of the matter which is to be adjudicated," and when Pawley began to argue that Mr. Bannerman had conceded from the very beginning of the interrogation that his client was the murderer, Bannerman broke in coldly to inform him that Mr. Bannerman was conceding nothing. "We have not admitted for one second that Sam shot anybody," he declared, and since that must have sounded just as odd to his own ears as to everyone else's he hastened to explain that Mr. Bannerman was charged with defending his client with every resource at his command. "I will remind Your Honor that the state will be charged with proving the fact of the murder, the identity of the victim and the guilt of the defendant, and I submit, avow and emphasize that when this venireman states under oath that his knowledge runs to not one out of three, not two out of three but all three of those facts, he has lifted from the shoulders of the state every burden the law has placed upon them. I further take the liberty of reminding the Court that I brought this vexing problem to the Court's attention in petitioning for a change of venue, averring at that time what we have proven so conclusively with the very first venireman—that Lowell is a contaminated and envenomed community."

"Aw, sit down!" Ambose barked. "I don't think it's going to come as that much of a surprise anywhere else in the state. Or the country either, for that matter."

"And that, Mr. Ambose," said Chobodian, like an auctioneer knocking down a sale, "will cost you $50. If that's not enough to encourage you to direct your future remarks to the Bench, the price can go up."

"With the Court's permission," Bannerman said, directing his remarks to the Bench, "I didn't quite catch the subtleties and nuances of this latest example of Mr. Ambose's legal scholarship. 'Aw, sit down,' was that what he said?"

Chobodian decided that the time had come to make a little speech of his own. If Mr. Bannerman, new as he was to this jurisdiction, had been told that the presiding jurist was one of those genial judges whose patience was nigh inexhaustible, then Mr. Bannerman had been badly used and sorely misinformed. With a curt nod of recognition toward Pawley, who had been standing through it all to respond to the motion, he warned the lawyers on both sides of the table that they would do better to tend to their cases and let the side-barring go.

Pawley waited, however, until the Court had gaveled for silence so that everyone (meaning the press) would understand that what he was about to say was of such importance that they should be getting ready to write it down. To make that point perfectly clear, he began by expressing his firm belief that the question that lay before the Court had a significance extending far beyond a single courtroom or a single case. Somberly, pulling at the skin under his chin, he said, "If it is not true that a jury can lay aside whatever they may have read or heard and judge a lawsuit solely on the evidence that is presented to them in a courtroom, if they cannot write off their earlier impressions despite their sworn oath to do so and follow the law as charged by the Court, then I submit that our remedy is not to be found in moving the lawsuit to another jurisdiction, whether that jurisdiction be twenty miles, two hundred miles or two thousand miles away. For we would be saying, Your Honor, that our entire jury system is no good and that we had better set ourselves the task of finding something else to replace it with."

Bannerman's rebuttal, delivered with zest, was that Mr. Pawley seemed to be arguing at this late date against the whole concept of change of venue, a concept Bannerman had up to this moment thought well settled in American jurisprudence. "As Mr. Pawley undoubtedly knows, and as this learned Court most certainly knows, the Supreme Court, whose confidence in the sworn oath of jurors is not quite up to Mr. Pawley's, has been overturning jury verdicts in lawsuits despoiled by publicity with a consistency that this advocate for one does not find so alarming." And overturning them on precisely those grounds that Mr. Pawley found so unnerving. "I could cite you *Rideau,* I could cite you *Irvin,* I could cite you *Estes* and *Shepard.* About the only thing I could not cite you, Your Honor, would be any collateral hints, fears or misgivings in either the majority or dissenting opinions that the death knell of the jury system is being sounded."

Muttering in his beard, far too softly to be hard by Bannerman, Ambose said, "If the silly bastards had any idea what they were doing, they would."

The afternoon session started slowly and plodded on, going downhill almost all the way. Bannerman was on his best behavior, Ambose wasn't there, and most of the prospective jurors eliminated themselves one way or the other before any argument could really be joined. The state used its first peremptory in midafternoon on a milkman who, upon being asked routinely whether he had worked at any jobs before coming to Lowell (Nevins having his full Lowell employment record right in front of him), answered that he had been a bootlegger back in Ohio, if that counted for anything. Nevins laughed along with everyone else and established that the milkman was now a good, law-abiding citizen with a fine family before he smilingly "excused" him. If there was anybody the prosecution wanted less than anybody else, it was he who had at any time in his life looked upon the law as an enemy.

Late in the afternoon, with the room growing stuffy and everybody becoming drowsy, there came to the stand one Amos Yorrash, a fifty-eight-year-old printer. Bannerman studied him with particular care as he was crossing in front of the defense table. "I like printers," he told Halpern, without taking his eye off him. "They've always been my good-luck charms."

This one undoubtedly wore a hat while he worked, his one distinguishing characteristic being a perfectly round indentation that ran like a tire rim around his downy-white hair. Considering his age, and considering that Bannerman wasn't going to take anyone today anyway, Halpern didn't look upon him as a serious candidate, although he did take care to notice that his hands and feet had remained motionless when Nevins asked him the capital punishment question.

Bannerman began to run through his routine questions very quickly, getting satisfactory enough answers, and then, in an abrupt change from the pattern, he was asking, "Are you aware of the great advances in the field of human behavior as pioneered by Lionel Allbright of the Allbright Institute and your own great trailblazer, Harmon Medellia, whose fame and accomplishments are viewed with as much pride here in Lowell, I am sure, as we in Chicago view the notable work of our great Nicholas Zacharias?"

"Well, I've heard the names."

Bannerman beamed at him, a sly, winking look, as if he loved him for that show of modesty.

And everyone became aware that something had changed, and this man was —just maybe—going to be the first juror.

"When you saw the picture on television did you notice the vague, stunned air of the man who is accused of doing the shooting?"

"Well, I noticed he didn't put up any kind of an argument. That surprised me sure enough."

"Just let himself—" Bannerman lowered his voice and waved his hand as if it were the trickle of a stream—"be led away?" Halpern wondered whether anybody else had noticed that Bannerman, with that perfect ear of his, had done a perfect imitation of Boris Karloff.

"Would you say, sir, that you are sufficiently open to psychiatric interpolation ... interper—" He withdrew the question with a little chuckle. What he had been *trying* to ask was whether he was sufficiently open to the latest psychiatric advances so that if he saw a man step out of a crowd "in that vague, dreamy way, raise a gun and fire it, you would consider the possibility, the strong possibility of insanity?"

"Yes, sir. I'd want to consider that possibility."

"And if the same man, having fired the shot, made no effort to escape, would you think that was further evidence to a finding of insanity as the most rational explanation for his strange behavior?"

He would.

"And you're not a man who would consider the life of a man of wealth and position, of honorable and greatly honored position even, more important than the life of the poorest among us?"

Of course he wouldn't.

"Tell me this, sir," Bannerman said, letting him know with his eyes how pleased he was with such democratic sentiments. "If it should happen that the defendant belonged to a religious order not usually thought of as among the Big Three would you hold that against him?"

"No, sir."

"Not for a minute even?"

"No, sir. A man's religion is between him and his Maker."

"And if a police officer is called as a witness for the state you wouldn't give his testimony any more credence than a defense witness who might have contradictory testimony as to fact or opinion?"

No, he wouldn't.

"If the defendant should choose to exercise his constitutional right not to take the stand—we're not saying he isn't going to, mind you, but as a hypothetical question—you wouldn't look upon that as an indication of guilt?"

"That's his constitutional right, Mr. Bannerman. No guilt attaches thereto." Yorrash made a face of his own at the kind of legalese he had found himself spouting, a face which said *thereto? I never used thereto in my life before!* As they grinned at each other again, Bannerman wanted this guy so bad he could feel it in his balls. It came to him at the same time that there was nothing to lose by sneaking in a quick feint. If he could get the state to wondering whether he planned to bring the trial to a dramatic end by calling Sam to the stand, they just might hold something back to hit him with.

He tried very hard to make it seem as if he were trying to sound casual. "On the other hand, Mr. Yorrash . . . if, for the sake of argument, the defendant did take the stand, would you think that because he was on trial for his life you'd have to expect him to lie if it would help him?"

Mr. Yorrash thought the only thing to do there was to listen to what he had to say and judge it the same as you'd judge anybody else.

He had him well primed, Bannerman was thinking, but, what the hell, why not one more big swing of the pump. "Would you think that if a man lost his temper and hit someone he loved—his wife, say—in a rage and was sorry afterwards, or had a fight with his best friend over something minor and inconsequential and afterwards, over a beer, neither of them could understand how it had happened or, as you yourself may have seen, somebody starts singing in the middle of the street and then seems to wake up and look around embarrassed, just as if he had gone up and hit a perfect stranger for no reason at all, or killed a perfect stranger . . . and it could be shown to your satisfaction that it had been a perfect stranger, a perfect stranger whom he had come across by a sheer accident of timing, do you think, sir, that all these sudden, inexplicable eruptions would properly fall under the heading of temporary insanity?"

Yorrash thought they very well might.

Nodding abruptly, Bannerman motioned everybody at the defense table together. "All bets are off," he said. "I like this guy." The four heads huddled together, looking up from time to time toward the witness chair. Bannerman, who had put his own arm around Tabor's shoulder, pressed hard enough to turn him toward Marma and although neither Marma nor anyone else had expressed any reservations about Yorrash, Bannerman said, with his face full of expression, "Sam and I like him. We don't care what you say, Alfred, we like him. Don't we, Sam? Let him see by your face that we like him so much, you and me, that we're fighting for him. Say to Alfred, 'I like him,' and be liking him better than you've ever liked anybody in your whole life while you're saying it."

Bannerman looked back to the stand. "If I may, Mr. Yorrash, I'd like to ask you one more thing. Do you willingly accept the principle that a man is innocent until found guilty? That means that if at the end of the trial you don't know which side to believe you will unhesitatingly find for the defendant."

Of course he would.

Much more softly, Bannerman asked, "If you yourself were on trial for your life, would you be satisfied with a juror in your present frame of mind? For your *life*, Mr. Yorrash."

"I'd be very well satisfied."

Bannerman asked the Court for a few more moments to consult with his client, and this time it wasn't for show. "Anything you're got against this one particularly, Sam? Any bad feeling? No matter whether you can put it into words or not. It's your ass they're out to fry, and if anything's twitching in there we'd damn well better listen to it."

Sam liked him just fine.

Amos Yorrash sat there as they talked about him, trying his darndest to look disinterested and failing completely to pull it off. To be accepted was to be honored and loved. To be challenged was to be rejected as unworthy, and he would go through the rest of his life never knowing what had made him unworthy or what he was unworthy of.

Bannerman said, "We want this juror, Your Honor. Sam likes him. I like him. We accept him."

Nevins said, "We like him just fine too, Judge. Welcome aboard, Mr. Yorrash."

A great sigh of relief swept through the courtroom. They had their first juror. The first milestone had been passed.

Amos Yorrash laid his head against his hand, looking suddenly ill. What he had wanted so badly only a few moments ago had become the worst thing that could have happened, and he looked for all the world as if he'd like to go through it all over again and maybe play it a little smarter.

—by Conrad Rittenhouse

The ninth and tenth jurors were picked in the Sam Tabor trial this afternoon. The first, a 28-year-old systems engineer, was taken with speed and dispatch by both Norman Bannerman for the defense and District Attorney Nevins. Observers of courtroom strategy believe this to be another example of the unorthodox thinking that has characterized the fabulously successful Bannerman career. Prosecutors traditionally accept engineers because of their systematic minds and thinking. Others saw it as somewhat more in line with the accent the noted defense attorney has been placing on youth and thought it significant that Mr. Bannerman had displayed a great interest in the fact that the juror had taken a course in abnormal psychology while in college.

The real shocker, in some regards the biggest surprise in the jury selection to date, occurred when District Attorney Nevins accepted Mrs. Ethel Bettlenork, a forty-year-old housewife who had worked until two years ago as a practical nurse. Mr. Bannerman left little doubt after the session that he felt he had scored a major victory in the long and arduous jury impaneling, which will reach the end of its second week tomorrow. The noted Chicago attorney, whose colorful antics have enlivened and on occasion heated up the proceedings to date, was ecstatic. It is Mr. Bannerman's belief that because of her extensive nursing background, Mrs. Bettlenork cannot help but be especially impressed with the array of experts the defense attorney has been promising to parade before the jury, including Dr. Lionel Allbright of the world-famous Allbright Institute.

District Attorney Nevins' only comment was, "She seemed like she'd make a good honest juror, so we took her."

With five jurors having been sworn in the past three sessions, the logjam seems to have broken and there is some hope for believing the final two jurors may be seated tomorrow. The defense has now used up 11 of its 12 peremptory challenges and Mr. Bannerman has been asking the Court whether he will be given any additional ones in the event all 12 are used up before a full jury has been impaneled. The prosecution, on the other hand, has . . .

Ruthie was there to pick him up at the airport, and while Hal knew he should head right for the motel to report to Bannerman or, at the very least, give him a call, he told her to drive him to the jailhouse so that he could talk to Sam Tabor.

Her mother had stayed on at the house just long enough to cook him supper, she told him, and seeing him begin to tighten up she changed her direction in midstream and said she was sure she'd be able to keep it hot until he got home. Timidly, in her teeny voice, she said, "You sounded so funny when you called that night. And then when I told you mother was staying with me, I couldn't make you out at all . . ."

He was just as glad he had taken the wheel because that gave him something to do with his eyes. He had been a damn fool to think she hadn't been able to see that something was wrong. What could he expect when he'd been such a damn fool as to call her in a sweat and panic like that. Rule Number Six: Damn fools do damn fool things. What a fool he had been only a week ago. What a child.

Grunting, looking mildly bewildered, as much at the effort of recalling which phone call she was talking about, it seemed, as the conversation itself, he finally remembered that it had been a bad connection on his end at first; and then, since he hadn't missed the emphasis she had placed on her mother's staying "just long enough" he performed the final little brush-up job on marital housekeeping by telling her that if he had sounded funny it must have been because it had made him think how much he wished he had been there with her instead of her mother.

To all appearances she was more than satisfied. Snuggling over to him, hugging his elbow possessively, she asked what he had found out that was going to set Sam Tabor free.

He saw Sam standing in the snow, crying . . . Well, he said, he had found out that the Redeemers didn't eat meat. Nor flesh, nor fowl. No milk, either.

When you came right down to it, how much did he really know? The Redeemers were such a tight suspicious sect that until recent years they hadn't even registered their births or deaths with the public authorities. It wasn't what he hadn't been able to learn that troubled him so much, though . . . let's not kid ourselves about that, huh? What troubled him was that so much of what he had been able to pick up at Twenty Hills was at such odds with the previous picture he'd had of Sam. Some of it seemed to throw Allbright's whole analysis, brilliant as it was, completely out of whack. *He saw Sam standing astride his father's grave shaking his fist at the heavens* . . . But who knew . . . who knew? The way those fellows' minds worked, it would probably all fit together like a dream.

The way things had gone at Twenty Hills, he thought, he wasn't sure of very much anymore. No, that wasn't so. *One thing* he could be sure of. He was sure as hell taking a lot on himself in deciding that he was going to see what Sam had to say for himself before he turned his information over to Bannerman.

Instead of swinging around to the Riverway entrance he pulled up to the curb at the corner of Baltan to save Ruthie the trouble of turning around. "I'll have mother gone by the time you get home," she said. "Whenever." There was so much not mistaking the message on her face that he leaned back in to kiss her. "Packed and gone," she said, moving her lips on his. "And the sooner the better."

"Horny," Harold Halpern said.

"They fight too much with Ambose," Sam Tabor said. "That's their trouble. I don't know why they do that. I've told them." Sam had lost weight. The skin hung looser on his neck and there was something else about him, too. A touch of the prison pallor. "If they'd leave him alone," he said. "If they'd leave me and Ambose alone we could work something out."

Sam was sitting in a rather odd posture behind the table in the Interviewing Room, his shoulders rounded over and his hands clasped together so tightly that the tips of his fingers stood out red against the white skin.

"Mr. Holden," he said. "Yes, he was always a very nice man. I'm glad he was of help."

Halpern had already told him that Mr. Holden wasn't running the paper anymore. It was being run by his niece. Emily Wolstenholme. "She said she went to school with you," Hal told him, trying to prod his memory. "One year." Julie had written her maiden name down, but Sam had already told him that Julie hadn't been in to see him. He hadn't even known she had come back to Lowell. Going to school together one year wasn't much of a help, since—as Mrs. Wolstenholme had already told them—every grade was taught in the same classroom from the little kids right up to the ones ready to go into high school.

Halpern had taken an envelope out of his briefcase as soon as he sat down and placed it on the table. Drawing out an old yellowed newspaper picture, he looked over at Sam with the kind of smug, tantalizing smile that told him he had a delicious surprise for him. "Maybe you'll remember this." It was a picture of a slim, boyish Sam Tabor in soccer uniform, a soccer ball crooked in his arm, his eyes upcast, shy but proud, into the camera. The caption said: LEADS REDEEMERS TO VICTORY.

"For pity's sake," Sam said. A pleased, crooked smile spread over his features. "Where did you ever find this?"

Hal smiled back at him, trying to look wise and competent, but in reality enormously pleased himself that Sam's lawyers would no longer be looking upon the defendant as a schlemiel but as the captain of the doughty little band of Emily

Wolstenholme's memory who had won the state championship by defeating the biggest high schools in Maryland. Mrs. Wolstenholme had told everybody, including the FBI, that her uncle hadn't saved the newspapers from those days. But then, the FBI didn't have Julie Elkins around to get next to lady newspaper owners. The back issues had been down in the basement, bound in heavy, dusty folders, five years to every folder and the pages brittle to the touch. Even as a little girl Mrs. Wolstenholme had been around the office whenever she could and she had remembered that picture very clearly because Twenty Hills got very little coverage. She couldn't remember anything else, and although they had spent the whole afternoon leafing through the brittle pages they had found nothing else about any of the Tabors.

"We were pretty good," Sam said. "They didn't think we would be, but we were. We won the championship." His shy, proud look was not so much different from the shy, proud look in the picture, even to the upcast eyes. "I knew we'd win. You know how in a game you sometimes know what's going to happen?" As he studied the picture it was all coming back to him. "It was more important to us that we win. They always thought we'd be so easy."

Hal understood what he meant perfectly. "You'd better take good care of me, Sam. I may be the only person outside of Twenty Hills who knows you were the captain of the team that won the state championship."

Sam shook his head. "The sectional champions was all. We lost in the first elimination for the state championship. Boy, were we ever slaughtered."

So much for Emily Wolstenholme's girlish memory.

It had been Mrs. Wolstenholme, Hal told him, who had given them the name and address of Ernestine Armstrong. *He saw young Sam standing in the snow, singing, crying* . . . She had been Ernestine Hartnett then, a young woman running a sort of nursery for the Quakers. "She's an old lady now, of course. You would have been about ten, Sam."

"Ernestine . . . ?" Sam frowned across the table, the name meaning nothing to him.

Hal didn't know why he had said nursery. A shelter for homeless children was what Ernestine had said it was. Orphaned children. Abandoned children. Children whose parents had to have somewhere to leave them for awhile. Sam had been there that week because his mother was heeding God's instructions to scour the mountainside and bring the word of Christ and Christmastide to—in Ernestine's tart phrase—"the religious needy."

Ernestine Hartnett had explained very carefully to Anabelle Tabor that it was the custom for the children in the shelter to be taken home by relatives or one of the kindhearted families of the region for the Christmas holidays. And Anabelle Tabor had assured Ernestine she would be back for Sam in plenty of time for him to spend Christmas Eve in his own home.

By three o'clock on the day before Christmas only two of the children had not been picked up. In front of the administration building (Ernestine said) had been a bench on which the spectators sat while the boys were playing soccer. A few minutes after three (Ernestine said) little Sam Tabor, all bundled up, was sitting on the bench alone.

At four o'clock the snow began to fall, a silent snow, wet and heavy. Ernestine called for Sam to come in. Sam had said, "I have to stay here. My mother is coming for me and she may think I have gone with someone else."

At five o'clock Mr. Armstrong came riding in on his great sleigh, pulled by his two great speckled horses (that was Mrs. Armstrong's girlish memory, for whatever it was worth), Mr. Armstrong having made his plans for their own Christmas Eve. Mr. Armstrong's solution, like Mr. Armstrong himself, had been simple and direct. They would take the boy along with them. The boy told Mr. Armstrong, as politely as he had told Ernestine, that he had to wait for his parents, else his parents would be so very disappointed.

Hal saw the time passing, the snow falling, the horses shivering. He saw Mr. Armstrong, at long last, going out to pick the boy up and carry him off under his arm if that's what it was going to take. He saw the boy fight his way free and run out into the deep, smooth snow. He looked across the table at the pale, pudgy, balding man and saw the sad, thin little boy standing in the middle of a great expanse of snow unbroken save for the trail of his own footsteps. He saw the sad little boy throw his head back and at the top of his lungs begin to sing, through his sobs, "Silent Night."

The Redeemers, Ernestine Armstrong had said, were a powerful people with the hymn book and there wasn't a one of them hymns Sam didn't know. Standing in the falling snow all by himself, singing and crying together, he had sung his way flat through the whole goldurn hymn book, from top to bottom, while his voice dwindled and grew hoarse and there was neither voice to sing with nor a single break in the smooth deep snow to tell a soul how he had got there.

The snow had near to stopped, Ernestine said, and the moon was out, when Sam came flailing back through the snow, falling and stumbling and crying, and pushed without a word past her and Mr. Armstrong, the snow stuck all over him like a woolly bear, and on into the barracks and to bed.

"Ernestine . . . ?" Sam frowned across the table, the name meaning nothing to him. "I remember Harley Armstrong. He was in the city council at one time, I believe. His wife . . . ?" You could see that he was trying to place her and failing. (Hal could see himself in the car trying so hard to recall the phone call to Ruthie that first night.) "I just can't seem to remember his wife at all."

"You were in there for a week or so, Sam. It was more like a home for children actually. Over Christmas. Your mother was supposed to pick you up and she . . . uh, didn't get back in time."

Not only didn't Sam remember, Sam didn't seem particularly interested. The scene which Ernestine Armstrong had remembered so vividly over the years and which had haunted Harold Halpern these past two weeks had meant not a thing to Sam. He turned the newspaper picture around and took another vaguely interested look at it. He was restless. He was bored. He was frankly unable to see why he was supposed to remember one week out of his life back when he was ten years old.

Because Hal felt like such a fool he also felt a fine malicious pleasure in seeing how quickly Sam would become unbored when he told him he had found Reverend McMannister. That's what had taken him so long; it had taken a couple of days to find him and then almost a week of waiting around while McMannister was making up his mind whether he wanted to talk to him. And then all he had done was to drive him down to a cemetery and show him Edgar Tabor's gravestone.

No, Sam wasn't bored anymore. He was watchful and waiting and wary.

Hitting him with it fast, Hal said, "When I asked him how he died he said, 'The same as everybody else—from living.' I wasn't sure that was worth waiting a week for. How did he die, Sam?"

Sam gave his neck a little twitch. "My father was an unlucky man. All his life he was unlucky."

"Did he kill himself, Sam?" Was that the big secret, Hal asked, trying to make him see how ridiculous it was to think there was anything to hide in that. "Is that why McMannister had to bury him himself and not the church?"

Sam gave his neck another twitch. "No, he didn't kill himself." His lips blew in and out, the way they sometimes did in court. His eyes were flat and distant. "Reverend McMannister must be a very old man."

Old he was. Kind of bitter, too. He had left the church, in case Sam didn't know. That's why he had been so hard to find. "What's the big secret, Sam? I'd just like to know. It can make you kind of curious, you know, waiting around in a strange town for a week wondering about something like that." A wholly unintentional rueful note had crept into his voice, elbowing aside the brisk, prodding tone he had been going for. Moving quickly to get his advantage back, Hal said, "His death wasn't recorded by the Redeemers, you know. That means it wasn't recorded anywhere."

"I'd just prefer that he be left in peace. Tell that to Bannerman. My father's got nothing to do with this." And there was just enough snap to it for Hal to see Sam Tabor once again as he had first seen him, as the old courtroom hand showing Bannerman who was boss. "Don't worry, Hal," he said, seeing his disappointment. "There's no secret." Sighing wearily, sick of it, he pushed the newspaper picture away from him, disposing in a gesture of the whole time, place and subject. "Let's leave him in peace, that's all."

The envelope from which he had taken the newspaper picture had been left lying on the table. Out of it, Hal took another picture, only this time it was a photograph. An old snapshot of Sam and his mother. The little boy was seated at the end of a table, looking younger and even shyer, his lips pressed together as if he were trying to prevent himself from giggling. At the side of the table, closer to the camera, was his mother, a woman about whom everything was cut to angles of the sharpest severity. Behind the table, in the space between them, was a rocking chair.

"That's Mama," he said, as if he wasn't quite able to believe that his mother had ever looked that young.

They had given the picture to him at the sanitarium, Hal told him. And then added, with perhaps unnecessary cruelty, "They still have all her effects there, you know." If Sam wanted to play so cute with him about how his father had died, Hal wanted him to know that he knew all about his mother.

It didn't seem to bother Sam at all, though; or if it did, it slid right off him. He was looking at the picture with such a fondness for the people there, nodding first at the memory of himself and of the table and of his mother and then shaking his head in a sort of disbelief that this record of those times still existed.

And something else, too. Sam had a way of adapting himself so perfectly to the coloration of his surroundings that Hal had always seen him as a prisoner in jail uniform, or as a murderer on trial. Drawn back by the old ties of blood, he had adapted himself just as completely to the smells, tastes and textures of the old cabin kitchen. What would he be thinking of? The thousand breakfasts shared long ago around a kitchen table that no longer existed except in this snapshot, breakfasts shared by younger, happier people who themselves existed only in this old, miraculous snapshot? (Who had taken the picture, his father? His sister?) How would he be seeing his mother here? As a cooker of meals, a washer of dishes, a soother of hurts . . . or as the street-corner preacher, the spoiled fanatic?

Hal, coming around the table behind him, called his attention to a sort of long shadow extending from the top of the picture halfway down to the rocking chair. He and Julie had gone crazy trying to figure out whether it was an imperfection in the print or some kind of religious artifact, and Sam, obviously puzzled by it too, squinted and grunted and turned his head aswivel until, all at once, there washed over him the expression of a man seeing a whole point in time and space made sharp by a taste or a smell or . . . well, a shadow. In that expression there was such a sweet scent of nostalgia that it was as if he were back in the kitchen soaked in its grains and temperature; such a sweetness of memory that it was as if he were looking at the giggly boy again and loving him for his innocence. "For pity's sake," he said. "Who'd have ever remembered the flypaper."

Closing his eyes, he began to rock back and forth, smiling. And then he wasn't smiling at all. His head fell back over the back of the chair, his body grew rigid and his knee began to jerk. Faster and faster and faster.

Recovering from the first shock of it, Hal reached down to grab Sam's knee, and grasping it heard him whisper, "I feel it, Mama. I feel the Power. The Power's in me. Praise the Lord."

Hal's throat was dry.

"Are you all right, Sam?"

Opening his eyes, Sam looked directly into—and through—Hal's. And if Hal's eyes were filled with alarm, Sam's passed in slow stages from exultation to wonder to stupor to emptiness. Vacant. Hollow. Nothing at all. "You don't see flypaper anymore," he said. "That's good. They're more humane today."

"Sam, why in god's name did you do it?" That was why he had wanted to talk to Sam first. That was what he had to know!

"Well, you know," Sam said as if it were the most reasonable thing in the world, "I guess it just seemed like something I had to do at the time."

He frowned then, as if he were thinking further on it. Puzzling it out. "Like raisins on a stick they were," he said. "Waving back and forth to make a soul dizzy. And there was always one, always one of them, with the wings still struggling. It's better this way."

Elijah Chobodian sat in the early morning darkness, drawing strength from the glass of cognac. And from the oak chair, stained dark brown (how many times?), the springs reset (how many times?), the upholstery replaced (how many times?) He found himself drawn more and more to this room ("Papa's room" once; the judge's study now) which had been decorated around this chair in damask and curlicues and old solid furniture; the solid oak desk in front of the window and the big full-faced clock standing alongside the fireplace.

Above the headrest, like a coat-of-arms, a bear's head snarled. The snarling features had been blurred and scarred through the years, mostly by nicks and scratches except for one great slash across the bridge of the nose which gave the bear a scuffed and vulnerable and therefore less ferocious look. It had been put there in unprovoked attack (how long ago?) when Joshua, scrambling through the house after his little sister, had tripped over a scooter which shouldn't have been there in the first place ("How many times have I told you to keep out of Papa's room?") and sprawling headlong across the chair had reached out for support and scarred both bear and chair for life with his Magic Somethingorother ring.

When was the last time he had seen a scooter? (When was the last time he had heard the rosy-cheeked whoop and clamor of children scrambling through Papa's room?)

Judge Chobodian took another deep draught of his drink. When had he ever had so much difficulty sleeping before?

Aram Chobodian had been a master carpenter and more. The hard wooden arms were rounded off at the ends into clearly delineated bear's paws, with claws unsheathed to match the snarling head. Along the arms the master carpenter had carved a pair of armrests as perfectly as if two arms and bear's paws had been pressed into cement. There, Eli Chobodian's arms lay. In the footrest, aslant, were two hugh bear tracks on which Aram's son (now older than his father had lived to be) rested his slippered feet. Aram Chobodian's friends had called him "Arche" (Armenian for the Bear), and it was not a nickname that had been given in jest. It was a title that had been earned, with honor, by carrying scores of old women and invalids on his back to the waiting barges and rowboats in the escape from the Turks.

"To my son Elijah," he had written in his will, "I leave the chair of Arche." It was all the father had to leave him, and that the son had kept it through the years as the thing he prized most in all the world showed how much more had been left to him by this fierce man with the walrus mustache whom he had never really known.

You could draw all manner of philosophy from that on the proper way to raise children, and on the proper father-son relationship, too, and all of it would be wasted effort, for all of it would be false. You would be comparing the same thing at different times, and that comparison could not be made. A logical fallacy. It was done all the time.

Except for this: In the end the blood discovers you. No matter how far the young man runs—let him declaim and disclaim as he will—if he lives to fill out the days of his allotted years he will find himself an old man sitting by the fireplace discovered by the blood he bears. Elijah's son Joshua would find that out in due time, and it was a thought to warm the blood of the father as he sipped the cognac (Aram's well-loved *Kinee*), the drink that had graced his father's table every night of his life and now graced his own.

And if he saw his father in these later years through the division of the young boy's fear and the old man's affection, in that vision he thought he saw him whole. His father would be pleased with him, he thought. Or (he now thought) did that only mean that he was pleased with himself? Or did it mean—ah, here was something to think about sitting by the fireplace on a dark and rainy morning— did it really mean that the Granite Judge who had been so pleased with himself until now, now . . . had . . . to . . . look . . . to . . . the dead for the approval he could no longer give himself? The dead made excellent character witnesses. They spoke as you commanded them to speak. Did he who was no more than a conduit for carrying the blood from his father to his son know the father? Know the son? Did he, Elijah Chobodian, drawing back to the root, know himself?

Ah, that was what it came down to always. What did Elijah Chobodian honestly think of himself here alone in the morning darkness where there was nobody to impress and no secrets to be kept. He thought of himself as tall timber among the scruffy pine—*yes, you do*—an image so noble as to erase all nobility from the image-maker. He who saw himself as a giant redwood, never compromising like Hilliard Nevins, never demeaning himself like Harry Davies, never corrupting himself like Foster McAlester up in Monroe, would be seen by them

. . . how? As a rigid, sanctimonious, overrighteous petty tyrant lacking in humanity, drained of all compassion, bereft of any ability to bend with the times? Was it the honest man's weakness (looking at himself with the honest man's coldness) that he had always looked upon himself, could not help but look upon himself, as the only honest man in town? Had not his own son been stultified by all that honesty? Had not his only son felt so oppressed by all that virtue that he had finally done the one thing he thought he could still do to please him, taken himself out of his sight?

Out of order! Objection sustained! No true bill could be issued here! Judge Chobodian stroked the smooth worn grain of the paws his father had carved out with such loving care. He was being too hard on himself.

The rain, no longer light, was beating against the roof and windows. The older you got the more you recognized that there were no rules, or that the rules kept changing. They changed with the weather, with the times. Youth, accepting what it finds, believes it has seized the times by the throat and forced change upon it; that was youth's greatest impertinence. Age, holding to what it had found and accepted, fights change, believing it can seize the times by the throat and choke it; that was age's greatest delusion. The law bends with the times, and he who administers the law must bend with it too. The bend of life . . . he thought, and knew better than to pursue this line of inquiry any further, lest in this dark, despondent mood that had fallen upon him he find that at the bend of life a man had become so brittle in the very structure of the bones that he was no longer able to bend at all. "The living law," Bannerman liked to say. It was possible that Bannerman had something there.

Not so! The prosecutor had slipped that by while he wasn't looking. No matter how he twisted or turned . . .

If values were relative, then what was truth? If truth changed with the weather, then where was right and wrong? It was an upsetting thought, going against the grain of his life, and he had forced himself to sit through the long morning hours to reach it.

Having reached it, he could now with safety discard it.

Granting for the sake of argument that what was right twenty years ago might not be right today—in human relations as in so many other things—he could yet maintain with vigor, citing such authorities as must send the opposition running for cover, that in the essentials the eternal verities remained solid and unchanging. Love, honor, respect and decency; those were truths to fit all times and seasons.

The light went on in the kitchen. He could see it faintly under the door. Straining to pick up the sound beyond the door and the empty dining room, he heard Katerine moving around preparing breakfast. Startled, he looked from his watch to the window. He had planned on slipping back into bed so as not to worry her. It wasn't even light out; the rain, that was what had fooled him. The raindrops swimming down the windowpane looked like frightened pollywogs. That was a depressing way to think of it, he thought. Why "frightened" instead of "playful"?

"Thank goodness," Katerine said, "there are only two more jurors and it will be done with today and over."

He could tell her on excellent authority they wouldn't get them today. Bannerman would have to run out all his peremptories to strengthen his change-of-venue appeal, whereupon he would ask for more and the Court would give him two; whereupon he would run them out and ask for more and the Court would give him one; whereupon he would run that out and the Court would deny him another.

From the stove, stirring the oatmeal, she gave him the woman's nonunderstanding, not completely resigned look which said: The games you people play. Didn't the judges in the appeals courts know that was what they were doing?

"Of course they do. They appreciate having us do it right." He wiped the milk from the edge of his lip. "Referees in all competitive sports will tell you, my dear, that it is easier to work with professionals than with amateurs. The professional can always be counted upon to make the play he is supposed to make." He coughed discreetly. "I take what compensation I can from the knowledge that if I play the game, too, I play it with the skill of a . . . ahem . . . veteran rock-faced jurist."

"You have no choice."

"Of course I do. I have the choice of playing or not playing. I seem to find it more politic to play. My only defense, before I throw myself on the mercy of the Court, is that the older I become the less latitude those choices seem to provide. You will note how insidiously I have played upon the sympathies and mature understanding of my audience who is, in the vernacular of a perhaps earlier day, no spring chicken herself."

Giving voice to that earlier look, she said, "I have observed, as what woman hasn't, that the work of the world is merely little boys, disguised as men, working their wills in public and convincing themselves in the privacy of their homes that their worst depredations are not only justifiable—everybody does it, don't they; if I didn't do it, they'd think I was crazy—but honorable and . . ." She brushed her hair away from her face. "Oh, I don't know, Eli. Honestly now, don't you sometimes get tired . . . ?"

How had he managed to get her so depressed so quickly, when it had been his intention to be relentlessly cheerful? Yes, sometimes he got tired, he said cheerfully. But not in this lawsuit. This lawsuit was better than a whole series of rejuvenating injections. "Do they still do that, with the monkey glands?" It might be described as a contest in oratorical cadence and cadenza. Ambose's cadence against Bannerman's cadenza. "I've always bet on the good strong slugger to get to the fancy boxer, the last legacy no doubt of my peasant background." (Yes, the blood discovers you.)

He was happy to see that he had brought a teasing smile to her face. "You've been known to do pretty well with the cadenzas yourself."

"The thanks I get." He made a face at the prospect of starting another day—and as miserable a one as this—with another bowl of oatmeal dissolved in milk. "I try to brighten your drab existence by bringing you along to grace countless sparkling daises and instead of admiring the tiaras of your betters you spend your time listening to me speak. What a waste! Nobody else does."

"I've always admired your mind," she said, setting the bowl in front of him. "You have a better mind than any of them." She was, he could see, in a mood to take on the world in support of that proposition. Good for her; he agreed with her.

"You think I sold myself short?"

The smile stuck to his face. What a thing to say! Immediately, before she could come to any conclusion that he had been sitting up all night regretting his misspent life, he threw her out something else for her to chew on. Lennard had been dropping in on him almost daily, he said, and he was really beginning to worry about him. "He always had that crazy way of talking. Now he's going around talking to himself."

"Lennard never talked to anybody but himself. He only lets you stay around and listen. Oh, when he's particularly pleased with himself he'll look to see if he's scored a few points with you." She sniffed derisively and an edge of almost comical exasperation came into her voice. "That's Lennard Swann."

Chobodian, hardly prepared to have such an obvious truth flung back at him when he had only meant to divert her, was for the moment speechless. He had never thought of it that way before. "You know something," he said, "you're right."

"Of course I'm right," she said, holding the edge to let him see that she was more insulted than pleased that he should be so surprised at her acumen. "A man of your advanced years should have discovered by now that women are students of every man who is important to them."

He raised his eyebrows. "Lennard?"

A steady look came back across the table. "Anybody important to you is important to me."

She had picked up her knitting, and she began to click away. He loved her that way, in the early morning, with her hair tied behind her neck and falling loose. Was it only that the faded print looked new to the fading eyes? No more than that?

But when he commented, mildly enough, that he had never looked upon Lennard as being important to him, she looked up, compressing her lips tightly, not quite sure whether he was being unusually difficult or unusually dense. "A psychiatrist in the circle, however much on the fringe, is, yes, of unusual interest to women, by which I mean, yes, wives. He knows about . . . things. I would imagine that knowing about those things, he fascinates men, too."

"*Those* things. Yes, I suppose so." He chewed it over, his mouth working on the thin, unchewable gruel, for he had honestly never considered it in that light before. He knew about those things, too, did he not? Was it possible that he had refrained from discussing these matters with her not because he was so sure they would both find that kind of conversation distasteful—there were at least two men they knew, his own age or not so very much younger, who had gotten themselves into that kind of difficulty—but because he wanted to spare her from wondering about him? Small worry there. They exchanged an understanding smile. Ho-ho, he had caught her wondering. Or, ho-ho, had she caught him wondering whether she was wondering? Did she know about those things, anyway? Did everyone? Was it only a pride of ownership—an insolence of office—that made him think they weren't known to everybody?

What worried him these days, he said, was that Lennard did ramble on about sex whenever there was a woman around. (He didn't add that he meant a young woman.)

She looked up over the needles. "He thinks he has to." (He hadn't had to.)

And when his fussy wrinkled frown asked what that was supposed to mean, her smooth, complacent brow answered that he knew very well. "My, my," he said. "I seem to be married to a psychiatrist. And after all these years, too."

She went back to her knitting, clicking the needles with precision.

"That's what he hides behind," Judge Chobodian said at last. (He saw Lennard now as a man of sorrows.) "He uses words as a wall around himself. He hedges himself in with words." (Hiding from what bitter wind?) "Do you suppose," he said, chewing on the milky gruel again, "that he's incapable?"

"My, my. Who's the psychiatrist now?"

Debility, senility and futility; the bitter end, the bottom line, and dismal trinity of man. There's another happy thought to start the day with. The worst he could accuse himself of, so far, was maundering, but then, the day had barely begun.

As efficient as he had always been about keeping his professional life out of his home, he had never been able to hold anything back from Katerine where his emotions were involved. He should have known that by now. Believing as he did in property rights, he recognized her holdings there. And so he was telling her soon enough about the wild-haired Negro venireman who had come in, dressed in African garb, and announced that he could not serve on the jury because he had no trust in the white man's law. "It was his particular complaint that since all white men were guilty of murdering the dignity and humanity of several million Negroes, he did not wish to waste his time on the murder of one white man by another white man. Somewhere along about there, there was a passing mention of the Nuremberg Laws, which he took, I take it, to be the only laws a self-respecting black man could have any truck with these days. And, oh yes . . . there was something about permitting us to cannibalize each other without any interference from him. I would say, to anybody soliciting a critical opinion from the presiding judge, that he had his piece to speak and he spoke it right smartly."

Before he was two sentences into it Katerine had put her knitting aside and folded her arms on the table. Through all his sardonic posturing her expression of deep concern never changed. "The times are dispirited and graceless," she said. "I hope you cited him for contempt of court."

"Not quite. The kindly jurist, tolerant some would say to a fault, inquired of him whether he couldn't take the oath to judge the case on its merits according to the law we happen to be living under as conveyed to him by the Court, who even the most wild-haired militant should have been quick to see deserved the love and respect of all men of good will, regardless of faith, creed, color or, if the previously referred to jurist can bring himself to the gravamen of the indictment, previous condition of servitude." He coughed politely. "He didn't think he could."

What the black man had really said was, "I am neither your dog to whip nor your dog to go fetch your papers. This Court is irrelevant to me as a black man, being that it is the means by which the slavemaster's lackeys serve the slavemaster by whipping all dogs who do not jump to do his bidding."

"That's insupportable, Eli." She was trembling in anger. "There was no need for him to be insulting. It isn't as though this country isn't trying. It isn't as though the opportunities aren't there. It wasn't easy for you. God knows it wasn't." The more she thought about it the angrier she became. She could have told his wild-haired African king something about living in a ghetto. Yes, she could have told him about people who had been put to the sword—a whole nation wiped out if the Turks had had their way—and escaping for their lives, penniless, with no more than could be carried on their backs, and nobody asking for welfare either. Home relief, did Eli remember that? She could have told him about her father, with five hungry children all in a room, weeping openly because he had to take one week's home relief and paying it back with the first money he earned so that his children would not have to remember him as a man who had to go to charity to feed his family.

"He has that," Elijah said gently. Dismayed as he was at causing her such pain, how else could he have expected this to turn out? What was it that was paved with good intentions? "Your father wanted that and my father wanted that, and both of them have it and both of them earned it richly."

"I don't understand you, Eli!" she cried out, near to tears. "It wasn't that they — It wasn't an— It was them! What they were! What they stood for!" Struggling to control her voice and succeeding only intermittently, she reminded him how he had gone to law school nights, earning his tuition by the hardest imaginable work in the daytime. "Lackey, is it?" she said, boiling over. "Well, damn him to hell! Him and everybody who thinks like him! No, Eli, leave me alone. I'm all right."

She wasn't all right, but she had composed herself. "I have that right. I can remember you coming home without any eyebrows, and that gives me a right. And your chest a whole mass of blisters from burning yourself in that damnable boiler factory. *And going to school right from the hospital because I was five months pregnant and . . .*" The tears were finally coming and with a sudden agitated jerk of the shoulder she turned away from him, almost as if she were warning him against any foolish effort to extend any comforting hand toward her. Rising, she turned her head away, dabbing at her eyes with her apron but determined to finish the story, as if he didn't know it, of how he had tried to slip into bed when he got home so she wouldn't see that he was bandaged up like a mummy, and that he would have, too, except that he couldn't keep from crying out in pain.

She wiped her eyes. She blew her nose. The tempest was over. "If it was a white man you would have dealt with him. Where's the equal justice there?"

Elijah was having all he could do to take hold of himself. The oddest kind of dizziness had come over him, and he'd had to hold onto the table to keep himself from just . . . dropping away. Thank god she had turned away from him when she did. And that his head had cleared just in time.

"The thing about that, dear," he said, "is that a Negro couldn't have got that damnable job in that damnable boiler factory and I'm not so sure he could have attended that night school either."

And that was supposed to be *his* fault? She looked at him as if she were ashamed of him for the first time in her life. "What right did that give him to call you a lackey?" She snorted in complete disgust. "Slavemaster! They repeat those words like trained monkeys." Having said it and having meant it, she was daring him to say that made her prejudiced.

"Why didn't I know if he could have attended that night school?" he asked her in careful, measured phrases that informed her she was missing the point. "Could it be possible that the question never presented itself to me as being worthy of consideration?" He hadn't had any sleep at all, Elijah remembered. He had better remember that. "The truth is that we looked upon them as less than human. Better than a dog but less than a white man. Facing it honestly, isn't that the truth? We men of good will must be given credit for facing such things honestly now that they are forcing us to face such things honestly."

"I deny that," she said fiercely. "I know you. I know what you've done. You're the fairest, most honorable man alive. How can you talk like that, Eli? I can see that he troubled you . . ." She slapped the table before she rose to go to the stove, letting it be seen that she was having no more of this foolishness. "You did what you could. Always. I don't know what's the matter with you this morning, but I do know some of the things you've done."

Judge Chobodian laughed. Through all his talk and all her indignation, an automatic timer within her, set with the coffee percolator, had been ticking away. Patting his stomach comfortably to let her know, in return, that the Hour of Contemplation was over, he stretched back and watched her pour. In round, oracular tones that asked not to be taken seriously, he said, "Yes, let it be said that I did what I could do without any great inconvenience to myself. A man less favorably disposed to the wise and wizened jurist might even say that it was not inconvenient and quite pleasing to the palate."

What is truth indeed? The truth was that the wise and wizened old judge being so philosophical and understanding—both to his undying credit—over the breakfast-table-and-will-you-pass-the-milk, had reacted to Katerine's African king exactly the way Katerine had reacted. And still he had not cited him for contempt. He had pondered that failure of will and duty through the evening and he had tossed with it in bed and he had sat up with it in his study, and if he had come to any firm conclusion it was that he knew now what had set off the loss of will and faith in the country. The faith of Americans in their natural superiority had always been fueled by the need of the newest immigrant group to be accepted as "real Americans," worthy of full membership, and there had always been a new group knocking on the door, hat in hand. And here was the Negro, the home-grown immigrant, saying he didn't want in anymore. Saying, those noisy few who spoke in his name, that he wanted out. How many didn't matter; they made a powerful lot of noise. And closer to home, across your own dinner table, the young were saying they not only wanted out, they wanted to scourge it in fire, plague and flood.

And where did that leave Elijah Chobodian, whose great accomplishment was that he had battered the doors down and forced them to accept him not on their terms but his own? Why, it left him right where he had been all along, full of pride in himself and his heritage. That being so, why had he felt called upon to do precisely what he had accused himself of doing in the no-longer-possible hypocritical past, by putting forth a veritable Fourth of July display of understanding and nobility? What was truth? The truth here was that the Giant Redwood presiding had thought of her African king as a black ape. Those were the words that came to his mind (unbidden and unwanted, to be sure, but still they had come) when he saw him strutting toward the stand in that outlandish get-up. Those were the words that had come to his mind again (could he still say unbidden? still say unwelcome?) as he was speaking the piece he spoke so smartly.

What was the greater truth that had been tracked down through the long watches of the night? The greater truth was that there was a great deal to be learned about hypocrisy even by a learned jurist who had rounded the bend.

Katerine had gone to the window to keep a sharp lookout for Hodapp so that Eli could invite him in for a cup of coffee. Hodapp wouldn't come at her beckoning; he always seemed to feel he was intruding. "He may feel that way with you, too, Eli," she said, "but with you he'd rather intrude than disobey. How did you ever make that poor old man think you were so ornery?"

Ambose and Pawley had been in and out of the voir dire from the beginning; Ambose had been missing for whole days, undoubtedly preparing his case. When the testimony began, the DA's office would have three relatively fresh men sitting at their table. Bannerman, the lone defender, would already be worn out.

Elijah Chobodian dreaded these long drawn out impanelings. In these long, drawn out affairs, the basic purpose behind it all, the delicate balancing of society's rights against the more heavily weighted rights of the accused, was subordinated, became obscured, and the dominant factor became, if only through repetition, the vast scheme of pretense by which it was made to work.

He passed a hand over his eyes, picking up the questioning. Bannerman now had the venireman under examination; Chobodian had not even noticed that he had been passed. He'd had a mild headache at noon. He had meant to take an aspirin, and as always had put it off, and now the pain was coming on strong. That little chill was still in his bones, too. How was it possible to pick up a chill just walking from the car to the courthouse stairs? What was it he had thought about Lennard? Debility, senility and what was the other one. Futility . . .?

Yes, that was it. Futility. The anxiety (amounting to an obsession?) that had been eating at him these past few days, that unreasonable despondency over the loss of will and faith in the country, had been scratching at him behind these more immediate ruminations, clamoring to be heard. This damnable impaneling had been sucked into that vortex, too—as everything and everybody was being sucked into it—for he saw the disparate elements of the country, the thicket patch of prejudices that the two sets of lawyers were picking at, as the basic weakness of the country itself. It seemed to him so very clear now that the much-celebrated strength of this nation, its diversity—its mixture of national strains and cultures, its open marketplace of ideas, and yes, its wide and generously flung-open arms —was the essential weakness that would destroy it. National purpose, brotherhood—fine words, fine phrases—had turned out to be nothing more than a thin surface varnishing to wish away the rot and turbulence underneath. Beneath the diversity were steaming hatreds. Out of the steerage holds had poured double loyalties. When the surface cracked, as it now seemed to be cracking, there was revealed a mongrel nation snarling at itself.

Out of the mix, when the heat was applied, would come not a melting but a final catastrophic explosion.

Why had it begun to crack and crumble now? Was Ambose right? If a homogeneous society was in need of the firm authoritarian hand of the law to hold it together, did not as heterogeneous one as this need an even stronger one to *bind* it together? If the bones were crumbling was it because David Boone Wilcke's Court had sucked the marrow dry?

Was Ambose right . . . ?

The cry from Judge Chodbodian's heart said *Nooooo!* The cry from Judge Chobodian's troubled heart said that if he had to stand with Jim Ambose to be right, he would rather not be right at all.

All at once he became aware that the courtroom had gone silent and everybody was staring at him. Bannerman and Ambose were standing. From the impatient movement of Bannerman's hand he could read his mind. Bannerman was thinking that they *always* told him their local judge had a mind like a steel trap and they always turned out to be wool-gathering old pensioners like this one. Dave Moore was moving toward the Bench, looking concerned. Below him, Marie was looking up, worried and embarrassed. Had he reached the point where his friends were becoming concerned for him? In an odd sort of way his ability to put that question to himself cheered and reassured him. As long as you can still observe your own fanaticism, Lennard liked to say, you are not an honest-to-god fanatic and don't let them lock you up.

With as much dignity as could still be mustered, Elijah Chobodian apologized to the attorneys, the venireman and the spectators for having lost the thread of the interrogation and asked Marie if she would read him back the pertinent Q & A's. Listening with attentive gravity, his hand at the hinged corner of his glasses, he heard that the juror had testified that he'd "have to put out of his mind what was already in it." Whereupon Bannerman, addressing the wool-gathering old judge, had said, "Your Honor, that's a burden the defendant shouldn't have to carry in a capital case," and Ambose had insisted that he'd already testified he had no fixed opinion, and "put it out of his mind or lay it aside, it's all the same thing."

Judge Chobodian couldn't remember that particular quibble coming up in exactly that way before. But maybe it had, maybe it had. The headache had become a steady pain behind his eye. A quibbling and a bickering, that's what a long drawn out jury impaneling became.

"*If* I may clarify this juror's thinking further," Bannerman was now saying testily. "*If* I may not be foreclosed from interrogating this juror at all. It has become perfectly evident that the district attorney is anxious to seat a hanging juror in this man, in which case we need not have any trial at all . . ."

A wave of nausea swept over Chobodian. With effort he kept himself from putting his hands to his eyes while the sickness took hold of him. Out there Bannerman's voice sang on. Chobodian opened his mouth to dismiss the juror, and nothing came out. He waved him out of the chair.

Out there he heard Ambose's voice coming from a great distance: "What? Is he letting him go? Christ . . ."

Finding his voice, Chobodian said, "Let's have the next venireman, please."

Her name was Holly Hansen, and goodness no, she didn't know any of those men at either of the tables. Heavens no, she had never been in any trouble with the law, she said in a sweet little frightened voice, the very thought of such a possibility alarming her. Her whole manner was so frightened and breathless that Judge Chobodian, who had poured himself a glass of water and felt the better for it, assured her with a grandfatherly smile that there was no need for her to be nervous for she was among friends here, and offered her a drink of water to prove it. "Oh no sir, Your Honor, sir," she said, widening her eyes, in innocence and hurt. "I am not nervous, sir. I have appeared before the public many, many times before in my career as a cabaret singer."

Having taken a closer look at her, Chobodian could see that the cute and breathless voice was far, far too young for her age (which she, with downcast eyes that confessed to her silly female vanity, begged off having to reveal). So was the little yellow cotton shift with the little dickie-bird collar, and the pointy white shoes she pressed tightly together on tippy-toe, and maybe even the huge white straw bag she hung on the arm of the witness chair. He could also see that she had brightened up his whole courtroom. There were smiles as far as the eye could see and a sparkle of interest in every male eye. Nevins, hardly able to restrain a smile, ran down his questions quickly, and to each of them she would answer with a childish eagerness and wistful appeal, Oh yes, sir; Oh my yes, sir; Yes indeed, sir. Or, sighing sadly, pouting somberly, Oh no, sir; Never would I, sir; Never, never, no indeedy, sir. And: "I have every faith, sir, that you gentlemen of the law will perform your duties as befits your high offices, sir."

Bannerman had whispered to Halpern, "Not a chance to get her on the jury, but at least I know who I'm sleeping with tonight." Seeing the question in Halpern's eyes, he chuckled, "I can feel the gentle fluttering of the womb and hear the eager twitching of the clitoris, a winning parlay, no pun intended, recognizable by the true connoisseur at thirty paces."

When it came time to question her himself, he was all smiles and twinkles. Walter Raleigh, on the best day he ever had, never treated Queen Elizabeth with more gallantry than he now extended to her. She leaned toward him, her eyes sparkling, and gave forth another series of cute and wistful and, yes, fluttering Yes, sirs; Oh my yes, sirs; even an Oh, indeed, sir, yes sir, upon my word and troth, sir.

As much as he was enjoying himself, Bannerman cut his interrogation well in half, and without even bothering to discuss the matter with his client announced with a confidence that was as convincing as it was fraudulent, "We will take her happily, Your Honor. The defense, the defendant and the chief defense attorney personally wish to submit for the district attorney's consideration that this young lady will lend to our deliberations a charm and beauty of such radiance and appeal as make the contemplation of each new day of the coming lawsuit an adventure in pure and wholesome delight."

Nevins, slouched deeply in his chair, didn't even bother to take his hands out of his pockets. "We'll excuse her, Judge. Thank you, Miss Hansen, for all your help and courtesy."

From the courtroom, as from the surf breaking on the beach, came the soft soughing moan: "Awwwwww."

Holly sat there, perched perkily at the edge of the chair, her mouth agape, unable to believe she had been rejected. Even after the Court told her she was free to step down and return to the Central Jury Room for possible assignment to another case, she sent a desperate pleading glance to Bannerman in the hope that he might still be able to save her.

Bannerman, as she should have been able to see, was at least as broken up over the whole thing as she was.

With Dave Moore preparing to draw out the next batch of veniremen, Chobodian announced they could all use a ten-minute recess. Catching Moore's eyes, he signaled him to come to the Bench when he was finished so that he could send him back to his chambers for a couple of aspirins.

With Bannerman taking a stretch and Chobodian occupied, one of the newspapermen in the front row was able to ask Bannerman why Nevins hadn't wanted her. "I can't imagine," Bannerman said, barely managing to keep a straight face. Seeing Pawley strolling toward him, he lifted his voice and said, "Unless he was afraid she'd distract Ambose and Pawley from the grim pursuit of their bloody work." Pawley threw one arm over Bannerman's shoulder and said, "Norman, that was positively indecent. If it went on any longer, it would have been the first voir dire that ever got an X rating." Since Pawley hadn't been in the courtroom the previous day and hadn't talked to Halpern at all since his return, he threw his other arm around Hal's shoulder. "Halpern, you are a magnificent and dedicated human being. On behalf of the National Hangmen's Federation, I welcome you back into the society of your peers."

Ambose and Nevins were both turned around talking to Jake Foxx. Alfred Marma had run out to the john. And so when Judge Chobodian turned back from downing the aspirins, there was nobody facing the Bench except Sam Tabor.

Their wandering gazes intersected and caught. Tabor, who would have wished to avoid that meeting even more than the judge, offered a strained and tentative quarter-smile, as if he were asking whether it was proper for him to communicate even that indirectly with the Court and, if it weren't, apologizing. For the first time in his life Elijah Chobodian, his own head aching, found himself filled with compassion for a murderer, and if he wondered on it, it was not alone at this latest example of how the foundations upon which he had built his life were slipping away from him, but also because he felt a sense of their common frailties, and in those frailties, of their shared humanity. This was the way things sometimes happened, the look the judge sent to the defendant said. Life was tragic, and what was there for any of us to do but accept the particular pattern of our own tragic fate.

It was Sam Tabor, not Judge Chobodian, who was at last able to break his eyes away. Judge Chobodian, coughing up phlegm, reached for the gavel and called the court back into session.

At the defense table a red check had been placed in front of the address of the upcoming venireman to alert them that he was from Paynter's Corner. Bannerman slapped Halpern on the shoulder and said, "OK, Harold, you're at bat. Get rid of him. I'm going out for a smoke." The next thing Hal knew, Bannerman was walking out of the courtroom.

Nevins propped the venireman up nicely in his own interrogation—he'd have liked a hillbilly on the jury—but as soon as he saw that Halpern was taking him, he made a flat, sit-down motion with both hands. All at once Halpern was their boy again. They were not at all averse to having their hand-trained boy look good, and they most certainly didn't want him to look bad.

After a hesitant beginning in which he had to rephrase his first question, Hal zeroed right in on fixed opinion and soon had the witness agreeing that there had been a lot of talk about the assassination at work.

"Did they speak of the murder with approval?"

"No, everybody thought it was a real bad thing." The witness looked at the lawyer as if he were crazy. "Especially for the country."

"And did you argue with them? Did you try to convince them it was a good thing for the country?"

"Good thing? How could it be that, a murder like that? For the country, that is?"

"What do you think should be done with the man who admits he did this terrible thing to the country?"

"Well, I think they should do something, I can tell you that."

"If the law said he should get off free, would you let him off anyway, or would you say the law's crazy, we've got to lock this guy up somewhere as a protection to the country?"

"Well, at the least that. The least they'd have to do is put him away somewhere. Anybody could tell you that."

Chobodian dismissed him. The juror gave Halpern a quick look as he passed by, showing very clearly who else he thought should be put away. Hal smiled at him anyway, to show him that he loved him. He even had a passing thought that somebody ought to do something for those hillbillies. Send their kids to a fresh-air camp or something.

Bannerman, having caught the end of it from the doorway, whacked Halpern on the shoulder and said, loud enough for everybody to hear, "Good work, Hal."

"Let's get on with it," Chobodian said, pounding the back of his hand with his fist. Moore had already called out the next venireman's name, and as Chobodian turned to the doorway to pick him up a terrible pain came into his eye, so sharp that the courtroom faded away and became dark. In the center of the blackness there was a small white light that seemed to be rushing away from him with great speed. He had a momentary thought of recessing early, but then the pain was gone and the courtroom throbbed back into view again. There was only an hour or so to go. With luck they might run out that last peremptory and get the final juror. Fight it, he thought, fight it! The poem popped into his head again. *You were ever a fighter, so one fight more, the best and the last.* The venireman being sworn, Judge Chobodian said, "I have a very few questions to put to you and then you —" and it all folded up in front of him, the courtroom folded up as if it were a paper picture being crumpled, spinning and disappearing into a receding whorl into which he himself was being . . . not drawn toward but blown away from rapidly. And then there was a surgically sharp pain across his eye, so painful that it cut his breath away. In the infinite calibration of time between the pain and the loss of breath it came to him that the poem was Browning's and that it was a poem about death. Not about fighting death but about welcoming it. In that same infinite calibration of time he sent out the thought, not in panic but only to keep the record clear: *No, that wasn't what I meant, Katerine.* He had already begun to turn to where he knew Marie would be, but the only sound that came out of his mouth was *Ooooooh!* and his head hit the Bench with a dull, sickening thud.

Norman Bannerman, standing tall amidst the gathering of lawyers in the cloak room, wasn't having any delay. "We're the side the Constitution says has a right to a speedy trial," he said with emphasis, "and we're not waiving nothin'."

"Now, Norman," Pawley said, asking him to be reasonable. "Even the Constitution has to make some allowances for an act of God."

"In the pig's asshole," said Norman Bannerman. "The Constitution doesn't have to make any allowances the Supreme Court doesn't say it has to make. And," he said, lighting up in anticipation of the rapier thrust that was coming, "the Supreme Court has risen up on its hind legs and ruled that God had better stay the hell out of it."

They had found out how much trouble they were in when Pawley called up to the law library to have Corinne bring down the *Manual on the Rules of Procedure* for the state Criminal Courts and discovered that Rule 11 provided that if a presiding judge became indisposed at any point in the trial, he could be replaced "at the discretion of the senior active judge," not as Pawley had always supposed (in that Chobodian had always made the decision) at the discretion of the appointments judge. The Rules of Criminal Procedure for the United States District Courts didn't help either, Rule 25 providing that "any other judge regularly sitting in or assigned to the court, upon certifying that he had familiarized himself with the record of the trial, may proceed with and finish the trial."

Harry Davies had not been hard to find at all. With his own court rendered inactive, he had let his people off to attend the trial or stay home as they pleased, and having nothing else to do himself, had volunteered to frisk the women spectators any time Miss Paskin, the lady bailiff, wanted to be relieved. Which was often. Miss Paskin had been complaining all along that this was a job for a dike. When Bannerman sneaked out for his smoke, just before Chobodian's collapse, one of the girls from the clerk's office, a little girl with the biggest boobs in the courthouse and the sweater to show them off, was trying to tell Davies that she had left the courtroom only five minutes ago to go to the ladies' room, as he surely must remember because he had asked her where she was going and could he go with her. Harry, bugging his eyes out, said, "Yeahhhh! I know who you are. I've had my eyes on you for a long time and I always thought you had a couple of concealed weapons on you." All Harry knew was that he had his orders, but to show her what a good fellow he was he was willing to leave it up to Bannerman, an acknowledged expert on firearms. "You take one cup," Bannerman said, smiling at her, "and I'll take the other."

Because Bannerman was looking on, Davies had probably done a more thorough frisking job than usual, and all the while she was submitting herself to it she was giving Bannerman the long, meaningful look and repeating that Harry knew her, her name was Dot Harbinger and she worked down in the clerk's office. Or, to quote Norman Bannerman after she was finally cleared for entry, "It never rains but it pours."

"Some of us," said Harry Davies mournfully, "should be so lucky."

Since Davies had accompanied the unconscious body to Chobodian's chambers halfway down the hall, a courtesy he seemed to feel one judge owed another, Bob Stringfellow was dispatched as a one-man delegation to inform him that under the Rules of Procedure the buck had been passed to him.

Nevins, balanced on the edge of the table, rolling his leg back and forth, was now suggesting that maybe they ought to just let the dust settle and then buck it up to Gardella, the presiding judge of the Administrative District, and have him appoint an outside judge.

"Gentlemen," Davies said, bringing the discussion to an end, "we'll continue to use Judge Chobodian's court in the hope and anticipation of his recovery. I will see you all in court tomorrow. Nine o'clock sharp." Stopping at the door, he rubbed his hands together heartily in anticipation of the great fun they were all going to have. "And you'd all better be there on time—hear?—or there's gonna be some learned and distinguished asses thrown into the hoosegow."

"Harry," Ambose said. When Davies turned a stubborn face back to him, Ambose just shook his head sorrowfully. "You're not good enough, Harry. David Wilcke deserves better. The people deserve better. Sam Tabor deserves better. Maybe Bannerman doesn't think so yet, but even he deserves better."

Bannerman arched his eyebrows at the "even." He was in too good a mood, you could see, to let "even Ambose" bother him. "Let the record show that Bannerman has expressed every confidence in the ability and sincerity of this judge. Let the record show that the defense team is in complete accord with his decision."

In invoking the defense team he had moved behind Marma and Halpern as if to show they were presenting a united front. The only problem that remained, as far as he could see, was how to inform the press. "For the good of the judiciary, the legal process, the flag and motherhood, I suggest that Judge Davies issue a statement under his seal and authority to which we will addendum our mutual desire to pick up the fallen banner and press on, with all parties fervently hoping and praying for Judge Chobodian's swift recovery and return."

Nevins bit down hard on his cigar. Bannerman could go out and tell 'em any damn thing he wanted, he said, with a clipt clarity so unusual in him that he was also saying that the state would do whatever speaking it had to do for itself. "Harry," he said, "I'd like to have a private word with you, if you've got another minute or two."

When they were alone Nevins didn't say a word. He remained right where he was, sitting on the edge of the table with one leg on the floor, rolling his cigar in his mouth, just looking at him.

"I'll tell you something in the strictest confidence, Hilliard," Davies said. "I need this."

"I want you to think about something, Harry. All you've got to do is sit still and keep your name out of the paper too much and you've got a lifetime job here with the electorate. You sit on this trial and you're liable to mess yourself up so bad you couldn't be elected dog catcher. Might not even get the nomination." Taking the cigar out of his mouth, he tilted the wet, scraggly, chewed-flat end toward him, squinting just a little as he spoke. "I don't agree with Ambose that often, but when he tells you you're a lousy judge, believe him." He drew the cigar aside, opening his arms wide as if he were stripping himself of all pretenses and defenses. "It surprises me, Harry, you never knew."

A blotch of red appeared high on each of Davies' cheeks. His chest heaved in and out with the effort of long, deep intakes of breath. "Mr. District Attorney," he said in a high, choked voice, "this is not the first time it has come to my attention that your estimate of my abilities is not very high. Perhaps you will think differently when this lawsuit is over."

Nevins gave him one last searching look before, in an obvious gesture of surrender, he pushed his glasses to the top of his head. "All right," he said, as much to himself as to Davies. "All right." He had done his best; he had let off steam. There wasn't anything to do now but resign himself to the inevitable. "Look, Harry," he said, perfectly composed. "We don't want a reversal, so we'll try to steer you straight. If you get into trouble look to us. When Pawley rubs his hand back and forth across his mouth a couple of times—like this—that'll mean you should rule for the defense no matter what we're saying."

"Like this." Dutifully, showing Hilliard that he understood, Davies drew his fingers across his lips.

Yeah, that was it. And if there was no rubbing of the mouth, he should be ruling for the state. "Ambose won't know anything about it," Nevins said, "and I've got a way of doing that without thinking. So just Pawley. Got it straight?"

"Well, gee, Hilliard," Judge Davies said, "that's awful white of you, knowing —uh—well, knowing how you feel and all. I just want you to know that I appreciate the gesture."

Judge Harrison T. Davies, the new presiding jurist in the trial of Sam Tabor, accused of the murder of Chief Justice David B. Wilcke, was perfectly serious.

"What a break," Bannerman told Halpern almost as soon as he jumped into the car. He threw back his head, in love with the world, and said, "Wheeee!" With Harry Davies they had a whole new shot at the Model Penal Code. A helluva shot. Pivoting around he hit Hal a good shot high up on the arm where it hurt. "I told you we were gonna make new law in this one, didn't I? Come on," he said, grinning broadly and feinting another punch at his arm. "Didn't I?"

Bannerman had been surrounded by newspapermen and cameramen when Halpern pulled up to the courthouse, and somehow Hal didn't think his glee had been running quite so unrestrained in front of them. To shut it off, he asked if there had been any later word on Chobodian.

Bannerman looked at him as if he had to be kidding. "Did you see the way he looked when they carried him out of the courtroom?" His eyes drifted beyond Halpern as they turned the corner, sweeping the street. "If you'd seen as many corpses as I have, Hal my boy, you'd have known that was an imminently-eminently dead judge they were lugging out of there. Holy mackerel dere, Sapphire, the way his head hit the Bench should have told you, if nothing else."

When Bannerman had asked him to drive him back to the motel, Hal had somehow got the impression that the sight of Chobodian keeling over like that had shaken Bannerman up far more than he now seemed willing to admit. Just in case he was wrong, though, he said, "Naw, I haven't seen many corpses, you're right about that. But I heard our statement over the radio. Y'know the one I mean? The one that says we're praying for his swift recovery. If it won't hurt our case too much, I'll keep on praying."

"Hey." Bannerman was looking past him and pointing. "Pull up over there. Over on the left." Over on the left a woman was standing alongside a car, waving. That Bannerman should be so chivalrous would have come as something of a surprise if Hal hadn't recognized the huge white bag against the yellow dress even before he recognized Holly Hansen.

In her sweet and cuddly voice Holly told Bannerman she didn't know what in the world could have happened but all of a sudden while she was riding along just as nice as anyone could want, her motor had just sort of plumb petered out. "My," she said. "Isn't it funny that of all the people in the world it should be Norman Bannerman of all people who happened along. I mean I feel so *funny* about it, don't you? It's a real Believe-it-or-not-Bob-Ripley."

Bannerman already had his arm around her waist. This kind of thing had a way of happening to him all the time, he told her, and it always seemed to turn out to be nothing but a clogged fuel line. If that was all it was, did she know what he was going to do? He was going to take her home with him and buy her dinner, because that would make it one Believe-it-or-not-Bob-Ripley on top of another, wouldn't it?

The preliminaries over, he snapped his fingers and held out his hand, appraising her so bluntly that there was very little for her to do but plunk the key holder down into his palm in a way that frankly conceded that the act was over for her, too. "How fortunate for you, my dear," he said drily, "that some miscreant didn't happen along and take advantage of your precarious situation."

Halpern, watching them drive off, had to admit that Bannerman could hear it twitching across a crowded room all right, all right. He also had to admit that he knew why Bannerman had asked him to drive him back to the motel, and it had not a thing to do with being all shaken up about Chobodian.

BOOK VI

The Big Show

"And wouldn't it be the final laughter of the gods if the last thing you discover at the edge of the graveside is that in all the things that mattered the fools were right and the wise men wrong?"

—*Judge Elijah Chobodian*

Lowell (UPI), July 30—The trial of Samuel Tabor, alleged assassin of Chief Justice David Boone Wilcke, will get under way tomorrow under the gavel of Judge Harrison T. Davies. Judge Davies is the last-minute replacement for Elijah Chobodian, the stern, 65-year-old jurist who was stricken at the close of Tuesday's session. The long and sometimes bitter jury selection came to an end at 10:47 A.M., less than two hours after the opening of Judge Davies' first session, when District Attorney Hilliard Nevins accepted a 42-year-old post-office worker, Martin Seidelman, as the twelfth juror. Red-thatched, velvet-voiced Norman Bannerman, who had used the last of his peremptory challenges earlier in the morning, had no alternative but to accept Mr. Seidelman also. Mr. Bannerman's motion that the entire panel be dismissed on the grounds that all 12 members of the panel had seen the assassination on television was overruled as Judge Davies upheld the earlier ruling of Judge Chobodian that anything seen on television was hearsay.

The bad blood that has been evident between Bannerman and hatchet-faced Assistant DA James Ambose flared up again after the first venireman of the day had testified to having a definite opinion about the case. Mr. Bannerman thereupon requested Judge Davies to ask the juror to state his opinion for the record, maintaining that if the juror was of the opinion that Mr. Tabor was not guilty the defense had every right to have him seated. "Over my dead body," Mr. Ambose declared, to which Mr. Bannerman replied, "Now that's the most tantalizing proposition I've had since I came to this fair city."

Otherwise, this 13th and final session of the jury selection was quiet and subdued as if the memory of Judge Chobodian's startling collapse still hung over the proceedings. Local observers had been telling the newspapermen who have descended upon this city in droves that Judge Davies was known to run a far more leisurely court than Judge Chobodian, and the change in tone became evident very early when the new jurist asked a 53-year-old housewife who was shaking so badly that she could scarcely make herself heard whether she would be more comfortable if she did not have to undergo any further questioning. The sigh of relief emanating from the witness chair brought such laughter from the crowded courtroom that

Judge Davies had no difficulty in getting both sides to stipulate that she be allowed to go.

According to the latest bulletin from the Phillips Brook hospital Judge Chobodian suffered a cerebral hemorrhage. The rumor that the opening of the trial would be delayed for one day or perhaps even until Monday as a gesture of respect to Judge Chobodian was shown to be without foundation when immediately after the swearing-in of the jury, Judge Davies announced that . . .

The line had started to form before dawn. By eight o'clock it wound all around the block and was beginning to lap itself like, to quote Conrad Rittenhouse's marvelously descriptive report in the early *Chronicle,* "a snake about to eat its own tail." (It was more descriptive than true actually, as the photograph just above his story showed only too well, the police having doubled the line back around the other way in order to keep the front entrance clear.)

Stringfellow's deputies had been reinforced very early by Chief Wilson's specially trained Crowd Control Squad, easily identifiable by the handsome brassards they wore around their arms (solid black with two yellow C's interlocked like horseshoes) and even more identifiable by their size, bulk and heft. Stringfellow had sent for help when he saw that something nobody had prepared for was occurring. Pickets were out in force. Some of them serious, some of them out for a lark.

There was, for instance, a youngish, rather good-looking, terribly intense evangelical couple, dressed rather shabbily and heavily tanned. The husband was slim and wiry and righteously overbearing; the wife, who was wanly pretty with long, long, *long* black hair, was sweetly supplicating. (As Bannerman would say later, "They work very well together as roundsmen for the Lord, the good guy and the bad guy. They missed their true vocation—they should have been cops.")

Each of them was parading a placard upon which messages were imprinted, front and back. The husband's messages were painted in defiant black, with the key words in the Devil's own red.

<table>
<tr><td>Sam *DeMon* Tabor
Is the *Hand* of God
to Save this *Country*</td><td>and</td><td>David Boone *Wilcke*
is Better *Dead*
than *Red*</td></tr>
</table>

They were joined, within a short time, by three college kids, two of whom were huge football types carrying a small sign on which there was printed the strange device: A FUNNY THING HAPPENED TO ME ON THE WAY TO THE ACROPOLIS.

Behind them, struggling always to keep up, trotted a little scholarly fellow lugging a huge sign that said: You mean APOCALYPSE, Stupid!!!!

When two representatives of the Homosexual Anti-Psychiatry League of America showed up with a large and interchangeable collection of signs attacking psychiatrists, judges and policemen, a quick call up to Pawley brought Stringfellow the offhand opinion that there were about ten constitutional rights involved. "About the only thing you can do, Bob," Pawley advised him, "is tell them that if they want to overthrow Harry Davies' court, they got here too early. Harry's hours are from ten to two thirty."

In due time a more conventional revivalist arrived upon the scene, a raunchy looking fellow who came equipped with a portable platform, a money bucket, a stack of pamphlets and a bullhorn. This time a call to Ambose brought the advice to send all the pickets across the street, preferably with a good kick in the ass—except for the queers, whom he was constitutionally entitled to knee in the balls since it would be impossible for them to prove damages.

With the weather reports predicting a record-smashing hot spell, the ice-cream peddlers had descended upon the scene also, and Stringfellow permitted them to park along the curb at carefully designated intervals. On the other hand, he ruled off the course all street peddlers who were hawking buttons, popcorn and American flags, and a sidewalk artist who had arrived ready to set up business.

The first of the people in line had already been interviewed to a fare-thee-well by the local press and by everybody who had come equipped with a tape recorder, and as the magic hour approached where they would be allowed to file up the flights of stairs "in a responsible, orderly fashion," a few members of the foreign press took a whack at them also.

Lenore was putting stamps on a stack of letters when Doc Swann came into the district attorney's office, an *icky* task she felt to be far beneath the dignity of the district attorney's secretary on this historic day (or any other day). But you could tell them and tell them down in Central Mailing and they'd promise and promise, but they didn't care when they got your letters out because *they* didn't have to explain to Mr. Nevins or Mr. Pawley why it had taken so long.

"Lenore," Doc Swann said while she was gawking at his black astrakhan hat, "have I told you it has come to my attention that despair and desperation being the lot of mankind, we derive what comfort we can by breathing heavily over other desperate and despairing men? I haven't? Remind me to bring it up sometime. I want it to have the widest possible distribution." Before he had stopped talking, he was past her desk and heading toward Nevins' office. Lenore, catching Corinne's eye as she emerged from the library loaded down with books, shook her head hopelessly and said, "Honest to god now, Corinne. I mean, honest to god . . . !"

Doc Swann came bursting into Hilliard Nevins' office just as Ambose was saying from the sofa that it was bad enough they'd given him a Jew juror, but at least they hadn't given him a nigger.

"Ambose," Doc said, "you'll never get on in the world unless you eschew prejudice and get that suit cleaned. I don't care what anybody says, I like you."

Ambose's cold, surly glare made it known that he was suffering neither the interruption nor the slight gladly. Which didn't mean that he didn't have to pause a moment to take a squint at Doc's astrakhan hat. "Look who's talking," he said, with a scornful toss of his head. "There at the hearing I was expecting a moth to fly out of your ear."

Immediately Doc's eyes lit up. So overwhelmed was he, in fact, at finding that Ambose was, for once, going to give him an argument that he did a little shuffle step that somehow gave the impression that he was spitting on his hands. "The invincible James Ambose, huh? You still ahead of the world, Ambose? Of course you are! I'd put the score this morning at Ambose three, World one." The malicious little gleam hardened to a fine malicious point. Bannerman had scored on Ambose, though, hadn't he? "Got one of those heathen Hebrews in on you while your back was turned, did he?"

Ambose was happy to be able to inform him that Bannerman hadn't stuck them; they had stuck Bannerman. He was even happier to inform him they'd sucked Bannerman into using three of his peremptories on guys they'd wanted to knock out themselves, if only Bannerman had known it. "One of them arrested five times and two convictions, only he was so busy listening to his silver tones, the fancy sonofabitch, he forgot to ask." The malicious gleam that had appeared in his own eyes came to its own malicious point. "The fancy sonofabitch, I bet he dyes his hair."

Nevins shut him up with a look. He had asked Lennard to drop in, he said, getting down to business, because Ambose had come up with information that Bannerman was subpoenaing some old records from the St. Cecilia Clinic to show that Tabor had got himself circumcised twenty-two years ago. And what did Lennard think they were going to try to make of that?

Swann's face twisted into about five different shapes, all of them showing distaste. "It means he pissed straight up in the air for three weeks. Jesus Hersholt Christ! The old witch doctors were supposed to read the future from the entrails of a goat—isn't that right, Ambose?—and all you're asking me to do is read a man's mind by the tip of his prick. To do that for you, I'd have to invent a whole new science." A faraway look came into his eyes. "I expect I could raise one hundred disciples and a government grant within the hour. It astounds me none of my colleagues has beaten me to it." He rubbed the edge of his thumb along the side of his chin like a man trying to decide whether he needed a shave, the faraway look becoming even dreamier. "Reminds me of a classmate of mine. Married an heiress to a shoe factory and retired to the Argentine to raise stud horses. Lovely little lady. Five hands high and broad across the withers. I'd had an eye on her myself. Dirty Louie we called him . . ."

The district attorney and his assistants had an eye on one another, too, every eye sagging and groaning under the weight of what they had somehow let themselves in for.

"Lennard . . ." Nevins said. "Some other time."

Bannerman had asked to be picked up around 7:30, but Halpern, with that habit of being ridiculously early for his appointments, arrived at the motel before the guests were up and on their way. Bannerman was not only up, though, he had already shaved, as could be seen from the flesh-colored little Band-Aid under his chin. (It came to Halpern that he had never considered the possibility that Norman Bannerman might conceivably cut himself shaving. It also came to him that he wasn't necessarily the only one who hadn't gotten any sleep last night.)

Bannerman was, as a matter of fact, already half-dressed. He had put on a pair of black pants and, Hal was happy to see, a shirt that was only slightly fluffed. The motel room itself was in a state of disarray, just like the hotel room used to be, and there was the same stale, pungent odor. The beds hadn't been made, of course, and it was impossible not to notice that both of the beds had been slept in. The top of the bureau was a mess, with books and briefs and telephone messages flung all around, a stack of keys (there must have been a dozen of them) piled in the middle, various vials and bottles thrown here and there, a couple of half-filled glasses, an almost empty pint bottle of Jack Daniels and, sitting incongruously in the corner, a pair of white carnations being kept fresh in a glass of water.

At the moment Bannerman was engaged in putting on his cummerbund and he had put on so much weight it was turning out to be a struggle. The only way he could do it finally was to put it on backward so that the clasps were right in front of him and then suck in his gut. Even then, his hands were shaking so badly that he fumbled a couple of times before he managed to get the job done. Having done it, he took an even longer and deeper breath while he twisted it around. "A little trick I learned from a ballerina," he grunted between twists. "Although needless to say she performed her calisthenics with her brah-sierre."

Perhaps Bannerman had only been making conversation. If that was all it had been at the beginning, the slyly spreading smile was all that was needed to announce that he had recognized it soon enough as a little trick that would come as no surprise to a gentleman by the name of Harold Halpern.

Speaking of ballerinas, he said (while he was adjusting the cummerbund to his satisfaction), Harold ought to have a go at Dot Harbinger, a little packet of dynamite from the clerk's office. Bannerman, good sport that he was, would give him her home phone number for the asking if he should ever develop a taste for trollop.

As he twisted his neck to loop on his necktie (a dove-gray cravat, he told Hal, as if he were passing on information of great importance), it could be seen that the shirt pinched into the flesh a little, too. Their client's wife had also paid him a visit, he said, inclining his head toward a folded document lying in front of the keys. "I thought it was about time for her to understand that with the trial getting under way we ought to professionalize the relationship, a procedure which in legal parlance is commonly referred to as a contract. Vera," he said, letting his eyes run to the bed, "was only too willing."

As unmistakable as the meaning was, Halpern found it almost impossible to believe that Bannerman would be interested at having a go at the middle-aged, marginally attractive wife of his client. Not even if that was what it took—and why should it?—to get her signature on a contract. Since he had no reason to disbelieve it, either, he said, "My, my. Between the little packet of dynamite and the willing client you had yourself a busy night preparing for the trial, didn't you?"

Bannerman chuckled just about the way Hal would have expected him to chuckle. He also sighed in relief at having got the cravat tied and ran his fingers around under the collar. They were going to need the blowup of Sam Tabor being taken into custody by Booker Phillips, a huge, five-foot cardboard blowup that Hal had been able to talk the television station's lawyers into providing. "It's in Room 10," Bannerman told him. "That's Julie's room."

If Bannerman was still playing games with him it didn't do him any good. Not because Hal had become particularly adept at hiding his feelings but because he didn't really have any. The only reaction he did have was that if Bannerman was telling him to add Julie to the list, Hal wasn't going to give him the satisfaction of keeping count for him. "Want me to call her," he asked. "Or what?"

Bannerman was looking into the mirror, alternately smoothing his hair back and probing unhappily at the Band-Aid. Hal would find the key to Room 10 somewhere in the pile, he said between grimaces, and all at once Hal found that he did have a reaction, and that it was a sharp feeling of disappointment at finding that Julie wasn't here, after all. Wasn't here and wouldn't be in the courtroom. He picked the key out of the pile and went out into the sudden heat of the morning.

Julie was there. She was in bed. Asleep. Turned over on her face. Right arm outflung. Thin blanket twisted and crumpled across the curve of her hips. Sheet twisted, strained and creased. Those damn sleeping pills of hers again, he thought.

The blowup was leaning against the far side of the bureau. Treading as softly as possible, he took hold of each edge. Treading softly still, he looked back at her and she was awake. So completely awake that it was as though the heavy sleep had been part of a light vigil she had been keeping since she heard he had returned.

They looked at each other. With fond and reminiscent little smiles, you would have thought from the outside. Tender and used-up smiles they were on the inside. The memory of pleasure that was not without pain, you would have thought from the outside. The memory of pain that was not without pleasure, it was on the inside. Hal held up the key. "I didn't think you'd be here."

"I'm here."

Her eyes went to the bureau to where her own key lay. "Bannerman likes to gather the slaveys around before the fray but he doesn't lock us in if that's what you were thinking." She had automatically brought the sheet up to her neck as she sat up. Looking at him, she let it fall away as if it were, under the circumstances, a wholly unnecessary gesture.

Julie in her pink silk nightgown.

"Bannerman," she said, looking at him, "has a thing . . . about . . . keys."

The blowup was cumbersome enough so that he put it down. "I looked for you in the courtroom when I got back."

She shook her head in the wonder of seeing him here, her eyes sweet and pained and apologetic. "I'm bad news," she said. "Haven't you heard?"

"You're bad news I heard you say."

She shook her head and sucked her lower lip in. The phone rang. If he remembered her one way more than any other it would be looking at him like this, in that way she had, with her lip sucked in. She let it ring a second time and, still looking at him, she picked it up and said, "Thank you," and dropped it back on its cradle. "It's a quarter to eight I heard them say. Time to be rising and shining. So if you will be a gentleman, love of my life, and—"

Say it lightly, say it mockingly, the words had a life of their own. Say it any way she wanted, once they sounded on the air they were as a mirror in which she was revealing herself. Once they sounded on the air they became a mirror in which Hal saw more than he would have thought he would see or wanted to remember.

"Never apologize, never look back," she said with resolve. "That's what I heard them say." Tossing the sheet aside, she swung her legs over the bed. Julie in her pink silk nightgown. "And I said to myself, and I heard myself say, those are words to live by."

She wasn't going to tell him whether she'd be in court today? He wasn't going to ask.

He picked up the blowup. "Goodbye, pretty girl."

"Good by, Lightning."

Bannerman was fully dressed. His jacket was cut to a modified frock coat, and taken with the gold watch chain across the front and the gray cravat it gave him a curiously old-fashioned look not at all in keeping with the living-law, progressive image he usually tried so hard to project. He twirled the white carnation he had selected under his nose, sniffing the fragrance, and very carefully drew it through his buttonhole. Taking a small strip of adhesive tape he had already attached to the side of his hand, he just as carefully secured the stem on the underside. "The white carnation," he informed Hal as he was examining himself in the mirror, "is the symbol of the pure, fragrant crusader. The knight-errant setting forth to tilt with giant or windmill in pursuit of virtue and justice."

Hal said, "The blowup is in the car. The car's waiting. And you're a prize prick."

Instantly, in the look of secret delight that came over Bannerman, he saw that he had told Bannerman what Bannerman had wanted to know. Almost as quickly, though, the interior laughter gave way to something else. An expression of complete surprise rose to his face—rose to it and rose to it—and sent him hurrying off to the bathroom. Halpern heard him throw up, heaving until he had emptied himself out and then retching and wheezing and gasping for air. Finally it ended. The toilet flushed. A short time later the water could be heard running in the basin.

"Well," Bannerman said, having emerged fully cleansed and curried save for the pale and clammy look that clung to his forehead. "That makes it official. No opening day would be complete without Bannerman puking up his guts to the martial strains of the marching Marine Band." His hand darted to the bureau for one of the vials, and in a quick, almost continuous motion he slipped a handful of Dexedrine pills into his hand, popped one into his mouth, gulped it down without water and dropped the rest of them into his pocket.

Half-turning, he cast a narrow, quizzical look at Halpern. "Wait until you hold the life or death of a fellow human being in your hands." Having said it he held his own trembling hands out for inspection, turning them over so that he could examine them, front and back, palm and knuckle, in all their terrible frailty. "Yes," he breathed, turning them slowly, flexing them lightly, "you just might find yourself killing a pint of Jack Daniels because your stomach won't hold food, and then you'll puke up your guts in the morning anyway." With an almost embarrassed little laugh and an almost horrified little shiver, he shoved his hands into his pockets. "I'll tell you one thing, kiddo," he said. "You won't be worth a damn if you don't."

He didn't have to tell him a thing anymore. Hell, Halpern was thinking, if drink and women got him through the long night and brought him to the starting line at a higher pitch, more power to him. And yes, if it helped him to know that they were the women the judge wanted and his client wanted and (he saw his own affirming smile) his co-counsel wanted . . . well, yes, even then. Because nothing mattered right now except saving the life of Sam Tabor. Nothing.

"Julie looked pretty good," he said. "I was glad to see her again." And if it was a peace offering Bannerman scarcely seemed to hear, he proceeded in his own way to acknowledge it. "A trial is like a Great Grizzly Bear," he said, staring off into space. Dreamily, his eyes half-closed, he began to waltz around in the open patch of space at the front of the room. "The Bear will devour you if you don't know how to dance with him, Harold," he said, holding the Bear with his eyes. "So dance with the Bear, dance with him. Lead him, but gently." With a sudden lurch and a whoop—with that exuberance that was built into his very structure —he grabbed Halpern around the waist and whirled him around and around and right out the door, and as he reached back to slam the door shut, there was a wild, manic glow of excitement streaming out of him, an all but audible hum of nervous energy building up to where it would have to be unleashed. Riding the crackle of that energy, he whooped, "Watch me, sit beside me, never take your eye off me. Take me to the county courthouse, Harold, and I'll show you how to dance with the Bear."

It had not been a good morning for Lenore. She had bought herself a whole new outfit in the expectation that the press would be buzzing all around, the way they had right after the assassination, but nobody had come in except Rich Caples, on his daily stop, and Mr. Nevins wasn't even in yet for him to talk to. Wasn't that just like Mr. Nevins, she thought, coming in late at the beginning of the biggest trial anybody had ever seen? And that was the whole trouble with this office, she had seen in one of those moments of revelation. There was nobody with glamor; nobody with a silver voice or golden tonsils. The trial was going to be just like the picking of the jury, only worse, with everybody buzzing around Bannerman all the time and nobody paying the slightest attention to the district attorney's office.

Usually Lenore did her nails at the desk when she came in, to give herself the extra fifteen minutes of sleep in the morning. But having gotten the full treatment at the beauty parlor the night before, she was mooning over the mailroom problem when Nevins came storming in with his head down and his eyes hanging low in their sockets like they sometimes did when he was sorer than usual at Ambose. Even the red tie made him look angrier than usual. (A red tie with a brown suit; she sometimes wondered whether he was color blind.) Putting on her brightest smile, Lenore opened her mouth to tell him that Mr. Pawley was waiting in his office and that Mr. Ambose had left word that he wanted to see him as soon as he came in, but before she could get more than two words out, Nevins bawled, "Get me Harry Davies on the gaw-damn phone!" and stalked past without so much as a good morning. It got Lenore so mad she did something she had never done before. She made a spiteful face behind the back of her boss.

Before the door slammed shut she could hear him yell, "Did that blooming idiot Harry Davies let us know he was gonna let them turn this courthouse into a gaw-damn moving picture studio? Gaw-damn . . ." Even after it slammed, if she had wanted to be the kind of secretary who had big ears for everything, she could have heard him bawl, "And did you see the gaw-damn menagerie they got parading outside? What are we gonna have here, another Monkey Trial? You gonna tell me we can't do anything about that?"

Yes, Pawley had seen them all right. And no, there was nothing they could do about it. The courthouse was under the jurisdiction of Davies and the streets were under the jurisdiction of Bob Stringfellow. "All we can do is exert our strong moral influence. I know . . . that and a dollar will buy you what fifty-nine cents bought you last year. It's a white-horse case of being out-jurisdictioned, but there you are."

The buzzer sounded. Lenore had Davies on the line. "Gaw-damn it, Harry," Nevins shouted into the phone . . .

Having got that off his chest, he hung up and glared at Pawley. "And what the hell have you got to say for yourself lately?"

From the look of him, anything Pawley would have to say was going to be cool and disapproving. All he had to do, though, was draw his hand across his mouth. "Lucky you're a friend," he said. "Otherwise he might get mad."

The buzzer had sounded again but before Nevins could pick up the phone

Ambose had already burst in on them. "Unless somebody wants to keep it a secret from me," he said, plumping himself down on the sofa, "what the hell we going to do about Karney?"

The problem was that Clougherty had asked Nevins if it would be possible not to put Karney on, since the old man was feeling particularly poorly in this hot weather. Despite Pawley's best efforts Bannerman wasn't willing to go along with the idea of accepting an affidavit from the only witness who had actually seen Tabor aim and fire. Bannerman had, in fact, served notice that if the state didn't put Karney on, the defense would subpoena him and, if it became necessary, demand to have its own doctor examine him.

Nevins tapped his teeth, thinking about it. The district attorney didn't see where it would be such a bad idea to make Bannerman force the issue if he wanted to. "After the jury sees Karney, Tabor is going to look pretty sane to them, wouldn't you think? I have a feeling Bannerman just might come around to seeing that himself if we give him a little time to think about it."

"Oh hell!" Ambose shifted in the sofa, recrossing his legs. Didn't Nevins understand that Bannerman had a five-way lock on this thing? Was he talking to himself, for chrissake? "The first question I'm going to be asking their psychiatrists is whether Sam was able to make a living, and they're going to have to say yes. If we get the kind of a report Bannerman's doctor will bring back on Karney, Bannerman's first two questions are: Do they know how much Tabor made and do they know how much the mayor makes, and he's established that you don't have to be in the best of mental health to make a living in this city."

Karney was going to have to take the stand as a state witness, Ambose said flatly, and that was all there was to it. "Myself," he said caustically, "I don't like eyeball witnesses put on by the defense instead of the prosecution. It goes against everything I've learned during my long and arduous training in the district attorney's office."

Nevins stopped tapping his teeth and flipped up his glasses. Well, well, well . . . And did Ambose have any other complaints he wanted to get off his chest? Were Nevins' better instincts right in telling him that Ambose wasn't happy in his work anymore?

He'd be a hell of a lot happier, Ambose told him in the same waspish tones, if he got a little more help from time to time. No, "help" wasn't the word he wanted. Consultation. "Like asking me about taking that Jew juror, seeing that I'm the guy who's going to be trying the case. Jesus, I walk out of the room for ten minutes . . ."

Sure he knew it was a Jewish *postman,* he said, throwing Nevins' emphasis right back at him. And normally he'd take a postman anytime. A Jew postman, a nigger postman or a kangaroo postman. But not as the number twelve juror in this case, after they had stripped the defense of their strikes, and after they had let Bannerman make such an issue of playing a WASP game of lawn tennis in the jury box. He thought they had an agreement, he said, bringing out his real grievance, that they were going to keep Bannerman on the defensive.

When Pawley found it necessary to point out that protecting the record was half the game, especially when you were on the attack, Ambose shot him his coldest, thinnest smile. Here they'd spent two weeks grinding Bannerman down. They'd had him on his heels. They'd had him screaming and floundering, ready to be ground into the dust. And then right at the end with the chance to pick and choose their own juror, they had given him a big psychological lift by letting him dictate their choice. "Everything considered—considering that we're dealing with an egomaniac here—I'd have to call it one of the dumbest stunts I've ever seen pulled in the courtroom."

With that last Ambose was setting it out clearly that he knew whose bright idea it had been. Just how right he was could be seen by the way Nevins swiveled around and frowned at Pawley while he was waiting for him to defend himself.

One thing you could be sure about with Pawley. Nothing was going to rattle him. Pawley thought it might be well to remind Ambose that Bannerman had not been making an issue over Jewish jurors, except what you'd want to infer from WASP. It was the Negro thing he'd made all the noise about.

"Yeah," Ambose said. "It's bad enough you gave him a Jew juror without giving him a nigger."

It was at that point that Doc Swann came swinging in through the door, wearing a crazy Russian hat. "Ambose," he said, "you'll never get on in the world unless you eschew prejudice and get that suit cleaned . . ."

Now that it had come to the bruising, Ambose had surrounded himself with his own people. Jake Foxx and Harvey Leigh, plus Bob LaRue, the cop who had ridden to the hospital with Wilcke's body. LaRue, who was sitting off in the corner in his sergeant's uniform, had testified enough to know that Ambose always liked the cops—especially the old cops he had ridden with in the old days —to come in early and hang around the office. Foxx had been waiting in the office, sucking on a mouthful of Life Savers, when Ambose arrived. Harvey Leigh arrived a few minutes later, in plain clothes, to give them a blow-by-blow description of how he had put Bannerman's wiretapper, Lew Brahms, on a flight to Chicago. Ambose and Foxx had both been informed immediately, of course, but with Harv having pulled more than a week of solid sixteen-hour shifts he had been furloughed to catch up on his sleep until the trial began and so they were hearing the story in all its colorful detail for the first time. "Seems like he just all of a sudden got tired of our company, Jake," Harv said. "I was downright hurt."

Yeah. Jake had seen he'd been getting kind of restless Sunday.

"Well, restless or something," Harv said. "Monday night, it would be—that's right, Monday—we're eating our supper at the Buckminster, just him and me, and he says . . ."

"He was eating at the Buckminster?" Ambose said. "That'll do it right there."

"So he says OK, how about getting him a broad for the night and he'd head on home, you know, in the morning. So I tell him poon-tang don't come with the service. Sorry about that. What he wants he gets himself, I tell him, only Section 532–6 of the Criminal Code, so he should know his rights, cites fornication as a felony punishable by a hundred-dollar fine, up to thirty days or both. And where I'm sitting, right outside the door, how the hell am I gonna miss it, right? What the law is in Chicago, I tell him, that's something we're in no position to know.

"You know what he says?" Harv began to chuckle to himself, his stomach bouncing gently under his jacket. "You'll never guess." From Harv's benign expression as he looked from face to face, Ambose figured it was going to be pretty good. "He says, 'A fine friend you turned out to be!' "

Ambose couldn't blame him for milking it. Poor Harv had this good story, and he could only tell it this one time.

Without putting it into words Ambose let them both see they had his thanks for a job well done. "Harv, you stick around here, general assignment. We'll find something to keep you busy." He could start making himself useful right now, as a matter of fact, by helping Foxxie on the telephone while Ambose got his exhibits ready.

On Ambose's desk were a stack of affidavits and interviews. He pulled out those of the witnesses who would be called today and read through parts of some of them, totally oblivious to the phone calls being made on the other side of the desk. When he'd collected them all, he slapped them into his old scruffy cardboard file holder.

Opening his drawer, he took out a small blue cotton bag on which the string was pulled tight across the top, the kind of bag a cigarette lighter comes in. In it was the bullet that had killed David Wilcke. Also a much larger white bag, of a thinner, coarser cotton, with the same kind of drawstring across the top. In it was the gun. Both bags were placed in a wooden cheese box that had been sitting atilt, in his Out box. Underneath, in the In box, were half a dozen glossy prints of Booker Phillips taking Sam Tabor into custody. He put them in the folder, too. Propped along the back wall were two diagrams. One of the City Hall stairs, the other of the route between the courthouse and City Hall. He took the diagram of the stairs back with him and placed it under the file folder. The other diagram he left right where it was. It didn't take any genius to figure out that the accident of timing that had brought Tabor face to face with Wilcke was the main weakness in his case. He'd let Booker tell it, but he didn't have to diagram it for them.

"Jake," he said, "you tell Booker I wanted him here before nine?"

Foxx's lazy eyes unhooded in mild surprise. He put his hand over the phone. "In court I told him, Jim. That's what you said." They were all going to be in by nine so far, Jake said, except for Sands, the ambulance driver, who had to take his wife to work and wouldn't be in until 9:30.

"He's got to take his wife to work?" Ambose yelped. One day in her life she couldn't take a bus? Or would it, for chrissake, be against her religion to get there half an hour early?

"Relax, willya?" Foxx told him. Even with luck he wouldn't be needing the ambulance driver until just before the noon recess. Never mind, it was the principle of the thing that bothered Ambose. One of his key witnesses and he wasn't going to be there on time, he said, shaking his head in utter disbelief, because he had to, for chrissake, drive his wife to work.

Cheerfully, in the tone of a man carrying good news into a bad situation, Harvey Leigh said, "The only one I haven't got so far is Doctor Price. The hospital says he'll call back."

Ambose just goggled at him. The medical examiner! The man he had to put on the stand to establish that Wilcke was, for chrissake, dead! *And he was going to call back?* He jammed one of his little cigars into his mouth. "Today, I hope!"

"Those things are no good for you, Jim," Foxx said. "Here. Chew on one of these." Foxx was holding out a fresh roll of wintergreen Life Savers. Now that Ambose thought about it, Foxx had been chewing on them all morning. Since when, Ambose wanted to know, had Foxx become queer for—Holy Toledo— wintergreen Life Savers?

"I'm trying to stop smoking," Foxx said smugly. "Haven't had a one in three weeks. With all this talk about lung cancer, you got to be crazy."

Ambose blinked at him, clearly unable to understand why the whole world had chosen this particular time and place in history to go crazy on him. Didn't Foxx know that if he stopped smoking and kept chewing those things by the ton like that he'd blow up like a house? Didn't he know that?

Sure Foxx knew it. Forcing patience into his voice, he explained, "There's a chance I haven't got cancer yet, at least. I *know* I'm already fat."

Thank god the phone rang. It was Lenore telling Ambose that Mr. Nevins had just arrived but had gone on by her like a mean old bear before she had been able to relay his message.

Judge Davies had waited impatiently for Marie to arrive, and when she came in, looking beat and complaining that she had never seen the expressway quite so bad, he remarked quite loudly that they both could use a long, cool drink. Immediately he buzzed Mrs. Coles to ask in his heartiest, bluffest manner whether now that he was such a Big Deal around here could he prevail upon her, as the Big Deal's secretary, to get them a couple of iced coffees from the cafeteria, and one for herself if she wanted.

As soon as they heard Mrs. Coles leave Marie pulled a chair over to the side of his desk. "On what you said," she reported in a low, conspiratorial whisper, "I spoke to that certain party and he said it would be better to just come up to your chambers afterwards, you know? All he wants is that you let him ask the Model Penal Code question on insanity, like Chobodian was going to. The Model Penal Code and the M'Naughton Rule both. And then, in the charge, you read them off both rules and give them their choice."

The judge's plain and honest face remained plain and honest. "Do you think Eli really told him that?"

For one second Marie's eyes moved away. Not long and not much. But enough. She shrugged expressively. "Well, like I've said about how much Eli told me . . ." She made up her mind very quickly. "I was under the impression, the last I heard, that Eli had promised to give it his serious consideration, and that's all." She made another rapid calculation. "If you want to know what I think, I don't think it matters what Eli told him. You're running the show now, Judge. I just have a feeling that if he could get the question asked and answered for the record, he'd be happy enough." She drew a breath, trying to read the judge's plain and honest face. "I wouldn't give him any more than that, Harry. On the charge, I mean. Unless he could really guarantee something . . . on that thing you want."

Behind the plain and honest face Harry Davies was thinking that Chobodian had promised Bannerman nothing of the sort. Dear Marie was selling him out, and what could that mean except that Bannerman had got to her through her— Well, how else did one get to dear Marie? That part didn't bother him one bit. Actually, he felt rather relieved. He could dump her when this was over and not feel a qualm. He'd be needing Marie through the trial, though. He would be needing her as a contact with Bannerman and he'd also be needing her advice. With all her experience, especially all those years with Eli, Marie knew as much as a lot of judges and more than a lot of lawyers.

"That's real good thinking, Marie. What's he ready to guarantee?"

"That he'd talk to his agency." Quickly again, gauging his reaction, she said, "I told him I didn't think that was going to do it. He'd have to be able to guarantee it. For sure."

"To stand behind it," Davies said firmly, sounding like nothing quite so much as a furniture salesman.

"That's right, Harry. That's what you've got to do. To protect yourself."

So she thought he was that dumb, did she? Davies leaned back in his chair, chewing on the rim of his glasses, more conscious than ever of the pictures of Eleanor and the kids. Yes, if it were possible for Harry Davies to dislike anyone, he might really have it in him to despise her. "You know what I think we'd better do, dear. We'd just better have the head of the agency here for a little talk-talk before our friend is ready to ask the legal question. *Wha—!*"

They had been talking so quietly that the ringing of the phone had cut through the air like a fire alarm. They stared at it, both of them, as if it were a witness in the room they had somehow forgotten about. Covering the speaker, he whispered, reassured and reassuringly, "It's Hilliard."

While Harry was doing his best to calm Hilliard down, Marie was wondering how even Harry could be that dumb. To talk to a lecture agency about becoming a client while the trial was still in progress could jeopardize everything they were working for: the trial, his career, everything. If Ambose found out about it Harry would be tossed off the case—and Ambose had a way of finding out about things. Still, the best course for Marie Pappas to take at this early juncture was to keep her eyes open, agree with everybody and carry the messages back and forth. The longer both Harry and Norman were in need of her services, the stronger she would be with both of them. The intrigue excited her anyway; there was a jingle and a tingle of Mata Hari about it and also, she thought with a warm little giggle, leave us not forget the reward that was waiting for her at both ends. Like a pat on the head and a cube of sugar to a faithful retriever. No one would ever know the part she had played in the Trial of the Century to save Sam Tabor's life and bring about a humane change in the law, unless she decided to write her memoirs late in her life and reveal to the world that Marie Pappas, whom history had looked upon as no more than the quiet and efficient court reporter, had in reality . . .

"That was Hilliard," Davies said, cradling the phone. "He's unhappy with the way I have chosen to serve God and mankind."

"So I gathered." She had begun to look upon Harry as fondly as ever. "I'll tell that party you need more collateral," she cooed. She puckered her lips coyly. "Lover . . . I need some collateral, too."

"Aw, honey," Harry Davies said. "Once I get that lecture contract signed and sealed, it's into the lawyer's for the settlement." His hands came crashing together like cymbals, one of them ricocheting high off the other. "Just like that."

Ambose, storming back into his office, passed on the news that Price wouldn't be in until noon, and in case anybody had any doubts how he felt about it he spat on the floor. With sound effects. "Sometimes," he said, "they tell me something around here."

Foxx was looking just about the way he had looked while he was wondering why Ambose was so upset about the ambulance driver. What Foxx wanted to know was what they were going to do about Karney. Ambose's face clouded over and he spat again. "We'll play that one by ear! We meaning *me!*" And turning his face to the general direction of the district attorney's office, he muttered something which, though generally unintelligible, left the clear impression that he had not turned there as toward Mecca.

Bob LaRue, who looked like an old welterweight fighter who was just beginning to go to fat, had settled back into his chair as a sort of amused observer, radiating his pleasure at having discovered that the district attorney's office was just as screwed up as he had imagined only the police department could be. "What's the matter with the doc?" he asked innocently. "He sick or something?"

From the doorway Caroline Beyner called in breezily, "Who's sick besides me? Would you think I was crazy, Jim, if I told you I didn't catch a wink of sleep all night thinking about what a fool I'm going to be making of myself in there?"

All of the men smiled at her except Ambose, who frankly looked as if this was one more intrusion he could have done without. There was not a thing for her to worry about, he told her shortly. He'd be asking the same questions they'd already gone over. Bannerman probably wouldn't ask more than two or three. She'd be on and off in five minutes.

"I know . . . But I've got to get up to the witness stand first and I keep seeing myself stumbling on that first little step and falling flat on my face." There was something so wistful and helpless about the way she said it that everybody could see she was only trying to coax some kind of expression from them that would tell her she was being foolish. Ambose knew what was really worrying her. Bannerman's investigator, Cowhig, had come around to interview her earlier in the week, and while Bunny had been smart enough to tell him exactly nothing, she had been able to see that what he really wanted to know was whether Sam had come smelling around the naughty little girls, and now that she'd thought about it, she had confided to Ambose, Sam did have a way of coming into the office from time to time and just standing around like a Dutch uncle, smiling at the kids while they were horsing around.

If she would be a good girl and leave him alone, Ambose said, taking her by the elbow and walking her out, he'd promise to put her on as early as possible. All she had to remember for now was to check with Foxxie outside the courtroom at, say, ten o'clock. "Foxxie will be running them in and out of the chute and he'll let you know how it's going."

"Sounds like fascinating work, Foxxie," she called back from the doorway. With a backward toss of the head that made it a very effective exit line, she added, "Like cows to the slaughter."

Just as they were leaving for the courtroom, exhibits in hand, Booker Phillips loomed halfway down the hallway with two middle-aged women rather uncomfortably in tow. With Foxx already holding the cheese box, Ambose handed the folder over to Harv and told them to go on ahead. And so it was that Jim Ambose found himself taking the shyly outstretched hand of Booker Phillips' sister Mady. The baby. This pleasant-faced, not unpretty but wholly indistinguishable woman who had been the central figure in that great drama that had taken place over their mother's coffin and determined Booker's fate and life. And (Ambose suddenly realized) in determining Booker's fate had also determined Wilcke's and Tabor's and the country's; and, to a greater or lesser degree, everything that was about to take place in the courtroom. The infinite weavings he had pondered over so laboriously before the bond hearing hadn't reached back that far or that tenuously, had they? He glanced down at Mady's left hand, knowing before he looked that there'd be no ring there; knowing without asking that she still lived with Booker. That was the way it would have to end. When Booker had taken his baby sister to care, he had taken her to care for life. No wonder he'd had to sell his car to give his daughter a wedding.

They had begun to walk down the hall, with Booker and his wife moving on ahead so that Mady and Ambose could get to know each other. "Well, well," Ambose said. So Booker had decided to bring her down to watch the show, had he? "I hope we can make it worth the trip."

Oh, she knew it would be, she said with her pleasant smile, which was really the anxious, eager-to-please smile of the spinster sister, the permanent house guest who could never afford not to be pleasant and accommodating. Even as Ambose was observing it, the smile turned over and became warm and candid. She had always known, Mady said, that Booker's true worth would be appreciated some day.

Huh?

"I always knew Booker had those qualities that would make him a well-known figure one day. I have a way about such things, I really do. ESP they call it . . ." Having stolen a quick look at him to satisfy herself that he understood what she was talking about and was suitably impressed, she said, positively glowing, "But I never thought he'd come to be recognized nationally." It had come rushing out of her all of a piece, as if she could hardly wait to hear how it sounded, feel the wonder of it as it bounced back; taste public recognition, as it were, in public. "My, no," she said. "I never doubted Booker's worth. I never doubted that he would be recognized one day but . . . nationally?"

Ambose could only tell her that they had always appreciated Booker's worth here around the courtroom. She could be sure of that.

As if in reaction to the eruption of energy upon leaving the motel room, Bannerman drew back into himself, totally preoccupied, during the entire drive to the courthouse. The closest he came to stirring to life was when he peeled the Band-Aid gingerly off his chin, wet the corner of his handkerchief and leaned over to adjust the rear-view mirror so that he could satisfy himself the bleeding had stopped.

As they were approaching the courthouse they could see the line bending around the block and then the pickets marching across the street, the three TV trucks pulling up right in front of the courthouse and, finally, the police gathered like a giant blue squid alongside the steps. "What in *the* hell is going on there," Bannerman said. "It looks like a trailer camp for fig-pickers." Although he smiled, it was a small smile, listless and mechanical. "If Nevins isn't careful he's going to end up with another Monkey Trial on his hands. Well, Darrow didn't do so bad with the original cast, did he?"

Since Hal didn't want to depress him any further, and since he didn't really think Bannerman had hired him as either a legal historian or a strict constructionist, he forbore from mentioning that while history had done very well by the memory of Darrow, Darrow had lost that case.

What was that fret of apprehension that crossed the handsome thickening features of Harrison T. Davies as he was being invested into his robes by the faithful Peterson? What could he be thinking of at this historic moment, this veteran judge who had been thrust, unprepared and unawares, into this awesome assignment? Could it be that Harry Davies was wondering—at long last, in all humility—whether he possessed the intellectual range and judgment to take up the reins of the case that was being called a test of American jurisprudence? Of one thing there could be no doubt at all. The judge was deeply troubled. No man stealing unobserved into the room could fail to see that he had fallen into a deep and brooding introspection; perhaps even a painful and penetrating self-examination.

But wait . . . ! The troubled judge has opened his mouth. Yes, the troubled judge is about to voice his innermost fears. "I want to ask you something, Pete," Judge Davies said, "and I'd appreciate your honest opinion. Do you think anybody would consider it in poor taste if I requisitioned Eli Chobodian's limousine for myself? God knows, the poor bugger's not going to have any more use for it."

Peterson cleared his throat and agreed in his quiet, ghost-like voice that it certainly wasn't doing anybody any good sitting there in the courthouse garage. "If I may offer a suggestion, Your Honor. I could call my friend in Judge Gardella's office."

Judge Davies didn't even bother to pretend that wasn't what he'd had in mind all along. "You might mention that your judge isn't thinking so much of his own comfort as how it's gonna look to all that out-of-town press, seeing the presiding judge drive up in a three-year-old Buick." Screwing his face up, Harry adjusted the crotch of his pants under the robes. His brow remained thoughtful and strained as with a couple of twists and wriggles he readjusted the robe at the waist. What new problem agitated poor Harry Davies' overburdened mind? What new doubt assailed him? "Don't call him until tomorrow, though, Pete. Late in the afternoon better. We don't want to look as if we're being ghoulish, do we?"

Conrad Rittenhouse was standing a few elevators away when Ambose and the Phillips family emerged. Hurrying over to Ambose, he said, "I was just on my way up to catch you, Jim. You got a few minutes?"

Ambose, looking at the mess up ahead of him, growled that by the looks of the damn place it was going to take him at least that long just to pick his way through to the courtroom. The whole corridor was a maze of wires and cables; some of them already covered over by metal shields, some of them still strung along the floor and being worked over by technicians. Spotlights had been attached to the ceiling at regular intervals, ready to be turned on at the flick of a switch. At the other end of the corridor—against the wall just outside the courtroom foyer—a small platform had been built. The platform was at that moment bathed in light, for Norman Bannerman was being interviewed by a network commentator. On an even higher platform directly across the corridor were three television cameras, manned by three separate television crews.

"Yeah," Conrad said, walking along beside him. "Did you see all those nuts out there? They'll be making this look like another Monkey Trial if we don't watch out."

Ambose was fully aware that it was a question rather than an observation. "I don't know about that," he said. "Just tell your readers not to bring their dog up here or they'll shoot a Lassie picture before they can get him out."

Although the greatest crush was around the TV platform the other news media people were everywhere; many of the younger ones sporting beards and even more of them supporting Fu Manchu mustaches. Half of the media people milling around in the corridor seemed to be carrying cameras, and by the look of them the word had gone out that the uniform of the day was dirty white pants and dirty white sneakers.

With Ambose not volunteering a thing, Conrad asked him how he viewed the state's case now that it was getting under way.

"You can say that I view the law against murder as a good one."

"You're gonna be like that, huh?"

"Like what? I just figured with you getting everything you need from Bannerman, it's only fair to spread the wealth around."

"I take it where I can find it, buddy. Just like you. All I got from Bannerman today is that he's going to see what you put on, and he's going to be firing from the hip."

"Well, that's all in the world I'm going to be doing, Conrad. Just going to put 'em on and let 'em tell their dirty little stories." A milky film came over his eyes. "And you can run on back and tell Bannerman that my daddy always told me to try to be a moving target."

Rittenhouse went pale. They had come to the edge of the crowd gathered around the TV platform and so he had to hold his voice down as hoarsely, breathing heavily, he warned Ambose that before he said anything he was going to be sorry for he'd better understand right now that Conrad Rittenhouse didn't go running to tell Bannerman anything.

Up on the platform the interviewer was saying that there had been a lot of talk among the reporters that the mob outside was reminiscent of the Scopes trial, otherwise known as the Monkey Trial, which held a not too happily remembered place in the annals of American jurisprudence. Would Mr. Bannerman go along with that comparison?

"Is that what they're saying?" With just a little more urging Bannerman would have been shocked. "No such wild and outrageous talk has reached my ears, Jack. I personally view the ferment and phosphorescence surrounding this lawsuit as a healthy resurgence of the basic American freedoms."

Somebody from NBC had Ambose by the elbow and was instructing him to stand by because they wanted him as their next interview for the *Six O'Clock News*. A short, husky man with a loosened tie and teeth that made him look very much like a beaver. Manfully resisting the impulse to wrench his arm away, Ambose smiled down at him and nodded.

Up on the platform stood Norman Bannerman, in his pool of light, smiling and smirking and dimpling at the camera that would bring his words to people numbering in the tens of millions. All around Jim Ambose pressed newsmen calling out questions. At Jim Ambose's side stood the Beaver shushing them, telling them to take it easy, they could have him after the network was through with him.

Bannerman was being thanked. Ambose was being pushed through the heavy traffic toward the platform. The Beaver was shouting to keep those lights on, he had the guy from the DA's office. Bannerman, having been helped down off the platform by warm and willing hands, looked up to see Jim Ambose only a few feet away, separated by the crush of news people between them. Across that wall Norman Bannerman smiled genially and, by virtue of his great height, managed to gesture most graciously toward the platform so that everybody could see that he was willingly turning the spotlight, the cameras and the great American public over to the opposition.

Jim Ambose removed the Beaver's hand from his arm. "You will have to excuse me, gentlemen," he announced in his measured courtroom voice. The babble that had welled up at the conclusion of the Bannerman interview fell away.

Everything touched by the circle of light fell silent. Jim Ambose surveyed the mob of newsmen with his cold, searching eyes. "You will have to excuse me, gentlemen," he said. "I'm on my way to Calvary to drive a couple of nails in."

Judge Davies called the court to order and announced that he had familiarized himself with every facet of the case and was ready to proceed. (Pawley, stretching his back, whispered to nobody in particular, "That's what's known in the law as an incontestable overstatement.")

The writers who had slogged through the jury selection could not help but be aware that a new feeling was in the air, crisp and astringent. The things that had seemed so important for three weeks now seemed like frittered effort. (Had it really seemed so important whether the prospective juror had recognized Sam Tabor on the television screen?) It was as if the X-rays and biopsies had been taken and they were finally wheeling the patient into the operating room. The instruments had been sterilized, the surgeons had washed down, the long blades were being drawn.

For Halpern, everything about the courtroom was so sharply in focus that it was as if he had turned a telescope on it and could see the shimmering of the rising heat. The colors of the flag behind Judge Davies had never stood out so vividly. Sam's color was high, as of a tautness of nerves. Ambose looked more ominous, more bred in the bone than ever. Marie was seated almost in front of the witness chair in her customary straight-backed chair, a fresh pale-green notebook sitting on the table in front of her and half a dozen newly sharpened pencils (four black, one red, one green) lined up neatly alongside. Five minutes after the trial started she would disappear into the background and become no more than another accouterment of the process, no different in kind than the microphone sitting in front of the witness or the tables or the chairs. At this moment she was the embodiment of every court of appeal, up to the Supreme Court itself, that might eventually read the record she would be preparing.

Even Hilliard Nevins somehow looked stiff and formal as he rose to ask that Josh Flowers, who would be a witness later in the day, be permitted to sit in the courtroom through the earlier testimony so that he could go on about his work as a television reporter. Bannerman immediately called out that he'd be happy to stipulate to that and asked the district attorney to stipulate, on his part, that the defense psychiatrists be permitted to remain in the courtroom so that they might continue to observe Sam Tabor as part of their ongoing examination. All of it pure play-acting. Judge Davies had already informed both sides that he was going to "waive the rule," by which he meant the rule that normally barred all witnesses from the courtroom until after they had testified.

Moving from the pre-preliminaries to the preliminaries, Bannerman made his motions for a mistrial, purely for the record, and Judge Davies, purely for the record, overruled them. And then, with the official recitations over, Norman Bannerman's voice turned rich and mellow. "Your Honor, by an accident of the calendar this lawsuit, which is of such a magnitude as to slice like a laser beam across the whole corpus of American jurisprudence, has spanned the Fourth of July, the birthdate of this great nation. It may be of interest to this Court to hear that upon leaving Lowell after my initial visit, I traveled across the several sections of this diverse nation, spending the Fourth of July in the little Kansas town of—"

"Hey," Nevins yelped, "he's making a speech there. If he's got any more motions, let him put them in. If he hasn't, let him sit down."

Ambose said, "Judge, if he's going to go on like that about the Fourth of July, I'm going to want equal time to tell how I spent my favorite holiday, Groundhog Day."

That made up Bannerman's mind for him. Yes, he did have one more motion. "There is an old Anglo-Saxon principle of law," he said solemnly, "that you cannot set a thief to judge a thief. I am invoking that rule at this time, Your Honor, to demand that Mr. Ambose be removed from this lawsuit, from the prosecution table and from the courtroom."

Judge Davies had mounted the Bench wearing an air of genteel weariness as befitted a man who had carried his several burdens with responsibility and dignity, a pose he had already managed to hold for a full twelve minutes. "Now what in the world," he asked, with the not so genteel weariness of a mother pleading with her children to play nice, "are you talking about?"

Ambose rose very slowly, unfolding in sections. Even when he was fully erect he flexed his shoulders three or four times before he said a word. And then he said with equal solemnity, "I move, Your Honor, that Mr. Bannerman be removed for reasons of clear and present insanity."

The Court let out a long, distressed sigh and asked the lawyers to approach the Bench. With no more than a lift of the eyes, Nevins signaled Pawley to let Ambose go up there alone. Their boy had got to Bannerman quicker than they could have dared to hope, and Nevins had every confidence that if it turned into a knockabout battle up there, Ambose would get in three blunt Anglo-Saxon insults while Bannerman was still conjuring up his first glittering multisyllable. But that wasn't the only reason. If Bannerman did have anything on Ambose, Nevins didn't want either himself or Pawley on record as defending him. Not now, he didn't.

Davies leaned over the Bench, tilted his chin to remove as much of the pouch as possible, and assuming his most farsighted and scholarly expression asked Bannerman what the hell this was all about. When Bannerman declared that he had reason to believe Ambose had put the idea of the assassination into Tabor's head and was now out to cleanse himself by nailing his accomplice, the expression became nearsighted and incredulous. "You have reason to *believe?*" He had made a statement like that in open court because he had reason to believe? And had he, as an officer of the Court, brought his evidence, if any, to the proper authorities? Confidentially, as if Ambose weren't there, he whispered, "Do you know how close you are to contempt, Norm? I've seen lawyers disbarred for less than that."

Ambose was there. Alive, well and smirking. "I'd still go for insanity as the proper grounds, Harry."

"You shut up, too," Harry ordered.

Still smirking, Ambose reminded him that Bannerman had never been admitted to practice before this Court. "You could bounce him easy, Harry."

"Aw, sit down," Davies said. "Get out of here, both of you. And cut out the crap for a change, willya?" (Marie was taking the testimony in shorthand rather than on the stenotype machine, because as wearing as shorthand could be over a long trial, she wanted to turn out as accurate a record as possible for Harry. In the interests of accuracy she had written: "The Court summoned Mr. Bannerman and Mr. Ambose for a Bench conference, censured them for their behavior and warned them against any recurrence. Whereupon the Court ordered both attorneys to return to their respective seats.")

"Mr. Halpern," the Court said. "Do you have a motion to introduce Mr. Bannerman for practice before this Bar?" Slamming his gavel down while Halpern and Bannerman were still rising, he said, "Motion accepted. Welcome, Mr. Bannerman. Mr. Nevins, will you step forward and arraign the defendant? Mr. Tabor, will you step forward with your attorney to be arraigned?"

Sam Tabor was about to play the only role he was scheduled to play in the entire trial. To speak his only line. Having been well briefed by Halpern he was ready. But instead of slipping between the tables as he had been instructed, he took the long way around, forcing Bannerman to more or less follow around after him. "Norman," he said, without looking back. "I want to talk to you about that."

Nevins was waiting for them directly underneath the Bench, hand in pocket and indictment in hand. He read off the indictment in a voice so bored and matter of fact that the word "murder" had almost no impact.

"How do you plead, Mr. Tabor?" the Court asked.

With Bannerman nodding encouragement Tabor said, "Not guilty, sir."

Both of Bannerman's hands were stuffed into his pockets, which told Halpern that they were shaking again. "If I may be heard, Your Honor," Bannerman said, in a voice so soft that he could barely be heard much past the press rows. "The defendant's plea is not guilty by reason of insanity at the time of the crime, and as he stands here now, with the supplementary pleas that he is incompetent to stand trial and—"

Davies had begun to bang his gavel, and when that didn't stop him he broke in to tell him shortly that the only acceptable pleas were guilty or not guilty, and that in a first-degree indictment it could only be not guilty. He glared at poor Tabor, who shrugged back at him as if to say, *What are you looking at me for, that's all I said, wasn't it?*

Hilliard Nevins wasn't going to let the incompetency plea pass unchallenged. "Judge," he said, "he had his chance to do that. He could have asked for a sanity hearing any time before his client walked up here, like everybody saw him do, and entered his plea for himself. He's about one second too late now. Tell him to cut out the act and start acting like a lawyer, huh?" Strolling over to the jury box he announced that the state was going to waive its opening remarks except to state that it was going to prove beyond the slightest doubt that Sam Tabor had willfully and with malice aforethought shot and killed David Boone Wilcke. He returned to his seat, crossed his legs, and threw one arm over the back of his chair. "OK, Ambose," he said under his breath. "Crank it!"

To the witness stand came Booker Phillips.

Ambose took Booker through the same story he had told at the bond hearing. When he introduced the photograph (along with the diagram of the steps) Bannerman graciously offered to let him put in the blowup as a state's exhibit "for the convenience of the jury," presenting Ambose with the unhappy choice of accepting something from the defense or rejecting it like a sorehead. And when Ambose said he'd go with his own evidentiary material, thanks, and let the defense go with theirs, Bannerman drew a laugh from the audience and appreciative smiles from most of the jurors by standing the blowup against the side rail where everybody on the jury could see it.

Within minutes the shoe was on the other foot. Ambose had reached down under the table and come up with the white bag from which he casually drew the gun. Approaching the witness stand in an easy, loose-gaited stride he read off the serial number and with a practiced little twirl that demonstrated his familiarity with firearms handed it, butt end first, to Booker.

"Is this the gun, Mr. Phillips, you took from the possession of the defendant, Sam Tabor?"

"It looks like it. It's the same kind of gun, a forty-five–caliber Smith and Wesson."

Ambose held out his hand to receive it back, and although he had hardly established that this was indeed the gun Sam had used and certainly hadn't shown that it was the same gun that had been issued to Tabor by the sheriff's department, he shuffled it over to Marie and confidently offered it into evidence as State Exhibit Number Three. Norman Bannerman, faced with a choice almost identical to the one that had confronted Ambose, played it entirely differently. He knew how eager the jury would be to see that gun. He also knew that it would come with exceeding ill grace for him to stand on a technicality so quickly after the gambit with the blowup. "Let's have a look at it first, if you don't mind," he said, holding out his hand. He smiled slightly. "I am sure Mr. Ambose will get around to laying the proper foundation later."

The first dramatic moment was, unexpectedly, at hand. Reaching across the table to take the gun, Bannerman fumbled it and the gun dropped right in front of Tabor. Sam picked it up mindlessly and started to hand it back. It was only when the whoosh of the audience washed over him that the awesomeness of the moment hit him. The murderer with the murder weapon. Dropping it as if he wanted no part of it, all but averting his eyes, he slid the gun over to Bannerman. Bannerman inspected it expertly and offered it to Halpern. Halpern turned it over as if he knew what he was doing and returned it to Peterson. It was a gun, that's all; no different from the guns on the hips of any of the deputies stationed around the courtroom.

And yet the moment it became an official state exhibit the gun did indeed take on an identification of its own. Ambose placed one foot up on the first step of the witness chair, held the pistol aloft, and with the identifying tag now giving it an ominous and historic flavor, he catalogued in his driving monotone the characteristics of a .45-caliber Smith & Wesson. "Will you now demonstrate for the benefit of the jury," he said, "exactly how Sam was holding it and how you proceeded to subdue him and take the gun away."

After Booker had obligingly shown how he had put a lock around Sam's neck with one arm and bent his wrist back with the other, Ambose sprang forward, clamped his forearm across Booker's windpipe and had his wrist turned back and the gun in his own hand in what seemed like one continuous motion. "That it?"

Booker looked back at him with a rather wry, not happy grimace. He rubbed his wrist and stretched his neck. "Yeah," he said. "Only not that good."

When Bannerman's turn came on cross-examination, he did it even better. Taking the gun from the exhibit platform, he stepped to the center of the well area (facing the crowded courtroom more than the witness) and delivered a brilliant portrayal of Sam Tabor stepping out from the crowd to shoot. In the Bannerman version, it was done with a dazed sideways stumble and otherworldly glaze that could have left no doubt in the mind of even the most confirmed skeptic that the unfortunate gunman was in the grip of some strange hypnotic seizure.

In reconstructing the arrest, he clamped his arm around his own windpipe and dropped unprotestingly to his knees, frock coat and all, from which undignified posture he asked the Court's permission for Booker to step down and demonstrate exactly how he had taken the gun away from Sam, and Sam away from the crowd. With Booker as his supporting cast, he then found it necessary to repeat the performance three more times, without any coaxing at all, before all the bugs were worked out. By which time, all critics present agreed, Bannerman was achieving dramatic heights of passive nonresistance hitherto undreamed of in a courtroom.

There being no rule in Judge Davies' court against lawyers roaming around at will, Bannerman had approached Booker originally with the warm and candid smile of an old friend. Booker had responded with the self-assured nod of a fellow traveler in the world of celebrities and the media. Mady wasn't the only member of the Phillips household who had been following his press notices, Ambose could see, and it didn't disturb him in the least. After some little debate with himself Ambose had decided against trying for the res gestae statement during his direct examination; first, because he was beginning to wonder whether it wasn't too borderline the way the higher courts were leaning over backward to protect the thieves these days, but mostly because he felt he'd have a better chance of getting it after Bannerman had got Booker good and mad in cross-examination. With Booker taking it this big, Ambose had a feeling that he was not going to be at all averse to building up his role.

Once the dramatic performance was over, Bannerman took Booker on the expected journey through the outward manifestations of Sam Tabor's frame of mind. Having been given the transcript of the hearing to study overnight, Booker was ready for him. He didn't know how anybody could tell what was in another man's mind, he said gravely, but as far as he could see Sam had not been "unusually nervous, distraught or emotional." And this time when Bannerman asked whether that wouldn't be abnormal in itself, Booker replied, "Not necessarily, Mr. Bannerman. Some are and some aren't."

He should have known by then what Bannerman did with that kind of an answer.

BANNERMAN: You wouldn't be able to say that he didn't look dazed, then?
BOOKER: I don't know that I'd be able to say that he did, Mr. Bannerman.
BANNERMAN: Then it would be fair to say there is a reasonable doubt in your mind as to whether he seemed dazed?

Pawley promptly objected that Bannerman was assuming as fact what the witness had already denied, and got himself a good laugh by adding that while "no" might mean "maybe" when it came to courting, it didn't mean "maybe" when it came into court.

"I have erred grievously," said Bannerman. "I was under the impression that this was cross-examination." He smiled over at Pawley, his eyes twinkling. "Or is it possible that my young friend, whose rich storehouse of romantic lore is the envy of all who know him, has thought it necessary to alert the witness?"

Not really. Because it wasn't really necessary. What had taken about thirty minutes to cover in the hearing took little more than three minutes in the actual trial. And that wasn't the only fallout from the hearing. Instead of pulling the answers out of him in a way that suggested Booker might well be holding something back, Bannerman had permitted him to come on so well prepared that he could answer quickly and straightforwardly. Ambose was pleased. Ambose was grinning.

310

The next question wiped the grin completely away.

Bannerman had walked back to the table to pick up his copy of the transcript, opened to a marked passage. He strolled up to the witness chair, started to hand it to the witness to read, and then checked himself. "Well, maybe there are better ways of going about this. Do you know what the Policeman at the Elbow Test is, Deputy Phillips? Good. Of course you do." And he would be stating it correctly, would he not, if he said that it was the routine question the state usually asked the defense's expert psychiatrist in an insanity plea to counter a claim of irresistible impulse? "Not the defense attorney, right? The prosecution. Thank you. Would I also be correct in stating that as usually phrased by the state's attorney it would go: 'If a policeman had been at Sam Tabor's elbow when he was getting ready to commit the act would he still have committed it?' "

Booker had heard it put that way, yes.

Bannerman thereupon hit him with a drumbeat of questions to impress its significance into the minds of the jury, and though his rhythm was rapid and insistent, the tone became increasingly teasing. As why shouldn't it be? With each of the questions Bannerman was yanking malice and premeditation farther and farther out of the courtroom:

The theory was that a sane man does not commit murder with a policeman at his elbow, was that right? (Objection.)

Would Deputy Phillips support the clear implication that an insane man therefore would? (Objection.)

Would Deputy Phillips support the theory that a man who did would have to be insane? (Objection.)

Would Deputy Phillips think that a man who did might well be insane? (Objection.)

Would Deputy Phillips entertain a reasonable doubt about the sanity of any man who did? (Objection, and instructions from the Court to move on to something else.)

Had Deputy Phillips himself ever been a witness in a case where that question had been asked by the state? (Yes, he had.)

"Isn't it a fact, Mr. Phillips, that it was a miracle Sam wasn't killed on the spot?"

Ambose hissed, "Let him answer it," and Pawley, who was on his feet doing the objecting, nodded in agreement. That was one Booker should be able to handle. Better to let him try, anyway, than to permit the bare assertion to go unchallenged in the jurors' minds.

"Well, he was in a crowd. And he wasn't resisting."

Bannerman looked surprised. "Was he now? While he was shooting . . . ?"

Returning from the defense table with a glossy photograph, he asked Booker to count the number of law enforcement officials on the portico. Booker counted eleven. While the jury was examining the picture, Bannerman produced a roster that listed the eighteen law enforcement officers from the police, the FBI and the Secret Service who had been behind Wilcke, every one of them armed.

"Would you not think, sir, that a man shooting directly into such an armed camp might reasonably expect to be shot back at?" (Objection. The witness was being asked to form a conclusion.)

Came then another half-dozen questions, all directed at showing that you're damn well right he would have. (Might he reasonably expect not to be shot at? Would it be unreasonable for him to suspect that he might be shot back at?

Wouldn't Booker himself have expected to be shot at? Etc.) Finally Bannerman asked whether it would be unreasonable for Tabor to have *suspected* the *possibility* that he might be shot back at, and to DeWitt Pawley's visible disgust Judge Davies decided there'd be nothing wrong about letting him answer that one.

Booker, no longer looking quite so confident, had to answer that it would not be unreasonable to suspect such a possibility. Pawley, knowing exactly what the next question was going to be, hadn't even bothered to sit down.

"And you are assuming, of course, that he is thinking as any *sane* man would be expected to think?"

"Objection!"

Bannerman had turned his back and walked away a couple of steps with the air of a man who knew he had scored heavily. From his bouncy step you could not have possibly suspected that his intestines were raw and burning. Wheeling back to the witness stand, he asked, "You did say this is a question that is usually asked by the district attorney when there had been no policeman or anybody else standing at the defendant's elbow, on the theory that if there had been a policeman there, the defendant would not have committed the act of murder with which he has been charged?"

Nevins said, "I heard him say it about seven times myself."

Ambose said, "I did, too, Your Honor. But I didn't hear him say even once that any policeman was standing at Sam Tabor's elbow."

Anybody observing Bannerman—which meant everybody in the courtroom—could shudder at the sheer revulsion with which he turned (in sinuous grace) his reluctant gaze upon Ambose. His eyes moved to him first; his head followed his eyes; to be followed, in turn, by his shoulders, waist, hips and body. Having been drawn, against his better instincts and innate sense of decency, by the horrible fascination of looking full upon the face of the gargoyle, he examined him with such infinite loathing that you had the impression—or at least Bannerman hoped you did—that he was, here and now, yielding up any last lingering hope that it would be possible to conduct a fair and impartial trial with this man. (And he was right, of course. If fouling one's own nest was unforgivable, then what Ambose had just done was unforgivable. There was not a lawyer in the courtroom who would not have wept with Bannerman if they had not known that Bannerman himself had just asked Booker about a dozen questions that had been every bit as illegal.)

"Your Honor," intoned the martyred Bannerman, "do you wish to condemn the shoddy tactics of Mr. Ambose?"

His Honor gave the matter his most earnest consideration. Maternal displeasure having failed so miserably, why not try an appeal to sweet reason? "If you have any questions to ask, Mr. Ambose, you know you're supposed to wait until you have the witness back on redirect. You know that now, don't you?"

Ambose scowled at him.

Back at his seat Bannerman looked down at his notes, which were nothing more than a laundry list of one-word reminders to himself, written out in his large ornate hand:

Elbow
Flashbulb
Timing
Rights

"The flashbulb popped just before the shot, is that right?"

"Yes. It was bang-bang, like that."

Bannerman looked off into space, visualizing the scene and encouraging the jury to visualize it with him. "Bang-bang. Let's see if we have this right." He slapped his hands together twice in rapid succession. "The flashbulb was the first bang and the discharge of the gun the second, is that it?" That being it, he thanked the witness with an expression of complete satisfaction and moved on.

Ambose leaned forward to peer across at Bannerman. "Now what the hell was that for?" he muttered to Pawley. "I hope the shithead doesn't think he can still go back to psychomotor epilepsy." Calling him that did not, for once, make Ambose feel any better. Bannerman had decoyed him so neatly on his cross-examination of Booker during the bond hearing that the possibility that he might be able to turn the Policeman at the Elbow Test around on them had never for one moment occurred to him. Could it be possible, he now had to ask himself, that Bannerman had something up his sleeve on brain damage as well? Was it possible, Jim Ambose was forced to ask himself as he watched Norman Bannerman step lightly between the defense table and the witness chair, that this guy was the kind of super-lawyer he was cracked up to be?

To cheer him not at all, Bannerman was finally moving into the area Ambose most feared; saving it, as he had known he would, for last. It wasn't enough that he had come in with his own chart of the streets between the courthouse and City Hall, he had also requested Stringfellow to have a blackboard available so that he would be able to choreograph the fateful journey of the murderer with the movements of his victim. Despite Nevins' strenuous objection that this was exactly the kind of thing that could turn the courtroom into a carnival, Harry Davies—who fancied that he had a nice little dramatic flair of his own—permitted him to use it. Given those kinds of props, Bannerman had himself a grand old time developing the theme that it had been only through the sheerest of accidents that they had arrived at City Hall before the Chief Justice left. Unless, of course, he suggested with a good-natured wink toward the jury, Booker had been in on the plot to get Sam there in the nick of time. "Don't worry, Booker," he said, smiling broadly. "We know that you got back to the sheriff's office when you did purely by accident yourself, don't we?"

And if Booker himself wasn't overcome by any particular feeling of relief at discovering that he was not being accused of taking part in any conspiracy, considerable relief could have been picked up in the general vicinity of the Bench and the court reporter's table at finding the stakeout being passed over that quickly. But then, Bannerman wasn't interested where Booker had come from; Bannerman was interested in demonstrating with a veritable plethora of questions that if Booker had come back only a few minutes later Sam would have missed David Boone Wilcke completely.

"And sheer accidents can't be planned?" (Objection.)

"If it was sheer accident it couldn't have been planned?" (Objection.)

"On your part there was no planning? You won't object if your friends let you answer that, will you?" (No, sir.)

"And so on Sam's part there could have been no planning?" (Objection.)

"As far as you know, there was no planning on Sam's part?" (No, sir.)

"Sam didn't say to you, 'Come on, I'm in a hurry. I've got to get to City Hall in time to kill the Chief Justice?' " (No, sir.)

"Isn't it a fact that he didn't ask to be taken to City Hall at all?" (Yes, sir.)

"It wasn't his idea at all?" (No, sir.)

"And that if you hadn't invited him, he couldn't have got there in time?" (Objection.)

"To your knowledge, did he have a car waiting out front, with the motor running?" (No, sir.)

"If you had decided to stop for a cup of coffee you probably would have missed Wilcke altogether?" (Objection.)

"Well, if you'd changed your mind en route and dropped Sam off downtown, he couldn't have got there in time? Could he?"

"If he hadn't been there, he wouldn't have been there. That's right, Mr. Bannerman."

"Well, don't get upset with me, Mr. Phillips. I'm just here to ask the questions. I wasn't the one who drove Sam there." (Objection and warning from the Court.)

Having apologized profusely to Booker and to the Court, Bannerman returned to his seat. It had been a good cross-examination. A hell of a cross-examination. He had yanked premeditation right out of the courtroom. At the prosecution table there were clouds of gloom, hanging particularly dark and heavy around Hilliard Nevins' chair. In Ambose's chair, there was no longer any question about going after the res gestae statement. The only question now was whether Booker was going to come through for him.

At the defense table Bannerman tapped his memo sheet, trying to decide whether to pass the witness back on that high note or take him through the drive back to the courthouse in order to reinforce the argument that Sam had been in a state of shock. In cross-examination, sequence was everything. Bannerman's plan here had been to open up the subject on familiar terrain by getting Booker to concede that Sam had been so docile that Booker hadn't felt it necessary to handcuff him or hold a gun on him, and then to hit him, fast and hard, with a question about whether he had informed him of his rights. All of it calculated to set Booker up for one question, the sixth or seventh question down the line: "And you didn't think to warn him of his rights because you could see that he was in such a state of mental paralysis that even though you—of all people—had every right to demand an explanation as a friend betrayed as well as an officer of the law, you could see that it would be a waste of time to even make the attempt to question him. Isn't that right, sir?"

He was sure he would be able to pick it up on recross, of course—and every instinct within him said that the most effective strategy now would be to let it go over to recross—but still . . . the time would never be so ripe. All the while he had been demonstrating that Sam couldn't have been planning to kill Wilcke, he had been pushing Booker further and further into a defensive stance, with this next line of questioning firmly in mind. That last snappish answer had told him how well he had succeeded. Goddamnit all, he had Booker set up so perfectly that he could hardly bear to let him get away.

All of this had flashed through Bannerman's mind in no more than five seconds. He rapped hard on the memo sheet one last time, the diamond sparkling back at him, his mind just about made up. You can't have everything in this sad world of ours and he had pretty much swept the boards clean as it was . . .

Halpern pulled his chair out and leaned far over behind Tabor's back so that he could whisper into Bannerman's ear. "Pass him back," he said. "Leave them with the memory of the blackboard."

Hilliard Nevins, who may well have been thinking that Bannerman was stalling in order to give the jury more time to contemplate that blackboard, asked the

314

Court in his most brusque and bumptious manner whether now that Mr. Bannerman was through with his drawing lessons they couldn't get the thing out of the courtroom and back to the little red schoolhouse or wherever it had come from.

And that was enough to make up Bannerman's mind for him again. "Was there any conversation in the car on the way back?" he snapped.

Booker shifted uneasily in the witness chair. "Well, there were a few things said. Not that I paid that much attention to it after the first thing, what with the driving and watching the prisoner. Not concerned, like I told you in the bond hearing, Mr. Bannerman, but just in case, you know. . . . My main concern, like I told you, was getting him back in a single piece, that was the main thing I was concerned with."

Bannerman caught something in the huskiness of the voice; in the slight catch, the extra explanation so unusual in an experienced witness; in the wandering focus of the hitherto unwandering eyes. *He had asked it wrong! He had let his mind relax for one second and he had asked it wrong!* How many times had he told law students—with his stupid, asinine grin; his preening, self-serving, capped-in-enamel grin—that a trial lawyer was a man on a trampoline holding a law book in one hand and a stopwatch in the other, while he was jumping through a hoop and rewriting an already carefully prepared play in which he was also the star and the director? How many times? Lose your concentration for one second, make one mistake in timing and you're flat on your ass with a broken neck.

They had planted something on Booker! His screen was sweeping the area around the witness stand, and his intestines were on fire. He had asked the same question at the hearing and they had played doggie on him, waiting for the trial, hoping for the mistake that would open it up for them. And just when—the words had been in his mind ready for transference to his lips: "Pass the witness." He had only had to say those three little words: Pass the witness. *Forgive me, Sam!* He had done it wrong! *Forgive me, father!*

To all appearances perfectly composed, Norman Bannerman slipped through the passageway between the tables, pulling the witness's eyes to him, and now that he had them—holding them, not letting go—he leaned back against the corner of the table, standing as much as sitting, and let Booker see that he knew him for what he was, a perjurer, a liar, a cheat and a murderer.

There was no forgiveness. For that kind of mistake there would be no forgiveness. *No, you don't forgive, do you? One little mistake, but not you! Never! To the deathbed, to the cemetery, to the will! Not you!*

"I want you to understand," Bannerman said, "that when I ask about the conversation, I am only interested in whether by tone of voice or facial expression he showed any more emotion than he had shown on the stairs." *Be careful, Booker,* his eyes said. *Be very careful.* "Confining your answer to that narrow area and without going into the conversation itself, would you respond, sir?"

Halpern, right with him, turned to that part of the testimony in the bond hearing and handed the folded transcript across the table. Without looking at it, Bannerman laid it aside.

Booker answered that as he had said at the hearing, there had been nothing of a nature to make him take extra precautions.

He admitted quite readily that he had not informed Sam of his constitutional rights. Not in the car. Back in the department when he was booking him, that was when he had advised him.

"When would you say he was under arrest? . . . Here, let me help you. Was

315

he under arrest when you took the gun away and bent his arm behind his back?"

Booker said, "He was under restraint."

Through the laughter Bannerman, not laughing, said, "That's good enough." The screen sweeping the witness box confirmed the earlier readings. Booker hadn't cracked a smile, either. He had stopped fidgeting. He took Bannerman's warning stare without flinching. His answers were the same answers he had given at the hearing.

It had turned completely around. Booker wasn't on the defensive anymore. Bannerman was. He scuttled the key question for the time being and turned the witness back.

From the moment he had let slip the fatal question Bannerman had never so much as glanced toward the prosecution table, and yet he could sense from the vibrations coming back from that sector of the battlefield that Ambose was licking his chops.

Licking his chops, Ambose said, "Deputy Phillips, Mr. Bannerman asked you on cross-examination just now whether there was any conversation in the car. Your answer was that you hadn't paid much mind after the first thing. I now ask you whether—"

Upon returning to the defense table, Bannerman had pretended to go into a quick huddle with Sam so that he would be able to leap to his feet in astonishment and outrage. "The state is intruding upon the defendant's constitutional rights," he shouted, appalled. "We object to that, and we object most vigorously!"

"Well, let him ask the question, Mr. Bannerman," Davies said. "My goodness . . ."

Ambose had pushed himself forward, far out in front of the two colleagues who flanked him, his head hunched so low into his neck that his jacket was riding high across the shoulders. Having come this far he was, by god, taking no chances. "I now ask you to tell the jury, to the best of your recollection, whether upon pushing the defendant into the car you told him you could kill him for what he had done and—well, will you just answer that part of it, Chief Deputy?"

Bannerman's lips had come together, tight and angry, while the question was being asked. "All right," he said, pulling himself up as stiff and erect as the pillars that kept the Supreme Court building from collapsing. "I now ask for a mistrial because of the grossly calculated misconduct of Mr. Ambose. He is leading the witness, Your Honor. The record will show that he has openly and blatantly instructed the witness as to the answer he wants from him."

Whatever it may have done for Booker, the question had most definitely activated Sam Tabor. Where his head had been cocked to the right, it was now cocked far over to the left, away from the witness chair, his eyes narrowed as if he were trying to get a better perspective on either the witness or the scene he was describing. "What the hell is this all about?" Halpern whispered. Sam hadn't told him about any conversation. Sam shook his head. He bit down hard on his lower lip and continued to stare out at the witness.

With the generosity of spirit for which he was so well known, Ambose had announced that if it would make Mr. Bannerman any happier he would withdraw the question. "Mr. Phillips," he said, rephrasing it, "did you make any comment to Mr. Tabor immediately upon entering the car?"

He had. "I said, 'Sam, I could kill you for this.' I said, 'Why in the hell did you do it?' "

"And what was Sam's response to that?" His eyes burned into Booker's. Would he or wouldn't he?

"That's it!" With a disposing back sweep of his hand, Bannerman spun toward the table and reached for his briefcase. And for one crazy moment it did seem as though he were going to scoop up his papers and stalk out of the courtroom. "Your Honor," he said, turning back, "I do not have to tell this Court that we are stepping off into the abyss." The witness was being asked to repeat a conversation he had held with his prisoner after he was under arrest, admittedly without having been advised of his constitutional rights. "I submit to this Honorable Court," he said, quivering with indignation, "that this is specifically forbidden by the Constitution of the United States."

DeWitt Pawley, the Great Conciliator, came to his feet, placing himself between Ambose and Bannerman. The state wasn't holding for one minute, he explained quietly, that it had any right to interrogate a prisoner without his permission, or to introduce such a conversation into evidence. "That is not the issue here. The only issue here is that Mr. Bannerman opened it up himself by asking whether there had been any conversation in the car."

Halpern had hardly missed the critical legal issue that was building up—how could he?—and yet he had an instinctive perception that Bannerman was fighting for something that went far beyond any mere legal point. Along with that perception had come an overwhelming urge to pitch in and lend a hand. As always, Ambose was taking a breather and allowing Pawley to make the legal argument. It was three against one, and even though he couldn't think of a thing he could do to help, Halpern came to his feet just to show Bannerman and the world that he was standing at his side.

He was, as it happened, dead wrong. What Ambose was thinking was that if Pawley would only stay the hell out of this, he might pull this thing off. Into Pawley's ear he growled, "Down, boy."

Pawley sat down. He sat down slowly, very slowly, his face reddening and his cheeks sucked in as if he were chewing on the insides.

Ambose said, "Just so there'll be no misunderstanding about this, we are not asking for the full conversation in the car, even though now that Mr. Bannerman has opened it up, we are fully entitled to it." All he was asking for, as a rereading of his question would clearly show, was a spontaneous remark made by Mr. Tabor immediately after being pushed into the car, in the course of a heated exchange that had occurred in the heat of the event and was therefore covered by res gestae. "As supplementary grounds—supplementary and complementary and cumulative—if further grounds are needed, which they are not, we say that it has been opened up by Mr. Bannerman."

"You see," Bannerman shouted. "They can't even get together on it!" Could anything be clearer, he wanted to know, than that his friends were engaged in a bootstrap operation to convince the Court that two transparently flimsy grounds could be magically entwined to form a single strand strong enough to defy the Constitution?

Poor Harry Davies. He had been confident that once the testimony got under way the importance of this trial would push both sides to reasonable and responsible behavior. Out of his natural optimism Harry had even managed to convince himself that if the judge showed himself to be a man of peace and reason a sort of contagion of Christian charity would radiate out across the Bar. Where were the fond, hallucinatory dreams of yesterday? All gone, alas. All shattered.

And on top of everything else, he had to have this!

Pawley hadn't rubbed his mouth, not even once, but Pawley wasn't looking very happy about it either. Now that he thought about it, what had made him think he could trust Nevins and that pack of jackals not to lead him astray the moment it served their purpose? There wasn't anything Hilliard Nevins wouldn't do to chalk up a win on a biggie like this one, and the only way he could win would be to get himself a nice fat death verdict, and to hell with the appeal!

Stifling a nervous yawn, he looked at Bannerman, who had become as solemn as a hell-and-brimstone preacher. (Davies liked that frock coat, though. As Bannerman began to address the Court again, the Court made a note to ask him where he had them made up and whether he could get him a price on one. The way they were dressing these days frock coats might come back and everybody would say that Harry Davies was a style-setter.)

"We have come this quickly to what may well be the turning point of this lawsuit," Bannerman said, his voice falling like a stone to demonstrate the depths of his concern. "I have not the slightest idea what this witness is going to say Sam Tabor said. I do know that if he is allowed to testify to it, we shall have flawed this lawsuit beyond repair."

The argument was on. The only specific question he had asked about the conversation, Bannerman kept stressing, was whether his client had been advised of his rights. "Are we saying that an American lawyer can ask an arresting officer whether his client was advised of his constitutional rights only at the risk of blowing those rights?" His voice rose with the wonder of it. "Because if we are, we have crossed the line of sanity and made a mockery of the Bill of Rights."

Nevins said, "We're not saying that, Judge. We'll stipulate to it right now that we're not going to make any mockery of any Bill of Rights."

But it was to Ambose that there fell the rare privilege of being able to cite Norman Bannerman as his authority. The attorney for the defense, he reminded the Court, had asked far more than the one simple question about his client's rights. Calling the Court's attention to page 21, line 8 of the transcript of the bond hearing, and savoring every word of it, he read, "It would appear that the state is now fully cognizant of the imprudence, the sheer recklessness of Mr. Nevins' question. Unfortunately, however, the state did ask the question, and when it got its answer it opened the door."

But it was on res gestae, Ambose wanted to emphasize, that he was making his main argument. "The classic definition, as this Court well knows, is that if you hit me on the nose and I say *Ouch!* that's res gestae." It was supposed to arise spontaneously out of the heat of the act. To have an exclamation point after it. The state, said James J. Ambose, was about to present a classic example of that classic definition.

When the argument came to an end the whole courtroom waited, silent and expectant, while the learned judge considered upon his ruling. Groaning inwardly, Judge Harrison T. Davies put on his most impressive and scholarly expression ("Every inch a lover and every hair a judge," Marie had once said about him) and asked Marie to read back the disputed questions and answers. Goddamn, but he'd have liked to call a quick recess, the learned jurist was thinking. Normally, he'd have already broken but with so much of the press having been broken in by Chobodian he had made a firm resolve to hold the recesses down to a minimum. This job was going to be as hard on the backside as on the mind, but nobody ever thought of that, did they? Oh no. They thought it was all milk and honey up here.

Bannerman had listened to the rereading of the record intently. The moment Marie finished, he turned to Tabor and whispered, "What the bejeebers is this all about, pardner? I told you I didn't want any surprises." Sam had been listening to the playback with a strained, grating expression, twisting his neck occasionally as if his shirt collar was too tight. He did seem to remember Booker saying something like that, he told Bannerman. But what he'd said back, he couldn't remember that. Over his head Bannerman and Halpern exchanged a dismal, unhappy glance. If Tabor could remember anything at all, he hadn't been as shell-shocked as they'd have liked. "I want you to think, pardner," Bannerman whispered urgently. "What did you say back?" Sam shook his head, pulling away from him much in the same way he had pulled away from Halpern. "I don't know that I said anything. Not that I can remember."

Bannerman looked across at Halpern again with a grim look of satisfaction. "Just what I thought. The bastards have planted something on your friend, Booker."

As soon as Davies called for a reading Nevins had made a peremptory motion calling for a quick huddle. "You just better know what you're doing," he growled at Ambose. "That's all."

Ambose was of a mind to tell him that if he thought he could do any better to just go ahead and try. All he said was, "I know what I'm doing. It's res gestae, and if it wasn't, the hotshot went and opened it up good."

Nevins wanted to know what Pawley thought. For while Pawley's brooding had been brought on by Ambose's insult, the silence that was so puzzling to Judge Davies hadn't. This had been the first either Pawley or Nevins had heard about any exchange between Sam and Booker, and both of them had a pretty good idea why. Jim was running the show, Pawley shrugged. It was too late, he pointed out, to back off it now, anyway. But with Nevins making it clear that he wanted an answer Pawley told him rather grudgingly that it was res gestae all right. "It was last week, anyway. The same for opening it up. If you're asking whether it's going to be any good by the time the Supreme Court gets it, I don't know that any better than you do."

Nevins gave Ambose another sour glare to remember him by. "It just better be worth it, that's all I got to say." It wasn't all he had to say, though. With Marie's voice coming to a sudden stop, his face wrinkled up and he revealed what was really bothering him. "I thought Booker was supposed to be a witness for the state, not the defense," he growled. "This has been a fiasco so far, I hope you know that." Having got that off his chest, his eyes went to the Bench. "What's the matter with Harry? Somebody oughta tell him he keeps trying to think like that he's gonna rupture himself."

Well, it was the state's baby, the learned judge was thinking, and he had two chances of being right —which was better odds than he usually got —and he was getting pretty damn sick of this argument, anyway. "Put the question to him again, Mr. Ambose," Judge Davies said. "The witness may answer."

Not yet, he wouldn't. Not yet, was Harry Davies through with it. Before the question could be asked Bannerman had sprung to his feet to beg the Court to reconsider its decision. Stalling for time while he ordered his thoughts, he moved behind Sam's chair and placed both hands on Sam's shoulders. He closed his eyes for just a moment, sighed heavily and patted Sam lightly and affectionately on the shoulder. Without raising his head he said, "Your Honor, this man's constitutional rights belong to him and to him alone. I, as his attorney, cannot waive them for him except on his permission after due consultation and only after I have convinced him that benefits will thereby accrue to him which will override the loss." Lifting his eyes, he said on a rising note of warning, "With all respect to this Honorable Court, this Court is not empowered to take them away from him either."

The plea itself was enough to tell Halpern that Bannerman had indeed opened the door. The pained, wounded eyes told him at what cost the plea had been made. Bannerman gave Sam one final little tap along the side of his chin and strolled across to the Bar rail, beyond his own chair, his fingers massaging his forehead. With his back pressed to the balustrade, he reminded the Court that the Supreme Court had already ruled in *Noia* that a prisoner could not waive his right to seasonable appeal, however consciously, except that he had an intelligent understanding of all the options and all the consequences. "The effect of *Noia* and subsequent decisions," he said, wondering whether he might not have something here, "is that the law will not permit a prisoner to surrender a right, even where the reasons were good and sufficient to his own mind, if the Court does not agree that they were good and sufficient in fact."

Could there be any doubt then, he asked, gaining confidence, in which direction the High Court was moving. "Your Honor," he said, "the High Court is marching to a drumfire of libertarian decisions and that is a march which once embarked upon can never be halted. The old injustices are being drummed, one by one, out of our jails and courtrooms and once we have had done with them not all the king's horses nor all the king's men will ever be able to put them together again." His voice had already taken on a martial strain and cadence. Unconsciously, he now edged away from the Bar rail to give himself room to rock to the rhythm of his advancing army. "I beg this Court not to close its ears to the rattling of judicial sabers. I beg this Court not to render these proceedings null and void here at the outset by allowing the attorneys for the state to lead it into such an untidy area of the law."

Suddenly he stopped. Watchful and alert. A hand lifted tenuously to ward off any potential distraction or interruption. What was he listening for? The call of the distant bugle charge? The rumble of approaching hoofbeats? Quietly and ominously he extended his arm full out behind him until it was pointing to the high arched windows in the rear of the courtroom. "Listen," he breathed. "Cannot you hear that outside this courtroom the wind is blowing?" His voice floated after it, eerie and prophetic. "Can you not feel the tremors that are shaking the very bedrock of the law?"

He was making a powerful if somewhat overblown argument, Halpern had no doubt about that. But wasn't there more to it than that? Watching him as well as listening, Halpern had seen Norman Bannerman come back to life. Had seen the spark kindled in the dull blue eyes, seen the ashen complexion take back its pink and satin glow. What more, then? At the deep of the sparkling eyes and the glowing complexion was the elation of a man fully engaged and deeply excited; a man buoyed up by the sound of his own argument. The wound had left him. He had talked it away.

Aaaah, there you had it. The sound as much as the argument. Was there any room for doubting, as Halpern had previously only suspected, that Bannerman's voice had such a deep and therapeutic effect on him that it had become an independent force that swept him along in its own deep-running, silent-running currents?

The gentle rocking ceased. Norman Bannerman was about to bring his argument to a forceful conclusion. "In these past few days I have become increasingly impressed by Your Honor's common sense and sound practical discretion. If I were trying this lawsuit with one eye on the appeal—and I say this frankly and without apologies—I would welcome an adverse ruling. None of us was left on the doorstep of this courtroom with the morning milk. We all know how the ball game is played. But I want this Court to produce an impregnable record. I am every bit as eager as the Court itself that this trial, which is of such a paramount concern to the entire legal fraternity, serve as a model for future generations of law students to study and marvel upon, so that they may say, in a pride of their calling, that here was the time and here was the place where American justice, put to its sternest test, never faltered nor was found wanting."

Having soared to such a high evangelical fervor, he took the long slide down the chute to tragedy. What could be more calamitous than to have this lawsuit overturned and remanded. The money wasted. The long, hard work of the attorneys come to nothing; the time and energy of the Court, whose good will was unquestioned, wasted. The time and effort of all these good jurors squandered. He had spread his arms wide to encompass the Court, the jury, and perhaps the entire civilized world, and however those who watched and listened might remember it, it was at the time enormously moving and effective.

A stronger note of warning slipped into the voice. A hint of menace. "But I say to this Court, which has my deepest respect and affection, that the time is past where state courts may feel free to trample upon the Constitution. I say to this Court that, Mr. Ambose's prejudices aside, some deference must be paid to the Bill of Rights. We are met here, Your Honor, under a stern constitutional mandate, and I must warn this Court that either here or at some higher level that mandate will accord us due process. I pray you, sir, that we may find it here, so that we shall not find it necessary to seek its remedy elsewhere. Let it be here, I say, Your Honor. Here in this great state, here in this lovely city, here under the guidance of this wise and benevolent Court."

The melodious voice, tailing off at the end, blended perfectly into the hushed and totally engrossed courtroom. Before the silence could be extended into a tribute to either Bannerman's argument or eloquence, Ambose's graceless monotone cut through the courtroom: "Do you want to answer the question now, Deputy Phillips, or do you want it read back?"

Bannerman's head shot up. "Hey, wait a minute there," he yelled. "We have a motion pending!"

"Oh, is that what that was? I thought you were delivering high unction."

Separated by no more than ten feet, naked hate met naked hate.

"I had thought," said Bannerman, "not even Mr. Ambose could escape some spray from the fountain of liberty." He glared at him with indescribable loathing. "I can see, however, that he has managed to face the ordeal squarely and emerge bone dry. Very well, Mr. Ambose," he said, setting the record straight, "it's not my job to sanitize the district attorney's office."

The words came out of Ambose, slowly and dangerously. "I sure do appreciate that, Mr. Bannerman. I just don't feel the need for a shower right now. But you just go right ahead and take all the showers you want. You must be plumb wore out from all that marching."

Halpern could have cried. How many times had he warned him? Before the effect of the long argument, so brilliantly and adroitly developed, was dissipated completely, Halpern jumped up and asked the Court for a ruling, and when Davies nodded to Booker and told him to answer, Hal demanded that the Court state the grounds on which the ruling had been made. Smiling benignly, grateful to Halpern for having brought the argument to an end, Judge Davies declared that he would be content to stick with the grounds that had been so thoroughly argued.

He did not remain benign or grateful for long. Little Halpern stood there, taking hitches on his pants, cross and abrupt, and insisted that the Court state for the record whether it was holding that the disputed statement was covered by res gestae or had been opened up by the defense, and then whether each provided complete grounds in itself or that there was an interlocking and/or intertwining which, taken in combination, formed one valid ground. After Davies had ruled that yes, each of the grounds was fully capable of covering the ruling by itself, he even made him say that no, neither of them depended on the other for any part of the ruling.

By that time Davies was looking at him sort of sidewise with a quizzical, not pleased expression that conveyed his downright disbelief that he was really being pressed this hard by this rank neophyte. By Harry Davies' lights he had every right to feel he had been betrayed. After the jury had been sworn Davies had summoned Bannerman and Halpern to his chambers with every intention of underwriting Chobodian's order that Bannerman add an experienced Lowell trial lawyer to the defense team. But with Bannerman expressing unlimited confidence in his youthful assistant and little Halpern looking so bright and bushy-tailed, Harry just hadn't had the heart to hurt his feelings. And so he had dismissed the whole thing with a broad smile and an indulgent wave of the hand and said, "Aaaaaaaahhh . . . stick with it, Harold. One day the law may become an honorable profession. That's what they told me when I was starting out, anyway."

And this was the thanks he got? Now he had *five* of them beating him bloody.

"Will you please note," said Halpern, "that we are taking a full bill of exceptions on the ruling in each, every and all of its parts. We now ask that the jury be excluded from the courtroom while the question is being answered so that if the Court should, upon more sober reflection, decide that the answer is so prejudicial as to be violative of the defendant's rights, the jury will not have heard it." Bannerman, who had been sitting by, silent and somewhat deflated, rewarded him with a nod and a smile and an "Atta boy, keep rolling," to let him know that it was an excellent motion. Hal already knew it. He saw the nod and the smile. He heard the words. But he saw and heard them as through a tunnel, dimly visible but outside his field of operations. Inside his field his mind was clicking along, sweet and clear; his voice was crisp, his command complete. To seal Harry up tight, he said, entirely for the record, "Once the jury has heard a statement as prejudicial as Mr. Ambose seems to believe this alleged statement of the defendant to be, it will not suffice to instruct the jury to wipe it out of its mind. Once you have rung the bell," he said, calling upon the lawyer's time-honored cry of outrage in these matters, "you cannot unring it." And then, feeling that he should, after all, throw Bannerman a bone, he said in ringing, not unmellifluous tones, "Once the banner has been run up the flagpole and allowed to fly over the citadel, you cannot hoist it down."

That didn't make a hell of a lot of sense once he began to think about it, but it was good enough for Ambose to hiss, quite audibly, "Hey, Halpern. You're beginning to sound like a poor man's Bannerman. He gonna give you one of his dirty old diamonds when he's through with them, too?"

Davies, hearing it clearly, was pleased to let it go. If Little Halpern wanted to play in the big leagues, let him find out how the big leaguers played.

Halpern stared straight ahead, not the least disconcerted. *Screw you, Ambose,* he thought. *You don't get Harold Halpern to bite.*

Malice was no part of Harry Davies' nature, though, and as soon as he had ruled on the last of the motions, his anger dissipated into the air. "Well, Booker," he said. "It looks like you're going to get to answer the question. I hope you remember it, because the Court sure don't."

Booker remembered it. "I said, 'I could kill you for that, Sam. Why in hell did you do it?' And he said, 'You can go to hell.' "

Malice had come back into the courtroom, with a curse on its lips. Norman Bannerman came to his feet shouting for a mistrial.

Sam Tabor started forward, his mouth falling open. He stared at Booker, mystified and hurt. "I never," he murmured. "That's a lie, Booker."

Halpern, who had just barely been able to make out the words under Bannerman's rapid-fire of citations, grabbed Sam by the elbow, pointed toward the jury box and shouted, "What did you say, Sam?"

But instead of repeating it loud enough for the jury to hear, Sam turned back to Hal. There was more than bewilderment on that pale, tense face, more than hurt. Behind the straining cheekbones, you could all but hear the hum of highly strung, tightly woven nerves. "I never said that," he said, in a wondering way that not only removed any question that might have been in Halpern's mind about who was lying but also told him that the lie didn't frighten Sam half so much as that it had come from a man who had no reason to lie.

In the afternoon the state proceeded with methodical, inventory-like thoroughness to lay out its prima facie case that Sam Tabor had, as charged in the indictment, shot and killed David Boone Wilcke. With the brick-and-mortar work being done, the trial settled down to the routine courtroom hum and rattle; the bleat and bay of question and answer, the orderly handling and mishandling of facts and the inexorable march of witnesses.

Ambose put Bunny on the stand first to put her out of her misery. (And if that meant the FBI and Secret Service agents, who had been accompanied to court by a huddle of upper-echelon officials from the Justice and Treasury departments, had to be kept waiting, wasn't that a shame?)

Bunny stumbled slightly as she climbed up to the witness chair, and to compound her embarrassment Judge Davies told her with his most comforting smile that there was not the slightest need for her to be nervous. "Why, we're all friends of yours here," that good gray jurist said. "You just sit back and be comfortable, and it won't hurt a bit." (At which point a dozen lawyers and perhaps eight court employees of varying sexes whispered to their neighbors that it was the first time Harry Davies had ever told a woman court employe to sit back and be comfortable instead of to lie back and be comfortable.)

Under Ambose's deft, impersonal questioning she told about the luncheon with Sam, and testified that he had not seemed any different from the Sam Tabor she had known for eight years.

When Bannerman got her he took her through a quick rerun of the luncheon so that he could say "Sam's friend, Mr. Ambose," a few times, after which he had her describe her work with the Young Adults Service so that he could stamp his personal seal of approval upon Lowell's most enlightened program for juvenile rehabilitation. He was well into the process of assuring her (and presumably the jury) that he would "spread the word around the darker, less enlightened regions of the country" when Nevins broke it to say, "Judge, I'm not sure I got the question."

"Well, stay loose," crowed Bannerman. "It's coming right atcha."

The digression, as Ambose knew and Nevins didn't, had been no digression. Coming at them, delicately disguised, was the question about Sam dropping in from time to time to smell around the naughty little girls. Bunny reported that if there were kids around and she happened to be busy, Sam would listen to what they had to say and be polite. Despite her best intentions she couldn't keep herself from smiling sympathetically at Sam. "He's a very polite man, Sam is."

Sam moved his lips politely. He was watching Bannerman with the same caught-bird expression that had come to his face so often during the hearing.

"Did he show any particular attention to the girls? To listening to their troubles?"

No more than the boys, Bunny said, too quickly. Not that he came in that often either.

"But he did try to be particularly helpful. . . "

"Well, if they talked he'd listen."

"Of course he would. That's what he dropped in for, wasn't it?"

With each question Bannerman's voice, his stance, his special ambience became a little more insinuating, creating the distinct impression (in Bunny's mind, at least) that he was wondering why *she* was making such an issue out of anything so harmless—*if* it was so harmless. It was perfectly amazing. She had said nothing, and still she had the awful feeling that she was saying everything he wanted her to say.

"If you were busy," Bannerman said, "he'd have seen that as soon as he came to the door, isn't that right?"

For the second time in the cross-examination Ambose placed his hand lightly on Pawley's elbow; he held it there while Bunny was answering that she supposed so. For the life of him he couldn't see quite what Bannerman had to gain in making Sam out a dirty old man. He'd have bet his life, though, that it was going to tie neatly into his psychiatric case.

"But he'd hang around anyway, talking to the girls, talking to the boys . . . talking to the girls and boys both?"

By the time Bannerman was through with her, Bunny (feeling sweaty, rapidly shrinking) was happy to see that Ambose didn't look completely disgusted with her. (But that was his job. He couldn't let the jury see that he knew she had destroyed his whole case. Wait until he got her alone, she thought with a cold shiver. Nothing he said would be too cruel for what she had just done to him; anything he did to her would be richly deserved.)

"Mr. Bannerman said something about Sam 'hanging around,' " Ambose said. "Did Sam 'hang around' your office, Miss Beyner, or did he just drop in for a neighborly visit when things were kind of slow there across the hall?"

With a dismally grateful nod to Ambose (what a good, kind man he was; he was still talking to her) and a dirty look at Bannerman (what a snake in the grass), she answered that Sam just dropped in now and then to pass the day and what-have-you.

"And did Sam ever do or say anything, within your sight or hearing or to your personal knowledge, that was the least suggestive?"

"No." (Why, it wasn't so bad, after all!)

"Or flirty?"

"No." (She wouldn't even know how to go about entering a convent.)

"Or was not in keeping with the way a man of his years would be expected to behave toward a girl in her teens?"

"Never!" *(Jim Ambose, you snake, why don't you ask me for a date?)*

Safe in the cool breeze blowing around her, restored to full size, Bunny stepped from the witness chair, caught her heel on the middle step and saved herself from the ultimate mortification only by breaking the fall with her hands. Recovering, she saw helpful males bearing down on her from all sides. Squeezing her eyes tight, she tightened her fists in a torment of self-disgust, almost—but not quite —stamping her foot, and having warned everybody away with a murderous glare, flounced out of the courtroom.

Through it all Harold Halpern's eyes had never left Sam Tabor. After each of Ambose's questions Sam had nodded in approval and snapped his alert and intense bird's eyes back to the witness stand. When Bunny stumbled, Bannerman and Pawley, being nearest to the passage between the table, had automatically rushed forward to help her, leaving nothing but open space between Ambose and Tabor. Catching Ambose's eyes, Tabor had thrown out a rather spinachy but quite explicit smile of thanks. And while Ambose's answering shrug could hardly have been more enigmatic, Halpern made a mental note that he had better sit Sam down and have a long, long talk with him. For it had come to Harold Halpern on the afternoon of the first day of the trial of Sam Tabor that when a defense attorney set out an insanity plea he brought about a complete reversal of roles. Norman Bannerman had become the prosecutor, accusing his client of insanity, and Jim Ambose had become the defense attorney, upholding to the death (Sam Tabor's death) his sanity.

Looking at Tabor, looking at Ambose, Halpern felt something dark and vizored brush past.

Neither Cecil Lewis of the FBI nor Sylvester Torgeson of the Secret Service, the agents in charge of their respective details, could add a thing to the account of the shooting, which did not prevent Sam Tabor, obviously feeling the power of the FBI, from turning grim and apprehensive the moment Lewis identified himself. Bannerman pleaded with each of them to turn their reports over to the defense so that "this defendant may enjoy his day in court." Each of them fell back upon departmental policy. With Agent Lewis about to leave the stand, Bannerman achieved one of the minor dramatic triumphs of the day by turning, full-face-and-throttle, to the jury and wailing, "Shall we, then, *spoon* out justice?"

Agent Lewis, disclaiming all responsibility, answered that *he* didn't make policy.

Josh Flowers came to the stand, and with him came a technician from WLOW– TV plus a projector, a screen and two cannisters of film. Hilliard Nevins, taking over the direct examination, told Flowers (whose full name turned out to be Armand Flowers) how much he and the whole family had always enjoyed him and sat back to permit him to relate the role he had played on the portico, a story he hadn't told more than a hundred times before.

When the first cannister turned out—to nobody's surprise—to contain the master film, complete with the twelve frames that had never been seen over television, Bannerman asked that the jury be retired. Once they were gone, he produced an affidavit from the station manager stating that upon his initial viewing of the film he had decided that the moment of impact was too graphic and horrendous for public consumption. "To show these graphic and horrendous frames to the jury," Bannerman argued, "would so inflame their minds as to make a fair trial impossible. I ask that they be excluded."

The audience groaned. Prematurely, they would discover. Rhetoric was fine, and bombast even better, but in planning his strategy Norman Bannerman was fully prepared to deal with the realities, and the reality of this situation was that every juror was going to feel that his service to the state entitled him to see the complete film. Bannerman, who had seen the full film at the station several times, had already informed the judge and the district attorney that he would not object to a new version in which only the middle five frames (one-quarter-of-a-second) had been removed. Knowing they could get that version at the very worst, the attorneys for the state were, of course, going for the whole thing. Ambose argued —and argued strenuously—that juries were very frequently shown material that for reasons of taste or privacy would never be exposed to public view. "Bullets make holes in people," he declaimed. "That's how it kills them! This jury is entitled by all the laws of man and God to see the unexpurgated version." And so by all the laws of God and censorship, he said (for whatever pressure it might exert on Harry Davies), was the general public.

The Court ruled, to renewed groaning from out front, that they'd all have to make do with the expurgated version. "Now hold on a minute," Davies told the audience with a smile that promised untold delights. "Just hold on a minute, willya?"

By the time the jury filed back in the screen had been set up at the side of the Bar enclosure, in front of Halpern and facing the jury box. Josh Flowers was standing alongside, pointer in hand, and Norman Bannerman, for reasons best known to himself, was reclining in the vacated witness chair.

In answer to Nevins' question Flowers (having been reminded that he was still sworn) explained that the film contained seven frames that had never before been shown in public.

Whereupon:

The spectators applauded.

Davies accepted his vindication amiably.

Bannerman stated in loud, magnanimous tones that he had no objection to having the jury see "this version," since he himself had suggested the five-frame formula "as a way out of our dilemma."

Ambose turned to Jake Foxx and said with enormous satisfaction, "And there goes his whole appeal on not wanting jurors who had seen it on television."

Nevins said, "We're not showing this through the largesse of the defense attorney," which, being a direct steal from a gambit used by Bannerman to great effect during the bond hearing, wiped the smile completely off Bannerman's face. "We're showing it," Nevins said, sounding more like himself, "as a state exhibit, which we have subpoenaed from the folks who own it."

The lights were doused, the blinds were drawn and the jurors settled back, like Saturday night at the movies, to view the film that, had they viewed it earlier—in a less graphic, less horrendous version—would have disqualified them from being in those seats if Bannerman's interpretation of the law had prevailed.

Sam Tabor pressed forward, half-sprawled across the table, with his right fist fitted over his mouth. The whole film was being run through once at normal speed, without interruption, and when Halpern, twisting his head around for a better angle, partially blocked Sam's view, Sam placed his free hand against Hal's chest and pushed him out of the way. It was only then that Halpern realized that Sam was undoubtedly the only person in the courtroom who had never seen the film before.

And then they played it back again, frame by frame, with Josh Flowers identifying the participants. Clougherty coming out of the shadows behind Flowers. Wilcke looking big and bluff and bursting with life. Karney being pulled into the frame to dispossess a gaggle of security officers. Everybody moving with the jerky, nightmarish, but somehow purposeful strides of the frame-by-frame projection that somehow made everything that was happening appear to be utterly predestined, a feeling that came through even more strongly when the film was backed up and everybody was forced to return to their marks and step through their paces again. When Wilcke's hands came spreading out wide, he had all the appearance of an auditioning actor. And then his hands were in his ears and coming right back out (just as if the projector had been reversed again).

"Hold it," Flowers said, and the image froze. Fixed in time and history forever.

"Now," Flowers said quietly, and the twelve men and women in the jury box bent forward like blown wheat. Twelve frames missing or five, there was still a definite break in the action as the upper half of Wilcke's body was jerked back through space, his left eye open wide, his right eye obliterated by what seemed to be a rapidly spreading blur, his lips forming a perfect circle as if he were saying, "Ohhhh."

Half the courtroom said it for him.

Caught up in the general lean and sway, Bannerman took hold of the microphone, turning it just enough so that it caught the one light that had been left on in the back of the room and reflected it back in a diamond glint. Tabor's energies were so completely concentrated on the screen that he did not move, did not even seem to blink his eyes. His mouth was still covered by his fist, and Halpern could only see one of his eyes . . . and so how could Hal say for certain—it wasn't fair to say for certain—that what he saw there . . . was what he thought he saw there . . . or only a random point of light that had been reflected off some metal object nearby—such as . . . well, to take only one possibility, such as a cigarette lighter one of the deputies may have suddenly decided to take out of his pocket.

The film backed up, bringing Wilcke back to life, reversed and ran on through, taking it away; the jerk, the blur, the "Ohhhh," and then, almost in defiance of the laws of gravity, his head and body rocked forward and crumbled, more or less sideways, to the ground. And then there was the dizzying shot of the sky as the camera swung crazily up and around, and came plummeting back down to pick up the back slice of the TV truck and the stairs; searching out, finding and finally homing in on the mob scene, the arresting officer and his prisoner. At that point Sam Tabor lost interest.

When the lights went back on Flowers resumed the stand for cross-examination, exchanging places with the cross-examiner. Bannerman's main concern, it became evident, was to establish the fact that Mayor Karney had told him he had seen the murderer in the act of shooting. And, of equal importance, that nobody else had.

Once that had been accomplished to his satisfaction, Bannerman congratulated Flowers fulsomely on his high degree of professionalism and informed him how much he—as a man not wholly unversed in the art of interviewing—was enjoying his newscasts during his stay in Lowell.

"Especially the ones that feature Norman Bannerman," Judge Davies said, giving everybody a good chuckle.

Put to his mettle as a gentleman and a host, Flowers responded, honestly enough, that when he had people like Norman Bannerman around the job was easy. Bannerman had topped Nevins easily, and Flowers had been a model of grace and modesty, but after it had all been said and done Harry Davies carried the day by rubbing his hands together in gleeful anticipation and crowing, "Well, catch me tonight, folks."

Robert Sands, the ambulance driver, was a good-looking, wavy-haired young man who came into court nicely decked out in a blood-red suit, a pink shirt and wrap-around sunglasses. He had barely settled into the witness chair before Judge Davies told him that unless he had some eye disease or allergy that made him sensitive to light the Court would appreciate having him take the sunglasses off. To Ambose, the fancy clothes were just another proof of his rare ability to judge people at a glance. He had disliked Sands when he first interviewed him and he disliked him even more for moseying into the courthouse an hour and a half late —the fact that Sands had now been waiting around for almost six hours being completely beside the point.

Sands identified the listing on the ambulance call sheet that showed he had received the call at 5:10 (while en route to a private home) and had called back his arrival at City Hall at 5:12. He and his partner had been rushed up the stairs by a platoon of officers, uniformed and plain-clothed, and once the body had been lifted onto the stretcher, Sergeant LaRue had taken Sands' end of the stretcher away from him and ordered him to get back behind the wheel and see how fast he could make it back to the hospital. The call sheet showed he had started back at 5:15 and arrived at 5:20.

On cross-examination Bannerman asked him if he had known Sergeant LaRue before. "Nope. We talked some outside number two while we were waiting but . . ." He toyed with the gold identification bracelet on his left wrist. "I wouldn't say that was enough time to . . ." He shrugged, either unable to complete the thought or unwilling to say what he was thinking. "He was DOA." He gave his wrist a little whirl. "He was a dead one when we got there. At City Hall. The hardest part of it was to pick him up without wading in the blood."

Judge Davies instructed the witness, quite sharply, to confine himself to answering the question. Jim Ambose was beginning to think he probably wasn't such a bad guy when you got to know him.

After asking a couple of more routine questions Bannerman suddenly jumped to his feet. "One more question, Bob. Who's your tailor?"

"Right off the rack," Sands told him. "Just like yours."

Ambose liked him just fine.

"What was the cause of death, Doctor?"

"Death was caused by a massive intracerebral hemorrhage, which is to say massive internal bleeding, which, of course—"

"And what you are saying, Doctor, is that the bleeding was caused by the passage of the bullet through his brain and skull?"

It was. The bullet had entered through the frontal lobe of the cerebrum, passing through the upper portion of the parietal lobe and exiting through the calvarium.

"The calvarium. In common usage would that be called the skull?"

"Yes, Mr. Ambose. You and I would call it the skull."

Dr. Price looked out into the courtroom, a dignified man with black, smoothed-down hair nicely lined with gray, and could not for the life of him imagine what all the laughter was about.

Jim Ambose would have been surprised, and somewhat amused, to be told that he made Dr. Price nervous, and he would have been even more surprised to be told that within his own small circle of friends Roy Price was known as a taciturn man with a rather sly and pleasing wit. Dr. Price would have been astonished, and somewhat disconcerted, if he had known that Ambose had his own considerable anxieties about him. Unless the doctor was watched very closely, Ambose had discovered, he could very easily turn into a human textbook, expelling thick, sleep-producing fogbanks of medical terminology around the courtroom.

This late in the day, with everybody half-asleep anyway, Ambose had been keeping his questions short and sweet in the hope of encouraging the kind of short and sweet answers that would send the jury off to their dinner with the picture of a bullet-torn brain impressed cleanly and neatly into their minds.

So far, so good. He had managed to hold Dr. Price in check while he was qualifying him as the medical examiner of Brederton County for nine years. In defining his specialty further Dr. Price had been brief and to the point in testifying that as a "forensic pathologist" he had limited his field of interest solely to the cause of death. The time of death had been set at 5:08, Sergeant LaRue having noted the time while he was feeling for a pulse.

The autopsy, he had testified, had been performed within the hour in the autopsy room, more commonly known as the morgue, and the protocol of the autopsy, and eighteen-page transcript of Dr. Price's running commentary, had been handed over to Bannerman prior to being placed in the record.

Bannerman was reading through the protocol so eagerly that you would not have thought it possible that he was following the examination (let alone that he'd had his own copy in his briefcase for the past two months). As casually as possible Ambose picked up some colored slides and headed for the witness stand. He hadn't taken more than three steps before Bannerman's head shot up. "Wait a minute," he yelled. "What have you got there? What's he doing there, Your Honor?"

(BENCH CONFERENCE: Mr. Bannerman objected to the introduction of nine colored slides, brought to the courtroom by Dr. Price and purporting to show the entrance and exit wounds and the damaged brain, citing his belief that such "overdramatic evidence" could only inflame the minds of the jurors. Mr. Ambose thereupon cited his belief that a murder trial tended to become dramatic. The Court ruled that the slides were to be excluded as "potentially prejudicial.")

"*Potentially* prejudicial?" Ambose protested. "What the hell does that mean, Harry? Is it all right if we say he's dead or is that going to get them all upset, too?" After a minimum of thought Marie decided not to put that in. As much as she'd have liked to stick it to Ambose, she didn't know what the hell "potentially prejudicial" meant either.

As long as he was there, Ambose stepped over to the witness chair and, positioning himself so that he was half-facing the jury box, asked the medical examiner to describe the passage of the bullet through the head of the late Chief Justice. "If it is at all possible," he said somberly, sending his own voodoo message (he hoped) to the jury, "will you try not to make it too dramatic?"

What he should have asked, he realized about ten seconds later, was whether Dr. Price might, through the exercise of superhuman effort, try not to make it sound as if he were giving the orientation lecture to the incoming class of meat cutters.

Dr. Price, who seemed especially nervous at having Ambose that close to him, began by saying, "The brain of a primate is, as we all know, subdivided into four major sections," and from there the jury was privileged to witness the miracle of a previously high-pitched, nervous voice settle into a low, steady drone. The bullet had entered the skull, just above the left eye, leaving a small, sharply defined entrance wound corresponding to the caliber of the bullet, around which there had been a narrow reddish rim of localized bleeding. Having pierced the skin and run into the increased resistance of bony matter, the bullet had, in a manner of speaking, been deflected from the pursuance of a clean and direct course, which was to say that it had begun to rotate and tumble—although speaking grossly, the bullet had continued to travel in a straight line, proceeding at a constant forty-three–degree angle. He had brought up the phenomenon of the rotating and tumbling so that the jury would understand that it had cut an irregular, ever-expanding path through the soft brain tissue causing considerable destruction of the tissue with accompanying intracranial bleeding. By the time the bullet had sliced through to the other side of the brain it had achieved a diameter of one and three-eighths inches (although he had seen .45–caliber bullet wounds even larger than that). When the already wobbling bullet had then met the heavier resistance of the opposite side of the calvarium or skull, a further rotating and tumbling motion had been imparted to it, causing a rather large and explosive exit wound, somewhat irregular in contour, which he would place, for the purpose of the trial record, at two inches if measured at the outermost extremes. "Examined grossly, as can be seen from a reading of the protocol, tiny fragments of bone were visible, along with the soft, spongy hemorrhic particles of brain tissue which had attached themselves to the spinous or jagged portions of the exit wound. There was also necrotic brain tissue visible in the clotted blood which had matted down the hair immediately surrounding the exit wound."

Ambose, with one eye on the jury box, had seen all interest fade away. Forcing excitement into his voice, he asked, "You said it was a small, sharply defined entrance wound, doctor. Would you give us a measurement?"

Dr. Price looked surprised. "Oh, I thought I said the size of a forty-five–caliber bullet, Mr. Ambose. That would be just under half an inch."

Bannerman rose, looking utterly fascinated with Dr. Roy M. Price and all his works—looking, in fact, like a man who had just enjoyed a good meal and was about to light up his after-dinner cigar. He began by informing Dr. Price, in slightly deferential tones, of the high repute in which he was held throughout the country and, lest anyone impute any devious motives to his expressions of admiration, very promptly put forth his own credentials by dropping the names of three of four other medical examiners with whom he felt they were both familiar.

"Let's see now," he said, returning with reluctance to the business at hand. "The bullet passed through the frontal lobe and the parietal but missed the temporal and occipital lobes completely, is that what you said?"

A welcoming smile, visible to the naked eye, flitted across Dr. Price's features. "Well, Mr. Bannerman," he said. "At a forty-three–degree angle. . . ?"

Through the rest of the cross-examination Bannerman continued to engage the medical examiner in technical talk, drawing unstintingly upon the extensive medical knowledge for which Norman Bannerman was so well and favorably known in better medical circles throughout the country. Ambose interrupted the lovefest only once, and that was with a wholly frivolous objection made for the sole purpose of allowing him to refer to the defense attorney as Dr. Bannerman. By the time the Drs. Price and Bannerman had finished their cozy little seminar, not one eye in the jury box was turned to either of them.

They sat, as they had sat so often, on opposite sides of the desk, Jim Ambose tilted so far back in his chair that he was looking straight up at the ceiling and Jake Foxx sort of settled down into his fat. "My boy," Foxx said at last, "I've seen you do better."

Ambose grunted. His eyes were on a spider dropping toward him on its silken thread, swinging slowly in the air currents, sensing every tremor in the air. To his positive knowledge he had never seen a spider in this office before (perhaps, he had to concede, because he so rarely put in a full day studying the ceiling).

"There's this about it, though," he said, letting his attention wander away from his friend the spider. "There's always another day, and tomorrow I could do worse."

Ambose not only appreciated Foxx's honesty, he insisted upon it. It was part of Jake's job to sit in the courtroom as a critical observer and give it to him straight. That was why Ambose had instructed him to stay in the courtroom as much as possible during the first day and let Harv Leigh ride herd on the witnesses. It was not part of his job to sit by Ambose while he was coming up out of the decompression chamber. That was friendship.

"I'll say this about your friend, Jinglebells," Foxx said. "So far he's been worth the price of admission."

The spider had made a quick drop down its cable and Ambose's attention was now riveted upon it. Other than making a small mouth of silence for Foxx to see, Ambose remained perfectly still and silent as down dropped the spider—down, down and down—in a plumb line straight for his mouth.

Down dropped his friend the spider, stroking liquid from his stomach and spinning it, by magic, into a silken cable to ride the air on. What a marvelous thing was the spider! The solitary hunter, sufficient unto itself, carrying transit in its spigot and death in its claws; the multieyed, multiclawed survivor of that feast on the cannibal ground where it had been spawned.

Down came his friend the spider, the beast of prey out looking . . .

Silent sat Ambose, no longer so much as blinking, holding his breath . . .

Lower and lower, testing the currents, a wary hunter with a headful of eyes . . .

Waiting and watching, gathering muscle, one lightning grab was all he would get . . . and . . .

At the first twitch of the shoulder—a mere tremor in the air flowing from the twitching shoulder to the silken cable to the sensing claws and his friend the spider was up the cable and out of sight, as quickly and completely gone as if it had been sucked up in an updraft.

What a truly marvelous piece of work was Jim Ambose's friend the spider.

"You can tell 'em for me if they should ask you," he said, invoking some wry, shorthand humor that existed between him and Foxx, "that I have always welcomed a new challenge." But only when he had to. He had entered the courtroom this morning thinking that Jake's friend Jinglebells had been underestimating him; he now had to consider the revolting possibility that he had been underestimating Jake's friend Jinglebells. "You can tell 'em that's sometimes known among us lawyer-types as a fatal miscalculation."

The phone rang. The private line. The eyes of the erstwhile hunter, drawn to the sound, showed absolutely no interest. In a weak version of his high falsetto Ambose said, "I've had a hard day at the office, dear. Jacking witnesses around this way and that." With Foxx rousing himself to take it, Ambose sighed, "You can tell 'em not too much cheese on the pizza." If that mystified Fox, it also mystified Ambose. "If anybody should ask," he muttered, "tell 'em that's what's known as ethnic humor . . . Huh?"

Foxxie was holding the receiver out to him, his eyes suddenly wide and full of meaning. "It's Ike," he said. "He's calling from the Annex."

The eyes of the two old friends held for a moment, and whatever message passed between them rode on the air currents, needing no words.

It was an expensive-looking two-story white brick home among the other Colonial-type homes on the wide, quiet residential street. The architecture, as much as the carpeted lawns and the lush, protective landscaping, labeled them as old homes in an old settled neighborhood. The proximity of the Medical Building at the corner—in whose parking lot Foxx had left his car—was evidence that it was no longer as exclusive a neighborhood as it had once been. The suburban crawl.

Like the homes around it, the Annex (also known as the Garden Building) was set well back from the sidewalk. They entered, without ringing, into a long narrow foyer. Off to the left was the living room, tastefully and unostentatiously decorated from the traditional furniture to the pleated satin drapes to the semi-impressionistic painting just above the fireplace. Down the foyer, just beyond the living room, was a long winding staircase. The second floor. That's where the action was.

Before going up, however, Ambose and Foxx turned, hard right off the foyer, into a small room that had probably been a waiting room (if the original owner had been a professional man) or a smoking room (if he hadn't been). Just inside the door a round-faced man behind a glass-topped desk was sorting out some file cards. The current owner, which happened to be the Lowell Police Department, used it as a kind of reception room.

Not that any of the neighbors knew who their neighbor was. Nor anybody else who didn't have to know. As the Supreme Court decisions had continued to come down, whittling away at their rights of interrogation, tying their hands, Chief Wilson and Ike Weiland had gone to their old friend Mike Karney to show them —as who could show them better—how to bury the cost and upkeep of a private little sanctuary in the annual budget. (It could be found there, if anyone ever got around to looking, by turning to the Maintenance section, flipping the pages until you came to the Warehouse & Storage listing, and running your finger down the page to the Storehouse division where among a solid block of subdivisions you would find, printed plain as day for anybody to see, the single word: Annex.)

The man behind the reception desk was occupied at the moment in sorting out the file cards and placing them into a small brown metal box which had an inordinately strong metal lock. Barely looking up at Ambose, he told him he'd be with him in a minute.

"That's all right, Condon," Ambose told him tonelessly. "I was hoping you'd take your time."

Condon's hand froze right where it was, over the cards. He breathed in deeply, letting it be seen with what effort he was keeping himself from being goaded. Condon knew what Ambose thought of him. An office cop. He knew what he thought of Ambose, too. If the baleful look he gave him as he reached for the phone was any indication, he did not feel any richer for having known him.

Having announced their arrival, Condon pulled open the drawer and held out a fistful of pawn tickets.

"Yeah," Ambose said. "Johnny McCullough told us all about them."

Maybe McCullough wasn't supposed to, Condon said tightly. He looked as if he were making a mental note of it. "The chief said I was to give them to you. Here. You want 'em or don't you?"

With one swing of his arm Ambose snatched them out of his hand and jammed them into his pocket. Who the hell did they think they were kidding here? he asked as nastily as possible. "The day hardly don't go by some irate citizen asks me how come we don't do something about that whorehouse out near Garden City." Puckering his lips together primly in obvious imitation of an irate lady citizen, he tucked his hands most daintily into his waist and trilled, "Why, all them depraved and dirty looking men sneaking in and out all times of the day and night, it's a shame and a disgrace."

They had stopped off at the police station on their way out to see Johnny McCullough of Theft and Burglary. McCullough had been waiting for them in Weiland's office, behind Weiland's desk, doodling impatiently on Weiland's note pad. "Actually," McCullough had made haste to point out in describing the arrest, "I was going off on a seventy-two–hour and if I could of ignored him I would of. If I'd known it was going to give me all this trouble . . ." Victor Hill, his erstwhile partner, had the right idea. What Victor always said was that he screwed his cop's eyes out of the socket when he went off duty and had nothing but love and understanding for his fellow man until he walked back into the locker room again. McCullough had been sitting a red light, minding his own business, and while he was waiting for the light to change the dumb bastard had come out of the building with a radio on his back and gone right into the pawn shop two doors down. He turned up his hands as if to say, *So what else could I do?*

"Two doors away?" Foxx said. He whistled through his teeth in admiration. "That's balls." You could see the aptness of it strike him right away. "Making five in all."

"Known as a cluster," McCullough said, smiling despite himself. "I say, radio. Remember those old console types?" He placed the pencil down across the writing pad and spread his arms wide to show how huge it was. "They made 'em solid them days," he said. "I got to say that for them. Your guy was so high, Ambose, he thought it was a television set. That's what he told me, anyhoo."

Big guy, Ambose said.

Scrawny little squirt, McCullough told him.

Yeah, Foxx said, but when they needed it they had the strength of thousands.

On the way to the station the squirt had started to talk about having something the "big boys" would be interested in, only he had to tell them personally. Johnny had figured the guy was feeding a pretty good habit and playing it cute, like all these characters, to see if he could maybe cop himself a fix. (That was when McCullough had told them the dumb bastard had ten pawn tickets on him, all of them dated over the past ten days.) Instead of booking him, anyhoo, McCullough had decided it wouldn't hurt to let Weiland's boy scrub him down.

"And you don't have to sit around getting him booked," Ambose said.

"Now that you mention it."

The next thing Johnny knew he was getting a call from Weiland telling him to drag his ass back over there on the double. He turned his eyes up to Ambose. "I guess the guy had something, huh? Sure could have fooled me."

Even through the ritualistic griping Johnny McCullough had been sending inquisitive, openly intrigued looks toward him. Perfectly understandable. Although Weiland wouldn't necessarily have told Johnny whom he'd be meeting in his office, it wouldn't have taken him more than a second and a half to realize that if Ambose had come down personally his pinch's information couldn't have been about anybody except Sam Tabor. McCullough had been balancing the loss of time and general inconvenience against the possibility that he had, in some small way—as yet unknown, possibly never fully known, to him—played a small role in the Tabor trial. And the more Johnny thought about it, the more he was liking it.

At the top of the winding staircase, there was an open door that led into a room that had been fixed up as a regular office, with a couple of desks and a row of file cabinets and phones and copying machines and typewriters. The guy behind the first desk jerked his head toward the next room, and as he was telling Ambose he was to go right on in, pressed a buzzer which not only alerted Weiland but released the lock.

"You know the script, Jake," Ambose said. "Let's put on a good show."

"I'll do my best," Foxxie told him. "And you just try to be your usual charming self."

The scrawny little man seated in the large white wooden chair was even less appetizing than Ambose had expected. Middling growth of disordered black hair. Old chino pants. Flimsy T-shirt hanging loose, pulled and tugged. Sharp, bony ankles surrounded by dirt.

Naturally enough the little man's eyes had gone to big Foxx first. Looking to Ambose, he uncrossed his legs in what seemed to be a gesture of respect. Otis Moscrip had been around; he could spot by instinct who the important man was here.

Ambose regarded him with loathing. "You ought to take a bath. You ought

334

to assert your constitutional rights to a free and equal bar of soap. What do you think you are, a second-class citizen or something?"

The scrawny little man smiled uncertainly. "I don't mind." Smiling was a mistake. When he smiled his lips collapsed, exposing the most rotted teeth Ambose had ever seen; black at the top and a kind of soft yellowish caries in between. They were so rotted away, those rotten teeth, that you could smell the fetid breath without having to smell it.

Well, Ambose thought. They say you're not supposed to look a gift horse in the mouth.

Across the large well-lit room was something that looked like a detached console from the engineer's booth at a radio station. Right alongside it, facing the wall, was a black leather-upholstered chair with particularly high and wide arm rests. A lie-detector machine. Of dubious value with junkies, Ambose had found, except that it could be hung over them as a threat. (As for truth serum, that was of no value at all as far as Ambose was concerned, period. A few years earlier they had almost killed a stoolie who had agreed to go under.)

On the basin counter, behind Ike Weiland, lay a hypodermic needle with a layer of white, milky fluid across the bottom. And a package of cotton batting pulled up to a wispy fluff at the top.

"Let's have a look at you, handsome." Ambose took Moscrip's chin firmly in his hand and turned his unresisting head from side to side. (Ho-boy, had he been right about the breath!) There was a brownish tint running through the whites of the eyes, much as if they were tobacco-stained. More to the point, the eyes were watery and the pupils dilated just enough to show that the last hit was wearing off. Stoolies had always revolted him. The scum of the scum; they couldn't even be loyal to their own kind. Ambose let the chin go with a little contemptuous shove and grasping him by the wrist turned his arm over so that it was fully extended. No tracks. That was a relief. Just one small scab at the bend of his elbow, and that would be gone by the time he had to testify. Increasing the pressure, he said, "So you know something about Tabor, do you, Otis? And you're willing to give it to us because you're such a law-abiding citizen and all we got to do is give you a hit." He snorted in complete disgust. "A false alarm, Ike. He's already been to the FBI with the same story and they threw him out on his can. That right, Otis?"

Moscrip hadn't moved his head one hair's worth from where it had settled when Ambose let him go. His eyes remained on Ambose, full of inoffensiveness and perhaps even mild regret that Ambose thought all these preliminaries were necessary with an old hand like him. Old hand that he was, he said nothing.

"Aw, Jim," Weiland said. "He needs a hit to stay in shape, that's all it is." He rubbed his hand across his big nose, a nose that showed all the signs of having been broken more than once. "How's he gonna testify if he ain't in shape?"

Oh, that was the ticket, was it? He was gonna move right in and become a star boarder, was he? "You know what happens to characters who try to get a hit from us under false pretenses?" Aghast at his own suggestion that such an effrontery might be lurking in Moscrip's breast, he kicked the chair right out from under him, dumping him on his backside. For just one second after he landed Otis began to skitter away on his backside and hands and then, stopping abruptly, he leaned back on his elbows and stared up at Ambose, slack-mouthed and indignant. "Have an open mind, why don't ya?" he yelped, with an absurd combination of

335

annoyance and dignity. "Ya could at least listen ta me, couldn't ya? Thass the leas' ya could do."

Yeah, why didn't he give the guy a chance, for chrissake, Foxx asked, and they were into their act with Foxx picking Otis up and brushing him off and asking Ambose why he had to go acting so tough when he had a good guy like this who was only trying to be cooperative.

As a man who had taken an oath to preserve our democratic way of life, what was there for Ambose to do but yield to the will of the majority? Otis barely had time to sit down and wipe his nose across the sleeve of his T-shirt before Ambose had taken him by the chin again to inform him that he was going to sit off there on the side and let him tell his story. "I don't want you to talk to me, I don't want you to even look at me. I want you to tell your story to Captain Weiland and Mr. Foxx because they believe in you. They have faith in you."

A polite and judicious silence ensued while Otis was permitting Ambose to make himself comfortable. "You wanna talk abou' drugs?" he asked in a politely inquiring voice. "Is drugs the subjec' matter? I could make so much noise there it's pitiful. Ya think it's jes' the kids? Some a ya leadin' businessmen in town. It's pitiful."

The first thing Ambose was able to see was that he had not really succeeded in striking terror into Moscrip's heart. Otis was sitting—his shoulders hunched but his back erect—with his elbows resting on the arms of the chair and his ankles comfortably crossed, pretty much as they had been when he and Foxx had come in.

Ambose wanted to know how bad his habit was.

"Not really," Moscrip said. With Weiland having wandered over to the window, Otis was talking directly to—or at least looking directly at—Jake Foxx. "I c'n take it or leave it." There was a slight English accent in there somewhere, barely noticeable before but coming out strongly in *take it or leave it.*

"But you'd rather take it, you handsome devil. Don't be modest."

"T'ree t'ousands once't a day," Otis said. He nodded toward the hypodermic needle. "Ya call 'at a habit?"

"You see?" The glow of pleasure lying not so deep within Foxx's lazy, hooded eyes was testimony enough that his confidence in Otis had been rewarded. So powerful was his faith that he announced in strong, firm tones that Otis was now going to tell them all about Sam Tabor.

Otis blinked like a dog, slow and sad, while he was absorbing the sudden change of subject. "Awright," he said at last, with an all-wise, in-the know look which he accomplished by pulling down on the entire bottom of his face. "Sam Tabor issa subjec' matter now. One thing atta time, right?"

Now that he had been set down so firmly on the track, he proceeded to tell them in his choppy, remarkably self-assured way how he had gone to work at BeeJay's Bowling Emporium, owned and operated by Mr. Howard Turner, right after he hit town about five–six months ago, as general maintenance man and house man on the pool tables, and how every once in awhile this guy Sam would come in. "Now, ya say Sam. Lardo was whad I callt'm."

It was a kind of hobby of his to hang a moniker on all the regulars, Otis explained, that being the way of poolrooms when you'd been around the big time. It made the customers feel friendly, see, like it was all one big happy family, and maybe they didn't think that was good for business, as Mr. Howard Turner (upon whose head he had hung the moniker Joe the Boss) could tell them, if they would excuse Otis for mentioning it. "Ya pin a moniker onna man, it's a responsibility on ya head it's gotta be jes' right. Not't I lay awake nights, y'unnerstan', see, it's jes' a talent I happena bin born wid." Twisting his face into that hideous look of all-purpose wisdom, he brought his thumb and forefinger close to his lips and threw a little kiss of appreciation to the gods who had so bountifully endowed him. "Well, ridaway we hid it off real good, y'unnerstan'? I c'n see ridaway he's crazy about me."

"That means you were hustling him pretty good, huh?" Ambose said.

"A Coke?" Otis squealed. "A twenny-fi'–cen' Coke?" Otis was so deeply wounded that he came dangerously near to looking at him. "An' I spot'm fi' balls'n shoot one-hanned'n bank de eid-ball. I gi' th' guy a real good shake, y'unnerstan', see? Alla time, always. He's a frien' a mine, y'unnerstan', an' I don' hussle no frien's. Whaddaya think?"

"You just turn 'em in, right? That's what I like about you, Otis, you're all heart."

From the original telephone conversation with Weiland, Ambose already knew that Intelligence had checked Otis Moscrip out with Turner. And also that Turner attached no significance whatsoever to the fact that Otis had left a couple of weeks after the assassination. Drifters like that came and went, Turner had said. The only thing that had surprised him was that Otis had lasted as long as he had.

What did Jake think of Otis Moscrip now, Ambose wanted to know. One friend in the whole world and he was ready to sell him out for three-thousandths of an ounce of crap.

As willing as Otis had shown himself to play it any way Ambose wanted to, this latest attack upon his character seemed to strike him as being particularly cruel and uncalled for. "I'm sufferin' from an emotional strain," he complained, the English accent coming up strong. "I gotta get it outta me, don' ya know that?" Suddenly wan and slack-mouthed, he fluttered his hand against his heart as tenderly as though it were a bird's wing. "The las' time I wenna see the doctor he tole me I hadda watch out fuh my high blood pressure."

As the failing man's one true friend and benefactor, Foxxie was moved to cluck sympathetically and utter a few wholly unnecessary words of understanding. "Alla my life I binna tough-luck guy," Otis said, and he was off on a heart-rending story about how once, across the bridge from Cincinnati, he had played another champion pool player who, like himself, happened to be on his uppers and after trailing 99–0, he had run off a hundred balls, nonstop, finishing with a three-ball combination. And did they know what he had won? One measly dollar. "An' this w'z a very well-known champeen, gennelmen, known as White Top, which innis day he's playt fuh t'ousan's on up, an' before some a the crowned heads a Europe by name."

"You never had a thousand dollars in your life, you creep," Ambose told him. "If you ever had to play for a thousand dollars, you'd shit."

Oh boy! Now he'd done it! Moscrip was so angry his lips went sucking in and out, making him look not unlike a fish at the top of the tank. "If you'll excuse me fuh sayin' so," he said, no longer able to suffer such indignities in silence, "ya c'n ast thuh offisuh that arrest't me is there anybody ta his long knowledge 'n experience could steal a television an' jes when Uncle Charley there is tellin' me how it's a radio an' thuh fucker don' even work, in come the offisuh to put the arm on'm? Ast'm 'at, why don'ya!"

Forgetting himself completely he was so riled up, Otis looked Ambose square in the eye—oh, Ambose had done it all right. "Lissen, why should I suck hind tit all my life? Y'unnerstan'?" Looking mean and determined (although he was quite good about directing the mean and determined look away from Ambose), he gripped down hard on both arms of the chair. "The things 'at happen ta me, I could writa book'd be onna bes' sellers."

"Hey, he's going to write a book, Jake. Otis has literary ambitions."

"Ya think so, huh? Nevva min'. My brother, he's a master in Ph.D. I on'y wenna public school but I'd go half-'n'-half wid some writer that wanna write my story. I'd give'm the title, too." Narrowing his eyes, his nostrils flaring, he looked from Foxx to Weiland with the half-pugnacious, half-injured air of a man who had been provoked so far beyond the bounds of reason that he was about to reveal to them, against his own interests and better judgment, a title worth a king's fortune. You could all but see the powerful invisible lean toward Ambose as he flung the magic words forth: "The Story of a Hard-Luck Guy."

Foxx nodded gravely. "The Story of a Hard-Luck Guy," he said. "That's it, all right."

"In Dulut'," Otis said triumphantly. The flaccid lips worked in and out, warming themselves up. "In Dulut' I played Russian roulette inna pool hall, thass how we'd start it, y'unnerstan', see, the openin' chapter . . ."

"Hey, that's good," Ambose said when the wondrous tale had been completed. "Otis figures his life is worth fifty-five dollars at five-to-one odds. The whole world would want to read about that."

"Fifdy-fifdy ri'down thuh line. Now y'unnerstan', Mr. Detective? Why should I suck hind tit all my life?" His lips went flopping in and out again. "In Bos'n, I wenna bed wid an actress. The leadin' lady in thuh Colonial The-a-ter. I was a fine a lookin' young man innose days as a duke." With a gay little roll of his eyes and an absurd little toss of his head, he reached up as if he were tapping a derby that was sitting on the side of his head. "Many'sa time my lady love tole me I had a career as a leadin' actor. An' I wouldn' wanya to get any ideas there, gennelmen, she was a real fine person."

Having paid such a touching tribute to the lady love of his youth, his face fell in grim and unmistakable forecast of the coming disaster. "In Pawtucket, Rhode Island, a week aftuh I give'r the go-by, I witnessta ganglan'-slayin', ganglan'-style, hidin' frum behin' a large iron barrel, fulla rust, inna very fear a my life. An' all I w'z wantin' w'z a slow freight outta town. Y'unnerstan' now?" He squinted at Foxx, one eye open, one eye closed, creating a total effect not of fear but of cunning. "Fifdy-fifdy I'd be willin' ta go widda writer who hadda proper flair fuh the words."

Drily but not completely without sympathy, Ambose said, "I'll tell you what your whole trouble is, Otis. You should never have left Boston."

"Many'sa time I had'at thought myself." Otis nodded several times; rocking, gray-bearded nods that didn't prevent him from sneaking a quick look around to case the reaction. "It was in Los Angeles, gennelmen, was where fickle fortune played the most crueles' of its many tricks on the Hard-Luck Kid." The deep and gloomy voice, taken together with the rosy pleasure that brightened his wizened features, informed his audience that they were in for a particularly satisfying chapter from his book of woes. "In Los Angeles, otherwise known as goodole L.A. or the gate-a-way uv thuh stars . . ."

Ambose's purpose had been to study his man carefully before he heard his story, and he had already seen and heard all that he had to. The little sonofabitch had a sporty little ego, which was all to the good. Unlike your average law-abiding citizen, he was used to being disbelieved, and that was even better. Whatever Bannerman threw at him, he'd stand up. Planting himself right at Otis's elbow so that Otis would have to crane his neck to look up at him, he informed him that the rules were about to be changed. What Ambose wanted to know now was exactly what Otis thought he could testify to about Sam Tabor, and as soon as Otis began to tell him, Ambose barked, "Look at me! I want to see the whites of your eyes!"

Otis, who had been looking right at him, continued to look at him, docile and uncomplaining, and yet somehow managing to let Ambose see that he forgave him because he understood perfectly well that he was only doing his job. His Adam's apple suddenly leaped into prominence as he took a couple of gulps of air. "He got ta talkin' aboud how he was gonna kill'm someday if he evuh got th' chanct. Wilcke, y'unnerstan'. Thuh Chief Justice by name."

Very deliberately, Ambose ground his cigar out against the top rung of the chair, inches from Moscrip's head. Otis continued to look right at him, not moving a muscle, his little eyes floating in their murky pools. "I want you to listen to me," Ambose said very quietly. "I want you to repeat exactly, word for word, what was said on both sides of the conversation."

"There wasn' no conversation on both sides. He was tellin' me how he work't wid the judges there, an' like the law wasn' no good no more 'cause this guy Wilcke ud ruint it good fer ev'ybody. An' that he's gonna kill'm some day fuh sure. If ya don' min' my sayin' it, it hurts my neck this way."

For that, he got a cloud of smoke in his eyes. Just so he'd understand that Ambose's tolerance wasn't inexhaustible.

The only thing that was bothering Ambose, frankly, was that it was almost too good to be true, but no matter how hard Ambose pressed him, Otis never wavered from his story that Sam had told him about his intention of killing Wilcke the very first time they'd got to talking, and a lot of times after. And that maybe a day or two before he did it—he couldn't be sure exactly—Sam had told him that Wilcke was coming to Lowell and this was going to be his chance, now or never.

And when Ambose demanded to know how come Otis hadn't gone to the authorities, Otis replied with great indignation, "Who'd a thought he meant it! If he tole you that, would you a believed 'm? Lotsa guys say they're gonna kill this one, gonna kill that one. Issat supposeta mean they're gonna *kill* him?"

As a final test Ambose gave out with a short, malicious bark of laughter, and sneered all over him as though he had finally forced him into making the one fatal mistake he had known he was going to make all along. And what would Otis say, he snarled, if he told him that nobody had known Wilcke was coming to Lowell until the day he arrived? And there being no way Sam could have known, what did that make Otis out to be except a goddamn liar? And what did that mean Ambose was going to do except bounce him out of there on his can?

Otis didn't bat an eye. "What would I say? Izzat the question you asteda me, Mr. Detective? I will say, pardonmepleez, if no one knew that then Lardo is one a them mediums as gets his messages from outta the air. I onc't worked wid one a them mediums inna carnival tourin' the Gulf from Galveston, on'y he was a fake. What I couldn' tellya about how easy people get fooled—it's pitiful. Thassa whole other chapter in my book. Or he was lyin', mister, an' it come true on 'm. Howda I know?"

339

Ambose was convinced. There had indeed been a paragraph in the *Chronicle* announcing that Wilcke had accepted the Bar Association's invitation. Otis Moscrip had dropped out of the skies to give them motive and premeditation, and that, Mr. Bannerman, sewed it up tight. And if Otis was an unappetizing witness —and Otis sure was an unappetizing witness—well, Ambose's business was putting on unappetizing witnesses.

He nodded to Weiland. He'd have Weiland book Otis for something a couple of days before the end of the trial, and they could tell the Court he hadn't come forward with his story until just before Ambose sprung him on Bannerman as a surprise witness. ("Surprise, No-o-orman!") By then, Weiland and Foxx would have him completely rehearsed.

"Otis . . ." Ambose said. Otis Moscrip's eyes had followed Captain Weiland through every inch of his journey from the window to the basin counter. They were now on the hypodermic needle in Ike Weiland's hand. "Otis," Ambose said. He patted him tenderly on the head, finding some previously unsuspected merit to him. "I just want you to remember that if you're lying to me I'm going to break off both your arms and beat you to death with the stumps."

"Lissen, I don' take somethin' fuh nuttin', whaddaya worryin'?" He was already flexing his fist to pump up a vein.

"Okay, Cap," Jim Ambose said. "Hit him."

Friday, August 1—

"There's this about money," Tommy Mallon said. "You can get used to it if you try hard enough."

"What?" Ambose said. "And break a habit of a lifetime?"

"Now, look," Tommy said. "I know I've hit you with it fast. But think about it, all right? We'll talk some more when this is over."

Ambose looked at his watch and leaned forward to grind out his cigar. "How's this, Tommy? When I get a little time, I'll think about it."

Tommy had hit him with it fast, all right. With Mallon and Gunderson down as the lead-off witnesses, Tommy had stuck his head into the office to suggest that the prosecuting attorney take his star witness to lunch. As it happened, Ambose was on the line with Jimmy Clougherty arranging to meet Mayor Karney for lunch so he could go over his testimony with him. "City Hall-wise," Foxx explained expansively, "Bannerman won't play ball on Karney, and that means we're going to have to put our dandy little mayor on ourselves." He stretched his hands apart, as if he were unveiling a banner headline. "Big Mike Karney Lives Again. Now that's what I call star."

Ambose held his hand over the speaker. "I finally won one with Hilliard. The Boss Man wanted to make Bannerman call him." He jerked his head in the general direction of Nevins' office to show in what high regard he held that brilliant idea.

The oblique look Tommy sent back gave every appearance of being both bored and amused to find *that* was still going on around here. As to Bannerman's refusal to play ball on Karney, *that,* you could see, hadn't surprised him at all. "We have a small, select coterie of distinguished attorneys around the country who don't." The boyish smile lit up his face. "If I were you, I'd want to put our falling-down-dead mayor on the stand, too. Anything for the chance to have lunch at City Hall.

According to the Women's Page of the *Morning Globe*, gourmets throughout the several continents vie for—"

As if that had been a signal Ambose stiffened to alertness. Mayor Karney had come to the phone to set up the appointment, and while Tommy stood by, leering, Ambose gave out with a series of "Yes, sirs," a "Twelve o'clock sharp, sir," two "On the dots, sir," and three or four "That's just the way I feel about it myself, sir."

"My, my," Tommy said. "Comes to the phone himself, does he? Talks and everything. That will come as a shock to the more gullible subscribers of the aforementioned pillar of civic virtue. By the way, James, I want to commend you on your telephone style while you are addressing your betters. I like a man who speaks up right servile." Flashing his most boyishly engaging smile, he ducked behind an upraised shoulder, as if he expected something to come flying at him. "Well, if you'd rather have lunch with a notorious pillager of the public purse than with a gullible reader of a pillar of civic virtue, I'll go where I know there is still some appreciation for the literate mind." The lovely Lenore had informed him on the way in, he confided, that Hilliard wanted to consult him on a matter of grave import concerning intradepartmental policy. A puzzled frown came over him. "I think she said it had something to do with disciplining unruly assistants."

Ambose, who had been frowning heavily at the notes he had just made, bared his teeth at him to indicate, ostensibly, that he was not amused but actually— as they both understood—that he had been happy to see him, even if it might not have seemed so. "Jim," Tommy said. He had stopped at the doorway with his hand flat against the jamb, looking quite serious. "I'll see you later, huh?" The slight, barely perceptible nod in the general direction of Jake Foxx made it perfectly clear to both of them that he wanted to see him alone.

Mallon didn't know how close he'd hit. Or maybe knowing as much as he did about the game they were still playing in that office, he had made a pretty shrewd guess. Earlier in the morning the lovely Lenore had informed Ambose that his presence was urgently required in Hilliard Nevins' office before Pawley joined them for the daily strategy meeting. Without saying a word Nevins had flung the morning copy of the *Globe* across the desk, opened to the AP roundup of the interviews with the various personages in and around the trial. The kicker was that while Bannerman had about five times more space in the body of the story than Ambose, the column carried the head: Lowell Prosecutor Wants New Judge.

Now that was pretty smart, Nevins scowled. "We've only got one judge on this case, so let's see how mad we can get him at us, is that the idea!" Well, just in case Ambose was suffering from any delusions of grandeur, Hilliard Nevins was there to remind him that while he was a useful man to have around, he was not by any stretch of the imagination indispensable.

None of it had come as a surprise to Ambose. He had read the story. The speech he knew by heart. He had been expecting, though not with wild anticipation, to be called upon the carpet, and he had intended to take his medicine without a word, as always. But somehow, despite his best resolve, he was unable to resist clucking sadly (he could only suppose that he had expected Hilliard to have *some* sense of humor about it) that you just couldn't believe anything you read in the papers anymore. "I didn't tell them I wanted a new judge. What I told them, if you'll read it, was that I wanted the old one back."

Oh, Nevins had read it. And it had ruined his whole breakfast. "I'm telling you right now that I'm not going to be reading any more of your wise-ass remarks about Harry Davies with my breakfast through the rest of this trial. I'm going to enjoy my gaw-damn breakfast through the rest of this trial. Do I make myself clear, Mr. Ambose? . . ."

As the loyal Peterson tried so hard to explain, it wasn't really Judge Davies' fault. There was no way Davies could have known that one of the lady jurors—which one he did not feel he, as a gentleman, could divulge—had been in the bathroom indisposed when the judge's order came up to him and (he shrugged helplessly) the lady had refused to be hurried. There had also been no way the judge could have known that it was going to take photographers of that caliber so much time to take a few pictures. Or that the directors of the television crews were going to refuse to roll their cameras until the still photographers were out of the way, let alone that each of the networks would insist upon shooting their footage separately. And with the judge himself inside the courtroom, there hadn't been any way for him to let the lawyers or the newspaper people know that the morning session wouldn't be starting until . . . well, the way it looked now it would be starting a good half-hour late.

All Judge Davies had been trying to do, after all, was to be courteous to the visiting photographers by letting them come into the courtroom early to get their pictures of the jury and the judge.

"It's never Harry's fault," Ambose snorted, loud enough to be heard about halfway down the long line of reporters waiting, in near mutiny, outside the locked foyer door. "Harry's like a cock-a-roach. It ain't that he eats so much, it's just that everything he falls into gets spoiled."

The damnedest thing about it was that in just that one split-second before he heard Nevins' voice boom forth he could feel Nevins' eyes burning into his neck. Nevins and Bannerman had slipped into the courtroom through the cloakroom door to find out what in the name of hell was going on in there, and Hilliard had, wouldn't you have known it, picked that precise moment to come back out. "Mr. Ambose is a great kidder," he heard Nevins say. "There's some even say he could die laughing one of these days."

A few minutes later Tommy had taken Jim aside and suggested that since they were in for a bit of a wait anyway, this might be an excellent time to go back up to his office and have their little talk.

"How would you like to come in with me," Tommy said, wasting no time. "The old partnership again, Mallon & Ambose." Ambose's look of astonishment and disbelief clearly pleased him. That was an ampersand between those two distinguished names, Mallon told him. Not a common conjunction, as in Pat and Mike. For Ambose's benefit he drew a rough approximation of an & in the air. "An ampersand is that curly-looking thing that looks like a dollar sign to the uninformed and has become accepted through time and usage as the bond that ties two attorneys together in the unholy pursuit of their profession. Which, now that you mention it, is the same thing." The light, bantering tone came to an end. "As partners we'll both take out two hundred thousand dollars per. Minimum guarantee."

It seemed to Ambose like a very good time to light up a cigar. Well, he thought to himself, he had two choices. He could say yes or he could say no. That wasn't so complicated. Not knowing what to say, he leaned back in his chair and pulled hard on the cigar. When the smoke had all drifted away Tommy was still beaming at him benevolently.

"They tell me you're a pretty good lawyer," Ambose said finally. "What would you tell a client if he told you someone had come up and offered him two hundred thousand dollars because he liked him so much?"

"Who said I liked you?" Despite the stiff, questioning look on Ambose's face and the gently admonishing one on Mallon's, it hadn't really been that serious a question. It was an old joke between them, actually, coming out of the Book of Wisdom of a con man they had both become rather fond of in the course of sending him to the slammer for from two to ten years. "I would tell him," Tommy said, by rote, "that when someone comes up and says they want to make you a lot of money, they don't want to make you a lot of money, they want to make themselves a lot of money. Right as, they say, rain." Look, he said, turning the benevolence off. Ambose was getting a national reputation out of the Tabor trial, and by a coincidence usually deemed fortuitous it had come at a time when Tommy had plans for spreading out nationally. "It also happens that because of my natural inclination toward sloth and lechery, a combination lesser men might not be able to handle, I don't want to strain myself. You'd be an asset in all ways." His contacts with the local politicos, Mallon was willing to inform him, had also been considered scrupulously and looked upon favorably. "Look, Jim, friends are friends but I make an annual donation of a hundred dollars to the Community Fund because I have it in writing that it will take care of all charities officially imprimatured as worthwhile. *Capice?*"

Ambose *capiced*. What he didn't *capice* was what had happened to a certain little friend of his who had always maintained that any lawyer who didn't start his own company and go it alone was a fool. "Travel light and camp alone, that was the way it went, wasn't it?"

Tommy didn't get this. He didn't get it at all. "So? I've *done* that! Is there some kind of a law now against changing your mind?" He glared at Ambose, daring him to answer. "I have reached that time in life where I want to enjoy what I make," he said, biting off each word clearly and emphatically. "And if there's a law against *that* I'm going to counsel myself to ignore it." Tommy was puzzled, and more than that, Tommy was hurt. He had come bearing gifts, glad tidings and news of great victory. And the recipient of it all was sitting back, stone-faced, thinking it over.

"You can always find an excuse, Jim," he said, letting his disappointment show. "You're a big boy now. It shouldn't be that hard to cut the umbilical cord." Across the desk, each of them leaning back, they checked each other out, Ambose looking to see whether Tommy had really meant what he thought he meant, and Tommy looking to see whether Ambose understood how much he had meant it.

How long, Tommy asked, making it as explicit as possible, were he and Nevins going to play that game of theirs, whatever it was? "What the hell did you do," he said, "take an oath of undying fealty or something? Do you think you're going to walk into the sunset together, him with his Boss Man plate welded across his chest, and you dragging your famous doghouse behind you?"

If that was supposed to get a rise out of Ambose he was in for another disappointment. Jim removed the cigar from his mouth and blew out a stream of smoke. The remote, standoffish attitude that had so disconcerted Tommy hadn't changed. "You keep talking about some game. I'm not playing any game here that I know of."

Tommy groaned. Tommy not only groaned, he went through all the preliminary symptoms of swooning right there in the chair. And then he laughed. There was something so brazen about anybody being so disinterested in all that money, so unwholesome really, that he just had to laugh.

"I'm not asking you to try criminal cases if that's what's bothering you," he said suddenly. Not unless a case happened to come into the office that he wanted to take. "And," he hastened to inform him, "there are some innocent accused, you know. Whether you want to believe it or not." The enthusiasm, never very far from the surface, came bubbling back. "Jim, take my word for it. You'll never know what the real pleasure of the practice of law can be until you've walked out a man you know is innocent."

What passed between them then had eight years of friendship—and sometimes less than friendship—behind it. "What makes you think I'd believe you less," Ambose asked finally, "if you said you wanted me in for old times' sake?"

Tommy insisted he had said that, and that it went without saying anyway, but Ambose was coolly shaking his head all the while. All Ambose had heard was something about the Community Fund.

"It goes with it, that's what I said. Look, I'm not pitching pennies against the schoolyard wall, James. If you didn't also happen to be the best lawyer I know, I'd still love you like a brother but I'd save the Auld Lang Syne for New Year's Eve. You want me to kid you? I'm talking two hundred thousand minimum, and an equity that will make you a millionaire." Having reeled off the kind of figures that should have had Jim's head reeling, Tommy gave him the kind of boyishly engaging butter-wouldn't-melt-in-his-eyes smile that made it seem all the more preposterous that he could be dealing in that kind of money. "What do you want to do, Jim?" He grinned. "Examine my books?"

Ambose shook his head. No, he didn't want to be kidded, that was evident enough. It was also evident that something still seemed to puzzle him. Or, at least, give him pause. "I've got to admit that it's a very generous offer," he said.

"Oh, for chrissake." Tommy was really offended now, though not as offended as he knew he should have been. First Jim had made it sound as if he was after his life savings and now he was sounding like a college girl giving some jerk the brushoff.

Ambose could appreciate that it had sounded that way. "It's a lot of fucken money," he said, considering both the money and his words with the greatest of care. "That's what it is. A *lot* of fucken money. And don't think I don't appreciate it." He still managed to sound polite. Removed. Disinterested.

"Well, it wouldn't kill you to make some money for a change, you know," Tommy said. "I mean doesn't it *kill* you to see these slobs you can tuck up your ass come into court and you *know* they're making five and ten times what you make? How can you stand it, Jim? It used to drive me right up the wall!"

Ambose was giving that his very careful consideration, too. He had never really thought of it that way before, because he had never really thought about *not* working in the DA's office.

"There's this about money," Tommy said. Snappishly. "You can get used to it if you try hard enough."

"What?" Ambose's mind was made up. "And break the habit of a lifetime?"

344

"All right, Dhalgren," Ambose said. "So Deputy Phillips sticks his head back through the door and asks Sam if he wants to come to City Hall with him and see the Chief Justice. And where was the gun all this time?" Bannerman and Halpern, who had both been tensing up hoping that the question wouldn't be asked quite that way, groaned softly together.

As far as Bannerman was concerned, Ralph Dhalgren was the only witness who was going to mean anything all morning. As brother attorneys, and host attorneys at that, Tommy Mallon and Bo Gunderson had been perfectly willing to be interviewed about the luncheon with Sam, and so Bannerman had known ahead of time that the state was putting them on only to fill out the chronology of Sam Tabor's day and establish that he had been acting perfectly normal. Dhalgren, though . . . As the only man who could have seen Tabor leave the office without the gun and then turn back to get it, Dhalgren could hurt him. If he had noticed and remembered, Bannerman was going to have to cast as much doubt as possible upon his memory and, while he was about it, make it seem as if it had been the natural thing for Sam to have done, anyway. He had sat up in the corner chair most of the night, with his eyes closed, considering every possible angle of attack, and during the drive to the courtroom he had fired a barrage of questions at Halpern. As he had known when he arose from the chair last night, it wasn't going to be easy. Especially since he had to treat Harry Davies with tender, loving care until Harry delivered on the Model Penal Code question.

As far as Judge Davies was concerned, the trial had been moving along beautifully all morning. Having had his picture taken from every conceivable angle by every kind of camera known to man (except possibly a Brownie), he had the gloriously heady feeling that by the time he mounted the Bench again on Monday he would have achieved a national reputation and social significance that would bring lecture agencies swarming to his door waving contracts. And then maybe he'd accept Bannerman's agency's offer and maybe he wouldn't.

Harry had basked in the warming morning sun, dreaming of the good life that lay ahead, while Tommy Mallon was telling Hilliard Nevins how Sam Tabor and Miss Beyner had joined his table and exchanged some good-natured small talk until Bo Gunderson came along to turn it into a good-natured conversation between lawyers. Yes, Harry felt so good about the world and all its manifold riches that when Bannerman broke into his reverie by objecting to the witness being asked what, in view of all that good nature, his reaction had been to the news that his luncheon partner had killed Wilcke, he ruled, with a lightheartedness unprecedented even for Harry Davies, "Aw, let's have him answer it and get it over with."

Thus did Thomas Mallon's not very astonishing astonishment pass into recorded history.

Since part of Bannerman's long-range strategy was to convince the jury through sheer repetition that Ambose and Tabor were bosom buddies, he opened his cross-examination by asking whether it was Mallon's impression that Mr. Tabor was meeting his friend Mr. Ambose for lunch. He knew, of course, that the answer was going to be that it had been Tommy Mallon himself—and, it seemed, Miss Beyner—whom Ambose was meeting, and he knew how he could use that to advantage, too. "We had just finished a hearing in front of one of the state's more distinguished jurists," Tommy said without so much as a glance toward Davies or the glimmer of a smile. "And we were getting together to talk the thing over."

"How'd you make out?"

"It looks like I've got a winner."

"My," Bannerman said with a glance toward Ambose and the glimmer of a smile. "And here I've been thinking that Mr. Ambose is unbeatable."

Although Tommy Mallon had testified, more in generosity than in truth, that he knew Sam fairly well and had always liked him (at which Sam had glowed), Bo Gunderson stated that he had no more than a dim memory of Tabor going back to his own service in the district attorney's office. To the best of his recollection, he told Ambose, Tabor had said very little during lunch, which shouldn't be taken as a commentary upon his conversational skills one way or the other, considering that there were three lawyers at the table fighting for the floor. "And then when you joined us, Jim, Mr. Tabor very graciously made room for you by moving to the table alongside."

On an impulse Ambose grinned over at the defense table. "Don't let it worry you, Sam," he said. "I couldn't get a word in edgewise either." What the hell? It wouldn't hurt to have Sam feeling friendly toward him, if only on the outside chance that Bannerman might be dumb enough to put him on the stand.

He succeeded far more than he knew. With those first friendly words from Ambose Sam's spirits soared visibly. He chuckled in appreciation at both Ambose (who had already turned back to Gunderson) and Gunderson (who was looking at Ambose), giving every appearance of a man who felt he had been accepted back into their company and was therefore entitled to share their insiders' joke about Bo's ability to take over a conversation. Unable to make connection with them, he turned full around to the audience and smiled at Vera.

Nor did the glow from Ambose's little pleasantry diminish markedly while Ambose was hitting Bo with a series of questions phrased to show that Sam had acted perfectly normal. "Taking into account your vast and varied experience as a trial lawyer, Bo," Ambose asked, bringing it to an end, "was there anything at all in Sam's behavior to lead you to look upon him as a prospective client?"

Never a man to be out-pleasantried in an open courtroom, Norman Bannerman arose to announce in grave tremolo—with a sly glance toward the witness chair—that while the question could be objected to on constitutional grounds he would never be able to forgive himself if he went on record as objecting to a free ad for a brother defense attorney.

Bo himself did not share in the laughter. Quite the opposite, he ran his hand rather vigorously over the hard bristle of his white hair, somewhat embarrassed, it seemed, at these testimonials to his modest skills. "I hate to disappoint you, Jim," he said. "But I'm afraid my experience is neither so vast nor so varied that I can spot a prospective client from the way he slurps his soup."

Through the fresh burst of laughter, building upon the laughter that had just died, Sam peered across at Bo. He was, it could be seen, somewhat hurt and rather anxious. Ambose had folded his arms and was looking up at Bo from lowered eyes, doing all he could to help Bo reap the maximum rewards of his real skill, which was in getting laughs. "From your vast and varied experience," he said, "do you now want to answer the question?"

It was all very first-nameish and neighborly, but it was a lousy examination he was conducting. Not that Bo was balky or that Ambose was stiff. It was just one of those examinations that never quite seems to take hold. About the only thing that could be said in its favor was that it didn't really matter. The lawsuit could have got along quite nicely without Bo testifying at all.

Bannerman asked only two questions. "You didn't pay very much attention to Sam, did you?" and "Was it your impression that Sam had come there to meet his friend, Jim Ambose?"

To both questions Bo's answer was a blunt "No."

To save something out of it, if for his own satisfaction only, Ambose rose again and with a great show of coyness and a voice full of delicate irony—the two qualities he was least equipped to get away with—asked Bo whether he had been under any impression that Sam Tabor and this mysterious Jim Ambose whose name kept cropping up all the time were friends.

"No, Jim," Bo said with the utmost gravity. "I had no such impression."

In a thin whine, clearing his throat constantly and compulsively, Dhalgren told the Court, the jury and the audience how Sam had appeared in the sheriff's office to have his gun checked out and, under Ambose's tightly controlled questioning, about the departmental policy that had happened to bring him there on that particular afternoon. Ambose was not afraid to linger over the sheer coincidence that the biannual gun maintenance had fallen on the same day as David Wilcke's visit to Lowell. So forcefully did he drive that coincidence home that every member of the jury should have been able to see that Jim Ambose was one prosecutor who could be counted upon to lean over backward to be perfectly fair and completely aboveboard in laying the facts before them, never minding whether his own side was helped or hurt; and every lawyer in the courtroom should have been equally able to see that Jim Ambose was not only leaning over backward but doing a backward flip off the high board to save Bannerman the necessity of lingering over it even longer and driving it home even more forcefully on cross-examination.

Ralph Dhalgren had more than the ordinary reasons of a first-time witness for being nervous, for although he was a prosecution witness Ambose's interrogation had not been at all sympathetic. Dhalgren had let his silky blond hair grow just enough in the week or so since Ambose had gone over his testimony with him so that the first beginnings of a mane fell down his neck. Just enough, it could be seen, to show on which side of the barricades he stood in the Revolution.

As with most witnesses, though, the act of testifying—of feeling every eye upon him and hearing reasonably literate English sentences emerge from his mouth— was enough to overcome his early nervousness. By the time Ambose got around to asking him where Tabor's gun had been through all the entrances and exits he had been describing, Dhalgren was perfectly at ease. Which was more than could be said for Bannerman and Halpern as they waited for him to answer.

Dhalgren's answer was that the gun had remained on the counter where Sam had originally placed it.

"And that's the little counter on either side of the swinging gate?"

"That's what it is."

"And then what did he do?"

"Well, he picked it up and put it in his pocket and left."

"Now let me see if I have this straight. Deputy Phillips came back and asked if Sam wanted to go with him, and Sam picked up the gun and put it in his pocket and left with him?"

"That's it."

Bannerman and Halpern hardly dared to look at each other. Dhalgren's memory of the way it had happened didn't hurt them at all. All Ambose was going for, it became plain, was the not very damaging fact that since Sam was going to have to come back the following day anyway, he could just as easily have left the gun there with Dhalgren. "But knowing he was on his way to see the Chief Justice," Ambose said, trying to make it sound as ominous as possible, "he carefully picked up the gun and took it along with him. Is that it?"

Bannerman objected. "The witness didn't say anything about carefully. I'm not sure how you pick up a gun carefully or carelessly. If Mr. Ambose will take that word out, Your Honor, we'll withdraw the objection and let him keep leading the witness to his heart's content."

The Court, amiable as ever, asked Ambose if he wanted to be a good fellow and take the word out.

Ambose, as unamiable as ever, said he'd be glad to if he could replace it with "premeditatively."

Before they could go around again, Davies took the word out for him, and Dhalgren answered, "Well, he just picked up the gun like anybody would pick up a gun that was going to put it back in their pocket. That's all I can tell you about it. I'm no mind reader."

The scornful turn of the lips had been barely perceptible, the surly little side-glance had been turned decorously away; but taken as a whole, taken with the last, gratuitous comment and that hair—that hair!—it was enough to make Bannerman wonder whether there might not be still a greater prize to be taken here. Instead of letting him go on cross-examination with one question and a hearty godspeed, he signaled Hal and Tabor in for a quick huddle. "Think fast," he snapped. He rapped his knuckles sharply on the table. "Do I let him go or do I try to hack a little more of it away?"

It was Halpern who was being asked, of course; Tabor just happened to be sitting in between them. (The question did have its effect on him, though, and Bannerman noted it out of the corner of his eye and filed it away in a corner of his mind. The glaze had come back over Sam Tabor's face; he had removed himself as if he had no idea what Bannerman was talking about.) "Let's be greedy," Hal said immediately. He sneaked a quick look up at Dhalgren, who was staring straight ahead, brushing the side of his hair lightly with his fingertips. "What's to lose, Norm?"

What's to lose? Bannerman's mind echoed. He remained where he was, facing away from the witness chair, twisting the diamond ring back and forth on his finger while he sorted out his line of attack. He would remind Dahlgren, in a tone of light bewilderment that would solicit his help in straightening him out, that he had testified that Sam had picked up the gun when Deputy Phillips invited him on the ride, thereby freezing the picture in the jury's mind—as his minimum goal—that the two acts had occurred simultaneously rather than consecutively (when was the operative word there) and then, firming up his voice, pitching it to a plane somewhat higher than mere suggestion if somewhat lower than flat assertion, would ask him whether it was at all conceivable that it might have been just a little before that.

If Dahlgren stated positively that it could not have been, that would be that. He'd thank him and run. If not . . . wouldn't it be something, Bannerman was thinking as he turned his eyes up to the witness, his forehead wrinkling lightly, if he could put that gun in Sam's pocket before Booker stuck his head back in.

Dhalgren's forehead wrinkled somewhat more heavily while he was considering it. "I'm giving it to you to the best of my memory, Mr. Bannerman," he answered.

Not very promising. On the other hand, the gate hadn't been slammed shut either. "I know you are." Soothingly. "I don't want you to take any of these questions as reflecting the slightest slur upon you, sir." Warmth. "I have every faith that you are a candid witness desirous of nothing more than to tell the jury what happened to the very best of your ability."

He came to his feet, rubbing his jaw. "Follow this with me, if you will. The deputies come in. You tell them Sheriff Stringfellow isn't there. Deputy Merck says he's put in a long day and he's going home. Deputy Phillips says he'll resume his post of duty at City Hall. All this time they're talking more or less to you, is that right?" His eyes remained on him. Admiring. Expectant. *See how important you are, Blondy. You're the man they're telling their troubles to.* "And so your attention has been diverted toward them. Away from Sam and toward them. Wouldn't that be so?"

"Well, I was talking to them and they were to me. Sure."

"And Sam was talking to no one, and no one was talking to him?"

Dhalgren thought that one over briefly and then, shrugging as if it were too trifling a matter for him to waste any more time on, agreed.

"Good enough." *Watch me closely, Blondy. Never take your eyes off me. See how I'm visualizing this right along with you.* "Deputy Phillips leaves for a brief moment and comes back. He asks Sam to come along with him, and Sam leaves, too." *You will notice, Blondy, the heavy cogitation that rests upon the famed attorney's brow as he struggles to aid you on your journey down memory's slippery highways and byways. Note now the hand extended fraternally toward you.* "Now, think about this." *Slow it down. Modulate. Let the picture sink in.* "Isn't it just as possible that Sam put the gun in his pocket in that moment when Phillips left . . . or was in the process of putting it in his pocket during the short interval when Phillips was out of the office?"

Dhalgren's fingers went to the side of his hair again as dutifully he reexamined the scene for Norman Bannerman. Concentrating deeply, he drew his bottom lip over the top one, which gave an odd turtle-like appearance to his sharp little face. "Well . . ." Uncertainly. "That's not how I remember it . . ."

"But isn't it possible?" *Take my fraternal hand.*

Nevins broke in, with unusual mildness for him: "Now we'll just have to object to this, Judge. The witness gave his answer. He gave it on direct. He gave it to him again just now. We all heard it."

Unfurl the indignation, mates! Hell hath no Wrath to match my Fury! "Your Honor, I must pro-*test* these scandalous and outrageous tactics most vehemently!" *Owwww . . . too much fury, damnit. That wrist still hurts; at my age these little things don't heal so quick. That round-round up round-round down little slut Dot whateverhername was. Another round?* "The district attorney has become so unnerved at the sight of an honest witness sitting here that he has been panicked into this crude and palpable attempt to influence his testimony!" *Are you going to let him do that to you, Blondy, an up-against-the-wall rebel like you? Naw, you're not going to let him turn you up, down and around. Not you!*

At the moment Blondy was so bug-eyed at the sight of this out-of-towner berating the district attorney that Bannerman decided to give him an eyeful. By which he meant that he would feed his eyeballs what they would undoubtedly expect to see coming out of the television screen. Staunchly righteous, stalwartly erect, Norman Bannerman leveled a finger of scorn at Hilliard Nevins and cried out that having already been hobbled by the antiquated rules that had denied him the opportunity to interrogate the police witnesses before they took the stand, he could only express his profound shock and dismay at the unsavory tactics of a district attorney who in order to advance his own selfish political ambitions would so shamelessly and cynically harass an American lawyer when the opportunity to question such a witness in the courtroom, under oath, finally came.

Out of his side vision he was able to see that Dhalgren had taken a small red comb out of his pocket and was absently and rather idly running it through his hair. Bannerman didn't have the foggiest notion what that meant, but when the tirade ended and Judge Davies told him he could answer, Dhalgren gave his hair a kind of toss, and there was something in that gesture, something determined and defiant, that told Bannerman it would be an excellent idea to approach the witness stand pronto. *I'm on your side, Blondy. Look at me. These guys aren't so tough. These guys can be beat up on just like anybody else. You and me, baby. We'll show them the way, huh?*

His hunch was right. As he was repeating the question from that close up Bannerman caught the mean, self-pleased glint of the man he was looking for lurking behind the window shade. The chronically disgruntled underling. *I should have recognized you from the beginning, Blondy.* He would have, too, if he hadn't been concentrating so intently on the question about the gun. Wasn't it remarkable how even Norman Bannerman, skilled as he was in the art of diverting a witness's attention from his true target, could himself be diverted from a witness's true nature by fixing his mind in a wholly self-induced hypnosis upon something else. He knew Dhalgren now. Knew him by the mean vindictive glint of the assassin who has his man between the gunsights and is like to pissing his pants at the thought of all the damage he could wreak if only he didn't have so much shit in his blood.

Be bold, Blondy. Us against the Establishment, huh, baby? "It's possible," Dhalgren said. "I don't think so but I wouldn't say it wasn't possible." He hesitated for a moment, thinking about it. "There wasn't much time, you've got to remember, between the one and the other.

Come on, Blondy, don't run out on me now. You can't beat these bastards if you've got shit in your blood. Do you want to be a clerk all your life?

Softly. "It is possible, though?" *We're two of a kind, aren't we, Blondy? Flashing and glittering like two comets through the universe. Can't you look into my baby blues and see the lively times we could have together, you and I? Grooving down life's lubricious highways, scattering our contempt for pigs like Ambose and Stringfellow to the round-round winds?*

"It's possible," Dhalgren said. "Yes, it is possible."

You see? Everything is possible. (If you'd have unbent enough to give me one more chance, I could have shown you that all things were possible.) Can I push this any further? What's left? Nothing's left. Too bad. (That's what's so tragic.) The way I've got this guy eating out of my hand I could have him swearing that Sam had left the gun there overnight. Hey . . . ! He'd almost forgotten. "I would imagine, Mr. Dhalgren, that there must be some kind of regulation in the sheriff's department against letting a gun out of your possession?"

There was. Most emphatically. It was a violation of departmental regulations punishable by a suspension of up to fifteen days.

Norman Bannerman passed the witness back, quite soberly, with a polite little nod and returned, quite soberly, to his seat. As Norman Bannerman sat back down, it was with a tranquil spirit and a low and throbbing sense of exhilaration. He had made it come out different. Where else but in a courtroom could you make it come out different?

What a marvelous thing was the law! The murderer was not a murderer (the jury said he wasn't). What had been done had not been done (the only witness said it hadn't been). What had been said had not been said (inadmissible evidence). Norman Bannerman had turned back the clock and put the gun in Sam Tabor's pocket fifteen crucial seconds earlier. Norman Bannerman had reached back into history and made it come out different. *(Didn't I tell you? And I didn't even have to tell you, that's what's so tragic. It was inadmissible evidence, but like a good boy I told you, and what did you do?)*

Nothing was sweeter than to make it come out different.

To make it even sweeter, Ambose became so overbearing while he was trying to get Dhalgren back to his original testimony that Dhalgren got his back up and answered that the more he thought about it, the more it seemed to him that Sam had put the gun back into his pocket just before Booker Phillips came back. "I'd say right now there's about as much chance of the one as the other," he said, and said it with a cool, challenging look that warned Ambose that if he wanted to keep pushing him, it was probably going to get tipped the other way pronto.

Of all the ways to abandon lost causes the best by far was to make it appear that you had achieved your purpose and were packing up to go home. To end it on something resembling a meeting of minds, Ambose tried to get Dhalgren to go along with the proposition that since Sam always kept the gun locked in his own desk, regardless of the regulations, Dhalgren could just as easily have kept it in his desk overnight if Sam had asked him to.

Dhalgren had to concede, after some hesitation, that he could have, but then, as if he were afraid Ambose might have tricked him, he lashed out spitefully, "But if he'd asked me I'd have advised him against it. They're pretty chicken in that office when it comes to regulations."

Ambose looked to the jury box to make sure they came to their own conclusion about the reliability of a witness who would talk that way about the man he was supposed to be working for and then, waving his hand toward the Bench as if he were dismissing him as too contemptible to waste any more of their valuable time on, announced that he was through with the witness—serving notice on Ralph Dhalgren at the same time that Jim Ambose wasn't ever going to be through with him.

But that only brought Bannerman back into action with an expression of hope, stated with just the right mixture of wistfulness and apprehension, that the witness was not going to be harassed for having had the courage to come into the courtroom and tell the jury the truth. And though he didn't quite petition the Court to place Dhalgren under its personal protection, he did express every confidence that if anything untoward occurred, Dhalgren would not falter in his obligation to inform the Court and, perhaps, the local watchguards of the press.

Dhalgren gave Ambose the hate-look right back before he deigned to leave the chair, demonstrating to his own and hopefully everybody else's satisfaction that he wasn't afraid of any of them. Just at the point where he turned to the door he had to walk right past Stringfellow who, by another of those coincidences, was the next witness. Ambose, who had been following Dhalgren's exit march dejectedly, watched even more dejectedly as each of them studiously avoided the other's eyes. He'd handled that with all the finesse of the village blacksmith. Now Stringfellow would never be able to get rid of the snotty little bastard.

Nevins' voice came to him as through a bale of sandpaper. "Nice going, Ambose." Nevins was slumped deep into his chair, with his hands shoved all the way into his pockets and his feet extending straight out under the table. "A few more like that and the jury will get to wondering which one's on trial here. That's what we're after, a nice confused jury." Looking right past Ambose, he rasped, "You take the next one, Pawley, and see if you can show him how the professional lawyers do it."

"Goddamnit," Ambose said. "Somebody should have told me the guy was a faggot."

Sheriff Stringfellow was being put on the stand to identify the receipt Tabor had signed when he had been issued the gun, and while he was sitting there Ambose had intended to give him his chance to set the record straight, all stamped and official, as to the purely nominal nature of Sam Tabor's connection with the sheriff's department. No problem there. Pawley knew all about it.

What Pawley didn't know was that Ambose also intended to qualify Stringfellow as an expert marksman so that he could ask him to estimate the odds on a man who had never fired a gun before getting off as perfect a shot as Sam Tabor had. (Stringfellow was prepared to put the odds conservatively at a thousand to one.) Ambose's thinking in that regard was that it would be far better, tactically, to discredit the weakest link in Sam's story before Bannerman's psychiatrists testified, on the theory that if the jurors had been preconditioned not to buy that part of it they would also tend to look with a somewhat more skeptical eye upon some of the other things Sam had told them.

All Ambose had to do, of course, was to tell Pawley about it, a temptation he was able to resist with ease. To hell with them! Ambose would put on an independent expert as a rebuttal witness later. He owed Colonel Chatnick of the National Guard a favor anyway, and he'd tell him to set his fee good and high.

Without a word to anybody, not even to Jake Foxx, Ambose got up and left the table. The final witness of the morning was going to be Sergeant Alvin Larino, who had been Tabor's contact with the police department for the past three years, and since Pawley had interviewed Sergeant Larino, Pawley would have been conducting that examination anyway. Nevins had released Ambose from active duty for the morning? Ho-kay, Ambose was now releasing himself from the courtroom. It was, after all, a lovely morning for a leisurely stroll to City Hall. As for Hilliard Nevins . . . well, Mr. Nevins would find out he wouldn't be back when he figured it out for himself.

Despite the parchment skin and bony hands, and the gaunt and still unhospitable angles that had been left behind when the character of the younger face departed, Mike Karney still managed to look, as far as Jim Ambose was concerned, as if he should be wearing a derby and smoking a cigar. Even lying on the old worn leather couch in his office, with a dainty little piece of pastry held daintily in his hand and a tall glass of milk on the platter alongside. What made it all the more remarkable was that there had also come into Ambose's mind the memory of the time his father had sent him on a trip upstate so that he would get to know his kinfolk, in this instance a granduncle who was supposed to be dying. The old man had a leech he kept in a bottle, like a pet, and every evening just as the sun was going down he would go out to the old sun-baked porch and set himself in his old rocking chair and clamp that leech onto his arm and croon to it all the while it was sucking out the blood that was poisoning his system. No sooner had Jim come back on home than they had received word that he had sure enough died, leech and all. He could remember about that so well—just where he'd been when he'd heard it—because his uncle had held the leech out to him the night before he left, and challenged him was he man enough to take it to his own arm without flinching and prove he was a real Ambose and Jethro's true son. Knowing all the time he was leaving Jim with naught to do but roll up his sleeve and hold out his arm—how old would he have been then, nine? ten?—and though his insides had fallen right out of him and he had been ready to scream from out of the top of his skull with fright, he had looked right back into the old man's cruel slate-gray eyes, never once flinching. And when at last the leech was pulled off him the old man had told him with approval, "You're a sure enough Ambose, Jamey. And I'll be right sure to inform Jethro he has no need to provoke himself on that account should he ever be of such a mind, and you have my word on that." And so Jim's first thought upon being told that the old man had gone and died on him was that it had all been for nothing to take that damn leech onto his body, because now his pa would never know. For if there was one thing his pa didn't hold with, it was those who were always bragging on themselves, and all the more if they were young'uns.

"Yes, go right ahead," Karney said. "I see by the newspapers where they're saying the fight between James Ambose and that behemoth of a clotheshorse from Chicago is to be likened unto a fight between a matador and a billy goat, and if I had my full strength about me, James, I can promise you on my solemn oath I'd write them back scathingly that a matador fighting a billy goat is liable to end up with his arse all colors to the wind like a reddy-arsed baboon." He cackled happily, just laughing away, with his eyes opened wide to see whether Ambose was laughing, too, when all of a sudden he stopped in mid-cackle, remembering something.

Up off the couch he jumped, over to the phone he chugged. "Clougherty," he shouted. "When I told you I would be accepting no calls today, you understood I wasn't referring to that certain call we were talking about, I trust? You're to put it right through to me, you've come to understand that by now?" He beamed his sweet old man's smile at Ambose from over the receiver. "But nobody else," he said in a voice to match the smile. "I don't want to be disturbed whilst I'm having such a delightful conversation with James Ambose from the district attorney's office concerning my testimony of this afternoon down at the new courthouse. Ah, that's a good boy. You're as bright as a new-born penny."

On his way back to the couch he tapped his head ruefully. "I got to be as loony as everybody says to be jumpin' up and down like this, a man with a heart attack and thousands of good years of prime living ahead of me playing bouncy-ball on the beaches of the Riviera, and I am imparting that information to you, James, only because I can trust you not to reveal the good news to the vituperative editorial department of the *Morning Globe* or the murthering professors of the city council. Eat your cookie, for the luv of heaven, I could never abide a picky eater."

With Karney standing sternly over him Ambose ate his cookie.

"Be patient and be kind," Clougherty had said as he was leading Ambose up through that incredible litter and salvage and red velvet and sticky heat. "If he wanders, let him wander. He'll get back to the subject in his own good time, and when it's over you'll find that as wild and disjointed as it may have seemed at times—and (he had smiled) as crazy—it will all tie together." Whatever other infirmities were on him, the old boy sure wasn't gone in the lungs.

While Karney was settling himself onto the couch, an operation of considerable magnitude, Ambose jumped the gun on him to explain that once they had got the little matter of his testimony out of the way, they'd have plenty of time to sit back and talk before they had to leave for the courthouse.

"Exactly!" Karney boomed. "It's David Boone Wilcke you've come to hear about, and not the memories that come howling at an old man in the night. What I can tell you about David Wilcke is that we both rose to the heights of our success because we were shameless demagogues, which is a word I neither disown nor disdain, for what does it mean, when you get to the gist of it, except a man who knows what the people want to be told?" Ambose crossed his legs and sat back. "It's all a matter of a smattering of knowledge about human nature and memorizing the slogans. Why, it's easy as pie once you get the hang of it."

The impressive, meaningful stare: "I'm going to let you in on a trade secret, Ambose, that all of us know and never get around to telling each other, and if I tell it to you at this time it's only because I hear you're a man of ambition for elective office and I've taken a small shine to you. You can write this down on that paper of yours. Are you ready now? No society can function . . . Is there no ink in that pen of yours, now? Ah, that's a good lad . . . No society can function for forty-eight hours—democracy included, and especially and in particular—unless the common man damn well does as he's damn well told—vote, drink your beer and shut your trap!—and he wants it that way nor would he have it any other, knowing as he does that he don't know beans about nothing, only he'll take to it more kindly if you'll keep reminding him every now and again as to how he's running the whole shindig from his job down in the boiler room at the gas works." He smiled wanly. "That's just a little of joke of mine, Ambose. Pay it no mind. Ahhhh, you wouldn't believe the things I've done for votes in my time, would he, Clougherty?"

Clougherty was coming through the door carrying another platter of pastry, and two more glasses of milk, but before he picked up the old platter and laid down the new one, he handed Karney a slip of paper, creased down the center so that whatever was written on it would be well shielded from anybody else's eyes.

Karney's head jerked up and a silent question flew between them. "Your friend decided to drop by," Clougherty said. "I told him Mr. Ambose was with you." With Karney continuing to stare at him, Clougherty found it necessary to add, in the kind of deliberately noncommittal tone that is used to mask the fact that information is being imparted, that he had suggested that his friend might want to phone up from downstairs but that his friend had preferred not to disturb him.

It was amazing how quickly displeasure could turn into pleasure. "These now," he said looking over the pastry, "they're turrible for me. But if I'm to drink their damn nutritional, vitamin-enriched milk, I'll plague 'em with my cookie jar. The doctors know what's best for you, for the luv of heaven, but to hell with them." Having finally picked out a cube of pastry with layers of fudge, he stopped it at the edge of his lips and with a fiendish little grin said, "You're wondering is the old man as loony as they say in the verminous, falsifying editorial page of the *Morning Globe,* that he's talking about getting votes instead of picking out his casket and making out the guest list for the funeral?"

The old man's quick, darting look caught him cold.

"Perhaps," Ambose said frantically, "we should get to your testimony while we still have time. I wouldn't want to rush you, sir, but it's getting pretty late."

"For the luv of God, man, the courthouse ain't going nowhere! I can tell you everything you have to know about that whilst we're driving down and we'd still have time to stop off at the Central Mall for a game of parchesi." Karney was regarding him as if he were wondering whether he had any brains at all. "You're to understand that if I'm impartin' to you at this particular time some of the political wisdoms and truisms I have garnered from forty years of public service, I have my reasons. Now do you want to know, for the luv of god, or don't you?"

Did he want to know? Did fish want to swim and did birds want to fly? With all his conjecturing—and all his impatience—the one possibility that hadn't come within voting distance of Jim Ambose's mind was that Mike Karney wanted to become his political sponsor and advisor. His own fond dream, his carefully guarded secret, come true! And Mike Karney had asked did he want to know! Breathing sincerity, exuding earnestness, Jim Ambose said, "Yes, sir."

Resuming his pacing, Mike Karney set off again on his free-floating monologue. "Now my father was only a poor hod-carrier," he began, "but I learned as a very young man that if there's something you really want in life, you got to lie and cheat to get it and keep on lying and cheating if you want to keep it. Like it or lump it, take it or leave it, that's the way of the world as I came to it, and just between me and you and certain sanctimonious despoilers of the public welfare well known to the both of us, I don't think it's going to get that much different just 'cause I'm leaving. Because I espied that philosophical truth early and took it to heart, I had some success in life, public and private." He had held the presidency in the palm of his hand early one morning in a Philadelphia hotel room, and he could go to his grave knowing that he had played that hand right. He had loved one woman and had the good fortune to marry her, and a fit wife she would have made for a king. The prowling stopped, the voice grew silent, and Big Mike Karney, all roads turned inward, looked back across the years to the golden days with their golden triumphs.

The moment passed and Big Mike Karney, come back home, turned his old and shriveled face to his hopeful protégé Jim Ambose and asked, "Now what kind of a God is that to get down on your knees to and say thanks for the past favors and would you please give me another sock on the snoot? Do you suppose Eli Chobodian is thanking God because he's so happy he finally got to be a turnip?"

Jim Ambose, who had been listening eagerly to this wondrous tale of power and romance in high places, blinked several times.

Karney was watching him like a hawk. "Eli Chobodian was a lean-eyed man like you, James. He had the good bones like you, and a good head to go with them." Like a hawk. "In this very room it was I told Eli I could get him the appointment as chief justice of the Appeals Court, young and Republican though he was. My May always liked him better than the others, she always had a taste for quality—God only knew what she saw in me. 'That nice Armenian couple, why don't we have them over to dinner again?' and never once saying, 'So I can have some people of refinement and honesty to grace my table for a change, and a conversation, if my luck is in, which holds more stimulating food for thought than whether McNamara or Granadella got away with packing more sand in their cement last week.' I've always thought it would have been different if the children had come, but who knows about such things anymore? Who can say yes or no?"

Turning on his heel so that his back was not entirely to Ambose, Karney pointed a lean, knobby finger toward his desk and intoned as if he were a keeper of the dusty books of history that it had been in this very office, at that very desk, that Eli had said to him, "No deal!"

" 'No deal,' he said to me, and him nothing but a foreign immigrant of a night school lawyer!" The unbelievable exchange of that day, capped by the outrageous rejection, rose up again to infuriate him. "And every other lawyer and judge in the state is willin' to get down on his hands and knees and poke the smallest peanut in all of creation by his nose through an acre of horse manure piled five feet high." And that, he said, sniffing around like a hungry dog, just to get a smell at it. "A hundred enemies I was ready to make, and more, and he gets up on his high horse like I'm insulting him for suggestin' it."

He had crouched down slightly, his knees slightly bent, and as each new word dropped heavily from his lips he cranked himself up a notch. "What . . . the . . . hell . . . did . . . he . . . think . . . I was . . . doing . . . it . . . for? The . . . Armenian . . . vote?"

Jim Ambose liked to think that if it was worth knowing, he knew it, and he had never heard that there had been the slightest friendship, or even acquaintance, between the Chobodians and the Karneys. Why would the Democratic boss have offered his number one patronage plum to a young Republican, and even more tantalizing, what in hell had gone wrong? Thinking back on some of the phony rulings that had come down since that drunken bum Foster McAlester had become chief justice—which was for as long as Ambose had been in the DA's office—it made him sick.

"McAlester?" Hadn't Ambose been listening to a single word Mike Karney had been saying? Had it all gone in one ear and out the other? "You don't suppose I could go home to my May and say, 'Well, what's for supper and did the President call and, by the by, I couldn't give the appointment to your handsome, dark-eyed young Armenian, he being too high-minded and stubborn a man, so I did the next best thing and gave it to a drunken, whore-chaser of a highway robber.' " The brogue, lilting: "It took a Republican governor, you'll be happy to know, James, to come up with the intriguing notion of trottin' down to the city dumpyard with a ten-foot pole and a chothespin on his nose to see if he couldn't dredge himself up a chief justice from out of the swill pile."

The chance to get a good one off at the expense of the enemy had left Karney in such a good mood that he scratched his jaw reflectively. "I wouldn't mind being a Republican myself right now, for that matter, with ivory tusks stuck out of my mouth. God gave the big dumb pachyderm the sense to find the burial grounds when his time had come, in compensation I would hazard as a guess, for making him so wrinkled and ugly." His prowling had taken him in front of his couch and, suddenly grown weary, he began to lower himself. "It's all in the size of the brain, don't you see?" he said, tapping his head. "God gave hisself the last laugh as always."

The small, crooked smile remained pasted to his face, like a self-inflicted wound, while he considered God's mean little wraths and petty malice.

"Oh, he was a better man than you or I will ever be, Ambose, J." But, he confided, as one political man to another, too damn honest in a hoity-toity, self-righteous way for Mike Karney's taste. "One small leetle matter of no consequence what-so-ever, and he'd have gone to the Appeals Court as chief justice and left his mark on his times, and so what does he do but get up on his high horse and end up in the Criminal Court, no better than a piece of pudden-pie like Harry Davies. Whilst those of inferior mental capacity are jumping up ahead of him so they can tell him what a dunce he is for saying 'Sustained' when he should have said 'Overruled'—tsk, tsk, tsk—and why doesn't he see if he can't get it right the next time."

While Ambose was marveling that the ghosts at that desk could still be clanking, Mike Karney's eyes came back to him. For all Mike Karney's weariness, which seemed as dry as dust, the gray slate eyes were purposeful and hard.

"Turnips or ivory husks, James," he said hoarsely, "it's all the same in the end. It's all ashes to ashes and dust to dust. What the hell's the sense of it? What's it all about, for the luv of God? We're born of the wild ride and a shaking of the salt and it's all up-and-at-'em and hurray-for-me, for they'll be shaking the ashes over you soon enough, won't they? Ah, yes," he said, taking comfort from a new thought. They'd be shaking the ashes over the malicious editorial writers of the *Morning Globe,* proud and vainglorious though they be, and who'd care or have known the difference? "David Wilcke left his mark, give the devil his due. Always give the devil his due, James. It's the wise course for a man who wishes to advance himself in politics to give every man what he has the power to take without you."

A look of extreme self-satisfaction slipped over him. He lowered one bushy eyebrow at Ambose and he was once again the wise pol of old sitting down to deal out the favors. "Though it might surprise you, James, I have my friends in places high and low. What I should know, they let me know, don't kid yourself about that, my bucko."

The shrewd, knowing look with its air of intrigue gave Ambose the feeling stronger than ever that Clougherty had been absolutely right—that all of this could be tied together, in some natural order, if you could pull it apart and sift it out and put the pieces back together at you leisure.

The little eyes were on him, gray as slate. "I speak of the pachyderm, in case you've taken to wondering, because he has other attributes which you might find worthy of consideration. You take the biggest, dumbest pachyderm and tie him to a truck to lug the lumber, and he's not so dumb he doesn't know he's no more than an instrument of labor and not a forest ranger with a hat on his head and a union card in his pocket and time-and-a-half for overtime." Gray as slate; intent and watchful. "Do you catch my meaning there? The one thing dumber than a pachyderm is the poor dumb beast, keen otherwise in mind and body, that don't know the difference between the carpenter and the hammer. The pachyderm, with a brain no bigger than a pea, is not so dumb as the hammer that thinks if it works hard enough and drives the five-penny nails straight, it's going to be turned into a dues-paying carpenter. Do you understand the gist of what I'm saying there? Do you perhaps catch a glimmer of my meaning?"

"Yes, sir," Ambose said, speaking up right sharply. For it seemed to Ambose that Karney was telling him that if he was going to help him become district attorney he had better not turn out to be as stubborn as Eli Chobodian, to whom he bore, in certain other regards, an unfortunate resemblance. The mayor wanted him to understand from the outset, it seemed to Ambose, that the political decisions and strategy were to be left in the hands of that master carpenter, Michael T. Karney. And Ambose was willing. Crazy as a loon Michael T. Karney might be, but he still had friends and he knew how to use them. If it should ever come to a quick showdown between himself and Dee Pawley, Mike Karney would be a powerful force to have behind him.

"We'll say no more about it then," Karney said. "Nor about Elijah Chobodian, either." As far as Eli Chobodian was concerned, Karney was willing to give Ambose his personal word that he was a good and saintly man, even though he had been done in by the one flaw in his character. "It stultifies a man, don't you see," he said, "to be stuck in a job beneath his worth?"

And now, he said, heaving a great, strained smile, he had better lay himself out and take a leetle nap to prepare himself for the coming ordeal before he dropped dead prematurely from old age and ruined the doctors' lunch for them. "They haven't found out that me and buffalo are extinct yet, so why tell 'em? They live in a world of their own, those fellows."

Mike Karney lay quite still. Not weary really. Floating in a void would be more like it. I'm talking too much, he thought. I don't have to tell him all of this. I've passed him the word, and now it's his turn if he's the honest man he's reputed to be by all reports. But what does it matter, for the luv of god? He thinks I'm balmy and he's probably right. *My ghostly father, I me confess, first to God and then to you. (Was I such a bad man, though?)*

"Seven children we lost, James. I had this feeling that my May was blaming me and that if I'd do this one fine shining thing . . . why, wouldn't that be enough to straighten it all out? Not that she ever said anything. It just kind of come over me one night that if her God, in His infinite wisdom and mercy, as she would say, was so set against blessing our home with children, good woman though she was, it could only be in the way of punishing me for my wickedness. And it come to me, that being the case, how could she not know it too? *Where are all our children, May? Where are the dear children to comfort me in my old age now that you have left me? (In all my life, with all my power, I only did a hurt to one man out of the maliciousness of my nature.)*

"It just kind of came to me in the dead of night that I could make it right with her and God both by taking the highest office I had and giving it to her dancing Armenian. Why, what merciful and forgiving God could ask a man—soaked as we all are in sin—for more? Just give it away in a way that would do me no good, and maybe a little bit of harm, as an act of contrition and charity." *One little baby to hold up by the feet, squalling. One little chick out of the brood of seven? That wasn't asking so much that I can see. (In forty years of public service—forty-four if you want to go back to when I was ringing doorbells for Shaper Dolan—did I ever once go back on my word? Doesn't that count for something?)*

"For if she was right, and while I'm a disbelieving man myself the possibility had to be admitted for the mere sake of argument, except that it was a curse on me and all of mine, what else could be the reason?" *With all the love and care we had to give them; with all the kiddoes running around barefoot and snotty-nosed in India and the like, without what to eat? (I had my commitment to keep with Fat-Arse Hawkins, I asked nothing for myself. It was not my fault our deal fell through. It was the fault of that black-hearted Armenian.)*

It was two months later, Karney said, peering at Ambose through the opening between his fingers, that the seat on the Criminal Court became open. He'd offered that one to Eli, too, which satisfied May, she thinking he was doing her Armenian a favor. " 'No deals,' says he. 'I'm my own man.' Oh, he was the great one for being his own man. 'No deals,' says I. 'Your own man you are.' " *And*

*good riddance, I've buried him forever, I showed him. (Hail, Mary, full of grace
. . .)*

"It was all those coincidences come together at once, like a black cloud had slipped down over our heads and all our luck was out together. "The caliber of judge we had in the Criminal Court those days—though not so low as now that they're elected—it was putting a giant in a hut with the pygmies. Oh, he was something to see in those days, was the young Elijah, come to clean up all the wickedness in the world once and for all." *You knew he was something special the first time you ever laid eyes on him, didn't you, May? There at Harry Buckern's First Ward Ball in the glittering, polished ballroom of the old Dubonier Hotel— it was the first affair ever held there, the original grand opening, and Harry Sylvester's orchestra with all them violins. And you hadn't even wanted to go. Do you remember how I had to coax and plead with you? "Your Dancing Armenian." We laughed about it all the way home. "I do believe that shy little wife of his was beginning to get jealous," I said. Do you remember that, May, and how we laughed? By god, weren't we all young together those days? By god, didn't we have some romps! And now he's nothing but a turnip, and there on Aspinwall Avenue where the Dubonier used to be there's one of them office buildings made all out of glass and such a pleasure to the aesthetic senses, but only if you should happen to be a member of the Window Washers' Union. (The Lord is with you . . .)*

"His own man. That's how you can always get 'em, Ambose, should the occasion ever arise where that bit of information might be of use to you. Just by being his own man he was going to wade into that stink-swamp and turn it into a garden paradise, the damn fool. For his good wife's sake, I hope he's got the good sense to get down on his knees and thank God he didn't end up with the stink all over him." *He was the only man I ever did a hurt out of meanness, malice and jealousy, and not the political exigencies for which it was nobody's fault but their own if they weren't fully prepared, and the will made out. (And blessed is the fruit of your womb, Jesus.)*

His own man, was it? And wasn't that a laugh. Who was their own man? Mike Karney, at the top of his power, had spent half his time tending to the problems of the people who gave him his power, and the rest of it, it sometimes seemed, tending to the people who wanted to take it away. You want to be your own man, go live on a desert island and pick coconuts. And even there you'll have to fight the monkeys for them.

"His own man" had sat on his little Criminal Court Bench like the King of the Gypsies and to-hell-with-you-all, until David Wilcke made the deal that put him on the Big Bench in Washington and turned the whole ball game around on him. Instead of being told to let a robber off here and there because the governor owed somebody a favor, "his own man" was told to turn the murderers and dope peddlers loose in the name of the law because David Wilcke didn't like the way they'd been arrested. What a laugh!

Chobodian and Wilcke. It had all been spinning around in his head these last few days, like one of those giant pinwheels they used to have in the Fourth of July celebrations back in the Third Ward. David Wilcke had fallen dead at his feet in a puddle of blood; Elijah Chobodian had been struck deaf, dumb and blind while presiding over the trial of his murderer; and to old Mike Karney it had all come full circle, with himself sealed off right in the middle, watching it spinning round and round, all running together in bright, blurry colors and spitting out sound and fire. Mike Karney could have made David Wilcke President of the United States, and did Wilcke say, "No deal"? *Anything you want,* Wilcke had said. *All you have to do is name it.* He'd have made him Secretary of State and, Holy Mother of Mercy, could you picture that? Holy Mother of Mercy, we'd have been at war with half the world in six months.

So the no-deal man ends up being the man of the anything-you-want man, and where was the sense to that!

"So where's the sense of it?" Mike Karney suddenly asked Ambose. "I offer the man the highest seat on the state Bench and practically unencumbered, and he has to get up on his high horse, and just the two of us here, because he's got to show me he's so much better than everybody else. My father was only a poor hod-carrier, but when I was just a lad preparing to go out into the world he said to me . . ." Vehemently, flinging it away, he said, "To hell with that! You're an honest man in your peculiar fashion, Ambose. You remind me of Eli just a leetle in that regard, though I know full well some of the turrible things you do." *(And give a hip-hip-hooray for all of them, you murthering barstard.)* "Ambose, J., the top-listed name on the roster of the district attorney's office. So tell me, Ambose, J., what was it all about, for godsake? Wouldn't it have been better for him to bend to the minimum necessities and know there was an honest man like his own self to oversee the courts of the state? Isn't that what he wanted, for the luv of god? Or was it better to get up on his high horse so that it goes to Foster McAlester, who does what he's told, when he's told to, and then goes into business for hisself like the bartender at the Parker-Haley saloon, one for you and one for me, until Hooley Parker caught him one night with his hand in the till and turned him arse over teakettle into the swill pail?"

A giant spider was clamped over Eli Chobodian's face.

It had been there from the first moment, preventing him from moving. He had a drifting, dream-like memory of Kenneth Kenworthy moving in and out. Of others with their peerings and their probings. He could remember Joshua tiptoeing in. Everybody tiptoeing. Nobody speaking. Nothing stirring. A cold clear morning. Earmuffs. Insulation. Silence. Drifting.

He tried to tell them to stop their damn whisperings and no sound came. No muscle moved. The iron spider held him tight.

They were leaning over him. Kenneth leaning over and peering into his eyes. Mouthing words to Katerine. Did they think he slept with his eyes open? Did they think he was a child? He tried to blink his eyes to show them he was awake . . . and alert . . . and they could speak up and . . .

What was happening here?

Katerine bending over him, moving her lips silently. Fluffing his pillow but . . . Kenneth propping his shoulders but . . . Raising his line of vision but . . .

He could not feel it.

He was a . . .

Nor hear.

He was a . . .

Nor talk.

He was a . . .

Nor move.

He was a . . .

I have been overrun by the barbarians!

He could remember now the searing pain of the last moment on the Bench. He could see Sam Tabor sitting at the defense table, the flesh falling from his bones. Didn't they know that only Elijah Chobodian could save him?

Who was going to save Elijah Chobodian?

Didn't they know he was the only judge in the history of Brederton County who had not paid for his appointment?

What are they doing to me?

What did it matter now, his epic conscience? His mountainous virtue? His invincible morality?

I have been young and now am old and dying!

For it all he had the hunched and waiting shadow of the gravestone.

I have been happy and now am sad and dying!

As his reward, the root had shriveled instead of snapping off clean.

I have fallen, cold and brittle. Cold and brittle I have fallen!

Something had been pledged to him and not redeemed. What treason had been committed here?

I did nothing to deserve this! I am innocent!

The mighty oak had been gnawed and riddled, shorn of its plumage, stripped of its boughs. What was it Jim Ambose had once said . . . ?

Why me? Of all people, why me?

He had been a judge, and a good one. He had been a man, and not a bad one.

I ask the Court for fairness. I ask the Court for a two-week continuance so that I may finish my work. I have served this Court well! I ask no more than is coming to me.

Something had been frittered away, something of value.

They had abandoned it as soon as it was challenged. Jim Ambose had said it, whatever it was.

What did it matter?

It had all been a fake.

Irrelevant, Your Honor. The Puritan Ethic is no longer relevent.

He must remember that. There was no right or wrong anymore. He was not supposed to make value judgments.

They had lied to him. The spider was out of the bottle. The barbarians had been let loose in the land.

The fakes!

Put the spider back in the bottle, damnit! Put it back!

The torque has been sprung, Elijah.

That's an order!

It's too late, Elijah. The bottle has been opened. (What's a torque?)

Get him the hell off me!

When the bottle is opened, the spider will crawl. (Was he going to have to die without ever knowing what a torque was? Was that fair?)

Now listen, I mean this! Get him off me!

> This one thing you know, this above all
> When the bottle is opened, the spider will crawl.

Only what I deserve! Right now! Off!

. . . and crawl and crawl and crawl and crawl . . .

Oh, how they had lied to him. The law stands like a rock, they had told him.

The law above all, carved in marble, writ in concrete, encased in the ages. All else is writ in sand, they had told him. They had told him that, and he had believed them. What a joke that he had been allowed to live just long enough to see the law sink into the sand and be covered over with spiders.

What did it matter now?

Katerine had moved back into his narrow lane of vision, and it came to him again how remarkable it was that the woman's flesh had ripened and bloomed while the man's bones had brittled and dried, thinking as he thought it that never again would he take her in his arms. Never again be warmed by hers. Never. That life was gone. Over. No more now than the sound of children at play as heard once, long ago, through an open window.

How much had changed so quickly.

Katerine keeps watching him, looking for some faint sign of awareness. The spider holds him tight. A cold and rusty wind beats through his cave; the sludgy fluids chug through the rusty lines. What was that you were saying, Elijah, about the efficacy of sheer will? *Can't, Joshua? There's no such word as can't. Won't, you mean!*

He could not will himself to move an eye. Wiggle a finger. Twitch a lip. Flutter a nostril. Nothing.

He could not will himself back to life. He could not even will himself to die.

So sad she looks. So troubled. So desperate to find some spark that she can fan.

In his wallet there is a snapshot of Katerine in the bathing suit of their era. A girl so young, so fresh, so innocent, so pleading to be found pleasing. He had taken that picture himself just before they were married, and when he traveled in these later years he somehow always managed to come across it as he was sorting out his credit cards, and there were times when he had foolishly and secretly and guiltily kissed it in the privacy of his hotel room and said aloud that there was still no fool quite like an old fool. He would never see or kiss that snapshot again. Never again to do so simple and loving a thing as that.

He had visualized so often these past few weeks how rich and ripe their final years together would be. Grow old with me, he had intended to say, the best is yet to come. (Yes, that was Browning, too.) The good ripe years. The flooded stream, the evening's wheel, the nest; the faintly beating wings into the dimly fading sun. The candle's end.

All gone.

And he had never told her.

Ah, if only he could tell her now how much he loved her, that was the thought that broke through the frost. For five seconds' worth of life right now, dear God, I will give you all of eternity with my immortal soul thrown in. Five seconds against eternity so that I may tell her—can't you see how unhappy she is?—that on the worst day of our lives together the good had far outweighed the bad because she was there beside me.

She never judged me, she never endured me. She celebrated my joys and comforted my sorrows. And I never told her.

The tears are running down both cheeks, loosening the spider's grip. They see. They start. They point.

Katerine looks into his eyes, only she, and, her own eyes never wavering, her finger goes to his cheek, takes up the tear and brings it to her tongue so that she may taste the salt. She knows. *Put thou thy tears into my bottle, and it shall be as wine.* From her dear lips the finger goes to her wet cheek and—with eyes that never waver—carries her salt tears beneath his line of vision to his cold lips. But he knows. *Put thou my tears into thy bottle, and it shall be as wine.*

All right. His life is over; he has absorbed that now. What is to be done now must be done for her. His liabilities were known. What were the assets that remained? A lane of vision that had permitted him to see her one more time. The tears to tell her that he had. And one thing more. His major asset by far. His judge's brain, which still was functioning with a surprisingly high degree of efficiency (although he had better assume, as a prudent man, too badly damaged to be functioning as clearly as he thought).

The well-trained judge's mind would now be brought to bear upon the situation:

(1) He had put his affairs in order, which was more than could be said for most judges and lawyers, and Harry Brandt could be trusted to administer his estate well.

(a) He had seen too many cases where the estate had been sucked dry by a long, lingering illness that was either terminal in nature or where there was no hope that the patient could ever function as a human being again.

(b) There was no hope he could ever function as a human being again.

(2) He would not have her dragging herself back here, day after day, drying up her own life in his dead one.

(a) He would not despoil the memory of the good life they had had together.

(b) He would not put her through the agony of fighting off—as eventually she would have to fight off—the wish that he would die.

Those were the givens. The question before the Court was what the Court, in its totally disabled condition, thought it could do about it.

(1) Was there any conceivable way of asking Ken Kenworthy to put him out of his misery, once and for all?

(a) No, there was not.

(b) Would he ask him if he could? An intriguing question. Purely academic, of course, but intriguing. No, he would not. The Granite Judge would not as the final act of his life make his entire life meaningless by asking another man to break the law.

His mind was very clear on that. He had lived his life by the values he had cherished, and if those values had fallen out of fashion temporarily or, for that matter, permanently—yea, if they were discarded and trampled and spat upon by every other man on earth—he, Elijah Chobodian, the Granite Judge, believed them still. Flat on his back, bereft of all movement and stripped of his senses, he would die as he had lived, his own man to the end.

Yes. Let it all fall to rack around him. Let the law turn to ashes and the barbarians take over the land, he was still the Granite Judge, and with his granite will he would will himself to die!

She sits on the side of his bed and will not be moved. He cannot see her but he knows she's there. It's better that she be here, he thinks, because she never would forgive herself if she had left his side on his last day.

Elijah Chobodian, down to the bitter root, in the dwindling length of his days, the dwindling light of his mind, breaks his concentration one last time to wonder what it was that Jim Ambose had said. Wouldn't it be the final laughter of the gods, thinks Elijah Chobodian, as the breath burns low, if the last thing you discover at the edge of the graveside is that in all the things that mattered the fools were right and the wise men wrong?

Michael T. Karney settled down into the witness stand gingerly, like an ostrich waiting for an egg to hatch. He smiled an awkward greeting at the jurors, all of whom were looking at him with open curiosity, and for one terrible second there Ambose was afraid he was going to go off on one of his rambling speeches.

"You can stop worrying," Clougherty had told him. "The mayor still has that way of rising to the occasion." Easy enough for Clougherty to say. During the short drive down Karney had sat beside Ambose in the back seat, off in his own little world, and every now and again he would mutter, "Damn . . . damn . . ." to himself. You'd have thought he would have known by now that where Mike Karney was concerned, Clougherty was always right. No matter how long they were in the teeth, these old-time politicians never lost that ability to tailor themselves to their surroundings. When the old man mourned that Wilcke's death should have come as the result of a courtesy call paid to an old friend as an act of kindness, his old eyes grew rheumy. In describing how, partly blinded though he was by a flashbulb, he had seen a man step out at the bottom of the crowd with a gun in his hand, it was with exactly the right tone of objectivity.

"Can you identify the man who stepped out with the gun?"

Karney, who had shown a remarkable lack of interest in Tabor from the time he had walked into the courtroom, barely glanced toward the defense table. "I couldn't do that," he said. "I know who it was, the same as the rest of you, but I couldn't identify him off what I saw just in them few seconds."

As Judge Davies turned to ask Bannerman whether he had any questions he wished to put to the witness, you could see that he was asking him to keep his cross-examination as brief and painless as possible.

Fat chance. Bannerman had brought a change of clothing with him for the second day of the trial so that he could change from the dark blue English-cut suit he was wearing for the morning session to a shimmering green. He had called the nearest florist to have them send over by special messenger "one perfect white rose" for his lapel. Bannerman's reasons for insisting upon Karney's appearance were not very complicated. Mike Karney's emergence from the tomb would make news, and in the management of the public relations side of his case it was important to keep the momentum of interest rolling until he could put his psychiatrists on. It was here in the courtroom, though, where he expected to reap the greatest benefits. Bannerman's strategy, just as Ambrose had surmised, was to lay an atmosphere of madness over the entire trial by showing Karney up for the crazy old man that he was. The eyewitness crazier than the murderer! How many times was that going to come up in a lifetime?

But Bannerman had another, and highly personal reason, which neither Ambose nor anyone else could know about. During Karney's tenure as governor, Bannerman had sent Karney a series of telegrams urging him to commute the death sentence of a college student who was being executed for the murder of his roommate, and as the day of execution approached with not so much as an acknowledgment from Karney, the telegrams had become more frequent and more urgent. Until finally he was wiring that he was going to give him only six more hours—and then five and four—before he took drastic action. Governor Karney had sent the whole file of telegrams to the Bar Association along with a note asking whether they felt a man of such obvious emotional instability should be permitted to practice law, and Bannerman had found it necessary to explain that he had been drinking.

Sooner or later, Bannerman always said, he paid the bastards back. Mike Karney's turn had come. Bannerman's simple, vengeful plan was to not only show that he was crazy but to drive him to a complete emotional breakdown right there on the witness stand in full view of the entire civilized world.

It was, perhaps, the single worst miscalculation Bannerman had ever made.

As always, he bowed politely to the witness before he said, "While I regret the necessity of keeping you from the strenuous duties of your office as mayor, I'm sure you won't mind a few more minutes of exposure before a jury of potential voters." He drew the small gold watch carefully out of his vest pocket, and holding it as if he were going to time him, he said, "I think the Court could be prevailed upon to allot you three minutes."

Judge Davies gaped out at Bannerman, unable to bring himself to believe it had been anything worse than a bad joke, made in the poorest possible taste. Although even there . . . to ask the man who had seen Wilcke fall at his feet whether he wanted to make political hay out of it was more than even Harry Davies could understand or find it in his heart to excuse. Befuddled as he was, Harry couldn't think of any way to censure Bannerman without somehow making the mayor look even worse.

Befuddled not at all, Mike Karney slid back into the witness chair, tucked his chin into his neck and measured his foe. A brisk, reckoning light animated his eyes, followed by a rush of sheer sporting glee. The clash of battle was tonic to Mike Karney; the rough-and-tumble of platform debate his favorite battleground. By the time Halpern had printed MISTAKE in huge block letters on his pad Karney had already turned to the jury with a happy little snort. "Nothing wrong with this city except they're taxing the wrong people. That's got me by for forty years, it ought to get me by an afternoon with a lawyer." He flashed the politician's wink of a smile, which was really a call to arms announcing that they were all in the fight for right and justice together. The jury smiled back.

Those answering smiles should have warned him off right there, Bannerman thought later. (Where he'd gone wrong, he decided, was in accepting the *Globe*'s word that Karney was a doddering old clown the city couldn't wait to get rid of. To think that after all these years he could have believed the penny press.) Instead, he had attempted to absorb the failure of his opening gambit by protesting, all dimples and airiness, that the mayor seemed to have misunderstood him. "You could search the whole country over," he said, his hand pledged to his chest, "and you would find no man who has followed quite so ardently or admired quite so passionately your brilliant malversations of public office."

That was his second miscalculation. If the clash of minds was Mike Karney's tonic, the flung insult was the music that called the cobra up from its nest. The man sitting on the witness chair was suddenly a different man than Jim Ambose had spent the noon hour with. (It was a worse miscalculation than that. Bannerman had half-expected Karney to take it as a compliment. He had slipped it in so the press could chuckle over it in the morning.)

"Young man," Karney said, chiding him, "I was using that trick when you were still stealing pennies from out of your mother's pocketbook." The brogue came floating out of him so lightly as to amount to a public announcement that he wasn't about to waste any more of it than was needed to dispose of such a poor opponent as this. "If you think you're going to bedazzle me with vocabulary, as wily an old dog as I've got to be, I'm here to inform you, Michael Timothy Karney in the living flesh, that you're suffering from a figment of the pigmentation." (Jim Ambose couldn't quite figure out whether Karney had meant to say "imagination," was making a comment on Bannerman's dress or was enjoying some kind of private joke. Not, as Karney would have said, that it mattered. Nobody else seemed to have paid the slightest attention to it, probably because they were laughing at Karney's deliberate mangling of Bannerman's name.) "Now you have me here under oath, Mr. Bannister," he had gone on, "and from what my governess told me whilst she was cleaning the beeswax out of my ears on the way to packing me off to kindergarten this morning, that means I've got to tell the absolute truth." He rolled his eyes rather playfully toward the jury and let them see by the droll pucker of his lips that he knew exactly what they would be thinking. "As a politician of the old school, that puts me under a considerable disadvantage, as who would know better than you, and though it's a sad fate indeed to come falling down on a man this late in his life, I promise you I'll bear up to it bravely. The question was asked about my malversations in office, and whilst I have expressed a suspicion that the . . . gentleman lawyer (no more than half a beat had been missed) doesn't expect poor, uneducated workingmen such as ourselves to know when we're being insulted, I will confess, under oath and of my own free will, that among my more routine malversations of office I have been buying up lawyers for forty years like bunches of bananas off a banana boat." The courtroom was suddenly as quiet as a tomb.

Bannerman, caught unawares, came strolling into the well of the Bar, rubbing the back of his neck. The frontal attack which was going to send Karney into a nervous collapse had already been abandoned. You were hardly going to traumatize a witness who gleefully accepted the very worst things you could say about him and more gleefully turned them back at you. Bannerman's new plan was simply to keep the garrulous old man talking until he became a tiresome old windbag. And he wasn't even thinking of his case anymore, he was thinking about how he could come out of this looking like something less than an ass. The way to go about it, he decided, calculating rapidly, was to lead him into talking about his great days as a behind-the-scenes national power—he could connect it in through the famous Philadelphia Convention where Mike Karney had stopped David Boone Wilcke—and with any luck at all . . . !

Bannerman's smile went out like a peace-feeler. Like everyone else in the courtroom, he said, he knew that Michael T. Karney was the past, current and aspirant mayor of Lowell, but he also knew, perhaps better than—

"Past and current," Karney said, finding it necessary to correct him. "Oh, I can swear to that part of it in the best of faith, since it's right there on the record. Aspirant is where the river parts and we go sailing off in opposite directions. He sighed. He brightened. "You mentioned in passing a whilst back there, Mr. Bannister, that you were an incorrigible admirer of my political rise and fall, and if it's political office you're aspiring to yourself, why, I can tell you there's nothing to it. For a fine-looking man like you, with the voice of an angel and the vocabulary of a professor . . ." He looked at Bannerman for a moment like a suit salesman who was adjusting the shoulders and studying the fit. "Why, pshaw, it's as easy as pie once you get the hang of it . . ."

Karney had taken the interrogation out of Bannerman's hands once before by using the politician's trick of staking out the new area of discussion at the end of his answer, and Bannerman most certainly wasn't going to permit him to do it again. "That's a most entertaining narrative," he said immediately, "and most enlightening." And before Karney could make any comment on that Bannerman was asking him whether he and the Chief Justice had discussed the famous Philadelphia Convention during their conversation.

"Now that you bring it back to mind, Mr. Bannister, that we did." While it couldn't be said that he actually turned to the jury, he alerted them with a little shift of his eyes and a twitch of his shoulder that was as good as a wink. "I happen to remember it so particularly because we were talking about political life and the need for fresh blood at the time, and seeing as how you're aspiring to a political career yourself, it might be of some interest to you what I told him."

To make it all but impossible for Bannerman to divert him for a second time from his diversion, Karney had turned full to the jury, taking them all into his confidence. "In politics, you whomp yourself up an emeny," he said, "and then you beat up on him for the people, and that's all in the world there is to it. You stomp him and punch him and put out his eyes, and if the people yell Hurrah . . . why, you know you're doing a good job at it. It you've got yourself a good ugly enemy to take a hold on, Bannister, that's as fine a beginning to public life as anyone could hope for, but if you ain't, and usually you ain't, why there's no need at all to lose heart. You build him out of snow, Mr. Bannerman . . ." He looked at him long and hard, emphasizing through his silence that he knew his name well enough when he wanted to, and also that the blow was about to fall. "Yes, you build him out of snow, Mr. Bannerman, and on election day he just melts away." Having let his voice trail away right at the end, he sighed again, in memory or tribute to all those snowmen to whose fallen ranks the name of Norman Bannerman could now be added. As Bannerman relaxed along with him for just a second, the old man's head came popping back up and he said, "Elective office, now there's a horse of a different color. Would you like to know anything about my experience as governor?"

Most decidedly Bannerman would not. What Bannerman would like to do now was to swallow his pride and concede defeat in as humorous and gracious a way as possible.

In the brief interval while Bannerman was formulating his gracious and humorous withdrawal, Judge Davies stepped in in his innocent, bumbling way to inform the mayor that the Court was always receptive to whatever wisdom Mayor Karney might be willing out of the boundless generosity of his spirit to impart.

Ambose had a distinct impression of Mike Karney's eyebrows thickening in wisdom. "When I was governor, Mr. Bannister, I had seven executions, and if you're wondering why I thought that might be of peculiar interest to you at this time, you might ponder a little on the intriguing fact that it is the only time the governor becomes the chief presiding officer of the courts, unless you want to count pardons in on it. Now, I had been told by the other members of the Governors' Club, which is a trade union of sorts, that executions were the special anguish of our calling." He closed his eyes for a moment and smiled angelically. "I slept like a babe. Read about them in the morning paper and turned right over to the funny page. They'd all killed people, they all got killed back. The only perfect retribution I've ever found in life." Seeing the distaste streaming out from Bannerman's face, Karney pushed his own pugnacious little face forward. "I always wanted to trot on up to see one myself, but my campaign managers thought it would be undignified. And dignity, as you might not be fully aware, being from out of state as you are, was always my main stock and trade."

Into Jim Ambose's breast there flowed a pride beyond anything he had ever experienced before. He had brought Mike Karney into the courtroom, had he not? He had vouched for him. He loved that old man.

Feeling anything but love in his breast, Bannerman had moved to the line of least resistance, the shooting itself. With an air of patience and fortitude, he was asking Karney for just enough added detail to justify having insisted upon his appearance in the first place, though not so much that he couldn't send him back to City Hall, with his thanks, as quickly as possible. That didn't turn out so well, either. In going for the extra detail he asked Karney to describe how Wilcke's body had hit the ground, and while that didn't seem to call for much more than a simple declarative sentence or two, Karney turned his answer into a lesson on construction. Just so that Norman Bannerman would understand that he knew exactly what he had been up to and everybody else in town would know that Mike Karney was still in control of all his faculties and then some.

In addition to detailing all the problems that had been encountered in the building of City Hall back in 1934, he referred Bannerman every step of the way to the relevant page in the Seaforth Investigation Committee report, which had been impaneled by the governor to investigate fraud and graft in the city, "meaning," he said, "me." When he was finished he found it necessary, for one of the few times Ambose could remember all day, to pause. "In answer to your question, Mr. Bannister, when a dead body hits reinforced concrete costing forty-seven cents a thousandweight back in 1934 it is with a dull thud such as you might expect to hear if you dropped a side of beef on it. It is not a pleasant sound to recall, which may be why Mr. Ambose didn't ask me, but being aware as I am of the necessities of your high calling, I know your task is difficult."

Bannerman had left the well and returned to his chair reflecting that there was nothing for it now but to grit his teeth and show the jury that he could accept defeat more graciously than defeat had ever been accepted before in the recorded history of man's stay upon the earth. With Karney's testimony at an end, he sat himself down on the edge of the table and—doing his damnedest to look pleasant about it—said, "I have just asked my young associate, Harold Halpern, how I can get myself out of this buzz saw, and he has advised me to apologize and run for cover. I consider that sound advice. Will you permit me, Mayor Karney, to apologize and run for cover?"

Who could ask for anything more gracious than that?

"Son," Karney said, "you don't have to worry about a thing. You just pick up the *Morning Globe* tomorrow and you'll see where you won yourself a famous victory over a doddering and evil old man."

Oh no! If Karney thought he was going to be more magnanimous-in-victory than Bannerman was gracious-in-defeat he had another thought coming.

"In which case," said Norman Bannerman, "the editors will be in instant receipt of a letter suggesting that they pay a call at City Hall one of these afternoons and win one of those victories, too."

Mayor Karney left the stand with the applause of the spectators ringing in his ears. Hilliard Nevins, having grunted himself to his feet in tribute to the mayor's departure, said, "The state rests, Your Honor. That's our murder case."

Ambose caught Clougherty off to the side of the crowd while Karney was shaking hands in the corridor and told him that if he were Karney he'd call a press conference in the morning and announce he was running for reelection.

Without taking his eyes off Karney, Clougherty shook his head. After awhile he said, "I told you he can lift himself up for the occasion. I didn't tell you what it takes out of him." Between the testimony and the long talk with Ambose, the mayor was just about going to make it back to bed and he would remain there in a daze for about a week. Before he moved into the crowd to ease the mayor away Clougherty turned to Ambose with a look that made it clear that Ambose was as much of an intruder as the rest of them. "Drop in for a cookie tomorrow," he said, "and see whether he'll be able to recognize you." His eyes went to the still open courtroom door. "The only reason I don't go in there and kill Bannerman myself is that he did give the mayor a chance for one last little rally to warm the old bones, didn't he?"

"You didn't miss a thing," Ambose informed a reporter who, having rushed off to file his lead, had missed Bannerman's opening remarks. "Bannerman got up and said his piece and the jury like to waltzed to the music of his words."

Bannerman had, in truth, described the wondrously coordinated psychiatric profile he was going to draw for them, with Dr. Harmon Medellia, their favorite son, laying a solid physical foundation; Dr. Nicholas Zacharias, who had so impressed everybody in his brief appearance in the bond hearing, constructing the basic psychiatric scaffolding; and Dr. Lionel Allbright, who stood astride the medical world like a colossus (and whose name Bannerman invoked with a reverence rarely heard outside a cathedral), then taking the stand to dissect the unconscious drives and compulsions.

His voice was low and throbbing and full of mystery. "With Lionel Allbright as our guide, ladies and gentlemen, we propose to strip the outer layer of skin and expose the deeper drives and swirling motivations that can compel an ordinary mortal to a mightier flood tide of passion than he would have dared to dream, from which flowed mightier consequences than he could have dared to plan." Spreading his hands across the jury-box rail, he promised them with a small, prim, come-to-the-churchhouse-meeting smile, that they were about to set forth on "an odyssey of our times, a journey into the mind and heart and—yes —the very soul of a fellow wayfarer, a brother human being."

He was in the process of reassuring them that they need have no fears because Lionel Allbright, the most famous navigator of those wild and churning seas, would be up in the wheelroom to steer them through, when Nevins broke in, very dry and terribly innocent, to ask, "Is it all right if I tell him he's making his summation a little early there, Judge? Will you tell him he hasn't Anchored-Away yet, and he's only supposed to be telling his passengers where they're going?"

Very virtuously and sorely tried, Ambose said, "We've already let him get away with bragging about who he's going to be calling on to testify. He's not supposed to do that, and if he's half the lawyer he's cracked up to be, he knows it. He's only supposed to be telling them what he's going to try to prove."

Harry Davies, however, had been listening in a very gog of admiration. Turning more gentle features upon Bannerman so that he would understand there was someone in the courtroom who could appreciate why Norman Bannerman rated top fees on the lecture circuit, he asked him—quite regretfully—if he couldn't possibly hold his statement more within the boundaries of what he was going to try to show.

That was easy. "I am going to show," Bannerman said, as if he couldn't imagine how anyone could have asked, "that Sam Tabor was in the grip of a compulsion arising from so deeply out of his unconscious that he was not in control of his mind or body during the act of shooting and could not possibly have known the difference between right and wrong."

There was another brief recess before Harmon Medellia arrived, wearing tennis shoes and the kind of old baggy pants and heavy-knit button-up sweater you might expect to find him wearing if you sneaked up behind him while he was raking up leaves. Frank Cowhig had found him out in front of the courthouse, engaged in zealous discourse with the evangelist couple, whose names—as everyone in Lowell knew by then—were Billy and Billie Hendinson. Medellia had managed to work Billy up to a state of apoplexy by setting forth his heartfelt belief that psychiatry and religion could be useful adjuncts to each other, a proposition which might not have seemed quite so inflammatory if the sign in Billy's hand hadn't read: Psychiatry is the WHORE OF BABYLON.

Medellia's testimony, which was also far shorter than Bannerman had planned, did succeed in settling some of the minor but by no means unimportant side issues of the trial. For one thing, it relieved Harry Davies of a considerable burden concerning his public image. For another, it let the lawyers know where the power lay in the jury box. Where Halpern was concerned, it stripped him, once and for all, of the fond illusion that he was going to turn the trial around by his brilliant concept (the only one of his suggestions Bannerman had incorporated into the basic defense) that it would be possible to turn a sedative into a stimulant by showing that Sam's failure to take the Librium pill that morning had left him in a highly excitable state of mind.

One thing it didn't settle. When Harmon Medellia stepped down from the stand Ambose was wondering more than ever just what the hell Bannerman thought he was doing.

Harry Davies took one look at Medellia while Peterson was swearing him in and decided that while he had been absolutely right in his decision to forego the pleasure of his pipe until the courtroom had settled into the kind of homey, casual groove where a pipe-smoking judge would go unremarked upon by the press, the courtroom had just become as casual and homey as it was ever going to get. As he turned back to the witness chair he saw Medellia going through his eye-rolling, slack-jawed routine, a sight so frightening in those normally dignified surroundings that he found himself asking, with real concern, whether he had anything in his eye. Medellia, not a whit offended, explained that it was a yoga exercise which relaxed the facial and neck muscles and left you instantly refreshed.

"Is that so?" As much to make the witness feel welcome as anything else, Judge Davies gave it a brief trial run, after which he commented for the benefit of the record—and the audience—that it could really make you dizzy till you got the hang of it.

The witness, having been qualified, identified a thick sheaf of papers handed to him by Bannerman as the report on the detailed physical and neurological examination that he and Dr. Allan S. Benswagner of the Phillips Brook hospital had conducted on the defendant over a period of three days, extending from June 29 to July 1. Reading directly from the report, Medellia testified that after Sam had fasted for a day they had collected blood and urine specimens and that all serology and urine tests had been negative. When he got to the neurological examination, the jury was privileged to learn that the subject had perceived the odor of tobacco in the right nostril and oil of wintergreen in the left nostril without difficulty, that his visual acuity was normal and that he had never used glasses or experienced ociplopia, blurred vision or visual defect.

With everybody at both tables and in the jury box sort of nodding along in the onset of the blanketing afternoon drowsiness, Medellia had practically tucked them in and sent them off to dreamland until Hilliard Nevins forced his eyes wide open and cried out, "Judge! Is he gonna read this whole twenty pages?"

The normal procedure, he pointed out hastily, was for the lawyer to just ask whether the vision and hearing and all were within normal range and have the witness either say that they were or tell them what was abnormal.

Well, maybe on your ordinary little murder cases. Grimly, and on occasion caustically, Bannerman argued that in order to fulfill his promise to guide the jury through the internal structure of a living, breathing human being ("an odyssey of our times," he intoned, as only Bannerman could intone), it was essential that he be given the widest possible scope in describing the physical plant with all its weaknesses and stresses. But Nevins had been stealing looks at the jury. Well satisfied that they were growing restive, he became, in turn, as homespun as only Hilliard Nevins could become. "These good folks," he drawled, "haven't been taken away from their jobs and families for any trip into outer space or internal combustion or whichever whichway he's gonna do it now." Putting on his glasses, he flipped the pages over aimlessly. "The tongue protrudes in the midline with free movements in all directions," he read, at random. "There is no atrophy, fasciculation or tremor." He let the pages fall back with a plop. "Now what do they care about that? Ye gods, we're conducting a trial here, not a college course in fasciculation."

"A show trial if the district attorney has his way!" roared Bannerman. "Well, I have more faith in these fine people than to believe that they can be hoodwinked into railroading this man to the electric chair without so much as a pause along the way stations to sip up a fact or two." The hard thin edge of moral censure that coated his features was visible throughout the entire courtroom. "The district attorney's idea of an intensive interrogation," he sniffed, lowering his gaze upon Hilliard Nevins, "is for me to put this witness on the stand and ask whether as a result of his extensive and detailed examination he found that everything was fine and dandy? A-OK? Hunky-dory?"

Now that the length of the report had been called to the Court's attention, Davies had been leafing through it with rising panic himself. As eager as ever to face up to his responsibilities, Harry swiveled around to the jury box. "Well, just how much education can you stand, jury," he asked, putting it to them fair and square. "Why don't you take yourself an informal poll and tell me which way you want to do it?"

As Number 11, the journalism professor, took a quick head count, draped his arm over the back of his chair and announced with practiced authority that they'd do it the usual way, the charade about the medical report was forgotten. For two days now both sides had been pestering the jury bailiff, Henigan, about which of the jurors seemed to be emerging as the leader, and now that George Washington Mondale had cleared that up for them so nicely he was going to find himself on the receiving end of a great deal of attention.

For the time being, he had managed to put such a severe crimp in Bannerman's time schedule that after Medellia had testified, in rapid order, that the cranial nerves, the motor system and the reflexes had been tested and also found normal, Bannerman tried to linger for as long as possible over the spinal tap. The lung puncture had been made on June 30, Medellia said, reading directly from the report again, and with the spinal manometer in place the fluid had been observed to rise and fall freely with respiration and coughing and straining. With a scornful side-glance toward Nevins, Bannerman then instructed Medellia to describe the laboratory procedures that had been followed in analyzing the two test tubes of clear fluid.

"Judge," Nevins drawled, with that maddening indolence, "just have him tell us whether everything was hunky-dory, huh?"

Apparently it was. Sam Tabor was just in tip-top physical condition for a fifty-two-year-old man who had been leading such a sedentary life, Medellia told the jury, and that took care of everything up through page 15.

Page 16 dealt with the electroencephalogram.

"We have come," said Norman Bannerman, "to a crucial moment in this trial. I will ask that the witness be permitted to describe the procedure in full before I ask him to give this Court his findings." Hearing no objection, he rubbed his hands together gleefully. "Are you with me, Doctor? Good. Let's go." And Bannerman did have a small surprise to spring on the prosecution. After drawing from Medellia the fact that the test had been conducted on a standard eight-channel Grass machine over two consecutive days, waking and sleeping both, Bannerman had him identify the EEG tracings, which were folded, accordion-like, in a cardboard stationery box. "These are definitely abnormal tracings," Medellia declared. "I found seizure discharges of a type and frequency which would be the equivalent of epileptic discharges, and of a type that are consistent with patients who have rage attacks."

"Rage attacks, doctor?"

"Attacks in which the patient is out of touch with reality and not responsible for his acts." The seizure discharges, he informed the jury, were in the form of abnormal peakings that had shown up on twelve different occasions while the subject was being recorded in the particularly sensitive slow-wave activity that comes when he is drowsy or in a light sleep.

At the first mention of rage attacks a small ripple of curiosity had passed down the prosecution table toward Pawley. Dr. Benswagner had reported to Pawley that the tracings were within reasonable limits. Nothing at any rate, that Bannerman was going to be able to make anything of after Zacharias' testimony.

Bannerman was pretty cute, though. Before he put the tracings into evidence, he had Medellia explain that in testifying that the abnormal peakings were the "equivalent of epileptic discharges," he had not been saying that Sam was an epileptic. What he was saying was that Sam had undoubtedly suffered a brain injury at some time in his life.

Q. And are you aware that Sam was a high school soccer player of outstanding ability?
A. Yes, I am.
Q. Is it possible, Doctor, that an injury rising out of that exceedingly rough and brutish game could have caused it?
A. Yes, sir, that is possible.

All of which meant exactly nothing. If it was possible that it was, it was also possible—as the state would bring out in cross-examination—that it wasn't. All

Bannerman had been doing with the soccer business was setting up a violent picture in the jurors' minds against which to view the harmless little squiggles he was about to show them.

Bannerman was more than cute. He was beautiful. Holding the stationery box in the palms of his hands, he marched to the jury box with the stiff-backed carriage and somber pace of the king's own pallbearer. He stopped. He looked. He held the open box out toward them for a long and trembling and historic moment. And no, it was not just a mile of graph paper he was about to unravel for them; he was, by god, about to reveal the unscalped head and exposed brain itself.

At the prosecution table the minds of the three lawyers were working in such harmony that while Marie had been marking the tracings for exhibit, they had come together for a huddle without anybody really having to call for it. As far as Pawley was concerned, Dr. Medellia had just given or been prevailed upon to give a highly insupportable opinion which Benswagner would dispose of in about two minutes.

Jim Ambose, who was hunched slightly over to bring his head down to theirs, clamped his jaw down and sniffed at the air. "We'll put Benswagner on," he said. "And maybe a couple of others, too." Maybe four or five. "He's played a bad hand there," he said with conviction. "He's handed us a weak spot we can attack."

Again, without a word being spoken, it was made clear that Nevins and Pawley were waiting to hear why. The one thing Bannerman had going for him, Ambose was only too happy to explain, was Lionel Allbright. By making Allbright's testimony part of a fancy three-pronged defense he was also making it dependent in some part at least upon the testimony of his other, not necessarily so credible, experts, the shithead.

And, he said, letting his eyes drift to Bannerman, the tracings were the only place where the evidence was right there in black and white. "The one place where you can put your finger right on it." He wasn't only giving them a chance to undermine the foundation of his case, he was giving them a chance to demolish it.

It would have been asking too much, of course, to expect that Nevins was going to be as impressed as Pawley so clearly was. "He's blowing smoke at us," the district attorney growled. How could they expect Bannerman to put Zacharias on the stand after this, he wanted to know, putting the question that had been sitting in the back of all their minds. Or did Ambose really think he was going to put a witness up there who would either have to contradict another member of the defense team or make a fool of himself by changing his testimony?

"You see what I mean?" Ambose said. "And he's impeaching his own expert witness in the bargain."

And yet, the feeling persisted, as it had persisted during Booker's testimony, that, as Nevins suspected, it wasn't going to be that easy. The feeling persisted, deep in his bones, that booby traps were being set up all along the way.

"This one," Bannerman was saying, "I won't even bother to mark, it's so prominent. Why don't you just pass it around and let everybody have a good look. I'm sure Nurse Bettlenork will be particularly interested in this one."

From the moment Ambose had heard that Bannerman had corralled Lionel Allbright he and Mollineaux had set about to meticulously research everything Allbright had written, always on the assumption that it was going to be a Freudian defense. Functional psychosis all the way. When Nevins and Pawley joined Bannerman and Dr. Medellia at the jury box, Ambose turned to Mollineaux and instructed him to get back to the office and scour through Allbright's works for anything that might indicate any interest, however remote, in any form of brain damage.

Unhappily for Halpern, the question about the tranquilizer came at the worst possible time. The audience had begun to fidget and cough during the complete lack of action while the lawyers were gathered around the jury box, and once the jury had come to understand that each of Medellia's "peaks" was going to look pretty much like any other, their interest had begun to slacken, too.

With the next question all that changed. The medical report had listed tonsillectomy and appendectomy as the only surgical procedures Tabor had undergone. "Wouldn't you call a circumcision after a certain age a surgical procedure?" Bannerman asked.

Medellia cleared his throat. Yes, circumcision was a surgical procedure although not normally thought of as such. The reason it hadn't been listed in the report was that Sam hadn't mentioned it while he was being examined, and though Medellia had found out about it subsequent to the examination he had not wanted to make any alterations or additions to the report as originally written. The distrustful sniff of a glance he directed at the district attorney could leave no doubt in anybody's mind why.

"As a psychiatrist, would you find that particular surgical procedure of more than medical interest?"

Gravely and wisely, Medellia answered, "I would find it of great interest, sir."

Pawley rose, none too certainly, to object that no foundation had been laid for that kind of testimony, and while Bannerman could have fought it through on two grounds—first, that Medellia was entitled to testify to what Sam had told him, and second, by promising the Court that he would connect it up later—he didn't. That last question had been planned as exactly that: his last question. Otherwise, he would have had the hospital administrator in Court to put the record of the circumcision into evidence.

Bannerman's scenario, as written for Medellia, had been to throw the tickler about the circumcision out for the jury to think about over the long weekend. Nick Zacharias was going to tantalize them a little further about Sam's sex life on Monday, and, if all went well, they'd be panting for Lionel Allbright to clear up the mystery for them when he strode to the stand, in all his magnificence, on Tuesday.

Bannerman glanced up at the clock. It was, goddamnit all, only 3:40. Ideally, if his time schedule hadn't been thrown off all afternoon, he would have asked the question at 5:00 sharp, wheeled lightly to the Bench and, with the merest pucker of a smile, moved for an adjournment. Bannerman had seen the snap and sniff that had come over the jury box. He could feel the tingle of interest in the courtroom behind him. *Goddamnit all,* he thought again. By the time the state got through with its cross-examination, the brief glimpse into the mysteries of the genitalia was going to be lost in a maze of technical jargon. Given this opportunity to turn the jury's mind—the whole damn country's mind—away from the horror of the murder and onto the strange behavior of the murderer for forty-eight full hours, would it not be negligence amounting to malpractice not to give them something more to slobber over?

Once more into the crotch, dear friends!

"As a psychiatrist, would it be of equal interest to you to know that Sam wasn't sleeping with his wife?"

No objection was forthcoming from the prosecution.

"Yes, it would."

Hearing the question, Sam had turned to Bannerman with the taut, high-strung whistling look that had become so familiar. Hearing the answer, he rubbed his hand over his eyes, almost as if he were trying to wake up, and, sighing heavily, began to massage the hard ridge above his left eye.

Bannerman was flicking his thumbnail off his teeth. His intention had been to open up one more corner of Sam's personality for public consumption over the weekend. No more. The problems of the marital bed or, at least, the first glimpse thereof, had been carved out for Zacharias, and who knew better than Norman Bannerman that these guys could be more temperamental than ballerinas? Medellia had been in on enough of the discussions to know exactly where they were going with it, of course, but he was also such a kook that you couldn't really be sure he wouldn't come popping out with some crazy theory of his own. *No,* he thought. *Let it go.*

"Would it be of interest to you as a psychiatrist," he said in a slow, wondering voice quite unusual for him, "in conjunction with and supportive of and in concert with what you know about the EEG tracings and the effect of the sudden withdrawal of the drug Librium that . . . uh, as a psychiatrist, Doctor, trying to determine the state of mind of the defendant at the time of the murder, would you find it of particular interest that he was no longer sleeping with his wife . . . that the reason for it was, because that had been a course of action, or lack of it . . . because he was following the advice recommended to him by a marriage counsellor?"

It was as if a wind had blown through the courtroom sweeping every eye toward Vera Tabor. Mrs. Tabor sat perfectly erect, a little stiff perhaps but no more than mildly ruffled. Alongside her Dr. Shtogren turned quite red.

Bannerman wasn't too happy about it either. That had been the most ungrammatical, disconnected sentence he had ever perpetrated in a public courtroom, and he would have given a great deal to have been able to expunge it from the record. His gaze, following his thoughts, fell not unnaturally upon the mature and buxom figure of the courtroom reporter bent to her notebook, and as it did he wondered—idly at first and then not idly at all—whether with a bit of romancing he might not be able to coax her into permitting him to edit it. And right behind that came the other thought—the dangerous thought that excited and stimulated him more than anything had excited or stimulated him in years. Once he had broken her in by getting her to let him edit something for grammar, why wouldn't he then be able to—you're damn right he'd be able to!—change something of more substantive value if the need should ever arise.

It wasn't the grammar that jolted Halpern, it was the whole line of questioning. Good god, he thought, they were going to get into that stuff, after all. And then he realized, with a sinking sensation, that the only reason he *hadn't* thought they'd be getting into it was that he hadn't permitted himself to think about it.

At the prosecution table Hilliard Nevins remained slumped in his chair, staring thoughtfully at the witness. "Let's find out what they've got," he grunted, just loud enough to be heard at the table. His jaws worked ponderously, much as they did when he was chewing on his cigar. "Until then, we don't touch this thing with a ten-foot pole."

Bannerman was debating with himself whether to lay the whole broad outline out for the press to feast upon over the weekend. Too many complications, he decided. Zacharias aside, Vera was in the courtroom, and it had been his intention to keep her and Dr. Shtogren away while her bedroom habits were the topic of discussion. Look at the jury, though. *Late though the hour be, no lack of interest could be discerned in the jury.*

"Dr. Medellia," he said, "do you know why the marriage counsellor thought it would be preferable for Mr. and Mrs. Tabor to sleep in separate beds?"

"Yes, I do."

"Tell us."

Dr. Medellia wrinkled his nose and sniffed rapidly, like a rabbit testing the winds. Bannerman waited stolidly, his arms folded across his chest.

"It was because of Mr. Tabor's sleeping habits."

"Tell us."

Dr. Medellia told them.

As he was telling them, the same common impulse that had swept all eyes toward Mrs. Tabor swept them the other way.

As he was telling them, Halpern gripped Sam's knee hard, under the table, to help him control the trembling.

When Bannerman was finished with him, Medellia was still so flustered that he started to leave the stand. Given that kind of opening, who could expect Ambose to resist the temptation to yell, "Whoa there!" or Harry Davies to have the strength of character to put aside the chance to get himself a cheap laugh by informing poor Medellia, however jovially, that despite anything he may have heard the Supreme Court had not yet gotten around to eliminating cross-examination.

Medellia, more flustered than ever, became embarrassingly apologetic. Judge Davies became gracious and indulgent and paternal. Ambose became sarcastic. In the general confusion hardly anyone noticed that at the defense table a grim and baleful Sam Tabor was talking to Bannerman, his head held so low that he seemed to be looking at him through the whites of his eyes. "I want to see you tonight, Bannerman," he said, in a high, strident voice. "And this time you'd better come."

Because if he didn't, Bannerman stood forewarned that Sam was going to send a note to Bob Stringfellow advising him that he had fired his attorney and wanted to talk to somebody about hiring a new one.

From Bannerman's easy, confident smile you wouldn't have thought he had a care in the world. "Why, sure, Sam," he said. "The time has come for us to have a little chat. You're absolutely right about that."

Ambose had pushed a note in front of Nevins:

Opening question. Is Sam able to exist in society and support himself and his family?

Nevins shoved the note aside without looking at it. His voice cracked out like a drill sergeant. "I take it you came running all the way down here in your track suit so you could show us the sockets of your eyes and tell us how come Tabor wasn't responsible for what he was doing?"

Medellia's whole body jumped in the witness stand. "My goodness," he gulped, holding his heart. "You scared me, yelling like that."

"My goodness," Nevins said, managing to mimic him and snarl at him at the same time. "Answer the question!"

That brought on a three-minute fight over courtesy, at the end of which Nevins, moderating his tone only slightly and his attitude not at all, scowled, "You're against capital punishment on principle, you gonna deny that, Doctor?"

It was just as well Medellia didn't, because Nevins was able to produce two papers Medellia had delivered at professional conventions, eight years apart, one entitled "Capital Punishment: Return to the Jungle," the other "Murder by the State: Last Vestige of the Jungle."

He knew Dr. Nicholas Zacharias, didn't he? "If you don't, I can have him stand up. I've noticed him hanging around the courtroom. Maybe you have, too."

Medellia had begun to clear his throat before every answer.

"Think he's any good?" Nevins barked.

Medellia cleared his throat five or six times. "I have a great deal of respect for Dr. Zacharias," he said, with a noticeable lack of enthusiasm.

Did he know what Dr. Zacharias had testified to at the bond hearing a little more than a month ago? "If you don't, he said there wasn't no chance at all this man had any organic damage there, anything wrong with his brain. No chance at all."

"Yes, that was before the recordings were made, Mr. Nevins."

"That isn't what I asked!" Nevins' voice had become a blunt instrument again. "Something wrong with your ears, too?"

Halpern slammed the table, enraged. "That's insulting!"

Nevins paid not the slightest attention to either Halpern or the Court. "Ya want to wiggle them or something to get them relaxed? We can wait."

To anyone who hadn't seen Hilliard Nevins in action before, the district attorney was a revelation. On the surface, he had no right to be in the same courtroom with Bannerman and Ambose. Where Bannerman's voice was full and resonant and, even at its softest, deeply penetrating, Nevins' voice came down with a heavy clunk. Unlike Bannerman, there were no undercurrents of excitement running in him. Unlike Ambose, he made not the slightest effort to engage the witness in civilized discourse, or even to elicit whatever information he might have. Still, as district attorney he came out of the gate with two enormous advantages. The first was that he was able to pick his spots, and in Harmon Medellia he had sniffed red meat. The second was that he was always seated directly across from the witness chair, on an eye-line covering no more than fifteen feet. His style was to slouch in apparent ease on the other side of the table and from that deceptively negligent posture pick the witness up by the scruff of his neck and beat him bloody.

Style aside, he was not only dogged but, when it became absolutely necessary, resourceful. Given his own track to run on, he didn't need very much more. Not for Harmon Medellia, anyway. When Nevins wanted to know how come Sam had never thrown a—what was it?—rage attack before, Medellia was emboldened to answer with a gently chiding smile that forgave him for not knowing what a district attorney could not be expected to know, "You don't throw a rage in that sense, sir. You have one."

Nevins all but jumped across the table at him. "Whatever it was," he shouted, "it never kept him from getting to work on time, did it? Did you ask him about that while you were at it?"

Medellia's reaction to being yelled at again (and right after he had tried to be so helpful, too) was to look hurt and reproachful and . . . well, kind of poutish and putterish.

When his hands had found their way into his sweater pockets, he turned to the Bench and asked if it would be proper for him to stand through the rest of his testimony. "I have always found when I was involved in the classroom situation that I felt much more at ease if I were on my feet when I was being attacked," he said. And with a great and simple and incredible naivety went on to explain that it probably had something to do with vestigial animal response, in the sense that the animal on his feet was that much closer to the instinctive response of flight, whereas the unnatural and restrictive sitting position left the vestigial animal feeling trapped.

Judge Davies peered down at him, genuinely concerned, genuinely wishing to be as accommodating as possible and genuinely mystified. Being mystified, he ran his finger around the inner shell of his ear, a not uncharacteristic mannerism that, under the circumstances, left the unfortunate impression that he couldn't quite believe what he was hearing.

Jim Ambose leaned back in his chair, hitched his pants and let his gaze rove in the general direction of Number 11. The others might be amused, and even reassured, at the picture of the professor whose head was so filled with book learning that on a practical level he was no more than a child, but to another professor it was a picture that should have made him cringe. While there was no discernible reaction from Number 11, Ambose did get eye-contact and a fleeting smile from Number 5, seated directly in front of him. Okay. Not bad for a beginning.

If the witness was ready to carry on, Nevins said caustically, he would ask him whether Sam had been having a rage attack when he killed Wilcke.

"It was consistent with it."

"That isn't what I asked."

"I couldn't know that."

"Well, you still haven't answered it, Doctor, but you're closing in on it. Why couldn't you?"

Medellia did look more in command of himself now that he was standing. To the astonishment of all five attorneys, he turned smartly in the witness stand so that he was addressing the jury directly. "What it is, you see," he said, taking them all into his confidence, "is that this isn't supposed to be in my part of the presentation. I'm supposed to be more like a technician, you see. Just laying down the foundation for Doctors Zacharias and Allbright to build on later."

The jury smiled back at him, letting him know that they knew all about that. A few of them even nodded. They liked him for it. Sure, they were a little embarrassed for him, but they liked him, that was the thing. And a jury that liked a witness wanted to believe him. Ambose and Pawley exchanged a helpless, groaning glance. Show them the lawyer who could find a way to stop a jury from believing what it wanted to believe, and you'd be showing them a lawyer who had a grand career in front of him.

But no. Ambose tapped Pawley lightly on the shoulder. Scanning the jury box, he had spotted one icy exception. Number 11. He had been right about that. Jim Ambose sat back in his chair, quite content that George Washington Mondale would chill the rest of the jury.

One accident had been neutralized by another accident.

Let the dice roll on.

Hilliard Nevins, whose attention never wandered far from the jury box, made a real effort to take some of the sting out of his voice. Now that Mr. Bannerman had brought it up, he said, putting the onus where it belonged, did Dr. Medellia happen to have an opinion on whether Sam had known right from wrong at the time of the act?

Dr. Medellia, of course, did not.

Ambose leaned over and whispered something into Nevins' ear.

Nevins pretended to brush whatever it was off. "Did you say he was taking a stimulant?"

"No, sir. I said it had the same effect."

"Just answer the question for a change, will you?" While Nevins hadn't exactly shouted at him, he did send him a sharp warning look, bringing to a premature end one of the shortest reconciliations in history. "What was he taking?"

"Librium."

Amidst the laughter, Bannerman called out, "Well, you did say to just answer the question, Hilliard."

Forced to be a good sport about it, Nevins pulled at his upper lip and admitted that he might have phrased his question poorly. "Is it a depressant?"

"Yes. I testified to that."

"You did, huh? I guess I didn't hear you. And is a depressant the same as a stimulant? I always did wonder about that."

"The same? Well, no. Of course it isn't."

"It isn't?" Having feigned surprise so badly, Nevins feigned curiosity even worse. "Is it the opposite of a stimulant, then?"

Medellia floundered and groped and flopped around. Nevins stayed right on top of him. Medellia tried to explain that what he had been saying was that it was the effect that had been comparable. And that if he had given any other impression, it must have been because he had been trying to avoid scientific language in favor of the somewhat looser usage of everyday speech.

"Tighten it up for us," Nevins commanded. "We're not all as smart as you are." By the time Bannerman got his witness back he was more than satisfied to settle for the simple statement that if Sam had taken his tranquilizer he would not have been as likely, in Dr. Medellia's opinion, to have committed the act of murder.

Even Halpern had to admit by then that his brilliant concept had been hacked away to practically nothing. Bannerman told him not to worry about it. Something about Sam having been on some kind of drug and not taking it on the day of the murder would remain in the jury's mind.

Nevins and Bannerman looked to the clock together. The time, Bannerman saw, was 4:40, which left little enough time to play with.

Grunting with surprise to find it was that late, Nevins instructed Pawley to wrap it up for him and, without a word to Ambose, went hurrying on out. Just outside the Bar gate he came face to face with Mrs. Tabor and Dr. Shtogren, who had, for obvious reasons, decided to beat the mob out, too. The district attorney greeted her solemnly, with sympathy and courtesy.

Judge Davies looked down to Bannerman, waiting to hear whether he was going to call another witness or move for an adjournment. Catching sight of Mrs. Tabor in the aisle, he gave her the kind of hard, lingering look, assessing her potentialities, that is reserved for a woman whose availability or bed habits have become known to you. Sam had fallen into something good there and all he wanted was the sugar titty, huh? Well, thought Judge Davies, puffing away at his pipe, there was no accounting for taste.

Vera Tabor glanced past Nevins, trying to catch Sam's eye, but Sam was turned completely around in his chair, talking in a low, excited way to Johnny Gerard. Gerard looked over to Mrs. Tabor, somewhat perplexed, and right back to Sam, his hands working in explanation and his eyes full of apology.

Bannerman's eyes, coming down from the clock, picked up every one of the exchanges. He had caught Sam's agitated ". . . and tell her I don't want . . ." He heard Gerard saying, much more clearly, "That's not up to me, Sam. You should have your lawyers tell her if you want."

Judge Davies raised his eyebrows and made a motion of impatience.

Bannerman narrowed down quite thoughtfully on the locked heads of Sam Tabor and Johnny Gerard. "Your Honor," he said. "The defense now wishes to call Deputy Gerard to the stand. We hope he'll agree to testify voluntarily." If necessary, he added, in a tone that established it was no idle threat, he could always send his associate down to the clerk's office for a subpoena.

From right alongside Bannerman, practically under his armpit, Gerard turned a slow, languid look up at him, and whether he was really that unapprehensive or just that frugal with his emotions was more than Bannerman could tell. If it was anything at all, he decided, it was the mildly contemptuous look of the man who wants it known that he is nobody to be trifled with.

Sam's reaction, as far as Bannerman was concerned, was more like it. Sam's whole body had stiffened, and he was sending a stunned and openly pleading look at Bannerman from around the back of the chair.

No, a little surprise never hurt. A great lawyer like Norman Bannerman walked into the courtroom with one great psychological advantage—a cultural advantage really—that far outweighed any mere geographic advantage the district attorney might have. Deep in the neural caverns where the conditioning process was ordered, the jury *expected* him—the residue of a thousand movies and television plays—to pull off an act of magic that would whisk his client off the stage and, at the snap of his fingers and the roll of the drums, present as the true culprit, the real murderer, who else but—

Until that moment of high drama arrived they would sit, patiently and gladly, through the early sequences. It was little enough they asked of him really, little more than a daily entertainment to remind them that he was indeed the Norman Bannerman they had read about and therefore the leading man in the high drama being enacted before them.

Bob Stringfellow, entertained not at all, came bouncing over to the side rail, chewing gum furiously and demanding to be told what was going on. It was Johnny Gerard who continued to fascinate Bannerman, though. Looking into those steely eyes, Bannerman had no difficulty casting Johnny Gerard as the gunman holding his gun on the dealer. What was not so easy to fathom was whether what he saw there was the icy glint of the born chance-taker or the cold menace of the natural hoodlum. Johnny Gerard's voice offered no clues whatsoever. "Why didn't you just ask me, Bannerman?" he said, without haste or excitement. "That's all you had to do." Holding his seat, he informed Harry Davies that he was on orders not to take his eyes off the prisoner at any time and "with the greatest of respect to the Court" he'd remain on his assignment until Sheriff Stringfellow, his immediate superior, relieved him.

No problem there. With one of those broad, theatrical gestures he was able to pull off so well, Bannerman invited the sheriff to find himself a replacement from among the hordes of deputies planted around the courtroom, and Stringfellow came slamming through the gate, with a growl and a snort, to relieve Gerard himself.

"Why like that?" Sam hissed at Bannerman. "Why? Johnny's my friend."

And that, Bannerman could have told him if it had been any of his business, was why. There had been something about the chumminess between his client and his client's jailer that Bannerman had found very disturbing from the first day. What he was setting out to do, as he also didn't bother to tell Sam, was to get his pal Johnny to say something that would make it possible for Bannerman to demand that he be relieved of his assignment immediately.

Sandy-haired, square-jawed, rugged and handsome, Johnny Gerard by his sheer physical presence seemed to dominate the witness chair. The answers to the opening questions, which dealt with his assignment to guard Tabor, came short and to the point, not grudgingly but with a reserve of disapproval. And yet always, as far as they went, rigorously honest. So honest that after he had answered, "Not to my knowledge," to the question of whether Sam had been booked before he was brought to the dispensary, his hand came shooting up like a traffic cop's: "Correction. No, he had not."

Sentence by sentence, tooth by tooth, Bannerman pulled out the story of Sheriff Stringfellow's reluctance to make any move until Tabor's lawyer was on the scene.

"When did you decide it would be such a good idea to strip down a man who hadn't been booked for anything?"

"I didn't."

"He did strip down, didn't he?"

"Yes, he did."

Bannerman knew all about the rectal examination, and though he put on a show of increasing horror as the facts were being developed, he was coming to the decision that it would do the greater cause no good at all to become indignant over submitting an unbooked man to such an indignity. Not when the jury knew that the unbooked man had submitted David Wilcke to the somewhat greater indignity of having his head blown off.

"And he was still in this unshorn condition when you discussed the shooting with him?"

No. Neither Gerard nor Blasser had discussed the shooting with him.

"That was big of you. Were you also thoughtful enough to inform him of his rights?"

"No, we did not."

Bannerman (slightly acerbic): "Why, pray tell me, did you not? And you can keep that answer as short as you like, too."

Ambose (slightly revolted): "He's answered all the questions, Your Honor. Full and complete. The jury's heard him. Best witness I ever saw."

The Court (slightly amused): "Now, now."

Gerard (impassively): "We were assigned as guards, not as interrogators."

"What did you talk about? The weather?"

"Some." There was a titter of laughter from somewhere out in the courtroom to which Judge Davies reacted with an unaccustomed sternness.

"When that subject of universal interest was exhausted," Bannerman asked, "are we to assume that you fell into a state of haughty and disinterested silence?"

"We talked about Tommy Mallon some. He had the idea there for awhile that Mr. Mallon was going to be coming along to represent him. Then we talked some, too, about how it had been a hard day on the sheriff's department. And there was a lot of talk about Deputy Blasser's dog."

With Gerard finally showing symptoms of loosening up, Bannerman had begun to edge in closer. He stopped in his tracks. "Deputy Blasser's dog?"

"Deputy Blasser has a seven-year-old police dog, name of Downtown. Deputy Blasser's dog, Downtown, gets talked about in the general conversation of the department because of his, uh . . . eccentric habits."

Since it was clear enough that he was going to make Bannerman ask, Bannerman asked, "Deputy Blasser has a dog in need of psychiatric care, maybe?"

Ambose (*sotto voce,* but not very): "Why? Is Medellia available, maybe?"

Without cracking a smile, Gerard said, "Deputy Blasser's dog, Downtown, has this habit of going into a saloon with Deputy Blasser and proceeding directly to the bar, of standing up to the bar on his hind legs and taking the bills, whatever bills might happen to be on the bar there. In his mouth, you understand? He'll pick up the bills in his mouth and bring them back to where Deputy Blasser happens to be sitting"—he glanced briefly at Blasser—"and drop them, you know, right there on the table in front of him."

The courtroom exploded into laughter, Bannerman along with everybody else.

"I've seen him do it," Davies chuckled, wiping the corner of his eye. "Dangest darn thing you ever saw. Stands there wagging his tail to beat all until Dick— Deputy Blasser there—gives him a sip of his drink. That right, Dick? And then that dang dog, he'll pick up the money and take it right back where he got it. Exact same spot on the bar. Smartest dang dog you ever saw in your life."

Bannerman, who had been shaking his head at the wonder of it all, beamed his appreciation at Blasser so that Blasser might be permitted to bask in the reflected glory of his remarkable animal (and so that the jury might be permitted to see Bannerman do it) and asked quite pleasantly whether the dog was for sale.

Blasser wiped the palms of his hand down the front of his jacket and waited until he was sure the sheriff wasn't going to place any restrictions on his answer. "I'd consider it," he said, with heavy deliberation. "But only to a person I knew could be trusted to get the money back to its rightful owners."

Bannerman made a helpless, disembodied gesture, and turning in the general direction of the witness said to nobody in particular, "Well, I seem to have angered the entire sheriff's department . . . and by pursuing my client's rights for him in the best way I know how."

From the witness stand Johnny Gerard said, "You haven't angered me, Mr. Bannerman."

For just the briefest of moments a smile came rising to Bannerman's face at having found a friend where he had least expected to. It had already begun to dim when Johnny said, "You disappointed me."

Bannerman looked into Johnny Gerard's eyes a second time. He had caught a glimpse of something sanctimonious there even as he had been turning. Something cold and rooted and disapproving. "I thought you were a man," Johnny Gerard said, delivering his final verdict on him.

Judge Davies was so startled that he didn't even reach for his gavel. "Johnny . . ." he said, looking wounded and concerned. Like everybody else around the courthouse, it pleased Davies to look upon Johnny as a sort of communal prodigal son. (Like most of them, if they had been up to admitting it, it was the legend of the swashbuckling, utterly fearless gunman that he really admired.) Unhappily for Harry, the high regard he held for Johnny left him in a very awkward position. While it was true enough that Harry Davies had to take a lot of crap from lawyers these days, there was only so much he could permit himself to take from a deputy sheriff. Or, for that matter, only so much he could take from Johnny without forfeiting the high regard he fancied Johnny had for him. "Deputy Gerard," he said, "you stand in contempt of court." There was a long silence, which rapidly became overhung with expectation before it dawned on Harry that having cited the witness for contempt he was now going to have to do something about it.

"Now, Johnny," he said, employing the first name this time so that he would understand the gravity of his offense, "if it's agreeable with Mr. Bannerman, you can purge yourself by apologizing to him and to the Court." The judge's soft, yielding face welcomed the prodigal son home again.

"If I hadn't meant it I wouldn't have said it." Square-jawed and uncompromising. "If I apologized for something I meant I'd be a hypocrite like the rest of 'em, and there's plenty enough of them around without me having to add myself to the list." He patted the arm of the witness chair. "With the greatest of respect, Your Honor, I've seen a lot of people sitting here, every kind in the book, and the ones I knew aught about, they lied when they had to. I always thought if I ever got to sit in this chair, I'd have enough respect for what it stood for to tell the truth. One way or the other."

Disbelief and dismay peered down from the Bench. What way was that to talk? There had been a million words spoken so far in this courtroom and there'd be a million more, God willing, and all he was asking Johnny to do was toss in a couple more.

To Harry's overwhelming relief, Sheriff Stringfellow came to his rescue by announcing that Deputy Gerard was being relieved of his assignment "as of this moment" and—since Stringfellow had nothing against words—that suitable departmental action would be taken.

Norman Bannerman strolled back toward Johnny Gerard, with a droll and skeptical smile curving across his lips. His original goal had been accomplished with ridiculous ease, but that didn't mean he was through. Not by a long shot. While Judge Davies was dithering, Bannerman had given himself an excellent line of vision on the witness, and he had seen—it had been impossible to miss—the fixed, self-righteous gleam, secure in its own unquestioned virtue. As Johnny patted the arm of the witness chair, Bannerman had caught the vengeful tightening at the corners of the lips. So that was it! The courthouse's prodigal son was blood-brother to the evangelists parading their hell's-fire, fundamentalist truth out front. Ohhhh no, it had not been by accident that Johnny Gerard had gone after the biggest card games in town. Not by accident and not for money. The only thing that puzzled him was how a clod like Stringfellow had been able to see that it wasn't a criminal he had on his hands but a natural-born, burning-up lawman.

A few strides short of the witness stand he planted his fists against his waist. "Well," he said, "everybody's so full of truth-telling around here. All right, Deputy Gerard, let's find out how much truth-telling you really want to do from that chair, huh? Is it or is it not true that you were arrested for armed robbery?"

Pandemonium in the courtroom! Ambose came zooming up off his chair, half a length ahead of Pawley and screaming twice as loud. The question was irrelevant! he roared. Libelous! he shouted. He wanted the jury to know that this officer had been pardoned by the governor, and that meant he had no record! And Bannerman knew it! Ambose's face was florid. His eyes were ablaze. "If we did something like that it would be an automatic mistrial! He's taking advantage of the state's statutory inability to appeal, and I want him censured by this Court and fined!"

In the midst of Ambose's ragings Sam Tabor tugged at Halpern and asked, in wistful and rather stupid wonder, "Why did he do that?" Harold Halpern could only shake his head to show that it was not only beyond his powers of analysis but beyond his powers of belief. Ambose was now demanding that the jury be instructed . . . no, not to disregard it, he didn't want it disregarded. He wanted them told flat out that Bannerman had told a lie! He wanted them told that Norman Bannerman was guilty of legal prevarication!

"Mr. Ambose," Davies said, "see if you can be quiet for a change, huh?"

In that one heightened moment when the room had gone absolutely silent, Johnny Gerard's calm, languid voice fell on the air. "Before anything else," Johnny said, "I'd like to answer the question that was put to me by the counsellor for Mr. Tabor, the defendant. He asked me was I arrested for armed robbery. The answer is yes, I was." Perfectly composed, never hesitating or faltering. "If he wanted to know how many times I committed the felony of armed robbery before I was arrested I'd have to petition this Honorable Court for time to think. I think I'd be able to count them up before I was through, probably, except it would take me a little time."

Judge Davies continued to stare at Gerard exactly as he had been staring at him through the entire recitation—as if he had just walked into a theatre and was trying very hard to adapt his eyes to the darkness. "I told you you're not to answer any questions unless—" Unable to understand him at all, Judge Davies gave up. Just waved the bailiffs back to their chairs and gave up.

Bannerman understood, though. Here you had the real fascination of the courtroom. Norman Bannerman had come strutting into the courtroom this afternoon, all spruced up and ready to pluck Mike Karney apart. Who would have thought the not-so-crazy old geezer was going to pluck him clean instead? Now enters Big John Gerard. In their wildest dreams, who would have thought the sheriff's pet rehabilitation project would be taking them into realms of truth-telling previously unheard of?

Nobody, that's who. No more than Bannerman or anyone else could have dreamed that they were about to witness one of Harrison T. Davies' finer moments in the service of justice. Addressing himself directly to the jury, Davies said, "This Court will now instruct you that Mr. Gerard has no record. I am going to inform you, on my own authority, that he has spent no time in prison and has a reputation equal to that of any law enforcement official in the city, state or country. As for the rest . . . well now, I will leave it to you, ladies and gentlemen, to draw your own conclusion on the kind of man he is."

That done, he shifted himself around and, drawing his gown across his knees, gazed reflectively out to the courtroom. At last, his eyes came to rest upon the men and women in the press rows. Leaning into his robes, his hands folded solemnly in front of him, he requested the press and media not to print anything of what had just transpired. As Harry Davies could do every now and then, he not only looked like a judge, he sounded like one. "I want to make one thing perfectly clear. I am not ordering you. I am making this as a request. I am not one of those judges, as you are probably aware by now, who believes that just because I happen to be sitting up here in a black robe somebody's given me the power to repeal the First Amendment or tell anybody what they've got to write." He pushed himself forward so that he was almost leaning against his folded hands. "Just between us here in this courtroom, the armed robberies were against Felix McPhait's card games, and while the law makes no distinctions . . ." He lifted his eyebrows meaningfully. "I just thought you ought to know that the robberies Mr. Gerard did commit, admittedly committed, back in his wilder days, that they were not against honest, law-abiding or, you might say, defenseless citizens. And," he said, glaring at Gerard with a strained affection, "if there were any, shut up. The Court is asserting your privilege for you."

Davies was finished. Ambose gave him an abrupt, congratulatory nod. From the press rows several reporters felt compelled to slap their notebooks shut in audible signal of their willingness to go along with the Court's request.

There could be no question but that it all added up to a stern rebuke for Bannerman, and as attention turned back to the attorney for the defense—there where he stood half-shadowed by the late afternoon sun—there was the illusion that he swelled up, grew taller, took up more space. Perfectly still, his arms crossed defiantly at his chest, he had all the appearance of a rider sitting high in the saddle. "Your Honor," he announced, "I now state for the record that these remarks, made by Your Honor in the presence of the jury, are so rankly prejudicial against myself as to eliminate whatever possibility may ever have existed that my client would be able to receive a fair trial. At this time, Your Honor, I move again for a mistrial."

"Mistrial?" Ambose squealed. "Why, you fat show horse, I'll mistrial you!" He laughed shortly through Davies' gaveling and gave his head a toss. "You and your dirty old diamond ring and your cockatoo haircut!"

Pawley hit him on the arm and whispered, "Relax." It wasn't really necessary. Judge Davies, his limitless patience finally exhausted, brought his gavel crashing down. The motion for mistrial was denied and Norman Bannerman turned, with relish, for his too-long-delayed confrontation with the truth-telling fanatic.

"We have come, unless I am mistaken, Deputy Gerard, to the fortuitous arrival upon the teeming dispensary scene of Sam's friend, your friend and the working girl's friend, Assistant District Attorney James Ambose?"

With Bannerman's questions assuming a heavy skepticism, Gerard estimated that Ambose's interrogation of Tabor had lasted for about an hour, that Ambose had warned Sam several times that he did not have to answer in the absence of his attorney, and that Sam had answered the questions quite willingly, regardless.

"All right, Deputy Gerard." The question came at him with a swift, business-like attitude that left no doubt they were right down to the burlap. "In your opinion did Mr. Ambose take advantage of their friendship?"

Pawley objected that Bannerman was assuming facts not in evidence, no such friendship having been alluded to by anybody except Mr. Bannerman.

"Good enough." Bannerman tossed his head at the witness. "Let's see what Mr. Gerard can tell us about that. Did it seem to you, Mr. Gerard, that they were friends?"

"They knew each other."

"Did they act like friends?" Bannerman demanded. Folding his arms across his chest, rocking back and forth on his heels, he added with a touch of glee that Gerard was the man who answered all questions truthfully, remember?

"They knew each other. I have no way of knowing how well."

Bannerman bore down on him. "In your o-*pin*-ion, Deputy Gerard . . . based upon your obser-*va*-tions, Deputy Gerard . . . did Mr. Ambose take advantage of their friendship or acquaintance or relationship or whatever mutual regard or association, however great or small, they may have had?"

Ambose didn't *exactly* look worried. But he sure looked interested. So did Pawley. The Supreme Court had ruled the use of psychological police techniques out of bounds. The very worst Bannerman would come out of this with, if he got the answer he was looking for, was a good-looking appeal. The best he could come out of it with was enough to make Ambose shudder.

Johnny hesitated. Whether the hesitation was involuntary (as Bannerman thought), the psychological block the mind throws up against a lie; or whether Johnny, as a conscientious witness, was giving a minimum of thought to a complicated question (as Ambose hoped the jury would think), didn't really matter as far as the courts of appeal were concerned. There were no pauses in the trial record. No facial expressions or patterns of speech. The record on which the appeal would rise or fall would show nothing more than Bannerman's question and Gerard's answer. ("You and Tommy Mallon are about the only friends I have left," Sam Tabor, that silly sonofabitch, had said. The hell of it was that Ambose had no way of knowing whether Johnny was aware that it was an old and lasting friendship that had come as a complete, if not unwelcome, surprise to Ambose. No, that wasn't the question, either. The question was whether Johnny had forgotten about it or would, perhaps, choose to forget about it.)

"I'll answer it this way," Johnny said. "Mr. Tabor did not display any reluctance in answering his questions."

"No! You'll answer it *my* way. The question, Deputy Gerard, is did Mr. Ambose take advantage of their acquaintance?"

"I've answered your question in the best way I know how," Gerard said, and the involuntary tightening at the corners of the lips rejected any attempt Norman Bannerman might ever make to make it seem otherwise . . .

. . . Confirming it to himself, Bannerman thought. (What a laugh!) These truth-tellers were all alike. Their lies were self-sealing and self-healing. "Does that mean you don't know whether he took advantage of their friendship?"

"Same objection," Pawley called out, forcing Bannerman to replace the word "friendship" for a second time.

In even, heavy tones, the bare outline of his resentment showing through, Gerard said, "You've got it now, Mr. Bannerman. I don't know."

Ah, the first onset of injured innocence. The odor of sanctity, was there anywhere a stench to match it? How dare I dispute you in your relentless honesty, Deputy Gerard, just because you happen to be lying in your teeth? What hypocrites these truth-tellers were! What fucken frauds!

Bannerman drew his lip back across his upper teeth to let Johnny Gerard see that he knew him for what he was. Fair enough, he said, easing the words out. If he didn't know, he didn't know. The leering, disbelieving smile spoke for itself. "Have you observed mayhaps the friendly smiles and gestures that have passed between them in this courtroom?"

There was no hesitation. "Yes, I have."

"All right, Mr. Ambose," Bannerman snapped. "He's all yours."

As Bannerman strode back to his own seat, five sets of eyes burned into him so hatefully that it was like walking into enemy fire. When he slipped into his center slot, with Tabor and Halpern clamped at his elbows and Bob Stringfellow and his two deputies forming an iron ring behind him, he might just as well have been in the middle of the enemy camp. (If hostility could burn up oxygen, he would have suffocated within the minute.) Fair enough. The courtroom *was* the camp of the enemy. If he had come to Lowell to fight them off again, it was only because he had met them on their own ground, at their own terms, through many another struggle to the death, and not only survived but conquered.

Only Frank Cowhig, out of the periphery behind Halpern, was on his side. A mercenary. You bought Cowhig's professional services if you could pay his price, and loyalty for the duration came with the package. Loyalty that was bought and paid for, that was the only kind you could take to the bank with you. It was the other loyalty, the loyalty of the clasped bosom, the loyalty of the blood, that was as delusive as Johnny Gerard's so carefully nurtured faith in his own impeccable honesty had just shown itself to be.

Well, Norman Bannerman had shown them that their diamond in the rough was only a handsome, well-cut hunk of glass.

"I'll take him," Pawley said, with a confidence Ambose knew damn well he didn't feel. "You're emotionally involved, Jim, and he's opened up a few things." Ambose gave him a sidelong who-do-you-think-you're-kidding look and, without rising from his chair, asked Gerard whether Sam Tabor had been orientated as to time and space while Johnny had been guarding him in the dispensary. Enraged as Ambose had been, he had not for one second lost the pulse of the courtroom battle. Crisply and methodically, he proceeded to establish that Sam had known what he had done and had shown no remorse.

"Did he know who everybody was?"

"Yes, he did."

"Were you there when I asked Mr. Marma, representing Sam temporarily for the Lowell Civil Liberties Union, if he'd let Sam take a lie-detector test?"

Objection.

"Did you hear Mr. Marma refuse to let him take a lie-detector test?"

Objection.

"Did you hear Dr. Swann ask him again the following day?"

Objection.

Keep objecting, sucker! By building up a relentless rhythm, Ambose had let his momentum roll right over Bannerman. Doc Swann hadn't asked Sam to take any lie-detector test, and even if he had, Gerard hadn't been there.

Ambose had put one over on Bannerman and suddenly he felt a lot better.

Ostensibly addressing the witness but not forbearing a sly, loping look of satisfaction over at Bannerman, Ambose pointed out that in that last question of his Mr. Bannerman had gone directly into the area of his client's alertness and responses. "The way the rules are written," he said, "I guess that means I'm going to get the chance to ask you whether Sam still knows who everybody he comes into contact is."

The only reaction at the defense table came from Halpern. Bannerman had a dreamy, faraway look about him. To all appearances he was paying minimum attention to the cross-examination.

Q. Let's back up just a bit first, Johnny. Is it a fact that you have been guarding Sam in the jail as well as in the courtroom?

A. It is.

387

Q. There in the jail, is he sensitive to his environment?

A. I wouldn't know how to answer that, Mr. Ambose. I'm not sure I know what you mean.

Q. Is he aware of what's going on around him?

A. He is.

Q. Is he interested in current events?

A. He is.

Q. Would you give us an example or two?

A. I don't think I'd want to do that. Anything we talked about, he thought he was talking about it in private. I know I did.

Q. Would you say he has a good mind?

Gerard had to think about that one. He shifted in his chair and tugged rather fastidiously at each pants leg. "I'll say this for him," he said finally. "He's shown me the best memory I've ever come across. Like when . . . well, he can rattle off all kinds of things from memory. And that's all I'd care to say about that."

"Do you get on well with him? Personally?"

Finally, a faint little smile. Even the voice changed. "Well, I got to get him up at six-thirty in the morning, you understand, and get him to shower and shave. And dress, too—get himself dressed." The witness and the defendant, returned of a sudden to their other roles as jailer and prisoner, exchanged a cozy smile full of shared memories and private jokes. "I sometimes get the impression, you know," said Johnny Gerard, looking at his prisoner with unmistakable fondness, "that he doesn't like me a-tall."

In case the jury had failed to pick out the truly significant part of that answer, Ambose helped them out by asking, "Oh? He's shaving himself these days, is he?" He still, Ambose was happy to see, had eye-communication with Number 5. "Thanks, Johnny," he said, before he turned him back to Bannerman. "You've been a real help to us here."

Although Bannerman came bouncing up out of his chair as if he were going to eat the witness alive, he only had one subject he wanted to cover on redirect. "You said, sir, unless my ears played me falsely, that Mr. Tabor here beside me has the best memory you ever saw?"

"Yes, I said that."

"Rattles all kinds of things off from memory was the way you put it, I believe."

"That's right. I think I said that."

Norman Bannerman sat down, looking very well pleased with both himself and his case.

Jim Ambose stood up to shake Johnny's hand as he came down off the stand, Pawley threw him a wink to set his mind at ease, and as Johnny was passing the defense table, Bannerman stood up and, incredibly, extended his hand. And looked very hurt when Gerard walked right on past him.

Before the door had shut behind Johnny Judge Davies' gavel brought the long session to a close. Jovially, Judge Davies announced, "And the Court hereby orders all within sound of its voice and sight to have themselves a real fine weekend."

Be that as it may, they had to remain in their seats after the judge and jury had departed, squirming restlessly while Stringfellow and his deputies were straightening out the sheriff's assignment in guarding Tabor through the corridor and into the jail elevator.

The first couple of dozen spectators had already filed out when Harry Davies came popping back through the cloakroom door, still in his robes and, if his high color was any indication, unusually excited. "For the benefit of the press," he called out loudly, "there's a news item just came in I thought y'all might want to know about." He cleared his voice. "The sad news has just come in . . . well, we've just been informed—my office has—that Judge Chobodian has passed away." He made a motion of helplessness to which nothing need have been added. "I just thought, you know, it was something you'd want to know."

You never know how anybody's death is going to hit you. Old Eli's death could hardly be said to have come as a surprise, and yet Ambose twisted away from it in an agony of gritted teeth and a slow, painful exhalation of breath. "Damn!" Damn, damn, damn.

Jim Ambose was, by his own admission, a lonely man, but he had always prided himself that loneliness was an old and comfortable friend, the walking companion of his choice.

He had never felt quite so isolated in his life.

Tabor had worked himself up to such a pitch of incoherence that at times the words would run together and at other times he'd stop in his tracks, his mind gone empty, and pull at a handful of hair as though he were trying to pull the next clump of words out of his head. His movements, in perfect tempo with his words, were abrupt and frantic: sudden stops and starts, quick turns and pivots within the narrow area of the Interviewing Room between the table where Bannerman sat and the door.

It had to stop, he told Bannerman. Flat-out stop, see? Johnny Gerard was his friend, and now he was going to be sore at him. The best friend he had. And Jim Ambose. He didn't want any more of this talk about putting his friend Ambose on the witness stand and what-not. "This game you're playing," he kept saying. "What is this you're playing, a game or something?" Well, it wasn't a game to Sam, you could bet on that. And no more of the fighting, either. He didn't want that. And this asking about private matters concerning his wife and what-not. His intimate marital relations. And the psychiatrists. He wasn't going to have anything more to do with them. And not on the witness stand, either. Whose business was that? What was that supposed to be? He had told Dr. Shtogren about that in the strictest of confidence. "The strictest of confidence," he kept repeating, and always with a sudden stop and a twitching, suspicious glare warning Bannerman or trying to trap him unawares. It got so bad that when he accepted a cigarette from Bannerman, he brandished the filtered end at him and said, "I just want you to know this is the first cigarette I've smoked since I've been in here," as if that were one more item to be charged to the account he was keeping against Norman Bannerman.

"And those psychiatrists, huh, what about them? You could see Ambose . . . Yes. Ohhh. Dr. Medellia, oh so nice, so soft and peddly. Freely and frankly, he said. In the *strict*-est of confidence. You told me they were there to help me and what not, and so . . ." He came spinning around on his heel to confront Bannerman, and there was a wild, secretive look about him. "Ambose thinks . . . He gave me a smile there once. Two, maybe three times." Sam tapped his head, closing one eye shrewdly. "Crazy. Hah! You could see. Easy." His nose wrinkled. The wild look receded. He was, for the moment, amused. "Crazier than

389

anybody. Naturally he couldn't say . . ." Without any warning the slides shifted across his face again, and the high, grating tone came back up underneath. "What about them is what I want to know. All the things I told them? No, *sir*. Not on your life. Absolutely, and not on your life. That's it! That's understood! Absolutely, positively, and . . . on . . . your . . . sacred . . . word of honor."

Norman Bannerman, sitting silently, watching imperturbably, found it unnecessary to answer any of the questions or make any comment. Sam was so wound up, his span of concentration so slight, that he forgot within the second that he had wanted one.

"You finished?" Although Bannerman had barely lifted his eyes, the metallic flatness of the question made it perfectly plain that he had made a calculated decision to let Sam get it all off his chest. Only that, and nothing more.

Even Sam couldn't miss it, and it threw him completely. Until that moment, you could see, he had never considered the possibility that when he, as Bannerman's employer, asserted his wishes, Bannerman wouldn't have to follow them —or else. As the sound of the words hit him, he flinched, turned halfway to Halpern and grabbed at a handful of hair, unable to think or, far more likely, unable to quite understand where his carefully thought out plan for bringing Bannerman to heel had gone wrong. His fingertips trailed down through his thinning hair and dropped away. "Or," he said, finishing his speech off anyway, "I'm just going to have to fire you . . . Norman . . . I'm afraid." He squinted at him, forcing confidence. "And that's all there is to it."

"That's it?" Imperiousness, an old habit, sat on Bannerman like a cat. "If you've got anything else to say, say it now. Come on. I want to hear it all. Every complaint. Every puling whine and whimper."

"Heyyyy." Hal found that his voice was unsteady. "What the hell, Norm," he said. "That isn't going to do anybody any good."

Sam's head was tilted to the side, his lips formed into such a perfect circle that you could see the breath being sucked in. Standing, he had become the same man who sat beside Hal in the courtroom.

"Stay out of this, Halpern," Bannerman said, so matter-of-factly, not even looking at him, that he might just as well have dismissed him as a presence in the room.

Just as coolly he said, "I'm going to tell you the facts of life like your daddy should have, Tabor, and once I've told you I'm never going to have to tell you again." The calmness of the voice was too much at odds with the words to last for very long, and as he continued to speak it took on the bite of a man who was laying down the law. "You're the biggest damn fool I ever saw, Sam. The first time I talked to you—it was right in this room, do you remember that?—I told you I was the only friend you had. You didn't choose to believe me. That's all right. I've had some who believed me right off the bat, and with some it took a while longer. But I never had a client before, and damn sure never a murderer, who didn't believe me by the time we went to trial. You're so dumb you think the man whose job it is to kill you, and whose pleasure it is, too—he'd have himself a volcano of an orgasm while you were frying, and you're so incandescently dumb you think he's your friend." A cruel, sardonic expression invaded his face. "How can one man have all that dumbness in him? God, how you disgust me."

"Now, goddamnit," Hal said, starting to rise. "That's enough."

Whatever Bannerman thought he was doing, the effect on Sam was odd. As insult followed insult, he had twisted his body away from Bannerman until he was watching him out of the sides of his eyes, like a man peering around a corner.

"Your friend, Johnny Gerard," Bannerman jeered. "Honest John, the last virgin in town. You poor goddamn fool, he goes running to Ambose with everything you tell him, don't you know that?"

"That's not so." Where Sam had not been able to rouse himself to the direct insults, he rose in childish indignation to that. "That's not so," he said, gathering his last poor shreds of dignity around himself. "That's a great big lie."

It was precisely the childish petulance of it that dismayed Halpern more than anything else. "Johnny's my friend," Sam declared, with the simple and desperate loyalty of childhood. With nowhere else to turn, he turned to Halpern, pleading with him to tell him it was so.

"Sam happens to be right," Hal said quietly. And then stupidly, knowing it was a mistake, Hal told Bannerman about the note Sam had given Johnny Gerard to be slipped to Ambose and which had been turned over to him instead.

The withering look from Bannerman, brief as it was, was to let Hal know that he'd have something to say to him about that later. That didn't bother Hal. He had expected that. It was Sam. What Bannerman hadn't been able to do with all his battering, Hal had done by trying to help him. Before their eyes Sam wilted, the fight gone out of him. Twice betrayed he would feel, Hal realized too late. First, by Johnny for not giving the note to Ambose, and now by Halpern for telling Bannerman.

While Halpern was berating himself—a lot of good *that* did—Bannerman was studying Sam like a fighter deciding where to plant the finishing blow. Totally involved in the problem at hand and yet emotionally detached. He began, methodically enough, by informing Sam that incompetent though he might be at the moment, he had signed a contract that was perfectly legal. Under the terms of that contract, which had become effective on the opening day of the trial, Sam was to reimburse Bannerman for out-of-pocket expenses, with no fee to be paid unless Bannerman was able to save his life. "In which case," Bannerman reminded him, "you are to pay me one hundred thousand dollars, with the proviso that any monies I might collect from Mrs. Tabor, through a private arrangement of our own, are to be deducted from the total sum owing."

It took all the willpower Hal had not to groan aloud. Poor Sam. In thinking he was protecting himself against the possibility of any double payment, he had, in effect, given Bannerman permission to draw up a second contract with Mrs. Tabor. Whether he remained on as Sam's lawyer or not, as Norman Bannerman now informed Sam Tabor with all the force and inelegance at his command, he was going to have to be paid.

The preliminaries having been disposed of, Norman Bannerman's mouth twisted the way it did when he was talking tough. "You keep wanting to know if this is just a game, huh? Well, I promised you I was going to tell you the facts of life, laddie, so perk up your ears and listen."

From the time Halpern picked Norman Bannerman up at the airport to the time (not so far off) when Bannerman would wing his way out, there was very little about the trial of Sam Tabor that Harold Halpern would ever be able to forget. But if through some miracle of time or drugs or a rap on the head everything else were wiped out, he would go to his grave with the next five minutes engraved upon his mind.

"Yes," Bannerman said brutally. "It's just a game we're playing, and, Sam, my boy, you're the prize. If the jury comes back with a death sentence, then Jim Ambose wins and he's going to walk out of the courtroom with your scalp hanging from his belt. If the jury says not guilty, or if I get you off cheap, then I'm the great big winner and that means I get to walk out of the courtroom with your hide. All Jim Ambose can get is a scalp to hang on his trophy-room wall, but if I win, Sam . . ." Smiling slightly, he gripped the outer frame of the chair and rocked himself back and forth. "If I win, laddie boy, I get it all. Everything you own or ever hope to own will belong to me. Anything you keep, that I *allow* you to keep, you will keep entirely on my charity and due entirely to my good will."

"Don't worry, Sam," Hal said. "I'm going to find out whether dual contracts like that are legal." The words, reverberating with a metallic clang through the iron room, rang so foolish even to his own ears—*Don't worry, Sam,* for the love of god—that with nobody paying any attention to him anyway he subsided into a rage of impotence.

Sam was standing in the middle of the floor, slack-mouthed and expressionless. Very slowly, as if it took effort, the corners of his eyes began to wrinkle and his mouth drew up in something resembling a wince of pain. The faintly muddied look of mystification and loss remained on Sam's face as Bannerman explained that if he didn't succeed in saving his miserable life for him he'd be working for nothing except Sam's insurance policy—a paltry fifty thousand dollars—which Sam's devoted wife had contracted to turn over to him. "A gruesome way to collect a fee, if you want to look at it that way," he admitted, facing the facts squarely for both of them. "And if it'll make you feel any better, sport, I'll feel even worse about it than you. It's been a pile of years since I lost a big one." If he did succeed in saving Sam's life . . . well, the cash value of the policy wouldn't do much more than cover the expenses. And as for Vera's earning potential as either a cocktail waitress or a receptionist? Norman Bannerman waved that aside, as hardly worth talking about.

The facts of life having been so bluntly set forth, the voice of the undertaker toted up the bill. "So you see, Sam, if I walk you out of here, I'll own you. And for the rest of your life you will do exactly as I say. If I don't walk you out, I'll still own your wife." That was the way it was, and there was nothing either of them could do about it. Well, one thing maybe. He did want Sam to know, if it would help to ease his mind, that he had not the slightest intention of depriving dear Vera of her car. Unless, of course, he happened to hear that Sam was trying to get in touch with Ambose again. "As much as I'd hate to do it, Sam, as much as it would pain me to deprive her of that last simple pleasure, I'd have no choice but to take title right there. You do see the justice of it, don't you? Well, don't you?"

Meekly and helplessly, Sam nodded.

"Sit down, Sam," Bannerman ordered. "Sit down and shut up."

Obediently, all will eroded, Sam moved to the empty chair on the opposite side of the table and slumped down, one foot extended and the other bent back under the chair, his eyes downcast and infinitely sad.

Across the table, Bannerman examined him as if, by god, he did own him. "You poor damn fool," he said. "You'd better get it into your head that you're nothing but the prize of battle anymore. This is a game of showdown between me and Ambose now, and all you supply is the ass! If they did it right, they'd put it in Yankee Stadium and sell tickets!"

Sam's hands curled up under the cuffs of his sleeves and out of sight. That was all. The smallest of movements. As insignificant as the sound of a wounded bird fluttering in the bush. Halpern moistened his lips and cleared his throat and sat there, powerless to intervene.

Well satisfied, Bannerman nodded slightly and gave himself a little backward push in his chair. "All right, then, I'll tell you what I'm willing to do for you. If you're a good boy and do exactly as you're told, I think I'll be able to see my way clear to leave Vera with enough money to live on until she gets back on her feet."

Sam's eyes remained downcast.

Bannerman tapped the table twice. Not loudly but with absolute command. "Look at me," he said.

Sam looked at him, his eyes dull and hollow.

In a heavy, disciplined voice that knew it was going to be obeyed, Bannerman prompted, "I'm going to do exactly as I'm told."

Sam Tabor said, "I'll do what I'm told."

"Say after me, I'm going to keep my mouth shut from now on and do exactly as I'm told."

Tabor said nothing. He didn't have to. A wall of ice had clamped down over him. Behind the ice he had capitulated completely.

Behind the wall of ice was a man with no life, no future, no money, no estate. All he had, Sam Tabor had just discovered, was whatever Norman Bannerman chose to leave him with.

Caroline Beyner marched into the elevator alongside Ambose holding a green wine bottle at shoulder arms. Seeing the full-length mirror along the side, she clicked her heels together, leered at herself inexpertly and in a deep-down, husky voice said to the image in the mirror, "Hey there, girly, howdja like to give a serviceman a good time tonight?"

Pleased with herself no end, she flung her big tan pocketbook around her neck with a hearty spin and, tucking her thumb cockily under the strap, proceeded to drape herself into sundry positions, hoydenish, touch-me-not and clownish, all of which clearly said, "Am I not preciously naughty, indescribably cute?"

A pat on her precious little head was exactly what she wasn't going to get. Jim Ambose, who had been listing dog-tired against the other corner of the elevator, made a sudden lurching, stumbling snatch at the wine bottle. "Ho, ho," she said. "Quicker than the eye am I. You shall not lay a hand on my fair body, mean man. I move with the grace and skill of a lady elephant. Arturo would be proud of me." Hugging the bottle to her as if it were a baby she was lullabying, she turned her shoulder to him and said, "He gave it to me alone because I am a sweet young thing and he likes me."

The elevator door was sliding open. "He's *my* friend," Ambose growled. "It's to the left there. *You* were only with me."

Bunny was not at all prepared for the handsome lithographic effect of the apartment. What struck her first when he switched on the lights was the modernistic arrangement of blacks and whites, spare and clean of line, and off to the side, covering one whole section of the wall, a charcoal mural of two mounted gladiators clashing in battle.

Bunny thought she had heard Ambose say something as they entered. Apparently she was mistaken because he met her look blankly. Having her there had sobered him up some; being there had sobered her up completely. To say something she said, "If you ever own a racing stable, let me guess what your colors will be." And there it was again, the inability not to be smart and brittle, a defect of character she used to cover up the fundamental defect of having no character. And all of it was spurious, faked, out of books, out of movies; the heroines she identified with in her cheap novels. As phony as the attitude of critical reflection she assumed when having examined the room, she found her attention drawn once again to the charcoal mural:

The gladiators were fully armored. Their steeds, powerful and muscular, glowed white beneath full battle array. One horse was just beginning to rear back to take the impact of the first powerful charge, mouth open and gasping, nostrils flared, the fragile forelegs bent and straining at the knees. The other horse was driving in off stiff, extended forelegs, its head tucked into its massive neck, the rear legs and bushy tail flying.

The riders in their metal helmets and closed visors were almost anonymous appendages to their mounts, indistinguishable except for the number of streamers flying back from the very tips of their helmets and the gray cloaks swirling below the saddle; the attacker's cloak blowing free in the full wind of the charge, the defender's flung back to match the rearing hind quarters of his mount.

The sense of impact was so overpowering that Bunny's first impression was that the artist had set the clash against a plain white background to permit the viewer's mind to fill in the colosseum and the crowd. But as she looked and as her focus widened, there emerged in the background, off in the distance, two bare, scrawny bushes—something more than clumps if less than trees—and up in the corner, closer in, a high patch of branches, wispy but firm. Along the ground, if you looked close enough, you could still make out the last faint signs of furrows, a grim reminder that someone had once attempted to work this hard, barren ground and long since departed.

No, this clash had been taken out of the closed arena, away from the roaring crowd. Here were two gladiators, bereft of all connection with humanity, battling to the death on some cold and Arctic plain. The fight was for the fight's sake. It was a battle without a winner, without in all probability a survivor. No eye would see them fall, no ear would hear them. The winds would freeze them in their metal shrouds, the snows would cover them over, and only the uncaring trees would remain.

She gave a shudder and turned away to hand him the wine bottle, holding on to it for a moment longer than was necessary in the hope he would read in her eyes the message which said: Let me take the winter from your wall, James Ambose. Come, let me make you warm.

The room itself had come as such a surprise, revealing as it did such an entirely unsuspected side of his personality, that she couldn't help but wonder whether he had done the mural himself.

"That?" His snort of repudiation, purely involuntary and therefore unquestionably true, let her know that he wouldn't want such a talent; wouldn't know what to do with it. "This character I sent to prison, he wanted to do something for me when he came out." It had finally got to where he was telling Ambose he could do murals and the like, and so Ambose had let him hang around to get rid of him.

"Con-man type," he said, setting her straight. "Sweet-talked old ladies out of their savings. *Real* sweet fellow." One of the old ladies had held up all the way to trial, more the tough luck for him. "Baker the Faker," he said, rolling the name out with a flourish. The laugh that followed came short and nostalgic. "Yes indeedy. Sweet-talked his way right into the can and, like most of them, sweet-talked himself right out again." Expansively, with an elaborate show of virtue, he laid the wine bottle across his chest as if the Pledge of Allegiance were about to be recited. "Straight and narrow forevermore, that was the road for him." He snorted again. The parole board! "Honest to god now. You ask them, 'How did the guy get into trouble in the first place?' and they'll say, 'He conned people.' And so you say, 'Then what the hell makes you think he isn't conning you, you simple-minded idiots? He's a professional teller-of-people-what-they-want-to-hear.'" But what the hell, it didn't bother him any. "I got a pretty good painting out of the deal," he smirked. "Once in awhile I look at it."

She still didn't understand why, if Ambose had opposed his parole, the con man had been so anxious to do something for him.

"Oh, come on." Ambose was peering down at her as if she were just too sweet and innocent to be true. "He's a *con man,*" he said, as if that explained everything. "He's thinking of the next time." But who knew, he muttered. Maybe Baker the Faker would amount to something yet. In rapid order he waved the wine bottle toward the mural, loosened his tie and indicated with his eyes that she was to sit down. "If he can stay out of jail. Which he won't. To hell with him."

"He'll stay out of jail." Her eyes were soft and luminous with the secret, intuitive knowledge cribbed from every actress whose eyes had ever shone with a secret, intuitive faith in the man she loved. Doing as she was told, like all good girls should, she perched herself sideways on the arm of the chair, paying particular attention to the line of her leg. Now that she knew so much about the artist, Bunny was examining the mural with an entirely different eye. Con men were in the business of telling people what they wanted to hear, Ambose had said. Not this time, buster. Recalling the sense of bleakness that had settled over her, remembering the chill, could there be any doubt that out of some extraordinary respect for the man upon whose wall he was leaving his permanent imprint this con-man-turned-muralist had discarded that original intention of doing himself a little good and, in what it pleased her to think of as a moment of rare artistic sensitivity and integrity—possibly because it made her feel so good—left him with a representation of the absolute truth as he had seen it.

As casually as she could manage, she asked, "Now why do you suppose he picked that particular subject?"

Aha. The very question Ambose himself had put to Baker as soon as the mural had begun to take shape. Nor had the answer been exactly fraught with high artistic sensitivity and integrity. Horses, it seemed, happened to be what Baker drew best. And yet . . . "Coincidence," Ambose murmured, frowning at the mural. "It's a remarkable thing." Sure death in a lawsuit, of course. Guaranteed to get you laughed right out of court. Juries wanted the lawyers to have the ducks lined up for them, all in a nice, neat row. Engrossed in his own thoughts, scratching his head itchily, Ambose set the wine bottle down on the low bench under the mural, stepped back and, with both hands now free, set them low on his hips while he pondered some more upon the gladiators and their horses.

Yes, he said again. A truly remarkable thing.

Before there was any law, Ambose informed her, people settled their disputes the same way kids fight for marbles. The kid with the bloodiest nose lost. That meant the barons, the warlords, did most of the bloodying because they were the guys who owned it all. On the really important issues, like who controlled the southern forty acres and got to tax the grain and deflower the little girlies they'd drag out their whole bloody armies and go to war. There was, he said, only one minor drawback to it. Since the opposing warlords had the best horses and the thickest armor and the strongest lances, the whole damn battle usually got down to a personal duel between them. The winner rode off with the spoils of victory, and the loser fell down and broke his crown.

In time, the sons and grandsons of the best fighters inherited the property, only they weren't the fighters their daddies were. Just like today. So they had to be smarter. "They were smart enough to see that while maybe it wasn't a good idea to give up the southern forty acres without a fight they had everything they'd ever need even without it and, anyway, you can get all worn out deflowering virgins after the first couple of hundred."

"My, they *weren't* the men their daddies were, were they?"

He gave her a look. "So when they got into a dispute over who owned what or who'd insulted who, they hired our friends there, the gladiators, to do the fighting for them." Either kept a gladiator around the castle on permanent duty —on a retainer, you might say—or went out and hired a hot-shot jouster when there was a job of work to be done. "From them to us," he said, with a noticeable lack of pride. "From the fighters to the talkers. Because let me tell you something, lady. When it comes to the bruising, that's all a lawyer is. A hired gladiator fighting somebody else's dirty little battle for him." A brusque movement of his hand informed her that the history lesson was over, and she could make what she wanted of the remarkable coincidence of Baker having stumbled upon that one subject to throw up there on his wall.

Invited to make comment, Bunny made bold to suggest that from fighting to talking had been a long way to come. "I know it's hopelessly decadent of me," she said quickly, feeling him withdraw. "And just like a woman. But it does seem better to have the verdict go to the one who's right. . . ? According to the law . . . ? Than to have it settled by who's stronger and can bloody the other's nose . . . ?" Even, she thought it wise to add in a teeny voice, if the way the laws were written left a good deal to be desired . . . ?

"The old way was better," Ambose said. "When one of those boys got himself run through, the verdict was writ in running blood and that took care of all the writs and briefs and appeals forever and a day." Reaching up, he patted the rear end of the charging horse with a wistful look that stretched beyond the mural and beyond the day. No sirree. You could bet those boys didn't go running around to find some referee who hadn't been there, so that some talking machine who probably wasn't there either could tell him why they ought to dig up the guy they'd buried and tell him how he'd really won. "In those days," he said softly, "only God could raise up the dead, and He only did it twice that I know of."

Still musing on it, he picked up the bottle and tilted it so that she could see how little was left. "You want to finish it off?" he asked absently.

She forced a smile and shook her head. As always, she thought with a sinking heart, it had gone wrong. The shifting associations in Ambose's mind having been hidden from her, she had taken his first withdrawal into himself as a sign that he was revising ais estimate of her. His deepening self-absorption was seen as a notice of disinterest. He had confided his innermost feelings to her and she had shown herself to be incapable of understanding them. He no longer wanted her; it was as simple as that. The old familiar sense of being herself at fault—not merely foolish or mistaken but inadequate—dropped over her (could it be that he wasn't looking for such pliable material, after all?) and with it came a desperate yearning to turn the clock back to the fetching girl who had amused and delighted him before the real woman was put to the test and the invisible flaw exposed.

"Aren't you going to show me the rest of the apartment?" She looked at him steadily with a warm and melting glow, her mouth slightly open, the invitation at once bold and timid.

The look was accepted in a swift and total recognition for what it was. "The kitchen's over there. I've been known to fry an egg in a hurricane. My so-called library is off the hall. I'm not of a mood to read a book myself but I'm willing to let you take a look in case you've never seen one."

"I've seen one."

"OK then, lady. The bedroom's right over there."

The living room, with its clean modernistic lines, had come as a surprise. The bedroom took her breath away. One look and there was no more need to wonder where the inspiration for the mural had come from. She hung at the doorway for a moment, in a trembling of wings, understanding perfectly why she had thought of Ambose as her punisher all these years. The shape of something not yet visible was, god help her, stretching out its arms to her. The breath of something not unlike the high, thin child-like reed of fear flickered on a screen. What was flawed would soon enough, thank god, be healed. Rejoicing with fear and trembling with hope, Caroline Beyner could tell herself that she was, at last, about to find out what little girls were made for.

Although it was their first real date, Caroline Beyner had met Ambose with that sense of gaiety and abandon of a woman who had held out for a reasonable length of time and has come to the decision, rather gratefully, that tonight will be the night and they both might as well know it and enjoy the tender, tense anticipation of it.

She could not have been more surprised than when Ambose had called her earlier in the evening to remind her that he owed her a meal. Or less surprised than when he had suggested The Seven Seas, an overdecorated, overpriced tourist restaurant that pegged him immediately as a man who didn't go out often.

"Good," he said. "I'll pick you up in half an hour."

"Oh gawd," she gurgled. "Do us both a favor, Jim. If you want me to look even halfway presentable you'd better give me a whole big hour."

In the elevator she squeezed his hand, clasping it tightly, placed both of their hands into the pocket of his light knee-length topcoat. With all the frantic rushing to and fro between bathroom and bedroom, her hair had come out well and lent a soft and shining warmth to her. Through some grace or premonition or luck she had bought a too-expensive tan tailored suit only last week (in her present light-hearted mood she had no memory of the heavy depression that had really been behind it), and it was even more marvelously flattering than she had remembered. Yes, with Ambose she'd had the premonition from the beginning that he had come to rescue her from the emptiness that had been closing in around her.

As soon as Ambose ordered the drinks he said, "Now, look. I want you to know what I have in mind for us. It's to take you home with me and show you my apartment."

"All right, I'd love to see your apartment."

There was an instant's flicker of doubt that it had really been that easy. "Listen, when I say I want to show you my apartment, you know what I mean, don't you?"

"Yes, Jim. I have an idea what you mean. I appreciate your delicacy but I do know what you mean. I'm sure you will conduct yourself like a gentleman."

He nodded abruptly. "OK, then." And she didn't mind at all, because the proprietary air he assumed over her was exactly what she wanted. Instead of taking her right back to his apartment, though, he dragged her around to a few of the bars where the criminal lawyers were known to hang out, and that didn't displease her either because it meant that he was showing her off. Coming out of the last one, he caught a cab on the fly, not the easiest thing in the world to do in Lowell, and instructed the driver to take them to Pinocchio's on the highway. He wanted her, he said, to meet the owner, Arthur Klein, an old friend who somehow never seemed to be able to make a go of his restaurants, and there was such a vein of affection running through the way he spoke of him that she took Klein to be a very close friend, quite probably the best friend he had in the world.

Pinocchio's turned out to be a huge restaurant, very tastefully and richly decorated in a quasi-Oriental style that fit the name not at all. The dining room off beyond an expanse of red carpeting was sunken two steps down and, dark as it was, she could see the remains of what must have been a pretty good Friday night crowd.

Arthur Klein was a middle-aged man of medium height, one of those men who never quite looks clean-shaven. He had come trotting over the moment he saw Ambose with his arms open wide and a big, welcoming smile on his face, a greeting that became all the more impressive as it became apparent that he was, while not a grave or sorrowful man, a generally unsmiling one. It also became apparent that Ambose hadn't seen his good friend Arthur for more than a year. And when Ambose kept insisting, with his standard quota of belligerency, that it hadn't been anywhere near that long, Klein told him that OK, if he wanted to be *that* way about it, he hadn't been there since the original Grand Opening, when it was called The Teahouse, which had been *two* years come August 17. Whereupon they were able to agree, in a rush of treasured memory, that time sure did pass—a sentiment to which Bunny was happy to lend assent.

Klein had taken over behind the bar by then, and settled in to spend the night with them. Ambose had been stealing looks into the darkened dining room from the moment they entered, and when Klein had to go over to refill the drinks of the two young couples at the near end of the bar, he took a good, long look. The only other customer actually seated at the bar, at that moment, was a beefy man a couple of stools away from Ambose, the kind of well-dressed, well-barbered man you could spot as a salesman from a hundred yards. The kind of guy who looked as if he boozed it up on the road and kept in shape by playing squash at the Y when he got home. His two equally well turned out companions were over at the cigarette machine alongside the checkroom, arguing noisily over whether the one in the white tie was going to accept the cigarettes the one in the red tie had already bought for him.

"Tell me, Arthur," Ambose said, "has Hilliard been in tonight?"

Hilliard and Lillian hadn't been in since the Tabor trial got under way, Klein told him, although normally he could count on them two or three times a week.

"Next time he comes in tell him I was asking, huh? Tell him Ambose and Carolyn Beyner were in here asking for him, will you tell him that? Miss Beyner works down at the courthouse with us, did I tell you that?"

"You told me, Jim," Klein said gravely. "But I'm always glad to hear it again."

Yeah, but Ambose wanted to make sure that he was going to *tell* him. He was so afraid, you could see, that Klein was going to dismiss it as just another of those amenities that Klein finally pointed to the phone in exasperation and told him that he could, for crying out loud, tell Nevins himself. "My hand to God, Jim! When did you become such a *noodge?* What's the matter, has Hilliard been after you to get out and mix more with the voters? Or to just enjoy yourself while you're still young and virile."

"Yeah bo," Bunny said, squeezing Ambose's arm. "I'm all for that."

The squash player said, "He's probably home hiding from Bannerman."

Bunny could see the line draw tight across Ambose's lips before he turned to look the guy over. She hadn't missed the hard, cold glint in his eye, either.

"That's the district attorney, isn't it?" the squash player said amiably, and there was something in his easy slouch and in the comfortable way he turned his glass in his hands that was meant to let them know that as a man who had held many a conversation in many a bar from here to the rocky coast of Maine he was not at all out of order in butting into their conversation. "I'm from Chicagoland myself," he said with a little chuckle, "and I hate to tell you, but there's none of these local yokels are in the same league even."

"What you drinking, Jim?" Klein asked desperately. "Gin, right? And you, Miss . . . ?" Their drinks had suddenly assumed an overwhelming importance to him. He had a new concoction he wanted them both to try. Specialty of the house, and compliments of the proprietor. A Pinocchio, he called it. Bunny, who had been drinking Brandy Alexanders, did her best (although she could tell from Klein's face that it was hopeless) by remembering, with a newly discovered vivacity of her own, that she did just happen to have a yen for a liqueur she had been introduced to a while back at a social gathering. The only difficulty was that she couldn't remember what it was. Not B & B, but something like it. "Something with a Frenchy name to it."

A peal of laughter came from the end of the bar as one of the women goggled, playfully aghast, at her escort and gave him a little love-tap on the side of his face.

"Chicago," Ambose said loudly. "That's where all the men are fat fairies like Bannerman and all the women are whores. That where you say you're from, Smitty?"

All by itself the voice would have been enough to alert the two men at the cigarette machine that something more than the usual barroom jollities were being exchanged. White tie put out a hand to accept the cigarettes and they came sauntering over together, swinging their shoulders and adjusting their neckties in the attitude of men who were positioning themselves solidly—and not for the first time, either, buddy—behind a friend who seemed as if he just might have a little trouble on his hands.

All things considered, their friend was remaining resolutely inoffensive, though not completely unoffended. "What's the matter with him?" he asked Klein. "All I said was—"

"Who asked you to say anything?" Ambose snapped. "You've got a big mouth. Didn't anybody in Chicagoland ever tell you that?"

Klein had reached down under the bar for his bar rag and was wiping the space in front of Bunny. Over and over and over. "Mr. Ambose is connected with the district attorney's office," he offered, as if he thought this might be an excellent time for them to meet each other formally.

The squash player made a noble effort at looking as if he were considering

Ambose's grievances in the light of this new information and—while not normally a man to let such insults pass undealt with—was finding them not wholly without merit. He tapped his cigarette pack on the bar reflectively, and then let it fall with a decisive flip. "No offense meant, fellow. I got a right to have an opinion, don't I? Even in Lowell."

One of the men behind him, the one with the white tie, said, "You having any trouble, Frank?"

"He's not having any trouble, Smitty. Not if he's willing to sit there and let me tell him his wife is a Chicago whore and he runs with fat fairies like you and that other queer with you."

Bunny couldn't believe it was happening. She heard herself saying, "Jim, please." She also found herself pulling her hand back before it touched his elbow because, absurdly, she didn't want him to take her for one of those women who would always be out to spoil his fun.

"Look," the squash player said, rising. "I didn't mean to insult your boss. OK?" His palms were turned up in what could be taken as innocence or apology or even evidence that he was unarmed. "Forget it, huh? Let's just forget I said anything." He pushed his stool back and started to leave, certainly more hastily than he'd have liked to, the man in the red tie right alongside him. The man in the white tie, more sensitive than his companions to the spectacle of three husky men being routed so easily, hesitated. Not exactly holding his ground but sweeping his eyes rapidly over the immediate environs to weigh their humiliation as seen through the eyes of others.

The two young couples at the end of the bar were very studiously looking into their glasses, pretending to each other as much as to anybody else that nothing of any particular interest was happening around them. The dining room was almost deserted, except for one waiter, who had his back turned to them, and a few widely scattered groups and couples sitting over their final cups of coffee and cigarettes. But then there was the hat check girl, wasn't there? And the hat check girl was looking right back at him.

"Kee-rist Almighty," White Tie said. "Now I can understand how Wilcke got killed in this town."

Everything seemed to erupt around Bunny at once. On one side of her, Klein closed his eyes tight, unable to bear to watch what he knew was about to happen; on the other side, Ambose's back went hurtling away from her, his muscles already bunching along the back of his shoulder. She saw the punch, incredibly short and quick, and heard the loud *thwack* of fist against flesh and the crunch of bone underneath it; not so much seeing and hearing as remembering it, in a single piece, a split-second afterwards, with the man's hands already covering his face and the blood spurting between his fingers and staining his neck and shirt and used-to-be white tie.

Another split-second and, in what seemed to be a delayed reaction—as of a gun recoiling—he went staggering back a couple of steps, his legs so wobbly that it didn't seem possible they could hold him up. They might very well have collapsed under him at that, if his friends hadn't rushed back and thrown their arms around him.

Ambose stood right where he was, his legs spread, his right fist cocked at the shoulder, a towering figure of menace. Ready for anything. "What do you say, Smitty," he asked the squash player. "Want to try for two?"

The third man, hitherto silent, looked back over his shoulder with what he obviously hoped he could pass off as contempt. He was, alas, unable to hold his voice, much less his eyes, steady. "Yeah, let's get out of here," he wheezed. "I told you we shouldn't have come in here, didn't I?"

"Yeah, let's," Ambose called after him with true and massive contempt. "Maybe you'd just better do that. Before somebody gets hurt."

At the end of the bar one of the young men hastily counted out some bills and dropped them on the bar. Before they left, though, they all sneaked a quick look at Ambose, men and women both. With the men, it was a furtive look, no more than a shift of the eyes. Innocent bystanders though they were, they knew they hadn't come off well. Their masculinity had been undercut in front of their women, cut through to the muscle in some way that they would never quite be able to put into words except that it was being compounded by the manner of their leaving—and by the furtive, sidelong glance itself.

The look from the women was something else. It was—and Bunny noted it with a feline, possessive pride—an upsweeping, appraising look which, though just as brief, left the impression of having lingered on him much longer. Long enough for Bunny to sense the animal attraction, as deep and bloody as the moon's, the ticking wound that wondered how it would be full of violence and cruelty and degradation.

The eyelids curling up, wondering how it would be with . . .

The eyes turning away, shivering with some delicious dread that wasn't so much known as half-remembered.

"Sit still," Bunny commanded, examining Ambose with a surgical eye. There were a few spots of blood splattered like perfectly round red polka dots across Ambose's neck and chin. Having sat him down, Bunny had commandeered his handkerchief, dipped one corner in his gin and was not too gently wiping them away. With Ambose submitting himself so docilely she finally felt that she was getting some idea of what he wanted her to be. Of service, but by no means a servant.

Klein was pouring a drink for Bunny and telling her that he thought this was what she had in mind, Grand Marnier. His eyes were on Ambose, though, restrained but perfectly candid, and there was something in them that was telling him he always had to make things tough, didn't he?

Ambose immediately laid down a twenty-dollar bill and insisted that Klein take it as compensation for the customers he had driven away. Klein just as promptly tore it into halves and quarters and eighths and let the pieces flutter from his fingertips, and it was hard to tell whether he was telling Ambose that he was insulted or that the touch of his money dirtied him. As the evening wore on and the glasses were emptied, the same curious combination of intimacy and antagonism ran through their entire relationship; a kind of jangling byplay which Bunny became aware of without being privy to. Bunny, who may have been a bit swoozled herself by then, found it all very charming, for it had come to her that she had always envied the rough devotion of men. Sipping on her drink and leaning on her chin, she was all but aglow with the good fortune that had selected her to become his companion for the night, for it had also come to her that there was a lonely strength about James Ambose and, now that she thought of it, a lonely splendor about herself that made her the perfect mate for him. (Mate as in shoes, she clarified for herself primly. Not mate as in bed. *But you can put your shoes under my bed anytime, baby,* she thought, feeling wicked but finding a happy portent in how neatly it all fitted together.)

When they were ready to leave, Ambose leaned across the bar and demanded with his standard quota of belligerency that Klein sell him a bottle of Grand Marnier for the lady. "That would cost me my license, Counsellor," Klein told him, and all the while that Ambose—who had taken to calling him Arturo—was denouncing him as a dirty spic innkeeper and an enemy of the people, the innkeeper was transferring the Grand Marnier from the liqueur bottle into a green wine bottle, an operation which required all the concentration he could muster. "On the other hand," he said, as he was tamping in the cork, "a lot of ladies are always asking me if I have an empty wine bottle around so they can dine by candlelight." He handed it over to Bunny, ignoring Ambose completely. "Only if I were you, I'd take my advice and find somebody with a little more class. You're too good for this bum, Caroline."

It was a waste of time to try to call a cab, he told them, because nobody ever came to Pinocchio's except by private car, and they could wait all night before one came. "I am," he said, as he handed Ambose his own car keys, "about to make another last of the great gestures." At least, he started to hand them to him. Then he took a good long look, shook his head sadly and gave them to Bunny instead. That last drink had done it, all right. As for Klein himself, he was going to drive home with the waiter and pick up the keys at the courthouse sometime Monday afternoon, being confident that his old friend Jim Ambose would get him in to see part of the trial.

It took a bit of doing, of course, for Bunny to hold onto the keys once they were out in the parking lot. She succeeded in the end only by reminding him how happy it would make Norman Bannerman if he should happen to be picked up for drunken driving and taken off the trial. Whereupon they headed back to Lowell, taking swigs from the wine bottle and harmonizing, more unharmoniously than seemed humanly possible, on a medley of songs, all of which Bunny —as if to prove what a good sport and gay companion she really was—would introduce with a bright and cheery: "And now, folks, here's another of your good old childhood favorites sung by your favorite boy-and-girl duo."

As he closed the door behind them in his apartment, Ambose breathed, under the tongue, "Screw you, Hilliard."

When she admired the mural so unreservedly, he began to see it through her eyes. Looking at it that way brought back the memory of how surprised he had been when it turned out that Baker hadn't been just running off at the mouth again. Although, he had to admit, no more surprised than he was a few minutes later when he realized how much he had been running off at the mouth himself. He hadn't brought her up here for any lecture on the history of the law nor, as she took pains to show him, had she come for one. "OK then, lady," Ambose said. "The bedroom's right over there."

"Done very tastefully in Early Roman Dungeon," Bunny said, hanging in the doorway. Her lips were dry. "Another gift from a grateful convict you sent to the bastinado?" (What in the world, she thought to herself, was a bastinado? If anything? Bastille was what she had obviously meant to say. Wherever had a word like that come from?)

The black-and-white motif had been retained in the bedroom, except that where white had predominated in the living room, black was the color of Jim Ambose's lair. The paneled walls were stained jet black. The bed was covered by a black bedspread. Two black pillows were plumped, points upward, against a wrought-iron post of interlocking fleur-de-lis–shaped sections. Since each of the sections was made of heavy interlocking links itself, the total effect was that of a continuum of chains snaking in and out of each other.

In the midst of all that blackness were two stark, dramatic splashes of white. Glowing from the wall just above the bed were a pair of battle-axes polished to a gleaming silver, the handles coming together at the bottom to form a V. At the foot of the bed was a fluffy white throw-rug—whiter than white—and whether that was Jim Ambose's lone concession to a world of softness and comfort or his daily reminder that he must always be on guard against the soft and debilitating influences of a crumbling civilization was more than Bunny would have cared to say. Or, in that trembling moment, dared to.

The high, thin reed of fear she breathed was not in anticipation of coming pleasure but more like the memory of a secret dread that had seeped back across some great distance of time from some childhood landscape to which she had always known she would return. In the scene she saw so dimly flickering there was the wide curved cutting edge of an axe, bodies hanging upside down from the dampish ceiling, and a bald torturer wearing a black vest-like garment waiting, with dull pleasure and watermelon belly, for his instructions.

As Bunny herself, her knees unstable as water, was waiting for her instructions.

Having closed the blinds, Ambose stopped at the foot of the bed and confided to her, with hesitant pride, that he had decorated the room himself. "Now, I say decorated. What it was—I told them what I wanted and they had some ideas, too."

"James Ambose, you are a man of unexpected qualities. And talents." She could no longer keep her voice from trembling. "What other surprises do you have in store for me?"

He drew his fingers down the side of his chin where the blood had been and looked her over like a drill sergeant sizing up a new batch of recruits. "You've got too many clothes on," the drill sergeant said, not smiling. "Get them off and put your ass down on the bed where it belongs."

Her instructions had finally come and she was not at all displeased that they had come in exactly that way.

"I'll make you a deal," she said, astonished at the cheery sound that was coming out of her. "I'll get out of mine if you'll get out of yours."

In his dark and smoky eyes she saw the gladiator on his mount. On the flickering screen, the barbarian could be seen galloping in with his equestrian hordes. "You heard what I said," the gladiator barked. "Move!"

Her hands jumped to the buttons of her jacket.

She undressed herself very quickly, as if her clothes were a burden she could hardly wait to be free of. And then, right at the end, in a final, unexpected flutter of modesty, she stepped out of her panties from underneath her half slip. With a few quick, practiced moves of her fingers she undid her hair, holding for a moment in what she somehow knew to be an unusually flattering pose, her body atingle, her skin tone softening, her eyes, wide and submissive, asking him the question that left her enslaved and in thrall.

Very deliberately, Ambose had begun to unbutton his shirt. He stopped, at the cufflink, to watch her hair come tumbling down as she shook it loose.

"That too. Get it off."

Her voice came cheery but strained. "Didn't you ever hear about the Irishman who always wore his derby to bed because his mother told him it wasn't nice to expose himself completely to the opposite sex?"

"Get it off!"

Poutish and a little shrill: Didn't he want to do *any* work?

He sat on the edge of the bed, keeping his back to her as he undressed. She lay perfectly still on her back, her arms crossed awkwardly and heavily at the waist.

He turned the table lamp off before he turned to her. He did not take off his T-shirt, and though she tugged at it, timorously, she was afraid to tell him right out that she wanted him the same way he wanted her. He removed her hand, quite brusquely, and pushed her, not too gently, back. His hand ran over and through her until, with a sigh, she shifted herself slightly, her legs moving slightly apart so that he could run his hand down inside her thighs. "Aaaaah," he said. "Smooth. Smooth like a Bunny." He cupped his hand over her. "Hairy as a bunny, too."

With a mewl of contentment, she crooked her arm around his neck, and, meeting resistance, lifted her own head to him. She kissed him, passionately, wetly, sloppily, turning her head slowly from side to side.

He placed his hand against her shoulder and pushed her back down. "Take it easy," he said. "We've got all night."

He was going to make her wait, and that was fine. He was going to do it in his own good time, and his own good way. If he did it at all. She had been primed, wound and sensitized to the nerve ends and now it was to wait. Her instructions, as she understood them, were to lie back and wait until he was ready or she was jumping out of her skin. Those were the conditions that were being imposed on her, and she understood—saw in the flickering on the screen—that it was just the way it should be. At his convenience. Not of service, but as a servant. A prisoner to be impaled upon the spike that little boys were made of. In the meanwhile, she would be tested to find out just how much she could endure. Set down, she settled back; her thighs trembling as she extended her legs and brought her feet tightly together, snuggling in for the excruciating wait. His hand began to move across her stomach again, in breathless, tingling arcs, dropping lower and lower and lower. The buzz saw flickered on the screen, spinning toward the soft, white neck; lower and lower and lower.

"Bunny," she sighed, when he got there. "I always hated that name when I was a girl." Ahhh. The rules were that she could talk, if talk could keep her from jumping out of her skin. He was so good to her. "I lived across from a park, and there were a group of neighborhood toughs of whom I was in mortal fear. It was their habit to collect by the water fountain under a grove of trees, and when I cut across the field it was the pleasure of these rude chaps to say, 'And speaking of Bunnies, how's yours?'" A rueful, reminiscent smile pulled at the corners of her lips. "I was told very early that men took any encouragement at all as an invitation to work their will upon my fair no matter how resisting body and, believe me, sir, I was prepared to believe it." The bus stop had been on the other side of the field from where she lived, and in the winter, when it got dark early, she had always walked the long way around, that's how frightened she was. "I'm not sure I really knew what terrible things I thought they were prepared to do to me if they should ever catch me in the field at night but I can assure you, sir, it had something to do with ropes and stakes and heavy boots and things too horrible for a refined and delicate young creature to contemplate." She stirred under his hand. "As a young girl, I had a headful of ignorance and a lively imagination. Between the two you can imagine."

"Sure can."

Ahhh. She had been right. She could talk, but only about herself. Ahhh, there was punishment enough. Her worthless self peeled back; her shameful past to be ransacked, plundered and cast aside. Betrayed by her own hand. (The heavy iron-ring rattles against the slimy stone. The trap door, opening, creaks. The body is dropped soundlessly into the swift, dark current below, while hunched at the entrance of the secret tunnel, there where the mossy growths hang obscenely from the slimier rock, a dark-caped figure wets his thumb, laughs evilly, and counts his ill-gotten gains.) "Something that would render me unmarriageable forevermore, no doubt. As a young lady, crossing dark fields, one fears it. In riper years, when all fields are dark, one fears that one will never find it." The tenseness had left her voice and in its place had come something sorrowful and yearning. "I was dreaming of a great romance, of course. At dreaming, as in English Lit., I had no peers." Her girlish reveries, as she recalled them, had run to long and companionate courtships from which she would emerge with the maturity and wisdom of a woman of the world, smoking perfumed cigarettes from a long marble inlaid cigarette holder. "Also a great deal prettier. I believe I saw myself most often as an international intriguer who won men over with the splendor of her mind and her cold, chiseled beauty. Oh, what a life of glamor would I lead if only I could pluck up the courage to walk across a neighborhood field in the dark." A low moan escaped from her, having not a thing to do with what she was saying. "Now how did I get to tell you the unappetizing story of my unappetizing youth? Oh yes." She placed her hand over his and pressed down. "I believe it all started with Bunny."

Jim Ambose had been listening to the unappetizing story unhappily. At first blush, he had viewed it as an attempt to draw him into her life as if they were new lovers who wanted to know everything about each other so they would understand what had made each of them such a marvelous person, what liens of past failures and present fears they could hold on each other, what miracle of fate had preserved them for each other. And then—and for some reason he found this more disturbing by far—he realized what she was doing to his theory, which he now passed on to her, that women who were nicknamed Bunny saw themselves as furry, cuddly creatures and were trying to make everybody else see them the same way.

"Some detective you are. I was a great, ungainly girl, the least furry, cuddly creature anybody could have asked for. Or did." The gentle, teasing note on which she had begun had been overtaken by a note of rebuke. And if it was self-rebuke, her apology for having begun to fail him that far back, so long before she knew him, it was also directed outward, toward him, urging him, as she pressed his hand, to take another look and see what one did not have to be any part of a detective to see; asking who was failing whom now. It had been natural enough, she sighed, solving what should have been no mystery for him, that with a name like Beyner the boys would see how unhappy they could make her by calling her Bunny. "The only girls who called me Bunny were the girls who most disliked me, they being the two best friends I had." Her eyes were glistening with tears. "Sugar and spice and everything nice, isn't that what little girls are made of?"

She moaned his name. Getting no response she remained perfectly still under his hand, tingling at the roots, breathing deeply until she was able to get the skin back over her. When she was able to speak again, her voice came trembling through a clench of hands and teeth. "The instinct to aggress shows up very early. How's that? I know that from my books. And now I know it good, do I not? Do I not sure as hell know it from my little monsters who like the Bunnies of your youth . . . oh, Jim . . . how I envy you the furry, cuddly Bunnies of your youth, damn damn them, who were not afraid to walk across the field at night, every one. *Jim . . . ?* And get caught."

She lay perfectly still, trembling in spasms, taking longer, deeper breaths, the skin gone and the bones melting. "The psychology is elementary." Her voice was tearful and beseeching. "The one purpose of their lives . . . our lives . . . is to get a man in bed, the marriage bed preferab- . . . and every one of us is every one of us's competition and each of us . . . *Jim . . . ?* becomes . . . *For godsake, Jim . . . !*"

He raised himself up on his elbow and patted her on the cheek to show that it was going to be all right, and was surprised to find that her cheek was wet. *Beyner . . . Bunny.* Once you were able to put them together it seemed so obvious. That's what was bothering him. How in the name of hell could he have missed it?

She was trying to fit herself into him. Her tongue was all over him, and her hands were running under his T-shirt. "A little more," she pleaded. "Oh gee, just a little more, honey."

Ambose pushed her back and got on top of her. As ridiculous as it was that he could have missed anything so obvious, what did it matter? Why did his mind cling to it? Unless there *was* something there that was important to him. A sympathetic chord that had been set to vibrating just outside his ear.

"I love you," she breathed, arching up to him—a barely audible whisper from the dreamer of the great romance. Her hands came down to guide him. He pushed them aside.

A sympathetic chord vibrating just outside the ear. Lapping at his consciousness. Yes. He had overlooked something that should have been just as obvious down where it *was* important. And what could that mean, he asked himself, becoming excited, except Norman Bannerman and the Tabor trial.

"I love you, Jim," she said, and this time it was no more than a simple plea for him to say something tender to her, if only for form's sake, as her need for kindness now that she was being embarked, some token words of wooing, rose up from the deeper coils to overwhelm the other need that had been so overwhelming.

"Spread yourself," he said.

She gave a startled scream as he entered, and then a long restorative sigh. "Don't go away," she said hoarsely. "Don't leave me." He had heard of screamers but he had never come across one before. Intrigued, he left her, ignoring her pleas, and upon his return got a plaintive, grateful whimper but no scream. That pleased him. If she had been a screamer, it would have been all over the courthouse. He could congratulate himself that nobody could make her scream but him. He experimented a few more times with somewhat inconclusive results, making her wait longer and longer until, her limits reached, she took him back with a fierce welcoming grunt and clamped her legs across his back to hold him there.

"All right, Bunny," he said. "I won't leave you. Just lay back and relax."

The business about the screaming having been settled to his satisfaction, his mind turned itself back to the more important question that had been lapping at the edges of his consciousness through it all. Something he knew and didn't know he knew. Something he hadn't permitted to penetrate.

What?

"O god," she said. "Where have you been all these years when you could have been giving me this?"

"That's funny, I was thinking the same thing." Holy Toledo, it was going to be hard to think straight if she didn't shut up. "I was thinking we've missed out on a lot of good—"

Tommy Mallon! Why had Tommy all of a sudden put the offer of a partnership to him? Because Tommy had all of a sudden missed him so bad after four years? Tommy had sure as hell been trying to tell him something and he had missed it. No. That was something to bounce around in his mind later, but it wasn't it.

What?

What? Lapping at the edges of his consciousness, like a wave at a sand castle. Washing up and fading away. Each time biting a little deeper before it receded, but always fading away.

Karney? Old Mike Karney, ridden with guilt. Couldn't tell his hammer from his carpenter, he'd said. Had he been right in thinking Karney had been offering to manage his campaign? Or had it been something else Karney was driving at there?

No! He'd been right the first time. It had to have something to do with that oily bastard, Bannerman. *What?* He'd been snatching at odds and ends. The right way to do this was to run the whole case through from the beginning, slowly and methodically, prodding his memory. Slow and easy, witness by witness, file by file. In box–Out box.

The waves came lapping up at him. Up and away. Closer and closer. Slipping away. He had it . . . he lost it. Cutting deeper and deeper. He knew that he knew it. Faster and faster. He knew that he *knew* it. Bannerman coming up and Bannerman sliding away. Bannerman, like a worm in his throat. What had he missed? What hadn't penetrated? Up and up and . . . and . . . aaaand . . . hold it, hold it, don't go away . . . the prickly heat on the back of his neck told him he had it . . . he *knew* that he knew it . . . over it lapped, over the hump, over the sand castle, the waves biting deeper and the sand castle crumbling . . . he *knew* it . . . crumbling to nothing in the pounding surf, crumbling like rotting teeth in a stinking mouth as the camera stopped on Otis Moscrip sitting in the police Annex as Ambose had first seen him: the smeared T-shirt, the socks falling down over the dirty ankles, the pale collapsible lips, the fetid breath.

Otis Moscrip, who had fallen to him too easily and too conveniently.

It was the teeth! "Never look a gift horse in the mouth," that had been the connection. The sum of his experience, all of his instincts, had been trying to warn him that this was one gift horse to be looked square in the mouth. He'd have to tell Doc Swann about that. He could just hear Doc saying, "I'd hate to ever get in your clutches, Big Fellow."

Bunny was in his ear telling him not to stop now, whispering what they had been missing and what she wanted him to do to her. "Bannerman," he breathed to himself. Emitting a low growl, he grabbed a fistful of her hair and yanked her head down to the pillow. Oh, what he'd do to him! Bannerman had sent him a phony witness, and how he must have chuckled when Ambose grabbed him. And —oh-oh? What about Lulu Brahms? Brahms, too? Yeah. Remembering the chronology. Sure. Bannerman had fed him Brahms, tipped all the way, to keep him and his boys occupied and off his own back while he and that Chicago investigator of his were scratching around for a phony they could send to him. And like a goddamn fathead straight off the farm, he'd let himself be sucked into that one, too.

Bunny's fingernails were running down his back, hard enough to scratch. *Damnit!* Before he could get around to telling her to cut it out, though, he began to chuckle, first to himself and then aloud. He had turned the tables on Bannerman. Now he was in the saddle. Now he had Norman Bannerman under his guns. It was only a matter of letting No-o-o-orman think he still had him sucked in and then—wham, bam and thank you, ma'am—and fat-faced Norman is caught—kerplunk—in his own trap. He could see Bannerman's soft and spongy face in front of him, splattering like a ripe melon that was being smashed . . . and smashed . . . and smashed. He could hear Bannerman scream.

Huh? He became aware that Bunny had begun to scream again. A throaty, keening scream wrung from the deeper coils, not wanting to hold on and not wanting to let go. The massed flesh under him was in the final throes. Thank god, it was almost over; how did anybody expect him to think? He went to work on it, to finish it off for them both, without wiping either Bannerman's face or his own chuckle completely out of his mind.

She lay across his chest, looking at him with a depth of love drawn from the drowsy, glandular, deep-seated contentment that had followed the long ride. "It was like a snowslide," she sighed. "An avalanche."

"Bunny," he said, with a contentment just as obvious and far more boisterous, "you don't know what you just did for me." To prove it, he rewarded her with a little pat on the backside and immediately pressed her face down into his chest to keep her from chattering on about it. All right, they'd sent him a phony in Moscrip, and from everything Ambose knew about big, bad Norman Bannerman, big, bad Norman Bannerman was planning to put on a fancy show, benefit for the world's press, while he was breaking him down. What better way to show Norman Bannerman to best advantage and, while he was about it, prove collusion between the witness and the prosecution. Once he came up with records to show that Otis had been hospitalized as an addict somewhere—and he would, he would —it would be a small matter to establish that Otis had been picked up on a robbery charge and been kept nice and cozy and well fed in his habit, courtesy of the Brederton County taxpayer.

"Me, too," Bunny had managed to whisper while she was being smothered against his chest. It had been in her mind to tell him that she had never known it could be like this, but some better instinct told her it would sound too much like her cheap romantic fiction. She could just hear what her rotten kids would say if one of their little tramps ever said anything like that. More's the pity for them. It was pleasant enough to just nuzzle against him, in a dreamy floating languor, reliving the long strenuous session in her mind. Wow! She had really been put through the paces. He had shown her who the master was, James Ambose had, making her wait, making her beg for it. And, hadn't it been worth it, every sweet, suffering second of it! The important thing was that Jim had enjoyed it, too. The way he'd laughed and gone crazy there. Like a madman. She'd be lucky if she didn't have a sore bottom in the morning the way he'd whacked away at it. A wild man! Grabbing her hair and bouncing her head up and down on the pillow with one hand, and whacking away at her with the other. Wheeee. Didn't he know she wasn't a kid anymore?

And while she nuzzled against his chest, grazing on it, there welled up in her such a longing to talk about it and have him talk about it to her. She longed to tell him what a great lover he was; how she had just kept coming and coming. She wanted to tell him he had taught her what women were made for, and the imagery for it just seemed to flow into her head. She had felt as the fruitful earth, she heard herself saying, spreading out her bounty for him. She would be for him, she wanted to say, as an ocean in which he would swim and which she, as ocean, would share the swim with the swimmer.

Pushing back against his hand, she was able to turn her head enough to look upon him. "Did I make you warm, James Ambose?" she asked, doting on him.

He grunted. Paying no mind to her.

The look became a little anxious. "Was it good for you, dear?" she asked timidly.

"It was good. Let's save the postmortems, huh? What do you want, a testimonial?" Oh, it was good, all right. The best. The jury never forgave a witness for lying, much less the prosecution for putting a lying witness on the stand. Bannerman would be punching a hole right in the middle of their premeditation case and, in the process, showing the jury that the state thought so little of their first-degree case that they'd felt it necessary to put a lying witness on the stand. *Mama mia,* was it good. Good and dirty. Good *because* it was so dirty. If he had been dumb enough to go for it, James Ambose, idiot prosecuting attorney, would have deserved everything he got.

"Damnit," he said. "Cut that out!"

There was still a lot to think about—like whether Nevins had to know about it right away—and although he had the whole weekend to plot his course, his mind was already alive with the possibilities.

Bunny was still grazing around his chest trying to get loving with him. "Can't you understand English," he said. In a sudden surge of annoyance he shoved her away from him and turned his back to her.

He woke from a light nap, so light that the after-image of his dream was still imprinted on his mind—the face of Norman Bannerman, battered to a pulp. His mouth was dry, and there was a strange smell, not unlike the odor of stale whiskey after the card game has broken up and everybody has gone home. He realized that it was Bunny's perfume just about the same time he heard her in the bathroom, urinating—that must have been what woke him up—and the picture that presented itself to his mind made him grimace. Not the vulgarity of it so much as the enforced intimacy. If she had to do it, and he supposed it was the hygienic thing to do, was it asking too much that she have the delicacy to do it *quietly?*

Bannerman had the right idea there. Call a cab and send them home. Bannerman . . . ? Comparing Bunny with the cheap tramps Bannerman ran with was so flagrantly unfair that the grimace was replaced by a twinge of conscience. He just wished to hell she'd get dressed and go home and leave him to his own bed, was that so bad? Giving women their due, they served their purpose, but he could have got that around town without all this crap about wining and dining them.

It had all been to the good, that business with the slut in the law library. Nevins had done him a favor there. It had cut him off from the wasteful, time-consuming pursuit of women and set him free to go on alone without encumbrance or illusion. He nodded to himself rather solemnly, his mind pleased and his conscience eased by the happy confluence of his current needs and his basic philosophy. Without illusion. Grant them their relief and their moment of given pleasure, but grant them nothing more. Anyway . . . The toilet flushed. Anyway. He had done as well for her as she for him. Hell, he thought, it had been an act of charity, a public service. She had been throwing those looks at him all night. If ever he had seen anybody asking for it. No, he decided, he didn't have to tell Nevins about Moscrip yet. He'd wait until he had a more definite idea about what he was going to do. She had, he saw as she came out of the bathroom, put on her brassiere and half slip.

Without looking at him—deliberately not looking at him—she sat down on the very edge of the bed and began to pull on one of her stockings.

"Hey." He rose up on one elbow. "What the hell do you think you're doing?"

In the dim light that came from the bathroom he could see the beaten, woebegone look about her. "It's all right." With a small, hopeless motion of her hand she released him from any and all responsibility. "I am well learned in the psychology of the post-coital revulsion of the human male. A one-night stand is a one-night stand." She lifted her hand and studied her fingernails without interest. "Just another experience in the fascinating daily rounds of your ever-obliging career girl." Her head moved just enough so that he could see her full profile. She looked older. Washed-out. Saggy. "I don't expect you to believe it but I get my information mostly out of books."

"Oh hell," he said gruffly. "Come on back to bed. It's late."

She didn't really resist when he reached out to pull her back in. She just let her dead weight be pulled back against him. "It's all right," she said. "Really." After awhile, she rested her hand along his arm. A sigh rose out of her, so deep and heavy that he could feel her whole body heave. Opening her eyes, she patted his wrist lightly and comfortingly. "We never expire of grief or shame. Being a woman is humbling work." She made such a brave effort at a smile that he was overcome by guilt. "Hey," he said, making a conscious effort of his own. "How come you didn't tell me you're a screamer? Goddamn, you like to scared the daylights out of me."

The whisper of a smile drifted over her, this time despite herself. Her fingertips went drifting back along the side of her hair in an unconscious tidying operation. "One does not expect nor is one looking for any unfelt words of endearment." Immediately, as good as her word, she placed a finger over his lips to spare him the necessity of looking for any. "You know what I admire about you?" In the effort it took to still his lips she had twisted around as far as her waist would take her, an awkward movement which left her cradled awkwardly against his arm and looking straight down at him. "You're a real man. You know what you want and you take it. And you know what you don't want and don't bother with it. I wish I could be like that."

"Ho-kay!" He slapped the bed so hard that she bounced. "What I want is for you to get that thing off and come back to bed. You said it yourself, so don't argue. And don't be so goddamn sensitive for a change, huh?"

Her eyes remained on him for another moment, but so blankly that it was impossible to tell what she was thinking. The stocking had fallen down around her ankles. She started, quite dutifully, to take it off, then stopped abruptly to rest her forehead in her hand for a long, long moment as if she had suddenly become dizzy.

The stocking was all she took off. She slipped back into the bed as gingerly as possible, tucking her feet under the sheet and sort of sliding in after them with the prim modesty of a well brought up young lady adjusting her skirts.

Ambose had the feeling that she was keeping the slip and brassiere on as a last small token of dignity and independence and he rather respected her for it. As it happened, he was wrong. She kept them on because she was afraid he might wake up before she did in the morning, and she did not think she was presentable naked.

When Ambose woke up, the slit of sun coming through the blinds lay across his eyes, and the space alongside him was empty. Her clothes weren't anywhere to be seen, either. Apparently she had slipped out during the night. As soon as he was safely off to sleep, probably. If she had, she had found the blankets in the closet before she left, covered him and—hell—practically tucked him in, a final, leave-taking gesture so thoughtful and maternal that he found himself enormously moved. The bedcover was folded neatly on the radiator box, the black throw pillows alongside it, and as his thoughts went back to when he had woken up during the night he could remember that her clothes had been folded neatly alongside them. For some unfathomable reason, the fact that he had treated such a neat women with . . . well, with less than scrupulous regard for her feelings left him saddened beyond measure.

And then he heard her moving around in the kitchen.

While he was washing up, she came to the bathroom door to find out whether he'd like to have her fry some eggs for him. Bent over the basin and rubbing his face briskly, he told her to scramble them. He also told her she'd find some bacon in the utility bin in the refrigerator, second shelf up from the bottom.

"I know, I looked. I know all about where you keep your coffee and your coffeepot and things like that, too." And then she said, "It all looks so good I think I'll join you if you don't mind having company." Looking up at her through the mirror, he understood that she was letting him know, just in case he might be wondering, that she had not been out to assert any squatter's rights to his kitchen while he was asleep and defenseless.

He liked her more all the time. Thinking back on it, he wasn't really sure why he had decided to call her, except that she'd been around him these past few days and he had found himself in such a gloom over Chobodian's death that for one of the few times in his life he'd found the loneliness of his apartment intolerable.

He stared at himself in the mirror. Maybe, he thought, shaving more slowly, it had been in the back of his mind from the first. He grunted, in audible surprise. Who knew?

Shaven but still shirtless, he slipped quietly to the bedroom door, just beyond the bathroom, and watched her across the living room and through the kitchen dividers as she moved around the stove. She wasn't young but she had a good enough body and she aimed to please. She thought he was King Shit, no doubt about that. He continued to watch her, quite thoughtfully. A little droopy around the breasts, as he remembered, but a good broad spongy bottom. And very neat, a very neat woman. You had to give her points there.

Maybe he had, maybe he had.

It was not until she was putting the first batch of eggs on the table that she became aware she was being watched, and as she looked up, back across the living room, her hand went to her hair in that unaffectedly helpless gesture of hers, and there was something in both her embarrassment and her shy pleasure that he found most appealing. She could be of use to him. Yes.

He thought about it all through breakfast. He continued to think about it while she was washing the pan and the dishes and the coffeepot, and putting them back exactly where she had found them.

Saturday, August 2

It was easy to pick out Jethro Ambose on the sunporch of the nursing home. Every other patient was sitting in a basket wicker chair, and every wicker chair was turned west toward the sun. Jethro Ambose, in his metal folding chair, was turned away from all of them in inviolate privacy. In all probability he would have been the first person any stranger's eyes would have been drawn to in any case, for amidst the general surrender to age and infirmity there was a fierceness about him that translated itself into a positive source of energy. His hair was still darkly brown against the gray all around him. His posture rigid against the prevailing softness. You would not have thought he was seventy-two. You would not have thought he was dying, either.

There was no change in his expression as he saw his son coming toward him, except perhaps for an all but imperceptible narrowing of his eyes against the sun.

"Sir," Jim said, "I happened to be up here in Monroe and I thought I'd drop on by and see how you were coming along."

The old man looked out straight ahead across the rolling well-kept field. "That's a mighty thoughtful thing for yew to do. Don't get any visitors here. Nor need them."

Hearing the deep and cavernous voice left you with the sensation of having been given a glimpse into the heavier bone structure and deeper tunnel in which Jim Ambose's voice had been formed. The features of the father and son were, in a manner of speaking, turned the other way around. Jethro's nose, more finely drawn, was a narrower replica of his son's. His eyes were deeper sunk within the withered flesh around the socket, and while there was little more than a hint of the high, flat cheekbones, that was more than enough, taken in combination with the sunken cheeks, to establish the same overall facial formation. And yet, such was the inner strength of Jethro Ambose that there was never any sense but that the older, fainter face was the original, and the younger one the copy. You had the feeling that if you could flesh those wasted features out and study them from any angle you pleased, you would find Jim Ambose crouching somewhere in his father's face, as in those childhood puzzles where, with a minimum of time and effort, you could find the cat the crafty artist had hidden somewhere amidst the leaves and branches.

When he indicated that he'd just as soon go back to his room, it could be seen that his bony shoulders were still square and, if such a thing were possible, even straighter across than Jim's. And though he moved with an arthritic stiffness, there was an effort to hold himself perfectly erect. Dressed as he was, in clean, neat brown work clothes (the shirt and pants of different shades), and with his black belt pulled tight, he could have just as easily been taken for a worker as a patient.

As they stepped up onto the patio, one of the old men, totally round, totally bald, totally smiling, asked, "Is this your son, Mr. Ambose? My, my." Jim's father didn't look at him or answer him. Not until they were in the room did he say, "Bad type of people they got in here. Don't bother me none, 'cause I don't pay them any mind. Parson Williams died, you know. Mealy little man you saw there, can't tolerate their own selves so they bow and scrape in the hope someone will be willin' to take them on for friend."

"Parson Williams? The parson? I didn't know that, sir. You should have wrote me, I'da come up for the funeral."

"He'd a been jes' as dead. I got my nap in five minutes but you go on, son. I'm listening."

"Well sure, Pa. You go on ahead with your nap and I'll go on about my business. I just thought I'd come by and see how you were doing, seein' I was up around these parts, you know?"

"C'n put off my nap. I ain't goin' nowhere I can think of or doing nothin' cain't wait. Wouldn'a done you no good to come up, they shipped his body back to where his folks be. Left me to thinkin'. Man oughta be buried in the ground he growed from. He's gonna be there long enough, he might jes' as well feel to home."

Although Jethro had seated himself on the side of his bed, just inside the door, Jim, of necessity, had remained standing. There were chairs pulled up alongside each of the other three beds in the room. Not Jethro's. The first time Jim had visited him, Jethro had said, "C'n git y'self a chair to sit on if it suits you. Don't cotton to 'em myself. Have a chair around, people git to feeling like it gives them a right to sit down." The tiny bureaus next to the other beds were covered with pictures of families and an assortment of radios, clocks, ash trays, tissues and candy bars. On Jethro's bureau there was only the tiny lamp issued by the nursing home and a well-worn, much-thumbed Bible.

The last of his father's short staccato fiats having being issued, Jim cleared his throat and said, "I didn't come down this time for any appeal, sir. In case you might have been wondering about that. They've been keeping me kinda busy lately trying this case, you just might have heard about it. This man killed the Chief Justice of the United States Supreme Court, David Boone Wilcke, and they're trying to say he's crazy." He smiled rather nervously to show what he and his father thought of them trying to get away with anything as shammy as that. "It's a real big trial, sir. People from all over the world been comin' in to write about it for their papers and magazines. From Germany and England, and there's a whole mess of them from France. I've been kept kinda busy trying it for the state to see they don't get away with saying he was crazy." He moistened his lips. "I thought you might have heard something about it, sir."

Jethro reached for his Bible, and holding it loosely ran his thumb along the side of the pages. "Nurse here come in one day and tole me I could come see yew on The Instrument. All red in the face and blowing—fat, buttocky woman who's a disgrace to the sight. Tole her I dis-me-approve of The Instrument and all those whose forms and faces appear thereon as she well knew . . ."

"I know, Pa . . ."

". . . Tole her I'd lived my three score and twelve without peeping at it but the once to make my determination and put my hand to it in wrath, as well yew know."

"What I'da been on, it would've only been a news show, sir. No different than if they were asking me for the newspaper, say."

"I have no fault to find in ye, son. Tole you when you went in to fight on the side of the law I was mighty proud to have you there." He tapped his heart. "Tole your mother I loved her when I asked her to be married, which was the fit 'n' proper thing to do. Never thought I had to tell her again." His eyes rose briefly to his son, conveying in his approval of the wife who didn't have to be told a second time his disapproval of the son who did.

Jim shifted awkwardly on his feet. "Well, sir . . ." He rubbed his hand across his eyes and, as he opened them again, back across his mouth. "I find myself thinking a lot of Ma from time to time lately. Those were hard days on the farm, you know, Pa. They was good days but hard. Just you and Ma and me. Remember the time when the man came down from the marshall's office with the attachment and you—"

"Your mother's always here," Jethro Ambose said, patting his heart. "I swore on the Book I was taking her to my bosom till death us do part, an' there's still my part of the bargain to be kep'."

"Hey, Pa. Remember the time we swapped that broken-down tractor from the elder Storey boy. We give our good milk cow for it and the first time you tried to start it up it went bucking all around like one of them Wild West rodeo horses, spewing black oily smoke all around, and you said—"

"The older Storey boy who got his throat slit for him in a honky-tonk on the way to Californy. Redmond was what his name was. I allow he was tryin' to cheat someone thataway, too."

"He sure didn't cheat us, Pa. Remember how you went over there with your double-barrel shotgun, and me right alongside with mah li'l squirrel gun, facin' the whole pack of 'em down, and you said—"

"I said, 'If yew fed mah milk cow ah'm much obliged and ah'm owing you the market price on provender. If yew milked mah milk cow yer owing me the railside cost per bucket.' "

"An' tole 'em they could pick up their tractor at our barn site any time they was of a mind, and if they were looking to pick up something else, now was the time to speak up smart."

A gentling reminiscence came over the hard, bony face. "Laws, I haven't thought of that in like to thirty years."

"They didn't have that much to say, them Storeys, did they, Paw? Remember how yew led the milk cow back down that little dirt road of theirs, with her tail swishin' the flies away and the old bossy-bell tinkling, and me right alongside acoverin' 'em with mah li'l squirrel gun that yew'd bought for me from out of Lame Henry's now that I'd come to my eighth year? How many of them Storey boys was there, Paw? Laws, there must have been a good six or seven. An' all of them full growed."

"The righteousness of our cause was what stayed the Storeys' hand, son. The righteous are as bold as lions, the wicked flee. Proverbs." As he held up the Bible for Jim to see and profit thereby, the crisscross of wrinkles on the back of his hand, deeply ingrained with their deeply rubbed dirt, was plain to see. "What was true in the past is true in the present and will be true forevermore. Yer Maw was never a woman to dwell overmuch in the past, son. Yer Maw and me were much alike that way."

414

"Me neither, sir. But they sure was hard times, wasn't they? I sure do think a lot about Maw these days." He licked his lips. "I tell you what, Paw. Why don't you come live with me and let me take care of you. I've got this big apartment, with all the room—"

"Tole you once, tole you five times. I don't aim to be no burden on my young. Don' know why I have to keep telling yew all the time."

"Well, yeah. The way it is, there's this, though. I'm getting married now, Pa. I've met this woman. I was going to bring her up so you could meet her. I think you're gonna like her. And now with the parson gone—"

"Why, shore. I c'n see yew cain't afford to keep up on the payments for me now yew've got the support of a wife on you, Jamey—"

"And now with the parson dead and gone, it just come to me how you don't have any real friends left here. She's a real intelligent woman, Pa. You're gonna like her. Graduated from college—"

"The ways of the Lord are wondrous to behold. Here I was thinking I jes' might want to pick myself up and go on back home and visit with some old-time friends before I die—"

"But not the kind to be show-offy about it, nothing like that. Yew don't have to worry none about that, Pa. Real homespun and down-to-earth. You're gonna like her. I was gonna bring her up for you to meet—"

"Jes' pick myself up, slow and easy like. And a voice shall say, This is the way, walk ye in it. Isaiah. No need for yew to fret none, Jamey. I wouldn't feel right in my mind burdening yew with my care, what with the support of a wife on yew."

Jim tried to tell him that the money wasn't any problem at all. Jethro, stern as a prophet of Israel, told him no woman newly wed and worth her salt would tolerate an old man traipsing around her house. It was downright indecent, just the thought of it.

"Pa! I want to take care of you! I want you to come live with me so you'll know the kind of work I'm doing . . . what I am . . . something about me. So I can get to know you some, too, Pa. There's plenty we could still do together. We could go quail hunting when you're up to it. We could . . . Why, I'll bet you'd . . . There's a lake I know, Pa, where the morning air's so sweet and clean, there in the reeds when the duck are flyin' and . . . there's so much, Pa!" In his desperation Jim had squatted down beside the bed and grasped his father by the shoulders, not realizing what he was doing until . . . "There's some farmland out not ten miles from where I live, and the soil so rich you'd . . . Why, we could buy us a piece of land if we were a mind to. What's to stop us?"

Not realizing what he was doing until he was struck numb by what he saw in his father's eyes.

Even as Jim's hands were being withdrawn, Jethro Ambose drew his shoulder away—the shoulder itself offended—never changing that look that was as cold as frostbite and as terrible to behold.

In desperation Jim rubbed the palms of his hands down the front of his pants, wiping them clean. Unable to think of anything else to do, he swallowed hard. "Like you say, sir, you don't have that much time left, and I just thought it would be kind of nice to spend as much of it as we could together."

Firmly and deliberately, Jethro lay himself down upon the bed and, just as firmly and deliberately, closed down his eyes. He was getting downright tired, he told his son from behind the shutters. He hadn't talked so much in he didn't know how long, and he sure did thank Jim for coming in to see him while he was passing through. "I jes' think ah'll do that. Jes' pick me up slow and easy like and mosey

415

on back home. I got some old-time friends will take care of me fine. You and your woman don't need to be worryin' yerself none there."

"Well, that sure does sound fine, sir." As tightly as he squeezed his eyes, he wasn't quite able to squeeze the mistiness away. There was something else he had wanted to say, but he wasn't quite able to remember what it was. "I'd take it kindly if you'd let me know where you were when you got settled," he said, speaking with difficulty. "An' who you might be staying with, if you would. I most surely would appreciate that, sir. Sure would."

"Why, shore," Jethro Ambose said, closed down tight and all shuttered up. "They's some good people 'round here. Ah'm shore the people here will tell yew right off I leave."

He had known there was something else he had meant to say, but he was out into the fresh air before he remembered that he had wanted to ask his father if he remembered the time they had shot the big ole grizzly bear.

Sunday, August 3

Harold Halpern wasn't exactly looking forward to seeing Sam again, and finding Johnny Gerard on the desk didn't make him feel any more comfortable. Quickly enough, if by indirection, Johnny let him know that he wasn't on punishment duty. Luke Okula, who had been down to work the desk today, had been assigned to take over Johnny's place on the guard detail, and it had been easier, it seemed, to have Gerard step into Luke's tour than to juggle the whole roster.

To Hal's astonishment, he saw that Johnny had made out the pass to Sam's cell up on the Catwalk. "It's Sunday," Johnny said. "Why not live a little? I'll let you in on a secret. That Iron Box up there always depresses the hell out of him." Gerard grinned at him then, the kind of sly, kidding grin Hal wouldn't have associated with him at all. "Of course, I never was able to what you might say straighten it out in my mind whether it was the Box or the lawyers." He said, "This way it will be more like a friendly visit."

Up to now, Hal realized, he had always seen Johnny under tension. With just the two of them there, on a lazy Sunday morning, he was an entirely different person. (The Relationship between Environment and Personality, with all its Infinite Variables, Hal thought. Now there was a doctorate paper for a sociology major to get his teeth into.) From what Johnny had heard from Dick Blasser, Sam was down in the dumps. Way down. Mrs. Tabor had taken a runout powder over the weekend, running away from the press. Not that he could blame her, he said, blaming her. But Stringfellow had been permitting her to visit Sam every day, and the way it had worked out she hadn't been in now since Thursday morning. "Two things worth thinking about. He lives for her visits. Maybe somebody ought to tell her." He paused just long enough before going on for Halpern to pick up the stutter that came when a client wasn't sure he should be telling you what he knew he was going to. "Luke Okula is a son. The kind that don't belong in the department. Nuff said?"

More than Johnny knew. Hal had been wondering how he could let Johnny know that he hadn't given Bannerman the note without sounding as if he were being disloyal, and Johnny had just made it easy. Confidence for confidence. "I don't know why I didn't," Hal told him. "I just didn't. If I had, I don't think he'd have done that to you."

"He'd a done it," Johnny said. "That's why you didn't tell him." By his matter-of-fact delivery, unclouded by any trace of bitterness or recrimination, he was saying that Bannerman's actions were so far beyond Bannerman's control that to blame him or set prior conditions to them was a waste of time. For the second time in a matter of minutes Harold Halpern had to tell himself that he sure had been underestimating Johnny Gerard.

"What do you think?" Gerard asked. "Anything that can be done for the little guy?"

"I am a very junior attorney on this. I just carry the bag."

"You'll do all right, Halpern. I've been watching you. Don't tell Stringfellow, though. Strict disregard to orders. That ain't what I mean, though."

Hal knew what he meant, and he could have told him that he didn't know the half of it. Halpern had come in yesterday all charged up by the knock-down, drag-out fight he'd had with Bannerman after they had left Sam, and fully prepared to set Sam's mind at ease. He had left shaken to the roots. He had begun by telling Sam not to take anything Bannerman had said the previous night too seriously because—and Hal could tell him this better than anybody else—the pressure of defending him was enormous. He had described how Bannerman was working twenty hours a day and living on Scotch, Dexedrine and the adrenalin flow. He had expressed complete confidence that after Bannerman got himself some rest over the weekend he would be an entirely different man.

Sam had listened silently, his mouth pursed in suspicion and accusation, and when Hal was finished, he had said cunningly, "No, Norman Bannerman knows what's best for me."

Through the rest of the visit Sam had been variously apathetic, sullen, cryptic, knowing, tense and, at times, seemingly on the edge of tears. At one moment he would be meek and anxious to please, and a moment later there would come over him that look that was not so much secretive as full of secrets. The one brief moment of lucidity had occurred when Sam came climbing back from out of one of his long silences to ask pathetically, "He doesn't want me to have one friend, does he? Not one."

The worst moment came shortly before Hal left. Pointing urgently to Hal's briefcase, making head-twitching, eye-rolling motions to warn him that the room was bugged, Sam had signaled that he wanted a sheet of paper. On the paper he had printed: MUST SEE AMBOSE.

Holding Halpern's eyes to his, he placed his index finger to his lips, laid it on the paper under Ambose's name, brought it back to point at himself and mouthed: *Friends.*

While Halpern was trying desperately to think of something to say (to agree with him was unthinkable, to disagree with him might be worse), Sam ripped the sheet of paper off the pad and dashed around to his side of the table so that Hal could watch over his shoulder while he printed in large, frantic letters: AMBOSE AND I CAN MAKE DEAL. FRIENDS. He underlined FRIENDS several times, thrust the paper into Halpern's hands, snatched it back again and tore it into small pieces. Whereupon, cautioning him once again to silence, he had stuffed the incriminating evidence into Hal's pocket.

The Catwalk was the name given to the top tier of the jailhouse where prisoners who were on trial, or awaiting trial, for murder were held. The jail elevator didn't go all the way up. You had to walk up about half a flight of stairs to a solid steel door, which was mechanically operated by a guard who, having been alerted by a buzzer that was activated the moment the elevator passed the fifth floor, was able to study you through a peephole as you approached. As a further security measure, you still had to pass through an electric eye that was so sensitive that Hal had heard Vera Tabor tell Bannerman how all kinds of bells and lights had begun to ring and flash around her the first time she visited Sam. The electric eye, it had been determined after a matron had been called, had picked up the metal support built into the brassiere of her foundation garment.

The Catwalk itself was exactly that. A narrow metal catwalk encircling the entire upper deck. Since the occupants of the Catwalk cells were not permitted to mix with the rest of the jail population during the regular exercise period, their cell doors were left open and they were allowed to roam the Catwalk pretty much at will. One of them, in fact, a young, dark-haired, good-looking fellow, was leaning over the rail off at the far curve beyond Sam's cell, staring down at nothing. It was odd, now that Halpern thought about it. With all the suicide precautions they took with these guys—no belts or sharp objects; shaving only under close supervision—there was nothing to prevent them from taking a header to the steel deck six floors below. A hell of a way to go, Hal thought. And a hell of a thing to be thinking about right now.

The cells were small, with nothing in the way of furnishing except a cot, a wooden table and a chair. And a commode in the far corner. The only thing that distinguished Sam's cell from any of the others was that there was an extra chair for the guard who had been assigned to stay with him from the time he was awakened in the morning until the time he went to bed at night. The one other minor difference was that when the guard left at night, the 100-watt overhead bulb was replaced with a 40-watt bulb, which remained lit through the night to permit the guard on duty to check up on Sam at any time.

Theoretically, a guard was with Tabor during all of his waking hours, at any rate. The head guard had been explaining to Halpern on the way down that Deputy Okula had been taken suddenly ill and—to hear him tell it—carted off in agony to a doctor. What that really meant, Halpern surmised, was that Deputy Okula had made a deal with him to leave early. Who, after all, could have anticipated that his lawyer would come calling on a warm Sunday morning and that he would be steered up to the Catwalk? From what Gerard had said about Okula, Halpern couldn't say that he was particularly surprised. From what Gerard had said, he couldn't say that he was particularly unhappy to have something on Okula, either.

Sam was in an odd posture, sitting up on his cot with his feet pulled under him, his shoulders rounded over and his hands clasped together in his lap. The top half of his coveralls were rolled down and tied around his waist, below the prison undershirt. The Sunday paper sat on one side of the table, apparently unopened. On the other side there was a cribbage board.

He said nothing at all as Hal entered. He said nothing when the guard told Hal it was customary to close the door when there were visitors. He did not alter his tight, prayerful position. He continued to stare wordlessly down at his hands after the guard left. About one thing Gerard had been both right and wrong. There had been something stiff and formal about the meetings in the Interviewing Room, but there had also been a sense of importance about them that had lent Sam stature. At home, in his tiny cell, he looked small and insignificant.

With a forced cheerfulness, the relentlessly false voice the adult uses to the child, Hal told him he had come by to find out how he was getting along and see whether he could do anything for him.

Sam blinked at him. Unshaven, his eyes looked pouchier. "I don't like to complain," he said, "but the coffee in here is terrible." The cunning look rose into his eyes, disappeared for an instant and then popped into place again. Loudly— far more loudly than was necessary—he said, "They treat me very well here, Mr. Halpern. They give me all the papers with only the stuff about the trial cut out. That's all right, I was there." The joke was encouraging, even if there was a rehearsed sound about it. It was, Hal supposed, the joke that was always passed between Sam and his jailers when the papers were brought to him. Sam had started to follow it up with a sly, underslung glance toward Hal, but halfway there his brows contracted in a vague, puzzled way. "You'd think they could leave the pictures, anyway."

Just like yesterday. Although Hal smiled back and said he wasn't missing much unless he was among the large group of admirers who couldn't see enough of Bannerman, he could see that Sam was drifting away from him, puzzling something out somewhere. Finding it at last, he said, "They won't give me my medication."

It was the tranquilizer he was talking about. Johnny had always brought it to him with his breakfast, and for two straight days now he had asked Blasser what about it and Blasser had refused to get it for him.

As, calmly and carefully, Hal tried to explain to him that Blasser didn't have the authority to go around giving prisoners drugs, that all medication was issued by the dispensary on a doctor's prescription. The quick, calculating movement of Sam's eyes told him that it was hopeless. Blasser had said that, too, and Sam knew better. He had been buying Librium without a prescription at Universal Drugs all the time, and they had never asked him for any prescription.

There being nothing to be gained by arousing Sam's suspicions any further, and nothing to be lost by humoring him, Hal promised to look into the matter and find out what had gone wrong. "It isn't Blasser, though," he said, wanting no difficulty there. "Believe me. It's out of his hands."

Sam gave no indication one way or the other whether he believed him. Or even whether he was listening. Sam was humming. Something generally tuneless and vaguely melancholy: long-held notes rising and falling from one plane to another.

"They're my friends," Sam said at last, so softly, barely breathing it, that he might have been trying it out on himself. "They're my friends," he said loudly, not looking at Hal. "Dick's my friend." He had been around cops all his life, working with them, and he knew how they thought. "They're out to show that smart lawyer it takes more than a big-time, expensive lawyer to save you. That's why they're withholding my medication." All at once he slipped his feet out from under him, thrust his head toward Hal and whispered, "They're trying to strip me of my dignity. They've got my body and now they're after my mind."

For that one second Harold Halpern could feel the hair come alive on the back of his neck.

"They're got my body locked up," Sam said hoarsely. "But nobody's going to get into here." He tapped the side of his head. "That's mine. The thing I got to do from now on is make sure nobody gets into here."

How could Halpern miss it? It was in the strain around Sam's eyes. It was in the panic lurking in the shadows. As Sam pressed forward, his knees wide apart and his hands pressed heavily on his knees, there was the sensation, stronger than ever before, of fine-spun, high-strung nerves stretching out to him. However close to the edge Sam might be, there remained in him a hard core of sanity that was fighting to preserve itself. The same hard core of common sense that had been reaching out so desperately for the tranquilizer. Sanity and common sense, the best of synonyms.

How could he possibly have missed it when the fear and the plea came streaming out toward him together, each at its separate pitch? Mind-to-mind resuscitation. "You can handle them," Hal said. "You just said you know cops, right? How their minds work. Deal with them." Nothing could have pleased him more than the soothing, confident sound of his own voice. "You can deal with them easy, Sam. You can handle them with no trouble at all."

"A hunger strike," Sam said, asking.

Hal's heart sank briefly. He shook his head and swallowed. "Up here," he said, tapping his head exactly as Sam had. "You're smarter than they are. You don't have to resort to anything like that. They have control over you, you've figured that out already. They can be generous or they can be tough. They can give you your medication or withhold it, just like you say. They regulate when your wife can see you. All kinds of things. You can make it easy or tough on yourself depending on how smart you play them."

Maybe Sam was, as Bannerman so frequently said, among the world's most suggestible people. But you couldn't have proved it by Halpern. There was no more way of telling what he was thinking than of making out the tune he was humming.

After awhile he said, "Did you see those pictures, Hal?"

It wasn't the pictures in the newspapers he was talking about this time, it was the TV film of the murder.

"Well, I've seen them many times, Sam. Sure."

"One second before you are dead, you are alive. Isn't that something?" He snapped his fingers, listened, and stiffening to attention, snapped them again. Fully alert, ardently attentive, he snapped his fingers again and again, the middle finger pointing straight out to Halpern at the end of each snap as if to adjure him to catch the sound before it died on the air. Over and over he snapped them, his chest rising and falling, taking more and more time between snaps as if he were succeeding, slowly but surely, in extending the sound farther and farther into the waiting silence.

It came to an end in a disconcertingly casual way when Sam's eyes fell upon the cribbage board. "Johnny used to come in and play cards with me," he said, shifting his attention as easily and naturally as a child. He was very anxious that Hal should know that Johnny had given him the cribbage board as a present. He showed not the slightest interest in hearing about how Johnny had been working the desk when Hal came in.

Sam had other things on his mind. Sam was busily occupied in stroking the smooth underside of the board, and as time continued to pass, there came to his face a peculiar inner smile that knew something inexpressibly secret and insupportably sad. In the next few minutes he spoke only once. "I've been with a lot of women before," he said, a trifle testily. "What the hell do you think I am?"

And then the small plump white hand went back to the cribbage board, and Sam Tabor, his eyes closed and his mouth slightly open, went traveling back down some bright tunnel of his past, stroking his memories and wiping his fears away.

When he opened his eyes again they were clear and rested. "Do you know what

420

I'm going to do?" he asked. He fixed a critical, not wholly unhumorous eye on Hal. "I'm going to outsmart 'em. I'm smarter than these cops. I've been around them all my life, I ought to."

If Hal's answering smile was uncertain, it was because Sam had been talking as if it was an idea that had just occurred to him. "I can feel the wall building around me," he said, awed by it all. "Like I'm not here. They have my body but my mind's still free." Smiling softly, he began to hum. "They haven't got my mind yet. Nor will they. You bet. Not a thing." Sam's humming floated across the room more lightly than before, alternating between the lower and the higher air. In his smile there was something inner and supremely private that he was not going to allow any of them, not even Hal, to touch.

It seemed to Halpern, listening to him, that he was beginning to recognize the tune, although he couldn't really be sure, to be truthful, whether it was because he knew it from somewhere else or because Sam's tune had, by now, become familiar.

Gerard had gone off duty. A new man, Baglio, someone Hal had never seen before, was manning the desk. Baglio didn't know from nothing about defense lawyers and doctors. All he knew was that he just worked there, and that was all he wanted to know. After a great deal of urging and, maybe, an implied threat, Halpern got him to call Stringfellow at home, and Stringfellow was only too happy to pass on the message that the word to cut off Sam's medication had come directly from Bannerman. And that if Halpern thought it was so important to start it up again, he shouldn't have any trouble in producing something in writing from a qualified medical man. Whether it was a prescription or a note, Stringfellow didn't care. Just so long as it was in writing.

Entering the cluttered motel room was like Bannerman revisited. The Great Man was perched up on the bureau, where Frank Cowhig had been sitting the first time, holding a drink in his hand just as Cowhig had. Since Bannerman was not Cowhig but inimitably and gloriously himself, he was wearing a red velvet smoking jacket over yellow pants, with a yellow ascot-like scarf and red bedroom slippers. The drink was in a silver cup on which was mounted a personalized insignia forged, it could be seen, from intertwined Old English script. "I greet you ceremoniously, Prince Harold," he boomed, holding out the cup. "Have a flagon."

The girl who was sitting in the chair where Julie had sat was a reporter from a French magazine. A thin girl in a plain white dress, straight-haired, strait-lipped, wearing thin-rimmed glasses and looking altogether like a college girl from Vermont. The one who got all A's.

In addition to the girl, there were also three men (just like the first time), seated around the bed. "I am touching bases with the international press," Bannerman announced gaily, but that was typical Bannerman hyperbole. Hal had seen all three of them around the courtroom, and they were all Frenchmen: Jacques, with the big teeth, was on one side of the bed staring up at him, and on the other side were Armand, with the gray streak up the middle of his hair, and the one and only Jean-Pierre, the excitable little fellow who was customarily sighted out in the corridor pulling at Bannerman's elbow, although most vividly remembered for that inspired moment when he had gone diving under the defense table to beat the other reporters to him.

For all the exuberance of the welcome, Bannerman was able to get across the message speedily enough that Halpern wasn't going to get to talk to him alone until the press conference was over. The defense had been getting an excellent press in France. Or, to put it another way, the United States as represented by Hilliard Nevins had been getting a very bad one. Norman Bannerman, you could be sure, had every intention of keeping it that way.

"At the time of your gloriously unfortuitous entrance," he said, sweeping the room with a wide, encompassing gesture, "my comrades from across the sea were attempting to convince me that Mr. Ambose constitutes an unsavory element in our legal process whom I have been dealing with no more harshly than he deserves. Given a little more time, I have every expectation that they shall succeed." He reached for the bottle of Scotch alongside him. "Patience and fortitude, Harold. And pluck. Pluck and fortitude always win out in the end. I never read a book that didn't say so."

Jean-Pierre scowled ferociously. "Monsieur Am-bose. *Boche!*" On the bare possibility that his opinion of Ambose had not been made lucid, he spat. Drily but noisily. "*Pas bon.* Fash-eest peeg."

"Yes," Bannerman said, determinedly misunderstanding Halpern's signals. "I seem to have fallen off the wagon." He frowned into the cup as if it were a prankish friend who had sneaked up on him when he wasn't looking. "But," he said, turning the cup so they all might see the insignia, "in what better cause than the cause of filial fealty? Dr. Everett McKinley Bannerman. A wintry, scalpel-sharpening, bone-sawing man. Father would understand. Father was a most understanding and forgiving man, a quality customarily found in such distressingly low yield in saints as to be commercially unfeasible."

His wandering gaze fell upon Halpern. "You would not believe it to look at Prince Harold now, Jean-Pierre, but Monsieur Ambose, whose call upon the services of the Holy Father's Good Offices may be viewed as otherwise problematical, is *Le Grand Boche* from whom Monsieur Halpern was untimely whelped." The brooding shadows that overhung Bannerman's eyes teetered for a moment and then fell back in, to be instantly replaced by a faintly flickering, faintly elfish smile. "But that was before I took him under my wing." He pressed the tips of his fingers together. "Observe him now," he said, his voice throbbing with insincerity. "Observe how he enters a room like a ray of sunshine, scattering joy and happiness around like dandelions. Behold the infectious high spirits and buoyant, boyish *bonhomie.*" He beamed at Halpern, bestowing his blessings upon him. "And when, at last, the Great Scorekeeper tolls off the final count, those who wish to glorify and make great my name need but to say that once there lived a man who took to his bosom an Ambose cub and raised him to become an unregenerate rakehell and gay drinking companion. That will be accolade enough."

Oh, he knew why Hal was there, all right.

The rest of the interview was completed in a mélange of English and French, with Bannerman, not really to Halpern's surprise, handling French quite well whenever he was of a mind to.

The three men got up to leave. Miss Jemaine didn't. Clearly, her male colleagues hadn't expected her to, and when Bannerman thought it necessary to explain to Halpern that she was going to interview him for a personality profile in order to bring new hope and inspiration to all French parents whose offspring were thought to be hopelessly retarded, they smiled exactly like Frenchmen were supposed to smile.

As Bannerman turned back from the door, having seen his guests off, his smile faded. "All right," he said, snapping his fingers imperiously. "Let's have it." And when Halpern told him, in his most astringent tones, that he had been waiting all that time because he wanted to talk to him alone, Bannerman said, "Oh hell. You're not worried about Colette, are you? Anything Colette hears she'll regard as strictly off the record. Won't you, Colette?"

"Strictly." Miss Jemaine sat, bored and impassive, blowing out smoke while she waited for Halpern to deliver his message like a good boy and leave.

"See if I can help you," Bannerman said when Halpern still hesitated. "You dropped in on Sam this morning, and have now come, O faithful Tonto, to deliver the minutes on his mental anguish. Sam is a virtuoso sufferer. I know." Cocking an eye at Halpern, he struck an extravagantly tragic pose. "He plucks at the heartstrings" he said in a voice trembling with passion, "with all the artistry of a Piatigorsky upon his Golden Cello."

At that moment Halpern loathed Norman Bannerman more than he had thought it possible to loathe another human being. Holding himself under tight restraint, he tried to impress upon him the absolute necessity of putting Sam back on the tranquilizer.

"No," Bannerman said. "Is that all?"

"No. It's not all. What do you mean, no?"

"I mean the best witness we have is Sam Tabor sitting there, visible to the jury at all times. For us to render Sam neutral and tranquil and just like the boy next door would, in my opinion, be benighted and counterproductive." His opinion, everything about him proclaimed, was to be accepted as infallible. All right, was there anything else? "If there is, please be more frugal of emotion. I've had a hard night." His features had already begun to soften as he turned away from Hal to contemplate with droll anticipation what unsuspected pleasures might reside within the bony frame and scholarly mien of the patiently waiting, indubitably willing Miss Jemaine. "And," he purred, strolling toward her, "if I don't watch my step I'm liable to have another."

Halpern took a couple of deep breaths to make certain he had himself under control. "I thought the idea was to get him through the trial."

"And so it is," said Bannerman. The surprise that Halpern would dare to question him about it was only slightly tinged with exasperation. "And so we are. While we're about it, we're going to do something else." Exultantly—the timing was masterful—he spun around. "We're going to win this lawsuit!" A delighted laugh broke him. "I'll let you in on a deep, dark secret, Harold. I have a ruse or two left in me yet by which to . . . catch justice by the throatlatch." His hand had gone curling out in a stealthy upcurving motion until right at the end, at precisely the indicated split second, it leaped for the throatlatch and closed tight. "We're going to *win*, dear boy. In the idiom of the street, we're gonna pick up all the marbles."

Over the closed hand his eyes shone in pure triumph. A smile curled across his lips, broad and confident. "And poor Sam is going to help us win." Poor Sam was going to help them win, he smirked, just be sitting in the courtroom "between me and thee" and giving his inimitable imitation of himself.

Behind Bannerman, Miss Jemaine was tapping the end of a cigarette with a no-nonsense briskness against her thin, flat, alien-looking cigarette holder. If he had been able to talk to Bannerman alone, Halpern couldn't help but reflect lugubriously, he would have been able to put up a much stronger argument. Whether it would have done any good or not, he'd never know. What he did know was that Miss Jemaine was Bannerman's audience now, his mirror, just as surely as Halpern had been when Bannerman was putting on his show for Sam Tabor.

Nevertheless, he tried again. Running his hand through his already tousled hair, knowing how hopeless it was, he made one last attempt to get Bannerman to understand how peculiarly Sam had been acting these past two days.

Bannerman remained completely, and even contemptuously, unmoved. His attention had been distracted by the image of himself in the bureau mirror, and all the while Halpern was trying to impress upon him how urgent it was to have Dr. Allbright examine Sam again, Bannerman was attending to the fit and set of his jacket.

"Prince Harold is at times insolent and at other times merely disputatious," he said, while he fluffed out his yellow scarf. "As you get to know him better, my dear, and I devoutly hope that you shall, you will discover that the most engaging of his many attributes is his happy-go-lucky refusal to allow his lack of experience to inhibit him from telling me how to try my case."

"We have this basic conflict," Halpern said, speaking to her for the first time. "I have this way of seeing Sam Tabor as a human being."

"Dear me." If the wisp of a smile was any indication, Norman Bannerman was going to be amused and grand and tolerant. Eyeing Halpern regally, he assumed his most mannered pose yet, one hand on hip and the other languidly extended. "How quickly we forget," he murmured. Having telegraphed that a curtain line was coming, he flicked his eyelids over him, little more than a quick dusting over. "And all the time," he said, "I thought you were the master tactician who wanted us to dehumanize him."

"Norman," Halpern said, "I don't know how much more of this he can stand. What I am trying to tell you, if you will listen to me, is that the way this is going I don't think he can get through the trial without losing his mind!"

"No tranquilizers!" Bannerman said flatly. "I said that before. I tried to make it trenchant. What am I doing wrong, dear boy? Why can't I seem to reach you?"

All right. Without saying another word, Hal warned him. Just by wagging a finger at him, too furious to say another word and acknowledging, in any case, that words had failed, he warned Bannerman to remember what he had told him in the car Friday about fighting him if he had to.

"I know," Bannerman said. "I know. The world is wickedness and strife." *Grow up*, he seemed to be saying. In case the message hadn't penetrated, he bent over Miss Jemaine and ran his fingers lightly through her hair. "We have a saying in this grand and glorious democracy of ours, Colette, that there is nothing quite so ridiculous as a young man wandering through a whorehouse protecting his zipper. Everybody laughs at him, for one thing, he misses all that available ass —and who does he think he's kidding anyway?"

He let his hand linger along the side of her neck, and by the way she covered it with hers and looked up into his eyes, Halpern could see exactly how he was looking down into hers (just as Bannerman could no doubt see—mirrors, mirrors everywhere, reflecting endlessly—exactly how Halpern would be looking as he watched them). "In such a world of wickedness and woe," Bannerman said, looking down, "how does the wise man pass the time except with a goblet of wine, a garland of roses and a wanton wench such as we have here to make the flesh merry? How long is it going to take to tumble you, Colette? Twenty minutes? Fifteen? Speak up. Time is passing. Life is fleeting. Do I hear ten?"

Although voyeurism did not rank particularly high among Halpern's big- or little-boy depravities, he remained rooted where he stood, held by the certain knowledge that Bannerman was talking entirely to him, that it had all been for him, that everything Bannerman had said and done from the time he walked through the door had been for him. That whatever role Bannerman was casting him in now, it was definitely not as a mirror.

It was Halpern himself who finally broke the spell by heading for the door, but not before Colette had sent him a brief, tormented glance. It was a look that had been meant for both of them to see, split neatly by her woman's talent for communicating along the full range of the spectrum. At head-on range, her prospective lover was supposed to filter out the delicacy of her position (*Not while he's here, please, Norman*), leaving nothing to be beamed across the room at Halpern but pure malice (*Can't you see where you're not wanted. Go!*).

Colette Jemaine's problems couldn't have worried Halpern less. It was Sam Tabor he was thinking of. Their best witness, Bannerman had said. How would the jury see the torment on Sam Tabor's face? As suffering or pure malice? "Thank you for arriving so promptly with your report," Bannerman called out. With Halpern at the opened door, Bannerman finally deigned to look at him. "In appreciation for your fidelity," he said, "I am pleased to inform you that the first of my clever ruses will be unrused at approximately eleven fifty-nine on the morrow. I will expect you at eight o'clock sharp, motor running and wheels ready to roll. Be here." He looked tired and haggard. He might have even looked— speaking of unprotected zippers—as if he were pleading with Halpern to get him out of the coming tumble with the perhaps wanton but most certainly unattractive Frenchwoman. Taking Colette by both hands, he pulled her out of the chair. "For now, be gone." He took her around the waist. "I'd tell you to be good," he said, looking at Hal while he was patting her like ask-the-man-who-owns-one. "But why bother?"

Monday, August 4

"Just who do they think they've got here?" Harry Davies exploded. "Little Ned from the *Third Reader*? You just go back and tell that certain party that you got into a conversation with an old Chinee friend of yours, and he told you, No tickee, no washee."

It was like Harry had always said—when things were going too good, you could expect them to take a turn for the worse, and when they were as bad as they could possibly get, you *knew* they were going to get worse. The morning had begun gloriously, and with the promise of glories yet to come, when Peterson had dropped the keys to the limousine onto his desk and—damn near to smiling— passed on the gladsome tidings that the papers assigning it to him officially would arrive before the day was over.

And so, before he'd had much more than a minute or two to picture the look on his neighbors' faces as he came driving down the street, Marie had come waltzing in with the news that Merril Hays, of the Merril Hays Lecture Agency, wasn't going to be able to rework his schedule so that he could come to Lowell, but that Bannerman was sending his personal assurance that there wasn't a thing for him to worry about, the deal was set.

"Now what the hell's the matter with *him,* all of a sudden?" Hilliard Nevins bawled. "Gawdamnit, you'd think we had trouble enough without Bob Stringfellow turning prima donna on us."

Ambose didn't quite smile, but he didn't quite suppress his smile either. "Well, he said it right in the memo. The drain on the manpower of his department in assigning permanent guard details to Sam Tabor and to the courtroom, too, is such that he can't spare more than one other man without seriously . . ." Before Nevins quite knew what was happening, Ambose had sprung over to the desk and plucked the memo right out of his hand. "If you ask me," Ambose said innocently, "our sheriff's got a hair across his ass."

The look Nevins gave him as he snatched the memo back told Ambose, and everybody else in the office, that it was just about all the help he might have expected from him.

Which made it even. Nevins' contribution to today's grand strategy meeting had been just about what Ambose had come to expect. Hilliard had been thinking on it over the weekend—see?—reading some of the Q. and A.'s in the newspaper, and he wanted Ambose to stop calling Tabor Sam, or else the jury was just liable to think there was something to all that stuff about how they were supposed to be such great friends.

"I think you've got something there, boss," Ambose said. "From now on, I'll call him Herman." Which was so far off Ambose's normal beat of humor that Hilliard hadn't been able to make his doghouse glare even remotely effective.

Ostensibly, Nevins had gathered the troops together because now that they had put the state's case in and got a smell of Bannerman's, he wanted to know how they thought it was going. Pawley, asked first, answered cagily that he thought it had gone about as well as could be expected. Foxx, from what he had seen, thought so too. Young Mollineaux, already overwhelmed at finding himself invited into the inner circle, endeared himself to Ambose forever by saying that if Pawley and Foxx weren't going to stick their necks out any farther than that, then he damn sure wasn't going to. Whereupon, Harvey Leigh, finding the district attorney's eyes resting on him, blurted, "What do I know, Mr. Nevins? I'm out more than I'm in. Of the courtroom. I just run the errands, that's all I do."

Nevins saw it pretty much the same way. They hadn't exactly come out of it unscathed, he said, summing up. "But, taken as a whole, I don't see where we've been damaged anywhere it could really hurt."

"Aw shit, Hilliard. If we were in any better shape, we'd be illegal." Ambose, not about to be ignored, was regarding them all with disgust. "You call that cross-examination? I'd call it a lot of whoop-de-doo and la-de-da. All our people held up fine. The shithead didn't budge a one of them." Leaning forward awkwardly, slapping his hands against the side of his knees, Ambose grinned over at Mollineaux. "Like I told you, Red. There's lousy lawyers and there's out-of-town lawyers. And poor Herman got himself one of each."

"Oh no!" Red Mollineaux flung up both of his hands, taking himself out of it. "Don't go looking at me. If I ain't arguing with them, I'm sure as *hell* not going to get caught between you two!"

426

With the defense about to put on its psychiatric case, the spotlight had turned once again to Norman Bannerman. The cameramen, retreating slowly down the corridor, were shouting and sweating, squinting and twisting; the reporters were crushed together, grunting and cursing. The spotlights, screwed and bracketed into the walls and ceiling, bathed the courtroom corridor in that otherworldly glare with which artificial light bleaches itself on top of daylight.

Norman Bannerman, moving against the tide within that pool of light, one arm around Nick Zacharias, was trying to make his way to the television platform; explaining, for the fourth or fifth time, that since Dr. Zacharias was about to take the witness stand it would be unethical for the good doctor to tell them that "the poor boy" had been particularly disturbed last night. Particularly disoriented.

Harold Halpern could have given them another reason why it would have been slightly unethical. Zacharias hadn't been to the jail last night. Zacharias hadn't seen Sam in two weeks.

Halpern had stationed himself alongside the water fountain, well out of the mob scene. "To look at them," he said to the perfect stranger standing alongside him, "you wouldn't think they already had a thousand pictures of Norman Bannerman, would you?"

Ridiculous it may have been to Halpern. Ridiculous, he could see, it was not to Zacharias. If the high, excited glow with which he looked upon the scene after Bannerman had been taken in tow by the television people was any indication, Dr. Zacharias was no longer quite so unhappy with the fate that had cast him as the lead-off witness on the first day of the final week of the Trial of the Century.

Up on the platform, Bannerman was answering that if all went well, and Mr. Ambose was able to curb his penchant for breaking into his examinations, he expected to complete his case in two days. Three at the most. The state would then put on its rebuttal witness, the local favorite, Dr. Lennard Swann, and there would then be, quite probably, a witness or two for each side on surrebuttal. "With luck, Dave," he concluded, "the jury should have the case by Friday, and we'll all be home with our loved ones in ample time to attend the religious services of the church of our choice."

That last, Halpern recognized as a private joke, the old interior laughter.

"You can take it from me," he rumbled down to his live audience as soon as the lights went out, "that Mr. Ambose is one swell guy and a compulsive do-gooder. The only fault I am able to find in him is that he has been endowed by a doting Creator with all the charm and allure of an elephant's scrotum."

All that came back at him was a sense of uneasiness and a few nervous laughs. Blinded as Bannerman had been by the lights, he had been one of the few people there who had not seen Jim Ambose come ambling down the corridor. "I'd hate to tell you what part of an elephant you remind me of, Fat Boy," Ambose called up to him. "But I'll give you a hint. I'm talking about *after* the hysterectomy."

You had to give Bannerman his due again. Surprised as he unmistakably was, he jerked his thumb toward the courtroom. "The Big Show goes on under the Big Tent in thirty minutes, which by my reckoning is less than one-half of an hour. Step right up, folks, and see the huley-huley dancer shake her tambourines! Watch the monkey scratch the monkey's head! See the elephant dance!" His face was radiant, his voice infused with the joy of the coming battle. "What I'd be worried about if I were you," he said, dropping his English accent, "is who's going to be giving it to whom in there!"

It took less than an hour after Judge Davies gaveled the Court into session for the fight to break out. It was, by unanimous agreement, the best and most satisfying one yet.

To save his life, Judge Davies couldn't have told you what they were yelling about this time. Nor could he have said that he particularly cared. Harry Davies had finally come to a decision on how to handle the Model Penal Code question, in the absence of Merril Hays, so that it would still come out to his own best advantage, and that was a far more important matter.

But once he had been shaken from his reverie by the clash of their angry voices, he could see that he had a lulu on his hands. There stood Jim Ambose, stiff and erect, his chair pushed back at an awkward, hasty angle, his horn-like fingernails exposing themselves to the Court's view every time he disposed of another point with a flick of his hand. "When Mr. Bannerman talks about modern scientific discovery," he was saying, dripping sarcasm and disdain, "a phrase that has been ringing through this courtroom like the trumpets of Jericho, he only means that his hired witnesses are trying to put across some crackpot idea from some other crackpot with a foundation grant."

Bannerman was out in front of the defense table, in the well of the Bar. "Pure essence of Ambose," he proclaimed. Distaste and hauteur stood forth on every line of his face. "I'm terrified at such a statement in an American courtroom, Your Honor. I can only hope that Mr. Ambose will one day avail himself of the opportunity of hearing a recording of what he has just said played back at the same pitch and decibel and, having with the passage of time become more learned in the law, be equally horrified."

"The only thing that horrifies me," Ambose snarled back, "is a lawyer so ignorant of the law, or maybe so indifferent to it, that he tries to get away with that kind of a question." He snorted in ill-disguised (he hoped) contempt. "There's a legal way to get the question asked, Mr. Bannerman, and I'll tell you straight out, that ain't it."

A lulu, Davies thought, settling himself in. A low-down, ring-tailed lulu.

Bannerman, going all lofty with superiority: "I must confess that I am drenched in admiration and envy whenever Mr. Ambose honors us with his breathtaking impersonation of a legal scholar. I can only imagine what prodigies of intellectual discipline were called upon for him to arrive at such an erroneous conclusion. For myself, Your Honor, I must confess that I prefer the simpler fare of constitutional precedent."

Ambose and his mirthless smile: "All Mr. Bannerman has been serving up so far that I can see is some second-grade hamburger from Dr. Zacharias' psycho-analytical meatgrinder."

Bannerman and the outflung arm: "Well, there he goes again, ladies and gentlemen. Ambose rampant on the field of unbridled ignorance."

Ambose, primping and mincing: "Well, there he is, folks. Bannerman resplendent."

Bannerman: "Why is it, Your Honor, that I keep having this strange feeling that something illicit is going on between Mr. Ambose and the Constitution."

"Gentlemen," Davies chided. "You want to keep this up or are you willing to settle for a Mexican standoff?" Truth to tell, Harry had been enjoying the give-and-take so much that if the sudden lull hadn't turned everybody's attention to the Bench, he'd have let them go on cutting and slashing at each other till the

428

cows came home. Harry had given the matter considerable thought over the weekend, and he hadn't quite been able to bring himself to believe that the luncheon stories that went over so well with Lowell audiences were going to make it all that good with an expensive lecture-agency audience. At those prices they'd be expecting some good fancy lawyer-language, and so the more of Bannerman's language *(pure essense of Bannerman)* he could get into the record, the better. Ambose could get off some good ones, too, of course, but he already had a goodly collection of Ambose stories that he was planning to use as comic relief. Nobody was going to believe half of them, but that would only make them better.

"Suppose I exercise my prerogative," Davies said reluctantly, "and call it a draw anyway, and we can get on with the trial here. Anybody got any constitutional objection they can find to that?" He had played that last line, as always, to the spectators and the answering laughter was as refreshing as a cool shower.

Instantly Bannerman became all apologies, announcing with a wholly excessive show of diffidence (since everybody had seen him go through the same act about six times by then) how ashamed of himself he felt when he lost his temper like that. "But I do get vexed," he said rather plaintively. "I do get provoked." And it was for that very reason, he declared, finally getting to it, that he would have to take exception to any ruling that might be interpreted as parceling out the blame equally. "Mr. Ambose marches to a malicious beat," he said maliciously. "My own poor song, I trust," he said, bowing to the Bench and readying himself to resume his interrogation, "is somewhat more gently orchestrated."

"Aw, and I thought Mr. Bannerman was going to behave, Your Honor. After all those good resolutions, and there he is, right back on the sauce again."

At any other time he might have let Ambose get away with slipping in the last word on him. But not today. Norman Bannerman's eyes moved back to him in such a slow and narrow compass as to leave you with the impression that they were not so much leaving the witness as being pulled to Ambose. So it wasn't over, huh? He looked Jim Ambose in the eye like a thoroughbred who had hooked a horse of inferior blood and breeding at the eighth pole and was saying to him, "All right, you sucker, here I am! Come on!"

"As much as I dislike exciting Mr. Ambose to any new fits of denunciation," he said evenly, "I can see that it has become necessary for us to curb his recklessness—"

"That's all!" the Court commanded. Frightened by what he saw in front of him, Davies forgot he had his pipe and not his gavel in his hand and sent burning embers of tobacco flying all over the Bench. "My goodness, Mr. Bannerman," he said, as, hastily he brushed off his robe, "we don't need such a harsh, unfriendly tone of voice, do we?"

With a backward wave of his hand that told the Court to stay the hell out of this, Ambose said, "Oh, let him rave on. He's out of control. He's breathing pure oxygen. As long as he's got his psychiatrist here doing nothing, why don't—"

"You see, Your Honor, how his litany of hatred rolls on and on. The prospect of not being able to deliver this poor sick boy to the hangman has so unhinged him that—"

"Those pretty words are what does it to him, Judge. He's like the burgomaster of our beer factory back home. A couple of sips and a couple of sniffs is all it takes, and he's high as a kite on his own brew. Now, according to Alcoholics Anonymous, there's only one known cure for—"

"Mr. Ambose, as the record will clearly show, erupts into these sporadic episodes of hallucinatory frenzy whenever he is able to gallop, whinnying sala-ciously, into the domain of personal defamation and abuse he finds so—"

"I wouldn't dream of entering your territory, Bannerman. Not without having you stamp my visa first. It ain't the water I'm worried about, speaking of the galloping whinnies, it's all those galloping syllables. You better be careful, Nor-man, or the common folk are liable to understand you one of these days."

"Oh-ho! Now I understand! Yes, I've heard you aspire to higher office, Am-bose. With the growing sado-masochist vote locked up, and the hard-core illiter-ates to build on, you may yet become a man for even Mr. Nevins to reckon with."

For what it was worth, that brought the briefest of smiles from Hilliard Nevins. And nothing at all from Pawley. Everyone else was fastened upon Ambose, in anticipation of another lightning—and possibly crushing—retort. The momen-tary hush extended into heavy silence. Jim Ambose, exposed for all the courtroom to see, had drawn a complete blank and before he had a chance to recover, Bannerman, never at a loss for words, was leaping in for the kill. Blood in his eye, and a curl upon his lips, Norman Bannerman drew himself to his full height, superior to the situation as well as to his opponent and fully prepared, one could tell as he began to speak, to bring this squalid exchange to a summary and, for him, wholly satisfactory end.

"The thought that I have displeased my friend has left me so depressed that had I been living in other times, in other cultures, I would be left with no alternative but to plunge a ceremonial dagger beneath my breastbone or, deeming that too small a price to pay for so flagrant an indiscretion, fling myself upon the first available funeral pyre in inconsolable grief and ignominy." He was rocking gently on his heels. "That I do not choose to perform either of the sacrificial penances for your delight and fancy this morning can only be because it has finally dawned on me that for all his feeble gropings toward humanity, Mr. Ambose remains singularly devoid of the most elementary understanding of the role assigned to the prosecutor under our system of jurisprudence." The rocking came to a sudden stop. The flaring nostrils detected something odious in the air. His voice, which had been so lush and melodious, turned abruptly and rancidly against itself, like a cesspool backing up: "Our system of jurisprudence," he repeated, raking Ambose with his most contemptuous stare, "which we hold forth as a model for the civilized world, but which in Mr. Ambose's grudging hands becomes transformed into a public abattoir."

In timing and control it was a marvelously accomplished piece of courtroom theatrics. As well it should have been; he had delivered that speech often enough before. If its effect was not all he might have wished for this time . . . well, that was only because of an accident of timing that had left him hurling his curtain line into a vacuum. At the very moment that Bannerman had been lowering his baleful gaze upon him, Ambose—resorting to maneuver where his tongue had failed—had begun to settle into his chair in a highly conspicuous pants-tugging, neck-twitching disposition of arms, legs and shoulders. Gesturing helplessly, raising his eyebrows in resignation, rolling his eyes—paying particular attention to Number 5 and Number 11 as he did—Ambose seemed to be saying, "You see? Just what I was telling you. I don't know *what* we're going to be able to do about this fellow."

The luck of the courtroom; the breaks of the game.

But listen. Any Bannerman-watcher could tell you that when the wind was up and the adrenalin flowing, Norman Bannerman was as resourceful a lawyer as had ever trod these courtroom boards. (If no Bannerman-watchers were around, Bannerman might even tell you himself.) As quick as ever, he lofted his own gaze of calm dignity over Ambose's head to those twelve Friends of Civilization in the jury box and waited patiently for them to come back to him. Displeased? Disheartened? The hell you say! He had already bested the lout in hand-to-hand vituperation, and if he could now move in and take over this new position Ambose had retreated to—beat him at his own game again—well, by jiminy (the thought alone had him giggling to himself), that would be as good as taking the oaf's girl friend away from him, right after he had upsy-daisied his wife.

"Very well," he said. He heaved an enormous sigh of resignation. "I suppose the law can survive even Mr. Ambose's most bacchanalian assaults upon it." Satisfied that he had them back, he bowed his head philosophically—it might even be said, chastely—in the direction of the Bench. "The law, as His Honor can tell you, has ever been a robust wench. As robust as life itself."

"Ye-e-e-e-essss . . ." said Jim Ambose.

He had barely breathed the word out, sailing it out onto the stream of air that rode between them. And wasn't it odd that with that one solitary word, he could have changed the momentum so quickly and so completely. And odder still that everybody should know it.

The fascination of the courtroom.

Perhaps it was only because he was so conspicuously welcoming, and so thoroughly relishing what his enemy had said. More likely, it was something darker and more menacing; some faint vestigial warning chime that sounded in the sleek and sinuous curve of Jim Ambose's spine as he turned, in his own good time, to narrow down upon Sam Tabor; some predatory instinct still visible in Jim Ambose that called to the deeply-embedded memories of a prowling world of heavy, mingled odors; of silent, rippling muscles. Of forest eyes.

"Ye-e-e-e-essss," Jim Ambose said, narrowing his eyes upon Sam Tabor. "And as cold as death."

Maybe Tabor didn't shudder, and maybe Norman Bannerman didn't, either. But Harold Halpern sure did.

Zacharias was the man in the middle in Bannerman's three-tiered medical defense. Medellia had set down the physical disabilities, Zacharias was to lay the psychological weaknesses on top of that and, as the grand climax, Lionel Allbright would come to the stand, rich in years and heavy with honors, and, in a display of psychiatric fireworks beyond anything hitherto seen in a courtroom, inform the jury of the strange and compelling forces that had been touched off in Sam Tabor by the sight and person of David Boone Wilcke.

A good analogy, Zacharias testified, setting the stage very nicely for Allbright, would be to picture Sam Tabor's mind as a faucet in which the physical damage might be viewed as a defective washer, and the psychological weaknesses as a corrosive acid that had been eating away at the inner lining. In such an analogy, as the jury could certainly see, the psychiatric pressure would act like a sudden burst of water that had blown right through the damaged controls.

Before they could get to the faucet analogy, though, it had been necessary for Bannerman to face up to the problem of disposing of Zacharias' previous testimony about the absence of brain damage without backing away from it so completely as to destroy his credibility as an expert. Engagingly, as if he were acting as nothing more than a conduit for the jury, Bannerman asked whether he had undergone any change of mind. Routinely, without any strain or apology, Zack testified that having had the opportunity to study the EEG tracings, he was now of the opinion that there was definitely some damage there. How much, he declared, looking the jurors squarely and soberly in the eye, was a question on which experts might reasonably differ. His own opinion was that it was significant —if it was significant at all—only as it had served to further weaken an already undermined personality structure.

Conspicuously, Bannerman didn't ask him whether the withdrawal of the tranquilizer had been a contributing factor. Medellia had already taken care of that. As long as it was in the record, Bannerman could forget about it until it was time to tie it into his total case during his summation. Instead, Bannerman had him rattle off the impressive battery of tests he had run on Sam and then took him through the passive character disorder and on into Sam's intellectual capacities.

"Mr. Tabor has a wide range of information," Zacharias said. "He is quite well read and has an excellent, I might say amazing, memory."

Jim Ambose, who had been hunched over, his arms flat on the table, was instantly alert. He had *known* the business about Sam's memory would be popping up again, and he had not for the life of him been able to figure out how.

Nicholas Zacharias said, "There is a phenomenon, which is becoming of increasing interest to researchers, known as identic imagery. The jury may be more familiar with it under the name of total recall or, as the popularizing press would have it, a photographic memory."

The jury, which had settled into its accustomed state of passive noninvolvement, began to show some faint stirrings of interest as Zacharias went on to explain that infants, being unable to translate their sights or sensations into words, were born "with the ability to store everything they see," an ability they began to lose when they were three and a half to four years old and began to develop some facility with words. "Adults who retain identic imagery have jumped the point of transition, skipped right past it, because something has happened there in what would normally be the period of transition that has left them so fearful, so perpetually on guard, that they have found it necessary to continue to store their memories as a way of warding off what is potentially dangerous in the environment."

When Bannerman asked whether he would consider that to be a healthy or unhealthy development, Zacharias turned once again to the jury, crossed his legs, perfectly at home, and with a wry lift of the eyebrows directed, first and foremost, at the journalism professor, allowed as how a photographic memory could be very useful, especially when you had to pass an exam. "But ask yourself this: Suppose you had to deal with every stimulus, attend to every noise in every nook and corner?" In an instant he had become the sober-minded professor himself, asserting the authority of his highly specialized training. "You'd be on edge all the time, don't you see? Everything and everybody becomes a potential danger. You're like a criminal who is being pursued." His gaze remained on the jury long enough to permit them to draw their own conclusions that however handy a photographic memory might be for parlor tricks, better that Sam Tabor had got stuck with one than they.

"It's a kind of voyeurism, don't you see," he said, turning back to Bannerman. "Because you have to see everything, hear everything, know everything."

"You say this is a known phenomenon in the field, Doctor?" Bannerman had begun to stroll around to the front of the table, rubbing his chin, puzzling it out. "You say that something has happened between the ages of three and four that forces the child to bypass the normal phase of development?" He leaned back against the edge of the table, his feet crossed at the ankles. "In your opinion, sir, in the opinion of the best minds in the field of psychological research—"

"We'll settle for the witness's opinion," Nevins rasped. "The best minds aren't here."

"The jury will ignore the best minds," said Judge Davies, and the ensuing burst of laughter left him so bewildered that he leaned over the Bench to ask Marie what the big joke was supposed to be. Upon being told, His Honor—never a man to stand on dignity—slapped himself on his forehead in sweet-natured rebuke at his obtuseness.

A few moments later any hint of laughter had been sucked out of the courtroom.

Dr. Zacharias had explained that he was talking about what was happening in the darkness behind the closed doors of the parents' bedroom, as translated in the confused mind of a three-year-old child. The jury leaned forward. A strained, queer quiet came over the courtroom.

"Let me be a little specific about this," Zacharias said, and his tone of professional detachment was reassuring. "It's not only the sexual activity of your parents. You get to be three years old and you have difficulty going to sleep, and the reason you have difficulty going to sleep is that you can't tell the difference between fantasy and reality. You're always afraid to let go, don't you see? You clutch tightly onto your hold on reality, or what you think is reality, because if you let it go away for one second"—his eyes swept the jury box from one end to the other—"then you are going to be overwhelmed by all the aggressive, dangerous fantasies."

Working quickly, Ambose scribbled "Identic imagery" on his pad, ripped the sheet off and turned around to send Mollineaux off to the medical library to find out everything he could about it. As Mollineaux was passing behind the defense table, he sought Halpern's eye in rueful admission from one junior attorney to another that his side had been disagreeably surprised. Halpern could keep to himself his own rueful thoughts that it had come as much of a surprise to him as to them. As for Sam . . . well, it was impossible to tell what he was thinking anymore.

Sam had come into the courtroom with a kind of tight, simpering smile that had made Halpern wince. In the exchange of greetings with his lawyers he had been meek and docile and—although the matter had never been broached directly —pitifully eager to let Bannerman see that he had taken their little conversation to heart. Even more unnerving to Halpern was the way he had seemed to have shriveled up over the weekend. His suit, the same brown suit that had fit him so snugly the first time he had entered this courtroom, now hung on him so loosely that it was impossible not to see how physically diminished the man inside it had become.

Through all of the earlier testimony that had revealed him addled of brain, psyche and personality he had sat there, blankly impassive. While Zacharias was splicing identic imagery into the medical case, he continued to sit there, so wan and, to all appearances, indifferent, that it was as if—or so it seemed to Halpern —he had pulled back to that final level of resistance where he was able to protect his integrity as a human being only by pleading a total lack of interest.

It was a frightening perception, which came through even more frighteningly

433

a few minutes later when the fight that had roused Judge Davies from his revery broke over them.

Ambose started it, routinely enough, with a routine objection, after Bannerman had asked his witness whether identic imagery and passive character disorder, taken together, might be looked upon as contributing factors to the irresistible impulse that had resulted in the shooting. Well, now . . . irresistible impulse happened to constitute the first part of the legal question, and since the legal question hadn't been put to Zacharias yet, Ambose was hardly going to let the shithead get away with slipping in as fact what was, at best, opinion, and, in any case, hadn't even been established as that.

With both of them panting to wade into each other, anyway, the routine objection, stated with Ambose's customary vigor, was all it took. And yet, once they had got in their first good blows each of them had his own good tactical reason for keeping it going. By challenging Bannerman to ask his questions in a legally acceptable way—*if he knew how*—Ambose was hoping to goad him into scuttling his carefully planned sequence. Bannerman would have been perfectly willing to exchange hit for hit all day because he saw it as an excellent opportunity to take some of the heat off Zacharias on cross-examination by showing Ambose up ahead of time as a coarse, ignorant lout who could hardly be expected to understand, let alone appreciate, the spectacular advances that were being made in scientific research.

And so, the lawyers railed, the battle raged and through it all Sam Tabor just seemed to recede from view, no more than the instrument around whom these winds were blowing.

"And as cold as death," Jim Ambose intoned, bringing it to an end. And having looked upon Sam Tabor and felt those chill winds blowing, Harold Halpern did —yes—shudder.

Whatever else Ambose may have succeeded in doing, he did not succeed in forcing Bannerman's hand on the legal question. Bannerman simply came at his target from the opposite side by asking, with the air of a man who wanted to be scrupulously fair with the jury, whether identic imagery was not, in fact, in direct conflict with the passive character disorder. As it happened, that was the identical question Bannerman had asked when Zack, looking awfully proud of himself, had first sprung identic imagery on him back in Chicago. Not, Zack had been able to convince him, if you did it right. Their whole defense, courtesy of Lionel Allbright, was geared to the Oedipal conflict. Identic imagery plugged right into the Oedipal conflict from one side; the passive character disorder, as he had testified at the hearing, flowed directly out it from the other. One was cause, the other was effect, and right in the middle, to loop them together, stood Lionel Allbright.

They were, Dr. Zacharias now testified from the witness stand, complementary.

With Bannerman still holding to his planned sequence, Zacharias told the jury about the one other sudden change in Sam Tabor's normal behavior pattern that had come to his attention, the emergence of Sam the Swinger on the night he met his wife. In a crisp, business-like voice that denoted he was dealing with fact not opinion, he went through the whole story of the Tabors' experience with the marriage counsellor, and into Sam's ultimate feeling of rejection upon discovering that his wife was "making out" with Dr. Shtogren, and that he wasn't.

Bannerman examined the upturned tip of one shoe. Gingerly he moved it back and forth. "You did say making out, Doctor?"

Although Bannerman left Sam's marital problems right there, it was only to make the vital tie to Sam's problems on his job. In a passive character disorder, Zack said, any slight, any loss of face or promotion, could become a crisis. And so, contrariwise, could the prospect of promotion to a job that had more responsibility than he thought he could handle. "Crisis is what they can't stand," he explained, speaking directly to the jury again. "And promotion carries within it the seeds of a future demotion, which, jobwise, constitutes the ultimate rejection. Rejection, in turn, constituting the ultimate crisis." From the witness stand Zack's high forehead was glowing with the sheer beauty of it. "Which is why, don't you see, they are so careful about placing themselves in the kind of humdrum work where they won't be placed in that kind of a bind."

The mixup about the gun, the fact that nobody had bothered to tell him about it, might not have been viewed as such an intolerable slight, in short, if Sam's personal life had not already thrown him into crisis.

The Chief Justice, then, had just happened to appear in front of Sam at a time when everything was going wrong?

"In my opinion," Dr. Zacharias said, "that is fairly put."

"And then the flashbulb popped in his face?"

"And then the flashbulb popped in his face."

As at the hearing, he diagnosed Sam as suffering from schizophrenia with paranoid features.

He defined schizophrenia as "a regressive psychosis in which an individual withdraws emotionally from a world of reality into a world of his own creation, a world of his own fantasy in which he is able to create everything he wishes by his own magical wishes."

He defined paranoia as "a well-delineated psychotic condition in which there runs a single delusional strain, which in this case—this is, of course, oversimplified—makes him dependent on stronger people in his hunt for authority, and therefore an easy prey to suggestibility."

At the first mention of Sam's dependency Bannerman had begun to smile at Ambose. "Thank you, Doctor," he said. The smile broadened. "I believe Mr. Ambose is waiting impatiently . . ."

If Ambose had been waiting for anything at all, he had been waiting, as Bannerman damn well knew, for the legal question to be asked. Bannerman's maneuver of passing the witness over without asking it left Ambose speechless long enough for Bannerman to be able to say, with beautifully contrived astonishment, "I've passed the witness, Mr. Ambose. Don't tell me you're at a loss for even one question?"

Judge Davies had been waiting far more impatiently than Ambose for the legal question to be asked, and with far more reason. In keeping with his well-established policy of what to do in times of utter confusion, he put on his brightest face and suggested that a ten-minute recess might be in order, a suggestion which, under the circumstances, earned him Ambose's very blackest glower.

The newspapermen were drifting out to file their reports on Zacharias' testimony, and Harry followed them longingly with his eyes. "If you're going for a beer," he sighed, "I guess you'd better make it a short one. And have one for the poor old judge."

While he was waiting Dr. Zacharias shifted in the witness chair, tugging at his cuffs and resetting his shoulders in what was not so much a redirection of position as of total perspective. Nobody had to tell Nick Zacharias that he was the man in the middle here in every sense of the word. The only reason he hadn't told Bannerman exactly what he could do with his case was that he wanted this return bout with Ambose so badly that he'd have . . . well, he'd have broken the rule of a lifetime and testified for nothing.

"Now, let me see . . ." Ambose scratched his head, almost shyly, as if he were having some difficulty picking up whatever thread he needed to begin his cross-examination.

It was an act, sure; but not wholly an act. The kick Ambose got out of cross-examination was to pick up a witness like this, on the fly, mobilize the main thrust of his attack—the target area, the strategy, the minimum goal—and then, with his mind at a high pitch, the filament burning at a high glow, develop his sequence of questions as he went along; moving from side to side as he advanced in order to pick off every advantage and close off every route of escape. Letting them tell their story, sure, but making them tell it more and more his way, until by the inexorable march of his questions he had turned them away from their own line of march and off toward Jim Ambose's target area.

The target area he would be driving toward was—what else?—the witness's contention that it had been Dr. Shtogren who had set Sam off. His strategy would be to make everything about their relationship seem as natural and normal as possible. A professional relationship between doctor and patient, that was all; not so much different from what the jury had experienced many times in their lives. As natural and normal, you might say, as a fight between husband and wife.

The limited goal Jim Ambose was setting for himself was to take Sam out of "crisis." Once that had been accomplished to his taste, he could pick up the other stuff, at his leisure, and touch upon each of the component parts long enough so that the jury wouldn't go away feeling that he had ducked anything.

Okay, Cap. Got it.

Despite the earnest head-scratching, his opening questions had been completely formulated in his mind before he entered the courtroom. Ambose had spent half the night turning through the pages of the hearing transcript (never doubting that Zacharias would be going over it, too), looking for a line that had been used with reasonable success. In cross-examination suggestion was half the battle. By hitting Zacharias right off with a line that would be reminiscent, but changed enough to make it seem fresh, Ambose was hoping to do two things. At the very least, he would be reminding Zacharias what had happened the last time and, if the Lord was good and the imagery given just the right half-twist, he would be preparing him, subliminally, to expect the same thing to happen to him again.

That was his maximum goal. Because, Mama mia, if he could pull something like that off against a psychiatrist-psychologist-trial horse, wouldn't that be points to put up on the scoreboard for Jamey Ambose!

Up on the witness stand Nicholas Zacharias waited.

"Now, let's see if I can remember any of this." Ambose screwed his eyes up in a painful effort to think. "You've diagnosed him as a schi-zo-phrenic with par-a-noid features, was that what it was?" Eyeing him skeptically, squinting the words out, he asked, "That's like a zebra, isn't it, Doctor? You've got this schizophrenic horse with lines of paranoia running through it from its hooves all the way up to its adenoids?"

Against his best resolve Zacharias found himself stiffening against that flat, driving voice. "Mr. Ambose," he said, "we have met before. Your show of small-boy bewilderment is most amusing, but we both know you have tried hundreds of cases of this nature before. And that you have a grasp of the field and its vocabulary which is more than adequate."

"No, don't stop him, Your Honor," Ambose said. "One compliment deserves another. You have sat in that witness stand in about a hundred cases yourself, Doctor Zacharias, and I want to say that I'd be a proud man if I knew your territory about half as well you know mine."

They nodded to each other in unison, like boxers touching gloves in the middle of the ring. In giving as good as he had got, Zack had served notice that he was no man to be trifled with. In getting in his blow, he had also given Ambose an opening to let the jury know, without being a lawyer about it, that they were dealing with a professional witness.

"Why, you're such an old hand at this kind of thing," Ambose said, nailing it down, "I'll bet you can even tell me what the next question is going to be." And perhaps he could have. For Ambose started out by asking Zacharias, as he had wanted Nevins to ask Medellia, whether the defendant had been able to function in the world and earn himself a pretty good living.

That led them directly into a lively little discourse as to whether Sam's faultless attendance record over seventeen years was proof of a well-adjusted personality or of exactly the opposite, with Zacharias holding that devotion to duty could, like anything else carried to an extreme, become the hallmark of the fanatic or the neurotic, and Ambose getting in a low blow by asking (you could see he didn't believe the witness could have really meant it) whether devotion to one's mother or country could be carried to an extreme.

"You're not seriously asking me that, Mr. Ambose?" Zack was regarding him with such profound astonishment and disappointment that Ambose, as a connoisseur of effective courtroom ploys, had to be impressed.

Impressed but not overwhelmed. "Oh, but I am," he shot back. To prove it, he repeated the question. Sternly.

Completely at ease now, his hand resting lightly on his knee, Zacharias replied that if a man's love for his mother was greater than his love for his wife, his wife might very well think so. And as for love of country . . . well, chauvinism was, by definition, exactly that, wasn't it? Patriotism carried to a fanatical extreme. "As I'm sure you know, Mr. Ambose."

"If you accept the definition," Jim Ambose said, showing the kind of stuff he was made of. And from the way he looked at the jury there could be no serious debate as to whether Webster's Collegiate Dictionary had been infiltrated by subversives. Nor, as he turned his incriminating gaze back to the witness stand, what well-known Chicago psychiatrist had been their technical advisor. "As far as you're concerned, Mr. Tabor's devotion to his job—wanting to give the county a good day's work for a good day's pay, not being late once in seventeen years —that was a form of false patriotism, is that it?"

Norman Bannerman's groan came forth as from a man expiring of six dozen buckshot wounds. His recovery was, as to be expected, rapid. "Your Honor," he exclaimed with elaborate distaste, "if Mr. Ambose wishes to etch his vision of a brighter, finer world onto our collective consciousness by leading us through a rousing chorus of 'Three Cheers for the Red, White and Blue . . .'"

Looking to the jury box himself, preempting their attention, Zacharias reminded the jury that it had been Ambose who had seen fit to introduce the flag and motherhood into the courtroom, not he. "I said, or at least such was my intention, that such faultless attendance, taken with the rest of his life history,

437

can only be viewed as one more symptom of the kind of anxiety neurosis I have been testifying to."

He admitted, in answer to a direct question, that he hadn't explored that particular subject with Sam himself.

"You never said, 'Hey, Sam, how come you never missed a day of work? Were you afraid they'd fire you, or something?' "

"No, it never occurred to me to say, 'Hey Sam, how come you never missed a day of work, were you afraid they'd fire you or something?' "

"Never occurred to you, huh?" Was it possible that there were other things that hadn't occurred to him?

"That is a possibility which always exists."

"Is it possible that it never occurred to you that a man who can go through college, perform in superior fashion in a sensitive and difficult job—his job was similar to your own, wouldn't you say, Doctor?—who could maintain a difficult marriage, so difficult that they decided to consult a marriage counsellor, is it possible that such a man is not only sane but maintaining his sanity under considerable stress?"

"In answer to the first part of that question, I believe I have already testified that I took his entire history into consideration. In answer to the second part, I will say this." He pressed forward in the witness chair to underline the importance of what he was about to say. "Until the stress got to be too much. That's the key to it, always. There is always the one straw too many. The one blow too many. That's what the straw on the camel's back means, Mr. Ambose. As you very well know."

"You keep telling me what I know," Ambose sighed. "And here the state's paying me all this money to try to find out what you know." The one straw too many, as Ambose understood it, was that the marriage counsellor was taking his wife's part instead of his. "If he hadn't gone to the marriage counsellor, the murder would never have taken place, is that what you're telling us?"

No, it wasn't that simple. They were dealing, Ambose had to understand, with an individual who was ready to break. "If it hadn't been that, it might well have been something else. There was a murder waiting to take place."

"Unless he took a day off from work, you mean?"

"I can't remember ever saying that Mr. Tabor's attendance record was a cause. I cited it, I believe, as a symptom."

"Was the Chief Justice a symptom, too?"

"The Chief Justice was a symbol. Symbol, symptom. They're quite different things, Mr. Ambose. Take my word for it."

By exercising heroic self-discipline, Ambose was able to resist the temptation to thank him for another vocabulary lesson. Soberly and courteously, he asked whether Sam had gone to the marriage counsellor voluntarily.

"He went willingly," Zacharias answered, granting him that much. "Not voluntarily but willingly."

"Thank you, sir. Now, is it a rational or irrational act, in your opinion, for a man whose marriage is in trouble to consult expert help?"

The graceful slide into respectful inquiry had been to give the witness something else to think about. Not in his wildest dreams did Ambose think he was going to pull the same trick on a shrewd old pro like Zacharias two times in a row. The shrewd old pro, remembering the last time, would be instantly on guard. And that was just it. Having no trap this time, Ambose was applying reverse

English. The outside possibility, if fantasy dreams were to be indulged in, was that the good doctor's concentration would become so divided that he would obligingly build a trap of his own. The odds against that happening were, Ambose would say, about a thousand to one. The odds that the good doctor would pull back enough to render himself less effective were considerably less.

Choosing his words carefully, Dr. Zacharias said, "In this case, there was the complicating factor that it was Mrs. Tabor who consulted help first. After which, Sam then made the appointment at her request. That was why I drew the original distinction, you will remember, between voluntarily and willingly."

"Rational or irrational, Doctor?"

"Well . . ."

"Let me help you. Is it unusual for one member of a marriage to consult a marriage counsellor, and for the marriage counsellor to then say that he has to see them both?"

"No, it's done that way as often as the other."

"Then just what are you saying here, Doctor? That it's irrational for a man to follow the advice of the expert he's consulted, him and his wife both? And was paying for? Would you say it was irrational for your patients to follow your advice?"

Bannerman pressed both hands down on the table preliminary to rising and then, changing his mind, sat back.

"No," Zack said. "I have never testified that it was irrational for Sam to have followed professional advice. His psychological disorder was such that it would be the most natural thing in the world for him to do. The only thing he *could* do. What I have been saying, Mr. Ambose, is that it was Sam's reaction to what ensued as a direct result of his having followed that advice—coupled, of course, with the purely accidental appearance of the Chief Justice—which led to the irrational act. Namely, murder."

"And if the Chief Justice hadn't happened along, and Sam Tabor hadn't happened to have a gun in his pocket for the one time in his life, he might have lived out his whole life harming nobody? Just piling up gold medals for attendance? *This insane man?*"

Nor had Zacharias ever said that Tabor was insane, insanity being an imprecise term never used in the field of mental hygienics. He lifted an eyebrow at him. "As you very well know."

"Use your own word, then. I don't care, I just work around here."

Zacharias took a long, deep breath, determined—Ambose was happy to see—not to allow himself to be baited. Exhaling, he closed his eyes and ran his hand up over his high, freckled forehead. "He was suffering from a deep psychosis. I have been saying, Mr. Ambose, that a mental instability, reaching back to his childhood and exacerbated by recent events, produced an explosion that rendered him temporarily unable to control his behavior."

"But he did control it . . ." This was what Ambose had been waiting for. He held his fire until he saw the expected look of apprehension come floating into Zacharias' eyes and then his voice exploded like the crack of a pistol: "He fired a perfect shot!"

Bannerman: "He's twisting the witness's words again, Your Honor."

"Am I? Am I twisting your words, Doctor? If I am, let's you and me just pitch right in and untwist them. How long was he unable to control his behavior?"

"That may have been a poor choice of words." The concession was so entirely uncalled for that Bannerman stood stock still. Unexpectedly, Zacharias had lost his bearing. He gazed down at his hands, his fingers interlocking and flexing. "When I say control . . . his behavior, I mean it in the sense that he was not responsible for his behavior."

"Thank you for clearing that one up for us." The thanks, by its tone, was an invitation (which he clearly did not expect to be accepted) to come clean on the rest of it while he was about it. "He was able to control it, but he wasn't responsible for it. That about the size of it?"

"He could control his motor faculties. Obviously." Just as quickly as he had lost his composure, Zacharias had regained it. A few hitches of the shoulder muscles, accompanied by a series of sharp, assertive sniffs, and he had taken on a new charge of energy. "He could not control, had no control over, his emotions."

"How about his intellect? His intellectual faculties? Did he have any control over them?"

"Well, now you're saying intellect. As I've already testified, it is my opinion that his emotions—the violent emotional storm taking place inside him—flooded his controls and overwhelmed his intellect."

"Yeah. I remember that, now. There was all that about the faucet, where he just turned it off and on whenever it suited him, wasn't it?"

The expression on the witness's thin features was not so much one of disapproval as of aesthetic revulsion. He had said no such thing. "Turning it on and off implies conscious control. The analogy was to a sudden, uncontainable eruption of water bursting through the damaged controls."

"Yeah." Ambose sent a grin over toward Tabor. "You ought to get a new washer put in, Sam."

The grin, wasted on Sam, went right on past him to Halpern. "I'll just have to object to that," Halpern said, glaring at him.

"I'll just have to withdraw it, then," Ambose said. Anybody could see that he wouldn't dream of hurting little Halpern's feelings, mostly because he couldn't be bothered. Leaving Halpern standing there, Ambose called a quick huddle.

As Pawley assessed the cross-examination to date, Ambose had done about as well as possible on the stuff he'd covered. Nevins' grunt was impossible to interpret, except that it had nothing in it that sounded remotely like approval.

When it came to advice, the only thing Pawley could offer was to lean some on the guy on identic imagery. Wherever the hell they had dug that one up from. Pawley would have thought he had come across everything by now, but, by god, if that wasn't a new one on him. Not that he was planning on losing any sleep over it. "I'd say that ought to be raw meat for you," he told Ambose, with his little pouting grin. "Better you than me."

"He's the second team," Nevins said. "I don't know that we want to waste too much ammunition on him." So why didn't Ambose just twist him around a little about changing his mind on the brain damage and throw him back to them until after he'd answered the legal question.

The fact of the matter was that Ambose had planned to hold his cross-examination over until after lunch so that he'd be able to see what Mollineaux had been able to dig up. Pawley, letting his surprise show, had to remind him that in holding the legal question over to redirect, Bannerman was also opening up his whole medical case again, identic imagery included, for recross.

He was right, of course, and it made Ambose's job a hell of a lot easier. It would have also made him a lot happier if only it hadn't been Pawley who'd had to remind him.

"Okay." Ambose scowled. "Okay. Only you don't have to be so proud of yourself. Jesus, all you do is sit around here. It's a wonder when you're any help at all!"

Many, many years ago Ambose had come to the conclusion that it was all in the barometric pressure.

Could anybody doubt that the prospect of having to defend such a complete turnaround in his testimony had been hanging like a sword over Zacharias all morning? Jesus. Ambose had damn near salivated every time he thought about it.

And then . . . a complete washout!

Zacharias admitted to his mistake with an expression of chagrin that seemed to reach out to the jury and make them all allies in their fallibility. There was no logical explanation for it. At another time, off a different sequence, the same expression would have looked weak and sickly; the same explanation would have fallen to the floor with a loud thud.

It still shouldn't have been that easy for him to wiggle away—that's what made it so galling—because Ambose was sitting with a trap in his back pocket, waiting to be sprung. The Piatrofsky signs.

The Piatrofsky signs were readings taken from the Rorschach. On each of the cards, as Ambose had Zacharias explain for the benefit of the jury, there was a well-delineated category of interpretations that was supposed to alert any competent psychologist to the possibility of brain damage. If the signs showed up on six of the ten cards, the balance was tipped and brain damage was definitely indicated. The trap Ambose was drawing him toward was this: If the Piatrofsky signs had been present, Zacharias certainly wouldn't have been able to so completely discount the possibility of brain damage, would he? And if they weren't present, wouldn't that stand in flat contradiction to his present testimony?

The trap remained right where it was. In Ambose's back pocket, unsprung. Firmly and with an air of uncompromising honesty, Zacharias declared, "I don't think you can diagnose organic damage from the Rorschach. Never did." Anticipating the next question, he forthrightly stated that there were some clinical psychologists who still did. (It was the "still" that did it.) "And," he said, scrupulously fair-minded to the end, "very respectable ones, too."

And somehow it played beautifully. Perfectly. Not only did it seem as if Zacharias was being unduly generous toward those stodgy old-timers who held stubbornly to such a foolish and outmoded test, but in some diffuse and incalculable way—listen, the barometric pressure would do until a better explanation came along—he managed to create the impression . . . But no, he didn't create it, that was the thing; it created itself. An impression arose in the courtroom, independent of anything that had been said, but *there,* like the ghost of Albert Einstein, that Zacharias himself had been in the small vanguard of rebels who had struck it down.

Well, Ambose had learned back there in the days when he was still getting his asshole twisted that a good liar was the most dangerous witness you could go up against. But still, if the air had been lighter or heavier . . .

He protected himself by putting the relevant pages of the hearing transcript into the record so that he would be able to quote from them in his summation. Who knew? If it happened to be a cold and windy day . . .

From that low ground there wasn't much Ambose could do except ask Zacharias whether he would have been able to pick Sam out as a potential murderer if he had conducted his tests twenty-four hours before it happened. And *that* was a question that did carry a money-back guarantee that he was going to have something to work with no matter how it was answered. Getting a positive answer, he reminded Zacharias, pointedly, that unless the test results had miraculously changed, too, he would still have to diagnose Sam Tabor as a potential murderer, wouldn't he? Right now, he said, pointing to Tabor. Right where he sat.

"We are all potential murderers . . ." Zack began. And that was as far as he got. Was Zacharias himself a potential murderer? Ambose asked, pulling back as if he were in mortal fear of being attacked.

Zacharias regarded him with delicious gravity. "Under the proper stimulus," he said finally. "Yes."

"My goodness. And would you hire Mr. Bannerman and plead temporary insanity?"

The voices of the potential murderer and his potential lawyer overlapped.

Bannerman: "This is getting to be a fiasco, Your Honor."

Zacharias: "I haven't completed my answer . . ."

He wasn't going to, either. Not if he was depending on any help from Davies. Although the word "fiasco" had been uttered with a laugh and directed at Ambose, Judge Davies had chosen to take it as a direct attack on his ability to maintain order in his courtroom. It was worse than that. It was just the kind of thing those pompous bastards upstairs picked on when they were out to tip you over, and which the newspapers, who god only knows, never got anything right, picked right up. And once that happened it was "Goodbye, Charley," it would follow you around for the rest of your life. "Judge Harrison T. Davies, who ran that fiasco in Lowell." Well, Harrison T. Davies might not be the most learned jurist to have ever mounted the Bench, but when it came to the clinches he knew how to protect himself. "This Court," he said savagely, "feels fully capable of making that determination. I will warn you, sir, that you have an unfortunate way of letting your words run away with you." He leveled his pipe stem at him. "Don't let it happen again!"

And don't ever think that it didn't do the poor old judge's heart good to see Norman Bannerman gawking up at him, dumbfounded. Probably the first time in his life the big-mouthed sonofabitch had his mouth open for five seconds running without having the dictionary come running out of it. "Are you objecting to the question?" he demanded. "If you are, say so!"

"Yes," Bannerman shouted. "I'm objecting!"

"Sustained!" Davies shouted back. "The jury will ignore it!"

Ambose was all phony innocence and confusion. "Wait a minute," he said. "Is Mr. Bannerman objecting to being hired by his own expert?"

Judge Davies bit down on his pipe and warned Ambose that he had better move on to another line of questioning. "I am a patient man," he said. "I try to get along with you lawyers, within reason, but I think we've just about exhausted this one." All it took was one more puff, and he had become the amiable old judge again. "And if you haven't exhausted the subject, you've sure enough exhausted this Court."

Having shown how easy it was to exhaust the Court, Ambose apparently decided to demonstrate how much easier it was to ignore it. "Is Mr. Bannerman a potential murderer?" he asked.

That brought Bannerman scrambling to his feet, laughing and posturing. "I'm really going to object to that one, Your Honor. I'm also going to take the Fifth."

Davies' eyes went merry with approval. "That's always the smart thing," he chortled. "But to save you the legal fees, I'm gonna sustain the first objection."

Amidst all the merriment Ambose's voice came through cold and toneless. "I thought we were all supposed to be potential murderers. All of us except Mr. Bannerman, is that it?" A different, colder light was shining in his eyes. An idea had come to Jim Ambose. An idea that reaffirmed his basic belief that the Lord watched over his true and faithful servants. "All right," he asked. "What about Sam Tabor? You never did get around to answering that."

Given a chance to, Zacharias was able to explain that the operative word was potential. Since Sam had already erupted, he said, there was very little likelihood that he would lose control again.

"He won't, huh? That's funny. He'd already erupted when you gave him all those tests, and you've just got done telling us how, off those, you'd have been able to predict he was going to lose control before another twenty-four hours went by."

Zacharias explained politely that he hadn't projected any time period at all *forward*. That it had been Ambose himself who had brought a time element into it, going backward from the time of the murder. "We are able to take these changes into consideration, Mr. Ambose, and make allowances for them."

"You can?" Ambose said, putting on a superb show of child-like gullibility. "How nice for you. Now that you've told us how you can do all those great and wonderful things let's try to find out why we can't get you to answer a simple question. A potential murderer, Doctor? Got it? Sam Tabor. Is he or isn't he?"

Unflustered, not a bit outfaced, Zacharias anwered that he would give the same answer as before. And with the same stipulation.

"And you have already said that knowing your own background as intimately as you do, you consider yourself a potential murderer. Is that right?"

Zacharias' reply was that he'd stand by his previous answer on that question as well. Also with the same stipulation.

Ambose came to his feet. Erect and confident. The overhead lights reflecting off his high-boned cheeks and forehead gave his craggy features the look of proud, hammered bronze. "Your Honor, I ask that this witness be impeached on the ancient precept of common law that says you cannot have a thief testify for a thief." He was looking right at Bannerman, and he was not smiling at all.

Across the prosecution table Pawley gave Nevins the kind of look that said, *Our boy, he never forgets.*

Judge Davies, looking as if he was wondering what Ambose was going to cook up in that diseased mind of his next, told him to stop horsing around and move on to his next question.

Ambose waved his hand airily. "You've got him back, Mr. Bannerman. Take him away."

Bannerman informed the Court that he could conduct his recross in a very few minutes.

He began by having his man state again that it was not within the defendant's power to turn his emotional outbursts on and off. Not because he feared that Ambose's attack on the faucet analogy hadn't been adequately disposed of, but only to give himself a chance to cross over to the corner of the jury box. While Zack was answering the legal question, Bannerman wanted him to be talking right to the jury.

Standing at a sharp angle from the witness stand, he asked whether in Dr. Zacharias' opinion Sam Tabor had been subjected to an abnormal impulse at the moment of the murder, and then whether he had been able to resist that impulse.

As he was putting the M'Naughton Rule to him, he retreated slowly, with his hand sliding along the smooth, polished balustrade, so that Zack's eyes would be moving across every juror's. "Based upon your examination of the witness and all the material you have seen or heard, do you have an opinion as to whether Sam knew the difference between right and wrong, and understood the nature and quality of his act at the moment he shot David Boone Wilcke?"

Like the veteran courtroom performer that he was, Zacharias projected his voice out to Bannerman at the far end of the jury box. "I have such an opinion."

"Will you at this time state what that opinion is."

"In my opinion, he was not capable of distinguishing right from wrong or understanding the nature and consequence of his act at the time of the murder."

Normally, that would have been the end of it. If there was anything to betray Bannerman's excitement as he put the Model Penal Code question it was, perhaps, a barely detectable shrillness that ran through the upper register of his voice: "Do you have an opinion as to whether as a result of mental disease or defect he lacked substantial capacity either to appreciate the criminality of his conduct or to conform his conduct to the requirements of the law?"

The prosecution wasn't going to let him answer, of course. The prosecution was going to object, routinely, secure in the belief that it had been nothing more than a routine stab which would be routinely turned back. Off to his side, Bannerman could see that Ambose was sneering at him. *Didn't anyone ever teach you not to reach for the chips until all the hands were laid down.* Within himself, he smiled. *Read 'em and weep, sucker.*

Pawley was already on his feet, arguing that the question was wholly irrelevant to any laws under which the suit was being tried. "That is *not* the test," he said, jabbing his finger toward the Bench with each of the emphasized words. "I move that the question is *out* of order and ask that it be *stricken.*"

During Pawley's argument Bannerman had stepped quietly away from the balustrade. Standing in the narrow aisle, almost against the back rail of the Bar, he began to argue, in strict defiance of proper courtroom procedure, that the M'Naughton Rule was medically unsound, legally obsolete and philosophically archaic. When—hallelujah!—no objection was forthcoming, he spoke with ripening enthusiasm about pumping life-renewing plasma into the standards of criminal responsibility before they expired of disrepute. "It is only because this Court is known throughout the land for the great courage and foresight it has shown in the past," he proclaimed, his voice soaring in tribute, "that I press upon Your Honor the urgency of taking the great leap into the future by allowing this witness to respond to the question."

Hilliard Nevins said, "Let's just stick to the law here, huh, Judge."

Whatever Bannerman may have thought he was putting over, he had been able to deliver his entire speech only because Hilliard Nevins, the man whose business it was to take the long, strategic view, had ordered Ambose and Pawley to keep quiet. There were all kinds of things that were supposed to influence the jury, and most of them, as Nevins well knew, were no more than theories made fact through an agreement reached by some long-ago judges in some far-removed chamber. Never mind. The wise elders of the appellate courts, made fat and powerful by nit-picking the transcripts in search of sin, had a vested interest in them. And so, to some extent, did we all. The primary duty of any court system being to legitimize the process, all theories being acted upon in the appellate courts carried the official stamp of revealed truth.

But the truth of the trial was something else again. As often as not, as Nevins had been able to observe over a period of twenty years, the revealed truths ran contrary to the observable facts. The fact in this instance was that the jury cared not a damn's worth about any abstruse arguments over the difference between the M'Naughton Rule and the Model Penal Code. Once all the testimony was in, they would listen conscientiously to the judge's charge and act according to it and their own good horse sense. If the M'Naughton Rule hadn't sounded eminently reasonable to them over all the years it had been in force, the juries themselves would have broadened the meaning of "knowing right from wrong" to fit their own sound rules of common sense.

Another courtroom truth was that the nit-picking theories had to be constantly combed through and dealt with, a process known to most trial lawyers as Protecting the Record, and to Jim Ambose as Protecting Your Ass. It was for just such a purely defensive purpose that Hilliard Nevins had given Bannerman all the time he could possibly want to decorate the record with so flagrant—and so meaningless—a transgression. For though the state had no right of appeal, Hilliard Nevins, the man who took the long, strategic view, was always willing to give the opposition its chance to balance off the state's own somewhat more effective, it was to be hoped, transgressions. To make sure the appeals judges wouldn't miss it, he went on, in his harsh, heavy voice, "I can understand how desperate Mr. Bannerman must be, making a summation like that, and with the jury in the room. He knows better than that, Judge. I think he does, anyway. I dunno, maybe his education was neglected up there in Chicago. Maybe you better tell him to make sure." Whereupon, he objected to everything that had been said, in whole and in part, and asked that it be stricken.

Harry Davies, a man whose time had come, lavished his sweet, grandfatherly smile upon Norman Bannerman. Harry Davies, seated upon his throne, could enjoy the spectacle of Norman Bannerman, all fluffed up but nonetheless the eager supplicant bending toward the Bench. The countdown was on, and Norman Bannerman was poised on the launching pad ready to be blasted off into the future.

Before he delivered his decision, Harry Davies assumed his expression of judicial wisdom. "The objection will be sustained, Mr. Distict Attorney. At this time." Quite unintentionally, he had found his gaze shifting from Bannerman to Nevins. He lifted his eyes back to Bannerman. "Mr. Bannerman's last remarks will be stricken from the record," he said equably, "and the jury will ignore them."

Mr. Bannerman's remarks were not the only thing stricken. Directly alongside Bannerman, Number 6's eyes flew open. Number 6 could have sworn that he had heard Bannerman hiss, under his breath, something that sounded very much like *sonofabitch*!

"Your Honor. . . ?" Bannerman said. His eyes were searching him out, beseeching but cautious. He took two dreamy, shuffling steps toward him. No sign forthcoming, he took exception to the Court's ruling and entered a formal request to "preserve the defendant's rights by making an offer of proof," either out of the presence of the jury or by means of an affidavit.

Nevins said, "There he goes, Judge. He's doing it, again."

In a queer, strained voice Bannerman requested permission to approach the Bench.

"Now there's no need for a Bench Conference," Pawley said persuasively. "Mr. Bannerman has knowingly put a question that is palpably not the test for insanity in this state, and the Court has rightly rejected it."

The extremely satisfied look that passed over Davies' face told Bannerman all he had to know *(like the old family lawyer, reading him the will, enjoying it)*. "The Court has made its ruling, Mr. Bannerman *(rejected him)*. I have every confidence that you understand it *(To my son, Norman, I leave the sum of $1 . . .)*. If not, I will repeat it for you *(To my son, Norman, I leave the sum of $1 . . .)* Your exception has been noted. *(From the grave, Papa? Why?)* You are hereby directed to proceed with your interrogation." *(As my last act on earth, I hereby forbid him to contest this Will.)*

As if I were ever able to contest your will, Papa.

His head lowered, Norman Bannerman trudged back to the defense table, digesting the sour taste of it *(from the graveyard he had beat him again)*, being careful not to send any betraying *(betrayed!)* glance at Marie as he passed the Bench. And yet, though his head was down, he had the sense of commanding a view of the entire courtroom. He could see them, sniggering and snickering, and they could see him *(the lights going on . . .)*, every one of them knowing that he had been tricked *(tricked)* by the friend *(friends)* whom he had trusted *(again!)*

Held up to ridicule; humiliated. *("It shows a contempt for you on the part of your fellows, Norman, a contempt which you proved to be merited by doing it.")*

Back at the defense table, he patted Sam on the back. "Don't you worry, Sam," he muttered. "Don't you worry. Norman Bannerman is a winner." Even allowing for the softness with which he had spoken, there was a hollow, faraway strain to his voice. Blankly, and to all appearances mindlessly, he cleared the space of table in front of him, pushing the unhappily evoked memories away. Without looking at Halpern, he said through his teeth, "That dirty, cocksucking, double-crossing, rat-bastard sonofabitch."

Unlike Juror Number 6, Harold Halpern showed not the slightest sign of shock or surprise. Just by looking at Bannerman as he was returning to the table, Halpern had been able to see that something extraordinary had taken place. His face no longer had that pink and pampered look; he looked—what an odd thing to think—as though his bowels had dropped out of him. No, Bannerman had not had to say a word for Halpern to understand that the "clever ruse" had not been, as he had supposed, the introduction of identic imagery. For reasons he had not chosen to divulge to Hal, Bannerman had fully expected that he was going to be allowed to ask the Model Penal Code question.

Because he was observing him that intently, Hal could actually see the private struggle for control taking place, the resolute play of under-muscles beneath the ashen mask, as Norman Bannerman girded himself for his return to the battle. Stubbornly, breathing deeply, Bannerman dug himself in. "In your opinion, Doctor, did the defendant have the capacity to appreciate that the law would regard what he was doing as wrongful at the time of the act?"

446

Pawley entered the same objection, and then, haltingly, chewing his words well, went on to say that since his friend was so determined to ignore the Court's rulings and instructions, it might facilitate matters if he were to be informed that the legal test was not, by any stretch of the imagination, a subjective one. "This defendant is bound by the law," Pawley said. "If he had the capacity to know what he was doing, and to control it—and if I have interpreted Mr. Bannerman's question correctly this is what he is conceding—the law does not concern itself with his opinion of it."

"I'll accept that interpretation," Bannerman said, pouncing on it. "The attorney for the defense will accept and embrace Mr. Pawley's interpretation, if Mr. Pawley will be good enough to reciprocate by withdrawing his objection."

Pawley hesitated long enough to look, in some confusion, to Nevins, which, as it happened, was about the same way Halpern was looking at Bannerman. For the life of him, Hal couldn't understand what good it was going to do to have Zacharias testify that Sam hadn't believed the law would regard what he was doing as wrong when, in the same breath, he would be pleading him guilty to the law as it happened to be written—until, that is, he realized how nicely that interpretation could be made to fit into Lionel Allbright's analysis of the subterranean pressures that had set Sam off.

Cut off from the Model Penal Code, Bannerman had set about to sneak a rough equivalent of it in through the back door and then leave it to the jury to decide whose definition of insanity they wanted to accept, the law's or Norman Bannerman's. It was such a bold approach, and such an imaginative one—the quickness of the man's mind, his maneuverability under pressure, was positively dazzling —that Halpern's confusion was transformed instantly into admiration.

Pawley gave a reluctant little laugh and told Bannerman that he supposed he knew what he was doing. "But," he said, "the question is still irrelevant and I'll just hold to my objection, if you don't mind. We object to it, Your Honor."

"That's right," Nevins grunted. "We'll stick to the law, Judge."

Though the deficiencies and derelictions of Judge Harrison T. Davies were manifest and manifold, it could not honestly be said that he was completely lacking in talent. Harry Davies, to give him his due, was one of the few men in the world blessed with the innate ability to frown genially. "Well," he said, frowning genially upon Bannerman. "It's beginning to look like nothing's going to work for you this morning. I guess you're just going to have to get around to following the Court's instructions, sooner or later."

Harry was also one of the few living jurists who could manage to sound faintly triumphant and faintly apologetic at the same time; and that was exactly the way he sounded as he told Bannerman to get on with his interrogation.

"I've got a better idea," Bannerman said. "It's twelve o'clock on the button. If it's all the same to the Court, I'd rather eat."

As soon as the door to the cloakroom closed behind them Bannerman said, "You were saying that I should have pushed the change of venue harder."

"And you were wondering why that slant-eyed Norwegian could have thought such an offhand observation should be worth hard money," Bo Gunderson said.

Bannerman conceded that the thought had passed through his mind. In all candor, he would have thought that Bo, as a knowledgeable observer, would have been able to see that, all things considered, his case was in pretty good shape.

Bo looked slowly around the room, in search of something that was very clearly not there. "All things considered," he said bluntly, "here we are."

Bannerman had found Bo waiting for him in the outer alcove. With him was a sad-eyed man whom he introduced as an old friend from his misspent youth in the DA's office. "And," Bo said, "a very good friend of Jim Ambose's. Mr. Klein used to run the Red Devil in those days, a watering place well favored by attorneys of all philosophical stripes and strains."

Bannerman had immediately instructed Cowhig to take the rest of the group over to Dorri's, and to have a shrimp and lobster salad waiting for him. "And if I don't make it," he told him, "sign for me."

And so, all things considered, there they were. "You are no mincer of words," Bannerman told him. He took out his watch. "I'll tell you what I'm gonna do for you. You tell me what you think is worth so much, and if it's worth it to me, it will be worth it."

After no more than a minimum of thought Gunderson said, "Foster McAlester, Chief Justice of State Supreme, has one great virtue. Just offhand, I can't think of it, but I can guarantee you that it isn't honesty."

Bannerman made no attempt to hide his disappointment. The assassination was no hoodlum rap that was going to be fixed for a thousand dollars. Or a hundred thousand.

Smiling wisely, Gunderson said, "Not at all like Hilliard Nevins. Hilliard Nevins, whatever you may think of him, is disgustingly honest."

Fully satisfied that Bannerman understood that the connection of those two names was by no means frivolous, he folded his topcoat neatly over the top of the chair and sat down, taking his own sweet time about it. "To illustrate how corrupt our estimable Chief Justice is, there was a time when Hilliard was preparing impeachment proceedings against him." He had his full attention now. "Just the two of us, Hilliard and me. Nobody else knew about it." His *full* attention. "Not even Jim Ambose."

"Keep talking," Bannerman said. He put away his watch. "I'm interested a thousand dollars' worth. American."

The case in issue had concerned a bank robbery Bo had prosecuted. The Sharkey case. "The jury came back with ten-to-twenty." He laughed shortly. Reminiscently. "Hilliard wasn't happy. We get thirty years here on bank robbery if we get it all, and Hilliard wanted to know what happened to the other ten." The wide-eyed stare, helpless and hopeless, said that Hilliard was like that; a hard man to satisfy.

A couple of days before the appeal was to be heard Bo had received a phone call from a contact of his who, in that well-worn phrase of their calling, "moves around town pretty good." His contact had wanted to know whether there was going to be a retrial, and Bo had told him they had enough to do without making those kinds of decisions until they had to. "I prided myself that it was a clean transcript. That was important to me once, you'd be surprised. And, damnit," he said, with sudden vehemence, "it was."

Bo's contact man had assured him he could count on this one because he had carried the biscuit up to Monroe himself. Five thousand dollars. He had been able to supply those little details that go so far toward lending authenticity. There had been a U.S. Senator, who would remain nameless, lying on the leather sofa in McAlester's chambers, and at the sight of Bo's man the Senator had said, "Oh, oh, this might be a very good place for me not to be, and so I'm not here, won't be and never was." What the boys were interested in now was finding out whether they had to prepare for a new trial. Instead, Nevins and Gunderson had persuaded Bo's informant to tell his story to the grand jury.

The grounds for reversal were that the money bags, which had been found in a ditch somewhere (and which Bo had thrown in just to round the damn thing off), had been manufactured ten years before the robbery and should not have been allowed into evidence because the statute of limitations had run on them.

That was so raw that even Bannerman made a face. "And you're telling me," he said, still not quite able to believe it, "that McAlester was able to get the other two justices to go along with him on something like that?"

The way they operated up at State Supreme, Bo explained, was that each of the justices took on the heavy lifting for one-third of the cases put before them. If one of them lobbied heavily for one of the cases he had read, the others generally paid him the courtesy of going along.

In all fairness, he felt it necessary to caution him that the Bar had been trying to clean the situation up. "Criminal cases are one thing. In civil cases . . . well, you're fooling around with money now." You spent months and even years preparing a case, you fought it through trial, you fought it through appeals, and then it went up to Monroe and they cut your balls off. "The old distinguished firms don't like that. You know how it is with those old, distinguished firms. They talk softly, but they're heard loud."

Okay. Bannerman could understand that. What he still couldn't understand was why they hadn't been able to get McAlester impeached.

"I don't want to oversell Hilliard here," Bo said. "He's honest, yeah. But Jim Ambose is the only avenging angel in that office." Hilliard had done a lot of thinking about it. For maybe a week after the reversal came down, every time Bo looked in on Hilliard, his glasses were up on his head and he was tapping his teeth.

"I've noticed that."

A bribery case, as Hilliard had explained to Bo, was never any picnic for a DA, and when a judge was involved, especially the Chief Justice of State Supreme, it could be a bitch. McAlester certainly wasn't going to take it without fighting back, and even if they won, all most people were going to remember when the next election rolled around was that Hilliard Nevins had been involved in some kind of case involving politics and courthouse graft. No, no picnic for anybody, and much worse for a DA who has his eyes set on the higher judiciary himself.

Nevins had pulled down his glasses and gone ahead with it, though. "And what do you think happened but that my friend—hell, I'll tell you his name, Coney Lewis. The damnedest thing you can imagine, Norm. The night before I was taking him before the grand jury, what did Old Coney do but up and die on us. And up to then," Bo said, dolefully, "he'd always been so reliable."

He shook his head, knowing exactly what Bannerman would be thinking. "No, nothing like that." Coney had caught himself a case of influenza and died in his sleep. Overnight. They had done everything with that body except dip it in sheep dip, and it was death due to natural causes.

Bannerman breathed out a long, sympathetic whistle in comment on the random, utterly unpredictable events upon which even the best-laid plans could founder.

Nobody had known about the grand jury presentment except Hilliard and Bo. And the clerk of courts. And the members of the grand jury panel. And the court reporter. And maybe any politico Hilliard had thought he'd better get ready for it. And maybe a leading light or two in the Bar. Or three or four. "You want to be a federal judge," Bo said, "you think a lot about things like that."

"That gets to be a lot of people," Bannerman agreed. "God so loved man that He gave him the power of speech without the compensatory power to keep his mouth shut. What more could any species, mindful of its place, ask for?"

Inevitably, McAlester had learned that Nevins had been out to get him. Bo could state that without equivocation because not long after he left the DA's office discreet inquiries had been made to him. "You know what I think," Bo said. "I think McAlester has been sitting back all these years waiting for the chance to hit Hilliard Nevins where it would hurt. You know what else I think? I think this may be the place."

What Bannerman was thinking could be seen in his sweet, angelic smile. "Nevins gets kicked in the balls," he said ecstatically, "and Ambose winces. The avenging angel."

A long silence ensued while Bannerman was considering the possibilities. Bo had been right about the change of venue; he had to give him that. If he'd hit the issue hard, made a real stink about the impossibility of getting a fair trial in Lowell, he'd have given them something where they could reverse without ever having to lay a hand on the trial record. It shouldn't have been tried in Lowell in the first place, so take it somewhere else, fellows, and try again. That was all water over the dam. From now on, he was in a position where he'd be able to try this lawsuit as much for Foster McAlester as for the jury. And if he could goose Hairbrain Harry into giving him any kind of a look-in on tipping over M'Naughton, the State Supreme would seem to be delightfully disposed to take that last, long leap to glory.

Bo moved his head in the general direction of the courtroom. "I don't envy you that jury," he said, rising. "Whew. The way they sit there, you can see the vultures circling overhead."

As Bannerman was making out the check, Bo told him to just put on the back: For Legal Services Rendered. Final Payment. "And," he said, peering gratefully over his shoulder while Bannerman wrote, "it was a pleasure to advise you on the intricacies of the local legal scene, sir. I'll be able to tell my grandchildren about it. Whoever they may be."

Cheap at twice the price, Bannerman told him. He waved the check back and forth as if he were letting the ink dry. "Although I will confess that I thought you were here to hawk information having to do with a certain ceremonial head-kicking featuring Mr. Ambose's toe and the late Mr. Zabilski's skull in an alley behind the Red Devil. Just what was all that palaver you were feeding me about that, sport?" The check stopped waving. "And waving Mr. Klein, the former proprietor of the Red Devil, in front of me like that."

Ruffled not in the least, Gunderson asked him if he hadn't ever heard the old joke about how to get a mule's attention. As for Klein, that had been sheer luck and, immodestly, opportunism. Bo had just happened to bump into Klein, coming out of the courtroom.

Bannerman held the check out to him. "I'm not even going to ask why you've been sitting back all these years waiting to hit Hilliard Nevins where it would hurt most. What business is that of mine?" Despite the pleasant tone, the insult was so studied that Bo Gunderson involuntarily withdrew his hand. But then, tossing it off with a smile, he said, "Just another fee, Norm. The way the price of milk has been going up, lately . . . you know how it is."

"I wouldn't think that would bother a man like you, Bo." As he handed over the check, he looked him steadily in the eye. "You've always struck me as a man who moves around town pretty good."

Back in the Cave, Jim Ambose had opened the top right-hand drawer of his desk and found, as he had expected to find, Deputy Blasser's handwritten report.

"The prisoner wont take sugar in his coffee any more. Says hes on a diet. He can be a kind of a funny guy sometime. Like where he says hes going to die on a diet. Ha-ha. He wouldnt let the mop boy clean up his cell last night which was Sunday. Wants to do it himself. No complaint from mop boy. Prisoner wouldnt put on his pajamas. Slept in his coveralls. Shoes and stockings too. Asked G about it. G said never happened with him. All sweaty this morning it being hot as all hades in the night. Had hell of time talking him take shower. He say thats what they told the Jews in Germany. Dont know is he kidding. He such a pistol. Sometime he acts real crazy. Dont know is he faking. I ask him how he feel about his shrinks like you say. He say he feel like Zacharias is real crazy and not responsible for the nature of his acts. And real cute smile like he watching me do I laugh. Wants to see am I laughing. Sometime I feel like he faking that he nuts like he watching me am I swallowing it. Is it an act? Sometime I think yes. Sometime I think no. Prisoner use to get all excited about the mail he received I forgot to tell you. And when FBI and Secret Service came to see him. Dont even open mail no more. Dont care. Not interested. Prisoner no like hammer killer. I ask why. He say anybody can kill a woman with a hammer and what so hot about that. A real pistol. He like crossword puzzle in morning Globe. Very fast. I ask him how cum he know so many words he say crossword is just knowing the trix of the trade. This morning after get him to shower no trouble about him shaving. What I tell him is he goes in or I throw him in. Thats the shower I tell him that about. Singing when he shaving. I say lets see can you do crossword puzzle again I am trying to keep him busy til we take him down. He give me crossword puzzle he make up for me out of his own head. Sonofabitch I cant finish it. He say tomorrow he make up easier one for me. Happy as pig in shit. I tell him go fuck hisself. This guy is going drive me nuts I am going be crazier than he is. More tomorrow if I am not crazy already this guy will drive me crazy thats for sure."

There was something about Cowhig that made him easy to talk to, and whether it was the result of a carefully cultivated facade or a naturally open and friendly personality, it was, beyond any question at all, one hell of a valuable asset for an investigator. As soon as Zacharias went to the men's room, Halpern was asking him about Julie.

When his chance finally came, after Zack had gone to the men's room, Cowhig didn't seem inordinately surprised. "You got a way of blundering into things, Hal," he said. "Because you've got a good heart in you, see? Sure. About things you don't . . . well, there are things you don't understand that much yet. That are outside your experience yet. You're how old?" His eyes went rolling across the ceiling. "Jeez, to be as young as you and as smart as me. I'd own the world." Just as quickly, he was serious again. Maybe Hal had noticed that their employer had his peculiarities. That was all right, he could afford them. "All of us," he said,

451

"serve our purpose." Julie. Halpern. Cowhig himself. He cocked a questioning eye at Halpern. "You're not going to tell me you've been around this long, a smart young fellow like you, and you haven't been able to figure out what mine is yet?" Thank god Cowhig himself did, he said gratefully, because it had taken him out of a flea-bitten little office and made him maybe the highest-paid investigator in the country.

Before he could say anything else, Bannerman's voice could be heard approaching just outside the doorway, a booming voice filled with merriment. Another moment and the Big Man himself was making a grand entrance with his arm thrown over the waiter's shoulder in his very best charm-the-working-man manner. Surveying the table, he transformed his posture instantly into one of regal disdain. "Remove this foliage with the *traif* remains of shellfish," he ordered grandly. "And in its stead, my steadfast friend, fetch me a generous portion of Jack Daniels, whose wise midday counsel has guided me through many a tighter pinch than that in which we now find ourselves."

Delicately, holding it between thumb and forefinger, he lifted up one of the shrimps. "We are one and all the creatures of a merciful and loving God," he intoned, and having pronounced his eulogy, let it fall, as a thing contaminated, back into the bowl.

As soon as the waiter left, grinning broadly, Bannerman sat himself down, all business, and told Frank that his new assignment was to call the office and have them stop payment on check number 4419, a three-zero job made out to Bo Gunderson. Meeting Cowhig's disapproving look head-on, he said with precise articulation, "Everybody's pal Bo has just sold me some information I trust no farther than I would trust Lout Ambose with a book of matches and the Bill of Rights. To hell with you, I'll do it myself." He had a more important assignment for Cowhig, anyway. He wanted him to find out everything he could about the death of Sandor Zabilski. Where and when and how and why. Everything that was known about it. The services of Hugh-bert Fletcher could be used on this one, he told him. For openers, it might be worth his while to find out what Fletcher knew about it himself.

"Schmuck," Cowhig said, "what do you think I'm going to find out in a couple of days that nobody else has?" Schmuck, Cowhig said, what made him think there was anything to find out?

That, glowered Bannerman, was why he thought he was paying him such usurious rates.

"Schmuck," Cowhig said, "can't you see that I'm trying to save you some money for a change? Act your age."

He wasn't paying Cowhig to save him any money, Bannerman scowled. And he sure as hell wasn't paying him to be told to act his age.

"All right, schmuck, I'll put it to you this way then. It's your money but it's my time. Go waste somebody else's, huh?"

Bannerman, looking not unpleasant about it, ordered him to just do what he was told and leave the thinking to his betters, huh?

Cowhig, reaching for a shrimp, told him with complete indifference to go fuck himself, schmuck.

And that, as far as Halpern could see, ended that. When the waiter came back with his drink, Bannerman put on another bravura performance for him, pampering and flattering him, handed him a five-dollar tip and insisted that he also buy himself the best cigar in the house and put it on the bill. "Booze for my friend,

Norman Bannerman, bartender!" he shouted, after he had taken his first stiff shot. "When Jack Daniels drinks, Bannerman drinks with him!" He took another stiff shot, trying to kill it before the waiter returned. "By the saints," he said, in an accent that sounded mighty like Mike Karney on the stump, "I think Lout Ambose may have hit it right on the noggin for once in his life. I'm out of control. I'm breathing pure oxygen. Victory is in sight!"

Well, if victory wasn't in sight, Nick Zacharias was. Zacharias was hurrying back in, drawn by the Bannerman voice, to find out how he was doing.

"Zack," Bannerman said, as if he had hardly been able to wait to congratulate him, "you are giving the performance of a lifetime." He lifted his glass in tribute. "A genius courtroom performer. A testifier touched by the celestial fires. And don't think I don't appreciate it. Know what I'm gonna do for you when we win this one?" he said, rolling his eyes at him. "I'm gonna send you a petunia to stick in your belly-button."

During the walk back, Cowhig fell in step with Halpern. "So now you know what my purpose is," he said. "See if you can figure out yours."

"Well," Pawley said, groaning himself out of the sofa, "the time has come once again to return to the arena in order to make this a better place in which to live."

Mollineaux hadn't come back from the library with anything on identic imagery and that could only mean he hadn't come up with anything yet. On their own, they had been able to find only one soft spot in it. How, after all, could they claim that Sam was a man who had to pay attention to everything in his environment and still hold that he had failed to take due cognizance of all those law enforcement officials up there?

"They can't," Ambose said. "It's got to be one or the other. They went to such trouble to dig up something nobody ever heard of before that they've knocked out everything except irresistible impulse."

Although God only knew that neither Ambose nor Bannerman was looking for it, the afternoon fight came almost at once, and it was Harold Halpern, of all people, who started it. And only—as he would reflect later—because upon picking up his pencil as the questioning began, he had discovered that the tip had been mysteriously broken off while he was out to lunch.

Ambose began his recross by asking when Sam's irresistible impulse had begun, fully confident that Zacharias was going to answer that it had started when Sam began to reach for the gun.

Zacharias said, "It started, I would say, somewhere in the third year of his life."

Holy Toledo, Ambose thought. They were going to try to push the noises-in-the-dark thing all the way. *Well, goody for them.*

"My goodness," he said. "You're giving us the longest-smoking kingsize irresistible impulse of all time here. Let me ask you this, Doctor. Did it ever erupt into murder before?"

"No. Not that I know of."

"Not that you know of . . . Don't know if he maybe cut up the family cat when he was five? You wouldn't happen to know anything about that, would you?"

In an attempt at being droll Bannerman suggested that if Mr. Ambose had any information to offer concerning the murder and dismemberment of any cats he would welcome the opportunity to examine it. "If not," he said, "may I suggest to him that he would do better to let dead cats lie." But the unnatural high spirits of Dorri's had drained something out of him and it came out all wrong. Poor Sam was looking from Bannerman to Ambose and, beyond both of them, to the jury, so utterly aghast, so hurt and pleading, that anybody in their right mind could see that he'd never do a thing like that.

Zacharias had waited the exchange out, grave and detached, tapping his foot gently. "All I am saying in trying to answer with exactitude, Mr. Ambose, is that I would have no way of knowing what I don't know. Any more than I would have any way of knowing whether the perfectly ghastly example you have chosen to pose came so readily to your mind because you happened to have cut up the family cat yourself when you were five." He forced his lips into a politely contemptuous approximation of a smile. "You see?"

No, Ambose did not see. "What I did when I was five is nobody's business, Doctor, because I haven't killed anybody—"

"Your Honor," Halpern sang out, "the distinguished assistant district attorney is stating as fact something not in evidence." Halpern had been leaning over the table, not exactly ignoring the testimony but primarily concerned with picking enough wood away from the lead so that he'd have something there to write with. It was precisely because he had been listening with only half an ear that the objection came forth so naturally and effortlessly, the first time since the trial began that he had not found it necessary to think about what he was going to say before he said it.

Judge Davies peered over the Bench and shook his head at him, much in the way a fussy librarian might deliver a warning to a generally well-behaved child. A rebuke so mild that it hardly seemed to call for Norman Bannerman to come rising to his feet, in all his impressive height and stature, to express his deepest and most profound apologies for the youthful excess of his assistant. If Halpern wasn't offended—and he wasn't—it was because Bannerman managed to make it abundantly clear, by the very extravagance of his apology, that the true reason for his rising would soon enough follow.

The real surprise was that it came in the oddly clacky voice of a man who did not have his breathing completely under control. "As the chief counsel for the defense," he said, "I am entirely prepared to stipulate that the assistant prosecutor has never, to my certain knowledge, actually pulled the switch on any of the scores of poor devils he has sent to their deaths."

"There was never a one I wasn't willing to, Mr. Bannerman."

Jim Ambose arose, purposefully but without haste. The answer had been set forth in simple, uncomplaining tones, without boast or anger, and when he spoke again it was with a kind of wonder that anything so self-evident, so patently right, should require an explanation. "There was never a one of them I prosecuted for the state, and that the jury after due deliberation convicted, that I wouldn't have pulled the switch on or sprung the trap, and done it gladly. And gone on home to sleep the sleep of the just for having rid society of another of its enemies."

"Oh, I know you would have, Mr. Ambose. I know. How unfortunate for you that you have been spared so heroic a diversion and denied so sweet a slumber."

As quietly and formally as it had been done on both sides, there was a trembling in the air. The very economy of words and emotion was proof enough that this was no part of the game of snap-and-bite they had been playing. Each of them had stated his purpose in life, and its justification, and with each of them it had been not so much *Here I stand* as *Here is what I stand against.*

And where they stood was at the opposite ends of the earth.

Watching the scene unfold before him, Harold Halpern experienced the intoxicating, liberating sensation that he was seeing the true nature of the struggle for what it was: It was the plea for mercy against the cry for vengeance; it was social order against anarchy; it was, from the first breath to the final gasp, belief against disbelief.

There; it was as simple as that. Once the true nature of the struggle had been revealed to him, the true natures of the combatants took shape. Bannerman was the village atheist and Ambose was the village priest, and, though they may have been traveling incognito to the rest of the world, they had recognized each other at first sight. Norman Bannerman would only have to hear Jim Ambose utter one sentence to see the Lord High Inquisitor touching the torch to the faggots. Jim Ambose had only to see Norman Bannerman come walking into a room, under his canopy of splendor, to see the pagan ceremony and sniff the pagan reek.

And what else? There was something else out there that wanted to come in and make itself known, and as his ever-expanding consciousness reached out for it, the old Dominion Street kitchen came swimming into focus, and he heard his father saying (and whether it was an old-country saying or one of his father's own, he had no way of knowing) that it was possible to argue religion with anybody except an atheist or a priest, because nobody except the atheist and the priest believed in God.

Not opposite sides of the earth at all, then; they had gone the whole world round in opposite directions to come back together as the opposite sides of the same coin.

Seeing that, Halpern was able to see much more. As they stood before him, stripped to their true identities, he had the illusion, in this moment of weirdly altered perception, that he was viewing them through a filtered, slanting light in which he could see the layers unpeeling. If it was more than a game these two were playing, it was more than a morality play he was witnessing. Each saw himself as the truly appointed protector of the weak and defenseless—*of course* —and what made them such implacable enemies—*of course!*—was that each would always see the other's victim as the true villain.

In Ambose's simple two-toned world the facts needed no character witnesses and spoke with thunder. The victim was David Boone Wilcke and, spreading outward, his family, his friends, his associates, and the whole society of which he had been a part; the villain was Sam Tabor, and anyone who pretended to think otherwise was a goddamn fool or a goddamn liar. Norman Bannerman, no fool certainly and no liar here either, lived in a world of myriad tints and shades, all merging, forever overlapping, in which no fact was fixed and it only seemed that the thunder called out the lightning. In Bannerman's world of infinite complexity the victim was Sam Tabor, and the villain—too cheaply identifiable as society— was the human condition.

There you had it. Each of them could say—and truly mean—that no man was an isle entire of himself, and they would be saying—and meaning—entirely different things. Any man's death diminishes me, Ambose would say, because the isle of which we were both a part has been made less. *Any* man's death diminishes me, Bannerman would say, because his death makes my death that much more certain.

The common enemy they shared was mortality. His father, the unschooled philosopher, had been right again. The village priest hated the murderer for hurrying death along by taking it out of the hands of He Who had created life and to Whom all life belonged. The village atheist hated God for the cruel trick of granting him the gift of life and taunting him with the knowledge of the cold void at the other end.

And so it was that in this moment of heightened sensitivity Harold Halpern could look across the few feet of polished mahogany table to where Norman Bannerman stood and know, at last, what the Itch was. It was an enduring rage which could be appeased only by rescuing one more victim from God's (herein called Society) mindless vengeance. Knowing that to be true, how could he doubt, as he lifted his gaze beyond Bannerman to where Jim Ambose stood, that just as the time would always come when Bannerman would awaken, with a start, and see the heretic waiting to be saved from the stake, the time would also come when Jim Ambose would awaken, in a sweat, and hear the bloodhounds baying.

Oh no, it was no mere itch that roused them from the deeps and sent them roaming into the night; it was an open wound that could be endlessly sutured but never healed.

And as that last layer peeled away to expose the bleeding, twitching wound that was at the core, he knew with that perfect pitch of certainty that knows what it knows who the real victims were that Norman Bannerman and Jim Ambose fought so desperately to save and to avenge.

And all in the matter of a few tightly-packed, runaway, mind-expanding seconds. No more than fifteen or twenty seconds had ticked away between the time he brought his father's gentle, well-loved voice back to life to philosophize on priests and atheists before he heard Lionel Allbright's bluffer, infinitely wiser voice at the motel saying, "The deformity can become the driving force . . ."

Jim Ambose and Norman Bannerman. This close to the end of the trial Harold Halpern, who had been little more than an awestruck observer with a privileged seat inside the Bar, could look at them plain and see them for what they were. Better lawyers than he could ever be, and then some, and lesser men. This close to the end, Harold Halpern was ready to move inside the frame of the trial and became an active lawyer in the defense of Sam Tabor.

Ambose resumed his questioning with a prodding, probing examination of "this kingsize, long-smoking irresistible impulse," until he had brought Zacharias to testify that "the eruption" had started when Sam's hand began to reach for the gun and had ended when he found himself on the stairs with his arm twisted behind his back. Halpern pulled his chair forward and followed the questions and answers closely.

Q. Now, sir. Let's get back to this irresistible impulse that was growing in him for forty-nine years, like a mushroom, waiting for the Chief Justice to come along and get killed. How come, after he'd waited all that long, he only shot once? How come he didn't keep shooting?

A. It is possible that his hand froze on the trigger. Or perhaps the one shot was release enough. Either would be wholly consistent with irresistible impulse. Or with brain damage.

Q. You're giving us a choice, huh? Or should I say both barrels?

Zacharias crossed his knees and bent his eyes down at him languidly. "I don't quite understand. Are you giving *me* a choice now, sir?"

Quick thinking. And beautifully timed. In any cross-examination there was a contest of personalities that ran parallel with the testimony. Zacharias had just turned the momentum of the testimony around so completely that Ambose dropped that whole line of questioning right there.

In a matter of minutes the momentum came back. Zacharias had been attempting to explain, as explicitly and forcefully as possible, that although Sam was most certainly going to erupt sooner or later, it had by no means been ordained to occur when it did, or how it did. It might have been only to hit his wife—something he assured the jury Sam had never done—or to commit some other act of violence equally precipitous in nature and yet so minor in the eyes of the law that they might not have thought it necessary to intervene. The important thing to remember was that to Sam the emotional release would have been exactly the same. "In either case, it was an act he wouldn't have felt himself capable of committing a second before he did it. In either case, he would have subsided just as quickly and been equally horrified."

Ambose had recognized the opening at once. And if he could get the right answers out of Zacharias on the next couple of questions, he could see where he'd be able to show the jury that this guy was not quite the honest, above-board witness they had taken him to be.

"How do you know he never did? Gained emotional release by hitting his wife, Doctor?"

A well-put question. Good misdirection. Zacharias would see the trap that was being laid for him. Ambose had dangled it in front of his eyes.

"She told me he didn't."

Good. For the first time all day Ambose slipped between the tables and approached the witness stand. "Oh, you asked her that, huh?" An insinuating note. An insinuating smile. *Of course you did,* Ambose was insinuating out every open pore. *Poor, gentle Sam, my eye. There's plenty you could tell us about "poor, gentle Sam" if you were of a mind to, isn't there?*

"It is my job to ask about everything."

"Except what you forget. We've already agreed on that, haven't we?" The tone had sharpened. He let a couple of beats go by, presumably to give the jury time to reflect back on the morning testimony. Excellent misdirection. What seemed to be a casual sarcasm, a momentary digression, was—in fact—an integral part of the sequence. The payoff question was about to come winging Zacharias' way, and it was vital for Ambose to be able to phrase it in a way that would lead the witness into giving him the answer he wanted. "You didn't bother to put that in your report, either, did you? We can agree on that, too!"

Not waiting for an answer, he strode back toward the table as if there was nothing more that needed to be said. A passably good performance, all things considered. Not brilliant, but passable. It would have been much better if he had been able to keep his ears from straining back to pick up what Zacharias was going to say in his defense.

"Among other things," Zacharias said, "I put in only what I felt to be significant."

Oh, beautiful. One stride short of the table, he came to a stop. He sniffed the air. Delicately, as if the first faint scent of crocus, heralding an early spring, was in the air. His head came around, ever so casually, so that he was looking back over his shoulder, one hand in his pocket, quizzical, amused, a bit debonair even. In three or four lazy strides he narrowed half the gap between them, leaning over from the waist as he approached, his head pushed far forward, his right hand extended and outspread. "Ahhhhh," he said, and the rebuke came so softly that it barely seemed to reach the witness stand. "But you felt it to be significant just now, didn't you? All right, Doctor."

The damn fool, Bannerman grumbled. All he'd had to say was that he hadn't asked Mrs. Tabor about it until later. He glared at Halpern. "Can't I even trust you to take a witness to lunch without letting him come back drunk?"

"Next time," Halpern said, "I'll make sure neither of you do."

Bannerman would have been even more incensed if he had known that "all he'd had to say" was also God's own truth. Zack's trouble was that he hadn't been able to remember offhand when he had talked to her about that part of it, and since it had seemed to be a matter of no particular consequence, he had, question by entrapping question, taken what appeared to be the easy way out.

Back in his seat, Ambose set to work to exploit his advantage; first, by trying to make it seem that in saying the shooting hadn't had to happen when it did, Zacharias had really been saying that Sam could have made a decision not to shoot, and then—after he had forced Zack to repeat his explanation about "the whole life span" and "the sudden eruption" for the jury to consider in the light of what should be their new misgivings about him—by fastening down upon that one day out of all the possible days of his life, and the one second out of all the possible seconds.

Left alone to claw over his story, Ambose would have beat him bloody, and nobody would ever be able to tell him different. Hell, he clobbered him pretty good as it was. There was, alas, nothing that said the other side had to sit back and let you destroy their witness. In rapid order Halpern, Bannerman and Harry Davies came rushing in to take the heat off him, and if that wasn't enough to make Jim Ambose wonder whether he was living right, they all made themselves look pretty good—goddamn good—while they were about it. Halpern and Bannerman, he didn't mind that much; they were only doing their job. But that goddamn idiot, Harry Davies . . .

Zacharias had given his opinion that Sam was probably still in possession of his faculties during the climb up the stairs, but he frowned so thoughtfully as he was saying it that Ambose asked, fully mindful that Zacharias was hoping that he would but still seeing more to be gained on his side than theirs, "Not sure, Doctor? Want to have him blank out all the way up?"

"The possibility exists," Zacharias said. "I'd say no more than the possibility."

"Just thought of that, too, huh?"

"No, I discussed it very thoroughly with Sam."

"Oh? and he told you that there was a possibility he didn't remember?"

"No, he thought he remembered it all. The mind fills in the vacuums—"

"Lucky for him you know better."

Halpern erupted out of his chair. "Let him finish," he shouted. "The witness has a right to answer without being interrupted and Mr. Ambose is cutting him off." He turned his fierce gaze from Ambose to the Bench. "And he's also being insulting."

Ambose gave him the side of his eyes. "Why, Harold," he purred, "you know I'd never do a thing like that."

Oh no! Halpern wasn't being dismissed that easily anymore. "Never mind that Harold stuff," he barked. "I'm Mr. Halpern to you. Got it?"

"Why sure. And you can just call me Jim." It got him his cheap laugh but, still and all, Halpern sat down heavily, more than satisfied. God save him from ending up like either Bannerman or Ambose but, by god, he had established his credibility and he knew which side he was on.

Mollineaux had slipped back into the courtroom, his briefcase dismally thin. While Zacharias was informing the Court that indeed he had not completed his answer, Mollineaux's eyes met Ambose's for a fraction of a second, all that was necessary to pass on the message that he had come up cold stone empty.

"The mind," Zacharias said, picking up where he had left off, "is disturbed by the absence of memory." His eyes went briefly to the jury box and back. Sam knew that he must have killed Wilcke, because he had the gun in his hand when consciousness returned. And because he was being placed under arrest. And because he was told that he had. "Once he had a rough idea of what had happened, his mind filled in the rest."

"And the walk up the stairs? He'd filled that in, too, maybe?"

"It's possible, I say. He knew he'd have had to walk up the stairs to be where he was."

"Oh, now I get it. You don't *know* he doesn't remember. You're just making out a case that he doesn't."

"Your Honor." Norman Bannerman's turn had come. You could see it in the graceful, indolent slouch with which he draped himself over the back of his chair and, even more so, in his faintly elfish, oddly horse-like expression of unexpected opportunity being gleefully welcomed. And though he made a truly impressive effort to trim his features back before he addressed the Court, the dulcet, richly modulated voice that was the Bannerman trademark rippled with an undercurrent that was unmistakable.

"Honesty, my father told me when I was but a lad, is good feed for the soul to grow on and, if his information was correct and his business acumen to be trusted, a sound financial investment." He folded his hands across his stomach. His voice dropped several octaves. "And so it is, Your Honor, that I beg permission to stand before this Honorable Court and, indeed, before all men, my peers (a nod to the Bench) and betters (a nod to the jury box), for I must put it to you fair, without further equivocation or flimflam, that while Dr. Nicholas Zacharias is a saintly man and an intimate friend of the Cardinal, we have made no claim that any powers of divinity have been visited upon him."

Although the bow he executed in the direction of Ambose was quite formal and courtly, his voice brimmed with the not unpleasurable effort of keeping the laughter from bubbling over. "On behalf of Dr. Zacharias, sir, the accolade is regretfully declined. Humble man that he is, he holds himself to be unworthy of enshrinement and, in deference to an excruciatingly low threshold of pain, ineligible." He paused skillfully, enjoying the audience reaction almost as much as Ambose's malignant glare. Resuming, he informed the Court—his voice hardening in mid-sentence—that he had called Dr. Zacharias to the witness stand to give an expert opinion, and that was exactly what he was doing. "My objection, since I can see Your Honor is growing impatient, is that the question is in no wise a relevant one. I will caution my friend, the assistant district attorney, that it is not even a legal one."

The Court: "The objection is a good one. The Court will sustain it."

Of all the idiocies and lunacies of the rules of evidence and procedure, there were few that enraged Ambose quite so much as the one that relieved a psychiatrist of any necessity to bolster his opinion with hard evidence. As, say, a ballistics expert might be called upon to produce a slide, or a medical doctor his charts and photographs. The reason was self-evident. Psychiatry was all web and no spider. Ask him to prove it and you drummed him out of the courtroom.

All he had been trying to do, Ambose told the Court in a bit of a sulk, was to bring the truth to the jury. If he couldn't tell them the rules of the game, he could damn well make them feel deprived. "We think the jury is entitled to know. And," he said, lowering darkly at Zacharias, "if Mr. Bannerman is worried that I'm attributing divine powers to his witness, you can tell him to just relax."

Bannerman: "I won't even deign to answer that kind of uncivil and unprofessional retort."

The murderous look Ambose would have preferred to have sent to Bannerman was directed instead to the witness. "When did he lose power over his limbs?"

Zacharias was slightly puzzled. "Do you mean his legs, Mr. Ambose?"

Ambose erupted clear out of his chair. "His limbs!" he bellowed. "Limbs means arms and legs, Doctor. I thought you were supposed to be the big expert on vocabulary around here, too!"

Out of the corner of his eye he could see that Number 5 and Number 6 were smiling at each other. They must be talking up in the jury quarters these nights. For the sake of those jurors who might have found Bannerman so entertaining that they had not been able to understand what he had been objecting to, Ambose went right back into the forbidden territory and asked Zacharias to tell the jury how he knew Sam's mind had been a vacuum. "What did you test it with?" He sneered. "A vacuum tube, maybe?" And then sat back and watched as Bannerman came grimly to his feet and moved for a mistrial. "The witness has testified how he arrived at his conclusion." His arms were folded high across his chest. "I repeat for the record that this is an expert witness giving his expert opinion."

"The jury understands that," Davies said sweetly. "These jurors, being unschooled in the law as they are, may not know when a lawyer is out of order, but they can tell when a witness is being badgered. Don't do it again, Mr. Ambose."

That was the trouble with trying a case before the Idiot King. There he'd be, farting along, paying no more attention to proper procedure than anybody would expect him to, and then, at the worst possible time, when your guard was completely down, he acted like he thought he was supposed to know what he was doing. The fact that Davies went on to deny the motion didn't mollify Ambose one bit. Jurors, being unschooled in what was expected of them, always looked to the judge for their attitudes as well as their instructions. The advantage that had been fairly won by all that hard work and adroit maneuvering had been whisked away from him in a matter of seconds.

Ambose could have kicked a lung out of him.

Nothing, Mollineaux whispered after Ambose had called for a huddle. "Zipped out." All the stuff on photographic memory had turned out to be freaky Sunday supplement stuff. Pawley suggested that he would put the whole office to work on it overnight. That would give them plenty of time to research it provided nobody had any foolish ideas about getting any sleep. Ambose nodded. On the spot he had decided to hold the idea that had been percolating in the back of his head for Lionel Allbright. He wanted more time to think about it. Pawley pulled his chair in even closer. The quip had been out of character for one of these huddles, even for Pawley. They weren't here to laugh. Pawley's job here was to give Ambose his best professional assessment of the battlefield situation before Ambose, the combat soldier, returned to the front lines. As far as the testimony that had been covered so far was concerned, Pawley thought he had covered everything more than adequately. "On the rest of it, two things." He glanced down the length of his arm to where his pad lay. Ambose had had something going for him with the "kingsize irresistible impulse," and then he'd just forgotten about it. "So just a tickler on that to pick it up again tomorrow with Allbright." Just "kingsize," though, he cautioned him, not "long-smoking." His eyes went flicking toward the jury behind Ambose. "You put in "long-smoking" and you're giving them the idea of something smoldering, and that's their ball game, not ours. OK?"

The other thing. "You're going too strong," he said earnestly. "Ease off a little." From what Pawley had been able to observe, a couple of the jurors were beginning to sympathize with Zacharias. "The women especially. Bettlenork."

"You hear that, Ambose?" The harsh way Nevins growled it out made it an order. "If Dee says lay back some, I want you to lay back. I told you that already, didn't I?" And Dee was right about Bettlenork, too. "She's the one that's going to be trouble if any of them. What the hell did you ever take her for, that's one thing I'll never understand."

"I didn't," Ambose said. Coldly and incisively. His upper lip pulled tight across his gritted teeth. "*Deeee* did. Once in a while *Deeee* isn't right." Ambose hadn't even been in the courtroom on the day they'd taken Bettlenork. He'd been upstairs preparing his case and being so all-fired confident that his associates were going to get him a couple of good jurors he could work with. "Tell him, Dee," he said venomously. "The boss wants to know what in the hell did you take her for. A nurse, for chrissake. You had to be crazy."

"Because once in awhile I ain't right," Pawley said equably. "Sorry about that."

It was more of an apology than he'd be getting out of Nevins. The district attorney merely glanced down at his watch and asked what he had left, if anything. "We can't spend all day with this guy, you know."

"Yeah, I know." Ambose's lip curled. "I haven't pinned him down on how come Sam had to see everything around him except that one time. Well, how about that? And none of you backseat drivers even noticed." Without giving them the courtesy of officially dissolving the huddle, without taking another breath really, he glared up at the witness from under his eyelids. "You have a pretty good private practice up there in Chicago, Doctor?"

"Satisfactory."

"All right, then." He pulled the chair around, and shifted back and forth in the seat to make himself more comfortable. "I will now ask you whether irresistible impulse isn't a legal gimmick which you are willing to testify to in a courtroom although it's something that never comes up in your normal practice. By which I mean outside the courtroom. Is that clear to you?"

From all appearances Zacharias had been considerably refreshed by both the drink of water and the delay. He opened his eyelids wide. "The answer is yes, it is clear to me, and yes, it comes up in normal practice. We see it all the time."

Ambose blinked. "Tell me about it."

Well, masturbation for one thing. "Masturbation is an irresistible impulse we are all familiar with at some stage of our development." The average teen-ager, he pointed out, adopting his smoothest professional voice, wanted to stop but found that he, or she, couldn't.

"Well, I don't know if I'd want to give you the Policeman at the Elbow test on that," Ambose said. "But suppose we give it a try." He was not completely successful in suppressing a snigger. "Suppose they had an irresistible impulse to masturbate at the A&P?"

From his right elbow Nevins said, "Drop it, Ambose. That's an order." He didn't whisper it, either. He said it in a normal, conversational voice that would have been impossible for the jury not to hear. That Hilliard might want to dissociate himself from this, or anything else, didn't come as any particular surprise to Ambose. But that he would do it at the price of hurting the state's case, that was something that had never happened before. Mrs. Brennan did look as if she had a bad taste in her mouth, but so what? Some of the men looked kind of amused.

There was no way to drop it, anyway; the question had been asked.

"There's those that do," Zacharias said. "As you very well know. The legal term for it is exhibitionism."

Kleptomania and arson were other examples that could be cited in this regard, kleptomania being of special interest in that it was characterized, in certain instances, by the desire to be caught. There had been many publicized instances of women of wealth and social position or public prominence who had taken some worthless item or other from a bargain counter under conditions where they could not help but be caught. He shifted completely around in his chair so that he would be addressing the jury directly in confidence—the same trick he had used in the bond hearing—while he was telling them about the many, many other cases, completely unpublicized, which ended up in the files of psychiatrists. Some of the names in his own files alone would make them gasp.

Ambose (loudly): "But none where the store detective had been right at their elbow, isn't that right, Doctor? Isn't it true that the desire to get caught is a purely unconscious desire?"

An extremely satisfied look passed over Zack's face. "Of course," he said. "That happens to be precisely the connection I have been seeking to make, don't you see? Wholly unconscious. The more enlightened store owners came to understand that many years ago. The major chains, in particular. Perhaps it would not be out of order to give them the credit they deserve." Back to the jury. "Understanding that these poor women are not responsible, they recognize how inhumane it would be to treat them as they might treat an ordinary shoplifter."

Because they're afraid some shyster lawyer and his psychiatrist will throw a million-dollar suit at them, you mean, Ambose thought in so many words, while in some higher part of his brain he was acknowledging that he had put Zacharias in a position where he could lecture to them.

On one side of him, Hilliard Nevins had turned his back on him. Just turned completely away from him to make sure nobody would miss how disgusted he was. That was Nevins, all right. Always right there when you needed him. On the other side, Pawley tilted his head toward him. "You're digging a hole for yourself," he said, without exactly looking at him. "Change directions."

Another precinct heard from. Well, Ambose wasn't so sure. Doggedly, digging himself in, he asked whether it wasn't true, whether it didn't necessarily follow that in every example he had cited, Dr. Zacharias had been dealing with an admittedly powerful force of nature which had been frustrated or perverted?

Except for one mild demurrer, Zacharias was more than willing to agree. He wouldn't have thought anyone looked on masturbation as a perversion anymore, he said, chiding him, but if the thrust of the question was whether they had all been examples of a sexual drive seeking an outlet, his answer would most definitely have to be in the affirmative.

In which case, said Ambose, scouring him with his blackest look, wasn't it also true that they could not be considered relevant, or even legitimate, examples of irresistible impulse in the same way he had been using that term in relation to the crime they were concerned with in this courtroom?

"I wouldn't say that. Not at all."

"You wouldn't?" The sweat was beginning to crawl down the inner lining of his stomach. The ends of his fingers felt numb. His every impulse was to strike out swiftly and scornfully by asking whether he was trying to tell the jury that the murder of the Chief Justice had come as the result of a perverted sex drive. Holding him back was the memory of all that earlier testimony about an unresolved Oedipal conflict and the "longest-smoking irresistible impulse of all time." Once he hesitated, the words caught on the roof of his mouth. Pawley had been right, and he might as well admit it. He had dug himself into a hole. To ask the question now would be to give Zacharias a chance to reveal just enough of the defense so that the entire civilized world would be panting for Lionel Allbright's appearance tomorrow. Not to ask it would be to leave the question as it was, implanted in everybody's mind.

How in the name of hell, he wondered glumly, had he let Zacharias lead him into this kind of blind alley when all he had been trying to do was ask a couple of questions preliminary to the identic imagery one? Well, one thing he was sure of. He might just as well throw that part of it overboard and give his mind over completely to the problem he was faced with. He couldn't ask the question and he couldn't conspicuously duck it, and that meant he would have to extricate himself by means of a particularly artful exercise of the lawyer's ancient and honorable device of making it seem as though he were following up hard on the question while he was assiduously evading it. One snappy question—inserted sideways through the horns—that would get him in fast, and out faster.

He eyed the witness critically, and then quizzically, and finally with amusement. "Then you see the murder of a Chief Justice as little different from, say, stealing a handbag down at Orean's bargain basement?"

"In certain respects," Zacharias said. If he was to understand that they were talking about this murder and this Chief Justice.

Ambose sat up straight and stared at him, unable, as anybody could see, to believe his ears. His senses returning, he flung up his arms and surrendered. "In that case, Your Honor, we have no further questions to ask this witness. We'll just hand him back to Mr. Bannerman."

Mr. Bannerman would just take him. Mr. Bannerman not only welcomed him back with open arms, he looked as if he was going to strike up the band and waltz him around the ballroom. He twinkled. He flounced. He positively glowed. Smooth as cream, deeply secure, he advised everyone within sound of his voice that he was so content with the testimony that had been elicited by Mr. Ambose's cross-examination that to ask one solitary question more would be to run the risk of earning himself a niche in the Legal Hall of Fame similar to the one reserved for that legendary artist who, unable to let well enough alone, had added the one extra brush stroke that had marred a perfect masterpiece.

"But," he said, smacking his lips, "I'll risk one."

Since nobody was ever going to accuse Bannerman of letting a dramatic pause go unpaused, he stroked his chin delicately, like a child sampling each piece of candy behind the glass counter before deciding which delicacy he was going to spend his last penny on. "In your opinion, sir," he said, at last, "did the assassination of David Wilcke come as the result, directly or indirectly, of a perverted or frustrated sex drive?"

"In my opinion, it did."

"Well, that wasn't so bad, was it?" He smiled skittishly around the courtroom until, his eyes falling upon Ambose, he passed the witness back with a wicked grin that amounted to an open challenge to jump right on in if he dared to.

"The state has no more questions to ask of this witness," Nevins said brusquely, so anxious to bring it to an end that he actually worked up enough energy to push himself up out of his chair. As long as he was up, he pulled gingerly at the seat of his pants. "You couldn't just ask about whether he forgot all those cops were there, could you?" he growled down at Ambose. "You had to be a lawyer about it."

While Ambose and Nevins were growling back and forth at each other, Bannerman was leaning over the defense table to shake the hand of Nick Zacharias and promise him that, win or lose, he had earned himself his petunia. Sam Tabor remained massively indifferent to both of them, and when Halpern intervened, confident that he could get Sam to understand how heavily they had scored for him, all he succeeded in doing was make himself painfully aware that it was the first time he had paid any attention to Sam all afternoon.

Bannerman had two quick witnesses to put on, both appearing under subpoena. The chief admissions officer of St. Cecilia's Hospital was called first to put the record of Sam's circumcision into evidence. Pawley took him on cross-examination and immediately drew out the fact that there was nothing in the records to explain why the operation had been performed. For whatever good it might do, he then had him list every possible reason, first and foremost among them being simple hygiene.

The other witness was Herb Jacklin, the intern who had given Sam the rectal examination. Jacklin was a young man with a long, sharp nose, and you could see from the first that he was unimpressed with Bannerman, unimpressed with courtrooms, unimpressed with the world. Bannerman's only reason for putting him on was, presumably, to get it into the record again—direct from the source, as it were—that Sam had been subjected to a physical before he had been booked. Beyond that, Jacklin had already told Bannerman everything he knew, which, to quote him verbatim, was exactly nothing, unless he wanted a detailed report on his client's hemorrhoids, which looked to hold up for a few more years if his client would cooperate by moving his bowels with regularity and staying the hell away from electric chairs.

Jacklin had been more than willing to testify as a defense witness if Bannerman thought he could do his poor bastard any good. The subpoena had been Bannerman's idea. "You've been so kind," Bannerman had told him, "that I wouldn't feel right about it if I permitted you to fall into the bad graces of those gorillas you have to work with." By establishing with his very first question that Jacklin had been subpoenaed, Bannerman would put him in the clear.

By the time Jacklin climbed down off the witness stand he knew what the real reason had been. Bannerman had peppered him with question after question purporting to show that Sam had been subjected to illegal questioning, and since Jacklin had already told him that he hadn't been, Bannerman had arranged things so that the jury would be able to view him as a reluctant witness who would be just as likely to be lying as not.

On the fifth floor of the courthouse building the lights in Jim Ambose's office burned far into the night. Ambose had already familiarized himself with most of the stuff Allbright had written, and Mollineaux had already catalogued, correlated and cross-filed it. Working from his file cards, they were now engaged in the painstaking, time-consuming job of breaking all the material down into six separate categories, each of them identifiable by its own color so that Mollineaux would be able to find any quotation Ambose asked for in the shortest possible time, under the heaviest courtroom pressure. The color-identification system had another and far more important value to Ambose. Just because it was such painstaking and time-consuming work it allowed him to absorb the material into his bloodstream.

"Suicidal ideation." He looked up from a book entitled *Man, the Irrational Animal.* "Think that's going to come up?"

Mollineaux looked back at him helplessly, his eyes bleary, his mind gone blank. Both of them were working in their shirtsleeves. Ambose's sleeves were rolled up halfway to his elbows, and his tie hung loose, in separate strands, around his neck. The younger man's collar was open, and his tie, which had been loosened only slightly, was tugged off to one side.

"Oh, hell," Ambose said. "Orange. Motivation. He kills him because he wants to die himself. Doesn't give a damn about the state's electric bill. Psychiatrists get all trembly in the knees over that one. The only thing about it is they love him so much they never want to oblige him. Or immortality. Out in a blaze. On the wings of glory. Then there's the messiah complex. They've got the word straight from God, see, and they're only doing His bidding. They think . . ."

Mollineaux, struggling desperately to follow what Ambose was saying, gave his head a shake.

"I don't know how you feel about religion, Red, but if you read your Bible—and whatever you want to say you're still going to find more solid, goshdarn, everyday truth in the Scriptures than you're likely to find anywhere else—if you read your Bible, you know that on the highly controversial capital punishment issue, we've got God on our side."

While Ambose had been talking, the flaming red hair had been slowly dropping, dropping, dropping, dropping. Mollineaux was fighting sleep. And losing. With one last, great, upheaving effort he jerked his head up. His eyes, showing mostly white, came stickily open and wavered upon a no-longer sympathetic Jim Ambose. "Go soak your head," Ambose ordered. "You'd think you were a hundred years old by the look of you. Well, come on! Hop! We've got a lot of work to do yet."

"Don't underestimate him, Norman," Marie said. "The only trouble with Harry is he's lazy. Lazy isn't dumb."

The sardonic look that was thrown at her from over Bannerman's shoulder was commentary enough on Harry Davies' unassailable dumbness, with more than enough left over to take care of anybody dumb enough to want to argue about it.

Bannerman was pacing up and down in front of the bed, in his red satin robe and bedroom slippers, pulling at his bottom lip. Marie, watching anxiously, continued to pull off her stocking.

"All right," Bannerman said. "You can tell him this. Tell him I can have Merril

Hays here to display himself and I'll have him make a sign, like blowing his nose three times or bidding three spades. Something juvenile enough to make your judge happy. But no conversation afterwards. That's out!" Again, there was the sour, oblique look that told her, more eloquently than words, how sick he was becoming of all these oafs and nincompoops who were complicating his life. "And if he won't take my word for it, he can go to hell!"

"He's really a very good speaker," Marie said meekly. "You'd be surprised." Another look. He sure would be. "Audiences love him, Norman. I've seen him. What I mean, I've heard him. Speak." She moistened her lips. "He relates to people very well."

A different kind of look; congratulating her. By god, he'd known she'd hit on something if she kept trying.

Harry's brilliant proposition had been that Bannerman would ask permission for a guest to be seated inside the Bar, whereupon he would introduce Merril Hays. After which, what would be more natural than for Bannerman to bring his guest around to chambers for a friendly chat, in the course of which Merril Hays could say, in a friendly, chatty way, that from what he had seen of the judge in action he liked his style and hoped he would be open to an offer to join his stable of highly paid speakers as soon as the burden of presiding over this current trial, which was being watched by the entire world, was off his shoulders.

"I know what you must think of me," Marie said candidly. "The first thing I've done every time I've seen you is see how fast I could jump out of my clothes."

Suddenly solicitous, Bannerman joined her on the side of the bed and began to stroke her back, smoothly and soothingly, expressing his surprise and personal dismay all the while that she, as a court reporter, could fail to understand that with his star witness taking the stand tomorrow, he really *did* have a lot of work to do tonight.

"I know, lover." She pouted at him mournfully, as much in sympathy at having to put up with her as with the long night's work that lay ahead of him. "I'd better jump out of the rest of them while you've still got time to fit me into your busy schedule," she said, and the way she pronounced the word "schedule," with the high-toned, very English soft "sh," turned it into a consciously tender acquiescence to her sad fate.

Since she was already down to her bra and panties, there wasn't much to jump out of, but, mischievously, in keeping with the spirit that there was not a second to be lost, she galvanized herself into action, flipping herself straight back on the bed, all the way back until her weight was resting on her shoulders and her legs high up in the air. There, at the top of her arc, she grasped the sides of her panties, slipping them off as she was coming back down, and, almost before her feet had hit the ground, reached back to unclasp her brassiere.

"Calisthenics," she said, stretching out her arms to him. "That's how I keep my girlish figure. Daily calisthenics with a little nighttime acrobatics thrown in to make it worth the while." She gave a little laugh, deep in her throat. "Not often. Only when I can get it." The suffusing warmth was already creeping over her. The serene, inviting smile. "I don't mind the robe, Norman, if you're so pressed for time," she said in a low, teasing voice. "But do me a favor and take your slippers off. There's something about shoes in bed that takes all the romance out of it."

A shadow passed over his face. *(His boots full of mud, kicking the door open.)* Deliberately, never taking his eyes off her, he pulled the robe back and let it fall.

Through the shadow came a warning, like a cold draft against the neck. If Harry didn't come through, where would that leave him? It would still leave him with Marie under his thumb, wanting to play games, and that meant she'd be willing to let him play games with the transcript. The shadow lifted. His whole body relaxed. He'd better do like the lady wanted.

Lying in bed beside her, he held out the prospect of two gloriously decadent weeks together on the Riviera, debauching and debilitating themselves. In minute and exquisite detail he pictured them sunning themselves on the glorious white sands of Cannes; standing on the fantail of their rented yacht with the pure blue Mediterranean spray in their face; cruising the gaming casinos and attending orgiastic revels where she would be priviliged to observe and perhaps participate in ancient sexual rites so arcane and perverted as to surpass the wildest erotic dream to have ever filtered past the sentries of her apple-pie American mind.

"Participate!" she squealed. "Participate!" Every American woman, she agreed enthusiastically, should be given two glorious weeks on the Riviera to debauch and debilitate herself in style before menopause set in. She kissed him warmly. "You ought to run for Congress, Norman. You couldn't miss with a platform like that."

As they were beginning to make love, he said wistfully, "Marie . . .?"

"Tell me, lover. Tell mama. Tell mama where it hurts, so mama can kiss it and make it better."

Maybe he'd marry her, he thought. He'd married worse. And for less reason. *How would Gwen like that!* "I was thinking of that exchange I had with the lout this morning. On direct." He worked on her a little. "Remember when I mean? I can't quite recall whether I got in the last word or he did." He worked on her some more. "I sure hope it was me."

"If that's what you hope, lover," she crooned, "that's what I hope."

"It's important to me."

"I'm the Good Fairy who makes all your hopes and dreams come true. Norman, do you have to keep that light on?"

"Our system of jurisprudence," he said, quoting himself lovingly, caressing each syllable as it issued from his lips, "our system of jurisprudence which we hold forth as a model for the civilized world, but which in Mr. Ambose's grudging hands becomes transformed into an arena having all the less desirable features of a public abattoir."

Directly above her Marie could see his face, upraised, staring vacantly off into space; staring, it seemed to her, directly into the light. She wasn't there, as far as he was concerned. *He* wasn't there at all. Inside her, he had shriveled. "That was beautiful," he breathed. "Wasn't that the most beautiful thing you ever heard?"

"Beautiful, lover."

"Beoooootiful." The word had been exhaled in one long sigh. "I do hope that's where it ended. I would find it beyond all endurance for that lout to have marred the majestic splendor of those words with some guttural caterwaul of hate."

"That's where it ended." She drew him down to her, and began to run her tongue around his ear. "That's where it ended, lover," she whispered, and clasped him tightly to her. "Ahhhh. Oh, that's beoooootiful. Oh, Norman. That's beoooo-ti-*full.*"

A couple of minutes later he said, "Marie . . ." They were lying side by side, with her back angled slightly away from him, so that he could come up and under and she could stroke him as he was moving in and out. "You'll make a note about that before you go, won't you? So you won't forget."

"You bastard!" Tormented, she turned her head away. Tormented, but gritting herself together; her eyes pressed tight, the knuckles of one hand pressed into her forehead. When she turned back to him her eyes were wet. "Why do you do that to me? You make me feel like a queen one minute, and a whore the next. Don't do that to me, Norman. Please don't do that to me. There's no need, Norman. Please don't."

"Now, now," he said, shushing her. Soothing her. Kissing her. Petting her. She had it all wrong. He had just been thinking, that's all. For later, he meant. She understood that, didn't she? Well, didn't she? Come on and tell daddy, didn't she?

That's a good girl. Of course she did.

A minute or so later, when he really had her straining for it, he said in a cold, demanding voice, "But you won't forget, will you?"

Tuesday, August 5

For whatever reason, Ruthie had been afraid that her presence in the courtroom would jinx Hal, and so despite his urgings she had insisted upon waiting for the great day when Lionel Allbright would take the stand. Maybe she had known something, at that. With Allbright having flown back into Lowell last night, the duty roster called for Cowhig to drive Bannerman to the Coronet for one last replay over breakfast. For the first and only time during the trial, Hal had been free to hang around the house so that he could escort her into the courtroom.

As they were getting ready to leave she took one last look at herself in the bureau mirror and, catching her husband's deeply preoccupied reflection behind her, asked with real concern, "Aren't you happy, Hal?"

Taken so completely unawares, he heard himself saying, "My father used to say, 'Happy is when you don't cry.' "

Through the mirror she gave him a briefer but more searching look. It was the third time he had quoted his father in the past few days, and until this darn trial he hadn't spoken of his father half a dozen times in the whole time they'd been married.

"What do you think?" She spun around with practiced grace so that he could look her over. "Am I a knockout? Am I the cat's pajamas?" Clucking her tongue, she kicked one foot across her body, punching the air in the same direction as she did, and posed there, like a Charleston dancer, with a fluttery, wide-eyed smile pasted across her bony, always mobile features. "Am I ready to go mix with the swells?"

The whole performance, precisely because it was intended to be so peppy and madcap, was exactly the opposite; as strained and feeble in its own way as Hal's reassuring smile.

"My father also used to say," he said, "that God picks out one man in every ten thousand and decides that he will be the one He will make happy by giving him the greatest gift within His power. A good wife. That's just in case you've been wondering why I snatched you out of the cradle before you could wise up and make yourself a better deal."

That's all it took. "Oh, I like your father." Except for a suspicious glistening in her eyes she was his old Ruthie again, all glow and sparkle. "Did he really say that? Oh, he didn't *really* say that. I know you, you're such a big fibber, you. You made it up. Did he *really?*"

"Would I lie to a child bride," he lied.

Bannerman was absolutely alone in the courtroom, in an unflamboyant black suit, turned sideways in his chair at the defense table, and so totally absorbed in Lionel Allbright's best-known work, *Man, the Irrational Animal,* that Hal went back and sat with Ruthie in the first row behind the press section until well after the reporters had begun to file in. Bannerman was about two-thirds through the book. Hal could guess that he had been up all night reading, and though he did find it momentarily unsettling, to say the least, to see how close to the edge of the brink Bannerman chose to work, he would have had to be pretty stupid not to understand by now that if Bannerman seemed to be deliberately courting danger, it was only because Bannerman functioned best—and knew he functioned best—when he could feel the sharp edge of the knife at his throat.

Still and all. If another breakdown in the air-conditioning unit hadn't delayed the opening of the session for twenty minutes, he wouldn't have come close to finishing the book. Giving him every possible allowance, that seemed to be cutting things too fine.

Immediately upon mounting the Bench, Judge Davies had announced that the maintenance people were right on the job and would have the air conditioning back on in a matter of minutes. While they were waiting, he did his best to carry on an intimate little chat with the jury by inquiring whether any of them had ever been on a jury before where they'd had to stay over a weekend, or overnight for that matter; and whether they were finding their quarters comfortable, small and cramped though he knew them to be. He assured them that the Court and the lawyers and the whole community, for that matter, appreciated the sacrifice they were making. He wanted them to know that if they had any thoughts among them about how anything could be made easier for them, they should send word to him right away, day or night. It wasn't through any fault of Harry's that the jury turned the intimate little chat into an intimate little monologue by responding to every question or comment with self-conscious little smiles and nods and shrugs.

"Well," he said, trying again, "I hope they let you watch the ball game on television last night, anyway," and the chorus of affirmatives encouraged him so much that he said, "That was a humdinger, wasn't it, though? I think we're gonna win it this year, when you win 'em like that, I really do. What are we behind now, four and a half? What are they quoting now in Las Vegas, two-to-one?" He drew the corners of his lips down into the thoughtful grimace of the self-acknowledged expert. "Friend of mine was telling me that this morning, two-to-one. Not that I'd encourage gambling, I want you to understand, but just to keep you up on current events. Although, just between us here, and I wouldn't want to see this printed in New York or Omaha, but if betting was legal in this state I wouldn't mind getting me a little of that."

Hilliard Nevins, who had startled the oldest courtroom inhabitant by coming into court in a brand-new blue suit, covered his face to hide a silent groan. "I wouldn't worry so much about Omaha, Judge," he said drily. "I'd be worrying if in the office of district attorney, Brederton County, anybody happened to read anything about it and thought they was gonna have to take action."

Through it all, Bannerman kept reading, lifting his eyes only to jot down an occasional note. He was still flipping through the pages when Peterson came in to whisper something into the judge's ear. The Court rapped for order. There had been a slight change in the original estimate, it seemed. They were now saying they had to send out for a new part that had broken down or blown out or something, and the best they'd guarantee was that they'd have the air conditioning working before the morning was over.

Well, Davies sighed, it looked like they were just going to have to suffer for awhile. "Unless," he said playfully, "anyone wants to leave. Now's the time, and no questions asked." He cast a long-suffering look at the jury. "Wouldn't you know today would be the day I'd forget my heat pills?"

"Your smart pills, too," Pawley muttered.

"I know it gets awful hot there in the jury box," Davies said in deep commiseration. "But if it'll make you feel any better, the Bench is the hottest spot in the courtroom." He loosened his collar underneath the robe. "Twenty degrees hotter by actual measurement."

"Oh, I don't know," Jim Ambose said. He was looking over at Sam Tabor. "What do you say, Sam?" he asked. "Want to get in on the bidding?"

The recitation of Allbright's credentials took twenty-three minutes by the clock, and the most striking thing about him was how ill at ease he was. As he went on from there to lay down the basic psychiatric profile Halpern had heard at the motel—the homosexual stance, the homosexual dilemma and the rest of it—it was in the same nasal tone and the same short, broken rhythm. By then, Bannerman had perched himself on the front of the table and was gentling him along in a confident, conversational tone that was very different from the orotund, hortatory style Bannerman-watchers had become accustomed to.

To that earlier material Allbright was now able to add the information Halpern had brought back from Cumberland, placing particular stress upon the traumatic incident of the Christmas "desertion" that had reinforced Sam's feeling of abandonment and worthlessness.

Ambose bent forward on his arms, listening intently. The only time he interrupted was when Bannerman attempted to introduce Mrs. Anabelle Tabor's "commitment papers"—which, technically, weren't commitment papers at all. They were the sanitarium records Halpern had brought back with him.

Sam himself had perked up at the sight of Allbright, visibly proud that such a famous man had taken the time to come and testify for him. But not for long. At the first mention of the strained relationship that had existed between his parents, his head popped back like a man who smelled trouble. When Bannerman held up the "commitment papers," he flinched and turned to Hal and seemed about to say something. And then his lips pursed and he was blowing a thin stream of air out between them. For the next hour or so his eyes went to the door every time it opened, as if he were still clinging to a last, forlorn hope that help would be coming from someplace in the great world outside the courtroom.

The change in Sam was no more than might have been expected. From the moment the question of Anabelle Tabor's records came into the courtroom a far greater and more puzzling change had come over Bannerman. Ambose's objection had been on the grounds that nobody from the sanitarium had been placed on the stand to identify them. Harry Davies laid his pipe aside long enough to ask, "Gonna connect it up, Mr. Bannerman?"

Bannerman ducked his head, played with the papers for awhile and, without looking up, said, "Nope."

It hardly mattered. Dr. Allbright had read all the reports and there was not a thing to prevent him from telling the jury everything Bannerman chose to have them know. And still, he sat there for an uncomfortable length of time with his head bowed and his hands gripping the edges of the table before he passed a hand across his eyes and muttered, so quietly that the jury could scarcely hear him, "Let us journey backward, Doctor, into the crucible in which poor Sam was formed and deformed."

The seconds ticked past. Bannerman's jaws worked meditatively. The stagnant air seemed to lay a dull and deadening hand over what should have been a moment of high tension. At last he closed his eyes and passed a hand across them. *(We're having fun, mama, aren't we?)* In his new subdued role he asked: "From your information, Dr. Allbright, would you relate for us the events which, in your opinion, caused Mrs. Tabor to end her life as a patient in the sanitarium?"

Lionel Allbright took a gulp of air before he spoke. His elbows seemed cumbersome and somehow in the way. Anabelle Tabor had received a blow on the head. A very bad blow which had split her head open and perhaps knocked her unconscious. From all the evidence, she had been hit by a swing while working in a playground. Treated with penicillin in the days before it had been discovered that many people could get an allergy reaction, she had broken out in a very bad blister rash. "As it happened," Dr. Allbright said, "her allergy reaction seems to have borne a remarkable similarity to the symptoms suffered by a mountain woman she had given comfort to—'sat over' is the term used—through her final hours. A woman who had been bitten by a snake."

Anabelle Tabor, whose faith in God had been the all-consuming purpose and passion of her life, had, to put it simply, gone out of her head with fear in the mistaken belief that she was dying and that the truth was being withheld from her. As she, perhaps, had withheld it from the mountain woman.

"For the benefit of the jury, Doctor:" *(Out of her head, what did she know?)* "You are not saying, are you, that this kind of mental affliction is inheritable? Or are you?"

Allbright wasn't able to say one way or the other. The statistics showed that children with schizophrenic parents were more vulnerable than others, but whether there was a genetic predilection involved or whether it came as the result of the shared environment was still a matter which, as lawyers would say, was moot. "The true significance of his mother's breakdown was in his discovery that the religion which she had called upon him to sacrifice so much for, his father's support and authority, her own warmth and sustaining presence, was, when it came to the crisis in her life, empty." For as long as Sam had been able to believe that her faith was real, there had been a meaning to all deprivation. With the collapse of his mother's faith, Sam's world had collapsed, too. On one level, the fact that her world—the very meaning of her life—had crumbled so soon after the death of his father, would be—to his way of thinking—her way of telling him how worthless she considered him as a replacement. On another level, if her faith was that frail a reed, she could never truly have possessed it. It had been no more than an excuse she had used to enable her to desert him.

"At a deeper level of the unconscious, the level at which the unresolved Oedipus complex had been slumbering, the nonexistent snake that had brought on the disaster, the snake that had never been . . ." Dr. Allbright's gaze went uncomfortably to Sam Tabor. "Well, there is a symbolism there I had rather not dwell on any further, if you don't mind."

Bannerman said, "Without going into it any deeper, it would mean, at that unconscious level, that he would feel that his shameful wishes, symbolized by the snake that had never been there, were the cause of her death?"

It seemed to be considerably more elaborate than that. It was the mother who gave the child his first experience as a trustworthy fellow being and thereby allowed him to spread that trust and friendship until it included the whole of human society. Sam had lost not only his trust but his connection—his life-line—to human society. "These things remain submerged. There are difficulties that can be well compensated for."

While the jury listened spellbound, Lionel Allbright expounded upon the meaning of Sam's job at the Missing Persons Bureau. "The poetry of the mind." He smiled; it was a phrase he liked so much that he relaxed and allowed his intelligence to come shining through. "Like so much about Sam Tabor, it satisfies on many levels. His father was always the missing person in his life, and because of that his life has been a constant search for the missing person in himself. His own masculinity." Again, the slight pause and the apprehensive glance toward Sam. "When the missing person returns to protect him against his incestuous impulses, he will no longer be forced to submerge his masculinity."

He sent a nervous smile in the general direction of the jury and went on to explain that by joining in on the search for the missing person in his job, Sam had put himself in a position where he was both controlling the situation and being controlled. "He must have authority. What better place to find it than in a courthouse? He must have approval. What better way to get it than by showing his good faith—indeed, his innocence—by being in on the search himself?"

The Sam Tabor who had met Vera Tabor at Kokoma Beach in an episode that seemed so completely out of character could, given that insight, be easily understood. Something would have happened, undoubtedly connected with his job, that had temporarily set him free. He had begun by taking the one vacation in his life. And how had he spent it? His activities over that brief span of time must have coincided very closely to the picture he had of his footloose father. The evil things his mother told him his father was doing would have been associated with sex. The footloose father, long before the son, had been the snake who wasn't there.

"Is that a guess, Doctor, or do you have independent support in the tests?"

"Well, yes." Very clearly, that was a question he had not expected to be asked. In some confusion he turned to the Court. Unhappily, the Court was too involved in a delicate operation of its own to offer any help. Harry Davies was happily blowing smoke rings. Tight-lipped but otherwise without expression, Allbright stated in the most general of terms that the Rorschach and Thematic Apperception tests had shown that Sam thought his body to be physically impaired.

Bannerman had already reached back and taken a single sheet of paper from his briefcase. He strolled over to the prosecution table and handed the paper to Pawley, not looking at him. Not looking at any of the state's attorneys while they were studying it; not looking at them when he took it back. Halpern, watching him at such a flat angle, had the weird sensation that Bannerman's breath was hissing through his lips in a thin, steady stream.

"Will you describe what the Draw-a-Man Test is, Doctor?"

"It's a test where you ask the patient to draw a man. And the way he draws it will reveal a great deal about how he sees himself."

472

Totally preoccupied, Bannerman strolled over to the jury box and handed the drawing to the printer, Yorrash. He turned back to the witness. "And what did Sam's Draw-A-Man tell you?"

Allbright took a deep breath. He gnawed at his lips. His answer, when it came, was spoken so directly to Bannerman that it could be taken as a rebuke. "It will be seen, Mr. Bannerman, that the lines do not quite meet at the crotch. That would be an indication, for reasons I have no intention of expanding upon in an open courtroom, of a man who sees himself as deficient in masculinity."

"Just so we'll understand each other, sir." *(Deficient in the moral character assumed in Ripon boys and demanded of Dr. Everett Bannerman's son.)* "You are not saying, are you, that it is customary to draw a male organ in the crotch?"

It was not. "It is common that the lines are joined. The joining stands for . . . it serves the same purpose, Mr. Bannerman."

"But wouldn't that depend upon the proficiency of the individual? An accomplished artist could be expected to draw a perfect picture under any circumstances, couldn't he?"

"That is taken into consideration, of course. It isn't a question of the drawing's accuracy, but of its validity. With experience, any competent psychiatrist or psychologist would be able to identify the various ways the patient might use his profession as a defensive tactic." He made a small mouth. "A homosexual artist, to give one example, would pay meticulous attention to the clothing of his people, and from that alone the knowledgeable tester would be informed that there was a kind of investment being made in the body. You see?"

Although the laughter that rippled good-naturedly through the courtroom was hardly unconnected with Norman Bannerman's own well-publicized delight in strutting his full plumage. Bannerman didn't even seem to hear it. Expressionless, moving (it seemed) within his own pocket of preoccupation, he ambled back to the Bench to enter the drawing into evidence and proceeded to guide Lionel Allbright through the accommodations Sam and Vera Tabor had made in their marriage. They were well into the dangerous role a marriage counsellor could play when Cowhig entered with Merril Hays, a small, wiry, tough-looking man with a fighter's nose and wishbone-shaped scar indented into his lower forehead just above the nose.

From the vacant, slightly annoyed way Bannerman looked while he was introducing him, it came as a relief when Harry Davies turned his most ingratiating smile upon Mr. Hays and invited him to take a seat inside the Bar as a guest of the Court.

Picking up where he had left off, Allbright said, "They were competing for the doctor's favor, don't you understand, and she was the better patient, *she* was the favored patient. Everything that was being done—the separate sleeping accommodations, the suggestion that she find a job—all of it was being done for *her* benefit." And now you had the childhood experience all over again. In addition to being the judging figure, the marriage counsellor was also playing a paternal role, the surrogate father regulating and ordering their life. "In the marriage, you understand, she had been playing the mother, giving him the breast and satisfying the incestuous impulse by sleeping with him."

Subtly, and in all probability unconsciously, Dr. Allbright had slipped into the comfortable, familiar deskside manner of his trade. "And now this fellow, Shtogren, having already given a shake to these long-banked and dormant coals, reenacts the boyhood struggle in its entirety. He steps between them, as his father had stepped between them, giving her more in those occasional visits than Sam, the dutiful son, can give her despite all his efforts to please. While on the other level, she, having already exposed his evil, dirty mind to the surrogate father, is also exposing to Sam his lack of attractiveness to other males. And he, having already championed her cause in the bedroom struggle, pronounces Sam so deficient in masculinity as to be unworthy of sleeping with his own wife."

Under the table Sam's hands unclenched. He never looked to the door again.

Dr. Allbright had the jury caught up completely in the sweep and momentum of his delivery which, while not exactly eloquent, brought to what he was saying not only the force of his authority but the ring of its own logic. "All streams are flowing together. As a final igniting incident, he is doing precisely what Sam's father has done. He is preventing him, by the exercise of his absent authority, from satisfying his incestuous wishes."

He brushed the hair back off his forehead and leaned forward. "What do we find? We find that the incestuous impulses, which have been so nicely repressed all these years, have come boiling very close, dangerously close, murderously close to the surface. He is ready to erupt. He is twisting and turning in an agony of resentment and evasion. He is balanced on the point of an explosive charge and the fuse is burning." His eyes sparkled. "And it is at this crucial moment that onto the scene, into his ambit, walks the Chief Justice, the guy who is supposed to be your superego—your conscience and your control."

They were into it now, and Halpern experienced a flutter of the heart, with maybe a touch of the giggly exhilaration and silly pride that come from knowing what nobody else knows. Lionel Allbright was about to whisk the veil away and reveal the anwer to the mystery, and Harold Halpern knew that it was going to knock their eyes out.

Allbright brushed the falling forelock from his forehead and his eyes rested briefly upon Halpern. "The supporting symbolisms are of interest to us only as they served to prepare the ground for the main issue." He turned back to the jury. "The Chief Justice is the guy who is supposed to protect you from getting seriously involved in the kind of thing in which you have to confront your evil impulses. And he hasn't done it."

In a sudden movement so physical and so emotional as to force the audience to view him in a whole new light, Dr. Allbright jerked himself erect in the witness chair and clasped both hands across his chest. *"It isn't my fault that I have these evil impulses,"* he explained, in a querulous, self-justifying voice that was clearly a reproduction of the inner voice of Sam Tabor. *"That's the kind of guy I am. I'm a pretty terrible fellow. Everybody knows that.* The Chief Justice has failed him, and what's worse, he has done it maliciously. There you have the grievance. He's letting him get away with it, just as he's letting other criminals get away with it all over the country. Sam has only to read the papers to know that."

"It's closer to home than that, Doctor," Bannerman said.

Allbright was so deeply immersed in the hypnotic swell of his voice and the sweet intoxication of his analysis that he scarcely seemed to hear him. "Sam is a man who can exist only by keeping himself under tight control, obeying strict rules—*that's the kind of a guy I am*—and in the permissiveness of the time, he has been permitted to bust loose.

"And that," Allbright said, coming back to them, "is overwhelming impulse. The conscious knowledge that it's wrong to kill may still be there. The ability to control his actions isn't. He is overwhelmed by forces he has no way of understanding or controlling. Overwhelmed," he said huskily, "overwhelmed."

Quietly, as if he were interrupting the witness with reluctance, Bannerman asked, "Did you discuss it with him, Doctor?"

"I have. David Wilcke doesn't exist for him as an individual."

"Did you find any remorse in him, Doctor?"

There were, as Allbright explained it, two elements in remorse: sorrow and guilt. "When he said he was sorry, he was telling the truth. When he said he didn't know why he did it, he was telling the truth. There is no way for him to feel guilty, because he did not know what to feel guilty about."

He stopped, not quite certain whether to go on. In the silence of the courtroom it was impossible for Halpern to tell how effective he had been, except from what might be detected from the quality of the silence itself. Number 11 seemed to be impressed, but he had seemed to like Allbright from the beginning. Bettlenork had put away her knitting. Number 5, smoking his pipe, was rocking and nodding; whether that meant he was agreeing with Allbright's analysis or merely considering it was impossible to tell.

In the silence Bannerman's smooth-textured, modulated voice filled every cranny of the courtroom: "In your opinion, Dr. Allbright, why did Sam Tabor kill the Chief Justice?"

And anyone who was not already aware that the Bannerman voice had become an integral part of the trial, soaked into its very bones, could not help but realize it then.

Allbright flicked away at his eyebrow. "On a conscious level," he said, "if there was anything remotely resembling a conscious level, Sam Tabor killed the Chief Justice for letting criminals get away with it. Because that made him feel threatened." He folded his hands in front of him, with his elbows on the arms of the chair. "Never dreaming that the criminal he had in mind was himself, Sam Tabor, guilty of the thought-crime of incest."

Bannerman nodded in approval. Halpern hadn't missed the insertion of the qualifying . . . hell, the disclaiming little adverb "remotely," either.

They were coming to the end. Allbright diagnosed Sam as suffering from chronic undifferentiated schizophrenia, which he defined as a psychosis in which contact with reality was intermittently disturbed. *Undifferentiated* because of the difficulty in distinguishing which of the three classic types—paranoid, catatonic or hebephrenic—was paramount at any given time. *Chronic* because it was of such long duration.

In an entirely different voice, brisk and business-like, Bannerman asked the legal questions on irresistible impulse and the M'Naughton Rule.

When Bannerman then put the Model Penal Code question to him, Pawley's objection was no more than perfunctory. They had, after all, been through all this once before.

Judge Davies said, "The Court will sustain the objection." There was the briefest of pauses before he added, "In its present form."

Pawley, who was in the process of sitting down, looked up, startled. Ambose started forward, his nostrils flaring. Norman Bannerman remained just as he was, his lips slightly apart, his head slightly slanted.

Legal scholar that he was, Judge Davies allowed as how he had some reservations about the word "criminality" in there, since it could be interpreted to mean that the defendant was expected to know the criminal code he was breaking. Frowning heavily so that everybody (meaning Merril Hays) could see how hard he was concentrating, he suggested that since Mr. Pawley had stated his objection so eloquently, he might be able to aid the Court by suggesting an appropriate word to take its place.

The likelihood that Pawley was going to suggest anything—except perhaps where Harry Davies ought to go soak his head—was so remote as to be negligible, but he didn't have a chance to suggest even that. The Court had not been concentrating so heavily that it had not been able to catch a surly movement of Jim Ambose's lips, and with that swift and terrible wrath for which he had never before been noted, Judge Davies wheeled on Ambose and demanded to know what he had said.

"I said I've got a word," Ambose told him, doing nothing to hide his disgust. "How about 'naughty?' "

"Naughty?" It was such a pleasure to have Ambose on the hip for a change that Harry Davies, bred and trained as he was in the infinite complexities of the law, wrinkled and puckered, pretending to give it careful thought. He sneaked a look at Merril Hays. An unimposing sort of fellow. Scrawny. Kind of beat-up looking. Looked more like one of the winos that used to come shuffling up in front of him. Which only went to prove, he reminded himself sagely, that you could never judge by appearances. Probably worth millions. Millions.

Out of the corner of his eye he had seen Pawley lean across to Nevins, and sure enough, up rose Nevins, like a great collie shaking himself free of water, to interject his authority as if he knew that good old Harry was just having his fun. Twirling his glasses, he rumbled that, as the Court well knew, the state had prepared its case according to the law as it was written in the books, and that to change the rules on them right there in midstream so to speak . . . well, that was something he knew this wise and honorable Court would never take it upon itself to do.

Wise *and* honorable, huh? Things sure were looking up in the world. Looking as wise as Solomon, and progressive enough to be trusted to take on any speaking assignment, even as the featured speaker at a convention of New York Jews, Judge Davies handed down his ruling. "Well, Mr. District Attorney," he said, "everything changes in this world, and so we'll just have to see what we can do about changing this now."

Now that he had taken the great step, a feeling of exhilaration came over Harry. See? All that worrying ahead of time was downright foolish. All in the world you had to do was make your rulings and plow on ahead because, when everything was said and done, nothing much was going to change in the universe. Or even in the courtroom. None of the reporters was leaping up and running for the wires. As far as Harry could see, surveying the long line of intent and innocent eyeballs in the press rows, there wasn't a one of them had the first idea that anything so very special was taking place. Courage was everything. Take the tide at its full flood, and you could stand astride the world like a colossus. Julius Caesar, another lawmaker of sorts, had said that.

Hilliard was sore as hell, of course. But, heck, he'd get over it. Pawley was up and pumping his arm at him, cupping his hand as he made each of his points the way you do when you're casting the shadow of a bird on the wall. Ambose, damn him and his little black bee-bee eyes, was slouched in his chair boring a hole in him. *I stick my tongue out at you, Ambose,* he thought. *I fart in your face. My thumbs in your eyeballs.*

He slammed his gavel down. "Overruled, Mr. Pawley, and let's get on with it.

How does 'impropriety' strike you?" Harry didn't think very much of that one himself. (The writers, no longer lined up in garden rows of eyeballs, were surreptitiously passing their own words around. During the noon break, it was decided, by acclamation, that "insincerity" was the winner.)

In the courtroom, where it counted, Harry Davies found exactly the word he was looking for.

"Wrongfulness!" he exulted, knowing a good thing when he hit upon it, and at the ready to pounce on Ambose and Pawley like a tiger when they came leaping up with their objections. "Don't shout at me like that," he roared. "Or I may have to invoke the Rule on the pair of you and nail you to your seats."

Norman Bannerman was a winner because he had the true killer's instinct. In his blundering way Davies had widened the distinction between the two clauses of the Model Code, and Bannerman had no intention of letting loose of it until he had squeezed everything possible out of it.

And so, after Allbright had responded to the full question, Bannerman brought a rancid look to Ambose's face by saying, "I will now ask you to specify, Dr. Allbright. Either, or." In breaking the question down, he put the unchanged part to him first. Had the defendant, as a result of mental disease or defect, lacked substantial capacity at the time of the crime to conform his conduct to the requirements of the law?

In Allbright's opinion, he had not. "To do that, he would have had to have the capacity to distinguish between reality, law and morality as seen by the whole of society. This he was unable to do."

The second part was for the whole ball game. Had Sam had the capacity at the time of his crime to appreciate the wrongfulness of his conduct?

He had, of course, gone over the Model Code with Allbright during breakfast. But that had been the code as written by the Legal Institute. He had to put the question to him without having the slightest idea how far Allbright would be willing to go in widening the gap between legality and morality.

For a few long seconds Lionel Allbright sat motionless, his chin resting in his hand, and his index finger pointing straight up along his cheekbone. The shock of hair fell unnoticed over his forehead. The furrows on his mastiff features deepened. A living lithograph of good, strong pioneer American stock.

Once he had sorted out his thoughts, though, the answer came forth with power and assurance. "In my opinion, he did not. Within himself, the defendant felt what he was doing to be profoundly right. Not transcendentally right. Profoundly and morally right. He was not attacking authority. He was, to his own way of thinking, upholding it. We are getting into something else here, Mr. Bannerman. In his own mind he was preserving the law by disposing of the man he considered the greatest of all lawbreakers. Both in the moral sense of blurring all distinctions between right and wrong and in the symbolic sense of 'breaking down' the law. No, Mr. Bannerman. He felt that what he was doing was the very essense of lawfulness."

As Bannerman returned to his seat the only outward sign that he was preening himself on his triumph was a broken gleam in his eyes. Like cat's eyes shining in the daylight. And why not? He had, as he had promised Hal at the beginning, made new law. He had struck down the archaic and punitive M'Naughton Rule and, with some unexpected help from the judge, he had extended the Model Penal Code to the outermost boundaries dreamed of by the drafting committee of the Law Institute.

He had made it come out different.

Even the timing had been perfect.

"Your Honor," he said, looking up, "I'm through with the witness for this go-around. How's about some chow?"

"When you want to know how you're doing," Bannerman said, "find yourself the best available expert in the field." His moving finger reconnoitered the entire table, bypassing Allbright, bypassing Hays, bypassing Cowhig, bypassing Conrad Rittenhouse (who seemed to be doing a long feature story on Allbright's day in court), and settled, unwaveringly, upon Ruthie, the only member of their party eligible to serve on a jury.

The question he was putting to her, as his only available expert, was how she would vote if he were to walk back into the courtroom right now and rest his case. "Don't worry about anything else. Based entirely on what you heard this morning, have we won?"

Ruthie clasped her hands out in front of her and squeezed them tight. "I think," she said with unmistakable conviction, "we've got a hit on our hands."

"We'd better," he grunted. To underline the importance of what he was about to say, he sat back enough to bring the whole gathering within his range of vision. "Right at this minute, we're as good as we're ever going to be. What you saw this morning, my dear. That *was* our case."

Up in his Cave Ambose was studying the Q&A's on those last two questions. While he was thinking about them, he took the Uher out of his bottom drawer and set it on the desk. Out in his office, on the other side of the closed door, the phone began to ring. He paid no attention to it. He read Blasser's new report, which was only about half as long as the first one. The only thing of interest was that Sam had climbed back into his coveralls Monday morning after he'd showered and shaved, and had absolutely refused to dress for the courtroom until Blasser threatened to call Bannerman.

The ringing of the phone came up, loud and pure, as Foxx opened the door and with a backward jerk of his head indicated very clearly who he thought was calling. "Mr. Nevins wants to know, wadayathink, the taxpayers are made of money?"

Ambose found that mildly amusing. Nevins had apparently just taken a look at the vouchers Mollineaux had submitted for the transportation, housing and estimated cost of feeding of the EEG experts who'd be coming in to testify tomorrow. "The kid doesn't make noises," Ambose said with approval. "But he gets the job done."

While Ambose was setting up the tape he asked Foxx if he'd been keeping in touch with Henigan. Knowing damn well that he had. The way Foxx heard it, the jurors had been eager to hear Allbright on Sam's perverted sex life. "Not necessarily impressed, just eager."

"Not necessarily impressed." He looked up sharply, letting the tape go. "What's that supposed to mean?"

It meant what it meant. He was passing it on to him exactly the way he had got it.

Ambose snorted to show what he thought of the way he had got it. Twice

478

removed. He threaded the tape through and gave the spool a full turn. "I'd like to know more," he said concisely. A slow grin spread across his features. "What do you say, Jake? Think we can do it?"

"Those days are over!"

Ambose wasn't accepting that for a minute.

"You want it once more with feeling?" Jake snapped. "Over!" He said, "Jeez, I wouldn't even ask him. You want to scare him off?"

"Who," Ambose said evenly, "said anything about asking him?"

Oh, he was crazy, all right. No doubt about it. "And if it's found? For what, Jim? Don't tell me you're worried about this one?" This new approach, he realized, was a good one. "Fish in a barrel. What's to be worried about?"

Worried? Who said anything about being worried? With a surly stare and a snarl of anger, Ambose punched down the second key on the tape machine. The voice of Marie Pappas came floating into the room.

Nothing. A couple of calls to her mother, and then a long, dreary conversation with her brother in North Carolina about the state of their mother's health, during which Marie complained more than a few times that he couldn't keep expecting her to do everything herself. After the next riffle of the dial, though, Harry Davies' voice came into the room, and Ambose leaned forward, straining to catch every undertone of meaning. Soon enough, he was sitting back again. Harry was only telling Marie he'd been a little delayed by court business and would be late maybe an hour, and whatever she had on the fire would she keep it warm for him.

The last call was from Harry to his wife, telling her he'd be home in half an hour.

"Half an hour," Foxx said, bowing politely toward the machine. "Slam, bam, thank-you, ma'am. Bannerman gave her more time than that last night and he's a busy fellow." He shook his head, finding it beyond his comprehension. "He sure goes for broads with class, don't he?"

"Pigs is pigs," Ambose said without interest. Nothing at all to give them a clue on why Harry had let the Model Penal Code question in. "North Carolina," he said with cutting disgust. "What the hell's a Greek doing in North Carolina?" He rubbed his jaw hard. "What the hell," he said, willing to be big about it, "I guess they're entitled to have a greasy spoon in North Carolina, too."

He sat there silently, hunched over his desk, his fingers tapping. One thing anyway. He didn't have to worry about the proper time to let Harry know that Bannerman was banging his girl friend. Marie was the courier, he should have seen that right away, and what would that mean except that Harry either knew or didn't care? A pig like that, he had probably set them up himself. What he couldn't figure out, he told Foxx, was what Bannerman had to offer Harry except cold cash. If it wasn't that Harry had turned Bannerman down on the same motion yesterday, he'd have said that Harry was just being cute. A grandstand play for the national press. But no, it had to be cash on the barrelhead. The overnight delay meant that Harry had been holding out for his price.

The tapping came to an end with a loud, decisive slap. "You're back on the street, Jake." His eyes flat and filmy, he barked out his orders. Everything there was to be known about Harry Davies he wanted to know. "Squeeze every snitch. Your whole damn staff, everybody you can get out on the street. And tell Harv it's time to get back to work." Since it had only been this morning that Ambose had sent Harv home under orders to take the rest of the trial off and get to know his kids, he felt constrained to explain that Harvey would never forgive him if he found out they had gone after Harry Davies without giving him a piece of it. "Tell him to get the old crowd moving on it. If they've got any leave coming, have 'em take a couple of days. Them that haven't, their own time. To tell 'em it's for Ambose, got it?"

At the mention of the old crowd a hard reminiscent glow had come into his eye. "Best roust artists in the country," he said, and for just that moment you could see how dearly he'd have loved to be swinging around town with them.

Foxxie didn't look all that thrilled. "The only thing I'm wondering, Jim, is it worth it, all of that?" The Model Penal Code question had already been asked and answered, hadn't it? "I've heard you say it a thousand times. You can't unring the bell, right? You can't produce an un-question or an un-answer." If it was just that Ambose wanted to put the screws to Harry Davies . . . well, Foxxie would put in his bid for a hunk of that, right now. But why not wait until the trial was over, and they didn't have to call up all of their credit?

Because the Idiot King still had to charge the jury, that's why. "And when he charges the jury it's supposed to be on the law. The law! What it is!" Considering the steaming look of hatred that was boiling in his eyes, it came as a shock to hear the words come out in such parched and decorous tones: "If we can show Harry what a mistake it would be to go beyond the law on his charge, all that crap about the Model Penal Code won't mean a diddly-doo."

Bannerman had spent the greater part of the lunch hour instructing Conrad on the significance of the Model Penal Code question, laying particular stress upon the truly historical breakthrough that had been accomplished, while being scrupulously fair about giving due credit to the courage and vision of Judge Davies.

By the time they were ready to break up Bannerman and Cowhig were amusing the others with a wholly frivolous argument about who was going to pay for a parking ticket Cowhig had managed to pick up at the airport while waiting for Merril Hays' plane. Bannerman was holding, with a severe and uncompromising air, that the "said five-dollar fine" was a wholly unauthorized and inexcusable expense arising out of the investigator's own palpable negligence. In submitting his claim to the final judgment of his luncheon companions, Cowhig came up with all manner of devious excuses, all of which he introduced by saying, "In all seriousness . . . now, come on, this is serious," the most imaginative, perhaps, being that the parking ticket had come as a direct result of the unfavorable winds that had undoubtedly delayed the plane's arrival, which made it an act of God and therefore beyond all human powers, including Norman Bannerman's, to contend with.

It was all byplay, of course. But byplay directed toward one man and for one purpose. The man being Lionel Allbright, who had been growing increasingly restive, and the purpose being to divert his mind from the cross-examination that was growing nearer and nearer. As for the parking ticket . . . well, the car being a rented one, the attorney and his investigator would, by long usage and mutual consent, let Mr. Hertz take care of it for them.

When Mollineaux stuck his head into the office he found Jim Ambose leaning all the way back in his chair, with his hands entwined across his stomach and his hat tipped, in typical Ambose fashion, far down over his eyes. Mollineaux had the definite impression that he was smiling.

Ambose had been sitting in the outer office for perhaps twenty minutes, putting together his strategy. The jury had been impressed with Allbright. So had Jim Ambose. Lionel Allbright was one of the few men Ambose had ever come across for whom he had felt an instant and genuine admiration, and Jim Ambose had been sitting in his outer office planning how to destroy him.

For all his eminence—*because* of his eminence—Lionel Allbright had a surmounting weakness. He was a sixty-six-year-old man who could never remember the time when he had not been treated with deference and respect. That it was an artificial and arbitrary weakness—a proof of virtue by any civilized standard —was wholly irrelevant. In a court of law there was no truth except the courtroom truth, and the courtroom truth was whatever Jim Ambose could make it. If you were Jim Ambose preparing your cross-examination, you were entitled to take the reputation that had been won through the accomplishments of a lifetime and show it to the jury for what it really was. A guilty secret. A secret vice.

The best of all courtroom strategies, on those rare occasions when all the tumblers fell neatly into place for you, was to lash out at a witness, fast and hard, where he was supposed to be strongest, because if you were able to take his strength away from him before he had caught his breath, the rest of him would crumble away to nothing. Ambose's plan was to strip away Allbright's credentials with a savage personal assault, long before he got around to dealing with his testimony.

The risks attendant to such an attack had already been explored. Tactically, it went against style and habit. Ambose's style was to badger a witness, sure; but always within the context of the examination, and always in support of the greater objective. Never before had he set out to villify a witness as an end in itself. That risk, as he saw it, was acceptable. If after all his years in a courtroom he should find himself less able to adjust to change than a sixty-six-year-old man fighting for his life in a strange and hostile environment, then as far as Ambose was concerned he would richly deserve to lose.

The real danger lay elsewhere. When you set out to kill a king, you had better get the job done. Ambose wasn't kidding himself. He was setting out to humiliate and degrade a giant among men, and if he failed, the jury would never forgive him.

But that was looking at it negatively. When you were dealing with a man of Lionel Allbright's stature and reputation, you degraded him by the very act of daring to degrade him. Looked at positively, if he pulled it off, the ball game would be definitely over, and Jim Ambose would have won it all.

The more he balanced those odds, the more he liked them. But then again, consider this: For all his lean-eyed scrutinizing, and all his orderly, meticulous mind, did he have any choice? It had come to the bruising in the most important trial in his life, and with everything on the line, what could be more exhilarating than to be sitting at his faithful, cigar-scarred desk listening to the tumblers clicking neatly into place. Underneath the tilted hat, his warm breath rising and falling, Jim Ambose was straining toward that rapidly approaching moment when he would be turned loose inside the courtroom to bring a giant down.

Mollineaux had not been mistaken. Jim Ambose was smiling.

They had gone only a few steps down the hallway when Ambose suddenly placed his hand on Mollineaux' shoulder and told him he'd be right back. Hurrying back through the office and into the Cave, he opened the drawer, drew the gun out of its holster and, with his lips pulled tight across his teeth and his eyes agleam, jammed it into his belt.

Jim Ambose, rising, bowed his head to Norman Bannerman. "It was with great pleasure that I sat here all morning and heard the defense attorney extol the several virtues of Professor Allbright and his splendid accomplishments." He bowed to the witness. "I would like to add my poor appreciation of his outstanding work and character. But . . ." Perplexity forged itself into his features. "There's one thing that puzzles me." He fingered the Xeroxed manuscript that lay in front of him on the table. "In listing those accomplishments, Mr. Bannerman failed to mention the brilliant work the professor has done in tracking and compiling the pertinent data on Boswell's Clap. Now, Professor, that isn't a subject that would normally be of that much interest to me, but seeing as how—"

Bannerman wasn't the only one who couldn't believe what he had heard. "Boswell's what . . . ?"

"Clap, Mr. Bannerman! The vulgar street parlance for gonorrhea." He was, he said (enjoying every sweet second of it), using it only because it was the title the witness himself had appended to his scholarly treatise. "I was saying that it wouldn't normally be of any interest to me, but now that Professor Allbright has brought it to our attention . . ."

"Oh, no you don't! You brought it up, Ambose!" He held out his hand for the manuscript and, having leafed through it with visible distaste, objected with exactly the right measure of contempt and hauteur that the manuscript was irrelevant and immaterial and had been introduced for purposes that were "salacious, prurient, degraded, scurrilous, lecherous, malicious, venemous, licentious, sick, provocative, perverted, insulting and altogether what might be expected of Mr. Ambose." Whereupon he took a breath and urged the Court to provide guidance to his wayward colleague by thumpingly condemning this latest example of his wretched vulgarity.

Ambose gestured toward the witness chair, dumbfounded. *I didn't write it,* he might as well have been saying, *he did.* What he did say was that Mr. Bannerman had sat there and reeled off about half an hour's worth of publications to impress the jury. "All we're doing here is our little bit to fill out the full picture."

If you were looking for someone to take a tasteless situation and make it worse, leave it to good old Harry Davies. Within full view of the entire courtroom, he leaned over to the witness and whispered loud enough for the jury to hear, "Who in the heck is this fellow, Boswell? I've only had it twice myself."

The manuscript had come to Ambose by one of those strokes of luck that wasn't luck. Mollineaux had dug it out of a carton of stuff that had been sent to them in the course of their investigation. A seventy-page manuscript, fully annotated and citing nineteen quotations from Boswell's *Autobiography* on what seemed to be abundant proof of a full, if somewhat precarious social life, complete with a bibliography of the ten other books young Lionel Allbright had researched. The crocodile grin chewed across Ambose's features. "You got 'em all listed, Doc. Didn't miss a one of 'em, I bet."

At the first mention of the manuscript, a sweet smile of reminiscence had come over Allbright. It had not been until Bannerman had objected so violently that he had come to realize that these people were trying to present him to the world, retroactively, as a dirty old man. And also, Ambose could hope, begin to understand, with some anxiety, that they had done one hell of a research job on him. An unexpected bonus came right away when Allbright thought it necessary to explain that he had been moved to write that paper, forty-three years ago, the same year he had switched from English literature to medicine, because it had seemed to him that the conventional view of Boswell as an unusually careless man who had been under some sort of a compulsion to prove his manhood to either himself or, more likely, to Samuel Johnson, did not fit the rest of his personality structure. It had been his theory, he said, feeling some sort of a compulsion to justify himself, that Boswell had been suffering from a single chronic case and was a victim not so much of carelessness or indifference as of the skimpy medical knowledge of the times. "From what we know today," he said, certifying himself as not only a man of science but as a prophetic one, "I would suspect that most authorities would now agree."

Ambose accepted his explanation soberly. "I hope you got that down, Marie," he said. "The jury might want to remember that the medical profession has been known to change its mind from time to time."

Two bonuses. Allbright's memory, as well as his need for self-justification, had led him astray. The opening paragraph, which Ambose now proceeded to read into the record, said exactly the opposite. That done, he went into a short conference with Mollineaux who, since Nevins had not yet returned to the courtroom, was seated alongside him. The women jurors, Mollineaux reported, hadn't seemed a bit offended. Bettlenork, in fact, had looked as if she could have pissed in her pants.

Ho-kay. He was satisfied that the shine had been taken off the illustrious Allbright's medals. Now the real lawyering, which would be to lead the inexperienced witness into devaluing himself out of his own mouth, could begin. A precise and delicate touch was called for, and for openers it was going to be necessary to have him describe Sam's symptoms as precisely and numerously as possible. Dr. Allbright had visited Sam Tabor four separate times over a period covering fourteen and a half hours. "What I want to know from you now is what there was in Sam's actions that led you to your diagnosis." Not whether his mother had left him alone one Christmas, and not what he had learned from any other sources. "I want you to tell this jury what Sam did or said while you were there observing him. Did he attack you? Did he froth at the mouth? Did he climb up the bars and tear his hair out and try to tell you he was the reincarnation of Richard the Lionhearted?"

"Sir, if even one of those symptoms had been present, Mr. Tabor would have been certified incompetent and there would be no necessity for holding this trial."

"Oh, you're a lawyer, too, are you?" *One more! Why not!* "In addition to being the world's foremost authority on Boswell's lifelong battle against those pesky little gonococci?"

Bannerman (fastidiously, above it all): "There is a chivalry in the conduct of a lawsuit which is regrettably beyond Mr. Ambose's beck and call. I beg this Court to instruct him to put an end to these random excursions into ghostly venereal revery. We have here as our guest one of the great minds of the Western world."

Ambose's narrow, rather amused gaze slid away from the witness chair. "He's not a guest. He's your witness." (If Bannerman thought he was going to help him rehabilitate his witness by asking Allbright how much he was getting to testify, he had another thought coming.) "How about it, Doctor," he asked, bringing him back to his diagnosis.

Dr. Allbright began with his first visit. "After the first half-hour or so, he became hesitant, evasive, confused, circumlocutory. While at other times, on subsequent visits, he was presumptuous, argumentative and, from time to time, even a bit hostile."

"All of those, was he? Let's just find out a little more about it, that all right with you, Professor?" He leaned back, so that he was balancing on the rear legs of his chair. "How was he evasive?"

"Well, Mr. Ambose. Evasive. He was guarded in his answers. Wary. Suspicious."

"Maybe he didn't trust you?"

"Well, that, too. That's quite consistent with schizophrenia. I was there to help him."

"Maybe he didn't think so."

"As I say, that's a symptom. His attorney, Mr. Halpern, had introduced us. Mr. Halpern told him I was there at the behest of Mr. Bannerman. And that he was to cooperate with me fully."

"Maybe he didn't trust Mr. Bannerman."

"Well, that would be the surest sign of all, wouldn't it?" Mr. Tabor had retained Mr. Bannerman. He had placed his life in his hands. "If he didn't trust him, the rational course of action for him to take would be to dismiss him and retain another attorney."

Ambose permitted a moment of anticipation to ripple through the courtroom. And then he fooled them. "Well," he said, "we wouldn't want that." He glanced down at the inventory of adjectives Pawley had copied out for him. "How was he hesitant?"

"He'd think before he answered. At times, as much as ten or fifteen seconds would slip by." Sometimes even longer.

"Wasn't it possible that your questions were vague? That he just didn't know what you wanted from him?"

"Oh no." Allbright could assure him that the questions had been framed for a limited response and toward a specific purpose.

"All right. You were there to help him, didn't you say? You told him that, didn't you?" He tapped the eraser end of his pencil on the table. "Wasn't it just the most natural thing in the world for him to think over his answers? Wouldn't he want to give you the very best answer that he could think of?"

In a tone of studied reasonableness Allbright answered that he had explained to Mr. Tabor at the outset that the best way he could help him was to be forthcoming with his answers.

Ambose nodded, accepting that. "And circumlocutory?"

"That, too. He'd feel his way all around the question. And if I pressed him, he'd say, 'You know what I mean,' or 'You know' or . . . something equally noncommittal." Only at times, though, he hastened to add. Not always.

"Presumptuous?" Ambose wrinkled his forehead and looked up rather fetchingly. "You've really got me on that one, Professor."

"Well, yes." There was that small, joining smile again, readily conceding that he had probably slipped into professional terminology. "You see, he would try to take control of the interview from time to time. In a superior and lordly way. This was in the later meetings." He cleared his throat, waiting for Ambose's eyes to come back up from the pad. "It sounds contradictory, I know, and yet it's quite characteristic. Believe me. He'd say, 'You don't have to explain,' or 'I know what you mean.'"

"Oh, I get it now." Enlightenment flooded his eyes. "It means he thought he was as good as you." He slapped the pencil down on the pad and pushed himself back in the chair. "That's a real bad sign, Doc. Real bad. I'm just about ready to throw in the towel right now."

Bannerman (bored, routine): "Now that Mr. Ambose's prurient interest in the venereal adventurings of the departed Mr. Boswell has been slaked, must he continue to pollute the record with his synthetic wit?"

The Court: "Let's clean up the pollution, Mr. Ambose."

"Leaving the field of humor in possession of Mr. Bannerman for the time being, and getting down to brass tacks, we covered your fee before, didn't we? So I will now ask you this: Does your willingness to testify in this case arise out of your opposition to capital punishment? It's sure been written up a lot these past few weeks in all the national publications."

The abrupt change of subject was deliberate. So was the quick (and, hopefully, mind-arresting) slide past the question about the fee. Jim Ambose was more than satisfied that the symptoms had been impressed upon the jury's mind with sufficient force that they would be instantaneously recognizable when he threw them back at him. It was going to work. The roiling in his groin told him that it was.

After a hesitation that was every bit as long as Ambose had been angling for, Allbright answered that it was a difficult question for him to answer with a simple yes or no, For although he was willing to admit that he could not conceive of any circumstance where he would testify for the state in a capital case, he would also have to deny, flatly and without reservation, that he believed all murderers were necessarily mentally ill.

"Not necessarily," Ambose said. "Let me read you something." He called for one of the books stacked on the empty chair behind Mollineaux, and in turning to take it became acutely aware of the gun in his belt. "Murder," he read, "is the most extreme example of an irrational act performed in a moment of high emotional stress. The corollary is that the murderer is passing through a severe psychotic episode." Holding his finger in place, he turned the binding toward the witness. *The Terrain of the Mind,* page seventy-nine."

Allbright could only suggest that he turn back to the flyleaf and read the copyright date, and Ambose, playing out the scene, conceded that the book had been written thirty-three years earlier. "Among your earlier works," he said with relish. "Are we to take it that your opinion has undergone another of those miraculous changes that occur so frequently in your imperfect science?" And then he had only to sit back and grin the grin-that-knows-better all the while the witness was trying to explain that they were into a very difficult area which went, quite frankly, to the difference between medical insanity and legal insanity, and that, yes, he would make that distinction more evident if he were to rewrite that chapter today.

OK, OK. And Sam, he took it, was among the truly psychotic. "Is he such an out and out psychotic that I, or a member of the jury, could have recognized the symptoms by talking to him for fourteen and a half hours?"

"The symptoms?" He peered at him. "No, sir."

"Even though you are aware that in my role as public prosecutor I come into contact with all manner of human aberrations on a daily basis." His voice turned brusque. "I've dealt with legal insanity for twelve years, and this is your first crack out of the box. Wouldn't you think that was a bit presumptuous of you, Dr. Allbright?"

"Oh? I thought you were talking about making a medical diagnosis. Are we talking about symptoms or diagnosis?" A slender reed of uncertainty had begun to run through his voice. "I thought you were asking whether anybody at all could have. . . ?"

Bannerman: "He was."

Ambose's leer grew broader. "Have it your own way, Doctor. Could I have seen that there was something wrong with him by talking to him for fourteen and a half hours?"

Yes, said the witness. A man of Mr. Ambose's experience most certainly could have. "I was wrong in my previous answer, if that's what you were asking."

Bannerman: "It wasn't. The question included both Mr. Ambose and the jury and went to the medical symptoms."

Ambose sent a sweeping glance along the jury box while he was asking the witness whether it would be fair to say that he had been confused and evasive in his answer. "Or would you say that circumlocutory might describe it better?"

"How, Your Honor?" On a note of outrage, nicely contained, Bannerman objected that Ambose had baited the witness with a general question based upon a single quotation which had been written thirty-three years ago, and then switched him to a vague and highly hypothetical question having no application to either the original question or the issue under discussion. Cheap shyster tactics, he said with blunt contempt. Just what they had come to expect from him.

"Let's see about that," Ambose announced. The machine had been loaded and the gears were oiled. From here the mechanism should practically run itself.

"Doctor, keeping the distinction you have just made in mind, will you tell me how many murderers you have examined who you did not find mentally ill?" He lifted his wrists and looked openly at his watch.

"Within the meaning of the law? Knowing right from wrong? Quite a few."

"Doctor," Ambose said, "are you aware that you delayed ten full seconds." It had only been five seconds, but who could tell?

"Mr. Ambose, you asked me to go back in my memory."

"Weren't you asking Sam Tabor to go back through his whole life?"

"Those weren't the types of questions I was referring to."

"You still haven't told me how he was evasive? You still haven't given me a single example."

Bannerman: "Your Honor, will you instruct Mr. Ambose to permit this witness to give these questions the concise, deliberate and careful consideration the Court expects from an expert witness."

Ambose: "Oh, now I get it. When a patient stops to think, it's a delayed reaction. When an expert stops to think, it's careful consideration."

Allbright's example was that when he had asked Sam why he had thought it would be helpful to consult the marriage counselor, Sam had hemmed and hawed and finally said that it was just something his wife had wanted him to do. What was the matter with that, Ambose wanted to know. "You were prying into his private life, and he was deciding how much he wanted to tell you. The way it seems to me he answered it truthfully and directly."

"No. It was an evasive, negativistic answer from a psychiatric point of view."

Ambose stared at him, incredulous. "It was?"

"Do you want me to elaborate on that?"

"No, I want you to be precise and to the point."

"Well, that's what I mean." As he saw the slow smile spread across Ambose's face, he dipped his head in rueful admission that he had been trapped.

"By golly," said Ambose, always willing to be generous, "the best of us can become confused in our answers. Go ahead, Doctor."

Allbright explained that Tabor had been turning all responsibility away from himself and that, even within that context, had evaded the essential question of why his wife had thought it advisable or why he had consented.

"And from that you concluded that he was mentally ill and not to be held responsible for the murder of the Chief Justice?"

"No, from that I concluded that he was being evasive. Nothing more."

It was at this rather uneventful juncture, curiously enough, that Norman Bannerman came leaping out of his chair, his arm pointing to the rear of the room. "I protest the indignity of that infernal air conditioner rumbling and squawking through these entire deliberations!" he shouted. "I want my objection noted for the record."

After the first dumbfounding instant Pawley, ever mindful of protecting the record, arose and said in tones bone-dry, "Mr. Bannerman is, as usual, unafraid of theatrics. I am sure there is nobody else in this courtroom beyond the last row who has been aware of the slightest gurgle."

Picking up the interrogation, Ambose asked Dr. Allbright whether it wasn't true that being opposed to capital punishment as he was, his examination had been directed toward the purpose of finding Sam mentally unbalanced?

"I deny that categorically."

"You really came into this case completely open-minded—honestly now, Doctor—to the possibility that normal people could go around killing a Chief Justice they've never met? All this stuff about the gown and the missing person, you didn't have that in the back of your mind, hadn't given it a thought, before you came in here?"

Bannerman: "The question is too vague and general. He can do better than that."

Dr. Allbright said, "I understand it. And I'll stand by my previous answer."

"You mean I know what you mean?" Everything about Ambose announced that this was just too good. "You know what I mean, and I know what you mean, is that it? What was the word again, Professor? Presumptuous."

"You're perfectly amazing, Mr. Ambose." As Dr. Allbright looked out upon the amazing Mr. Ambose his mouth opened in a kind of brooding reflection. Lionel Allbright's whole life had been devoted to communicating abstruse and sensitive concepts of human relationships on an infinitely precise scale and he was only now beginning to find his bearings in a world where the most clear and simple statements were deliberately spun around on their axis and hurled back at him as their opposites. "Your tactics are so shamelessly partisan and manipulative that . . . I see exactly how you do it now. You haven't from the time we started made the slightest attempt to question me on my opinions. You see me as no more than a marker in your game."

James J. Ambose said not a word. As close as he was to the jury box, he had only to pick up his pencil alongside his pad and, with a large and sweeping gesture, check off the last two adjectives on the list. If the jury didn't remember that they were "argumentative" and "hostile," he would have plenty of time to remind them of that later.

Now that he had ringed the illustrious Allbright around with his own words, he had something else to try on him. Suppose Sam Tabor had run a red light on the way, been stopped and given a ticket, and before he got there the Chief Justice was gone? "What I want you to do, Doctor, is to suppose you had been called in to examine Sam Tabor, who is pleading not guilty by reason of insanity for running through a red light."

Halpern: "Mr. Ambose's imagination is running through all the stop signs."

"Let's see if it is. Running a red light is a criminal offense for which a defendant is entitled to plead insanity. You do know that, don't you, Doctor?"

Allbright was willing to take Ambose's word for it. But it wouldn't be very practical, would it? "By pleading insanity, he'd be going to great effort and expense, and if he won he'd be locked away for an indeterminate time." He spread his hands out. "For going through a red light?"

"You see? You're making out a very good case for him already."

"It's not my case, it's yours." He turned rather stiffly to the Bench. "I wasn't trying to put forth a tenable case, I was explaining why the hypothetical case he was putting forth wasn't tenable."

"Ahhhh," said Ambose. "But to make out an insanity case for Sam Tabor when he is on trial for his life, that's quite tenable, isn't it? Thank you, Doctor. You've cleared that up for us very nicely."

At last, a good hour after the cross-examination had begun, Ambose was ready to bring Dr. Allbright around to his diagnosis of chronic undifferentiated schizophrenia. He began by asking whether it wouldn't be fair to define it as "a kind of wastebasket in which you psychiatrists file all the scraps and overfill of schizophrenia you haven't been able to fit into your file cabinet," and Allbright showed every willingness to accept that definition. "Where you say wastebasket, I would say 'file under miscellaneous.' That's all."

"Thank you. And do you expect that before the world comes to an end, much of the behavior which is now called undifferentiated schizophrenia will be reclassified so that it can find a home in a separate drawer in that cabinet under a name of its own?"

Dr. Allbright was willing to accept that, too, with one clarification. "It would still be a mental illness. What it was called would be a matter of convention. You could differentiate it seven ways to Sunday—you could isolate one syndrome, say, and call it ego dysfunction—and you would still be talking about an individual who has difficulty with reality."

And ego dysfunction, said Ambose, snatching it right up, wasn't considered schizophrenia anymore, was it?

"Let's say a near relative. The nomenclature has changed. The label has changed. But, I will repeat, it's the same individual behaving in the same way."

That was all Ambose had been going for, but something else—something far better—was beginning to take shape in his mind. In one of the more bizarre forms of schizophrenia, he reminded the witness, the individual could suffer from delusions. "The man who goes down the street yelling he's Richard the Lionhearted ain't just funning, is he? He really thinks he's Richard the Lionhearted."

"That's one of the possibilities."

"And you'd say he was schizophrenic because this theory of his about who he is is wrong."

"Well, I don't know if I'd say it was a theory." He had agreed only that he could be suffering from a delusion. The difference, he explained, was that a theory wasn't accepted as a fact by even its most ardent advocates. It was merely an educated guess based upon a whole mass of accumulated knowledge. "You see," he said, "we're getting into the purpose of a theory here. The scientist who takes a theory and sets out to prove or disprove it is not a very good scientist because he has limited the scope of his exploration to the limits of the theory itself. The true scientist accepts a theory as a starting point for his investigation and permits it to take him where it will. If it takes him into areas far beyond the original field of inquiry, so much the better. That's how the barriers get pushed back."

Ho-kay. "Is schizophrenia a fact or a theory?"

Dr. Allbright was so startled that he drew back and sneaked a look at Bannerman. "Schizophrenia is the name by which we identify a particular type, or types, of mental illness. I thought we had been through that."

"And mental illness is itself a theory?"

"Mental illness is a fact. We see it all around us."

"No, Doctor. Odd behavior is what we see all around us. An inability to cope with reality. That's what we've been through, if you'll remember. Wouldn't it be more accurate to say that *in your opinion* mental illness is a fact."

"It's a very certain opinion, Mr. Ambose."

"All right, a very firm opinion. But still an opinion." Wasn't it true that the whole concept of quote-unquote mental illness was subject to further experimentation? Wasn't it true that old theories gave way to new theories? Firm opinions were shaken and, finally, changed. "Wouldn't it be fairer, really, to say that it is only for the sake of convenience that you operate on the principle that this accumulated mass of knowledge, observation and theory can be added up to turn mental illness into a fact?"

A startled little laugh escaped from the witness. "I see where you're going, Mr. Ambose. But I disagree."

Ambose dug around for a moment in his bulging file folder of clippings. Finding the one he was looking for, he said, "Do you happen to agree with the wise man who said, 'We lack the exactitude of the physical sciences. We have an art, a sense of the direction, and we are just not ready to take over the field of the mentally-ill offender.' "

"Indeed I do." He permitted himself the wisp of a smile. "I might have even said it myself."

"You did, Doctor." He held up the clipping. A symposium in Milwaukee. Not thirty-three years ago. Less than two years ago.

Under the table his feet began to move up and down in quick little tap steps. "In your firm opinion something which lacks the exactitude of the physical sciences and which you choose to call mental illness does exist, always keeping in mind that as a true scientist you are always ready to discard old theories when confronted with new discoveries and concepts. Keeping all that in mind, I will now ask you, sir, how you would diagnose a legal system which accepts the theory of mental illness as a fact?"

Pawley's head came jerking around. "Knock it off, Jim."

Ambose responded to Bannerman's objection by arguing that he was going to the credibility of the witness. But before Judge Davis could react to Pawley's signal, Bannerman had thought better on it and the objection had been withdrawn.

Pawley, looking more than ever as if he wished Nevins were there, whispered, "I don't know that this is going to do us any good, Jim. Be smart."

"Wouldn't you say, sir, that a legal system which accepts the theory of mental illness as a fact, not as a basis for experimentation but as a basis on which to determine the guilt or innocence of acknowledged murderers, meets the basic definition of schizophrenia? That by treating a theory as if it were an established fact, it has lost all contact with reality?"

Bannerman: "Hah! You'll notice, Your Honor, how quick Mr. Ambose is to reestablish diplomatic relations with psychiatry whenever it serves his purposes."

The Court: "You don't have to answer that question if you don't want to, Doctor."

Ambose still wasn't giving up on it. "I put these questions to you, Doctor, because you're the only expert we have sitting here. If the chief of state were schizophrenic you'd fear for the country. If the whole legal system is sick, wouldn't you consider it your duty to sound the alert?"

"If I thought that, I most certainly would."

Ambose leaned forward and rested his chin in his hand. "But you do, Doctor. You think the system is insane that allows the type of cross-examination I have submitted you to. You've as much as said so."

"There is the system, Mr. Ambose. And there are those who pervert the system."

"What do you think of a system that can be so easily perverted?" Ambose shot back. "No, Doctor. I'm serious."

"Mr. Ambose, I have expressed a healthy skepticism of that system on numerous occasions, as you have been very good about reminding me. But having made the decision to appear, I can only say, one more time, that you can call it anything you want. It's what it is. It's what we see. Whatever you choose to call it, we have found ways to recognize it and to treat it."

"No, sir," Ambose said. No. "Because if it's not an illness, it's something else. And it's on the basis of calling it an illness that the law says an individual is not responsible. Where if he just doesn't give a damn, he is. You have seen people from time to time in your practice, Doctor, who just don't give a damn, haven't you?"

"Yes," Dr. Allbright said, looking right down the barrel at him. "I come across them all the time, Mr. Ambose."

Bannerman seized upon that moment to object that this farce had gone on long enough. "If Mr. Ambose is attempting to put the legal system itself on trial here," he said, before he sat down, "I will warn him here and now that he is courting a mistrial." Bouncing right back up again, he said, "Dr. Allbright, like the Court, the jury, and perhaps even Mr. Ambose himself, is bound by the law as it is writ."

Ambose said, "Why?"

"Why?"

"That's right. Why?" Hadn't Mr. Bannerman done that very thing this morning? "With the permission of this Court, and over our objections. The word he used was 'obsolete.' "

The defense was entitled to, Bannerman said, because the defense, in a capital case, was entitled to everything. "You are not entitled to, Mr. Ambose, because the prosecution is charged with proving guilt beyond a reasonable doubt according to all the rules of procedure and rights of due process."

The startled look that came over Ambose had not a thing to do with what Bannerman had been saying. (He had, in fact, been thinking, Keep mouthing off, shithead, that's just what I want them to know.) In taking a hitch on his pants, his hand had closed over his gun and he had damn near come out with it.

Readjusting both his jacket and his seat, he swung his big shoulders and snarled, "You say Sam killed Wilcke because he thought the Chief Justice should have been keeping him from thinking about how he used to want to sleep with his mother when he was a boy, only he didn't know it even then, and that was something like forty or fifty years ago, and she's been dead for twenty years. Is that about the size of it, Professor?"

Dr. Allbright took his time about answering. "I believe I gave the full explanation on direct examination," he said finally. He sounded as if that had been a long, long time ago.

"This is cross-examination now. And you're telling this jury that every boy wants to do that, only Sam never got over it because his father wasn't around that much and his mother didn't show up there one Christmas to get him. Are you telling this jury that everybody who has a father who isn't around and a mother who disappoints him, disillusions him even, shouldn't be held responsible for anything he does?"

This time the answer took even longer to come. The final transformation in Dr. Allbright was taking place, an ingathering of his resources and his integrity by which he was removing that essential part of himself he held to be inviolate. "I don't believe I've ever said that. It is not the child's experience that dictates his actions. It is the conclusions he draws from his experiences."

"Let's talk a little about drawing conclusions. Do you think he knew that if he aimed a gun at somebody and pulled the trigger, one possible consequence was that he could kill him?"

"If he had not been deprived of the ability to consider the consequences. If he had been consciously aware of what he was doing."

"Let me read you something else." He reached for the file folder holding the clippings. "Temporary insanity," he read, "is a rare mental disease which can best be found while seated in a courtroom, since as far as I have been able to discover it has never been found anywhere else." Disgust was written all over him. "Now, Doctor, would you or would you not say that what you have just tried to palm off there amounts to pretty much the same thing?"

Allbright brushed the loose lock of hair from his forehead. "I really don't recognize that quotation as mine, and I'm not sure I'd hold to it, in toto, today, but if what you're asking is—"

"Hey!" Norman Bannerman had come alert. "What was the citation for that quote?"

"It was just a quote," Ambose said. He smiled broadly at the jury. "Something I remembered from somewhere." When Number 6 not only grinned back at him but shifted forward in his seat as if he were being drawn to him, it seemed to Ambose like an excellent time to pass the witness back.

"From everything you know about Sam Tabor, from your private interviews with him and from all the other sources that went into the forming of your opinion, I will now ask you the following question." The Bannerman voice was clear and resonant and compelling. "If you had been in possession of the same material twenty-four hours before the murder would you have been able to prognose a murder?"

"Yes," said Lionel Allbright, in the sixty-sixth year of his life. "I would have."

"A week before?"

"Yes. I would have."

"With certainty?"

"Yes."

"Without reservation?"

"Yes."

Norman Bannerman had just won ten dollars American from Cowhig.

The timing was so perfect, Bannerman's command so complete, that it would have been impossible, Halpern could see, for Allbright to have answered any other way. "Why does the ripened apple fall from the tree?" Bannerman had once asked him, quoting somebody or other on the mysteries of life. "Is it because it is drawn by gravitation to the earth, because its stalk has been withered and dried by the sun, because it grows heavier, because the wind shakes it, or because the little boy is standing under the tree with his hands held out waiting for the apple to fall?" That was what a good trial lawyer was, Bannerman had told him. The little boy standing under the tree drawing the apple down into his hands when the time was ripe.

As easily as that the apple had fallen to him.

Now that they had the answer Bannerman felt they so desperately needed, Halpern found that he was dismayed by the ease with which the best of men could be brought to betray themselves. As the examination continued, he watched the old man on the witness stand as if he were an extension of himself. He heard him answer a few questions; saw him turn to the Bench; saw the affirmatory nod from the Court; saw the old man take out a cigarette, light it and hold it between the second and third fingers of his left hand, low in the chair, all but shielded by his right hand.

Alongside Halpern the silken thread of Bannerman's voice unwound; up on the stand the old man's cramped voice prodded itself on. But that wasn't what held his attention. His attention was fixed on Dr. Allbright's left thumb, which was going through a strange, repetitive ritual. Rubbing first against the little finger, stealing over to the cigarette and making its way up to the tip of the index finger for one hard, quick surreptitious flick. As if, it seemed to Halpern, he were trying to flick away a speck of dirt over and over and over. Once the index finger has been flicked, the thumb rests momentarily, then starts again, like a little animal, rubbing first against the little finger, then working forward nervously like a mouse sniffing for food—until it reaches the cigarette, taps the end of it, manipulates it as if it is testing the texture, crawls (tap . . . tap . . . tap) up the cigarette until, growing impatient—agitated, really—leaps up for that quick furtive flick of the index finger. And drops back, as if sighing. Rests again, content for perhaps three or four seconds, before it starts off once again on that same, restless, never-changing journey.

Everybody in the courtroom saw it and like Halpern, was both fascinated and disturbed by it. Here at the moment when the psychiatric case for Sam Tabor had been unveiled, they had been given that classic figure of contemporary literature —the psychiatrist with a compulsive neurosis.

Harold Halpern closed his eyes. Something had gone very wrong here. A hunched and brooding beast had taken over the courtroom. It had slipped past the guards on the first day, scarcely noticed, and slowly, steadily succeeded in sucking the breathable air out of the courtroom. The newspaper reports written by the more cerebral and self-assured journalists that Sam, miserable specimen though he be, was entitled to his day in court—that was part of it. To Harold

Halpern, Sam was not a miserable anything. He was a man who despite what now seemed to be almost disabling personal problems had girded himself up to fight the world through an entire lifetime, without ever begging off for a single day. When he opened his eyes it was to study Sam's guards in an entirely new light, for it seemed to him that he had finally come to understand the true basis for the feeling of kinship that existed between the prisoner and his jailers. In a day or two the trial would be over. The script would be put away, the footlights would fade, the lawyers, the newspapermen, the spectators would go home, and only Sam Tabor and his jailers would remain. Sam Tabor, his jailers and the odor of sanctity.

Leaning over to Tabor, he asked, "You all right, Sam?"

"I feel much better now," Sam said. "The blood has flowed away."

The *what?*

"The blood in front of my eyes." He flapped his hand, limply, like a semaphore. "It flowed away."

The beast that had taken over the trial.

Across the table Ambose was firing questions at Allbright from the books he had written and the little furry animal crawling up the cigarette was no more than a pale reminder of the beast that had been consuming them all. The trial itself.

Pleading the need for a little air himself, Halpern accompanied Allbright out of the courthouse. During the fifteen-minute recess that had been called while Bannerman was preparing to put on his final two witnesses, the manager of the bowling emporium and the girl at the drugstore counter who had usually sold Sam the Librium, Allbright had politely declined Bannerman's invitation to stick around for the victory party. They were down the elevator and walking across the lobby when Allbright said, "All these years I thought it was professional pride that kept me off the witness stand. It took sixty-six years to find out what it was."

Hal told him he had done just fine. He had given them a case Bannerman could present to the jury, that was the main thing. "The cross-examination always takes something away." He tried to smile. "That's why they have it."

When they were out in the air Allbright said, "There comes a time in a man's life when he shouldn't discover a basic defect of character." He was looking off down the street. "Once the arteries begin to harden, it's not so easy to make the necessary accommodations." He winced with the effort it was taking at that moment, and for the first time Halpern could remember there were no laugh lines in the wrinkles around the eyes.

"For whatever it means," Hal said, "Bannerman knows how to do these things. That's why he's up there where he is." For whatever good it would do, he told him how Dr. Shtogren had flatly refused to testify under any circumstances because it was like playing in the other guy's ball park with the other guy's rules. (He didn't bother to tell him that Bannerman had said afterwards that he wouldn't have put him on on a bet, anyway.)

"I'll let you in on a secret, Halpern. For a long while there I couldn't understand what Bannerman had you around for." Finally Allbright was looking at him. "I understand now. For Sam's sake I hope you do."

When Nevins was grumping and growling over his glasses it usually only meant that he was getting ready to let Ambose have his way about something and didn't want him to go getting any wrong ideas. This time it was different. "I've been giving some thought to offering them a plea and getting this farce over with," Nevins rasped. "I want to hear what your ideas might be on it, so you won't think you have any cause to come yelling around later!"

"Why would we want to do anything like that?" Ambose asked, treading gingerly. "If you'd been there this afternoon, you'd have seen their whole case go up in smoke. Didn't Pawley tell you?"

Pawley was going to do the talking, it seemed, and Ambose took special note of the conciliatory tone. All the usual crap about the appeals dragging through the courts forever if they got the death penalty and, even if it wasn't overturned, how they'd never get a chance to strap Sam into the chair.

"We sure won't," Ambose said. "Not if the prosecutors are so quick and ready to run out ahead of time." Or maybe there was some mitigating circumstance Ambose wasn't acquainted with? "Did you happen to find some mitigating circumstance in the testimony this afternoon, Hilliard?" he said, looking right at him. "I mean, from not being there?"

By all rights, Nevins should have erupted all over the place, and Ambose would have felt better about it if he had. Instead, Hilliard shoved a UP story, torn from the teletype machine, across the desk. It was a news item, under a Washington dateline, reporting that the Supreme Court had agreed to hear a case challenging the constitutionality of capital punishment.

"Well, well," Ambose said with a little crooked smile. "The Asshole Court having farted fitfully for years has finally let go with a firecracker, huh?"

"That's the Supreme Court you're talking about," Nevins said, not smiling. "And as long as I'm still running this office nobody's going to be referring to the Supreme Court with disrespect."

Pawley hastily cleared his throat and began to cough. The Court, he was finally able to point out with all the graveside solemnity Ambose could have hoped for, had not granted certiorari so that they could turn it down. There was something else, too. They didn't want Tabor carried out of the courtroom in a basket, did they? "I was watching him today, Jim, and you can see the little flies gathering around the carcass, know what I mean? It gives you the creeps."

Momentarily, Ambose felt relieved. If that was all it was . . . "That's Bannerman's worry! He wants to petition that his client is no longer competent to stand trial, let him." Fat chance. If Bannerman did that without Tabor throwing a falling-down fit, he'd be admitting that he wanted to throw in the towel. "We're dealing with the assassination of the Chief Justice of these United States," he found it necessary to remind them. "I just happen to think it's important to get it on the record that an American jury found for death. And if those nine distinguished shitheads whose feelings you're so worried about want to come along later and say he shouldn't pay for it with his life, then it's on their heads, not ours. You wanted to know how I see it, that's how I see it. That it's our job to make them!"

Again, he would have felt better about it if Nevins had jumped all over him. But although Hilliard did fluff himself up like an angry bird, for the second time running he left it to Pawley to do the talking. "It's the best thing that could happen to us, Jim," Pawley said quietly. "Not to them. To us."

Huh? Were they by any chance talking about the same thing?

They were. "Think about it," he urged. As long as capital punishment continued to exist, the defense attorneys were going to be able to distort the issue by throwing great clouds of humanitarian rhetoric over the most heinous of murders.

Pawley was serious about this, and he made a better case than Ambose would have thought possible. As chief administrative attorney, Pawley knew better than either of them that the justices of all appellate courts were setting such impossibly high standards for upholding a death verdict that it was getting to be more trouble than it was worth, and if Pawley's troubles didn't exactly move Ambose to tears, then perhaps he should be reminded that every time the courts found it necessary to dig up some brand-new grounds for a reversal, the prosecution found itself weakened in damn near every other area of the criminal law as well.

"Putting our emotions aside and looking at this thing dispassionately and practically," Pawley said, "every district attorney in the land should be petitioning the court to put an end to capital punishment, and all the hot-shot defense attorneys like Norman Bannerman and Tommy Mallon should be doing everything they can to stop us."

The listening mind could hardly miss the tempting dish that Pawley was serving up to him. And yet, in his other mind, his monitoring mind, Ambose could not shake the nagging sense of unease that something was not quite kosher here. Something had changed in this room. The monitoring mind kept pushing the picture of Tommy Mallon at him. Tommy Mallon sitting across the desk from him, asking whether he thought he and Nevins were going to walk into the sunset together.

A coded look had passed between Pawley and Nevins. They wanted his approval, and that could only mean they hadn't approached Bannerman about a deal yet, thank god. It could, just possibly, mean something else. All the while he had been listening, Ambose had been thinking furiously about what he could do to stop them, and that was a question that called back and finally identified the original gut-feeling that something wasn't quite right in this office. Stop *them*. That was the thing. Not Nevins. *Them*. Pawley was no longer acting as a go-between. It was them against him. Thinking back rapidly, he could see that they had been paired off against him ever since they had come back from the weekend break.

Whatever it was, Mallon knew. Oh no, it had not been by accident that Tommy had offered him a partnership at this particular time. The little sonofabitch knew something and he hadn't told him. He'd have to see Tommy fast. Tonight. Before they could do anything.

Foxx's note read: "He'll meet you at the Bankers' Club at 9." While Ambose was crumpling it, the phone rang, and that was Foxx, too. He had been calling for the past half-hour because he had some information he was sure Ambose would want. He was right.

The Bankers' Club was still the place where the leading political and financial figures met when there were matters of importance to be discussed. For Tommy Mallon to have arranged to meet Jim there was as good as telling him that he knew what he was going to ask, and that he had the answer.

Given the lateness of the hour, the dining room was practically empty. It was also so dimly lit that Ambose had followed Ramon, the headwaiter, halfway to Tommy's table in the rear corner of the room before he could see that Tommy was already there.

Tommy had taken the liberty of ordering cream of turtle soup for both of them. The specialty of the house, as he made known to Ambose, by kissing his fingers more gauchely than seemed humanly possible.

Ambose came right to the point. "What the hell's going on, Tommy?"

"I got Jake's message and I thought to myself, Thomas, Jim wants something from you. Without giving you so much as a chance to slurp your soup, he's going to sit down surly and ask what the hell's going on." Forcing a smile, he plucked a sugar cube out of the bowl, held it up to show he'd won and dropped it into his pocket.

"I got to thinking you were trying to tell me something when you offered me a job."

"A job? When did I ever offer you a job? I offered you a partnership." He leaned across the table. "You got to thinking, huh?" Completely serious now. "You tell me and I'll tell you."

When Ambose told him, Tommy drew his lips down, considering it. Two thoughts came to his mind. One: What was Nevins selling? Two: What would Bannerman be buying? "Bannerman's only reason for taking it would be that he doesn't want to hear them come back with the death verdict. An eventuality, Mr. Prosecutor, which I take it you view as a distinct possibility."

Ambose plucked a cube of sugar from the bowl, and held it up as his own prize. "You want to try for 'foregone conclusion?'" Which brought up the question Ambose was really interested in. What would Nevins be getting out of it? "All right, the Ladies' Auxiliary would vote him their Pinup Boy of the Year. But Hilliard gets elected because the folks know he gives them law and order. That, he's smart enough to know. That's the only reason he puts up with me."

Mallon examined him with an incisive eye that let Ambose know that Tommy had always wondered just how well he did understand that. "Maybe he thinks his days as district attorney are drawing to a close. Maybe he's afraid the Tabor trial could end up being an embarrassment to him. Embarrassing if he loses it, and embarrassing if he wins it." Mallon had caught the last part of Allbright's testimony. Bad witness. Bad break for Bannerman, but bad investigation, too. "Didn't he bother to read what his man had written? Didn't he care?" Never mind. Bad witness or not, Allbright's name carried weight within the journalistic-intellectual community, and the wrath of that community did not fall lightly upon those who had displeased it. "The *Chronicle*, as you may have noticed, has been taking on a definite Bannerman hue. The Monroe papers would similarly hail it as a statesmanlike act worthy of a federal judge."

He handed Ambose a big, thick cigar. "Try one of mine," he said. "You may need something solid to bite on, and I don't have my bullet with me."

Ambose put the cigar aside. "What do you know for sure?" There was a screeching sound in his ears. His voice came out of the deeper caverns of his chest. "There. Did I ask it nice enough for you?"

Tommy's eyes hadn't left him. "Just that T. Richardson Cox is thinking of stepping down in the full flowering of a glorious career. It's come to him in a flash of wisdom that he don't hear too good anymore."

"T. Richardson, hell! He ain't heard thunder in twenty years! Or seen lightning in ten."

None too happy now that they had come to it, Mallon crumpled his napkin and set it on the table. The deal was that T. Richardson would step down on condition that his grandson, Halsey, be appointed attorney general. "That's what I heard," he said gently. "I got it good, Jim."

The screeching sound grew shriller. His breath came hard. He had been waiting for ten years, and if no one had told him—

"Halsey Cox," he spat. Viciously. "That pusscat. That dreamer. Between him and his grandfather, they haven't raised a respectable hard-on in thirty-five years. Why don't they just hand it over to the ACLU and be done with it?" Already, though, a soothing thought had come to him. If that was the deal, it couldn't come off until the next election, and the election was fifteen months away. Carter Prescott sure as hell wasn't going to hand in his resignation just so the federal bench could get rid of T. Richardson.

Working rapidly, Tommy Mallon cleared everything away from the space between himself and Ambose, including the red candle-lamp. Then he took four cubes of sugar out of the bowl, lined them up in front of him and numbered them from one to four. Number 1, he announced, slapping the first cube down on the table, was Hilliard Nevins. Number 2, T. Richardson Cox, was placed alongside Nevins, and the other two were placed directly underneath them to form a perfect square. Number 3 he identified as Carter Prescott. Around Number 4—he drew a big, bold question mark. The mystery contestant.

From his pocket he drew out the cube he had awarded to himself earlier, and with a deft disappearing-coin-trick pass transferred it from his right hand to his left. "Halsey Cox," he said, holding it up. "Watch." With his right hand he picked up the Number 2 cube. "We take T. Richardson"—he flipped it away, over his shoulder—"and retire him to a home for the deaf, dumb and blind. Into his place we slide Number 1, Hilliard Nevins." *Capice?* So far, so good? "We now send Halsey Cox in from the sidelines, where he has been warming up for fifteen years." Making the exchange, he was left with the ex-Number 3 hitter looking for a new spot to step into. What other high judicial post could Ambose think of that happened to be open? Aha. By a coincidence that was in no way coincidental, the death of Judge Chobodian had left the county Criminal Court in desperate straits for an appointments judge.

"And that's the deal, Jim. It's all been done under the chandeliers."

Ambose's eyes remained on the table. Three cubes where there had been four. He started to speak and had to stop to clear his throat. When he began again his voice came hoarse. "There's one post that still hasn't been filled. Hilliard's."

Mallon ducked his head and dipped his spoon into the soup. Neither man spoke. Ambose finally got around to lighting the cigar Tommy had given him. He followed the flight of the smoke as it dissolved into the air, not wanting to let Mallon see how desperately important the answer to the next question was going to be. They both opened their mouths at the same time, and they both spoke the same word:

Mallon said only one word: "Pawley—"

Ambose said, "Pawley's getting it."

Pawley's name, spoken in a high, reedy voice by Mallon and covered in a low, throbbing voice by Ambose, seemed to reverberate in the air.

"They could have at least interviewed us both," Ambose said dully. "Had the courtesy." He sounded empty. He looked empty. "They could have asked Nevins for his recommendation."

Mallon was in pain. "Jim . . ." he said, and it was as if he were telling Ambose that he knew better.

In a strangled voice Ambose asked whether Nevins had appeared before the committee.

"It's all over, Jim." Tommy Mallon was watching him with deep concern. "It was only a formality."

"This afternoon," Ambose said. He nodded to himself. Not completely able to accept it yet, but making an appointment with himself to accept it later.

Mallon gave it to him straight. The whole package had been laid out the day before the trial began. Hilliard had seen his chance to put it together as soon as it became certain that Chobodian was gone. The only thing that had been holding it up was that Prescott's wife wasn't that anxious to move out of Monroe, and Prescott was the key to the whole package.

"Yeah. Prescott's the key, all right." Ambose dipped his spoon absently into his plate, brought it to his mouth and, becoming aware of what he was doing as he took his first swallow, made a face and dropped the spoon back. "He promised me, Tommy."

"I know he did." The shrug was not unsympathetic; it simply asked: *So what?*

Ambose had to ask it, though. "Did he bring my name up? Did he give them a choice?"

All Mallon could do was look back at him, and hope that no answer would be answer enough.

"I want to know," Ambose said doggedly. It was all right. He was going to be all right. He'd do what had to be done. But something that went to the core of whatever Jim Ambose was demanded that he hear the words spoken.

Gruffly, with the attitude of a man who has finally come to the conclusion that he might as well get an unpleasant job over with, Tommy spelled it out for him. "I could tell you that Hilliard didn't want to rock the boat, that there's people who don't like you." But that wasn't it. Pawley had been part of the package from the beginning. Everybody liked him. Hell, they liked the whole deal. Why shouldn't they? They'd been living in fear for twenty years that somebody would print they had a vegetable up there in the District Court. "Do you know the last appeal I took up there I had to hold his hand while he was signing the order?"

Ambose continued to stare at him. Waiting for the words. Exasperated, Mallon said rapidly, "The name of Jim Ambose was never mentioned. Don't ask me if I asked. Don't ask me if I'm sure." He paused. "I told you the time was overdue to cut the umbilical cord."

"You told me."

A lawyer as brilliant as Tommy Mallon would know when the time was ripe to press an advantage. "What do you say, Jim? You and me. We'll laugh at them all. For every dollar Pawley makes, you'll make ten. Guaranteed minimum."

Ambose shook his head.

"What is it? Are you too proud to come in with me? Is that it? Because I was once a snot-nosed kid you used to know? What the hell do you think you're going to do? You're not going to stay on under Pawley. I know you better than that."

"I told you what I'm going to do. I'm going to burn Tabor."

"That's this week. What are you going to do, like on Monday?"

"Well, I'll tell you. I've got a strong back. I can always dig ditches."

Mallon twisted his head away so that he was facing him obliquely, the expression on his face asking whether that was any way for a presumably intelligent man to face a problem.

498

"What's so bad about digging ditches? It's better than being another pig at the trough."

Mallon took a deep, deep breath. "Oh boy! You've got to do it, huh?" He peered across the table at him as if the idea, long seeding, had finally taken root. "You know, they're right about you. They're right. You're off your fucken head! Jeez!" The rising wonder gave way to rising anger. "OK, pal. Okay! Go stake out a campsite and shake your fist at the world. You've been living in your own fucken world, anyway." He said: "So you're gonna burn Tabor, are you? You're gonna do exactly nothing." Was he so fucken *dumb,* Tommy asked with what was supposed to be annihilating contempt, that he couldn't see that the Tabor case was going to be taken out of his hands along with everything else?

"Nobody takes the Tabor case away from me." His eyes were absolutely flat. His lips barely moved. Everything about him—the stiffening set of the shoulders as much as the impact of his personality—set forth the picture of the sentry guarding the gates. And while they were about it . . . since Tommy was so hell-bent on making Ambose's future secure, Ambose was going to let him book a three-horse parlay for him. To get the action under way, he was going to bet Tommy that before another hour went by DeWitt Pawley would come traipsing through the door arm-in-arm with Norman Bannerman. Having won that one, he would double up on his winnings by betting that whether Bannerman was willing to cop a plea or not, the Tabor trial would go to a finish. Because if it didn't, Hilliard Nevins was never going to get to sit his fat rump on the federal bench, and they both knew better than that, didn't they?

Tommy shook his head in a kind of mordant disbelief that he could have heard what he had been hearing. "In case I forgot to tell you. If you get to be too much of a nuisance, they'll ship you off to Algonquin. Who the hell do you think you're playing with?"

Who the hell did *they* think they were playing with? Let Mallon think he was spinning his wheels. Both of those bets were sure things. Foxx's phone call had been to forewarn him about the meeting between Pawley and Bannerman. As far as Hilliard Nevins was concerned . . . well, Ambose had the leverage to use on Hilliard Nevins and it wasn't a question of whether he had anything to lose anymore, was it?

The final bet was going to be far more of a sporting proposition. If Tommy would wander into Judge Davies' court sometime Friday or Saturday, Ambose was willing to bet the whole bundle that he would hear the jury come back with the death sentence.

And what did Tommy have to say about *that,* Ambose as much as said. From all appearances, Tommy had very little to say. A moment of revelation was upon Tommy Mallon, and it had nothing to do with the Tabor trial. "And I'm the guy who's been telling you to cut the umbilical cord to Nevins," he said at last. "It's just about time for me to cut the cord myself, wouldn't you say?" It wasn't said in anger or self-rebuke or malice; it was no more than a statement of fact, too long deferred. "I'd have beat you on this one, James. If Hilliard had come around looking for a deal with me, he'd have had to go to voluntary manslaughter. Because I'd have heard the jury come back with, at the very worst, second degree."

Correction: It had everything to do with the Tabor trial.

Ambose had all he could do to work up a decent snicker. "And that's why you ran away from it like a yalla' dawg." With the hounds of hell yipping at his heels.

Mallon shook his head. "Not ran away. Walked away. Believe it. I'm the last of the red-hot patriots." His lips moved in a secret, sheltering smile. "I will now ask you, Mr. Ambose, had you not been in the state's attorney's office, would you or would you not have leaped to volunteer your services in the defense of Sam Tabor?"

Jim Ambose, his interest stirred, narrowed his eyes down. The thought of how he'd feel about defending Tabor had, you could see, simply never occurred to him before.

"Jesus, you do get involved in your job, don't you? Never take your eye off the ball for a second." All right, let's see if Tommy could help him out. "How many times have I heard you say they ought to impeach the bastard. That's what Sam did. He impeached him. With a gun. An effective majority of one."

Tommy was right, of course. Ambose had to give him points there. No, he wasn't sore at Sam. "Before I burn him, I'll pin a medal on him. *Then* I'll burn him."

Mallon smiled a nasty smile. "I've got somebody else to put on trial. The Supreme Court. And," he said, "I've got a patsy."

When Ambose reminded him how he had specifically ducked out on the grounds that it would be impossible to put the victim on trial in this one, Mallon reminded him right back that he'd had eighteen hours to figure out the best way to beg off before Ambose had showed up at the apartment. "Before you make a fucken fool of yourself, ask yourself one question. What was my primary goal with you, teacher? I got you off my back, that's all I did. I didn't want to torture you, you poor sonofabitch, by making you defend Wilcke and the Supreme Court. You'd have never been able to live with yourself."

"You know better. It's just a game with me, and I play it. The way it falls."

"Ha!" Slumped as he was in the chair, small as he was, Tommy's eyes tilted up at him, exposing, for just that moment, the wound that had been inflicted on him. "You're a fanatic there, don't you know that yet? Jeez! One word is all it takes. You're about the worst fucken bore I know." The wound, brought to the surface by the snort of derision, had melted away. "No, I guess you wouldn't know, would you? Unless you decided to make a crank of yourself on purpose."

A horseshit defense, Ambose told him loudly. He'd be making the malice case out of his own mouth. He'd have turned it into a cakewalk. His lip curled. "I'll say one thing for Bannerman. He's a horse's ass and he's as queer as a cucumber, but at least he's making a fight out of it."

Not from what Mallon had heard, he wasn't. From where Mallon sat, Bannerman's defense added up to accidental homicide, and that just wasn't going to do it. "I could have mounted a defense," he said longingly, "that would have been a wonder of modern advocacy." One psychiatrist to answer the legal requirement. On and off. Screw the childhood. Screw the Freudian crap. "I put in a case that looks to the naked eye like basic courtroom insanity. Straight and simple and everybody gets home for the weekend. And then I walk to the jury box to make my summation, and that's when I put in my case for second-degree and manslaughter. And when I sit down, pal, you have to stand up there and defend yourself. I'm not trying Wilcke, you shithead, I'm trying you. You're my patsy. And when you sit down, you're out of the DA's office. Win or lose. Believe it."

Well, it wasn't Ambose's job to save the boy from his delusions. "So you'd have called me to the stand, huh? It would have been interesting, I'll say that for you."

"Not you, you idiot. Sam."

Ambose couldn't believe his ears. "Piss to my paddle," he snorted. "I'd have beat him bloody."

Mallon didn't have to say a word. His ever-broadening smile, inquisitive, was plenty good enough to send Ambose scurrying back to think more on it. Having thought more on it, he retreated to more tenable grounds. Well, he'd have destroyed Sam as a credible witness, that's what he had meant to say. Always being careful, of course, to stop short of having Sam foaming at the mouth.

No good. Mallon puffed on his cigar, his head thrown back, and breathed out a long, lazy stream of smoke. "You're forgetting Part One. The jury knows by now that you've been putting ideas into his head." In addition to the cooperation Tommy could have expected from Sam's loving spouse, he would have had Samuelson (that was the kid from Washington) testify to what Ambose had said at lunch less than five hours before the murder. Bo, too. And don't think Bo wouldn't have. There were too many things Tommy could do for Bo, the way things were with Bo these days. And once Samuelson and Bo had testified, it would have been very difficult for that little Bunny of his to maintain a loss of memory. "That's a good thing you've got going there, Jim," he said. "What the hell's the matter with you? She's ready to fall over when you walk into the room, and I'm giving odds you've never tipped her."

Ambose told him that when he decided to, he'd let him hold the stopwatch.

The most tantalizing and provocative part of his defense, Tommy now informed him, was that the more forceful and compelling a courtroom performer Jim Ambose proved himself to be the more credible he would be making Tommy Mallon's defense. "It doesn't matter whether you think you were friends or not," he said, anticipating Ambose's objection. "Sam thinks so. You ought to know how it is with these schizoids. They lead a rich fantasy life."

With Ambose continuing to muse upon it—*Goddamn, but it was good*— Tommy proceeded to tick off the approaches available to Ambose on cross-examination. In just about the same order, as it happened, that Ambose had been thinking of them.

Break Sam down, and he'd be showing the jury he was insane. And after all the nice things Sam would have said about Ambose they'd hate his guts for it.

Go easy on him, after the jury had seen him in action against the other witnesses, and he'd be confirming what dear friends they were.

Don't ask any questions, same thing. Plus they'd think he was afraid to.

Go straight down the middle, conning Sam along while trying to get him to put himself in the chair, and the jury would despise him even more.

Same thing with Sam. If Sam tries to make a fight of it and gets beaten down, they weep for him. Whether he collapses or not.

If Sam agrees with him, putting up no fight, trying to please him, Ambose is worse off than ever.

"There's no way out for you, James. It's a Gotcha!"

Apparently, that was it. He brought his lighter up to his cigar, but, capping the flame for a moment, he directed his eyes back across the table. "Granted that counsel for defense would have to be a prick," said Tommy Mallon. "Please be advised that small though this one may be of stature, he learned the art of pricksmanship from a master."

The light was shining through from Hilliard's inner office. Ambose had guessed that Hilliard might have come back to clear out some of his personal effects while he was waiting for Pawley to call. He had sure as hell hoped so, anyway.

Back at his desk, under the cone of light, he studied the three photographs, one after the other. Although he was perfectly aware that Hilliard might be leaving at any time, he spread them out on his desk and gave himself one final chance, his fingers drumming, to change his mind.

Making his decision, he took a fresh envelope out of his desk and placed the pictures inside. He sealed the envelope tight and placed it in his inner jacket pocket.

Nevins was so startled that he actually jumped. "Oh, Ambose." The first expression of relief changed immediately into the customary grouchiness. His voice took on the customary edge. "What are you doing back here so late? I thought you'd gone a long time ago, hadn't you?"

Ambose almost had to smile. Nevins almost never wore a hat, for the very good reason that they always looked about a size too small on him. He looked ridiculous.

"I thought you'd want to know I'm taking over the Tabor trial from here," Ambose said. "Your presence isn't going to be needed in the courtroom. That's up to you. You're welcome if you want to show yourself. Pawley, I'm going to need. He'll be some help in the legal side of it. I expect he'll want to be seen by the people, the way it is, now that he's moving into elective office."

You had to give the old man credit. He'd hit him with it like this, fast and hard, and Hilliard hadn't twitched a muscle. The reaction, when it did come, was nothing more than the same old surly growl. "He hasn't moved in yet. I'm district attorney until you're officially informed otherwise, Ambose. So if you know what's good for you, you'll just keep on doing like you're told."

Ambose took out the tin of cigars, making a major production of opening and shutting the packet and putting it back into his inside pocket. When his hand came back out, the envelope was in it. He held the envelope up long enough for Nevins to see that this was what it was all going to be about. Then he placed it down on the edge of his desk so that Nevins could continue to look at it while Ambose was shielding the match with his hands.

In an entirely different voice Nevins said, "My door's always been open when you wanted to talk. And it always will be. Whether I'm here or not . . . you understand? I'd hope you'd know that."

Holy Toledo, Ambose thought, Hilliard thought he was handing in a letter of resignation or something. Well, that was one way to look at it, at that. Ho-Kay. He reached for it. "I hold here in my hand an envelope which contains three photographs, taken on separate nights, variously and widely spaced, by means of an infrared camera, Model M-27, which is the property of the district attorney's office, Brederton County, investigative branch."

The expression on Nevins' face changed as rapidly as lights rippling across a screen. From incomprehension to caution to wonder to remembering to understanding to outrage to—as his eyes went to the leather couch and then beyond it to the door—a sharply-scenting fear. He looked from the couch to the door twice, measuring the lane of vision in what must have been an overwhelming compulsion—dead giveaway that it was—to see for himself whether it was conceivable that anyone could have taken a picture without his knowing. And, undoubtedly, whether he could have been stupid enough to have left the door open.

"You happened to be otherwise occupied at the time, Judge. When I say 'at the time' I am referring, generically, to all three times." He brandished the envelope. "Both of you."

The neural paths that controlled Jim Ambose's relationship with Nevins were undergoing a rapid and highly satisfactory reordering. For the first time in twelve years he could honestly say that he was wholly free of any apprehension. The matching neural paths on the other side of the desk were undoubtedly undergoing a reordering that was every bit as basic. But that was supposition. You sure couldn't tell it by looking at him. Knowing, as he certainly must by now, what was in those pictures, Nevins waited with dignity, quite steadily, to hear whatever else Ambose might have to say. That was the kind of self-control Ambose could observe with respect. The old man was tough. Good.

"You forgot that I sometimes work very late. All hours of the night. That late at night, with nobody around, voices carry. Even when they're soft, lovey-dovey voices." He frowned, working his lips out. "I think," he said, "it was the giggling that first attracted my attention. It just happened that I had to go to the library to look up a citation."

Nevins opened his drawer, saw that he'd long since smoked his daily cigar, and slammed the drawer shut. Ambose permitted himself a meager smile. The involuntary need, the reaching for comfort that wasn't there, the momentary loss of control, all these had been noted with satisfaction. That small comfort was being denied to Nevins, as the district attorney's job had been denied to Ambose.

"I put your names up to the committee, Ambose. Both names. I did what I could."

"You know what I'm going to do for you, Hilliard? I won't count that, because you're not a judge yet." A stupid lie. Ambose was disappointed in him. "From now on, they're going to count."

Nevins looked at his watch impatiently. Just as impatiently he held out his hand. "All right, Ambose. Let's see what you think you've got. That seems to be what you're here for."

Ambose shook his head. Although that was exactly what he had been waiting for—for Nevins to ask—the peremptory tone and manner were something else again. If Nevins was interested in seeing what he had, Mr. Nevins was going to ask like a man needful of favors. "You're willing to take my word what I got," he said. "And you know why? Because I've been such a true and faithful servant, that's why. Like a hammer to a carpenter."

Mike Karney's words had popped into his head at the very last second. What he had been about to say was that if Nevins wasn't willing to take his word, maybe Mrs. Nevins would be. He wasn't here to sound like a cheap blackmailer. It wouldn't alter the situation, nothing could alter that. What would be altered was the delicate balance of their still-developing relationship. For despite his reflections on the reordering of their respective neural paths, Jim Ambose knew very well the powerful role that habit (by whatever name you chose to call it) played in such things. That being so, the power he held over Nevins was still new enough to be a chancy thing, and it was precisely that—the reordering of their relationship—that Ambose was after as payment for twelve years of his life.

He held up the envelope so that Nevins could see it one last time before he tucked it away. "The Tabor trial is mine," he said flatly. "No deals and no interference."

Pawley had drawn the straight-backed chair up to Nevins' desk. He had not taken off his topcoat, and he sort of gathered the bottom folds around his lap. "He didn't know I'd already called you, then?" Since Nevins had already made it as clear as humanly possible that not a word had been said about Ambose's encounter with Pawley and Bannerman in the Bankers' Club by either of them, Pawley's question was being directed to himself, for further consideration.

Nevins was following a somewhat different train of thought. "I've been thinking that maybe he got wind of it before," he said. "And that he was hitting up his old friend, Tommy, to see how he'd feel about talking his old boss into his office." What else, his suddenly elevated eyebrows seemed to be asking, would be important enough to have them meeting at the Bankers' Club?

Pawley was growing more dubious by the second. "You'd think he'd have guessed I'd be calling you as soon as he left, though. Now, wouldn't you?"

Nevins hadn't been idling away his time while he was waiting for Pawley to return. His briefcase was now bulging with so much sentimental value that it was a struggle to shut the clasp. For no discernible reason he strolled over to his book cabinet and opened the doors as if he were airing the rows of thick, tightly-packed law books (which, god knows, hadn't been exposed to very much air or anything else over the past few years). "I hope Tommy said yes," he said, looking back at Pawley. "I'd feel better in my mind knowing old Jim was settled in somewhere."

Pawley grimaced, not with any particular asperity, just giving up. The relationship between Nevins and Ambose had always been beyond him. Why should he expect to start understanding it now?

"Anyway," Nevins said, "I'm glad he knows." Rubbing the back of his neck thoughtfully, he strolled back to his desk. A sly grin came drifting across his face. "What was worrying me so much, you see, was how I was going to go about telling you that I was leaving it to you to break the news. I'd just about decided that seeing how the best way was the honest and direct way, I'd put on my hat and coat and, in the most direct and honest way I know, run out." His eyes went, with instant pain, to the couch. "On that, too." They remained there for a long while, unable to understand how he could have allowed himself to get involved in anything so messy at his age.

"Anyway . . ." He heaved a small sigh, pulling himself out of it. Anyway. "If there's one thing you don't have to worry about, it's that his word is good." No, Hilliard Nevins wasn't going to complain because Ambose hadn't got around to asking whether Bannerman was willing.

It was easy enough to tell when Pawley was troubled these days. He had developed a habit of picking gently at the by now practically invisible scar with his thumbnail. "The thing I find so vexatious here, Judge, is that he never asked. If Bannerman's turned me down cold, you've got to know by then. And if the deal has already been turned down, he's trading you those pictures for nothing. Does that sound like anybody you know by the name of James J. Ambose?" It wasn't that Pawley didn't have any explanation, it was that the only explanation he had been able to come up with was even more vexatious than the question. "It means he's got those pictures, and he's been waiting to use them and he knows that time is running out on him." It still didn't make sense to him. "What do you think, Judge?"

Nevins gave him a look of approval. "I think I'm leaving this office in good hands," he said. "Among other things." One of the other things was that by making his move when he did, Ambose had given himself a free hand over what was left of the trial. Be that as it may, Nevins was just as glad Ambose hadn't known that Bannerman had already turned them down. "I'd hate to think of him holding anything like that over me until he had a bad case he wanted reversed. That would have been something to see, wouldn't it? Jim Ambose trying to fix a case for the defense?"

"What would you have done, Judge?"

"Danged if I know." It wouldn't have meant that much, really, once he was safely on the Bench, except that he'd hate to have those pictures turn up in Mrs. Nevins' mail some morning. "That possibility having been averted," he harumphed, "I can tell you in all confidence that I'd have booted him out of my chambers and halfway into tomorrow. No question about it." He drew himself erect, the very picture of the judicial rectitude he was describing. "As long as the matter has been broached, Dewey my boy, I have a feeling I'm going to be powerful tough on you prosecutors, knowing as I do the lengths some of you fellows will go to get the harshest possible verdict."

The last item in Jim Ambose's Journal read: "The gretest illusion a man can have is to believ he is without illusion. Having such an illusion (delusion?) he will be sure to buld his life and good name upon it, and when the hour of disilusioment strikes, his life will be without purpose."

It had been written in a fierce and fearsome doomsday scrawl that bore no resemblance to the passages written elsewhere in his small, neat hand. The last item in Jim Ambose's Journal had not been set down by a composed and orderly mind; it had been blown across the page by a raging tornado.

The former keeper of the Journal was swung halfway around behind his desk, staring intently into the fireplace, his hands clasped low between his knees. For more than an hour now he had been staring into the fire, mesmerized by its power and energy. In the eye of the fire, his overheated mind was being cooled.

As he watched his Journals being consumed, he was able to visualize the final passage exactly as he imagined he had written it (in his normal hand, without the misspellings). Had it been possible, he would have called it back from the fires just long enough to add: "To have no purpose is to have no identity."

He had built his life upon an illusion.

Tommy Mallon had done everything except draw him a blueprint, and he had willed himself not to understand.

Mike Karney had set it out in front of him in so many words. "The dumbest thing in the animal kingdom is the poor dumb beast who doesn't know the difference between the carpenter and the hammer." What could have been plainer than that? He had his sources of information, Karney had told him. Who would have better ones? And instead of hearing what Karney was trying to tell him, he had thought . . .

As the memory of what he had thought came back to him, his insides writhed in a convulsion of self-loathing. He had been perfectly willing to let Mike Karney make all the shady political deals he scorned other men for making, hadn't he? He had been ready to turn himself over, lock, stock and barrel.

Been willing to. . . ? Come on, now. Was overjoyed to! Leaped at the chance for! Congratulated himself upon! Slobbered over! Would have crawled on his hands and knees to! Blessed the day!

All the while Mike Karney had been telling him how honest and noble a character Elijah Chobodian had been (and Ambose had been preening his feathers —don't forget that!—on the remarkable similarity Karney must be finding in the noble character of Ambose, J.), Ambose, J., had been prepared (in his own mind had already agreed) to do just exactly what Chobodian had refused to do.

Pride and ambition!

Jim Ambose, who had been so sure he knew the way and was as corrupt and contaminated as the worst of them.

To still the clamoring that was inside his head, again he stared, more bleakly than ever, into the fire. Behind the grating the Journals burned. Through the night, Jim Ambose watched his Journals burn.

In the morning there was nothing left except one tiny section of twisted spine.

When Jim Ambose arose, the road he must travel from this point on had been set out very clearly before him.

After he had cleaned up the little matter that lay between himself and Norman Bannerman.

Wednesday, August 6

"It's all right, Marie," Ambose said. He shut the door behind him. "It's personal, kind of, but I think it would be all right for you to hear it. I think you should." He motioned for them both to sit down. "Yes," he said, after he had dragged up a chair for himself, "I think you should hear it. If my friend is right."

Now, he knew he was sticking his neck out here, Ambose said, taking them into his confidence. But he'd had this piece of information brought to him. And —his gesture was modestly disclaiming—what were friends for. . . ?

Harry made a notably unsuccessful effort to smile back.

"This friend of yours. . . ?" Marie asked.

A snitch, he informed her. An informant. Harry could tell her how it worked. "He owes me this favor from way back and . . . happens all the time, right, Harry?"

By the simple act of lowering his voice, Ambose was able to draw them into a tight conspiratorial circle. This friend of his who sometimes did a little work for Felix McPhait had been tapping the phone of a distinguished citizen. For reasons having to do with a gambling debt. This distinguished citizen had a— what would you call it? . . . an arrangement? "Well, hell, they had an apartment there, a regular love nest. Him and a woman there who worked with him." Ambose's friend had apparently thought he could do himself more good by turning the tapes over to Ambose than to McPhait. "You know how these guys are, Harry," Ambose said, grimacing. "We got to use them, but—Harry can tell you how it is with these guys, Marie. You can't trust any of 'em."

"Oh, I know that, Jim." Davies was trying desperately to remember what the hell he had said over the phone that could be used against him. He couldn't think, period. His mind had gone blank.

"A love nest," Marie purred. "My." She had always wanted to know what went on in a love nest. "You bring the tape machine," she said, turning it on for him, "and I'll bring the broads."

A mercilessly blunt look, carrying a message direct from the spleen, warned her never to try to pull that kind of crap with him again. A second or two later and he was their friendly native guide again, reluctantly confessing that he still hadn't heard the tapes himself. His friend had brought them in a sealed envelope, and Ambose—delicate soul that he was—didn't think it was his place to, you know, to listen in on private lovemaking.

Oh my god. Did he have the apartment bugged, too? A wave of nausea swept over her. Her insides shriveled. *The bed???*

Her insides could damn well have shriveled up and fallen out of her, and she still wouldn't have given him the satisfaction of seeing how he had shaken her. "I wonder what kind of a sick, perverted mind would want to go sniffing around in someone else's bedsheets." And though she succeeded quite well in sounding amusingly horrified and faintly repelled, there was not a blessed thing to be done about the overwarm coloring that had swept over her immediately after the nausea. "It would have to be some kind of sexual frustrate, wouldn't you say that, Ambose? Some kind of a dirty-minded little faggot with a disabling problem where his . . . uh, normal sex life was supposed to be."

Ambose was perfectly delighted. "Just what I told him!" You could see how delighted he was by the air of cordiality with which he studied her. "My very words," he crooned. "What kind of a sick, perverted sonofabitch would do a thing like that, poor devil? The poor devil needs help, that's just what I said." He stopped smiling. "The way I look at it, a little pussy never hurt anybody. So what if he's married? Whose business is that? A little pussy on the side can do a married man a world of good." How many times had they heard Bo Gunderson say, from out of his vast experience as a divorce lawyer, that a "piece of strange" at the appropriate moment had saved more marriages than all the marriage counsellors in the world, laid end to end.

Satisfied that a mutuality of interest had been established, he felt free to confide that he was bringing the problem to Judge Davies' attention because of his confidence that, as one swordsman to another, Harry would be sympathetic toward the poor fellow's plight.

Against all reason and logic, Harry had been clinging to a slender hope that the plight was going to be somebody else's. That hope having collapsed, he was ready to suggest that while he would be more than happy to help out any friend of Jim's, it would be a waste of time for him to do anything until he was sure there were no other copies of the tapes around. Ambose was in the fortunate position of being able to guarantee—his word for his snitch's word—that the bargain would be kept.

Still, something did seem to be troubling Ambose. There was, they could see, a minor difficulty which Ambose was finding it rather awkward to have to bring up. "He's willing to do this for me, this snitch of mine, because he owes me such a big favor. But he wants to wait until the jury is out on this case we're trying now. He wants to hear you charge the jury on M'Naughton." Jim Ambose was every bit as mystified about it as they were. This snitch of his was just one of those crazy guys you kept running into in his line of work, that was all. Some guys loved music, some guys loved sports, some guys loved to sit in duck blinds and shiver. "My friend, he just happens to love sitting around courtrooms listening to M'Naughton being read off." Jim Ambose spread his hands out helplessly and heaved a great philosophical sigh. There was, it was clear, no accounting for taste.

Casually, the smile still pasted on his face, he turned to Marie. "Speaking of ass, dear, you want to play house with Bannerman, that's your business. But if Bannerman should happen to get wind of this, that's going to make it my business and your ass."

Leisurely, he headed for the door. Leisurely, he turned back. "Oh, by the way,

Harry, I've been meaning to tell you. You're doing real good so far. Real good. Keep up the good work. The entire legal profession is proud of you."

Lowell, August 6—In a foreshortened session of the Sam Tabor trial, Mr. Tabor's insanity defense was heavily attacked by four distinguished neurologists and electroencephalographers from various parts of the country.

Beginning with Dr. Allan S. Benswagner of Lowell, who conducted the medical tests on Mr. Tabor two weeks after the assassination of Chief Justice David B. Wilcke, and continuing on through the testimony of Dr. Serge Simonowitch of Yale University, Dr. Richard M. Lerber of the Mayo Clinic and Dr. Harmond Calienda of Chicago University, the witnesses were in substantial agreement that the readings of Mr. Tabor's brain waves would not support a diagnosis of brain damage.

Dr. Simonowitch, a gray-haired, well-groomed neurosurgeon who gestured frequently with his hands, graded the brain waves as, "Normally abnormal, and mildly so."

In answer to the question put by Asst. DA Dewitt Pawley, Dr. Simonowitch stated that more than 40 percent of the entire population had brain-wave patterns with similar minor and nonspecific abnormalities.

Dr. Lerber testified that of the more than 40,000 EEG's he had studied, he has never seen a tracing similar to Mr. Tabor's in a brain-damaged or epileptic patient.

Under the gentle cross-examination of noted attorney Norman Bannerman, Dr. Lerber readily admitted that the "state of the art" was still in a post-primitive stage of development. "We have come a little distance." Dr. Lerber smiled. "There is always a greater distance to go."

Q. Nonspecific means you don't know what it is, doesn't it? If you don't know what it is, you can't say positively that it isn't brain damage, can you?

A. All I can say is that it is not the pattern found in patients who are known to have brain damage.

Q. Bear with me, Doctor, please. If you can't state positively that it is not brain damage, then it follows that you cannot, as a true scientist, eliminate the possibility that it is brain damage?

A. May I answer that in two parts. The first answer is that as a scientist I can and do eliminate the possibility that Mr. Tabor has any form of brain damage currently translatable from EEG tracings. Consequently, he does not have any form of brain damage that has ever been identified by any neurologist. The second part of the answer is that I cannot eliminate the possibility that such a connection will never be discovered.

Q. New discoveries are being made every day?

A. Allowing for the hyperbole of your profession, Mr. Bannerman, I will agree.

While no official reason was given for the sudden cancellation of the afternoon session, the best indications were that Judge Harrison T. Davies had become indisposed. Judge Davies assumed the role of presiding judge during the final days of the jury impaneling following the dramatic court-room collapse of the original presiding jurist, Ebenezer Chobodian.

Unlike the previous sessions, which have been highlighted by frequent

508

and at times vituperative exchanges between Mr. Bannerman and Asst. DA Ambose, this morning's session was marked by the good humor and good will that obviously exists between Mr. Pawley and Mr. Bannerman. Under Mr. Pawley's direction, this phase of the state's case moved with unprecedented swiftness. Mr. Pawley was assisted by a youthful colleague, Asst. DA Robert X. Mollineaux. District Attorney Hilliard Nevins was not present in the courtroom. Mr. Ambose, though present, was a silent observer.

Asked whether he expected that the good spirits evidenced in this morning's session would continue to prevail through the remaining days of the trial, Mr. Bannerman answered that it would depend upon whether Mr. Ambose was "back in his pulpit tomorrow."

Informed of Mr. Bannerman's remark, Mr. Ambose replied, "Tell him I've never missed a roll call yet."

Dr. Lennard Swann, the chief psychiatrist for the prosecution, is expected to take the stand tomorrow as the final witness for the state.

Thursday, August 7

The pouched red-rimmed eyes opened wide upon DeWitt Pawley, standing behind Nevins' desk. "Where's Hilliard?" Doc Swann demanded. "I always said he'd be late for his own funeral, ask him if I didn't. It wasn't in the bargain he was going to be late for mine." Charley Curran, whose conversation with Pawley was being interrupted, smiled the broad, bemused smile Doc knew so well; a tolerant smile acquiescing to Doc's view of himself as a crazy old coot. Looking from one to the other—explaining to Curran, complaining to Pawley—Doc protested, "He's supposed to chuck me under the chin and tell me how I'm the only gaw-damn genius he's ever come across. He *knows* he is, that's a *rule.*" Red-eyed or not, Doc still had what it took to turn giddily reminiscent. "Gawdamn, but that's the kind of good, tough criticism that makes me feel beloved all over."

Pawley was breaking it to him gently that Hilliard might not be in all day when Jim Ambose came bustling in to spare him the necessity of further evasive action.

"Here comes Ambose," Doc blared. "With the sirens blowing and the red light revolving. Heyyyy . . . you're looking good in there, Big Fellow. Damn me with faint praise if I don't go to sleep every night feeling safer just knowing you're standing guard." In another second he had turned all meek and sniffly. "At least I would be if it wasn't for this pesky little case of insomnia that's been hanging on the last coupla-three-four-five years. Don't know what it is. The weather, I guess."

The moment Doc relaxed, the suffocating weariness could be seen in his hollow eyes and sagging jowls. The bone-weariness. It was because of Doc that yesterday afternoon's session had been called off. Not Doc himself but trouble at his Children's Home. Bad trouble. The old man was so completely beat that, as was to be expected, he tried all the harder to be his usual rambunctious self. The first time Ambose made a passingly slighting remark about Allbright, he became indignant. "Let me tell you about Allbright. One word is all. The man has done just a terrific job in taking all the known facts and jigsawing together a picture of how it's possible to kill a Chief Justice without knowing a thing about it. Terrific! If I was him I wouldn't settle for nothing less than the Nobel Prize in Jigsaw."

And when Ambose finally suggested that they retire to his office to run through his upcoming testimony about what crap this undifferentiated schizophrenia was, Swann turned upon him a look that was supposed to curdle him in his tracks. "Crap, is it? What do you know about anything, you three-bit law-school graduate? Pure schizophrenia, that's what he's got. Lot of that been going around lately." An innocently scampish look took brief hold on his features: "He's two of a kind, that's what I always say about Sam Tabor. Haw! Double or nothing. Hangs on worse than amnesia."

Pure babble. Even while he was being so perverse vocally, he was following Ambose docilely out of the office, muttering away about how he'd rather be a schizoid than a masochist any old day, in fair weather or foul. Going out the door, he looked back over his shoulder. "Schizo gives you something else to think about, but masochism *hurts!*"

The door, gently shut behind him, opened again immediately. No more than enough to allow Doc Swann to pop his head back in. His eyes went darting around the room in fear and suspicion before settling, in balmy ecstasy, upon its two occupants. "Paranoid's the thing to be these days," he whispered. "Got it? Paranoid's good for you. It . . . keeps . . . you . . . on . . . your . . . toes." He brought his finger to his lips, cautioning them to secrecy, and having swept his eyes around the room one last time, checking every corner, he very carefully withdrew his head, pulling the door shut behind him.

Pawley stared blankly after him. "He's going to crack up one of these days," he told Curran grimly. "It's *got* to be. Wouldn't it be great if today wasn't the day?"

Ambose didn't waste any time. "Let's put an end to the suspense," he said crisply. "Do you have an opinion as to whether the defendant knew right from wrong when he took the gun out of his pocket and killed David Boone Wilcke?"

As always, all was cold calculation with Ambose. Right up front, he was out to demonstrate to the jury that the state's expert did not have so much as a second's worth of doubt about the sanity of Sam Tabor. Once that little matter had been taken care of, the questioning could proceed, in rapid and relentless order, to refute, ridicule and otherwise dispose of the main items of Bannerman's defense. And *only* the main items. Cut the roots and the branches will die, that was Ambose's philosophy.

The risk you'd normally be running with that kind of rapid-fire assault was that your expert could end up sounding like a yapping dog. Not with Doc Swann. Doc Swann—as Ambose had said so often—was the best forensic psychiatrist he had ever come across, because he could always be counted upon to give "the folks" a lively, illuminating presentation of life over myth. The risk you ran with Doc these days was exactly the opposite. Lose control of the examination for even one second—and with the latitude allowed to an expert witness, that risk was always present—and he was just as likely to go rambling off to god only knew where.

It came, therefore, as no small relief to Ambose to find Doc so manageable in the early going that he was able to take him through the circumcision, the Oedipus complex and the identic imagery at a brisk and easy canter.

The circumcision at the age of thirty? All Sam had told anybody was that he had been advised to have it done. "Lacking any proof to the contrary," Doc sniffed, "I wouldn't go constructing any cockeyed theories that said different." And when he added, almost as an afterthought, that if you wanted to play Freudian strip poker you could just as easily interpret it as a symbolic act by which he was cutting himself off from his religion as one binding himself to its teachings, it was done with the kind of offhand shrug that told "the folks" he could come up with a dozen other interpretations if he put his mind to it—all of them equally persuasive and equally unreliable.

The Oedipus complex was dismissed out of hand as nothing more than a theory that had been put forth by Dr. Freud as a stage all boys went through during their first growing awareness of sex. A theory so fanciful that Freud had found it necessary to dip into mythology to find an appropriate name. "I've always wondered," he said drily, "whether Freud's own unconscious wasn't playing tricks on him there."

It wasn't until Ambose introduced the phenomenon of identic imagery, however, that Doc seemed able to shake the weariness off his shoulders. (And it was more than just weariness, as Ambose had discovered during the run-through. It was a festering deep within himself that wasn't going to be cured by a good night's sleep.) "With all respect to Zacharias," Doc said, "there is an internal conflict in his testimony you could drive a milk wagon through." The personality Zacharias had constructed contained features of identic imagery but, as he now reminded the jury, it had been dominated by a passive character disorder. Both revolving around an unresolved Oedipal conflict. "To which I say, one or the other, Doctor. One or the other."

The change in him was so marked that as he moved on to explain why there were two abso-lutely different perso-nality patterns involved, he adopted an aggressive, pattering rhythm that amounted to an open attack upon the pitchman who had tried to tell them different. "On the one hand, you have a man who is so passive that he allows himself to be shaped en-tirely by his environment. Goes wherever the four winds blow him. Is self-pitying and self-justifying. On the other hand, you have a tense, alert and overstimulated personality who reacts to the dangers he senses all around him by sniffing at the winds so that he can antic-ipate anything that's going to happen and deal with it ahead of time." One was dominated by his environment, the other shaped his environment to his will so that he could dominate it. "Couldn't be more different if you tried."

In separating them at Ambose's request, he was willing enough to grant that Sam most certainly did have a passive personality—and if anybody wanted to get fancy about it and call it a passive character disorder, you could see that it was perfectly all right with him. When it came to identic imagery, though, he shook his head so decisively that he might just as well have been saying *not even close.* "When you talk about identic imagery, you're talking about a man who feels he's constantly in danger from unseen forces out there who are out to get him, and so he keeps putting himself in dangerous situations to prove to himself that he can lick it. You see? He has to constantly reassure himself that the forces of death and retribution that dominate his fantasy world haven't got to him yet."

That such a personality came about as the result of noises in the dark at a critical time in a boy's life, that was theory. That such a personality existed, that was fact. He sat back and snorted. "But you don't find that kind of a personality working in the civil service, you can bet on that." You found them working for themselves, in dangerous professions. The kind of profession where they could be constantly proving to themselves that they still had everything under control. He was speaking now in a careful, measured cadence, as if he wanted to make every word count. "They're so alert to protecting themselves at all times that they've developed a special kind of . . . tuning in that lends itself to professions like high finance and psychiatry."

"Excuse me." Bannerman, asquint with innocence, was leaning across the defense table with one hand cupped near his ear. "Did you say psychiatrists?"

Given the opening, it was a routine enough ploy. Clever enough to get him the laugh he was reaching for, but essentially harmless. He could not possibly have anticipated what he was letting himself in for.

"Psychiatrists, Mr. Bannerman!" Swann said, coming down hard. "Psychiatrists are fellows who are able to peer into those closed bedrooms like that theory of yours says, huh?" They were fellows who were able to play God with other people's lives. Turn them inside out and find out what makes them tick. "What could be more control than that, huh? And what," he asked, pulling at his nose, "could be riskier?" He eyed him, coolly and knowingly. "And lawyers. Oh yes, Mr. Bannerman. Trial lawyers more than anybody. We have more in common that you might imagine, my dangerous profession and yours." Correction: He was eyeing him coolly and merrily. Lawyers were given a license to open those doors, too, huh? To pry and probe for those hidden secrets. The difference was that a lawyer wasn't restricted to his private office. A criminal lawyer's license put him right out in the spotlight where everybody could see him and hear him. And where he could see and hear himself being seen and heard. You betcha. Television cameras, pictures in the paper and everything.

"And every client in clear and imminent danger," he breathed. What could be more dangerous than that? Or god-like? His eyes came to life. "You and me, we've been given a license to handle those murderous impulses that sit across the desk from us, huh? Pure dynamite!" The sense of something being held in abeyance came through so powerfully that Bannerman merely continued to watch him, with a quizzical half-smile that never changed.

Doc Swann, who was watching Bannerman every bit as closely, conceded, with a generous bow to both him and his profession and a becoming humility toward his own, that since a psychiatrist was usually dealing with the ones who hadn't lost control yet, while as great a criminal lawyer as Norman Bannerman almost always got to handle the ones who had, Doc could be compared, more realistically, to a child who was being allowed to play with matches, and Bannerman to a demolition expert. "But," he said, brightening, "we both make them jump through the hoops, don't we? And like it so much they'll pay the fancy fees we bamboozle 'em out of. Now, that's what I call keeping the situation *well* under control. That's what I call *really* showing 'em who's still boss."

To give Bannerman one last thing to think about, he warned him that before he got too stuck on that noises-in-the-night theory of his, it might be well for him to consider that words were nothing but grunts cut to order. And that a good lawyer had to be alert to every possible meaning of the words spoken in the courtroom in order to make sure that nothing was being put over on him. "Why, there are some lawyers so sensitive to sound," he said, lifting his eyes to the air-conditioning grating at the back of the room, "that they're even aware of the sounds coming from outside the courtroom. Those little everyday sounds the rest of us automatically filter out."

Languidly, complacently, Ambose said, "Too bad I don't have it."

Stung, Bannerman snapped, "Now, there's a self-serving statement if ever I've heard one. But on the weight of the overwhelming mass of evidence, I'll accept it."

Ambose just kept looking at him, giving him every opportunity to make the same self-serving statement himself, until Judge Davies broke it up with the cheerful observation that everything had been going along so well all morning that he didn't want anything started now.

Minutes later Bannerman was leaning across to Halpern, more heavily flushed than ever. Swann had just brought the first phase of the examination to a close by delivering his opinion that "that particular theory," the Oedipus complex, had been "grossly misused by Zacharias and carried to the ends of the earth by Allbright," a personal attack upon a colleague's competence and/or honesty that Bannerman found so incredible that he had turned his back completely to the witness stand. "And Zack didn't want to question this guy's credentials," he hissed at Halpern. "Too bad he didn't stick around. He might have learned a thing or two about professional courtesy."

"Yeah," Halpern grunted. "He could have seen our whole identic imagery defense blown out of the tub, too." How in the hell, he demanded, could they have missed that?

Bannerman, not deigning to answer, shifted his attention to Sam. "Don't worry about a thing," he told him with absolute confidence. "I'll take care of everything." He might as well have been talking to the wall. With Ambose having moved the questioning to Sam's marital problems, and specifically to his preferred mode of sleeping with his wife, Sam had already waxed himself over.

Up on the witness stand Doc Swann shrugged expressively. "Well, you know, so what? People do that. People are like that. People have all kinds of sexual habits and preferences, and they're not always in the strictest keeping with what we pretend. We all know that." He skimmed his gaze out over the audience. "We know it," he said, indicting everybody out there for hypocrisy and cant. "In ourselves."

Now that he had everybody ashamed of themselves, he was able to assure them that there was not a thing in Sam's relationship with his wife that had not been entirely consistent with his normally passive behavior. Or anybody else's. "Look," he said, "marital happiness in this country depends upon the male's willingness to accept monogamy, which means his willingness to renounce connection with other females. Not because he prefers it that way. We know better than that. Because his wife prefers it that way. Because it's a woman's view of happiness." He wasn't talking to the courtroom audience anymore. Nor even to Ambose. By nothing more than the direction of his mind, he had narrowed the field of communication down to a small circle of interest between himself and the jury box. To the extent that any man acceded to the practice of monogamy, he told them, he was passively accepting the environment he found himself in. A note of studied reasonableness came into his voice. "Sam seems to have carried it to its extremity. If we are to credit the data, he was willing to go along with forgoing connection with his wife herself when that was what she preferred."

Like hell I did. On the outside, Sam Tabor was impenetrable and imperturbable. Inside, he smiled. Behind the battlements, Sam Tabor saw himself betrothed and bestride. Atop the rampart wall, he saw himself strutting, top-hatted, cock-of-the-walk. It was almost too good. He had slipped through the walls of time, and none of them suspected. *Like hell you do.* No more than they suspected the other thing. On the outside, Sam Tabor remained sealed tight. Inside, the single eye crouched at the secret outlet and smiled the sly, secret smile that knew what nobody else in the world knew. Not even Bannerman. *Like hell you will.*

Doc Swann was saying that it was altogether in Sam's personality pattern that he should have gone along with whatever he was told would help his wife, whether it was sleeping in another bed or becoming a patient himself. "You see it all the time," he said, turning at last to address the jury directly. "Men who become martyrs to their wives' neuroses. There aren't many families without one."

It was right here, in his ability to come riding in on just such commonplace, everyday truths, that you were seeing what made Lennard Swann the best forensic psychiatrist Jim Ambose had ever seen. In turning to address the jury, Lennard Swann had not been offering them the benefit of any special professional insight so much as joining them in somber reflection upon the unforeseeable turns of fate that brought such tragedies down upon a marriage. He knew so well what he was doing that he could have choreographed the heaving sighs, tightened lips and clouded eyes that materialized across the jury box. And why shouldn't he? It was his business to know. They'd have only to close their eyes for a moment, he knew, to see the bride and groom at the altar, bright of eye and brimming with the invincibility of youth. They'd have only to open them again to see the creeping erosion that had been wrought by life's steady load of wears and tears—and then, like a thunderbolt from the blue, the final havoc wrought by the glandular upheaval imposed upon women. (What bridegroom had ever thought of that at the altar? What bride?) Never mind. By what the bridegroom, plucked and nicked by time, then chose to do, you knew him. *For better or worse* was the bargain he had made that day. The man's part, if he were a man, was to take the affliction of her sex upon himself as he had taken its sweetness and its comforts. Hey! Viewed in such a light, youth's promise of invincibility had perhaps not been so foolish, after all. No? Consider this, my friend: Through all the days and nights that Time, that deadly spider, had been silently spinning the web in which they were now entangled, the bride and groom had, unbeknownst to themselves, been weaving something a thousand times stronger. Under the battering, deep in the bone, they had been weaving a bond that would hold until hell froze over. Could anything be more miraculous than this: That Love, grown dim of eye and vague of memory, should have been transformed into something rarer and finer. Loyalty. *For better or worse* was not an oath that had been taken lightly. Down at the heels and needing a shave, the creaking bridegroom wheezed and slogged through the hopeless days and nights, and stuck. A man as common as clay, but a man. Indomitable and—yes, by god!—invincible.

And most remarkable of all, there weren't, as Lennard Swann had said, many families without one.

The real world out there had come back into the courtroom, lugging its bag of troubles and its Cracker Jack prizes.

Sure, Sam would have been upset about being dispossessed from his own bed. But, to be practical about it, married people sometimes did sleep in separate beds, didn't they? And when you came right down to it, how much trouble was it, really, to take a couple of steps across the room? "For all I know, that's just what Shtogren may have had in mind. To force Sam to the gesture of coming after his wife, and by making her just a little more . . . uh, inaccessible, getting him to appreciate her more."

"But didn't he also tell her to go out and get a job and become independent?"

"She didn't, did she? That showed more than anything else."

"Yes, sir. What does it show?"

"Well, it shows that she didn't want all that independence, or it shows that whatever had been wrong was working itself out. Probably a little of this, and a little of that, and"—he shrugged—"a little of something else we don't know anything about."

"You don't agree, then, that the advice was all that disastrous?"

Doc gave an involuntary little snort. "Well, when the patient goes out and kills somebody, anything you do can be considered wrong. When the patient comes along, anything you do can be considered right. Who knows whether the treatment had anything to do with it? In other words, nobody has any magic wands. In other words, how smart can any one man be?"

How smart? The rapport between the witness and the jury was running so strong that four or five of them forgot themselves long enough to smile at him, and Bettlenork, with her intimate knowledge of the medical profession's failings, nodded in emphatic agreement. Here was one psychiatrist who didn't fill their heads with fancy words and fancy theories. He made people sound like the people they knew. *People act this way,* Doc Swann kept saying. They do the craziest damn things. And if you wanted to go a little nuts yourself, the easiest way was to try to figure out why.

What better frame of mind could any jury possibly have been in at the climactic moment when Ambose came to his feet to launch Doc on the attack that would dismantle the intricate Oedipal superstructure that had been contrived by the amazing Allbright?

"Dr. Swann," he said. "I will now ask you . . ."

The jury leaned forward. The low hum of the air-conditioning unit could suddenly be heard throughout the courtroom.

The ground had already been prepared. It had not been on any mere whim that Ambose had solicited—and Swann delivered—that earlier blast at the "fanciful theory." Expanding upon that theme now, he stated in tones of purest derision that to leap from the original theory to the even more fanciful theory that a boy who was unable to make the assumed transition harbored a lifelong, severely repressed desire to sleep with his mother was nothing more than guesswork piled on top of guesswork, and to then make the further leap that he hated her so much because of this presumed failure of his own that he wanted to kill her—conjecture upon conjecture upon conjecture—was piling it so high that you had to call it scholarship or you couldn't get anybody to listen to you.

"But to then take one last, great, bullfrog leap out into the void—not bullfrog, mountain goat. Kangaroo. And say that the grown man, being unable to face his desire to sleep with his mother—and never mind that she's been dead twenty years, either, that doesn't—and so he symbolically kills her by putting somebody else in her place so that . . . a man no less, because he's a judge and sometimes wears a robe, it's . . . uh, well, it's . . ." To pull himself together he took a deep breath and then gave his little potbelly a kind of truculent, upward flip. "It's like building a castle in the air and then sending out engraved invitations to the Grand Opening."

Not entirely by accident, Jim Ambose's hands were clasped together in loose and prayerful attitude at his chest. "Yes," he said, slanting his gaze piously at the jury. "I guess all us folks get to wondering who's the sicker sometimes, the patient or the psychiatrist."

One loud, raucous guffaw from a spectator who had quite probably put in time as the first and was very clearly no admirer of the second drew everybody's attention from the witness stand for the briefest of moments. Not Bannerman's, though. Bannerman's eyes went groaning straight up to heaven, and finding little to encourage him there, come rolling in a wide, down-sweeping arc to the press rows, where his prospects for finding a sympathetic audience were undoubtedly more promising.

Well satisfied that he had the finest flower of the nation's press solidly behind him, he pushed himself back onto the rear legs of his chair in order that he might look with as clear an eye as they upon the ignoramus who had perpetrated this new affront upon their common sensibilities. "Coming from Mr. Ambose, who has polluted the stream of justice and poisoned all constitutional wells, this oafish sampling of the anti-intellectual bias that runs so strong and deep within him is no more than we might have warranted. Congratulations, Mr. Ambose . . ." It was really remarkable how through nothing more than a sudden pinching of his voice and nostrils Bannerman was able to create the impression that he was holding a soiled tissue delicately between thumb and forefinger. Dropping it, his voice dropped, too. "You have finally succeeded in touching the bottom rung of judicial tolerability and, as water seeking its own level, plumbed the lower depths of civil discourse."

"Pollution, is that what you call it in Chicago, Norman?" The lazy, hound-dog smile that had not been in evidence for a couple of days was already curling itself around Bannerman. "The way we like to think of it around here is that we are simple field hands irrigating the processes by which justice is served."

Bannerman thought about it. Harry Davies thought about it. Halpern thought about it. The same image came to everybody in the courtroom, in all probability. "Mr. Ambose," Mollineaux whispered, "you sure do take chances."

The payoff on Allbright's reconstruction of the murder—the Big Casino that all the Oedipal crap built up to—had been the dramatic unveiling of the Unconscious Motive, and however Ambose might scoff at it publicly, or for that matter privately, he didn't underestimate its importance. Everybody's first reaction had been that there had to be some connection between Tabor and Wilcke. It made everything so much simpler and safer. Allbright had given them one. Considering that it was a motive compounded of suppositions, theories and surmises—meaning, as far as Ambose was concerned, thin air—Ambose felt that Doc was going to come about as close as was humanly possible to blasting it to smithereens.

For openers, Doc went after the weakest point in the Allbright defense, the concept of the Unconscious Murderer, with heavy sarcasm. "It wasn't Sam who killed him—and this is exactly what Allbright's testimony comes to—it was his unconscious that did it. Consciously, Sam didn't know a thing about it. He was just kind of standing around there on the stairs with his skin wrapped around his unconscious. An innocent bystander, that's all he was. Nobody could have been more surprised."

And if in the subsequent interweaving of Doc Swann's testimony the jury came to confuse the Unconscious Murderer (who almost certainly did not exist anywhere) with the Unconscious Motive (which existed in everybody, everywhere, always), it could very well be because that was exactly the way Ambose and Swann had planned it.

What they mostly had in mind, though, was to show them that there was an internal conflict in Allbright's analysis, which lay so close to the heart that it could never be resolved. "The question I'd have wanted to ask Allbright," Lennard Swann said at length, "was how did this unconscious, which needed a lawful, orderly society so bad, think it was going to make this one more lawful by committing the ultimate unlawful act, which is murder, and the ultimate offense against order, which is the striking down of a high government official?"

To wrap it up Ambose reminded him that Allbright had diagnosed the defendant as schizophrenic, and Zacharias had added a pinch or two of paranoia. Based upon Lennard Swann's own interview with Tabor less than twenty-four hours after the murder, plus the evidence that had been introduced into the courtroom, Jim Ambose now wanted to know how Lennard Swann would diagnose him.

Lennard Swann pulled at his nose and scratched his ear. "I'd say without any hesitation at all," he said, after all that hesitation, "that the defendant, Sam Tabor, is what we'd call a kind of queer duck."

"Damn," Pawley groaned. "Here, right at the end . . ."

Ambose, taken completely off guard, had to ask whether queer-duckism was a form of behavior that fell short of mental disease.

Norman Bannerman and Lennard Swann quickened to each other from the beginning. Bannerman was positively exuding confidence. Doc Swann was so frisky and peppery and up-and-at-'em that after only two exchanges Pawley was sighing to nobody in particular, "It's no good. Doc still don't like him from the last movie."

By the time they had done with it, the exuberance of the one and the friskiness of the other were gone. The cross-examination of Lennard Swann turned out to be the strangest, most improbable one that Bannerman had ever been involved in, or that Jim Ambose and DeWitt Pawley had ever seen.

Bannerman had opened it up on a low, needling key by laying bare his mortification at finding Doctor Swann so monumentally unimpressed with Allbright after he had gone to such effort and expense to bring him to Lowell for his edification. Immediately, he had expanded it into the question of whether Doc had been in the courtroom while Allbright's professional honors and attainments were being recited, and, answering in kind, Doc had confessed that while he had missed the first fifteen minutes worth of medal-rattling he had somehow been under the impression that they'd just piled them all up on top of a scale and weighed them to save time, and they'd come to about the tonnage of a light destroyer.

"Little bit jealous, maybe?"

"At my age . . ."

Accepting with gratitude the reminder that the doddering old fellow's memory might be failing, Bannerman reeled off a list of Allbright's more imposing titles and honors. "As a purely hypothetical question . . ."

The record would also show that Bannerman's cross-examination began and ended with a hypothetical question, and that the witness won them both, hands down.

The first hypothetical question went like this: If a psychiatrist, otherwise unidentified but carrying those same commanding professional attainments, testified under oath that a murder for which there was otherwise no readily identifiable motive had, in fact, been committed under the compulsion of an irresistible impulse, would Dr. Swann be inclined to accept it?

"In this hypothetical question, have I examined the patient or not?"

"Let's say you haven't."

"Then I'd have to answer it this way—"

"No. Let's answer my way first. With a yes or a no. Then you can answer your way. Fair enough?"

"Fair enough." He nodded as if he were in complete agreement with him and went right on, doing it his way, to say that if a meteorologist who had every degree and award known to the world of meteorology, and a Nobel Prize thrown in for good luck, had studied his charts and come up with the conclusion that it was a warm and sunny day outside, he would be absolutely inclined to take his word for it. "But," he said, holding up a finger, "if I happened to take a look out the window and saw that it was raining, I'd be even more inclined to believe what my own eyes told me. So the answer to your hypothetical question, I guess, is that I'd bow to the authority of those professional attainments but I wouldn't go out without a raincoat."

Ambose was so elated that he took a big hitch on his belt and hooted, "That was an awful big cloud you whipped up there, Bannerman, for such an itty-bitty fall of rain."

Ignoring the laughter, Bannerman reminded the witness that it wasn't rain, or the harbinger thereof, that he had asked about. "Do you think there's such a thing as a motiveless murder?"

"I think there's such a thing as a murder where we haven't been able to discover the motive."

Bannerman was willing to accept that. "Do you think there's such a thing as an irresistible impulse?"

"I think there's such a thing as an impulse. I also think there are impulses that are not resisted. People steal penny candy all the time. They do it because they have a sweet tooth and they think they can get away with it."

Without looking at Halpern, Bannerman snapped his fingers and asked for the transcript of the hearing. "And you can tell whether he's sane or insane just by talking to him." He held up the transcript, daring him to deny it. "Just by conversation, isn't that what you told us?"

That's what he had told him, right enough. "If he can talk to me in a reasonable, rational manner, I say he has no mental illness. If he says he's Richard the Lionhearted and orders me to go saddle up his horse, I'd want to dig a little deeper into the possibility that he'd lost touch with reality before I went around looking for any stables." That was one place where he wanted Bannerman to know he was in complete and total agreement with Allbright.

The laughter from the audience came easily, for by this time they were cued in perfectly to the unfailing rhythm of the scientifically precise answer followed by a delightfully roguish or—depending on which side you were rooting for—overly flippant commentary. Bannerman didn't mind. A little farther up the trail he was waiting to ambush him with a question that bristled in his mind's eye like a spear held at point in his hand. The cockier the old coot showed himself to be, the deeper, Bannerman was sure, he was going to impale himself upon it.

The pattern continued to hold, after Bannerman asked, with lordly disdain, whether in view of the "lordly skepticism" Dr. Swann had displayed on direct examination he was willing to accept the fact that a mental illness known as chronic undifferentiated schizophrenia did, in fact, exist. Doc raised a few eyebrows by answering that it was immaterial whether he accepted it or not. "A man who is disoriented is disoriented. If you want to call it schizophrenia or tic-tac-toe or a bag-of-beans, those are words, they're marks on a piece of paper. If he's disoriented, that's a fact. You don't have to be a psychiatrist to see it, and you don't have to give it a fancy name."

It was quick-decision time for Norman Bannerman. The examination took its first sharp turn while Bannerman, having opted to pin the old coot down to as many of these wayward opinions as possible, was trying to get him to make some kind of distinction between the assassination of a Chief Justice and a common, ordinary, run-of-the-mill murder that might take place, say, during the holdup of that confectionary store that suffered such severe and steady losses from petty pilferage. Swann made it explicit that the only distinction he was interested in drawing was the one between the mentally ill and the mentally disturbed. Categorically, he was willing to state that all murderers were mentally disturbed. "They're angry and frustrated and distraught, or they wouldn't have done it. I don't even have to have a conversation with them to know that. Happy people just don't go around killing other people. It could ruin the rest of their day." He also wanted to say that he didn't think unhappiness removed the responsibility for murder, a wholly gratuitous observation that Bannerman, with his constitutional inability to resist an opportunity to show off his medical knowledge, expanded into a learned discussion as to whether the degree of unhappiness didn't have to be taken into consideration, also. Specifically, whether unhappiness didn't merge into depression, and depression into melancholia, which was a recognized mental disease.

"Now you've got it," Swann beamed, welcoming him aboard. People could indeed become so unhappy that they became disoriented, ceased to function effectively and withdrew from life—although the final descent, he advised him, wasn't melancholia but a form of catalepsy in which they ceased to function so completely that they ceased, to all intents and purposes, to exist. He was able to advise him further that nonfunctioning people had an identifiable characteristic that made it easy for an expert like him to spot them after all his years in the field. "They don't function," he said triumphantly. "In other words, they don't get up every morning and go to work for seventeen years and, one fine day, go out and shoot themselves a Chief Justice for dinner. That just ain't the way it works."

"Let's see how it does work." Flashing his teeth and ring and dimple as he ticked each item off on his fingers, he forced Swann to admit that he had never come across a case before where: (1) the murderous impulse had not been resisted; (2) he had been unable to discover a motive; (3) the murderer, had he been in full control of his faculties, could reasonably have expected to have been killed.

"Thank you, Doctor," he said with the solid satisfaction of a man who was finally getting somewhere. "What you are saying is that you don't have the foggiest notion why this murder was committed but you are going to refute the explanation put forth by the glittering array of defense experts, including even Lionel Allbright, because that's what the state is paying you to do. I'm sure Mr. Ambose is very, very proud of you."

"What I am saying is that man is an instinctive murderer. It's part of the legacy, it comes with the blood." His look was rancid. "The murderous impulse. Remember?"

But Bannerman had already lost interest and was rustling aimlessly through the papers in front of him. Even as he was asking Doc if it wasn't true that in his work with disturbed children at the juvenile home he was always faced with the limiting factors imposed upon the children's personalities by their early environment, he had opened his briefcase and was alternately peering in and fishing around. Absently, almost mindlessly, he asked, "Did you have an incident at your home yesterday where two of the children placed in your charge went after each other with knives?"

It had come at him so unexpectedly, so casually, and from out of such a harmless-looking box that . . .

Stricken, Swann didn't move. His mouth kept opening, and every time it did his tongue bulged out to fill the opening, leaving you with the weirdest impression from out in front that he was working a wad of bubblegum. When at last his vision cleared, he saw that Bannerman was holding up an affidavit. "If it will refresh your recollection, Doctor," Bannerman said, "I have a witness whom I can summon to the stand."

Doc continued to stare at him wordlessly through a wall of resistance. The craziest thought came into his head: *He had used "whom" correctly in ordinary conversation. There weren't many people who did that anymore.*

He was only dimly aware that Ambose had set up a small diversionary flurry by demanding that this purely irrelevant matter, having nothing to do with the lawsuit or issue at hand, be stricken from the record. The question wasn't at all irrelevant, said Bannerman. It went directly to the witness's credibility. "My witness is right here in the courtroom. I ask you again, Doctor . . ."

On the witness stand the tongue came into view. Not looking at him, and in a faraway voice, Doc affirmed that the incident he had spoken of had taken place.

That was plenty good enough for Bannerman. Now that he had the dotty old coot ready for a fall, he would have to be particularly careful not to cast him as the mangy little homegrown Jehovah of troubled and troublesome kids being pitted against the much-honored, world-famous psychiatrist and the golden-throated, world-famous lawyer. "Yes," he said, assuming a posture of exquisite and delicate fair-mindedness, "I see what confused you." More accurately put, only one of the boys had used a knife. The other had used a sharpened beer-can opener.

Bannerman put the question to him directly. "In your opinion, sir, did either of the parties to the outbreak of violence that erupted on the second floor of the Number One Barracks late yesterday morning have it within his power to control or limit his action?"

There was a scrubby, stunted look about Doc as he sat there pondering the carrot that had been dangled in front of him. And also the stick. Bannerman had shown him that he was in a position to let the whole city know that a black boy and a white boy entrusted to his care had sliced each other into ribbons.

The tongue. Like bubblegum. Mechanically and tonelessly, he said, "In troubled children the controls are notoriously tenuous. In adults controls are assumed. Otherwise, you don't have a civilization."

He would give him nothing!

"Excuse me." Bannerman had to ask whether he was saying he didn't believe adults had irresistible impulses or he didn't believe they were entitled to have them, and when Swann answered that he did not believe a society could exist that told men they would not be held accountable for what they did, Bannerman could only wonder if they were talking about the same thing. "I submit to you, sir, that the liberating concept of the twentieth century is that a person who is so mentally disturbed that he is unable to fully understand the difference between right and wrong is not to be held legally responsible for his acts."

520

Life came drifting back into Doc's eyes, as he was making it plain that he considered that to be the most dastardly and illiberal development in the history of law and medicine. "We are all responsible for what we do. Yes, I do believe that. That is the hellish burden a man must bear, and it is that burden, sir, I submit back to you, which is the civilizing influence and the liberating concept." He paused. "I have great sympathy for Mr. Tabor. I think he is a troubled and damaged man. Less than some. More than most. But he knew what he was doing when he did it. He knew it was wrong. To say that some life-pattern renders him nonresponsible degrades him. You do him no honor with such a defense, Bannerman. You degrade him." His eyes flashed. "You degraded yourself by placing a spy in my home. In my midst."

Decision time again. Bannerman hesitated for only a moment. "More than the electric chair would degrade him, I assume you mean."

"Yes!" He flung the word out at him recklessly. Yes! Better to walk to the electric chair as a man. Better even that than to renounce your humanity. "I sympathize with you, Bannerman, because you have been cut loose from the responsibility for what you do." He was seated more erect in the witness stand. His voice had taken on a hiss. "You have been turned into a moral eunuch, and I'm not the one to say it's entirely your fault. The society which sets you to the task and grants you the immunity is partner to your corruption. You undergo a frontal lobotomy in law school."

Above him the gavel banged. Behind the gavel an unexpectedly severe voice warned him that it would tolerate no more of that kind of talk.

"No, do go on," Bannerman urged. "I don't often have the enlightening experience of meeting a psychiatrist who finds the tools of his own profession so devoid of merit as to urge the superior therapeutic and rehabilitative benefits to be derived from a short squat in the electric chair." Or perhaps, he said, finding a place at last to bounce a carom shot off Doc's "queer duck" answer, the good doctor's budding interest in ornithology had usurped the function of the psychiatrist.

Too readily Doc agreed that he didn't often see eye to eye with his colleagues. "It doesn't make for a life of uninterrupted frivolity," he said, not unproudly. "But I watch my step at all times. The trick is to proceed with caution and duck for cover whenever you hear a 'peer group' or 'usurped function' come flying at you."

Not that it mattered but the "duck for cover" had been a purely accidental pun. Doc wouldn't have paid any attention to the laughter, in any case. Having satisfied the basic requirement of courtroom etiquette by answering the question, he was already turning to the more important matter of meting out a public tongue-lashing to that insufferable popinjay, that primping, prancing fop who had the audacity to think—who probably didn't have to think twice about it—that the commission he had been given to defend the legal rights of one man had given him the right to plant a spy on another. *On him.* His bones ground together every time he thought about it. Like a thief leaving his shadow and smell in your home. Whisking your privacy away. He'd sent him a spy. To smile at him every morning, to win the affection of his boys, while all the time she had been . . .

Meanly, spitefully, he said, "I'm sorry for you, Bannerman, I truly, truly am, because after the original choice you had no choice. To blame society is no good, you know. It is you who bears the stain. To be a human being and a free man is to accept individual responsibility. You, as much as your client. You, even more than your client."

Really out of countenance now—judging from his florid face alone he had never been this angry—Judge Davies rose up on the bench, fully prepared, as everybody in the courtroom could see, to make the witness feel his terrible wrath. But as Harry Davies glared down at his old friend Lennard, he saw such anguish in him that he could not bring himself to go any further than to warn him that . . . well, that this was the last time he was going to warn him.

Bannerman could. Easy. "You'd put a crazy man to death!" he shouted, springing to his feet. His arm shot straight out, and his finger was pointing dead-center. "You'd kill a lunatic!" he roared, as if it was beyond all belief that such a man could call himself a psychiatrist, and when Doc growled back that he'd better hold onto his hat because an even choicer blasphemy was coming, the most spirited exchange of the morning was under way.

"Given any choice at all," Doc said, blaspheming grandly, "I, for one, would infinitely prefer to put an insane man to death than a sane one." When he added, with sudden thoughtfulness, that he couldn't imagine anyone in his right mind who wouldn't, Bannerman went scooting backward, chair and all, and all that ever need be said about the personal magnetism Bannerman was able to project when he put his mind to it is that you somehow had the feeling that the better instincts of all mankind were riding with him.

"That frightens the beejeebers out of me," he gasped. As in faultless proof of his fright—or possibly to remove any doubt as to where his beejeebers lay—his hand clutched frantically at his heart. Could it be possible, he croaked, that Dr. Swann didn't understand how close to euthanasia he was getting there?

"I thought that was going to get you to sparking all over the place," Doc sniffed. Not to let Bannerman get too much mileage out of that euthanasia stuff, though, he took care to point out a few minutes later that he had only been batting back a philosophical observation on health versus illness, not putting any bills into the legislative hopper. Not to sound too apologetic about it, either, he doubled back and picked up the topic closest to his heart. Responsibility. First, the criminal's and then, needless to say, the lawyer's. "You are responsible for every guilty man you send back out to bloody up the streets," he informed Bannerman smartly. "For the perversion of truth that set him free in the first instance, and for every crime he commits thereafter."

As it happened, Bannerman was every bit as anxious to remind Doc Swann that it was Sam Tabor's responsibility that was at issue and, of far vaster importance at this trembling moment of history, Dr. Lennard Swann's responsibility to assess it with reasonable regard for the standards and criteria that were accepted as the norm. "As much as it seems to distress you," Bannerman said, going right to work on him, "we do have to work within the limits of vocabulary, Doctor, and . . ."

The wheel had finally come around full circle to the question that had been pushed aside back there in the early smelling-out phase of the cross-examination. Bannerman had been trying to steer the interrogation back onto that track from the time it became evident that the failure of the ambush had—as so frequently happened when these well-laid plans misfired—put him in a new and better ball game. Instead of traumatizing the old man as Bannerman had planned, the ambush had raised his hackles. (The old buzzard did have a categorical gaminess about him that Bannerman had to admire; you had only to look at him to see he was one of those nuts who went stalking through life angry at the world.) The new game, then, was to give Swann all the room he needed to carry his disregard for psychiatry and psychiatrists far enough and deep enough to discredit his entire testimony. And if, perchance, Bannerman's guardian angel happened to be on the job, ready to snatch his feet from the fire one more time, the old coot just might be driven far enough off his rocker for Norman Bannerman, that little old magician, to pull off yet another courtroom miracle. In what other courtroom, in what other trial, had an expert witness ever accepted an invitation to impeach himself for professional heresy?

Knowing how eagerly Bannerman plunged into the question, who would have believed that the crazy old buzzard would whisk it cleanly out of his hands—Houdini couldn't have done any better—and, speaking of magicians, turned it into something else that had never before been seen in an American courtroom.

The question, as Bannerman had finished putting it to Swann, went: "We can only seek the testimony and opinions of respected and qualified psychiatrists. And vocabulary being all we have, they can only define for us the harvest of their own and the communal storehouse of experience." Oh, it was easy enough to mount one's disapproval and call a plague down on the whole house, he said, laying it right in his lap. But could Dr. Swann suggest any better way of helping a jury to reach a just and reasoned determination on the state of mind of the accused?

"Sure. Put him on the stand and let the jury have a look at him."

Bannerman-watchers were fond of boasting that given a minimum amount of encouragement, nobody—but nobody—could be more scandalized in a courtroom than Norman Bannerman. Ten thousand times Norman Bannerman had risen to shake his locks and shiver his timbers and cry out in a voice that rang through the air with the purity of a Chinese gong, "I am scandalized, sir! Scandalized and shocked . . ." For the first time in his life Bannerman was authentically scandalized in a courtroom, and it was an experience he found so unsettling that it never occurred to him to tell anybody about it. "You don't believe in the Fifth Amendment?" he asked in a rising crescendo of disbelief. "You don't believe in the Bill of Rights? *You don't believe in the Constitution of the United States?*"

"*Believe* in them? I didn't know they were holy documents. You asked me what's the best way for a jury to find out if a man is crazy, disoriented or whatever you want to call it. I can't think of a worse way than to get a couple of psychiatrists to parade their vocabularies back and forth while the only man who really knows what happened sits there and isn't allowed to tell the jury a thing. That's all."

He was asking the question now, then, Bannerman told him. "You don't believe in affording every American citizen the shelter of the Fifth Amendment?"

In rapid succession Pawley (unable to contain himself any longer) rose to state that he had been practicing law for twelve years in the happy confidence that the Bill of Rights was well settled in the law, and that if he had been living in a fool's paradise, it was not, in any event, a question germane to the issue at bar and that, the witness not being a legal scholar, his opinion on such matters was neither competent nor relevant; Ambose came rising right behind him to announce that while the state did want to have the witness's lack of legal training placed into the record, it had no objection to his answering legal questions if he wanted to help Bannerman out; and Bannerman extended his hand toward the witness stand, as if he were saying, *It's your move, Doc.*

Lennard Swann was willing, and the result was a lively exchange between himself and Bannerman, and a brief, decisive one between Ambose and Pawley.

"If you really want to know what I think," Doc said, "I think it's a lot of damn nonsense."

"Oh, you do? You believe your wisdom to be superior to that of the founding fathers and to the best legal minds of the time?" He pulled the corners of his lips down in a kind of rueful consideration of such incredible but, considering the source, not really *surprising* news. "You've already told us you believe it to be superior to the best medical minds."

Swann told him not to bring the founding fathers into it. "The founding fathers wouldn't recognize the Fifth Amendment, such as it is today, if they were hand-cuffed to it. On the other, that was about my superior wisdom, wasn't it? Yeah." His eyes opened wide. He had said he thought it was nonsense, and since only fools could believe in nonsense and he didn't consider himself a fool, of course he believed that his wisdom was superior to the best legal minds of the time. "Assuming," he said, "that any of them really believe it, which of course, they don't."

"He's making him out a crackpot," Pawley groaned. "Come on, Jim. We'd better start building a fence around him."

Ambose looked him squarely in the eye. Finally. "Sit down," he said. "I want to hear what the funny little man's got to say."

Not any more than Bannerman did. "If you are telling me, having read my mind, that I don't believe in our legal system, I will have to tell you that you are wrong. Perhaps not for the first time this morning."

"As a courtroom technique. As an aid to the defense. But as a means of separating actual innocence, meaning he didn't do it, from actual guilt . . ." He pulled his head back and sent him a sidelong *who's kidding who here* look. "You know better than that. It's a protection for the defendant, you've already said that. A shelter. At no time is it aimed at finding the truth. Or looking too hard for it. Or at it. It's a way of averting one's eyes." Not averting his own eyes, his look turned scornful. "Our legal system," he jeered. "It's aimed at putting as many obstacles as the minds of clever lawyers can conceive in the way of the state. Weak laws, weakly enforced, you make your living that way, Bannerman. Weak laws, weakly enforced," he repeated, more slowly and emphatically. "You make your living that way, Bannerman." And by the weight of the repetition alone, he was setting forth what a vile and uncivilized way it was, to his way of thinking, of making it.

How the jury was taking all of this Bannerman had no way of telling. Every jury eventually found its personality, and this one had the personality of a cold fish. They had warmed to Swann on direct. Like a miser having spent too freely of his affections, they had put it all back into the vault.

And right there, Bannerman could tell himself wryly, was where he and they parted company. Bannerman, who hoarded nothing, was brushing the sides of his hair back briskly to hide how chagrined he was. He still didn't know how he had let the thing deteriorate into a haggle on the law, but to get into a haggle on the law and lose . . . ? Courtroom miracle, huh? In what other courtroom, in what other trial, had an expert witness ever psychoanalyzed the law instead of the defendant?

Didn't the old buzzard know that it was psychiatry Bannerman wanted him to psychoanalyze, not the law?

In his second crack at it Bannerman set out to lash him to the mast right away by asking straight out whether he did or did not believe that such a thing as mental disease existed, and though it seemed for awhile that he was going to get another of those "yes and no" answers, by the time the answer was completed, Doc had given him just what he was looking for. What his answer came around to was this: If Bannerman was asking whether a direct parallel could be sustained between a disease of the body and what was sometimes referred to as a mental disease, the answer was a flat and unqualified no. If it was something else he meant —a figure of speech, a metaphor—then yes, Swann would be willing to accept that for what it was worth, and you could see that he didn't think it was worth anything.

"I mean disease," Bannerman shouted. "D-I-S-E-A-S-E. Disease."

Then where was the etiology? Swann shouted back. And where were the symptoms? Was the patient running a temperature? Were there any bones that could be set? Any germs or cells to be studied under a microscope? Bacteria to be sliced and stained and classified? He challenged Bannerman to cite a single identifiable characteristic that, if isolated, would stand as an absolute proof that any disease, let alone the indicated disease, existed. No, the best they could come up with, Doc said, answering his own question, was to take a set of reasonably similar symptoms, isolate those that formed a recognizable pattern, call it a syndrome and announce the next time they spotted a similar pattern that they had reproduced the syndrome in accordance with the best traditions of the scientific method. If they were suckers enough to fall for it, he told the jury— and why shouldn't they, what did they know about it?—they'd believe it. "But between you and me and the lamp post"—without any warning his head snapped around to Bannerman—"and you know the symbolism of a lamp post, Mr. Bannerman, it just ain't so."

It was one of those rare occasions when the witness and the lawyer were equally pleased with themselves. "Hand me my sand-wedge, Harold," Bannerman said in a loud stage whisper. "I'm going right for the pin."

The question was whether it was possible, in Dr. Swann's opinion, for any psychiatrist to have a valid opinion on whether any patient suffered or had suffered from what was known, in accepted medical and legal terminology, as a mental disease.

Pawley sat back and clasped his hands behind his neck. That was the question he had known Bannerman was going for, and there were so many traps bristling around it that it almost didn't matter whether Doc answered yes or no.

Doc handled it, almost without breaking stride, by taking a giant step backward. Sniffing the air, he looked Bannerman shamelessly in the eye and agreed with him that unless the patient was—as he had said—disoriented, they were most certainly dealing in opinion. "That's what I've been saying all along. You might call it a valid opinion, and I might call it an educated guess and the other fellow might call it a stab in the dark. But you're absolutely right, Mr. Bannerman, any competent psychiatrist can take a stab at it."

Forced to take a giant step backward himself, Bannerman adopted his best sneer and swagger and put in the form of a question, for the edification of the jury, what he had been hoping to prove through the witness's answers. "I will now put this question to you directly, sir. Do you believe that holding the heretical views you have been giving voice to all morning—and you have been delightfully unreticent in confessing how far you have removed yourself from the mainstream of thought in your profession . . . ." He cleared his throat decorously. ". . . Up to now. Do you believe that you are willing or able or capable or qualified or disposed to or of an equitable frame of mind to answer the right-or-wrong question, in all due conscience, sir, according to the high standards of objectivity to which this Court, this jury and this defendant are entitled?"

"Why, sure," Doc said. "I can take as good a stab as anyone else."

"Take a stab at this then!" Bannerman roared, and, rocking on his heels, he reeled off a hypothetical question that ran trippingly off his tongue for nine full minutes by the clock and summed up all the facts of the murder as seen by the defense. "Assuming all this to be true," he said when he had finished, "would you rule out the possibility of irresistible impulse?"

Doc told him that was like drawing an elephant on the blackboard and asking him whether he'd rule out the possibility that it was an elephant. "Well, a drawing of an elephant isn't an elephant, it's a representation of an elephant. Any *school* child can do it." Bannerman had drawn a very respectable representation of irresistible impulse, Doc told him generously. "If your facts had been true, so would have been your conclusion."

That was what Bannerman had been waiting for, and the questions came popping out of him in rapid succession. "Are you denying that he had the gun by sheer accident? Are you denying that he got to the scene on time by sheer accident? Are you denying that he had never met or seen the Chief Justice before? Are you denying that it could not have been planned?"

"You say planned, Mr. Bannerman . . ."

"Yes, I did." Pouncing on this unexpected chance to pin him down. "Are you saying that it was?"

Lennard Swann scratched the side of his nose. His tongue appeared between his lips. The courtroom waited expectantly. To judge from Bannerman's alert and pressing stance he thought he had the witness on the run. He couldn't have been more wrong. Doc had ducked the chance of answering that question once before, because he had a theory that he was sure would be so persuasive to a jury that he would be driving the last nail into Sam's coffin. Doc Swann had played the game of experts often enough to know it for the game of bay and honk it was, but he flattered himself that he played it on his own terms. His game was knocking down the other side's fanciful baying, not honking out equally fanciful, and just as unprovable, theories of his own. On the other hand . . . to duck it again would be taken as more backwatering and an invitation for Bannerman to press him further.

He sat there scratching his chin and asking himself whether he really hated Bannerman so much that he'd be willing to drive the last nail into that poor slob Tabor's coffin.

"Have you ever played stud poker, Mr. Bannerman?" he asked. Well, with a good stud poker player, there came a time when he saw something developing. "You have a jack of hearts in the hole and an ace of hearts showing, and one of the other players has a king showing, and he raises, so you know he has kings back to back, and you raise him right back because you have the feeling that it would be a very good idea to have him think you have aces." On the third card the queen of hearts falls to you, and now you are sure of it. You know you have a situation developing where you are going to improve your hand all the way, and the other guy is going to improve his, too, and it doesn't much matter much how because you know in your bones that you are going to draw whatever you have to. A straight or a flush if that will do for you, or if the other guy fills up or even better, draws four of a kind, a straight flush. Whatever you need, that's what you are going to get, and all the time you are betting as if you have the aces wired so that when you push all your chips into the pot at the end, he is going to have to go all the way with you, and more, because he knows you have to be bluffing.

"I think Sam Tabor, knowing he had a gun, saw the situation developing, not even thinking about it that consciously, where he was going to get the chance to kill the Chief Justice under circumstances that would have to look unplanned and unpremeditated, and he rode along with it—he's a passive man, Bannerman, he goes where the wind blows him—until seeing the Chief Justice standing there, and himself with a clear, open shot—just like he'd known it was going to be—he made his final big bet and pulled out his gun and fired."

"In your opinion, he was just playing a little game of stud poker?"

"I was drawing an analogy. A-N-A-L-O-G-Y."

"Do you know, to your own knowledge, whether Sam plays stud poker, had ever played stud poker or even knows how stud poker is played?"

"I'll try it again. A-N-A-L-O-G-Y. Analogy."

The jury was impassive. Stolid. Inscrutable.

"And the winning pot is the electric chair?"

Up on the witness stand Doc shook his head. Slowly. Like he *knew.* So sure of himself that you could damn near see the interior smile.

The air-conditioning unit could be heard humming. The clock could be heard ticking.

"The winning pot was having it work out as he had imagined it was going to work out. The winning pot is the trial. The winning pot is his name and picture in the papers. The winning pot is you there, and me here, and the jury over there." His expansive gesture embraced the whole courtroom. "This is the winning pot. It's all of us gathered here saying, *Look what Sam done.*"

"And wouldn't that be irresistible impulse? Wouldn't that be the act of an automaton—no, let me finish the question, I want you to listen to me—wouldn't that be the act of an automaton swept up in a drama that had taken possession of him and overcome his will to resist?"

"No more than anybody else who takes a gun and goes out and kills somebody."

"I put it to you fairly, Doctor. Listen to me. Isn't one an act of premeditation and the other an act of fate, of chance, which by your own dramatic reconstruction . . . You said it yourself—listen to me—*Just . . . like . . . he'd . . . known . . . it . . . was . . . going . . . to . . . be.* I put it to you, Doctor. Haven't you drawn us the picture of a man caught up in the sweep of an inevitability so terrible and awesome as to constitute an invasion upon his total being and a preemption of rational control?"

"I wouldn't say that at all. I would say that it was a particular kind of premeditation more closely comparable to a thrill killing."

Right there he could see the wind go out of Bannerman's sails. Blanked and deflated, he sat down. Absently, he examined his ring. And then Norman Bannerman said another of those strange and inexplicable things that dotted the entire trial. "Tell me, Doctor," he asked plaintively, "do you think we're all going to end up psychotic from that air conditioning?"

Across the way Jim Ambose was exultant. Thrill killing! Why hadn't he thought of that himself? That was the bulletin that would soon be flashing across the entire country: TABOR A "THRILL KILLER" PSYCHIATRIST SAYS.

"Shall we take a break here?" Ambose suggested in the hope of getting all those typewriters and telegraph lines singing right away. "Or is Mr. Bannerman about to wrap up his examination?"

Mr. Bannerman stated that he had many, many more questions to ask this witness. Plenty more. And that he would vigorously protest any interruption. He didn't have many questions left, though, and none of any importance. A few more faltering, dispirited minutes on both sides, and it was over.

Ambose was content to leave it right there. "No questions," he said.

As part of the agreement to cut short the previous day's session with the nonappearance of Dr. Swann, the state had agreed to permit Bannerman to put Mrs. Tabor on the witness stand for the limited purposes of qualifying the second-degree and manslaughter pleas, whenever she was available, in turn or out. Cowhig had come into the courtroom during the early part of Swann's cross-examination and passed Halpern a note saying that he had her outside.

Vera Tabor looked older. She wore a wide-brimmed black hat to shade her eyes from the spectators while she was testifying and carried a small and dainty handkerchief, holding it genteelly at the corners with one or both hands until it became necessary for her to use it, and then folding it neatly over twice and touching it lightly to each nostril. Before every answer she took a long, deep breath. In the short time she was on the stand the Court had to instruct her to speak up three separate times.

The violation that had been done them in exposing their private life to the world was there for anybody to see. Never once did they look at each other. She stared straight ahead, he stared straight ahead.

After she had answered the technical legal questions she had been put there to answer, she testified that Sam had never struck her, that he had enjoyed his work, was a good provider, contributed to the Community Chest and—Halpern had to wonder whether this last was true—that he tithed regularly to the Children of the Redeemer.

Not looking at her, Sam was aware of nobody else. Erect in his chair, staring straight ahead, he heard every word she spoke, and her voice had become a conduit to her body and her rhythm. For one last time, he would allow himself to taste the biscuity odor she had brought to his kitchen and the musky odor she had brought to his bed. For one last time, the damp tropical heat, the swamp, the rolling underbelly. For one last time, her warmth and nourishment. (He had been warped and havocked. Mischiefed and havocked. Wreathed and havocked. But if he did not look at her, he would hold her safe. If he pretended that they did not know each other so very well, they could not blame her, and he would have fooled them again. He was too smart for them. None of them knew that beneath the sheath of skin, behind the battlements, he saw every move they made, read every thought.)

Ambose asked a couple of meaningless questions, thanked her politely and hurried out of the courtroom.

Mrs. Tabor started to leave, too.

She was a couple of steps from the witness stand when Bannerman, who had been watching Ambose's exit, asked her if she would wait another minute while he was deciding whether to ask another question. Utterly confused, she remained where she was, directly in front of the Bench, waiting to be told whether he wanted her back on the stand. It was as if an unseen director had suddenly taken over to bring the scene into sharper focus. That touch of having her stand there, that final indignity . . . wow, there was the touch of the master. *There is no escape,* it said. *There is no place to hide.*

For in facing Bannerman at that flat an angle, she was, by necessity, also facing Sam.

In one stricken moment it was all there for everybody to see. The doomed man and the rapidly aging woman who had once meant a great deal to each other.

One stricken moment, and then Sam turned to wax. Halpern saw it happen before his eyes; the final enmeshing of that protective fiber that had began to form with Hilliard Nevins' so casual announcement so long ago that it was the state's purpose—and his—to put Sam to death.

All Bannerman asked her in the end was whether she was familiar with the many brain injuries Sam had suffered in his youth. "That's it for us," he sang out, when Pawley's objection was sustained. "We'll just turn it back to the state before we make a determination of whether to rest our case."

In the next few seconds, a succession of small things took place, all minor, all connected, that sent Halpern running out to the street. As Davies was turning to Pawley, Mrs. Tabor paused at the door to see whether Cowhig was following behind to escort her home. Bannerman made a motion for Cowhig to stay where he was, and Halpern, looking to Cowhig for the same reason, saw it. While all those looks were being exchanged at the defense table, Pawley asked, uncertainly, for a brief recess in order that he might confer with his associate, Mr. Ambose. Looking to the door, along with everybody else, to see whether Ambose was on his way back, Halpern could see a photographer come leaping into the foyer in one orangutan bound and sight his camera on Mrs. Tabor. A blink of the eye, and three other photographers had come in behind the first, hemming her in. Surrounding her.

All Mrs. Tabor had to do, of course, was to permit them to take their pictures and go their way. But Vera Tabor was in an emotional turmoil. She did the least wise thing she could have done. She panicked, and ran.

Halpern flung one look at Cowhig, and hurried out of the courtroom and on through the foyer in time to see her disappearing down the stairs, followed by a clutch of photographers and reporters. He'd have probably been able to get to her earlier, in the lobby at the worst, except that Jim Ambose had him by the arm and was telling him all in a jumble that he wanted him to meet somebody.

He'd have still got to her earlier, after he had disengaged himself from Ambose, if he hadn't felt it necessary to stop at the first landing to tell Rich Caples what he thought of him: "You didn't *have* to do that," he snarled at him. "What did you do, see it in a movie somewhere that you're supposed to do things like that?"

Caples, who had stopped to jot down some notes, looked up from his notebook, surprised. "You know it and I know it. But my editors don't know it. They've been screaming for a take on her all morning."

As he raced on down the stairs, feeling foolish but taking them two at a time, he heard Caples shout after him, "Hey, I said it was my job, I didn't say I liked it. Bannerman double-crossed us . . ."

Once he was down in the lobby he didn't feel at all foolish. Two photographers had preceded her through the revolving doors to get the conventional frontal shot of her coming down the courthouse stairs, and when they continued to circle around her after she had reached the sidewalk, she panicked completely and began to run down the street. By the time Hal caught up to her she was running blindly, all out of breath and wobbling dangerously on her high heels.

"It's all right," he said. "It's all right. I only want to get you a cab. Come on, now. It's going to be all right."

The elevator opened and there in front of him was Julie Elkins.

The man and woman who had been in the elevator with her had to push around him, one on either side, each with an automatic dirty look which became, as their eyes wavered back and forth between him and Julie, an automatically knowing one.

Hal remained right where he was, in front of the open elevator, transfixed by the warmth of the affection he felt toward her. Julie slipped off to the side, away from the traffic, and leaned back against the glazed stone wall between the elevators.

The elevator doors slid shut.

"Does it go well?" she asked him in her low, throaty voice. She was looking at him the same way he was looking at her. A tenderness but with the quills out. It was look but don't touch. Remember and don't spoil. Both of them knowing that by the luck of this accidental meeting they were going to remember each other always in a way they hadn't known until this moment they wanted to.

"I looked for you," he said. "In the courtroom."

"I stayed away."

"I noticed."

Green and deep were the color of her eyes. "I did get called back, you know. That much of it was true."

"I know you did. By telegram." His lips pushed out ruefully. Hers, too. Both of them coming close to laughter at such a shameless confession that he had checked.

"Don't worry, I've had my spies out. I know how well you're doing. Clear brilliant."

If he had ever doubted how she felt about him—and he had—the pride that glowed in her in this moment was enough to dispel it forever.

Saying nothing, he studied her from a succession of slightly different angles, his head moving this way and that so that he could catch her in every dimension; remembering everything about her as she had been in Cumberland—the bad as well as the good—even while he was imprinting her into his mind, indelibly, as she was now. He would always remember her with a mosquito bite at the upper right-hand corner of her lips. And with the tip of her tongue—just the tip—showing between her lips.

"You're lucky, you know," Julie said in her low, shivery voice.

"Boy, am I lucky."

"Bad News Julie, that's what I'm known as. All the way home."

"Bad News Julie."

She had that way of sucking in on her lower lip. "You've got a lucky wife, does she know that? She'd better." The mischievous eddies were playing around in the depths of her eyes. "You know what I'm going to do for you, I'm such a good kid? To make sure you're appreciated at home, I'm going to call her up and give it to her straight, woman-to-woman. I'll say, 'Hey, the present Mrs. Harold Halpern, I just happened to be passing through, and I'm going to slip you the glad word. That husband of yours, he sure knows how to deliver the lightning.' "

They smiled at each other, both of them happier than they could have dreamed they'd be at the discovery that they felt such an affection for each other.

The elevator on the other side of Julie was emptying, and a trill of artificial feminine laughter floated around the outer edges of their ambit. A large man hurrying toward the elevator from the other direction stopped long enough to ask whether either of them could tell him where the Tabor trial was being held.

Neither of them looked at him. "Third floor," Hal said. "Judge Davies' court."

The elevator doors closed immediately behind him. "I wonder what he thinks that line is for?" Hal said.

"He thinks they're waiting for the ball game to start. Somebody should tell him."

Hal's hands didn't move from his side, but he might as well have reached up and touched her on the cheek. "Pretty girl."

She looked at him from way down under. Shyly. "Have I still got a friend in Lowell?"

"You've got a friend in Lowell. Always."

"That's a very nice thing to know. You don't know how nice a thing that's going to be to know when the dog nights come and nobody in their right mind will put up with me." That was all. With a self-conscious little laugh that was like a sleepy poodle giving itself a tiny shake, she brought the mood right back to where it had been. "You will always be my rising young barrister," she said. "Rise, young barrister."

In much the same way as he had imprinted her image in his mind, she took her own last long look at him. "Not that I'll ever think of you," she said, looking. "The memory has already grown dim. What did you say your name was again?" Turning abruptly, she took the elbow of a bewildered old gentleman who was waiting for the elevator. "Sir," she said, bringing her warm, grave gaze back to Hal, "this young man keeps bothering me. You have been pointed out to me as a man of substance and no little influence. See if you can make him stop."

The way they were looking at each other was such a dead giveaway that the old gentleman suddenly looked about ten years younger himself. It didn't matter. He had already passed outside their ambit.

"Goodbye, pretty girl."

"Goodbye, Lightning."

Her heels sounded across the marble lobby floor like bullets. Click . . . click . . . click . . . and she was through the revolving door. As she neared the bottom of the stairs, her hand went shooting up to signal a cab, and from the narrow change in her direction Hal knew he'd only have to move back a step or two to watch her climb into the cab and disappear from his life. It didn't matter. He knew she wouldn't be looking back. "I'm a clear bitter broad," she had told him on the bad, bad night. "I never apologize, I never say thanks and I never, but never look back." But that was all right. By then, he understood.

It was hours before it came to him that Julie was the witness Bannerman had planted on Doc Swann. That was all right, too. She was an investigator. It was her job. She'd do anything for the Jolly Red, and Hal knew why. No matter how infuriated he might become at Bannerman, he would always remember that on a not so jolly night it had been Norman Bannerman who had saved Julie's life.

For an hour or so after the accidental meeting things were popping so fast around him that he didn't have time to think of anything.

The action began with Ambose grabbing Halpern in the corridor, at the top of the stairs, to tell him that Bannerman had been out there a few minutes ago looking around. And then he kind of had him by the elbow and was telling him to say hello to Otis Moscrip, who was a great admirer of Bannerman's. Moscrip turned out to be an ugly little guy sitting on the bench next to Jake Foxx and so uncomfortable in his new blue suit that he kept rubbing his hands across his lap as if he were trying to wipe out the creases. Asked whether he had enjoyed Bannerman's performance of the morning, the little man made a weak effort at an ingratiating smile. "Excep' I'm inna kinder blue momen' a my life adda presen' time," he told Hal.

"The thing is," Ambose said, "Otis would like to stick around to watch his idol in action, but he's got this train he's gotta catch, and he wants to be especially remembered to him. Isn't that right, Otis?"

It was. "I hadda broke pocket uptada presen' time, sir," he said with a kind of squinty, sidling-up look that gave Hal the damndest feeling that he was about to be hit for a touch. "I al'ays bina tough-luck guy."

"The way I heard it, Otis," Ambose said, "I was under the impression you were traveling for your health. To a climate more healthy for your lungs."

"It's my legs," Otis said mournfully. He stuck his sticks of legs straight out. "On accounta I do' wanna faw down widout any a my lungs and ge' me legs all broke up, Mr. Ambroze, if da's wha ya mean to say."

Just before they returned to the courtroom Ambose looked down at him, almost affectionately. "Hey, Halpern," he said, "you've come a long way. Sure could have fooled me." He considered him for a moment longer. "Look me up at the end of the day," he said. "I've got some information about a deal for Sam I think is going to interest you."

Ambose wasn't two steps into the courtroom before Judge Davies called him over to the bench where he was chewing the fat with Bannerman and Pawley. "It don't look good to let it get this sloppy here at the end," Harry whispered to him. "We're all agreed on that. So let's shit or get off the pot, huh?"

[Bench Conference: The Court inquired of Mr. Ambose whether the state wished to call another witness or rest its case. Mr. Ambose replied that he had just come into possession of information that had forced him to consider the advisability of calling one more witness and prayed the Court's indulgence.]

"Did you say something, Sam?"

Sam, seated in that odd sideways position of his, had seemed to be paying absolutely no attention when Hal told him he had put Mrs. Tabor in a cab. Although Hal felt a small tug at his elbow a few seconds later, Sam still wasn't looking at him. He thought he heard him whisper, "He's one of them."

Sam's eyes shifted warningly. To him and away. His mouth barely moving, he said, "D. B. He doesn't think I know." The eyes turned back toward him just enough so that Hal could see the grim warning look. The old sensation of grating bones, and when he smiled it was like splintered glass. And then Sam turned around in his chair and he was smiling broadly at his guards. "Dick Blasser's my friend, out of all of them."

"Sure, I am," Blasser said. "Better be good, Sam. The judge is looking this way."

The smile became crafty. "You too. You're OK, Okula." He jabbed his elbow surreptitiously into Halpern's side as if he had scored heavily.

"Come on," Okula growled. "Just knock it off, huh?"

When Bannerman returned from the bench his hand fell triumphantly upon Hal's shoulder. "I told you I am admired and respected in Chicago, my home-town." He drew out his gold watch. It was already half-past twelve. "While I do not mean to in any way disparage your efforts, in about thirty minutes I am going to give you the opportunity to make humble restitution for the insufficiency of faith which has on occasion been evidenced." His eyes were sparkling. There were promises of great happenings in the air.

"What the hell is all the waiting around for now?" was all Halpern said.

As soon as Ambose and Pawley were back at the prosecution table Pawley said, "I stretched it out with Colonel Chatnick for as long as I could. The jury was ready to throw rocks at me."

Mollineaux didn't think so. From the way Mollineaux began to praise what could only have been the most routine kind of examination, Ambose began to suspect that the news of Nevins' upcoming appointment and the resulting change in command was already getting around.

Pawley may have been wondering the same thing. "It's known as grace under pressure." He laughed. "I don't mind, Jim. Just let me know what I'm doing, that's all."

"It's known as stalling for time," Ambose said. For Mollineaux he had some very specific instructions. He was to go out to the foyer and wait for Harv Leigh to come back and give him the nod. At which point, he was to come back into the courtroom, station himself against the wall and keep his eyes open. "In due time I am going to rise and recite my eight or nine dirty little words. Whereupon, Norman Bannerman is going to turn all shades of green and, if it's my lucky day, grab at his heart and keel over. It's what is known as grace under pressure."

While Mollineaux was heading for the door, Pawley never took his eyes off Ambose. Neither of them said a word until Ambose asked him whether he hadn't even wondered just a little bit why Bannerman hadn't jumped to make the deal. "Some day, if you're real nice," he said, meaning never, "I'll tell you."

For perhaps twenty or thirty seconds after Mollineaux had stepped back into the courtroom Ambose continued to sit motionless, pretending to make notes. And yet, the change in him was so perceptible that Judge Davies was moved to say, "Well, Mr. Ambose, do you have any more witnesses or don't you? Do you want another recess or what? We're all at your disposal here."

Jim Ambose came very deliberately to his feet. He rubbed his chin, hard and reflectively. For the briefest of moments his smoky eyes moved toward Norman Bannerman. And then he ducked his head and dug his finger around the shell of his ear as if he were cleaning it out. "We have no more witnesses, Your Honor," he said. He looked up and raised his voice. "At this time, Your Honor, the state rests its case."

Harry Davies turned at once to Norman Bannerman and saw that the blood had drained from his face. With every eye in the courtroom on him, Bannerman's own eyes went to the door and beyond; he started to turn to Cowhig and then, thinking better of it, threw back his head almost—it seemed—as if he were laughing. "Your Honor," he said, "we have many, many motions." But before he made them, he felt it necessary to remind the Court that he had not yet rested his case. He looked at Ambose as if he were thinking about it. Not with any particular hostility, just thinking about it. Ambose, looking back, tilted his head toward the witness chair as if he could hardly wait. His lips formed a word that not even Pawley was able to make out. "The defense," said Bannerman, "has one more witness. At this time I call to the stand Assistant District Attorney James Ambose."

It was no good. The sense of the end of the affair was too much in the air for even Norman Bannerman to pump new life into it. Harry Davies took one brief look at Marie and shook his head, and although Bannerman complained that the refusal to allow the jury to hear Ambose "constituted an unprecedented shackling of the defense, amounting to juridical vasectomy," there was, as anybody could see, very little conviction in it.

Before retiring the jury to their chambers, Judge Daviès informed them that with the testimony now completed, they would be returning one final time to hear the summations and the final charge of the Court. Whether that would be later that day or early Friday, he said, frowning at the clock, would depend upon the speed with which the Court and the attorneys were able to settle the mechanics of the thing. "Which is nothing for you to be concerned about," he told them amiably. "And which the Court will keep you informed about."

Somehow everybody understood what he meant.

In theory, the judge drew up his charge and submitted a copy to both sides in order that they might make whatever objections or suggestions they had ahead of time. He then either made the requested changes or gave the defense its opportunity to introduce them into the record in the form of objections.

As with so many other elements of the trial, the practice was altogether different. Since it would take even a good judge a day or two to draw up the charge from scratch, and Harry Davies forever, it had become the accepted practice for the DA's office to dig out the charge on the last case where the same legal issues had been involved, submit it to the judge and allow him to make the very few changes that were necessary. (It was also customary, part of the game, for the defense to cite this practice as proof of the complicity that had existed between the judge and the state throughout the entire trial. And for the appeals court, which understood that both the practice and the horror were purely automatic, to ignore it.)

The defense would petition for as many changes as it could conceive of, which from a lawyer of Bannerman's fertile imagination would be the rough equivalent of one petition per paragraph. The judge would allow one or two of them entirely for the sake of form, and the defense would be able to add a dozen or so entirely worthless items to its appeal.

1:03 P.M.

In the *People* v. *Samuel Tabor* there was the entirely new factor of whether the Court was going to charge the jury on both the M'Naughton Rule and the Model Penal Code, and also whether he would charge them on the Model Penal Code both as it had been written by the Law Institute and as it had been extended by Harrison T. Davies. And yet, somehow or other, as the lawyers gathered in the judge's chambers, that was a subject that never came up in the discussion.

Norman Bannerman wasn't anxious to discuss it because he was planning to enter an objection on having the M'Naughton Rule in there at all, on the grounds that it was tantamount to giving the jury a choice of legal alternatives. And while any other judge would have understood that he was, in the best tradition of the Bar, acting solely in the interests of his client, he wasn't going to take any chances with Harry Davies—particularly since the dual charge had been Bannerman's idea to begin with—until the final charge had been written out, put through the Xerox machine and slipped to the press.

With Ambose so sure that it was he, not Bannerman, who was sitting in the catbird seat, he was more than willing to let Harry handle it however he wanted to. As a result, the discussion in the judge's chambers had turned, almost from the beginning, to the advisability of having the lawyers sum up before the jury that night and put over the battling over the charge until the morning.

And on the surface it made a lot of sense. If they did it the usual way, it was going to take the rest of the day to hammer out their briefs on the charge and they'd probably still have to return in the morning to argue the final version with the judge. With the evidence already in, as Ambose had pointed out, the jury would have had practically a full day by then to sort it out in their minds. "And once they've done that," he said unhappily, "the summations aren't going to be worth a piss-all. I've got enough healthy egotism, as long as there're no psychiatrists in here to call it megalomania, that I want to take my best shot at them."

There was still another reason why the testimony had come to an end at the worst of all possible times. The word, undoubtedly coming from Henigan, had been around the courtroom all day—even the press had it—that the jury was very interested in getting home by Monday, and the jury had been assuming such importance in everybody's eyes over these last twenty-four hours that everybody was very anxious to fall over backwards to oblige them. "If we go right into the summations," Ambose suggested, "you can have the jury sleep on it, and we can all get together and tangle assholes over the charge first thing in the morning."

And even there, Bannerman was quick to observe—giving voice to what was uppermost in his mind—there was going to be enormous pressure on the jury to arrive at a verdict by Saturday, unless they were told that Harry Davies would reconvene his court to hear their verdict, if it should become necessary, on Sunday.

All Harry had to say to that was that one thing he was sure of was that he wasn't going to have any jury coming in on a Sunday when there was a possibility of having a death sentence handed down, for the love of Mike.

"Who are you kidding, Harry?" Bannerman chuckled. "Henigan will be letting you know what it is three seconds after they knock." More likely, he amended, being even more practical about it, three minutes before.

"You said it," said Judge Davies, that soul of discretion. "I didn't." Judge Davies wasn't supposed to know until he heard the foreman say it, and what he wasn't supposed to know, you could be damn sure he didn't.

That left the question of the summations still squarely in Bannerman's lap. And the problem, as he saw it, was that if they took the afternoon to prepare their summations they wouldn't be starting until well into the night. And while he was enough of a night person himself so that the idea intrigued him, he wondered whether the jury would be alert enough to follow the arguments.

"They'll follow my arguments," Ambose said, narrowing his eyes. No juror had ever gone to sleep on him, he wanted Bannerman to know. And he'd be going

535

on last. Nevertheless, it seemed to give him something to think about. Giving them six hours to prepare their summations, they'd be starting at something around 7:30. And since they had already agreed that each side was going to have two hours to sum up, that would run them to midnight. "If he wants to go midnight, I'll go midnight," he told Davies, making up his mind. But not any later. If they couldn't get started by eight at the latest, he said, nodding his agreement to Bannerman, they should put it over for the morning. "We can agree on that, anyway."

Halpern, who had been sitting back quietly, came forward as Ambose was making that final heart-rending plea. "You're all heart," he said.

They all turned to him, astonished.

"You're all heart," he repeated with emphasis. "But we'll just wait for the morning and start fresh."

Judging from the small smirk that played around Ambose's lips as he looked from Bannerman to Halpern, Ambose could see who had taken over the defense. "Then the morning it is," he said, starting to rise. "Fine."

Judging from the grim set of Bannerman's mouth he still hadn't made up his mind. Obstinately, in the face of Bannerman's clear disapproval, Halpern reminded him that he had been hired to instruct him on the local laws, practices and customs. Including the practices and temperaments of the prosecutors. He looked directly at Ambose. "I've seen him argue cases at night before. I've never seen him lose one."

For although Halpern couldn't have said why he was so sure that Ambose was trying to con Bannerman into making their final pleas at night, he knew that he was. He had come to trust himself on certain things these last couple of days, and this was one of those times when he was absolutely sure.

And he was right. Ambose always did try to make his plea for a death sentence at night when the conditions fell just right. The later the better. Like most great discoveries, he had come upon this one by pure accident—he had, indeed, been forced into it the first time at the insistence of a defense attorney who had felt, with reason, that he had a sure acquittal coming up. When, instead, the jury came back with death, Ambose, with that methodical mind of his, had pondered upon it so carefully that it had taken up two full pages in his Journal. "The idea of taking the life of a fellow human being is so abhorrent to the average man," he had written, "that as much as he might have accommodated himself to that possibility during the trial, the awesome responsibility, when it comes to the bruising, is something he would ordinarily draw away from. But not at night. Night is the time when he is accustomed to thinking about death. It is part of his experience that he has lain awake in bed at night and seen his own grave. Death does not seem unnatural at night, for darkness is death's natural habitat."

It was an insight he considered so valuable that he had not passed it on to even the brightest of his boys. That Halpern should have figured it out for himself made it necessary to upgrade him several notches. The kid had good instincts. The kid, he was beginning to see, was going to be one of those late bloomers.

It was Harry Davies who, for once in his life, came to the rescue by suggesting that Peterson call up to Henigan to find out how the jury wanted to do it. As if there was any question about that. "What the gentlemen of the jury want," said Bannerman, summing it up neatly, "is to spend Saturday night disgorging great gouts of sportively liberated spermatozoa into the grateful vaginal canals of their spouses." Unless, he smirked, Bottleneck was taking them all on up there, one at a time, whenever the prim-lipped Mrs. Brennan made one of her interminable visits to the can. All at once, he became completely serious. "If this lovely land of ours should ever become truly civilized," he said, "all prospective jurors would be asked, as the very first question, whether they thrive upon continence."

2:15 P.M.

"All right, you've told me," Ambose said. "I want to do it." His lip curled. "If you can't fade the heat, I'll give you a note for the teacher saying it was all my idea. Absolving you from any responsibility."

And how was he going to absolve him from blame for committing a felony, Foxx wanted to know. "That I didn't know?" He was insulted. Also incredulous. As for fading the heat, Ambose knew better than that. "But where's the good of it?" he asked for perhaps the fourth time. Ambose still wouldn't be hearing why the jury decided to vote the way they had until after the verdict was in. "What's the good of it, that's what you're not telling me." He wasn't going to be prosecuting any more cases, so what was there to learn even?"

There was no risk, Ambose told him. "Bannerman sits down. I get up to start my summation. And that's when you slip out. Everybody's watching me. If anybody asks, you're going out to take a crap. Been holding it in, waiting. Then when the jury comes back, while they're filing in, you go back up and slip it out. Nobody's there. They're all in the courtroom." And anyway, what did Foxxie think he had to lose? Did he think Mr. District Attorney DeWitt Pawley was going to be keeping him on there? "You're right out on your ass, the morning after. I'm giving you your one last chance to go out in a blaze."

Foxxie was shaking his head. "You have to know that bad, huh? You hate him that much, that you have to know the wheres and the whys and the wherefores?"

2:43 P.M.

Halpern, rather surprised to find Ambose sitting there in Hilliard Nevins' office, said, "Lorna said you had the charge ready. To pick it up here."

Ambose pushed a Xeroxed copy across the desk. "Lorna said right." There was no smile, but his face was friendly. "Good hunting," he said. "What's your quota? The record is forty-eight."

Halpern had to laugh. "A respectable showing. I'll settle for half." Bannerman, after all, would be doing the final filigree work on it in the morning.

"Just do us all a favor, then, and don't tell Bannerman about the forty-eight. If your man knows there's a record, he'll go for it and we'll never get started." Under Ambose's intent stare Halpern's quizzical look became even more so. "What's the matter?" Ambose said. "Haven't you figured it by now? I'm never wrong where your man is concerned. I've made him the object of a personal study. I can program every move he's going to make." Like the night summations, he said, just in case Halpern didn't know what he was really talking about. "It had to appeal to him. It's different. A real, live courtroom drama. And he knows I want it." He hesitated long enough so that Halpern would understand that he could strike all the other reasons. "If he didn't know it, you told him. That's enough right there. He's got to beat me at my game." Moving his lips in the attitude of a smile, he made as if to tip his hat to him.

"Speaking of abnormal psychology . . ." Halpern said, tipping it right back to him. "Who had to let whom know that he knew just how Bannerman thinks?" He was enjoying this, the byplay of lawyers. Harold Halpern against the great Jim Ambose. Enjoying it so much that for once the thought didn't come filtering in that nobody was paying much attention to Sam Tabor in this game the lawyers were playing.

It was Ambose who brought Sam Tabor into it. "Take a load off, Halpern," he said, "I am going to tell you about a deal that was offered by the deal-making folks around here to your deal-making man . . ."

3:25 P.M.

Cowhig had hired a public stenographer, a youngish, well-built woman with glasses, who was waiting for him in Chobodian's old office. Rather sweet-faced and thrilled to death at being in on the trial, at even this peripheral, mind-dulling level. At about a quarter to five Marie called to tell Halpern that Davies was going out to dinner and wanted to know how he was coming along. Before he could even ask why the hell Davies should care, she lowered her voice. "I was thinking about what you said, and I can't remember Ambose losing one of his night summations, either, now that I think of it." Lowering her voice even further, she told him she had been trying to get in touch with Bannerman, but the switchboard had told her that he wasn't taking any calls from anybody. "I just thought you'd want to know, in case you have any way of reaching him, that Harry's set to have it tonight no matter how late they're ready. Know what I mean?"

"I know what you mean," he told her, not knowing anything. "Tell Judge Davies to enjoy his dinner."

Halpern was frowning when he hung up, and because Sondra was so enthralled by his fascinating work that he had been explaining all manner of things to her and because she had told him, during their one coffee break, that she was divorced and had a son to raise and there were no *men* around anymore, if he knew what she meant, he told her what the call had been about. And when Sondra, misreading his bewilderment, interpreted it to mean that Marie was rooting for them, he scoffed, "Yeah, she's rooting for us!" And because it was, after all, her field, he informed her that court reporters made their big scores by selling the transcript to the defense for their appeal. "A buck and a quarter a page," he said. "Three thousand dollars on this one easy." If it came back not guilty she'd think they were stealing money from her.

Sweet-faced Sondra let out the vilest kind of oath. She had been typing them up for them at ten and fifteen cents a page. And for Marie Pappas, too. "Why, that dirty little bitch!" Her voice went hard as stone. Her lips all but disappeared. "No more. You can count on that."

6:45 P.M.

Marie hung up the phone with a shrug. Nothing there either. Just like she had said. She looked at him. "What are you going to do about the charge, Harry?"

Davies held onto his head and looked unhappy. "As if I didn't feel bad enough already, you've got to ask me that." He gave himself over to some heavy thinking about it. "What I'm going to do is this," he said with determination. "I don't have the slightest idea what I'm going to do."

Actually he did know what he was going to do about it. He was going to worry about it tomorrow. What did she think he was going through this whole goldurn waiting-out for a night session for if he was going to have to think about it anyway? This way, he wouldn't have to go over it with the lawyers until the morning, and then it would be too late for whichever of them got stung to scream for more than a couple of minutes.

Under the robe he scratched himself. "Goddamn," he said, looking without affection toward the sofa. "Either I'm getting a nervous condition or the crabs."

"Thanks," Marie said, letting him see how good he had made her feel.

"Goddamn," he said. "Have I got time to take a shower? I've got all the troubles, with none of the pleasure." His eyes lit up. "Hey! Let's try it in the shower one time? Have we got time?"

"Harry," she said, giving up on him completely, "you sure do take chances." She thought, however, that she should call it to his attention that it wouldn't be a matter of jumping up and pulling on his pants this time if someone came in. "How do you explain being stark naked with a naked lady? And all lathered up, too."

"Well, you're a court reporter, aren't you? All you got to do is go down on me and I'd just say you were taking dictation when I got to feeling like I had the crabs and—" Already Harry had lost interest. "Maybe something will come to me when I'm listening to the summations." He scratched good and hard underneath the robes. "Goddamn," he said. "I hope they don't talk all night. I'm tired enough already. Too pooped to pop." He rubbed his eyes. "What the hell," he said, looking on the bright side of it. "I don't have to listen. I'm not on the jury."

At 7:15, they were finished. She had been instructed to send her bill to Norman Bannerman at the Coronet, but Halpern decided it would be easier and safer if he just gave it to Bannerman himself. He made it out from 2:30 to 7:30, adding enough on each end to give her an extra half hour to pay for her taxi home. She gave him her card, "in case you should ever want me again . . . for anything." The look that accompanied it meant just that. In case he had missed it she added, with the same open, direct look, "I do good work, Mr. Halpern, I try very hard to please, I really do, and I've never had any complaints yet."

Her parting words as she left, though, were, "A dollar twenty-five a page. My god, how do you get to be a court reporter? Do you know?"

Darned if he did. But it didn't do any harm, he imagined, if you knew somebody.

She nodded grimly. "I'm going to know somebody."

7:48 P.M.

Just outside the courthouse a car pulled up alongside him and he heard someone yelling his name. "Hey, Halpern," Johnny Gerard said. "Are you deaf? Can I give you a lift somewhere?"

He sure could. "You could drive me to the Coronet if it isn't out of your way."

Nothing, it developed, was out of Johnny's way. Johnny was on the midnight shift in the sheriff's office, and he was spending his own time, as was apparently his habit, cruising around town, looking for trouble. He had been touring the night clubs, he said, his disapproval showing, and they were all jammed. With newspapermen, a lot of them, and their dates. And spectators who had remained in the city waiting to hear whether the night session waa going to go on. He even insisted that they stop at one club on the way, just so Halpern could see for himself. A middling to fair club, neither the best nor the worst, and it was jammed to capacity. From the way the manager came hurrying over to Gerard, probably beyond. A couple of reporters, recognizing Halpern, came over to get the latest scoop and when they went back to their table Hal could recognize a couple of the girls from the courthouse with them. One of them from Judge Parks' office. And at the next table, Lorna from Hilliard Nevins' office.

Back in the squad car Gerard said, "I could have hit him with three violations just standing there not looking." But what the hell, he couldn't blame the club owners for cashing in on a good thing. Any more than Halpern could blame the reporters who, having been kept busy through the trial, were relaxing and solidifying the friendships that had been developed.

And both of them recognized kindred spirits through every word of it. "It's barbaric," Halpern said, when he finally exploded. Barbaric. "A man's on trial for his life up there, waiting to find out if he's going to live or die, and they're part of it. That's the only reason they're in town, because they're here as part of it."

Barbaric, Gerard said, tasting the word and liking everything about it. And at last they were able to talk about Sam. For although Gerard had been ordered not to even go close to the little guy, Blasser had kept him informed. "I don't know that it isn't the best that they do it tonight and get it over with," Johnnny said. "The little guy's in bad shape. This way at least, he's had his day in court, and it's over once and for all. See what I mean?"

It was the first time Halpern could remember that the door to Bannerman's suite hadn't been wide open, and it was easy to see why. Bannerman was slumped in an upholstered chair in the far corner of the room with his head hung down on his chest and his arm draped over the far side of the chair. The only light in the room came from the dim floor lamp just behind him. Norman Bannerman was all decked out in his red velvet robe and bright red slippers, and he was also, to all appearances, sound asleep.

And yet, as Halpern came down the stairs from the bar platform, there was an odd, unidentifiable sense of movement in the air that directed his eyes straight down to the carpet, and to the dark stains splattered all over it. And to something shining on it, too. Glass. Scattered everywhere. As Hal bent down to pick up the jagged neck of a broken whiskey bottle a coldness hit the back of his neck, drawing his attention upwards. On the ceiling directly above him was a dark stain, so freshly made that beads of liquid were still coming together within its surprisingly symmetrical design.

Sombody, it was clear, had very recently heaved a bottle of liquor against the ceiling, splattering it to smithereens. Bannerman and his faithful companion of the long night had apparently had a falling out. Broken up was more like it. All broken up.

Whether Bannerman was sleeping off a drunk, or was pretending to be asleep because he was in no mood to talk to anybody, it was all the same to Halpern. His natural instinct was to get the hell out of there.

He was neither. "Mr. Bannerman is awake, Harold." His eyes remained closed. His voice was a distant rumble that was and wasn't the voice of Norman Bannerman. "Mr. Bannerman is preparing his summation. Or was so engaged before you chose to frivolously intrude upon it."

If so, the damage had been done, and Hal wasn't going to be put off now. Respectfully, but all the same determined, he put the question to him. "Ambose says you were offered a deal. I feel I have to know if that's true."

"I feel you don't have to. Had I felt otherwise, you may rest assured you would have been admitted to the inner councils for advice and consent." It was like another voice, functioning independently of the main supply of energy which was, even as he was speaking, directed to the organization of his summation.

"Why did you turn it down, Norman? I have a right to know."

Bannerman opened his eyes, and immediately it was Norman Bannerman speaking. "What difference does it make now, Harold? I had a plan. We suffered a setback. A minor setback but a setback." The lurking chagrin came through more strongly than he could have intended. "Don't worry, my boy," he said, straining to brighten things up. "Norman Bannerman will save the day yet. If you will now cooperate with my day-saving endeavor by removing yourself and your censorious vibrations from the premises, I will remain, your ever humble servant, eternally in your debt." He closed his eyes. The recording machine turned inside him. "You play an important part in my plans, Harold. Faith is the virtue to be clung to for the next few hours." His head slumped back down onto his chest. "I have to fight with everybody. Do I have to fight with you, too?"

Once it was put that way, Hal would have removed himself immediately, except that at the mention of the minor setback something in his mind had stirred. "Ambose introduced me to a man named Otis Moscrip. He said to tell you. He didn't tell me why."

"Mr. Ambose has spent a busy afternoon sowing his seeds of discord, I see. What did you say the gentleman's name was?"

After Halpern had described Otis Moscrip in all his skinny, wasted glory, Bannerman opened his eyes only long enough to say that he had never heard of him. "No," he said, as he closed them, "I cannot say I have run across anybody in my intercontinental gallivantings among the Smart Set with a dental problem as fraught with pathos as the one you have described." The Bannerman vocabulary droning on in the non-Bannerman voice was more disconcerting still. "If you should happen upon the unfortunate gentleman again, you might make discreet inquiry whether there is a malpractice suit in the offing. From your moving description, the poor man would seem to be afflicted with a rare case of terminal tooth decay, an excruciatingly dismal way to go. For the mental anguish alone, fifty thousand would be a poor and paltry compensation."

He opened his eyes. "We could work together again, Harold. I'd like that. You have done very well for poor Sam. You have fought hard for him. And while it has not gone completely unnoticed that you became convinced all too readily that I was the enemy to be overcome on his behalf, I will here and now withdraw any complaint I may ever have had." And, he said, with the same grave dignity, if Hal would hold himself ready to come back and pick him up in the morning, he would reveal how he intended to reward him. "We shall walk into the courtroom together, arm in arm, shoulder to shoulder, shan't we, Harold? Partners again, and friends. We shall present them with a united front. Would you like that?"

Hal nodded dumbly.

"I'm glad, Harold." He closed his eyes for the final time, like a child about to drift off to sleep. "Yes, I would like that very much, too."

The echo-chamber voice came drifting after him again as he was departing. "You won't have to worry about poor Sam anymore. Norman Bannerman will save him for you."

Under the dim light, Norman Bannerman is organizing his final plea. His mind is functioning at a familiar pace. His memory system is to drop a keying word from each of the items he plans to cover, and string them together into a lucid, colorful story line that will cue him back in, word by word, while he is addressing the jury. If his story should happen to come out a little racy . . . well, that's the way things go sometimes, and it doesn't make it any harder to remember, does it?

Even if you have been blessed with a memory like Norman Bannerman's, the concentration must be total. Each time he drops in a new keying word, it is necessary to implant the expanded story solidly in his mind before he is ready to move on to the next item. Occasionally a word turns out to be so obstreperous that the whole story line has to be revised. From time to time, when he finds it advisable to rearrange the whole sequence, he must be able to scatter the words across the table of his mind, shuffle them around, bead them back together and systematically reslot them.

If you happened to be Norman Bannerman, you accomplished it with the ease and confidence with which those old-time jugglers kept the balls and candlepins circling through the air while reeling off their snappy monologue and breaking every now and again to show their medals. Why shouldn't he? He had done it often enough.

He is never in a hurry to finish, and that helps, too. He lingers over it, enjoying the mental stimulation of the game of words, the quiet exuberance of the mind's clear functioning. The total concentration. The solitude.

That's not the only reason, though. The concentration is so intense, the solitude so complete, that when it is over he will be overtaken by an exhaustion of the mind and spirit that will leave him powerless to resist the wave of loneliness and desolation that will come closing in over him. He knows. It has happened a hundred times before. It will happen again.

He knows: Through all his preparation of another man's plea, a riderless horse has been coming at a gallop across the ghostly plains to keep its appointment with Norman Bannerman. It will arrive on time. It always does.

He knows: When he is done with this, the other will have stepped into the wings, only a remove away, to cast its shadow across the stage.

His hand goes slack; it's done. His mind is spent. His spirit is drained. It always happens this way. It is happening again.

As Bannerman rose to address the jury there was the old sense of expectation cocked. In just that moment he was once again the man who had dominated the courtroom in those first early days. The man who has won all the blue ribbons and is expected to win them again. It was almost 9:30 when he stepped to the jury box and he used the lateness of the hour to the best possible advantage by stretching his arm out to the clock and intoning, "What is the truth of midnight that is not the truth of noon? That is the vexing problem, ladies and gentlemen, we have been wrestling with together in this courtroom for a full week."

For a full week, he said, in his deep, melodious voice, they had been living within the shadow of the midnight darkness that had fallen upon Sam Tabor's mind while he was pulling the trigger and shooting David Wilcke.

"We are all the playthings of fate," he was proclaiming a few moments later. "Destined to live out our lives tracing and retracing a single circle. Is he the most heinous murderer of the century, as you have been and will be told? I have tried hundreds of cases, my friends, and I have yet to defend a man who has not been described as the most heinous murderer of the decade, the century or the era." Was Sam Tabor a heinous murderer or a poor mad fool? "That was the question that hung over us all as I rode into this fair city. That is the question which, after the most searing months of my life, still curls over this courtroom like a giant question mark as I stand here in these last agonizing hours before I take my farewell."

Under his expert hand the three-tiered psychiatric defense reemerged, neatly ordered and artfully compressed. At times, he paced up and down in front of the jury box; at other times, he spread his hands across the railing and wrapped the entire jury in his steady gaze. As the medical case was coming to an end—it took a full half-hour and more—he hammered hard at the accident of timing that had brought Sam Tabor to the steps of City Hall just as Wilcke was coming out. "What did he represent to Tabor that wired the mind to the hand and squeezed the fingers on the gun—he's an automaton now, remember, a robot—it couldn't have been planned. You heard the testimony of Allbright. You saw the film. The question has never been whether but why." His head bent to the jury; his voice turned low and intimate. "We can only guess. We can only surmise. Does Sam Tabor know? Ladies and gentlemen, I wrestled with that question for a month, and I still don't have the answer. How can you get the answer from a diseased mind?"

That had been the task that had been set before them. To find the twist in the brain that had impelled Sam to the deed. In search of that twist, he said—twisting his hands as if he were squeezing a wet towel—he had brought to them the greatest array of experts ever gathered in a courtroom. Against this constellation of dedicated scientists, the state had chosen to bring them . . . who? "You saw him. The jailhouse psychiatrist—I do not mean to say that unkindly. A man brought to you in an insanity case who admitted he did not believe in insanity." He shrugged. Expressively. Dismissing him from their minds forever. But there was one man, he reminded them, whose testimony had not been heard at all. "I cannot help but wonder along with you," he said, "what was said in that interview in the dispensary during those critical hours immediately following the murder that the state does not want this jury to know."

Pawley: "Your Honor, there is nothing in the testimony about anything being kept back. Mr. Bannerman called Deputy Gerard to the witness stand himself, and if he had wanted the jury to know what was said during that conversation he could have very easily asked him."

But Bannerman was smiling down at him sweetly. "Oh, I don't wonder that my friend rises in such perturbation to interrupt me. The failure to permit the jury to hear Mr. Ambose constitutes an insult to due process of such major proportions as to lay a cloud over the entire trial." All the while that Davies was warning him that such remarks were out of order in a summation, Bannerman's eyes were fixed solidly upon Ambose. Not until he was sure he had Ambose glaring back at him—and directly into the jury box—was he ready to pronounce his final verdict. "Mr. Ambose is a man who enjoys his work. You have only to look into his eyes to see the crematorium's glow." The eyes held for a long moment. "I wonder," Bannerman mused as he turned back to the jury, "what in his enthusiasm for his peculiar art form he did manage to accomplish during those crucial hours of that critical day?"

And then he was doubling back to Sam Tabor's background, not as it applied directly to the medical case this time but in a far more general, philosophical way. "I entered into a covenant with this jury," he began. "I promised you that we were going to peel the layers of his mind like an onion, and I can tell you now that I have kept that promise." You could recognize immediately that he was about to enter into a new area. Not so much from the suddenly erect form, or even from the quick look toward the clock—he had already been going on for more than an hour—as from the voice, which had suddenly seemed to go one tone higher. A tone that somehow didn't seem to accord with his words as he said, "To keep that promise we went so far as to elicit ghostly testimony from the grave." And then he was talking about the wandering wastrel father, and the religious fanatic of a mother who had raised her son to believe that he was a messenger from God, a savior with special powers for healing. "The mother who died in an asylum bitten by the snake and could not be saved by the special powers of her son, who found himself, when put to the test, unable to save this one person he loved most on earth. The only person he ever loved."

So far was that from the story that had emerged during the trial that everybody waited for a clarification or an explanation. Including Ambose and Pawley. But Bannerman merely nodded to himself and ran his hands through his thick mane of hair. "What happened, I had to ask myself," he said at last, "to the issue of this monster and this madwoman."

What had happened to him, as far as Halpern was concerned, was that he was sitting there beside him like a wax figure. "Like all dug up," was the way Julie had described him that first day, and that seemed to describe what was happening perfectly. They were disinterring the bones of his life. It was not for this that he had killed David Boone Wilcke, Harold Halpern was thinking. And right there, it now seemed to Harold Halpern, was where this whole thing had gone wrong. If Sam had a message he considered so imperative that he killed a Chief Justice to make the world stop what it was doing and listen to him, who had a right to stop him? Crazy or not. Psychopathic or what. Who said that the law had the right to shut him up and force him to sit there like this, no more than a poor, scarred, wounded animal, hearing his lawyer tell the world that rotten people came from rotten stock. What the hell kind of protection was that?

Halpern was not alone. The jurors were shifting uncomfortably in their seats. The spectators, lined up along the walls, shuffled their feet and twitched their necks and shoulders. "Yes," Bannerman said, unable to ignore the heavy, oppressive atmosphere that had settled over the courtroom, "it makes you uncomfortable. I want to make you uncomfortable. No great advances have come from soft, comfortable minds. The Reformation was not comfortable, and we are being presented here with a golden opportunity to set upon a reformation of the law." (During the fifteen-minute break between the summations, Ambose asked Pawley, with a smirk, how he thought those Catholics on the jury felt about having the Reformation cited to them as one of the great advances of mankind. "I told you from the beginning, the guy hasn't got it.")

As Bannerman went on, leaving the particular and becoming ever more general, he began to ramble back and forth so much that it was impossible not to come to the conclusion that he had completed the prepared portion of his summation and was merely running out the clock. "You have been told, over and over again," he said, "about the fancy Chicago lawyer who came here with a forked and guileful tongue to try to fool you good people. It is an insult to your intelligence and your integrity and your sound common sense." Nevertheless, he was willing to plead guilty to coming from Chicago. "I will also plead guilty to having achieved some position in my profession, and I say that proudly, for I believe it to be a noble profession." And to bringing before them scientists of an equal stature and nobility. "We held nothing from you. I had not the resources of our opposition. Against me were arrayed the full might and the unlimited resources of the state, in money and manpower and investigative technology, and they did not hesitate to use them against me. I tell you that they did not hesitate to use against me any tactics that came to their minds, and I will say no more about it than that."

Very quietly, without moving in his seat, Pawley said, "I am going to object to all of this. I will ask the Court to remind Mr. Bannerman that it is Sam Tabor who is on trial, not Norman Bannerman."

It was apparent that Bannerman was very tired. As his presentation became increasingly ragged, he found himself defending the same psychiatrists whom he had been extolling so lavishly. "The real heroes of these courtroom dramas, I sometimes think," he said. "They come in here knowing they are going to be ridiculed." To demonstrate the problem they were confronted with he searched the very arir around him for some tangible evidence of the psychiatrists' prey. "You can't see it, you can't hear it. It is absent to the smell and elusive to the touch." But there nonetheless. The twist of the brain. "Our appeal had perforce to be not to your senses but to your intelligence. If there were some among you who may have thought I was unduly harsh on you in the voir dire, you know the reason now. I could not afford to settle for anything less than the most intelligent twelve individuals who were on the panel." He was satisfied, you could see, that he had found them. "We all know that insanity exists. We've all had crazy people on the block. We have all seen people who acted bizarrely in their daily lives, said wild, unbelievable things on their death beds, things that nobody present could believe. We've all had experiences such as that."

He looked at his watch. "I have only a few more minutes of time allotted me. For the rest of my life I will have to ask myself whether I have used these final minutes to the best possible advantage." He directed their attention—finally—to Sam. "You have seen him, sitting there daily, with all his infirmities upon him. You see him here now, sitting calmly." And why? Because he knew he was out of life. His life was over. The beast within him had been penned. "Penned, ironically, by the very act of having broken loose. You heard Dr. Zacharias explain how that can be true. No matter what happens to him he is free from life, because if you set him free, as you know you must, he is not free. His life will be a carefully regulated one. He will go directly to a mental hospital, and you have my word that he will remain there, at my personal expense if necessary, until he is certified as wholly and completely sane."

With less than fifteen minutes left, he brought himself erect and rocked gently on his heels. And when he spoke again there was a sense that he was swinging back into his prepared text, his prepared ending. "The great miracle of this case, ladies and gentlemen, is that there is a trial at all. For it is a miracle that Sam Tabor wasn't cut down on the stairs at City Hall with the gun still smoking in his hands." Perhaps, he said, musing on it, that would have been kinder. Most certainly, it would have been cleaner. "The automatic reaction of the policeman hearing the shot, seeing the gun, shooting, killing. The policeman in pursuit of his duty, who could have blamed him?" (In Bannerman's reenactment the automatic reaction of the policeman in pursuit of his duty bore a remarkable resemblance—all things considered—to his somewhat riper reenactment of the equally automatic and, needless to say, blameless actions of his client.) "And perhaps one of the army of police officials in the immediate vicinity would have done exactly that if Sam had not been so quickly enveloped by the crowd. Thrown down, pummeled and kicked."

Yes, perhaps it would have been kinder. Sam Tabor would not have had to endure the agony of this trial, and the jurors would not now be charged with the terrible responsibility of debating whether to kill him, two months later, with no shot ringing in their ears, no gun smoking. "Not as an uncontrollable muscular twitch, an irresistible impulse, but as sensate, sensitive, thinking human beings." In a wholly unexpected change of pace he thundered, "There has not been a shred of evidence cited in this court that Sam Tabor murdered in cold blood. It is the prosecution which is asking you—you good ladies and gentlemen of the jury—to kill Sam Tabor in cold blood."

Ambose said, "We object to that, Your Honor. We have never asked them to do anything in cold blood. We're asking for reason and justice."

Although the objection had been made more to break up Bannerman's peroration than anything else, it was an interruption Bannerman welcomed. He had been wondering how he was going to be able to work Ambose into his next line. "No animal has ever killed as an act of vengeance," he said, letting his gaze remain upon him. Only man. "Mankind," he said, "which operates on both a higher and lower level. Man who invented the wheel and broke men on it. Who discovered fire and burned men at the stake. Who unleashed the power of electricity and burns men in the chair." The death of Sam Tabor, he reminded them, would not bring David Boone Wilcke back to life. How much better, then, to put Sam where he could be studied than to kill him in a mindless act of vengeance.

With time running out, he reminded them that the burden of proof was on the state. "Burden of proof," he said, dropping his voice to a whisper, "means the weight of a feather." The defense did not have to prove that Sam Tabor was legally insane. The state had to prove that he was legally sane. "But enough of that," he said. The Court would instruct them on the law.

At 11:31, two minutes over his time, Norman Bannerman went to the jury box and spread his arms across the rail. "As the night gathers around us, and the time for the terrible meditation begins, I give into your hands the loneliest job any man or woman can ever be faced with. The life or death of another human being. I have done my best. I know you will do yours. God bless you."

"I am my brother's keeper," Ambose shouted. "The voice of my brother's blood crieth unto me from the ground." That was the Bible, as he was sure most of them knew. Genesis 6:4. "It is my job as attorney for the state to ask you, as David Wilcke's brothers and sisters, to hear the cry of his blood."

Being aware that the cozy, intimate approach was not exactly his strong point, Ambose's style was to stand back a good ten to twelve feet from the jury box and shout it out to them. Having transmitted the call of the blood, he set himself to the task of dismantling the psychiatric case. "Sam Tabor," he began, "went to work every day for seventeen years. He married, and if it wasn't a marriage to write TV commercials by, it was a functioning marriage. The man could function fine. He could make a living which sixty-six percent of the people in the country would envy. But he walked from that courthouse where he had been making a living for all those years, doing difficult work, and from one second to the next, a flashbulb went off and because of that Mr. Bannerman is asking you to believe that he was driven insane."

Yes, he knew he was simplifying it somewhat there, but that was what it came down to in the end, and he'd be getting back to that a little later. But first he wanted to talk a little on the subject of responsibility. Norman Bannerman had chosen to ridicule Dr. Swann, but as far as Ambose was concerned, and he kind of thought the jury agreed with him, Dr. Swann had made a lot of sense. "If we are responsible, we have dignity. We are masters of our fate. We say, I am man or woman enough to do what I do and accept the consequences for what I have done. If we are not responsible, we are automatons. Less than human beings." He squared his shoulders. "I'm not going to try to tell you that I hold an especially high opinion of the defendant, Sam Tabor, but I have enough respect for him to be able to say that the Sam Tabor who walked from that job and into the sheriff's car and up the stairs of City Hall was a man and not like his own lawyer tries to call him, a vegetable. I never knew before that vegetables went around hiring lawyers and psychiatrists to work for them, and expensive ones at that."

Listening to those psychiatrists who had come snowshoeing in there at Mr. Bannerman's invitation he had wondered whether he was listening to *Alice in Wonderland.* Like that fairy tale about how Sam had been walking around for forty-nine years with a trigger cocked in him. "And maybe they really believe that. I don't think you people, picked for your common sense, will." Because, he said, all that amounted to was accidental homicide. "But while they are saying it was accidental, they're also saying he was insane all the time. Think about it, and ask yourself if that isn't what they're saying. They're saying that all over this country there are people, living side by side with you, passing you every day on the street, who didn't get over wanting to go to bed with their mother—I know that's offensive to some of you, it's offensive to me—but that's what they said. I don't think that's the kind of a world we're living in, and I don't think you want to tell your fellow citizens it's the kind of a world you think you are."

Against that, he could remind them of the picture Dr. Swann had drawn for them. Why couldn't Tabor, knowing that the gun maintenance was due just the day that Wilcke was going to be there, have planned it, if he got the chance, and if the chance had come by accident—well, wasn't that just what the defense claimed, that he was an accident waiting to happen? And if it hadn't come by accident, then, couldn't he have got him at the hotel later or at the Bar Association dinner that night or at the airport the next day? "He had the gun with him, didn't he? Maybe he was just dreaming about it at first, sure, but then when the invitation came from Deputy Phillips, which seemed like even more of an invitation from fate . . ." He let his eyes run down the entire jury box. His voice turned scratchy. "This man who the defense's own expert said was a man who allowed himself to be controlled by the whims and winds of fate."

In a way, he had to confess that he was kind of disappointed in the case Mr. Bannerman had presented in that courtroom. Mr. Bannerman had told them how he was going to bring in his great array of psychiatrists, and how famous they were supposed to be, and all they had said was that if you killed somebody you had to be insane because if you weren't why did you do it? "And if ignoramuses like you and me don't believe them . . . well, what school did we ever go to?" He flicked his thumb along the side of his chin. "Some of these psychiatrists don't think other people know what they're doing, because they don't know what they're doing about half the time themselves. Allbright certainly didn't remember what he had said from one minute to the next. He sure did get himself all balled up. I don't know, you just heard Bannerman over there tell us about all the money he spent, his own money, to get the best he could afford, maybe even the best money could buy. And I have to wonder now if he didn't get cheated. He comes in here with this cock and bull story about the man was insane, and then, when he doesn't prove a thing—and that was the sorriest psychiatric case I've ever seen and I've seen a few. I might even go so far as to say that for every insanity case Mr. Bannerman has tried I've tried twenty. They come in here and say that it was predestined and accidental at the same time. It had to happen, and it was pure accident. I don't know."

And they'd heard a lot about the unconscious. How the unconscious is responsible for it all. "They're not responsible, they must have had unhappy childhoods. Well, we all had our troubles growing up. You heard Dr. Swann say that. Puberty is never easy. Adolescence can be counted on to bring a heap of trouble. Some of you who are parents yourself have probably heard the old saying that goes, 'Little children, little troubles; big children, big troubles.' Life isn't easy for any of us. We can all make excuses. Oh sure, they say they've got it all down to a science now by all those tests and inkblots, but if they know so much about him, this golden vein they struck, how come they want to spend the rest of his life still studying him? I never could quite figure that one out. They could study him all his life, they say, and not plumb the bottom of him, but after two or three hours —fourteen at the most—they're ready to come in here and put their hand on the Bible and swear they know all about him right now, and tell us just about everything Sam and his unconscious did over his whole life."

But that, he took care to remind them, was only if he was to be found permanently insane. "They gave us both barrels on that. Mr. Bannerman said you could find him not guilty by reason of temporary insanity and set him free and he, out of his good nature, would have him looked at for awhile before he set him out onto our streets again. Mr. Bannerman didn't say he was going to stick around because it would make him feel so safe, maybe you noticed that. But, Mr. Bannerman said, that's all right, leave it up to me, I'll set him free when it suits me."

But, he said, it was getting late and he'd already spent more time on that sorry excuse for a medical case than he had intended. "Mr. Bannerman says what good will it do to put Sam Tabor to death, it won't bring David Wilcke back to life, will it?" And that was one place, anyway, where he had to agree with him. "If Sam Tabor goes to jail for life it won't bring him back, and if we give Sam Tabor a medal or a vacation in Acapulco it won't bring him back. If we killed Sam Tabor five times over it won't bring him back. Nothing can bring David Wilcke back to life," he said, and suddenly he was wheeling around and pointing. "Because *you*, Sam Tabor, killed him, and if the blood of David Wilcke doesn't cry out for vengeance, then the society from which he was torn does."

"You do, Mr. Ambose," Bannerman said, setting out the lines. "Not society, you." He lifted himself to his feet. "The Supreme Court, I must remind Your Honor, has never made any such concession. The law specifically excludes vengeance as a significant or admissible element under our system of due process."

"Yes," Ambose said, addressing himself directly to the jury. "We've heard a lot about due process. And I want to say this to you. Due process is only that, a process. Not an end, a process." The lines had been drawn and he was accepting them. "The purpose of due process is to punish the guilty and free the innocent. That's why we have it. Just as the purpose of a schoolhouse is to teach children, not to see how clean and shining you can keep the classrooms. The best way to keep a classroom clean, if that's what you want, is to keep the children out of it. The best way to make sure nobody ever gets some right taken away from him under due process is to keep everybody out of jail. You won't have any education one way, and you won't have any justice the other."

Bannerman couldn't believe his ears. Was Mr. Ambose really coming out against due process? "I warn you, sir," he said, looking grim. "Be wary. I warn you now, for the record, that you are entering into a very dangerous area."

Ambose, being wary, pointed out that he had restricted his remarks solely to the subject as it had been opened up by Mr. Bannerman. The counsel for the defense, he then said, not being wary at all, had also seen fit to question Dr. Swann on the Fifth Amendment, and since that had come up in the testimony, too, he would deal a little with that.

"To impeach him as a credible witness," Bannerman shouted. "to attack his credentials." But, he said, showing his utter disbelief, if Mr. Ambose wanted to impeach himself on his own, he was perfectly willing to give him all the latitude he needed.

"You will notice," Ambose said with satisfaction, "that Mr. Bannerman's mind still finds it difficult to accept the idea that it makes any difference whether the man did what he is charged with doing. Perhaps there are some of you who will find it just as difficult to accept the idea that a man can kill a Chief Justice and you can't ask him about it. It's in the testimony, Your Honor, he held a colloquy about that with Dr. Swann. Or can kill your wife or your child, and nobody can ask him about it. Or can kill you. Perhaps you'll find that stranger than Mr. Bannerman seems to find the fact that I am pointing that out to you, after he himself brought it up in the testimony, and he didn't seem to think it was so strange then."

"Only because you're supposed to be a lawyer," Bannerman snorted. With a wave of his hand, he signaled for him to go on. "And that," he said, folding his arms, "is the last warning I am going to give."

Ambose studied the ground, studied the toe of his shoe. He looked up at the jury, turned to look at the clock, and turned back. They had heard a lot tonight from Mr. Bannerman, he said, about how far the law had taken us from the jungle. As his glance ran to Bannerman, he saw that Foxx had returned and that made up his mind. What the hell did he care? This was the end of the line for him. What did he even care whether Sam Tabor fried, as long as Jim Ambose heard the jury come back with a verdict to fry him. It was that first half-step you took backward, he had often said, that killed you. Almost as a symbolic act, a gesture of defiance, Jim Ambose took a full step forward. "I wouldn't normally burden a jury, especially this late at night, with any history of the law, but now that he's seen fit to bring it up, let's talk a little on it." He took a deep breath, and the face he turned to them was like hammered bronze. "When the first savages came out of the jungles and forests to huddle around a fire and form into the first tribes, they discovered quick enough that there were those among them who meant them no good, who stole and raped and murdered, and so they decided they needed some laws to protect themselves. And that's just what they did. They got together, the good people who wanted to be let alone, and codified —drew up—the first rough, primitive set of laws to protect themselves against those who meant to do them harm. And a court system of some sort—the wisest old man, the elders—to make sure they didn't have the wrong man and hear what kind of excuse he might be able to make for himself." And that was all. "It had to wait for the twentieth century, in this poor bleeding country of ours, for David Boone Wilcke to come along with the idea that the tribesmen—the society—had written out a set of laws to protect the lawbreakers, the people who wanted to destroy them, against themselves."

At one o'clock in the morning a spry little glint, as of the stirring of hope, arose in Sam Tabor's eyes.

"I say that," Jim Ambose said, "although David Boone Wilcke, lying in his grave, is my client. Because," he said, wheeling and pointing, "when he was killed by *that* man, it was up to me, as the representative of the law in this county, to exact society's vengeance." And why did he say that? Well, they had heard Mr. Bannerman say that no animal had ever killed out of vengeance. And Mr. Bannerman was right. Vengeance was purely a human emotion. The purest and most human of all emotions. "Vengeance assumes memory. It assumes love. It assumes pride. It assumes outrage." And that was why if you were going to have any kind of civilization at all, the individual had to be willing to surrender his natural desire for vengeance to the more neutral vengeance of the state. Otherwise, the society was going to be split apart by an unending series of family vendettas. His brow darkened. "When the state becomes so soft or so corrupt or so decadent that it is no longer willing to fulfill its part of that compact, then there is nothing left for the wronged man to do but take it back upon himself or be forced to admit to himself that he does not have the courage or strength to do it. And when that happens, I say to you that the law-abiding citizen of the community has been twice wronged."

They had all heard him ask Dr. Allbright whether a law that was based on a theory called mental illness wasn't schizophrenic by his own definition. Well, Jim Ambose said, throwing caution to the winds, perhaps he had stopped too short. "I wonder what he would have said if I had asked him whether a law that protects the murderer at the expense of the victim and the victim's kin isn't as good a definition of insanity as we're ever likely to come by."

He shrugged as if to say that it made little difference anymore. Everything had got so turned around that the verdict they were going to be directed to bring back if they should find for the defense was "not guilty by reason of insanity." Not "guilty but insane" like every other civilized country in the world, but "not guilty." The Court would instruct them that they could bring in a verdict that said he had killed the Chief Justice of the United States but was not guilty. "I asked you before, I think, whether you didn't get the feeling listening to Bannerman's psychiatrists that you were listening to something out of *Alice in Wonder-*

land. For those of you who might not remember that fairy tale from out of your childhood, that's the one with the Cheshire cat that just keeps on disappearing slowly until there is nothing left of it but the smile." He stood for a long, long moment, just looking at them. "The law is like the Cheshire cat," he said. "There ain't nothing left but the smile."

It was amazing how habit held. Instead of turning slowly to look at Sam Tabor, as the contemplative, carefully considered approach he was now taking called for, he found himself wheeling around as always to point that accusing finger. "If he can walk out of here free, what's so bad about killing a Chief Justice? If he can kill a Chief Justice and be given a sentence that might one day allow him to walk out free, what's so *bad* about it?" If a man could kill a Chief Justice and live, he said, making a titanic effort to get them to understand, *what was so bad about it?* Nothing was so bad about it! That was the message that would be going forth from this courtroom. For the first time in the entire summation he lifted his hand and wagged a finger at the jury box. "Any nation," he said, measuring his words, "which cannot put to death the known assassin of one of its political leaders within forty-eight hours is in a stage of terminal decadence. We used to be able to do that in this country before David Boone Wilcke came along."

The internal conflict that was contained within those two sentences, the opposing tensions, came through so plainly in those early morning hours that it could be felt through the whole courtroom. Jim Ambose, suddenly made aware that in making his own case against the state of the law he had come full circle around and was making the defense's case, too, twisted his lips wryly and said, "And if Sam, poor Sam there, thought it was up to him to set it aright himself, then I'll say to you that it was not up to Sam Tabor to appoint himself the judge and the jury. If that's why he did it, and that's the defense they made when you cut all the unconscious and subconscious away from it, I want to make the case for him flat out. The flat bottom. And it just ain't good enough." The habits of seventeen years were holding. "We do it by the law or we're back on the stairs with Sam Tabor, and it's every man with a gun and every man for himself, and that's the choice."

He looked the jury square in the eye. They had been getting a lot of sympathy from everybody about the hard task that was ahead of them but they would be getting no sympathy, he told them bluntly, from him. "We asked you all, first thing, were you in favor of the death penalty if the facts so dictated. You all said you were, and we believed you. We believed you then, and I believe you now. You swore that you were willing to take on the responsibilities of citizenship without mental reservation or a feeble heart. You swore it and I am holding you to it. I will tell you, though it might not be of that much interest to you, that this is the last case I am ever going to be prosecuting because I will be leaving the district attorney's office two seconds flat after you come in with your verdict."

Sam Tabor looked stricken. A low moan escaped from him.

Jim Ambose said, "I have every confidence that it will be with the death penalty I am asking you for because if ever a man richly deserved to be sentenced to the electric chair, this is the man. A coward shot a defenseless man, that's the truth of it. A man who wasn't even looking at him, didn't know where the shot that ended his life was coming from. You saw that in the films. David Wilcke never knew who killed him, or why. He lived a good life—I wouldn't want to say he didn't believe in what he was doing—and he was shot down in his prime by an unknown murderer. I'd hate to have to die that way. And so would you."

A deathly quiet had come over the courtroom. At 1:26 in the morning Sam Tabor's mouth began to work spastically, as if he were gasping for breath. Under the table Halpern squeezed his knee.

"You may be thinking that, sure, it's easy for him to stand up there and tell us to do it. He just told us that he isn't even going to be working here anymore." Slowly and purposefully Jim Ambose turned full around and looked Sam Tabor in the face. "I tell you now," he said. "And I tell Sam Tabor now, and I tell this Court and the whole wide world, that if you come back with the sentence that you must come back with, I will ask the governor to permit me to be the one who straps Sam Tabor in the chair and pulls the switch."

Sam didn't move; didn't so much as blink. He no longer seemed to be breathing. A river of liquid from beneath his pants cuff formed a dark puddle at the side of his shoe, and it was Halpern's first insane impression that the wax was melting. That his very bones had begun to disintegrate.

And then, as the puddle expanded, he understood what it was. Sam was pissing in his pants. In that stunned moment, with his hand going out to make contact with him, he looked into Sam's eyes and they were as dead as the crematory ashes. At the first touch Sam toppled straight over, stiff and unmelting, into Bannerman's lap.

Into Bannerman's lap . . .

After that it was kaleidoscopic. A tumult of the mind that slowed everything down. Did he see a first start of distaste in Bannerman at the foreign hulk in his lap? Did he see a ripple of an undersmile, so slight that it dissolved as it was being formed?

He would never know for certain. He was never able to separate what he had seen from what he had imagined. He did know that Bannerman's eyes flew open, and there was pain there, a limitless tunnel going back into pain and desolation. And at the end of the tunnel . . . what? A plea for forgiveness? Or a blanking out?

Halpern could never remember how it had come about but he had his arms around Sam's head, and he was cradling him in his arms, and Sam was perfectly stiff and frozen except that his head was lolling back and forth.

And then the camera was running again at normal speed. Stringfellow was jumping over the Bar gate, and in what must have been an emergency plan going into automatic operation, the deputies were piling in behind him and blocking off the rails, inside and outside. It was only because Bannerman was right there beside him that Halpern was able to hear him murmur, as if in a daze, "What are policemen doing inside the Bar of an American courtroom? I protest this outrage, Your Honor. I must protest . . ."

And then it was all lost in a babble of voices, a convulsion of movement streaming inward. A crush of deputies. A straining of reporters being held outside. A gavel banging. A wall of deputies thrown around them.

Looking back on it later, Halpern would remember Jim Ambose elbowing his way past the deputies, the one man who seemed the most at home. Not excited. Leisurely, even. Jim Ambose looking down at Sam from high above as if he were inspecting a hunk of meat. "Oh well," Ambose said, sniffing at it. "Another shitty victory."

He would remember Bannerman, standing right at Ambose's side, so close together that he couldn't point at him without also jostling him. "You did this," he said in a hoarse, unnatural voice. "You're the murderer. I knew it the first time I laid eyes on you."

And then the professionals were there. There were people peering down at him, reasoning with him, prying his arms loose. A doctor shining his light into Sam's unresponding eyes. And then Halpern was helping to load him onto a stretcher, and holding onto the side tightly while he accompanied the stretcher bearers out the door, and Johnny Gerard grasping him by the shoulder as they were backing through the foyer out into the corridor. "What happened to the little guy?" Johnny Gerard was shouting, pointing down. Halpern looked down at the hunk of meat on the stretcher, and in the next second they were being buffeted by the deputies encircling the stretcher and swept out of the way. It was only when Johnny Gerard gave him a good hard shake that Halpern realized he was in mild shock.

"Well, it's like this, Johnny," he said. "Sam Tabor just had his day in court."

BOOK VII

The Curtain Falls

"A fellow named Neville Chamberlain made a contribution to the sum knowledge of mankind equal to that of Isaac Newton. Neville Chamberlain discovered that when you carry an umbrella you bring on the rain."

From Ambose's Journal, page 21.
Also used effectively in a television debate
on WLOW-TV, on the topic: "Does Our Legal System
Meet the Needs of a Changing Society?"

Booker Phillips first heard about it over the radio.

Booker had been asleep all day, having worked the night shift, and when he woke up he turned on the radio and heard it as the lead item in the news summation. He heard that in a sudden and unsatisfactory ending to the Trial of the Century, Sam Tabor had gone insane.

Nobody was home. He roamed around the house with nobody to talk to.

He called the office, and was told that Stringfellow wasn't there.

He called Arch Merck, and nobody answered.

He drove to the courthouse.

Avoiding the elevators, he walked up to the third floor. The outer door to Judge Davies' chambers was locked. The corridor was empty. It was already past six o'clock. Everybody had gone home.

There was one person he could think of who still might be around. From the pay telephone booth in the corridor he dialed Jim Ambose's direct line. The phone rang once . . . twice, and as he heard it being picked up, he hastily hung up. What did he have to say to Jim Ambose?

In the foyer, under the table in the corner, there was a pair of fur-lined galoshes, zippered down to the bottom. On top of the table was a deck of cards. Behind it, sticking up, was one ski.

The courtroom was empty. It was empty as only a stadium can be empty after the game, with the peanut shells and scorecards scattered all around, and the sound and semblance of great events still echoing from the field.

The courtroom had not been cleaned. The seats at the prosecution table were in disorder. One thing. Out of a decent respect for appearances, someone had set the chairs at the defense table neatly into line. With Bannerman's chair turned to the witness chair, as always.

The room was quite dark. Gloomy. Something else. Someone had pulled the blinds down. As if there had been a death in the family.

Booker Phillips peered at the chairs, as if there was something waiting to be said. Heavily, not sure of his purpose, he moved to the witness chair, and the courtroom was so empty that his shoes squeaked.

Before he mounted the stairs to the witness chair his gaze went to the side, as though he expected to find Peterson there ready to swear him in.

He settled himself in laboriously, trying to make himself more comfortable, his elbows resting on the arm rests, his hands clasped in his lap.

It had to be done just right.

His eyes, moving briefly to the bench, saw Judge Harrison T. Davies limned in his black robes, and, moving on, dropped down to the defense table. To one chair. In the near darkness he gazed steadily at Sam's empty chair until he could see again the whole tableau take shape, as it had been on the first day of the hearing. And it seemed to him that though it had not been long ago, they had all been younger and gayer and happier that day.

He waited until once again Sam turned to him, in pain and apology, for putting him in the uncomfortable position of having to testify against him. Never dreaming that Booker Phillips, who had never borne false witness against any man, was going to nail him where it counted. The trial.

With his hand upraised, he said, "As God is my witness, Sam . . ."

And wasn't it amazing how clear his mind was and how choked his voice (though, secretly, he took comfort that Sam, hearing his voice, would know how sorry he was).

"As God is my witness, Sam," Booker Phillips said, "I never thought it would come to this."

Bunny crept into the Cave and sat down in the corner, her knees tight together, her toes barely touching the ground, taking up a minimum of space, breathing a minimum of air.

Ambose said, "Was it you who called?"

She shook her head.

He went back to cleaning out his desk, throwing everything away.

Bunny said, "Where are you going from here?"

"Who knows?"

"You could always marry me."

He gave a short, dry, snorting breath.

"I'd be good for you."

"I'm a casualty."

Her eyes moistened. "I am old and ugly, Father William, and I am afraid of the dark. Please marry me."

Ambose was studying some photographs. "Still afraid to walk across the field in the dark, are you?"

"All us casualties are."

"Here. Pornography is big this year."

She looked. Surprised, she looked back up at him and looked again. "Anybody I know?"

"Sure do."

She looked again, and gasped.

"That's Mr. Nevins," she gasped. She couldn't tell who the woman was from that angle. "That's the angle from which they all look alike, isn't it?" She was blushing. "Oh, Jim, it isn't . . ."

He held the other two photographs out to her. "You can make her out better from these. If you really want to know."

She was dying to know. But she did the right thing. The right thing to do was to shake her head, quick and determined.

"You wanna blackmail them? Big money in that."

"I'd be afraid. Please marry me."

He ripped all three pictures up and dropped the pieces into the carton with the rest of the trash.

The cabinets he studied without appetite. To hell with it. He'd leave it all there for his successor, who probably wouldn't bother to look at any of it. He sure as hell was in for some thrills if he did.

"I'll cook and I'll clean and I'll never speak unless spoken to," she said.

He weighed the bust of Winston S. Chirchill thoughtfully.

"You won't have to take your hat off in the house," she said.

"I thought you didn't speak unless spoken to."

"Only when I'm trying to get myself married."

He dropped Winston S. Churchill regretfully into the carton. She was over in a bound to retrieve it and, sitting back down, hug it to her. "I only said married because you're so big for the legalities." She cleared her throat. "As far as I'm concerned . . ."

Ambose hunkered down, reached in under the bottom of the desk and, straining, yanked at a wire until it broke. He opened the bottom drawer, lifted out the recording machine and dropped it, with a splash, into the trash carton. There was only one thing he was going to take out of here. The only thing he needed. Paying no mind to Bunny, he took out the gun and holster. He was about to take off his jacket but, changing his mind even about that, flung the holster across the floor and jammed the gun inside his belt.

He'd be traveling light. As light as he'd be traveling, any excess baggage was too much.

"I've got a road to travel," he said, and lets her see that he has no choice but to travel it, and that she is wasting her time.

"Speaking of blackmail, mister," she says. "Have you got a permit for that gun?" In the gloaming they look at each other and he knows that she understands exactly what road it is. And that on such a road any woman would be both excess weight and hostage.

Her mouth is dry. She has never been so afraid. "Every illusion," she says. "Every illusion except that last little one."

He doesn't understand.

"Except that last one," she says. "That last little illusion about how you're going to save the world."

He says nothing.

"Oh, Jim," she says. "I'm so afraid for you."

She had, for once—not trying to say the right thing—said the right thing.

Saturday, August 10 . . . Lowell
10:45 A.M.

The office looked different. It had changed character, like a suit of clothes to fit its new occupant. Clean-cut. Crisp and efficient. The slack taken out.

By calling his key assistants in on a Saturday, Acting District Attorney DeWitt Pawley was wasting no time in letting them know who was in charge and how different things were going to be.

"Right down the fairway," he was saying to Charley Curran. "One time. You're sitting pretty because I need you so bad. You can have my old job or

Ambose's, pick the title that will sound prettiest to your wife. Combine them if you want. No matter how you decide to shuffle it, you'll be second in command, whatever you want to make of it." They'd pick the new chief investigator together. Charley would be in charge of training the new assistants, and that meant he could bring his kid brother in, in whatever capacity he wanted.

Charley's expression of canny interest pleased him.

"I want them young and fast and tough," Pawley said, "and I want to play the game within the rules." He could promise him that there would be no more of Nevins' country-boy stuff and no more of Ambose's strong-arm. They were going to make it an office any lawyer would be proud to work in. As he outlined his plans, he kept coming back to the same refrain. The necessity of bringing modern management and public relations techniques into the field of public service. "I tell you, Charley, we can get the bright kids out of law school, if we can get across the message that our aim is to protect society without ever, ever losing sight of the rights of the individual. And I think we can show our sincerity in that regard by letting them know they'd be free to campaign against capital punishment under the aegis of the office."

In the same regard, he could guarantee them, and Charley too, that there would be no more pig-stickings like the Tabor trial. One of the top-priority items in Pawley's progressive, farsighted regime was to arrange for the university to set up a pool of psychiatrists out of which all future expert witnesses for the state would be taken.

"I'll let you in on a secret, Charley. There's a U.S. Senate seat up in four years, and if you're not ready by then, I'm still not going to lose any sleep, because there'll be another one coming along two years later."

Having promised Charley that he would be district attorney in four to six years —without actually promising it—he ground out his cigarette. "I don't expect an answer right now. Don't want one. What I do want you to do is talk it over with your wife and brother." His smile puckered out, and for the first time all morning you could see the old Dee Pawley. "I've got until Monday," he said and, pushing himself up, began to walk to the door so that Curran would have to walk with him.

"All right, Lorna," he said after Curran was out of earshot. "Cliff Hargan will be in next. Keep 'em coming." He was going to have to do something about Lorna. She was a good kid and he liked her, but she didn't have the class for the kind of office he had in mind. The secretary was the first thing anybody saw when they entered the office. The secretary set the tone.

"Mr. Stattanius is on the phone," she said.

Stattanius was publisher of the *Globe,* and, back at his desk, Pawley set a tone of his own—a nice blending of respect for age and power with the vigor of youth and confidence of position—as he suggested that it would be helpful all around for him to get together with the *Globe's* upper-echelon editorial people for an informal luncheon. "I anticipate absolutely no difficulty in working out the fair trial–free press conflict to our mutual satisfaction," he said. "And if, out of that, we can work it into a standing monthly or bi-monthly backgrounder, so much the better." He waited patiently through the not unanticipated reception. "I quite agree with you, sir," he said. "I think it would be of enormous benefit to this office and to the people if we could arrange to keep them fully informed at all times."

Bannerman was holding a final press conference and the door was wide open.

The room was a mess. The blowup Hal had got from the television station had magically reappeared and had been tossed out onto the floor with the general drift and debris. The television set was on, with the sound turned off, and what made it especially disconcerting was that Judge Davies' handsome and benign face was smiling noiselessly behind Bannerman all the while Bannerman was attacking him for having displayed open bias.

They had all seen it, Bannerman kept saying. Just as they had all heard Bannerman warn, time after time, that poor Sam was teetering on the edge of insanity. "With any kind of a shake," he said, "I'd have walked the guy out. I don't have to tell you guys that. You all know it. You all saw. I warned everybody from the beginning that we were all teetering on the edge of the abyss."

Forgetting how sure he was of walking Sam out, he was saying in the next breath that if poor Sam hadn't flipped out, he'd have got a reversal for sure. Never had he seen a trial record so thoroughly impregnated with error and prejudice. He had a list of 105 appeals ready to go with, and at least 10 or 15 of them were solid. "And, gentlemen," he said, "I use the word impregnated advisedly. For the slow learners, that means we were fucked, and fucked, I might say, right royally."

It was the kind of performance where the kindest thing you could do for him was to avert your eyes. The district attorney's office was dismissed as "the flabbiest competition I have ever come up against." Both newspapers were attacked for being openly prejudiced and hostile, and Conrad Rittenhouse was singled out for special attention for having quoted Bannerman as saying that Ambose would be spending his time during the break before the summation "drinking from his pint of Old Bigot." Well, Mr. Rittenhouse and the *Chronicle* were going to wake up in the morning with a million-dollar libel suit on their hands for that little gem, and maybe—he grinned—his listeners could guess who his lawyer was going to be. Since half the people in the room, Halpern included, had heard him say it, there was an embarrassed silence. The reporters stopped asking questions. They put away their notebooks.

As Hal was calling out his goodbyes at the door, Bannerman came back and slipped two envelopes into his jacket pocket. One of them had a check for the two hundred dollars he still owed him. The other one was sealed, and he insisted that Hal give him his word not to open it until 3:30.

It was no coincidence at all, Hal suspected, that Bannerman's plane was leaving at 3:30.

There was no bluff and bluster as Bannerman held out his hand for the final goodbye. He looked ill. Worse yet, he looked at Hal as if Hal could say the words that would make him feel better. A month ago, a week ago, three days ago, Hal would have said them. Not today, pal. Not today. "I'm driving up to Algonquin," Hal said. "I'll give Sam your regards."

It was the kind of fog that descended so quickly and so heavily that you could feel it clogging your nostrils and clotting your eyebrows.

Harold Halpern, shaken to his roots, had stopped on a small arched brick bridge at the edge of the main hospital grounds to gloom over the dismal future that, lacking a miracle, lay ahead for Sam Tabor. Sometime in the early morning hours of August 9 Harold Halpern had stopped believing in miracles. The diagnosis was catalepsy. They moved Sam's head, it remained where they placed it. They lifted his hand, it remained where they dropped it. Stick a needle in him, and he did not flinch. He was putty. Whatever you wanted to do with him, you could do.

I think, therefore I am. A nice philosophic fancy which, turned around, became a hard medical truth: *I do not think, therefore I am not.* Or: *I do not exist, therefore I do not have to think.* Take your choice, and what the hell did it matter?

What mattered was that these next twenty-four hours were critical. What mattered was that if Sam didn't come out of it by then, the chances of his ever coming out were not very bright. Since Harold Halpern carried the germs of Sam's disease—the trial—the doctors had been afraid that the sight of him might break whatever frail connection with reality might still exist and drive Sam the last, soundless fathom under.

The implication that he had been a contributing factor in Sam's breakdown was a bitter pill for him to swallow. But swallow it he did. To cry out, as he ached, that he—he alone!—had been Sam's friend would have been unseemly, would have been wasteful, and, worst of all, would have been irrelevant. He—he alone! —had seen what was happening and he had waited too long. Norman Bannerman, driven by whatever interior furies drove him, had counted upon him—him alone!—to step in and stop him. Bannerman had as much as told him. Cowhig had as much as told him. Lionel Allbright had as much as told him. Ruthie, even Ruthie, had told him.

There was blame enough to go around, you'd think. And, in all honesty, he couldn't find anybody to blame. Bannerman couldn't help himself. The only verdict he could hand down on Bannerman was not guilty by reason of . . . what? Irresistible impulse? Harold Halpern had started from too far back. The only verdict he could hand down on himself was not guilty by reason of inexperience and incompetence. Harry Davies? Blaming Harry Davies was like blaming the wind for blowing. It had started to go wrong when Judge Chobodian had died. An act of God. You didn't have to be a lawyer to know that nobody could be held responsible for acts of God.

The bridge was set across a small gorge. Immediately beyond the bridge was a steep and narrow drop of stairs leading down to the dirt road which ran behind the administration and hospital buildings. Facing as he was, his car was visible about thirty yards down the road under the light of the lone street lamp. With his ridiculous sense of direction, Halpern had taken a wrong turn out of town and approached the hospital from the rear entrance, and after a few trips back and forth the full length of that road had made it clear—even to him—that it was going to be impossible to get to the administration building except on foot, he had parked the car under the lamp post where even he couldn't help but find it.

Below him, on the other side of the road, there was a greenhouse and a scattering of old barracks-like wooden buildings set up on piles. The only other light came from the barracks building almost directly across from where he was standing. The first few people trickling out the door barely attracted his eye, and then the building began to disgorge people, a great gush of people pouring out in a steady flow. Hal had just about realized that it would have to be the dining hall for the ambulatory patients when the fog descended with such suddenness that it swallowed them all in a gulp and turned the window lights into distant beacons on a blurry sea.

Even then he was still so deeply immersed in his own brooding thoughts that it did not occur to him that they would be coming up the stairs and over the bridge until the first hulking form materialized from out of a gust of fog—a giant of a man, he seemed to be, with massive, heavy-knuckled hands and a long, prognathous jaw—and then they were upon him and swirling around him; singly, at first, and then in pairs, and then as one great polluted stream of humanity.

By a trick of the air, a delusion of the fog, they came looming over the rim of the bridge like a marching army of the misshapen and misbegotten. Damp-faced men and scale-skinned women washed up by the sea, and the fog swirled around them like seaweed. Bred on the fog, they were distorted by the fog; swollen and stunted, pitted and waffled. Wobbled and wadded and welted. Their mouths moved without flesh or backing. Their eyes were dead in their sockets.

Weightless creatures from a remote age, they floated by without stirring the air, without rippling the pond. Up, through and gone; up, through and gone. Whoosh . . . whoosh . . . whoosh . . . whoosh. Their footfalls cushioned, their breath feathered. Whoosh . . . whoosh . . .

It was the end of the world he was witnessing, a glimpse into the Apocalypse.

On the other screen he saw the rowboats on the beach, and their oars were dead in their locks.

Not a man or woman looked at him, not a head nor an eye was turned. They were substance, he was air. The nightmare fantasy which was fleetingly his was the nightmare world they inhabited always. No, Harold Halpern had not been placed upon the bridge to bear witness to them, they had been brought here to bear witness to Harold Halpern that something had gone terribly wrong in the world. He was a spy in their encampment. They were doing him a kindness not to notice him.

"Someone has to love it or it will die," he father had said. He longed to make them understand that he was their friend. Their protector. It was all he could do not to shout out that he, Harold Halpern, would save them.

The last stragglers loomed, trundled past and faded into the fog from which they had come. And when the last of them had gone, it was as if they had never been there.

As quickly as the fog had come, that quickly the fog went. A curtain had been dropped. The curtain was raised.

Or, there on the bridge, the other way around: A curtain had been raised. The curtain had fallen.

There on the bridge Harold Halpern wiped his face and found that it was dripping wet. Coolness was everywhere around him. His face was numb. His skin ached.

Below him, across the yard, the dining hall came back so sharply defined against the crisp, bracing air that the window lights sparkled forth like Christmas without wreaths. Outside, one lonely figure was dumping garbage in a ten-gallon iron can. Inside, they would be washing dishes and wiping down the tables.

Down the road the street light had turned his old car new.

Halpern was down the stairs and standing alongside the car when he remembered, from out of nowhere, the sealed envelope Bannerman had left with him. Tearing it open, he twisted around so that he would be able to read by the light of the lamp post. Two words, printed large: BANNERMAN HURTS.

A wince of laughter escaped from him. And yet, knowing as he did, the enormous effort it would have taken Bannerman to put those words down, what could he do except shake his head. Leave it to Norman Bannerman to put Sam Tabor's ordeal in true perspective.

He tore the letter up into small pieces and flung them high into the air. A fitful draft of air caught the scraps of paper as they were being carried aloft, churned them around for the briefest of moments and then they came drifting down like snowflakes as Harold Halpern, under the lights, opened the door of his car.

7:47 P.M.

A snowstorm was raging in Sam Tabor's head. An electric storm sheet was wearing him away.

The chaste white walls had hemmed him in. A flaccid, convex world, curving outward, collapsing inward. Keg-shaped, as seen through a fish-eye's total 360-degree vision.

A million lock-bolts had already closed on Sam Tabor's memory. A million more were closing. Outside his windswept cave, there were sounds still struggling to be heard. Through every crack and fissure, the image-heads poked and the image-eyes peered.

The shutters keep banging. (So sad.)

The dove wings flapping against the windowpane.

The falcon's wings, the falconer's cry.

The slamming shutters in the ripping wind.

Logs in a swift current, roaring, rearing up in the white froth to become alligators, mouths yawning, voracious, ferociously snapping down upon . . . CLICK!

The world is white and beautiful and soft again. A snowy world, fleecy soft, technicolor white, a white more beautiful than any white that has ever been seen before. A summer shower of sparkling light. (Ah, beautiful. Oh, sad.) A sunburst of color, fragmenting into brightly-colored needles as it whirls; crystalline needles, prickly with radiance. Around and around they go—whirling, whirling— a rotating globe, sprayed with color, strewn with light. A whirling of color as seen through a diamond's gloriously diffusing glow. Warm and tingling, and trimmed with intricately lace-like beadwork. Every pattern of such ingenious design and configuration as has never been dreamed of before. Each of the luminous contours constantly flowing away from itself and catching up to itself, like a fan being riffled in the hands of an expert, opening and weaving and closing in a miracle of precision tracery. Truly prophetic. Divinely inspired. A great breakthrough has been accomplished and he is its agent. Who would have thought? Who could have dreamed?

A grateful world has erected this monument to Sam Tabor. A monument! Spired and fluted and trellised. A balustraded terrace, surmounting all, sits atop his monument like a crown, spinning round and round and round . . .

The glory of his life. So glorious and so sad. Who knows, even now, the real Sam Tabor, the secret Sam Tabor, the Sam Tabor of his solitude and dreams? Ladies and gentlemen of the world . . .

A stuttering of the heart warns him. The diamond's glow has flared too hot, too bright. (Mustn't touch; burns. Mustn't look; blinds.) Faster and faster the monument whirls. The central spindle cannot hold. The beautiful colors, whirring and whirling, spin off from gravity, fly off into space as coveys of frightened sparks and speckles holding to a tight flight formation against . . . Oh, my god! They're being shot at! One falls, plummets to earth. (The falcon is tearing at the dove's soft throat.) The others, scrambling for safety, swoop down into the bushes, scurry for cover. Become seed burrowing into the earth. Become spore, corpuscle and sperm. The weak cluster together into no-color blobs of nothing things. (So sad.) Excrement. Fragment themselves until they are pollen poised to ride the wind to the safety of the unfolding flower. Too late. The wind is empty, the flowers close.

The earth is barren, the river dry. The enemy is powerful; the enemy is sly. The enemy is a white, antiseptic laboratory, where they are terrified viruses squirming under a microscope. Caught. Held. Found out. The enemy is a white-masked scientist turning the black wheels with black gloves. Seen. Gonococci. Dirty . . . CLICK!

    The shutters banging. So sad.
    The ocean is calm. The ocean flows serene.
    Beside the dike, the windmill's blades, catching a stir in the air,
        move from a clover to a circle of turbulence.
    Overhead, the scudding clouds warn that there is a turbulence
        gathering in the air.
    Comes the crack of thunder. Comes the flash of lightning from
        cloud to earth.
    (The falcon diving toward the falconer's black glove)
    Down comes the downpouring rain
    The ocean gathers into one rip-roaring, earth-buckling wave
    Which tosses the ships like driftwood in a cyclone
    And breaking, in a sea of froth, upon the shore into a bucking
        bronco upon which,
    Betrothed and bestride, Sam Tabor rides.
    Rides the kicking, twisting, rampaging stallion across the
        tumbleweed plains; gentling, spurring, digging in
    While overhead, the Shadow's Wings ride with him,
    Following every twist and turn. Dips lower and lower,
    The rider, desperate, tries to buck the Shadow off
    And is himself thrown down to earth,
    The rustler's leader stands astride the unhorsed rider
    The brand glows red in his black-gloved hand
    (The dove is in the falcon's throat)
    The Tyrant's Paw
    Ths hiss of fire
    The Brand is on him. He bears forever the Mark of . . . CLICK!
    The winds turn cold, the rains turn white
    The shutters are banging, the window holds tight
    The windowpane is etched with frost
    Down comes the sheet of snow, a snowslide, tumbling white on
        white
    Becomes a long white strand unraveling into a longer streamer,
        which unfurls in flaps and patches.

A flag. A standard. A banner.
Poking its head up, jagged and proud
A banner to be rallied around.
Down comes the smothering avalanche. Caught. Drooped, dipped
    (tired), buried (sad). Gone.
The shutters banging (barely heard)
The logs rush on, the logjam breaks.
The river runs swiftly, dead ahead lie the falls.
The lumberjack, bestride, leaps bravely (too brave) from log to log
The lumberjack off on a jaunt (too jaunty) doesn't know (nobody
    told him)
That the river runs swiftly, dead ahead lie the falls.
The ice is cracking up into floes, fragmenting, melting.
The white world, crumbling, is dirty, slushy
The lumberjack, bestirruped, leaps here, leaps there
Full tilt against the current from log to log.
The edges are slippery, the stirrups won't hold
The river runs faster (swept toward the falls)
A slash of green along the slippery-elm bark
Another. Another.
He stumbles, loses balance,
Tumbles
Into the river (swept toward the falls)
Over and down and into the falls
Down, flailing, tumbling
Down and down and down, without a parachute
Like a piece of driftwood sucked into the cyclone
Deep down into the receding whorl. Down toward a distant,
    ever-receding point of light.
All his dwindling energies gathered to hold onto one point of light
The shutters bang softly, the wind is dying
The wings tap lightly against the windowpane
The light is fading.
Wind: Off
Dove: Gone
Shutters: Silent
CLICK! CLICK! CLICK!

The whole world is squeezed down to the tiniest pinpoint of light, which at the deepest bottom unravels, spiral-like, into a long, thin floating strand, which at its other end dissolves, losing itself in the all-enveloping, all-encompassing, all-engorging all-black-and-total darkness. And when, at last, the point of light has spun itself away, and there is nothing left but the last curling, floating strand—it holds itself intact just long enough for him to see it for what it is, a strand of pure, white cloth to make a turban of.

Swami . . .
CLICK!